"Brilliant."

"Szwed reveals the breadth and depth of Sun Ra.... It's more than a biography. Reading this book, like encountering Nietzsche or Zen, can make you rethink everything."
                                                                —*L. A. Weekly*

"The achievement of this biography is that it carefully articulates Ra's views of life and art at the same time that it provides hard data and analysis to locate his theories in historical context.... [Ra's] story is told with brilliance and grace in this deeply simpatico biography."   —*Washington Post*

"[A] model of creative criticism, cogent writing, and scrupulous research.... [The author] deftly catalogs the myriad ideas that fed [Ra's] philosophy with scholarly insight and narrative panache.... It's Szwed's ultimate triumph that his book will almost certainly send its readers to the record racks to sample the work of this magnificent enigma."   —*Newsday*

"The value of giving shape to the life of a great and neglected 20th-century musician is inestimable, but perhaps the *true* force of Szwed's book is its archaeology of the rich environment in which Sun Ra developed.... Szwed carves out a central image of Sun Ra as a man whose sincerity was unquestioned, whose heart was pure."   —*Village Voice*

"[This] long-awaited biography fills in many of the substantial gaps in the long, apparently lonely life Sun Ra spent in pursuit of secret knowledge and immortality. Szwed is best on Ra's jazz roots and early years of bitter struggle in Birmingham, Alabama and Chicago."   —*Spin*

"The definitive investigation into the mysteries of Ra.... Szwed's challenging biography ... is highly literate and exceptionally thought-provoking. [He] offers the reader cogent insights into Ra's music.... Szwed's scholarly tribute to [Ra's] undeniable originality is both timely and fascinating."
                                                                —*Jazz Report*

"Sun Ra is vividly and respectfully portrayed and defended against those who thought [he] was a crackpot.... As elucidated by Szwed, Sun Ra's seemingly outlandish ideas make a certain sense.... Szwed also makes a strong case for Sun Ra as creative genius."   —*Kirkus*

"If *Space Is the Place* teaches us anything about this complex individual, it is that Sun Ra was an American original [of] considerable artistic accomplishments.... [A] memorable portrait."   —*Chicago Tribune*

SPACE IS
THE PLACE

THE LIVES AND TIMES OF
SUN RA

JOHN F. SZWED

DA CAPO PRESS

A Member of the Perseus Books Group

Library of Congress Cataloging-in-Publication Data

Szwed, John F, 1936–
   Space is the place: the lives and times of Sun Ra / John F Szwed.—1st Da Capo Press ed.
   p.   cm.
   Previously published: New York: Pantheon Books, 1997.
   Discography: p. ****
   Includes bibliographical references (p. ****) and index.
   ISBN-10: 0-306-80855-2   ISBN-13: 978-0-306-80855-5
   1. Sun Ra. 2. Jazz musicians—United States—Biography. I. Title.
ML410.S978S73   1998
781.65'092—dc21

[B]

98-15303

CIP

Grateful acknowledgment is made to the following for permission to reprint previously published and unpublished material: *Jack Cooke*: Excerpts from review of "Sound of Joy" by Jack Cooke (*Jazz Monthly*, May 1970). Reprinted by permission of the author. · *Eddy Determeyer*: Excerpts from "Sun Ra: Verleden, heden, toekomst" by Eddy Determeyer (*Jazz Nu*, July 1982). Reprinted by permission of the author. · *The Estate of Sun Ra*: Various material authored by Sun Ra. Reprinted by permission of the Estate of Sun Ra, Marie Holston, Administratrix, Birmingham, Alabama. · *Jazz Magazine*: Excerpts from "Il sera temps d'édifier la maison notre . . . Sun Ra" by Philippe Carles (*Jazz Magazine* no. 217, 12/73). Excerpts from "L'impossible liberté" and "Un soir au Chatelet" by Philippe Carles (*Jazz Magazine* no. 196, 1/72). Excerpts from "L'Opéra Cosmique du Sun Ra" by Philippe Carles (*Jazz Magazine* no. 159, 10/68). Excerpts from "Visite au dieu Soleil" by Jean-Louis Noames (*Jazz Magazine* no. 125, 12/65). Reprinted by permission of the editors of *Jazz Magazine*. · *National Interreligious Service Board for Conscientious Objectors*: Records of the National Interreligious Service Board for Conscientious Objectors, Swarthmore College Peace Collection. Reprinted by permission of the National Interreligious Service Board for Conscientious Objectors. · *The New York Times*: Excerpts from "Sun Ra: I'm Talking About Cosmic Things" by John S. Wilson (*New York Times* 4/7/68). Copyright © 1968 by *The New York Times* Co. Reprinted by permission of *The New York Times*. · *Robert Rusch*: Excerpts from "Sun Ra: Interview" by Robert Rusch (*Cadence Jazz Magazine*, June 1978). Copyright © 1978 by *Cadence Jazz Magazine*. Reprinted by permission of the author. · *Phil Schaap*: Excerpts from "An Interview with Sun Ra" by Phil Schaap, which appeared in *WKCR* 5, no. 5 (January–February 1989) and vol. 5, no. 6 (March 1989). Reprinted by permission of the author. · *Straight Arrow Publishers, Inc.*: Excerpts from "Sun Ra" by John Burks (*Rolling Stone*, 4/19/69). Copyright © 1969 by Straight Arrow Publishers, Inc. All rights reserved. Reprinted by permission of Straight Arrow Publishers, Inc. · *Bert Vuijsje*: Excerpts from "Sun Ra Spreekt" by Bert Vuijsje, which appeared in *Jazz Wereld* (October 1968) and in Vuijsje's book *De Nieuwe Jazz*, 1978. Excerpts from "Sun Ra: nar van de schepper" (*Haagse Post*, 11/25/70). Reprinted by permission of the author.

First Da Capo Press edition 1998

This Da Capo Press paperback edition of *Space Is the Place* is an unabridged republication of the edition first published in New York in 1997, with several minor textual emendations. It is reprinted by arrangement with Pantheon Books, a division of Random House, Inc.

Copyright © 1997 by John F Szwed

Book design by M. Kristen Bearse

Published by Da Capo Press, Inc.
A Member of the Perseus Books Group

TO SUE AND MATT

AND

TO THE MEMORY OF

ANN ELIZABETH ADAMS

(1952–1996)

"Our music is a Secret Order."

LOUIS ARMSTRONG, 1954

CONTENTS

ACKNOWLEDGMENTS

THE GENEROUS HELP I received from so many people in working on this book was overwhelming. My indebtedness to them has been a secret source of pride to me, and I take this opportunity to go public with it and to thank them all.

Since Sun Ra left the planet just as I was beginning work on this book, interviews with him which had been done in the past were especially critical. Fortunately, I was given access to dozens of tapes made by fans and journalists, many of whom also shared their notes and memories with me. And every musician, family member, or associate of Sun Ra's that I approached spoke to me and treated me with such courtesy and kindness that my life has been enriched and even changed by the experience.

Let me first off thank Sun Ra's family: his sister, Mary Jenkins, his nephew, Thomas Jenkins, Jr., and his nieces, Marie Holston and Lillie B. King. Among his associates and musicians from the Birmingham years I want to acknowledge Frank Adams, Melvin Caswell, Johnny Grimes, Jessie Larkins, J. L. Lowe, Walter Miller, and Fletcher Myett. From his time in Chicago and later there was Marshall Allen, Richard Berry, Phil Cohran, Vernon Davis, Alvin Fielder, John Gilmore, James Hernden, Art Hoyle, Tommy Hunter, Harold Ousley, Lucious Randolph, Eugene Wright, and of course Alton Abraham, the cofounder and force behind Saturn Records. From the New York years there was Ahmed Abdullah, Amiri Baraka, Paul Bley, Jothan Callins, Verta Mae Grosvenor, James Jacson, Wilber Morris, Olatunji, Pharoah Sanders, Danny Ray Thompson, and Richard Wilkerson; and from Philadelphia onward there was

Rhoda Blount, Craig Haynes, Tyrone Hill, Michael Ray, Spencer Weston, and Dale Williams.

The return to my hometown of Birmingham was made easier by the graciousness and guidance of Ann Adams, L. Wade Black, John Cottrell, Jimmy Griffith of Charlemagne Record Exchange, George Mostoller, the staff of the Alabama Jazz Hall of Fame, my Eutaw connection Davey Williams, and A. J. Wright.

For help with translations from French, Dutch, German, and Italian I counted on Amy Reid, Anti Bax, Dorothea Schulz, and Christina Lombardi.

Music critics, writers, and jazz historians were especially important, since they were often the only sources for locating Sun Ra's work and whereabouts during various periods of his life. Bill Adler, Joseph Chonto, Hugo De Craen, John Diliberto, Hartmut Geerken, Gary Giddins, John Gray, Hans Kumpf, Art Lange, Howard Mandel, Francesco Martinelli, Robert Palmer, Lewis Porter, Paul Rubin, Bob Rusch, and Phil Schaap were my sources.

The Sun Ra cognoscenti—those who were touched by the Arkestra early in their lives and stayed with the maestro—were critical sources for me: Ken Ashworth, Charles Blass, Tom Buck, Alan Chase, Gerry Clark, Byron Coley, Jules Epstein, Yale Evelev, Rev. Dwight Frizzell, Bruce Gallanter, Don Glasgo, John and Peter Hines, David Hight, Rick Iannacone, Ademola Johnson, Kidd Jordan, Alden Kimbrough, R. Andrew Lepley, Eliot Levin, Christine Lippmann, Robert Mugge, Alan Nahigian, Roy Nathanson, Jim Newman, Pat Padua, Ralph Plesher, Paul Sanoian, Thomas Stanley, Bernard Stollman, Rick R. Theis, Mark Webber, Russ Woessner, and Peter Wilf. Thanks, too, to the Saturn internet group, from which I learned much as an eavesdropper.

For a thousand other favors and insights, thanks to Ira Berger, Carol Blank, Dave Brubeck, Dave Castleman, Irwin Chusid, Selma Jean Cohen, Janet Coleman, Jeff Crompton, Margaret Davis, Jennifer Dirkes, Craig Dorsheimer, Leo Feigin, Harold Flaxon, Harold Gold (of Plastic Fantastic Records in Ardmore, PA), Jane Goldberg, Ernst Handlos, Gail Hawkins, Malcolm Jarvis, Kathy Kemp, Miles Kierson, Jorn Krumpelmann, Jan Lohmann, Judy McWillie, John J. Maimone, William Allaudin Mathieu, Jonas Mekas, Ivor Miller, Thurston Moore,

Dan Morgenstern, Phil Niblock, Tosiyuki Nomoto, Robert J. Norell, the Hon. Deval J. Patrick, Bruce Perry, Gloria Powers, Robert Pruter, Ron Radano, Pat Reardon, Ishmael Reed, Bruce Ricker (of Rhapsody Films), Thomas Riedwelski, Michael Roberts (of Custom Photo Art, Birmingham), Robert Schoenholt, H. Sigurdsson, Jack Sutters, Archivist of the American Friends Service Committee, Allan Welsh, and L. William Yolton.

This book required considerable help from librarians, and I was fortunate to have access to some of the best: at Yale, the staff of Interlibrary Loan at Sterling Memorial Library; in the Birmingham Public Library, Marvin Whiting, head of the Henley Research Collection; at Rutgers University at Newark the wonderful Institute of Jazz Studies staff, and especially Ed Berger, Don Luck, Dan Morganstern, and Vincent Pelotte; at Swarthmore College Library, Wendy E. Chmielewski, curator of the Peace Collection; and at Alabama A & M College, Mildred L. Stiger.

I tested my friends' goodwill even more than usual: Roger Abrahams, Jack Ferguson, Joe McPhee, Karl Reisman, Dan Rose, David Sassian, Susan Stewart, Robert Farris Thompson, and Alan Tractenberg. I owe you all, big time.

Let me single out a few people for special thanks. First, members of the Arkestra: Jothan Callins welcomed me back to Birmingham by buying me lunch at the best hotel in town and taking me along on his gig at the United Mine Workers' buffet at the Best Western motel in Bessemer. In our many talks he brought his considerable knowledge and scholarship of Alabama to bear. Tommy Hunter was a principal source for Sun Ra's life from Chicago on, the maker and keeper of many priceless photographs, and a treasured dinner companion. And James Jacson, a man of great charm, intelligence, and talent, put up with many visits and calls from me, always with a scholarly patience. All three of these men have taught me much beyond the life of the Arkestra. As with all the members of the Arkestra, I am proud to have known such exceptional people and to call them my friends.

Professor Robert L. Campbell of Clemson University is of course the master discographer of Sun Ra, but he was also an essential source for interviews, and was helpful in many, many ways. John Litweiler, a jazz scholar of note, shared his Chicago interviews with me and gave me a sense of the Chicago scene. Graham Lock and Val Wilmer, two of the great jazz writers of Britain, gave me access to their files and tapes, and more important, offered their wisdom on many matters. Victor Schonfield, the person most responsible for Sun Ra's first European tour, likewise was generous with his collection and his memory. Roy Morris of Homeboy Music came out of the blue from Scotland to surprise me with press clippings which I would have otherwise never seen. Warren Smith, one of the former owners of Variety Recording Studio and a scholar in his own right, loaned me his files and gave me counsel, which has been invaluable. Sally Banes, Wade Black, Francis Davis, Gray Gundaker, and Daisann McLane have all put up with me through the work on the book, and aided me immensely. Anthony Braxton and Michael Taussig offered me encouragement and opportunities to talk about the work publicly at early stages; and Michael Shore, Jerry Gordon, and Trudy Morse—true believers in Sun Ra's cause—have helped me in ways too numerous to list, but the book would be inconceivable without them.

Throughout the work Sara Lazin kept the faith cheerfully and did exactly what I always thought an agent should do. Among the wonderful folks at Pantheon my editor Erroll McDonald encouraged me at the right moments, managing editor Altie Karper kept me more or less on track, and copy editor Maud Lavin and production editor Susan Norton saved me from ignominy time and again. Nara Nahm, who does everything, did it better than anyone.

The book is dedicated to my wife, Sue, and my son, Matt, who as always carried me, and what's still surprising to me, shared my enthusiasm; and to Ann Adams, my research assistant in Birmingham, friend of Sun Ra, and true Angel of the New South.

INTRODUCTION

CLOTHIER HALL, Swarthmore College, in the high-sixties: a school where the students are as tuned in and turned on as any in the country; the site of major draft resistance and antiwar organizing, hotbed of civil rights agitators, the home of the first rock-and-roll magazine.... The students enter the auditorium joking, or distant and cool, wearing retro evening gowns, granny glasses, work clothes, military-uniform detritus from wars before their times... one boy is naked except for the American flag draped around him. The lights dim for the concert to start. And they continue to dim, dimming below Quaker gray, until total darkness covers the hall. Minutes pass and nothing happens, the audience is subdued, trapped in their seats. Then a faint sound in the aisles, a rustling, a sense of movement. Someone whispers something about rats and nervous laughter follows.

So slowly that it seems not even to be happening, the lights begin to come up. A single drummer in dark glasses, hood, and sparkling tunic, who can just be made out standing behind a six-foot carved drum, raises two strangely shaped sticks and begins a rhythm; others who can now be seen around him, in robes, weird hats, all in dark glasses, take up his beat and add to it until the rhythm becomes a polyrhythmic snarl. And as the lights continue to rise it becomes clear that a kind of procession is under way: dancers in flowing gowns hold richly dyed silks in front of changing colored lights; others parade before the audience paintings of Egyptian scenes or of monsters coiled around their victims. A conversation of flutes begins; the musicians sway in fabulously shimmering robes; tinted lights scatter amorphous shapes across the walls and ceiling; a film begins, projected silently on the wall behind them, showing the same musicians on some other occasion. Now the horns are heard, one by one, then all in a knot of dissonance, a trumpet piercing the air above them. Smoke begins to slither across the floor as a dancer enters carrying a large glowing ball like some turn-of-the-century art study. A woman with a beatific smile seems to float to the front, and begins to sing until she is joined by others who look like some crazed monks lost in time:

> When the world was in darkness
> Darkness is ignorance
> Along came Ra....
>
> The living myth, the living myth
> The living Mister Re

And there in the middle of it all, his face impassive, sits a stocky, middle-aged black man in a cockpit of electronics. On his head is a cap which appears to be a working model of the solar system. He fingers, then thrashes the keyboards around him with his fists and forearms. And so it would go for the next four or five hours, though a generous number of students have fled the hall immediately and would not know this.

Sun Ra was in the house and in his universe.

Even in the excesses of this era there were few audiences prepared for an ominous, ragtag group of musicians in Egyptian robes, Mongolian caps (Mongolian, as from the planet Mongo of Flash Gordon), and B-movie spacesuits who played on a variety of newly invented or strangely modified electronic instruments (the sun harp, the space organ, the cosmic side drum) and proclaimed the greatness of the most ancient of races (this, the Sun Ra of the Solar-Myth Arkestra); or, on yet another night, a merry band in jester's motley, jerkins, and pointed caps (à la Robin Hood or perhaps the Archers of Arboria) who marched or crawled through the audience, chanting cheerful songs about travel to Venus. It was intensely dramatic music, moving from stasis to chaos and back, horn players leaping about, or rolling on the bandstand, sometimes with fire eaters, gilded muscle men, and midgets, an all-out assault on the senses. At the end of the evening the musicians and dancers moved among the audience, touching them, surrounding them, inviting them to join the Arkestra in marching off to Jupiter.

As much as these spectacles were a part of the times, they were far from what hippies called freak-outs: Sun Ra's performances were shaped by a rationale and a dramatic coherence drawn from mythic themes, Afro-American liturgy, science fiction, black cabaret, and vaudeville, yet strangely open to free interpretation. Depending on who you were and under what circumstances you heard Sun Ra live, you saw him as a traditionalist, an aggressive and threatening magician of black arts, a laissez-faire multiculturalist, or maybe an avuncular but eccentric senior citizen.

Some years ago a German journalist headed his review of a Sun Ra performance, "Genius or Charlatan?" He might well have added "madman" to his question, because these are the roles in which this legendary and semireclusive American jazz musician was cast, and part of the mystery of one of the strangest artists that America has ever produced. Yet for well over forty years he managed to successfully hold together the Arkestra, his band of dozens of musicians, dancers, and singers, which performed in every conceivable venue, from conservatory to country-and-western bar; his longevity as leader was longer than most symphony conductors', longer even than Duke Ellington's; he recorded at least 1,000 compositions on over 120 albums (many for his own company, El Saturn Research), and his hand-painted records have long been high-priced collectors items, with arguments over even the existence of some of them becoming the basis of legends. And in spite of being the quintessential underground figure, he managed to turn up on *Saturday Night Live, The Today Show, All Things Considered,* and the covers of magazines and newspapers like *Rolling Stone,* the *Soho News, Reality Hackers,* and *The Face.* Sun Ra created an Arkestra which became the most continually advanced and experimental group in the history of jazz and popular music. And by locating himself in Chicago, New York, and Philadelphia, the major centers of jazz, he affected all of the music of his time.

Yet there was a curious tension between the musician and the mystic in Sun Ra, something very *"National Enquirer"* about his synthesis. The far-out gave way to the merely old-fashioned at a moment's notice. His obsession with the links between the universe and the musical had its basis in pre-Newtonian physics, and at some instants seemed not so much mysterious as simply out-of-it. Yet he also had an uncanny ability for making the everyday seem strange. As personal as his vision was, it was nonetheless drawn from many currents of Afro- and Euro-American thought, most of them unknown to the public. He spoke from a long tradition of revisionist history by way of street-corner Egyptology, black Freemasonry, theosophy, and oral and written biblical exegesis, all bound together by a love of secret knowledge and the importance it bestows upon those excluded from the usual circuits of scholarship and power.

This is the biography of a musician who confronted the problems of creating music for an audience who expected nothing more than to be entertained, but who at the same time attempted to be a scholar and a teacher, and to take his audiences beyond the realm of the aesthetic to those of the ethical and the moral. It is then also a biography of his music as a living entity, a music which had its own role to play in what he would have called the cosmic scheme of things.

SPACE IS THE PLACE

CHAPTER ONE

You might have seen him on the street any day, an august young black man with a slight smile and a distant stare, wearing sandals and wrapped in a sheet like a prophet from the Scriptures.

It was Birmingham, Alabama, in 1940, the most segregated city in the United States. A city so racially possessed that black businesses were legally enclosed within a downtown grid, and local custom set aside a day for blacks to shop outside of it—a day on which, whites complained to each other, they'd be shoved off the sidewalk if they dared to venture out. This was the city where the Robert E. Lee Klavern boasted the largest KKK membership in America, and was so bold that they murdered a Catholic priest on the steps of his own rectory. A city where violence seemed so imminent that President Harding (who some said was a Negro himself) had once given a speech timorously pleading for an easing of segregation.

You might have seen him strolling down that wide street, past the splendors of Hotel Row on his way from Terminal Station to Forbes's Piano Company. You would have seen him, maybe laughed, called the police, or shaken your head over the sorry state that things had come to.

But if Birmingham was racially demonized, it was also extraordinarily tolerant of individuality, of eccentricity and personal excess. This was the city where an ex-mayor had built a home on Shades Mountain in a fantasy of the Roman Temple of the Vestal Virgins, and where His

Honor and his servants dressed in togas—a different color for each day
of the week—and his guests were entertained by wispy young women
who gamboled across the lawn between three miniature garden temples
which served as doghouses.

ARRIVAL

He was born on May 22, 1914—a Gemini, on a day with a doubled
number. His mother named him Herman Poole Blount. "Herman" was
inspired by Black Herman, the most famous of many early twentieth-
century Afrocentric magicians. Claiming a lineage that reached back to
Moses, Black Herman was said to be able to raise a woman from the dead
at every show; and as an associate of black cultural nationalists like Marcus Garvey, Booker T. Washington, and Hubert Fauntleroy Julian, the
Black Eagle of Harlem, he seemed capable of raising a mighty race as
well. Since there were several magicians with the same name, Black
Herman himself appeared immortal, and like Marie Laveau, the voodoo
queen of New Orleans, able to succeed himself.

"Poole" was the name of a railroad worker his mother knew from her
job at the Terminal Station restaurant. There was talk, but his mother
said Mr. Poole just wanted to have a child named after him. Years later in
Chicago it amused him to think that he might be distantly related to Elijah Poole, a man from Georgia who changed his name to Elijah Muhammad and founded the Nation of Islam after meeting another magician
named Wallace D. Fard, who was said to be the reincarnation of Allah.

"Blount" was his patronymic, a connection to a father's line of kin. But
somewhere in his childhood the name began to seem strange, ill-fit: it
had no potential, no rhythm. " 'Blount' did not equate," he said. South-
erners pronounced it "Blunt," and it was sometimes spelled that way, or
"Blondt," or even "Bhlount." He began to feel that his real father's name
had been taken from him and that he bore another man's. Even though it
was not unusual for young black people in the South to take other relatives' names if they were raised by them, for Herman this seemed an unbearable fraud. From then on "Blount" would be a cover for a name so
secret that even he did not know what it was. For years all he would say
about it was, "I had some relatives named that."

> Man that is born of woman is of few
> days and full of trouble.
>
> JOB 14:1

Birth dates, names, addresses, documents, the remembrances of family and friends, these are the makings of biographies, the truth about a person's life, the elements which keep fact from fiction. But at the heart of everything that Sun Ra did or said was the claim that he was not born, that he was not from earth, that he was not a man, that he had no family, that his name was not what others said it was. For almost fifty years he evaded questions, forgot details, left false trails, and talked in allegories and parables. Just as artists and composers destroy their early works to protect the present moment, Sun Ra destroyed his past, and recast himself in a series of roles in a drama he spent his life creating. And in the end he almost succeeded. Files and certificates had been destroyed or disappeared or never existed, photos vanished, and early recordings and compositions were lost in fires or deceased musicians' attics. Gone were most of the family members, school friends, teachers, and musicians who could testify to his past, and the memories of those who were left were reshaped and clouded by his shifting biography. He had succeeded in erasing a third of his earthly life.

Sometimes he said he had no mother; or he implied that he was from Saturn; and by evading dates—like a Frederick Douglass or even a Booker T. Washington—he became ageless and timeless. "You can't ask me to be specific about time," he said.

> Me and time never got along so good—we just sort of ignore each other.... I came from somewhere else, but it [the Creator's voice] reached me through the maze and dullness of human existence. But if I hadn't been, it couldn't have reached me and I'd be like the rest of the people on the planet who are dancing in their ignorance.... I came from somewhere else, where I was part of something that is so wonderful that

there are no words to express it.... I arrived on this planet on a very important day, it's been pinpointed by wise men, astrologers, as a very important date. I arrived at the very moment, a very controversial arrival...in a position where a spiritual being can arrive right at that particular point.

At three, the Creator separated me from my family. He said, "Well, I'm your family." And from then on, I was under his guidance. I was there but I wasn't there.... I remember things—images and scenes and feelings. I never felt like I was part of this planet. I felt that all this was a dream, that it wasn't real. And suffering...I just couldn't connect.... My mind would never accept the fact that is like it's supposed to be. I always felt that there was something wrong. I couldn't explain it. My people kept saying, "Why are you unhappy? You never seem to be happy." And that was true. I had this touch of sadness in the midst of other people's parties; other people were having a good time, but I would have a moment of loneliness and sadness. It puzzled me, therefore I had to analyze that, and I decided I was different, that's all. I must have come from somewhere else. I wasn't just born; I had been somewhere before I was born.

I'm not a human. I never called anybody "mother." The woman who's supposed to be my mother I call "other momma." I never call anybody "mother." I never called anybody "father." I never felt that way.

I've separated myself from everything that in general you call life. I've concentrated entirely on the music, and I'm preoccupied with the planet. In my music I create experiences that are difficult to express, especially in words. I've abandoned the habitual, and my previous life is of no significance any more for me. I don't remember when I was born. I've never memorized it. And this is exactly what I want to teach everybody: that it is important to liberate oneself from the obligation to be born, because this experience doesn't help us at all. It is important for the planet that its inhabitants do not believe in being born, because whoever is born has to die.

Years later, after he had become knowledgeable in cabalism and etymology, he would say that birth was the beginning of death, a "berth" being a place for sleeping, to "be-earthed" was to be buried ("A true birthday is the day of your death"). A man who was not born, who was made, as Mary Shelley suggested of Frankenstein, was without original sin.

[Man] has to rise above himself... transcend himself. Because the way he is, he can only follow reproductions of ideas, because he's just a reproduction himself.... He did not come from the creative system, he came from the reproductive system. But if he evolutes beyond himself, he will come up from the creative system. What I'm determined to do is to cause man to create himself by simply rising up out of the reproductive system into the creative system.... Darwin didn't have the complete picture.... I've been talking about evolution, too, but I'm spelling it e-v-e-r.

So it went with Sun Ra. Yet once in a while the mundane would creep into his talk, and a hint of nostalgia for the prosaic would surface, if only for a moment. He would say that his father left when he was small, and his mother remarried, giving him his new father's name, "but I knew neither name was mine.... My father just took off when I was very young," and his mother kept him away from him. Once he allowed as how his father had made several attempts to kidnap him, but then he quickly added, "It's not good for me to be remembering all that." Yet he saw his father in visions: "I really believe my father was not a man. The last time I remember him I was in his arms, and I don't think of him as being a man. He was another kind of spirit, a dark one. And I was a baby in his arms.... I was really raised by the creator of the Universe who guided me step by step."

His older sister Mary was far less circumspect: "He was born at my mother's aunt's house over there by the train station.... I know, 'cause I got on my knees and peeped through the keyhole. He's not from no Mars." Cary and Ida Blount and their firstborn son, Robert, moved to Birmingham from Demopolis, a trading center in the large plantation area of west-central Alabama, near the Mississippi line, a town which had once been a French utopian community. Cary Blount had four children from an earlier marriage, Margaret, Della, and George, who stayed behind in the country when he took Ida and went off to work for the railroad, and Cary, Jr., who also went with them. Ida separated from her husband when Herman was still young, and when her house burned down she moved with Robert, her daughter Mary, and Cary, Jr., into a house on the north side of town. Herman was raised by his maternal grandmother Margaret Jones and his great-aunt Ida Howard in a large two-story house at 2508 4th Avenue North, in an area that was largely commercial. A block away was Terminal Station, a massive domed Beaux Arts structure flanked by oversized wings which at one end housed baggage and at the other the colored waiting room. It was the largest train station in the South, where eleven railroad lines converged, and where people crisscrossed the state and flowed back and forth to Chicago, the closest northern city. All of them passed under a huge sign at the front of the station which read, in 10,000 lights, "Welcome to the Magic City."

Lionel Hampton remembered that station as a major site of entertainment in Birmingham, where people perched along the tracks watching trains like The Black Diamond Express, The City of New Orleans, or The Sunset Limited—all memorialized in songs—coming and going; where crowds applauded the performance of the waiters setting tables in the dining car and the porters making beds, cheering the engineer blowing the whistle and the fireman ringing the bell. When the train pulled out of the station in slow motion, the fireman pitched spare shovels of coal over the side for the spectators to take home, and the cooks tossed out food.

Herman's mother and great-aunt were employed in the restaurant at the terminal, and when they were at work he was taken care of by his grandmother. He never cared for her cooking, so as often as he could he walked to the terminal where his mother and great-aunt fed him in the kitchen of the big railroad restaurant. Afterwards he'd stand in the dining room and listen to the player piano, hearing the latest rolls, like Fats Waller's "Haitian Blues" and "Snake Hips."

They called him Snookum as a child—a name that remained with the family, so that years later his nieces and nephews called him Uncle Snookum. He was a pleasant child with an agreeable smile and a quick mind, but distant and quiet. His recollections of his mother were few, but her character was well etched in his memory: he recalled as a child traveling to Demopolis with her, where she shared her whiskey with him at a party, sending him reeling across the floor. When the other adults chastised her, she explained that it would be hypocritical of her to deny him when she drank...besides, she said, this way he wouldn't be interested in liquor when he grew up. Most of all he remembered that his mother was not especially religious ("she said you make your own heaven and hell"), and never went to church, which put her at odds with his grandmother, a very strict and pious woman, who saw to it that he went to Sunday School and accompanied him and his great-aunt to services at the Tabernacle Baptist Church. He took these services seriously, the somber prayers of the deacons during the devotion, the rich argumentation of the sermon, the ecstasy of the women in the service, the power and terror in the idea of the Old Ship of Zion. But by the time he was seven, he was secretly posing questions to himself: "I never could understand if Jesus died to save people, why people have to die. That seemed ignorant to me. I couldn't equate that as a child." When the congregation joined in the hymns he was very careful about what he sang. One line he refused to sing was "I will help Jesus bear the cross": "It asked you to make a declaration, and you never knew who might be recording it." It was not so much that he was an unbeliever—what tormented him was the question of *what* he should believe in.

When he entered the first grade at Thomas Elementary School he was a teacher's delight: a polite, studious boy who already knew how to read and who was devoted to his studies from the first day. Often while other children played games during recess in the field that served as a schoolyard, he read, and the teachers said that he soon had read everything in the school. And so it went for the first three grades, and then the rest of grade school when he moved to Lincoln School: a child who no one knew well, but who all recognized as exceptionally promising.

He stayed close to home, mostly playing alone or with his cousins, and had no interest in sports. A protected childhood, he later called it, free from violence and even the sting of race, he said, for he had little contact with white people. But at age ten, Herman was persuaded to join the American Woodmen Junior Division, a group of boys who met Saturday mornings at the Knights of Pythias Temple. He surprised everyone by becoming deeply involved with the group, and remaining a member until he entered high school. There he received training in woodcraft, camping trips, precision marching, and oratorical contests. A veteran of World War I named Grayson was the leader, and he drilled the boys in military routines and much impressed Herman.

The senior Woodmen group who sponsored them was a beneficial organization created by white people for blacks, and provided health and life insurance and volunteer help for members and their families in times of trouble. Their rituals and emblems were centered on the idea of life and work in the forest, part of a larger reaction against the growing commercialism of the United States. Along with a faint identification with American Indians, there were the symbolic trappings familiar to all secret societies—handshakes, tasks and trials, pranks, and a drama of initiation with a cast of stock characters: a cold-hearted banker, worthy beggars, and Death speaking from behind a screen, surprising and then threatening the initiate, and reminding him of mortality. The Woodmen made a commitment to Nature and Nature's God, to the forest as temple, to the wilderness as an alternative to the corruption and inequities of cities, and to rejecting wealth and status. "They showed me discipline . . . all about secret orders . . . and how to be a leader."

When he reached adolescence various physical problems began to plague him, especially a severe hernia associated with problems of testicle development, cryptorchidism, an affliction whose name alone was a scourge. He concealed this as best he could, but it was a source of constant aggravation, a weakness that left him feeling that at any moment his internal organs might shift or drop, and forced him to be constantly wary; his body became a nuisance and an object of scrutiny to him, and left him fearful that others might find out and that he might be treated as a freak, like the carnival sideshow anomalies he saw every year at the Alabama State Fair. It was a secret affliction which became an obsession and a curse, but yet also an emblem of his singularity.

When his grandmother suddenly passed away, Herman was solely under his great-aunt's protection. He was her favorite, her joy in life, and she refused to let anyone discipline or correct him. She devoted herself to his welfare, and was proud of his accomplishments and his talent.

Once in school, he stayed with the same classmates all the way through. "It was a setup for me to know nothin' about the world. . . . If I had known about the world, I probably wouldn't be what I am today."

I've never been part of the planet. I've been isolated from a child away from it. Right in the midst of everything and not being a part of it. Them troubles peoples got, prejudices and all that, I didn't know a thing about it, until I got to be about fourteen years old. It was as if I was somewhere else that imprinted this purity on my mind, another kind of world. That is my music playing the kind of world I know about. It's like someone else from another planet trying to find out what to do. That's the kind of mind or spirit I have, it's not programmed—from the family, the church, from the schools, from the government. I don't have a programmed mind. I know what they're talking about, but they don't know what I'm talking about. I'm in the midst of what they're doing but they've never been in the midst of what has been impressed upon my mind as being a pure solar world.

MUSIC

His first memory of music was that his older brother Robert had phonograph records, and that he loved every one of them. The adults laughed because when they called out requests he ran back and forth finding the records, even before he could read the labels. In a few years his brother was bringing home new records by the father of swing, Fletcher Henderson. Herman was entranced by them, charmed by the musicianship and the flash in the tricky shifting rhythmic figures of "Whiteman Stomp," the luxurious chinoiserie of "Shanghai Shuffle," the Latin exoticism of "The Gouge of Armour Avenue." He remembered that composing tunes seemed natural to him—"like a bird in flight." "When I was a child I sang melodies while I walked in the street. But at that time I couldn't play them. I felt like writing down the melodies which came into my head, but I didn't know how."

On what he later guardedly called his eleventh "arrival day" his great-aunt Ida bought him a piano for a present. Since his sister already played piano, it was an immediate source of friction between them, and one that became all the worse when Herman began to play without lessons. He was not just playing by ear, which is the claim made for so many great musicians, but also with the ability to read music. He had already learned the names and locations of the notes at school; now he secretly borrowed his sister's *Standard Music Book,* and taught himself to read. This was too much to believe even for those who already thought he was exceptional.

> My grandmother liked church music so she bought a book with religious songs because she couldn't believe it either. I played everything in the book. Then my friend William Gray came, who played the violin, and he didn't believe in me. He said, "I have to study every day. I know it's impossible just to play music without reading it. You play it like you hear it, and that's it!" He went home to get sheet music and I played everything that he brought, Mozart, everything, I played it. So from that day on he brought sheet music every day to find out if there was something I couldn't read. I had to play everything by sight. He couldn't find anything that I couldn't read.

Within a year he was composing songs. Soon he began writing poetry as well.

Every week his great-aunt took him on the streetcar to one of the black theaters to see a stage show. He saw Ethel Waters, Ida Cox, and Clara Smith, bandleaders like Duke Ellington, Fletcher Henderson, Fats Waller, and Bennie Moten, vaudevillians such as Butterbeans and Susie. Once, on his way to Bessemer with his great-aunt, he saw Bessie Smith, her long boa streaming behind her, leaving a nearby boardinghouse popular with touring performers.

Herman began to practice with other children who played musical instruments, especially Avery Parrish, a boy at his school who would later become the pianist and arranger for the Erskine Hawkins Band. It was Parrish who first gave him a book on chords and helped him expand his piano skills. They talked every afternoon about careers in music, but Herman resisted the idea: "I had read about poets and writers and wise men all having a difficult time as human beings, so I didn't intend to get into that.... I never wanted to be a musician because I heard that musicians died young."

∎ ∎ ∎

Like most Southern black cities in the 1930s Birmingham was flush with music, in the streets, the clubs, the churches. On a walk downtown you could see blues singers such as Daddy Stovepipe, who had drifted in from Mobile and played in opera hat and tails; or Jaybird Coleman, who answered his own field-holler blues cries with yelps on his mouth-harp; or you could drop by a picnic and find the Birmingham Jug Band huffing and buzzing. At a tent show or vaudeville there might be boogie pianists like Cow Cow Davenport, who found his way to Birmingham after being expelled from the Alabama Theological Seminary; at a house party you might spot Robert "Cyclone" McCoy, who had migrated from Aliceville and was an accompanist often favored by strippers; and if you were lucky you might run into Lucille Bogan, conceivably the nastiest of all the blues singers, accompanied by pianist Walter Roland, whose right hand tapped out powerful but fastidious rhythms against her bawdy laughs and cries.

Every church had a choir, and sometimes several to a congregation, but it was the gospel quartets which were the jewels of black Birmingham's religious music. Baptists especially encouraged these a cappella quartets, providing them with "trainers" who operated like medieval traveling scholars, arranging and teaching parts to one group of singers, then moving on to another. Every Sunday the radios of Birmingham were saturated with quartets, their double-lead singers dramatically entwined together, challenging one another like jazz soloists; their bass singers whomping out wordless sounds; all of them together singing sharply accentuated, percussive melody lines. Before its efflorescence waned in the 1950s, the Birmingham quartet style had spread out to the countryside, to New Orleans and then on to pop culture.

For sophisticated nightlife, the big dance bands were the choice. Outside the reach of whites, a rich network of black nightclubs, theaters, and social clubs formed an alternative world of entertainment. There were nightclubs like the Owls in Woodlawn, called the "little Masonic," since the elaborate events it staged rivaled those of the Colored Masonic Temple; Bob Savoy's, the only club which stayed open twenty-four hours a day, every day, and was a favorite after-hours hangout for musicians; the Rex Club on the other side of Shades Mountain; the Grand Terrace in Pratt City, named after the fabled Chicago ballroom; or the

Thornton Building at Tuxedo Junction, a streetcar crossing in Ensley immortalized in a hit swing tune by the Erskine Hawkins Band. Black theaters like the Frolic, the Famous, the Carver, or the Dixie regularly presented nationally known singers, comedians, and bands as part of vaudeville shows or as acts between sepia films.

Then there were the parties, holiday festivities, coming-out balls for teenage girls, picnics, and weekly dances put on by every type of social club—protective societies, card-playing clubs, savings societies, arts and literary clubs. And no admission was required of those with an invitation. For women there were clubs like the Sojourner Truth Club, The Progressive Culture Club, and the Alpha Art Circle, and sororities like The Courts of Calanthe or Eastern Star. For men there were protective societies like the Elks, the Knights of Pythias, and the Masons. All were sources of pride in the community. The Masonic Temple, for example, was a monument to black achievement: designed and built by African Americans, it was seven stories tall, and housed many of Birmingham's black leaders in business, medicine, and law, but also contained the largest dance hall in the city. These societies had select memberships, but nonetheless reached across social class and religious lines and laid the basis for the unity of black Birmingham, a unity that would later give birth to the civil rights movement of the 1960s.

The protective societies gave annual balls which were elaborate affairs, displays of elegance and dignity, where foundry workers could move in the same circles as the small number of lawyers and doctors (especially as some foundry workers at times made more money than the professionals). Manual laborers by day could assume positions of great respect at night. As with the Krewes of New Orleans before Mardi Gras, these balls were worked on for months ahead, and professional costume and set designers, lighting specialists, and choreographers developed within the black community to meet the demand for these spectacles. Each ball was thematically keyed to a current hit song, and the "Club Special"—the dramatic introduction of the members—was the highlight of the evening. In the 1920s, for example, the elite Shadows Club introduced its members from behind a lit screen, throwing shadows of themselves in advance of each person's entry to the music of "Me and My Shadow," a 1925 pop hit by Ted Lewis. The effect was stunning (though some of the more progressive in the community grumbled that it was in questionable taste, since Lewis, a white man, sang and danced this song with Eddie Chester, a black man, shadowing his every movement). The Knights of Pythias once introduced their members to the music of "Stairway to the Stars," each of them descending from the ceiling, stars sprinkled through their hair.

These club dances were far more influential as entertainment in Birmingham than the nightclubs. "I played for social clubs," Herman recalled:

> Black [people], who had their social clubs, and they'd be together, and they'd rent a place, and every week you'd have a social event with the tuxes and the eating and the drinking. It was another kind of society. It was in the white world, but it was some people who were together and they were very beautiful. But when I came to other cities, they didn't have what Birmingham had. They had taverns and all that—nightclubs—and I wasn't used to that.

The black orchestras were themselves showcases of splendor and of gentility, and to the degree that some were often as much in demand by whites at wealthy hotel and country-club gatherings as they were among blacks at the black clubs, they had an aura of acclaim that gave them some protection from the disrespect of everyday life. On stage the musicians were rakishly attired in freshly pressed suits, starched shirts, and patent-leather shoes. Drummers sat amidst gleaming foliage of cymbals and gongs, the heads of their bass drums painted with tropical scenes which were lit softly from behind. Spotlights bounced off gleaming brass through the smoky haze in a phantasmagoria which transvalued the nights of those who spent the days serving the blast furnaces of North Birmingham and Bessemer. The music could be a solid wall of sound, every voice as one; or a single section—of trombones or trumpets or saxophones—could suddenly go into sovereign motion, their instruments lifted and swaying, choreographed against other sections, their physical movement miming the call-and-response of the music. Soloists rose from behind the anonymity of music stands to step up to the microphone with personal style, and whole theories about the nature of black masculinity were refuted in a single chorus of the blues. Behind the soloists there were testifying instrumental riffs and verbal cheers of praise and support. Bands were models of how it was possible to be an individual in the midst of a demand for absolute group discipline and unity, utopian images of racial collectivity. It was a life of elegance, of pride in craft, a life that mocked the social limitations placed upon them.

Away from the stage, life in the bands was not always so glorious. Dance bands were often loosely strung together bodies of men, many of whom shared little more than music, and on long trips on the road the personal habits of individual players, their differences in age, education, and class, sometimes added up to a chaotic existence. Younger members were often exposed to the most dangerous and destructive elements of life and to cruel pranks. The organization of bands was paternalistic, modeled on the family, some leaders often demanding absolute loyalty and single-minded obedience while giving back little. Once on the road a musician could have his pay cut, or be dropped without notice, with no means of getting back home and without even a change of clothing. If it was an occupation to which many aspired as an escape from an existence which they felt to be a kind of slavery, life in the bands was nonetheless a form of feudalism.

Teenagers were discouraged from attending dances at clubs, but like other young musicians, Herman found ways to slip from the house at night and stand outside of clubs listening, where he heard all of the bands from the Southeast—so-called territory bands—that came through Birmingham as part of their touring loop: C. S. Belton, from Florida, the Duke Ellington of the South; Doc Wheeler's Royal Sunset Serenaders, the band who sang the melody of "Marie" in unison long before Tommy Dorsey turned the idea into a hit; and the Carolina Cotton Pickers (originally Band No. 5 of the Jenkins Orphanage fundraising enterprise), a band so poor that they wore coveralls when they traveled on their aged bus, but who soon were so successful that they took off on their own and became renegades, only returning to the school several years later. "When I heard Charlie Parker it struck me because he sounded like the alto player from the Carolina Cotton Pickers, Lew

Williams.... The world let down a lot of good musicians. But I saw and heard them all."

> I never missed a band, whether a known or unknown unit. I loved music beyond the state of liking it. Some of the bands I heard never got popular and never made hit records, but they were truly natural black beauty. I want to thank them, and I will give honor to all the sincere musicians who ever were or ever will be. It's wonderful to even think about such people. The music they played was a natural happiness of love, so rare I cannot explain it. It was fresh and courageous; daring, sincere, unfettered. It was unmanufactured avant-garde, and still is, because there was no place for it in the world; so the world neglected something of value and did not understand. And all along I could not understand why the world could not understand.

> What happened is that, in the Deep South, the black people were very oppressed and were made to feel like they weren't anything, so the only thing they had was big bands. Unity showed that the black man could join together and dress nicely, do something nice, and that was all they had.... So it was important for us to hear big bands. That's why big bands are important to me. We had trios and stuff like that, but the big band was something else.

"My grandmother called this music 'reels.' But she was right. It was real music."

'FESS

This was the Alabama of Booker T. Washington, who advocated vocational training as a means of survival within a segregated society. But music was not one of the studies that Washington promoted from Tuskegee: like all cultural activities, it was too impractical, too emotional, perhaps too stereotypical. Only by the methods provided by the sciences and mathematics could the race gain the machinelike precision and discipline necessary for its development and for its opposition to the irrationality of racism: anything else was a distraction. So it was that in Birmingham's first schools for African-American children, music was a functional and social activity, but not a subject for instruction. Yet with-out teachers, even without a source of instruments, a guild system de-veloped in black Birmingham, with older musicians tutoring the young. Most children who played in school bands had mastered the basics of in-struments before they reached school. Volunteer school-band directors squeezed rehearsal time in where they could, and they organized pro-fessional groups which used students when they played at nights.

Some of these teachers became legendary for their accomplishments. Sam Foster, for instance, the first school-band director in Birmingham, worked at Tuggle Institute, a school funded and run by Birmingham's fra-ternal organizations and their women's auxiliaries, providing housing and education for homeless black boys. Tuggle, like other such schools—the Jenkins Home for Boys in Charleston and The Waifs' Home in New Orleans—became a crucial source of professional musicians from the South.

In the public schools the first music teacher was John T. "Fess" What-ley, Foster's student, who had replaced Foster at Tuggle, and had been so successful there that he had taken his grade-school orchestra on tour. Later Whatley was hired to teach printing at Industrial High School, but in his spare time he also organized a marching band and a concert band. By his second year he added a dance band. In 1922, his fifth year at In-dustrial, Whatley had developed a group of current and former students who were musically strong enough to form the Jazz Demons, still re-membered as Birmingham's first real jazz band.

Whatley was tough and autocratic, rigid and demanding, sarcastic and occasionally abusive. He is remembered for his fanatical insistence on punctuality, abstinence, neatness, and mastery of fundamentals. Perfec-tion was his goal, and he enforced standards by threat, ridicule, praise, and example. From his printing shop downstairs he could hear students rehearsing in the bandroom during lunchtime, and one wrong note would send him racing up the stairs and straight to the culprit. If stu-dents played in his band they were expected to play perfectly and to be attentive to his lectures in class, even if they had been out until three o'clock the night before. Those who failed at either were disciplined both at the school and on the job. His students recall the extremes to which he would pursue a student's failures, and for the colorful language with which he drove home his points: "If I had an appointment with the devil, I'd be there fifteen minutes early and ask him where the hell he had been." His sense of discipline extended even to seating in the cars in which the band traveled; he assigned certain seats to those being punished.

He was completely committed to his work, and spent all of his days and free evenings in the school. In his own way he was a race man, and urged all black musicians—especially his students—to join the Union. There were not many full-time musicians in Birmingham, and white musicians regularly came to hear the better black musicians perform (though the reverse wasn't possible); so Whatley saw the Union as a means of protecting the music as well as the musicians. The Musicians Union was segregated, but within a segregated society this sometimes worked to their advantage.

Whatley's reputation as a music educator spread nationally, and bandleaders such as Lionel Hampton, Louis Armstrong, and Duke Ellington called on him for musicians. His influence was especially strong in the black state universities, Alabama State Teachers College and Alabama A & M, where his recommendation was enough for his students to get scholarships. Black-college dance bands were usually a means of fundraising for the schools, and some of them were so successful and traveled so often that the students seldom attended classes. In Alabama the most famous was the 'Bama State Collegians, which at one point turned into the Erskine Hawkins Band, a group especially popular among black dancers in the 1930s and 1940s. The Hawkins band at some points was huge for bands at the time, with as many as ten brass and six saxophones, and it set the standard for bands from Alabama, appealing to dancers' tastes with well-rehearsed and crisply played instrumental compositions such as Avery Parrish's "After Hours," a song so popular that it was once semiseriously suggested as a replacement for "Raise Every Voice and Sing" as the Negro National Anthem.

In 1929, Herman entered Industrial High School, the only black secondary school in Birmingham, and the largest in the United States. He moved quickly ahead of others in his class, earning top grades in everything (everything but Business, in which he received a "Satisfactory"), his record sprinkled with comments of "brilliant" and "apt," a term which has over the years lost most of its force, but once was reserved for the very best. Most of his classmates knew him only as existing quietly on the margins. Once, however, on March 13, 1931, he surfaced briefly as a reporter on the front page of *The Industrial High School Record*, the student newspaper. In an article titled "The Value of an Ideal Theme in Capt. Max Wardell's Talk," Herman exuberantly summarized a talk given at a student assembly the month before. Wardell's message was motivational, and dwelled on the importance of character and the need for setting high ideals. Herman was deeply impressed by the stories Wardell told in service to his themes, and he recounted them enthusiastically:

A man was going across a river once on a ferry. He asked the ferryman, "Do you know any Biology?"

"No," said the ferryman.

"Then," said the man, "you have missed one-fourth of your life." Pausing, he asked, "Do you know anything about Astronomy?"

"No," said the ferryman.

"Then you have missed one-half your life."

Then, again he asked a question: "Do you know anything about Mathematics?"

"No," said the ferryman.

"Then, you have missed three-fourths of your life."

Suddenly, the boat turned over. "Do you know anything about swimming?" shouted the ferryman.

"No," said the man.

"Then," retorted the ferryman, "you have missed all your life."

Another of Wardell's stories concerned a king in ancient times:

Once a king, becoming disgusted with his wise men, asked an artist to paint him a picture of a perfect man. The artist did what he requested and presently brought the picture to the king. The king took the picture and hung it in his room where he looked at it every day.

One day he noticed something curious about the picture, something familiar. Then, concentrating deeply, he discovered the brow was that of one of his wise men, the eyes that of a child, the mouth that of his wife. Thus, we reached the conclusion: no one is perfect, all of us together would make a perfect mortal.

A third story led Herman to understand that whatever you think about, you become: "Turn our nature into radiance and beauty, for as a man thinketh in his heart so is he." The speaker then concluded with his personal creed, "to be ever mindful of my duty to my God; to listen to his voice and hear no other call and rise each day with a wise sense of life and love." Herman ended the article by saying, "I went into the auditorium almost indifferent because I had never heard him lecture. I came out different—or shall I say 'glorified.' "

There was material here that would recur again and again later in Herman's life: the nature of true knowledge, the possibility of perfection among humans, the power of the spirit, the proper relationship to God—but, characteristically, it would recur with perversely different conclusions.

It was his constant and serious reading by which he was known in school, and by which he is remembered by surviving classmates. They speak of it in almost legendary proportions: he read while waiting in line, on the streetcars, before rehearsals, during meals. And as soon as he'd finished a book he'd ask others questions based on it; and when they didn't know the answer he'd tell them what he'd just read. There is genuine admiration in these memories, for serious reading could be a feat for a black person in Birmingham: during the Depression books were beyond most people's means; libraries were segregated, and to use the Birmingham Public Library meant going to the back door, ringing a bell, and counting on black aides to slip books out the door. Yet he read copiously: novels, poetry, science fiction, world history, and religious tracts; magazines of popular science and comic books; travel and art books. He plumbed the science and technology section of the public library (which in those days was also deep with books on psychic phenomena and the occult), and at the colored Masonic library he found the literature of Negro achievement and the mystical and biblical bases of Freemasonry.

Since he was a pianist who could read music at sight, Herman was immediately added to the school orchestra, which played a repertory of classical and salon favorites for marching in and out of assemblies. Every day after school he rehearsed with them in the bandroom, quitting just in time to get home before dark.

White musicians had not yet replaced black musicians in playing for polite white society, so by the 1930s Whatley also had several bands outside of school, each of which was especially active in the summer when students were free to travel. The cream of the three was the Sax-o-Society Orchestra (later renamed the Vibra-Cathedral Orchestra) which played mostly for country-club and other white social-club affairs, dressed smartly, and traveled in Cadillac limousines. It was this group in which Herman first worked as a professional musician during his senior year, filling in for the regular pianist, Curley Parrish, the brother of Avery. Most pianists in the Birmingham dance bands were women, but the three who played for Whatley at this time, the Parrish brothers and Herman Blount, were the exceptions. Though he often resented Whatley's insistence that there was only one way to do things, Herman took pride in being the only student member of this band.

Most of the bands which developed in Birmingham in the 1930s—such as The Black & Tan Syncopators, The Fred Averett Band, and The Magic City Serenaders—were made up of Whatley students, many of whom by then were teachers of music themselves in other Birmingham schools; some, like the Society Troubadours, organized in the late 1920s, were even financed by Whatley himself. In the summer of 1932 Herman went on the road with the Troubadours. In their little Eton jackets ("waiters' jackets," he called them), with just enough money to pay for lodging and food, they toured throughout the Carolinas, Virginia, Wisconsin, and Illinois. When they triumphantly reached Chicago for the first time, the bus broke down, and many people came up and asked about relatives in Alabama when they saw the banner on the side of the bus.

It was on this tour that Herman began to keep a diary of his experiences, and some remember him as writing down his thoughts on segregation and the indignities he suffered. Only on rare occasions did he tell the other musicians his feelings about these incidents, but trumpeter Walter Miller recalled that he was particularly disturbed by an encounter with a policeman as he was coming home late one night. The officer blocked his path, and whichever way that Herman tried to pass, he stepped in front of him. Herman finally implored him, "Officer, why are you doing this to me? What have I done to you?" His notebook was his means of recording and totaling up these injustices.

J. L. Lowe, a debonair and distinguished saxophonist, recalls that book:

> I remember we played in Anniston at one of the hotels. He carried this notebook. I presumed he was writing down things he felt were wrong... things he was opposed to. He was not a talkative person by any means. One of the things would be that you had to enter buildings by different places from white folks. You couldn't enter the front door. We would enter from an alley where the freight elevator would be. I could tell from the expression on his face that he was concerned and objected to it. None of us liked it, but we had a job to perform. We knew in Birmingham there might be ten elevators, but one was always for "colored." We were not bitter and didn't carry a chip on our shoulder. But it didn't sit well with him.

Black musicians in the South had always been given a few liberties which allowed them access to areas of white privilege, but their presence at white social events invariably exposed them to indignities and even danger. Once when Herman played a dance in the elite Five Points section of Birmingham, a scuffle broke out when a policeman objected to some of the white guests socializing with the musicians. On another occasion he filled in as a pianist with a white orchestra which was playing for a ballet company in Scottsboro, Alabama, in 1933, just as the second "Scottsboro Boys" trial was underway. "The South had put a beating on him, and he hated it," said Birmingham trumpet player Walter Miller.

In January of 1932, in the depths of the Depression, Herman graduated from high school in a class of 300. He had been discussed as possible valedictorian, but he had no interest in it because he said he wanted nothing to do with leadership. He had requested that his transcript be sent to Miles College in nearby Fairfield, but with no tuition and without a regular job, he never applied, and instead continued to practice for three to four hours a day with some of the musicians he had played with in high school. He spent the rest of each day arranging music and reading. Gigs were hard to come by, and crowds were small, but they put together a band which had a steady spot at the Masonic Temple every Monday night and kept them afloat by earning three to five dollars a night.

Over the next year and a half they began to have some success. Under the name of The Nighthawks of Harmony, they played on radio station WAPI a few times, worked fraternal clubs like the Owls and the Elks Rest, and nightclubs such as the Grand Terrace and Bob Savoy's. They even played a concert for one of the Baptist churches. Meanwhile Herman continued to work as a sideman in other bands such as Paul Bascomb's and the tap dancer Prince Wallace's. For a while he was hired as an accompanist for J. William Blevins, a well-known gospel soloist and the first black singer on radio in Birmingham, for seventy-five cents a service.

Bill Martin, a local trumpet player who played with Count Basie, encouraged Herman to try arranging by first transcribing a record onto paper. Herman protested that he knew nothing about it, not even transposing, or the range of instruments. But Martin explained the different keys of the instruments to him and how to transpose them, and Herman copied the whole arrangement of Fletcher Henderson's "Yeah Man!" from the record. Some say he was the first musician in Birmingham to try this. Just as he had quickly learned to play the piano and to read music, he felt that he was to be a natural arranger.

Many days he stopped by Avery Parrish's house to play four-handed duets. When Parrish dared Herman to try and write something, Herman not only composed several pieces, he promptly mailed them off to Clarence Williams's music publishing company in New York. Years later he claimed that he was never paid for these pieces, but that in 1933 Williams had nonetheless recorded one of them with his own band for Vocalion Records—"Chocolate Avenue," a thirty-two-bar pop song phrased behind the beat and played at a walking tempo.

In 1934 Ethel Harper, a favorite English teacher at Industrial High, decided to give up her job and organize a band. An elegant, refined, well-dressed woman in her thirties, she was an actress and a singer with a pop and light classical repertoire. She approached Herman about writing arrangements for her and helping with the band, and after a few rehearsals they became the Ethel Harper Band. She bought them uniforms and got them booked into showcases such as the Masonic Temple, and then took them on the road to the Carolinas and Virginia. The idea of a woman leading a group of men created a buzz, but her voice was ill-suited to arrangements which were keyed to scat singing and jazz phrasing. So when summer came she gave up the idea and left for New York City where her sister ran a nightclub, and where she joined the Ginger Snaps, a vocal group that went on to some modest success.

In the fall of 1934 'Fess Whatley decided to test this same group of musicians, using his name on the band, to see how well they would do out of town. Riding in a limousine and wearing uniforms paid for by Whatley, they toured the same route that Whatley's own band had played the summer before. Iva Williams, a bass player who was somewhat older than the others, was put in charge of finances. Herman reluctantly agreed to be the acting leader of the group. Traveling with a tap dancer and a male singer, they went as far south as Florida, and then north to Columbus, Ohio, Indianapolis, and on to Chicago. When they were required to join the Chicago Musicians Union in order to play the Savoy Ballroom, the band suggested that Herman declare himself as the leader. Reluctantly he agreed, but saw this as an opportunity to bury "Blount" behind a stage name, and decided to place himself within the royal lineage of jazz Dukes, Counts, Princes, Earls, and Kings, and call himself "Baron Lee." But he heard that another bandleader had the same name; worse, there were Barons all across the music world, including Lee Baron, Blue Baron, and the Melody Barons of Tuskegee. "Sonny Lee" might have worked, because the musicians had taken to calling him "Sonny," but then he thought of General Robert E. Lee, a white southern hero, as well as a loser. "Lee Son" was considered for a minute, then rejected as too passive. Finally he dropped the idea and resigned himself to the name of "Blount," but treated it as if it was a stage name, blaming it on the band, saying, "I said don't use my name, I don't want a band... So they took the name of Sonny Blount. This was not my name, but the name of my half-brother and half-sister. They knew my brother and he was good at making candy. He was very popular, so they took his name." In an age in which bandleaders were the local equivalent of movie stars, Sonny literally stayed out of the spotlight, concentrating on the piano as if he were a sideman. He was keeping what he called a "low profile," but what others laughingly called "no profile."

After leaving Chicago they went on to Wisconsin and back south to the Cotton Club in Kentucky, and then to New Orleans and Big Stone Gap, between Virginia and Tennessee. One of their biggest engagements was at the Coconut Grove in Cincinnati, where the booker arranged to have Ernie Morrison, Sunshine Sammy of *Our Gang* fame, billed to dance, sing, and front the band as if it were his own. But the turnout was small, and their stay in Cincinnati was cut short. Even though they were more often than not sleeping in their limousine, they made only enough to cover expenses, and returned home with no money left.

HUNTSVILLE

Sonny continued to think about going to college. There was some prospect of a scholarship at Florida A & M, one of the great southern schools for music. Some of the members of his band wanted to go as a group to Bishop College in Dallas, and the mother of band member William Reed made some efforts to get them scholarships, but they lacked money even to get there. Sonny then requested his transcript be sent to Alabama State Agricultural & Mechanical Institute for Negroes. Drummer Melvin Caswell (who was already in his second year at A & M) recalled that a neighbor, Dr. Sam F. Harris, heard them rehearse, and was so impressed that he convinced the dean at A & M that they should have a dance band, and so the dean gave ten members of the Birmingham group scholarships. In exchange for playing for school events they were given tuition of thirty dollars a year, three dollars a month to cover music lessons, and room and board of seventeen dollars for the year.

But Sonny remembered all of this differently. For him, college was a way of escaping the band. But the band followed anyway, and when he got off the train at Huntsville and discovered them there, he complained to the dean of the college. To his dismay, the dean gave them all scholarships, uniforms, and a bus, and made them an official band of the college. "So there they were up there with me. I couldn't get rid of them. It seems like fate just stepped in or something. I was trying to avoid it, but there I was in music again." Whatever happened, at the end of the first term there were only three other band members listed as part of the freshman class of 1935–36, trumpeter Charles McClure, saxophonist John Reed, and Iva Williams.

A & M was a two-year college, geared to vocational training, with a 250-acre farm, and its own elementary and high schools, and with an enrollment of 224 students and a faculty of twenty-five. Sonny enrolled in the teachers' training course since it was a way "you could major in everything... most of the fellows in the band were majoring in liberal arts. But I took teachers' training because I made good marks all through school. I could cover the range of everything with teachers' training. You could teach anywhere from the first grade on up. You had to be good at outlining, which I was good at. So I can teach people. I don't care how difficult others feel it is, I can teach people things because I got the training for it."

On the first day he registered as Herman S. Blount and was assigned to live in a room with nine other students in Langston Hall, a temporary dormitory which also housed the kitchen and the dining room. Sonny was displeased by this arrangement—there was no room for practice, no privacy for dressing or sleeping, no quiet place for study. So, much of that year he spent in the library or the rehearsal rooms.

He signed up for courses in English composition, social science, biology, drawing and art, music appreciation, music notation, and music history ("I think I studied everything at that school except farming"). At the end of the first term he made the honor roll with a 3.14 average, and was eighth in the freshman class.

Sonny also began his first formal study of piano with Professor Lula Hopkins Randall, a pianist who had studied at Chicago Musical College, and who was also responsible for teaching voice, directing the chorus, and teaching all of the music and music education courses. In his private lessons with her he worked on compositions by Bach, Haydn, Mozart, Beethoven, Mendelssohn, Schumann, Chopin, and Samuel Coleridge-Taylor. One day when she arrived to begin the lesson, Professor Randall was impressed to see Sonny transcribing music from a record. She asked him if he would assist her in her theory course ("She was so nice, people would be talking during her class. When she put me up there, they wouldn't talk, they'd be listening"). Though the curriculum stressed European classical music, it also exposed students to contemporary African-American composers like Nathaniel Dett and Will Marion Cook. And in spite of the classical course of study and Sonny's lack of formal training, Randall encouraged Sonny to go beyond the curriculum, to find his own way, to discover what was unique in himself, cultivate it, and let it emerge in his performances. In her music appreciation class "I studied Chopin, Rachmaninoff, Scriabin, Schoenberg, Shostakovich...."

THE CALL

The school work, as always, came easy to him, but throughout that year Sonny was wrestling with questions that had stayed with him since childhood: who he was, his place in the world, his relationship with God. "The next thing, I decided since I was making such good marks, there wasn't no need being an intellectual if I couldn't do something that hadn't been done before, so I decided I would tackle the most difficult problem on the planet. I could see how I was progressing on the mental plane, on the intellectual plane, but the most difficult task would be finding out the real meaning of the Bible, which defied all kinds of intellectuals and religions. The meaning of the book that's been translated into all languages. They could never find the meaning and that's what I wanted to do."

He withdrew into himself more than ever, and began to spend more time in the library, poring over commentaries and concordances to the Bible, atlases of the Holy Land, biographies of great preachers. He flirted with joining a church, perhaps the Seventh-Day Adventists, since he was attracted to their prophetic and utopian tradition, their drive for physical health, the importance of angelic guidance, and the role of Satan in human life in their doctrines.

Then I decided to try and reach God to find out why you have to have funerals in church. What they were teaching in churches—was it true?

What did he want? Because I met some good people on this planet, unselfish, and they still died. So I wanted to know what he wanted. I asked him that as a child. He told me he wanted to find one pure-hearted person on this planet. Just one. Someone with no ulterior motives, just simple, natural, pure of heart. I had this all written down. I used to keep a diary.

One day in the spring Sonny returned from class and found his roommates huddled over his bed, reading his diary and laughing:

They were having a good time. So then I abolished the diary. But I still retain the memory, and in there I said that these space men contacted me. They wanted me to go to outer space with them. They were looking for somebody who had that type of mind. They said it was quite dangerous because you had to have perfect discipline.... I'd have to go up with no part of my body touching outside of the beam, because if I did, going through different time zones, I wouldn't be able to get that far back. So that's what I did. And it's like, well, it looked like a giant spotlight shining down on me, and I call it transmolecularization, my whole body was changed into something else. I could see through myself. And I went up. Now, I call that an energy transformation because I wasn't in human form. I thought I was there, but I could see through myself.

Then I landed on a planet that I identified as Saturn. First thing I saw was something like a rail, a long rail of a railroad track coming out of the sky, and landed over there in a vacant lot.... Then I found myself in a huge stadium, and I was sitting up in the last row, in the dark. I knew I was alone. They were down there, on the stage, something like a big boxing ring. So then they called my name, and I didn't move. They called my name again, and I still didn't answer. Then all at once they teleported me, and I was down there on that stage with them. They wanted to talk with me. They had one little antenna on each ear. A little antenna over each eye. They talked to me. They told me to stop [teachers training] because there was going to be great trouble in schools. There was going to be trouble in every part of life. That's why they wanted to talk to me about it. "Don't have anything to do with it. Don't continue." They would teach me some things that when it looked like the world was going into complete chaos, when there was no hope for nothing, then I could speak, but not until then. I would speak, and the world would listen. That's what they told me.

Next thing, I found myself back on planet Earth in a room with them, and it was the back room of an apartment, and there was a courtyard. They was all with me. At that time, I wasn't wearing robes. I had on one of theirs, they put on me. They said, "Go out there and speak to them." And I looked out through the curtain and people were milling around in the courtyard. And I said, "No, they look like they're angry. I'm not going out there." So they pushed me through the curtain, and I found myself on a balcony, people milling around in the courtyard. They said, "They aren't angry, they're bewildered."

All of a sudden, the people were turning around, looking up to me on the balcony. (I was living in Chicago at that time.) I saw that I was laying down on a park bench, a stone park bench, in some park, near a river. There was a bridge. I knew it was New York City. I had done very well in Chicago and I thought that was one thing that could not happen. I looked and saw the sky was purple and dark red, and through that I could see the spaceships, thousands of them. And I sat up to look, then I heard a voice [say] "You can order us to land. Are conditions right for landing?" I think I said yes. They started to land, and there were people running to come to the landing, and they shot something like bullets. But they weren't bullets. They were something that when they hit the ground they were like chewing gum. It stuck people to the ground.

I came out of that. But [later] when I got to New York City, I was up near Columbia University. I saw the bench, I saw the bridge, so those things have been indelibly printed on my brain. I couldn't get them out if I tried.

He told this story many times, unembarrassed, ingenuously, and with remarkable consistency of detail. In another age it might be called a visionary tale, a story in which unacceptable ideas are placed within the framework of a benign account of an encounter with an angel or some otherwordly beings. But now we see it as a classic UFO-abduction story, from the beam of light which transported him, to the warnings of the moral chaos which lies ahead, to the power and wisdom offered him, to the curtain or veil through which he passes. Yet in other respects it seems oddly divergent—the robes, the calling of his name, the aliens as guides rather than abductors, the railroad track in the sky—and given its date, anachronistic as well. It might be Velikovsky revised by von Daniken—*Worlds in Collision* reimagined through *Chariots of the Gods?* And if this experience took place in 1936, it came far before the date of what some say was the first alien contact, that of George Adamski in California in 1952—the year in which Air Force investigators recorded the largest number of UFO sightings. Sonny's account seems all the more enigmatic since the location of the contact shifts from Huntsville to Chicago, where he didn't live until 1946; and those who knew him best in those years say that he never mentioned it before 1953.

In one retelling of this encounter, years later for the MTV cameras, Sonny softly added his own brief interpretive comment at the end (then, characteristically, quickly changed the subject): he said that the people who were milling about in the courtyard were the gentiles. The gentiles? The people outside the covenant? The people for whom Luke says Jesus will be a light for revelation, the people for whom Paul is the apostle? Now it seems less like a UFO story than it does a conversion experience and a call to preach in the Afro-Baptist tradition, where God calls the chosen by means of lightning bolts, shafts of sunlight, moving stars, and celestial music, where the elect are dressed in robes and lifted to heaven by railroads, ladders, and chariots. Alien abductions and conversion experiences both result in ontological shock, a revelation that there are forces at work larger and more direct than had been imagined, but UFO experiences leave the victim traumatized, full of fear and a sense of the cosmological emptiness through which we are all doomed to wander. Conversion, though, connects the chosen with the African-American sacred cosmos, and gives rebirth by awakening an inner self, the whole experience occurring within a tangible spiritual community. When conversion occurs combined with the call, it may be a command to preach in the licensed, orthodox, sense of the word, or to be a messenger, an exhorter, a role large enough to include a Nat Turner, a Father Divine, or an Elijah Muhammad—all of whom were at one time Baptists. Even if this story is revisionist autobiography—explaining his past in terms more appropriate to the present—turning his encounter with God into a trip into space with aliens, Sonny was pulling together and connecting several strains of his life. He was both prophesying his future and explaining his past with a single act of personal mythology. "This was in Huntsville, where the government developed the space-ships."

At the end of the school year Sonny went home to Birmingham, and when fall approached he traveled down to Montgomery with a vague idea of going to Alabama State Teachers College at Montgomery, and joining one of the 'Bama State Collegian bands with which so many other musicians from Industrial High School had played. He auditioned during registration (his sister recalled later that after the audition the professor told him that they had nothing to teach him there), and then went out on a trip with one of the dance bands and missed registration. He returned home and never went back to college, putting behind him the chance to assume a teaching position, one of the highest and most secure positions available to a black person in the South.

> In a sense I gave up my life. Most men give up their life and die. But any-body can do that. He ain't got nothin' to worry about. But if you give up your life and you're still livin' and you see the world passin' you by—all kinds of persons getting famous, making money, and you're told by the Creator, "Don't have nothin' to do with that. Stand your ground." You have all kinds of difficulties that other folks don't have. But that's a test.

He came back to Birmingham with a new vision of himself as a teacher more than a leader. Slowly he began to assemble a band for re-hearsal only, a band that would play for the sake of beauty and enlight-enment. He recruited musicians who he felt were spiritually compatible; and if some of them lacked the necessary musical skills he trained them himself.

Over the next few years Sonny was acknowledged to be the most seri-ous musician anyone in Birmingham had ever known. He did nothing but think and play music, day and night, sometimes all night. His great-aunt's house became a rehearsal hall, where furniture and Sonny's books and records were moved out of the way in the large downstairs room in which he lived. From the piano bench he instructed musicians on their parts, the individual style they were to play in, sprinkling his talk with anecdotes, maxims, and jokes on any subject. Saxophonist Frank Adams said, "Sonny's whole life was in that room, that room on the first floor of the house—his books, records, instruments. It was where he ate. It was his whole world." Local and out-of-town musicians dropped in at all hours, having heard that there was a kind of perpetual rehearsal going on there. Stories are still told of the characters who showed up, such as the midget saxophonist from the Carolina Cotton Pickers whose horn was held together with rubber bands, but who played so well that Sonny suggested that all the other saxophonists break their horns. His rehearsals became a stopover for musical drifters and hustlers who were seeking to make a reputation, his house a kind of pool hall for the metaphysically minded.

Most days he followed a familiar routine. Mornings he listened to records—Ellington, Art Tatum, Earl Hines, Fats Waller, Teddy Hill, Chick Webb, Lionel Hampton, Tiny Bradshaw, Louis Armstrong, Henry Red Allen, and Jay McShann, mostly—then he practiced a bit, and did some composition and arranging; afternoons he strolled the streets of Birmingham, looking in shop windows, visiting the library or the Modern Bookshop, a rendezvous for intellectuals run by the Communist Party, where he browsed through books about African Americans or examined their exhibition of paintings by black artists. Often he would end up five blocks away from home at Forbes's Piano Company, a store filled with instruments, records, sheet music, and band arrangements. Forbes had never practiced Jim Crow policies, and black musicians always entered by the front door—an indulgence whose importance is impossible to fully grasp today—and were treated with courtesy. Instruments and music were available on an easy-payment plan, and months could pass between payments without a word. Forbes was just as generous with his instruments, allowing musicians to try them out, even take them out of the store. In the phonograph record department new releases were played for black and white alike. It was a haven in a storm of exclusion.

Sonny sampled the pianos on every visit, sometimes playing for an hour at a time, gathering a small audience of clerks and customers who requested he play new pop tunes. He often studied sheet music and stock dance-band arrangements in the store, sometimes sitting for half a day, copying them into notebooks. He kept up with new developments in music technology, especially those involving electricity, and dreamed of the possibilities of composing for instruments with new musical timbres. Knowing this interest in new keyboard inventions, Forbes loaned Sonny a celeste—a keyboard whose hammers strike metal bars instead of strings, and produces a delicate ringing tone. And when the Hammond Solovox—a small add-on electric keyboard—first appeared in 1939, Sonny was among the first to buy it.

When the steel tape recorder became commercially available in 1937 Sonny bought one of the first models—the Brush Development Company's Soundmirror—and in spite of its short recording time, used it to record his own band at rehearsals and performances, as well as to record bands like Henderson's and Ellington's when they were in town. Sonny's speed at copying arrangements from these recordings amazed other musicians. Trumpeter Johnny Grimes once asked Sonny to help him create a book of arrangements; Sonny agreed, and they went to see Earl Hines's band at a concert, where he made wire recordings from in front of the band stage and then stayed up all night transcribing seven of them into arrangements. He then gave them to Grimes for nothing. Some said he could reconstruct an entire arrangement after hearing it played only once.

Of those who came by Sonny's house in the late 1930s, almost none remembers ever seeing his great-aunt there. And many never knew that he even had a sister. If he was asked about his parents, he had nothing to say. None of his friends had ever seen his mother, and didn't know whether she was alive or dead; and he never mentioned anyone else in his family. Yet he visited his relatives from time to time, especially his cousin Carrie Lear, who lived two blocks away, and his brother Robert's family. He played piano for family gatherings, good-naturedly putting up with their teasing about not drinking or smoking, or not having a girlfriend. "He wasn't one for talking," said his niece Marie Holston. "He'd come in, say a few words and go off and read a book or play the piano. He played the piano *all* the time."

In order to keep a band together, Sonny was forced to find regular jobs for them, playing the blues and the pop tunes of the day requested by dancers, original arrangements of standards like "After You've Gone" and "Embraceable You" and copies of hits like Erskine Hawkins's "Don't Cry Baby," Coleman Hawkins's "Body and Soul," and Benny Goodman's "Serenade in Blue," or merely simple riff tunes such as his cover of Charlie Barnet's "Ponce de Leon," with an arrangement done by Fletcher Henderson's brother, Horace. He also played a few pop songs of his own, such as "Alone with Just a Memory of You" (which he copyrighted in 1936 with Henry McCellons).

Swing music was by now easy for him, formulaic and predictable. But he had another book of arrangements which the band rehearsed but never performed and whose purpose he never explained. Was he writing for another kind of audience? Waiting for the right moment? The compositions and arrangements in this book were inspired by dreams or made up of ideas derived from reading *Popular Mechanics:* pieces like "Thermodynamics" and "Fission" were built on complex and oddly shifting rhythm patterns ("Sonny got rhythms going so you couldn't tell where the beat was," said trumpeter Walter Miller). They seemed to celebrate new technological systems, new ways of organizing energy. The arrangements in this book were all his own, except for a single one written by Don Michael, a one-armed pianist who played and recorded with Erskine Hawkins in the mid-1940s.

Once when Duke Ellington was in town, Sonny took his book of arrangements backstage to show him. They talked for over an hour, Ellington gracious and regal in his black silk dressing gown. At one point the Duke pulled out his own arrangements. He saw that Ellington also used dissonance in his writing, only it never seemed dissonant. Sonny was thrilled to see his own ideas confirmed.

His uniqueness was a source of pride, but at the cost of loneliness. He enjoyed the presence of people, but at a distance, on his own terms. Long walks through town, staring in store windows, walking through Pizitz Department Store, dropping in at dances and walking home alone late at night—these were his daily social rituals, the rituals open to a black man in the segregated South. But they were rituals of the *flaneur,* the watcher, not the participant. There was a fascination for him in the frivolity with which people squandered their lives, and in the evil of which they were capable.

He dreamed of owning a house big enough for all of his musicians to live in together, monastically, devoting themselves to the unified study of music, clean living, and spiritual matters. It was not to happen here, but he got as close as he could with what he had. His rehearsals became virtual lectures, illustrated and inspired by music, and often filled with rhetorical shock tactics to focus his musicians. One day at a rehearsal Sonny casually commented from his piano bench that he was neither black nor white. In a world defined by race, it was the most radical claim a person could make. Frank Adams remembers:

He wouldn't argue the point, just said he was describing the situation. It wasn't hype, because in those days he had no reason to do it for musical work. Sonny never sought publicity for his band: he just responded to bookings. And he was booked by a blind man named Barker.

No one said Sonny Blount was crazy: he was different, they said, and no had approached his degree of difference. Birmingham could tolerate a lot of strangeness. And even in slavery there were some blacks who defied all kinds of rules. And no one dared burn a cross to control them. And Sonny was no threat to anyone—especially other musicians—he never threatened to become "successful."

Sonny was a genius. He turned us on to Bird and Diz. But he was weird—and for a while, a vegetarian. None of us had seen anything like that before. There was nothing in which Sonny was average. One night the band was booked into a gig in Gadsden. We pulled a trailer loaded with instruments so as to get everyone there in one vehicle. But when we got ready to come back we had one extra person, so Sonny insisted on riding in the open trailer for the sixty miles back to Birmingham. When I looked back, there he was with the wind blowing him, reading a book.

"He didn't smoke, drink, or use drugs," Melvin Caswell remembered. "He became interested in health foods, and he ate a lot of grapefruit, vegetables, and the skins of fruit. He told the musicians that he was eating pills which were food. He would eat a pill and say it was a pork chop. They were really food supplements, like vitamins, but we had never heard of them then. He had read about them in books he borrowed from the Hillman Hospital library."

But for all of Sonny's talk of health, he was a puzzling exemplar. He had developed insomnia, and seemed to never sleep except for brief moments of napping, usually at the keyboard in the middle of rehearsal. Instead of a handicap, he saw it as a sign of potential greatness, and cited Napoleon and Thomas Edison as fellow nonsleepers. Sleep took too much energy, he said, it was a waste of creativity. His short moments of sleep—especially when others around him were awake—put special emphasis on the waking state, and deepened the mystery of sleep with a suggestion of death. "To be asleep" was a figure of speech by which he represented the state of somnambulism which plagued humanity, an unnatural state, an early death. For the rest of his life he was notorious among musicians for calling at all hours of night with new musical ideas or solutions to musical problems, and he sought musicians who could be free to rehearse and try out new compositions as fast as he wrote them, no matter the time.

Sonny's days blurred into nights, and he held to his regimen of reading, music, and strolling. He now referred to himself sometimes as a scholar, sometimes as an artist. He dressed casually, even shabbily, his only sense of vanity being the waves he put in his hair, a small ritual he did when he visited his brother Robert's family. His interest in the Bible had now become a passion, and he was making marginal notes and cross-referencing his reading with different versions of the Bible and other holy books. Occasionally he walked the streets in sheets and sandals. His research into music grew deeper, and his room was littered with classical sheet music and records, and a stack of books on the lives of composers stood in the corner.

THE WAR

Some older residents like to romance about life in Birmingham during the thin slice of time when the Depression eased and World War II began. When war was declared Birmingham's iron and steel plants rose out of a long stupor, and were reborn as defense plants, producing mortars, bombs, and shells, and work was plentiful and well paid. But life in Birmingham was never idyllic. It had a long, strange history of unresolved industrial strife and racial conflict ranging back to the days before there was a city, when the coal, iron ore, and limestone mining camps in the hills were staffed with prison laborers, relocated white farmers, and blacks only a generation out of bondage. When northern capital financed the building of railroads to haul the minerals, mills and foundries began to flourish in the late 1800s, and thousands of immigrant workers arrived from Europe and the North. It was this strange ferment which gave rise to the third largest city in the South.

It became an industrial city which never lost touch with its origins. Despite city planning, beautification campaigns, and a history of private patronage, it never settled comfortably into the gentility of an Atlanta or a New Orleans. And even after American deindustrialization set in and brought Birmingham to a halt in the 1960s, many families could still find the odd stick of dynamite or blasting cap around the house, reminders of the speed and fury with which Birmingham had been wrenched from the soil.

There had been efforts to organize labor along racial lines as early as 1870, and a long line of unions had used racial discrimination as a basis for their recruitment drives among blacks even before the Communist and Socialist parties began organizing. Labor organizing in Birmingham set at odds not only labor and management, but also groups as different as the Ku Klux Klan, the NAACP, the United Mine Workers, and the CIO, not to mention the police and the Democratic Party. But the interlock of churches and fraternal organizations in Birmingham reinforced union organizing and eased the transition away from the old-style organization of southern production. Birmingham's famed gospel quartets were typical of the new spirit: groups like the CIO Singers or the Bessemer Big Four (a group formed within the Steel Workers Organizing Committee out of the former West Highland Jubilee Singers) were using older religious songs as the basis for commentary about workers' solidarity.

As World War II began, defense plants fell under federal guidelines, and progressive groups saw new opportunities for social change. On top of this, the spirited messages of patriotism coming from Washington had the unintended effect of rekindling the struggle for civil rights and emboldening black workers.

Birmingham was overcrowded, jammed with newly arrived workers and with soldiers coming and going from nearby Fort McClellan in Annistan. Railroads, streetcars, and buses often became the locations of intense conflict long before Rosa Parks refused to accept the line drawn on segregated buses in Montgomery. African Americans in Birmingham were resisting segregated transportation by means of individual complaints, rock throwing, fistfights, and sometimes gunplay on the buses. Weekend travel to black social functions became moments for displays of racial unity. Stylish clothing, overcrowding, and even normal socializing began to annoy whites who felt their control over blacks eroding. Black soldiers saw their uniforms as the basis for making claims for justice and equality, but to some whites they marked black men for attack.

Sonny had very little interest in the politics which surrounded the labor movement—he was a member of the Musicians Union, and went to meetings, but usually sat through them quietly; he later said the Union had never treated his band fairly. The ideology which lay behind these movements and their cultural consequences did not escape him, however. In 1941 he was reading the Southern Negro Youth League magazine *Cavalcade: The March of Southern Youth,* where antiwar sentiments were expressed in blues form by poets like Waring Cuney or Eugene B. Williams, and where editorials drummed up support for anti–poll tax legislature and against police brutality. And as war was declared, Sonny noted the efforts of Louis Burnham, the Southern Negro Youth League's organizational secretary, to redirect interest in the war to a renewed battle for civil rights by drawing attention to the works of Gandhi and W.E.B. DuBois, and by proposing a new black political party under the slogan of "Non-Violence and Non-Cooperation."

Sonny immediately felt the effects of the war when musicians began to be drafted, and he found himself having to fill in with high school students that he had to train himself. A man who was relocating to Nebraska suggested to Sonny that he could get a choice job as an entertainer in a Martin Aircraft defense plant in Omaha, but he pre-

ferred to maintain his teaching and rehearsals. Though he saw the goings and comings from the railroad station every day, he went on as if
nothing would ever change, as if he would remain the center of a musical universe.

Then he received his induction notice—addressed to Herman P.
Blount (col.)—a letter that he kept as evidence of the continuing discrimination which lay behind the pieties of the war effort. He ignored it,
thinking that it somehow didn't apply to him. They wrote again. Meanwhile, he met members of the Fellowship of Reconciliation, the Protestant pacifist group founded when conscription first began in World War
I; and following their suggestion he requested a hearing with the draft
board. His family was bewildered and mortified; none of them could
comprehend his thinking. Neither they, nor none of the musicians, had
ever known a pacifist, and they asked him to explain himself. He would
only say, "I don't have the right to go and fight with those people." He
made no effort to convince others to follow him.

On the evening of October 10, he walked to the Brown-Marx Building at First Avenue and 20th Street and gave the board his reasoning:
they had made a mistake in listing him as twenty-five (he was twenty-
eight); his seventy-five-year-old great-aunt was dependent upon him; he
was in poor physical condition; and, in spite of not being a church member, as a Christian he opposed fighting and killing of any kind. Somehow,
against reason and all odds, they granted him a 4-E classification as a
conscientious objector opposed to both combatant and noncombatant
military service, and on October 14 a report was filed with Selective Service in Washington to determine where he would spend the duration of
the war. He had joined the ranks of a very small number of African-
American pacifists which included A. Philip Randolph, St. Clair Drake,
C.L.R. James, Bayard Rustin, Jean Toomer, and 200 members of the
Nation of Islam.

Sonny completed a questionnaire to the National Service Board for
Religious Objectors requesting to be placed in a Civilian Public Service
camp rather than in a prison. A system of CPS camps had been established by Selective Service as a means of offering alternative public service to conscientious objectors to keep them out of federal prisons. The
camps were administered by the three pacifist churches without any fi-

nancial support from the government, and though they did agricultural, medical, and other work of national interest, each CO was expected to be able to pay for his own keep or have his family pay for it. Sonny suggested on his questionnaire that he could support himself by selling arrangements and compositions. Under "skills" he listed writing poetry, composing, arranging, and playing the piano and the Hammond Solovox. Under "physical defects" he listed a hernia associated with problems of his left testicle, and indicated his plans for an operation. But even as he was formally requesting alternative service, he added several pages pleading for a temporary deferment in order to have the operation. He wrote in a clear and steady hand, confident that he would be understood by northern pacifists:

> At the present moment my whole left side from head to foot is burning and aching. I am subject to such attacks without warning. During the last ten years I have visited several doctors and even sought aid and advice at a local hospital which the records will show, but after x-rays and other examinations doctors were still puzzled as to why....
>
> Do you know how it feels to be numb from head to foot? Have you ever been awake all night in too much pain to lie down, too much pain to walk and as a result could only sit and wait until dawn? I know how it feels.
>
> I don't see how the government or anyone else could expect me to agree to being judged by the standards of a normal person.

He was speaking to another outsider, and his secret frailties and anxieties poured forth.

> I have never been able to think of sex as a part of my life though I have tried to but just wasn't interested. Music to me is the only worthwhile thing in the world, and I think of it as a full compensation for any handicaps I have. I am sure no one could begrudge me this one happiness. Of a truth it is all I have in the world, being motherless, fatherless, and friendless, too, for that matter. Unfortunately, I have learned not to trust people. I am a little afraid of normal people. Their greatest desire in life seems to be to maim and destroy either themselves or others. A mali-

cious pleasure. This war, for instance. Only yesterday, a woman in attempting to shoot her husband shot her three-year-old child through the heart and killed him....

My orchestra and the management of it, the arranging and composing, the rehearsing, the developing of potential talent, that is my work and the only earthly pleasure I love. To separate me from music would be more cruel than standing me by a wall and shooting me. I think I would prefer the latter. I hope you understand why I am so staunchly against being in any kind of camp where one must live according to certain rules and regulations and requirements. I myself am puzzled about my case. If it were possible to be in civilian life and be of help I would appreciate greatly this consideration.

It seems too much to ask for or hope for, however being a Christian, I have never hesitated to ask for the things which I felt were mine. I do not think I ask too much, being as I am through no fault of my own.

Although I do not know you, I feel more at home writing to you than I would anyone nearer to me in vicinity.

Near the end of November he was ordered to appear on December 8 at Civilian Public Service Camp No. 48 in Marienville, Pennsylvania, a camp run by the Church of the Brethren in the middle of a forest in the northwestern part of the state.

In the meantime, the National Service Board replied to him, suggesting that he appeal his case to the local draft board, and even cited him the section of the Selective Service Regulations which he might use on his behalf. Again, he appeared before the board. His appeal was rejected, and he wrote back to the National Service Board describing his experience:

The local board would not consider my case at all. One could expect that, they being prejudiced in the beginning. They went through the farce of having me before the appeal board which consisted entirely of white people, and after hearing part of my story, told me that they had no jurisdiction over the matter despite the fact I showed them your letter.

They would not even look up the Selective Service Regulations, Paragraph 652.11 which shows conclusively their malice before thought.

If they had been sincere they would have investigated same and at least discussed such with me.

I, feeling that I am not well and that any doctor will substantiate my claim, told them that I would probably not show up at the designated time, which of course was amusing to them. They spoke of jail which amused me. Gandhi, Stalin, Christ, and a lot of people who fought for right know of jail.

There can never be any fairness in dealing with Negroes unless one Negro is involved in the deciding. I must say that your board has been very fair. This one smacks of Hitlerism. Have you a suggestion?

Three days later he wrote them again:

Enclosed please find two letters or rather envelopes which speak for themselves [again addressed to Herman Poole Blount (col.)], if there was any doubt in my mind concerning the prejudice in my case and the unfairness of my board, who as I wrote you, refused to even look at the paragraph you told me to refer them to. Unfortunately, I am not living in a part of the U.S. but more a section which seems a member of the Axis and which is determined that no Negro will ever receive justice.

I had thought my case would be dealt with in understanding and sympathy; rather it has embittered me to such an extent that I am wondering whether a Negro has the right to be a Christian or whether it is even remotely possible that any white man can ever be expected to deal fairly with my race.

Heretofore I have avoided joining any organizations for any cause whatsoever. Now since circumstances force me to forsake what I at last realize to have been a selfish attitude, I shall in all probability be a Seventh-Day Adventist, which church has always had my admiration and contributions. If possible I would like for you to call me at my expense Wednesday or Thursday morning before twelve so that any suggestions you have to offer will receive my immediate attention.

On December 2, he received a sympathetic note from J. N. Weaver, head of the Camp Section of the National Service Board for Religious Objectors, telling him that he would be given another physical examination when he reached the camp, and that he would be discharged if he was not physically qualified. He concluded, "I suggest that you report to camp and we shall do everything in our power to see that you get justice."

On December 8 Sonny failed to appear at CPS Camp No. 48. A week later they came after him, and took him away to holding rooms set aside for malingerers and subversives at the old post office building not far from his house. His family, still humiliated and angry, refused to have anything to do with him. Only his brother Robert's wife and daughter came to visit him, where they found him spending his days writing letters to his bedridden great-aunt, the FBI, and President Roosevelt.

A hearing was scheduled after Christmas, and Sonny came prepared with Bible in hand. He argued his own case, citing chapter and verse, standing against war and killing in any form, still without declaring membership in a church or belief in any conventional religious doctrine.

It was a brave and audacious act. Black men in the South did not go to court readily, and certainly never to argue against the United States government. It was such a daring act that the judge found it interesting, even challenging in a perverse way. He countered Sonny's exegeses with his own, in southern Protestant fashion, and for a few minutes a strange intellectual encounter woke a sleepy court-room. The judge granted Sonny his knowledge of the Bible, but found his lack of church membership all the more puzzling. The outcome became clear within minutes, however, and so Sonny upped the ante, threatening that if he was forced to learn to kill, he would use that skill without prejudice, and kill one of his own captains or generals first. The judge now grew tired of the byplay. "I've never seen a nigger like you before." "No," Sonny said, "and you never will again." The judge ordered that he be held in Walker County Jail in Jasper, Alabama, until further disposition of his case.

On December 29 he was placed in a long cell filled with cots covered by gray blankets, not unlike his room at college. He requested an interview with the warden, then with an agent of the Federal Bureau of Investigation. On January 31, 1943, he typed a letter to the U.S. Marshall, now pleading to be released to the CPS camp:

> I write you this begging you not to think of me as just another legal case,
> but rather as a helpless victim of circumstance, for I am so unhappy and

bewildered that I am almost crazed. If there ever was a person who had reason to commit suicide, I feel that I am that person. A month ago I had my music and a good name. Things which I had to be true to, and never, regardless of temptation, commit any deed or discuss any personal feelings or desires which would harm these most important things in my life. If I could only talk to you and others face to face, I feel sure that you would understand a lot of things which I mistakenly felt you would know without my telling you.

He expressed his fears of institutional living, of being under the control of others, of life without art, of human cruelty, of imminent sexual assault, of his fear of being considered a freak among men:

This morning I took a razor and started to slash my wrists or mutilate the one testicle I have, but I thought of the wrong of murder in any form and hesitated. Yet some things are worse than death. Please forgive me for writing you such a personal letter, but I know of no one else who might help me as soon as possible. I dread tonight and the days are so lonely, being musicless.

> Sincerely,
> Herman Blount

P.S. If I am to go to camp wherever that is, I would appreciate your allowing me to go immediately because I hope you understand what I have to face here.

Probably my physical condition is aggravated by easily excited nerves or worry because this morning my whole left side seemed to have been paralyzed and my heart beat so that it seemed to shake the bed. I sent for the doctor.

It would probably be more merciful to be killed than to be as I am.

Sonny later said that the warden of the jail complained that he had been unable to sleep during the thirty-nine days that Sonny had been a prisoner there. "I don't care what you do with him, but get him out of here!"

Though no records of it exist, a grand jury was apparently called, but failed to indict him. He was released from prison on February 6, and this time they put him on the train to Washington, D.C., with a ticket which took him to Kane, Pennsylvania, where the director of Camp 48 picked him up in a truck.

Camp life was a daily routine of forestry work followed by evenings of rest, discussions of religious matters, and reading. Because of the hostility towards COs in communities near the camps there was little contact with civilians.

Sonny pleaded with the camp director that he was not physically fit for the conservation work done at the camp. He was suffering from heart palpitations, headaches, backaches, stomachaches, and the continuing sense of paralysis on his left side, and was given occasional sedatives. He had tried everything now—pleas of conscience, practical need, illness, physical disability, threatened suicide, physical and sexual fears, mental instability—so when his records arrived and the camp director saw his letter to the U.S. Marshall from Walker County Jail, Sonny was recommended for medical examinations. In a psychiatric report with elements which echo those of Lester Young, Charlie Parker, Charles Mingus, and perhaps hundreds of talented young black men of the era, he was described as "a psychopathic personality," but also "a well-educated colored intellectual" who was subject to neurotic depression and sexual perversion. Five days later the camp physician and the psychiatrist both recommended him for immediate discharge for reasons of physical disability.

Sonny was meanwhile assigned to practice piano during the day and play for the men in the evenings. The camp at Marienville was not segregated, and for the first time in his life he had daily contact with white people, and he joined in the nightly discussions of the evils of war and the morality of resistance.

At 9:53 on the morning of March 22, Sonny was put on a train and sent home with a 4-F classification.

Ask anyone who knew him then and they'll tell you that he came back changed. They had never seen him angry, but now he was furious, enraged at the city, the government, and at his family and his friends for not visiting him. The musicians explained that they had no idea of where he had been, that Joe Alexander, a Birmingham tenor saxophonist who moved in hip circles in New York City, had come back and told them that Sonny was in the army. When they asked him to talk about camp, he said there was nothing to tell. "A white man heard me play, and said 'You don't belong here.'" Yet the experience affected him deeply. He wrote a letter to the National Service Board for Religious Objectors on November 9, 1943, requesting a subscription to their newsletter. In it he recalled that

> a fellow from camp (a soldier Afro-American) remarked that people in general are rotten to the core, but that there are one set of people who are men in mind and deed as far as the treatment of the black man is concerned. I felt very proud as he said 'the C.O.'s.'

Certain of a sympathetic audience, he went on to talk of morality, and the role of teacher he was assuming in civilian life:

> At all my band rehearsals I talk to the fellows and try to make them see the point of knowing and admitting to oneself whether he is right or wrong and how fine it is to know the ecstasy of being right. Due to the many aspects which discourage, the young Afro-American often loses initiative and other valuable principles of life.
>
> I never speak of conscience, which makes them listen more eagerly as they think I will. I am beginning to wonder if conscience isn't like intellect—you either have it or you don't. The majority of people in the world don't think, they dodge social problems and many other things which puncture their ego. Is it because they don't have the brain? Some of them, maybe? Then what about conscience?... Sometimes I think it is an abnormality to want to help others and to care about anything but self. The world is so selfish that sometimes I don't care whether I live or die. I've tried to be selfish and unthinking, conscienceless, but I can't.

Back in his house on 4th Avenue, the rehearsals resumed as if they had never stopped. There were new opportunities to perform provided by the war effort, and Sonny took his twelve-piece band to black USO clubs and to military bases. And there were even more community-center dances and picnics in the parks. Yet he felt he was being blackballed by the older musicians because of his war resistance. He would have to count entirely on younger musicians.

Rehearsals were now more intense than ever. New compositions were brought in every week, and were rehearsed over and over for hours. Sometimes they rehearsed so much that they were late for the performances. But then on the job Sonny called for music that they had never rehearsed. Or they'd arrive only to find that there wasn't any performance scheduled. Many times the new pieces were too difficult for them to play, and Sonny patiently rewrote them, or coaxed the music out of them. Frank Adams recalls his first public performance with Sonny's band:

> I was taking the place of Roosevelt Smith, who was a first-rate alto saxophonist—there wasn't any better in Birmingham. I could read what he was putting in front of me all right, but I had never taken a solo, much less improvised. Sonny called on me to take an ad lib solo. I got through a chorus or so by running scales, and when I turned to sit down, he said, "Keep playing." I kept on playing scales and running up and down the chords, but I had nothing to say. He made me play for chorus after chorus, and I felt terrible. When I did finally sit down, he turned to me from the piano stool and said, "That was nice."

Sonny began giving private lessons, though never for money, as he was looking for promising members for his new band. Walter Miller, one of his students, said "that way, he taught them what he wanted them to do in his band; he didn't want perfect musicians, but those he could develop. Sonny bought them tuxedos and had them looking good. He was well organized. The band was tops! Other bands couldn't make a living out of music, but we were." For the next year the band played every Monday night at the Masonic Temple, and during the week they worked at various spots in and out of town such as the Madison in Bessemer. They played only once for a white audience, at a club in Cullman, Alabama, a town with no blacks, and a stronghold of the Klan. The musicians stayed close together throughout the night, and there were no incidents.

His musicianship had never been doubted, but now local musicians were also marveling at his creativity. Sammy Lowe, another arranger for the Erskine Hawkins Band, said, "Sun Ra would go into chords that nowadays are pretty common, but back then were in another world." Flatted fifths and augmented ninths had been used "to enhance an ending or get to an interlude where people would look up and say, 'What's happening now?' But [Sonny] used them all the way through." Like Duke Ellington, Sonny felt that each musician should play in a manner true to himself, and he should sound like no one else. It was the arranger's job to find a way to bring idiosyncratic sounds together. "He felt that certain sounds could be made by certain people that showed their true selves," said Frank Adams.

> He thought of musicians as troubadours, as traveling poets with a higher calling. He felt greed was the cause of musicians' downfall. There were physical attractions that can destroy you—women, alcohol, drugs—sincerity was the key thing he sought, not technical ability in a player. He explained that about Teddy Smith—a man who had no technical ability on the alto saxophone, but had a great ear. Sonny said that the devil didn't want Smith to speak in his own voice and so led him to destructive forces. Sonny was metaphysical that way.

One night in 1944 Frank Adams and Sonny were listening to a radio broadcast of a jump band led by trumpeter Red Allen. The new jazz called bebop was in the air, and the tone quality of individual musicians was changing, and melodies were becoming angular, sharp-edged, lightning-fast, the harmonies strange and unresolved. Some said it was crazy people's music. "I told Sonny that the way Allen and alto saxist Don Stoveall were playing together sounded weird. But Sonny said, 'Listen. They're talking to you: just listen to how they communicate.' "

He had always been interested in space travel, and news of research on rocketry and the development of atomic energy was suddenly everywhere. His talk at rehearsals increasingly turned to future technology, all of which fascinated the musicians, even when they thought he didn't know what he was talking about. Even musical instruments, he said, would some day soon be electrical, and be capable of producing sounds they hadn't even dreamed about. But they were incredulous, and argued that horn players at least would be electrocuted.

When his great-aunt Ida passed, Sonny saw no reason to stay in Birmingham any longer. Once when he was talking about the possibility of leaving Birmingham, someone had scoffed that he would never leave until his last friend was dead. Sonny took it as a prophesy. Her death freed him to look north to Chicago, like the countless number of other black folks who had been drawn by the flame of the promise of jobs and dignity in the weekly pages of the *Chicago Defender*. Since he never disclosed his reasons for leaving, his musicians—like Frank Adams—were left to speculate:

> He hated Birmingham, yes, and never got over Birmingham for racial reasons...but that's not why he left. He was drawn to the big bands, and Birmingham was not where they were. But years later he was still sentimental about Birmingham.
>
> He had no best friends, but he had no enemies either.

So, at the start of 1946, at the age of thirty-two, Sonny left his orchestra and music in the hands of Fletcher Myett, packed up a few things, and walked down the street to Terminal Station and bought a ticket to Chicago. He was not to return to Birmingham for another forty years.

A xerox of a photo of his band exists from Sonny's last year in Birmingham. Eleven musicians sit in front of a shimmering curtain, posed for the photo as if they were playing. They are wearing smart pin-striped suits and bow ties, and every instrument is held at the proper angle. A male singer sits to the right of the band, looking into the camera as if waiting for his chorus to begin. At the edge of the picture is Sonny, standing, dressed like the rest of the band, except that he is wearing a striped boating shirt beneath his suit coat. He is expressionless, and is looking off into the distance, away from the camera.

CHAPTER TWO

He arrived in Chicago, and stayed for a while with an aunt who lived there. He looked up a few acquaintances from Birmingham and reactivated his Musicians Union membership, and began signing his name "Sonny Bhlount." And even before he had a place to live the Union had found him a job with Wynonie Harris, who was about to leave for Nashville. Harris was a flamboyant figure who had begun as a vaudevillian—a buck dancer, drummer, and comedian—and had just begun singing the year before with "Who Threw the Whiskey in the Well," a huge rhythm-and-blues hit he recorded with Lucky Millinder's Orchestra. Now billed as "Mr. Blues," Harris cultivated a particularly aggressive form of singing, punctuated by leers, swaying hips, and double entendres, and was a pioneer in popularizing vulgarity. He was just beginning his career as a solo singer when Sonny joined the band. During the three months that he spent in Nashville working with the house band run by saxophonist Jimmy Jackson at the Club Zanzibar, Sonny appeared on his first commercial recordings, two singles cut by Harris for Bullet, a new local label. The song titles said it all: "Dig This Boogie"/"Lightnin' Struck the Poorhouse" and "My Baby's Barrel House"/"Drinkin' by Myself."

One night Sir Oliver Bibb dropped in to the Zanzibar. Bibb was a Chicago musician, a drummer, who led a blatantly commercial band with a book of tunes and arrangements written by Zilma Randolph, a songwriter who had created the hit "I'll Be Glad You're Dead, You Rascal You" for Louis Armstrong. Bibb's band dressed as eighteenth-century gentlemen, precursors to Liberace, with tricornered hats and

foppish handkerchiefs draped from their sleeves. During a break Bibb
told Sonny that he was reorganizing his band and asked him if he wanted
to join them for the last leg of their tour. When he learned they were
headed back to Chicago, he quickly agreed, and left Harris's band. Sonny
took Bibb's costumes in stride: "Being black, you don't get no jobs unless
you're a freak or something...people just don't understand that."

Back in Chicago, Sonny found himself a small apartment at 1514
South Prairie, next to the Johnson Park–Englewood "El" near 54th
Street, in a neighborhood of migrants who had found their way north to
the South Side. While he never denied that he was from Birmingham, he
mentioned it less and less as time went on; and though he occasionally
wrote one or another of the Birmingham musicians, he completely lost
touch with his sister and other family members.

The Union found him another job with the Lil Green Band. Green
was a Mississippi-born singer who was a bridge between country blues
and rhythm and blues, and who had some hit records in the black community, including "In the Dark" and "Why Don't You Do Right?", a song
later made famous nationally by Peggy Lee. On Sonny's first night the
band came by to pick him up, and as they drove to the club there was the
usual storytelling and joking in the car, and a bottle was passed around.
Sonny sat quietly in the back seat until the bandleader—Green's husband Howard Callender—turned around from the front. When Sonny
saw that he was wearing a very large crucifix around his neck, he suddenly became agitated. Drummer Tommy Hunter recalls that night:

Sonny started on Howard right away, saying, "How can you wear that
cross, glorifying what they did to Jesus? It's one thing to kill the man, but
to wear that symbol to remember it by is something else...!" He kept that
kind of thing up all the way to the gig. Howard was getting mad, but he
couldn't get at Sonny in the back seat on the other side of the car. We got
to the club and were setting up when I heard screaming, and I saw
Howard chasing Sonny around the club with a rusty old gun. When they
ran past the stage, Lil—who was a *big* woman—grabbed her husband by
the neck and told him, "Now, baby, be quiet and let the man play." She
calmed him down enough that Sonny finished the night and even continued to play with the band. In fact, he played with her band a number of

times, and was with them long enough to make some changes in the arrangements Green had in her book, and improve them.

He [Fletcher Henderson] was undoubtedly reincarnated
from another age or planet. He was too gentle for his time.

REX STEWART,
Jazz Masters of the 1930's

Chicago was just as Sonny had heard: there were so many bands, so many places to play that it was possible to go to a different club every night and never see the same band twice. But on nights he wasn't working the only place he went to was the Club DeLisa, where Fletcher Henderson, the father of swing music, had an orchestra in residence. Henderson's career had been in decline for many years, his reputation tarnished by an aloofness which bordered on carelessness, and this was to be one of his last opportunities to play a decent club. But none of this made any difference to Sonny. He knew every record Henderson had made, the steam engine riffs which had driven young Louis Armstrong's hell-for-leather solos, those rich chords which framed Coleman Hawkins's majestic tenor saxophone. And here the man was every night, looking elegant and suave, standing in front of his band at the elite club of black Chicago.

The club was opened in 1933 by the DeLisa Brothers, who ran it as a nightclub and gambling operation until it burned down in 1941; and a few months later they opened the new DeLisa at 55th and State Street, a couple of doors up from the old place. The new club was spectacular: faced with glazed white bricks on the outside, it was lit inside with red fluorescent bulbs, and had a dance floor which was hydraulically raised up to the bandstand when the floor show began. It held over a thousand people, and ran four shows a night, Sunday shows starting with a matinee at 5:00 P.M. and running continuously until the breakfast show from 6:30 to 8:30 on Monday morning. And through it all, yet another crowd was gambling downstairs in the basement casino.

In many ways the DeLisa was the Chicago equal of the Cotton Club in New York City: though located in a black neighborhood it drew a wealthy white clientele, and the house bands' leaders and the dancers in the chorus line recruited for the club were all light-skinned. But unlike the Cotton Club the DeLisa had no Jim Crow policy, and was popular with celebrities and show-business folk who enjoyed the black-and-tan atmosphere. Bob Hope, Paul Robeson, Gene Autry, Joe Louis, George Raft, Mae West, and Louis Armstrong were steady customers when they were in town, and John Barrymore was often seen there with his regular drinking partner, blues singer Chippie Hill.

On the first night Sonny went to the club he introduced himself to Henderson, telling him how much he admired his music, and connecting himself through musicians they knew in common, like Nat Atkins, a trombonist who had once played with Henderson, and also in Sonny's band in Birmingham. Every chance he got over the next couple of months he came in and chatted with Henderson, asking him questions and telling him about his own music. Then one night in August—like a scene out of a thirties musical—Henderson's regular pianist, Marl Young, a law school student by day, fell asleep in a car outside the club during a break and missed the show; and since Sonny already knew the band's repertoire and was able to sight-read, Henderson asked him to fill in. Afterwards, he offered him the job for the rest of the engagement. Sonny was to play piano while Henderson led the band (except on two piano features, "Humoresque" and "Stealin' Apples"), and to serve as music copyist for the arrangements used with the floor shows and visiting acts. Then each evening after the show he was to work with club choreographer Sammy Dyer as the rehearsal pianist for the chorus line.

After we'd get through playing at four o'clock in the morning I would stay there and the producer would be teaching the girls the show for the next month. We might stay there until twelve o'clock the next day. He'd be telling me things according to the way he was dancing when he showed the girls. I'd sketch out the whole thing, the chorus and all, and give it to another arranger, so when the show came out they'd be dancing right with the music.

Five nights a week the Henderson band played for dancers in the audience and then stayed on stage to accompany acts in the floor shows.
These shows were elaborately staged and built around themes which
changed periodically. That first week the theme was "Lime House
Nites," a show centered around the pop song "Limehouse Blues," one of
the many "Chinatown"-type songs then in vogue. On the bill with Henderson were rhythm-and-blues singer Little Miss Cornshucks, comedian and impersonator George Kirby, house vocalists Lulean Hunter
and Willard Garner, and several vocal groups, shake dancers, and a chorus line of fourteen led by dancer Freddie Cole. The range and breadth
of these DeLisa shows, their lavishness and grand theatricality, all made
a deep impression on Sonny, and they were one of the sources for the
elaborate "cosmo dramas" he would later stage with his own band.

This was by no means the best band Henderson had ever had, and he
made few concessions to showmanship. On the bandstand he seemed to
be listening to the band more than leading it, as if he were surprised they
could play at all. But his aura was still there, and he could draw a crowd
and even occasional name musicians like trumpeter Freddie Webster. In
any case, Sonny was thrilled by it all:

> That band was like a powerhouse. Fletcher had a very good education and
> his father also played the piano. Jazz came to him through the intellect.
> But Fletcher succeeded in forming a big band. Fletcher was able to take it,
> to coordinate it very well. Fletcher told the musicians how to attack the
> notes. And when he played he always had people who were swinging. He
> himself was always in the background.
>
> The bass part was written out, so that if someone tried to play Fletcher
> Henderson arrangements he had to play the bass parts, too. The bass part
> sometimes was written as "anticipated" [as in Latin music].

Sonny talked to him about some of his own musical ideas, and Henderson encouraged him to bring some arrangements in to rehearsal.

> …but I told him if I brought in what I had, no one would be able to read
> them anyway. The boys thought that was crazy because they'd been read-
> ing Fletcher's arrangements easy, so how could they not be able to read

mine? He called a special rehearsal, and I brought in two charts: "Dear Old Southland" and a ballad called "I Should Care".... The notes were there, but they couldn't play them right. They couldn't read them. After three hours Fletcher gave up. It was a different kind of syncopation, and they didn't have it.

This was not the first sign of friction between the musicians and Sonny. He used unusual voicings and chord inversions which had them objecting loudly to Henderson: "All of the people in the band were my enemies. They wanted me to play like other piano players." Henderson ignored them, but after a while their constant slights and jibes reached Sonny and led him first to set a razor on the top of the piano as a warning to his critics, and then finally to give his notice to Henderson and quit:

... Fletcher didn't say anything, he didn't say he accepted it, and he didn't say he didn't. The next night the band played, I went, and they didn't have a piano player. He was up there directing and they [the band] realized he meant it, so they told me to come back on stage, so my notice was over. After that the band didn't bother me because they realized that Fletcher meant it.

The Henderson band had been hired for a six-month stay at the DeLisa, and Sonny had joined it just at the point where the contract ran out, but the success of the band got them extended into 1947. Over the next nine months they played for a series of floor shows advertised as "Early Fall Capers," "Sound Off," "Romance & Rhythm," "Bronzeville Holiday," "Bag O'Tricks," "Favorites of 1947," "Copper-Cabana Revue," "Spring Fest," and "Drumboogie Revue." In these shows they accompanied blues singers like Big Joe Turner, Gatemouth Moore, Dr. Jo-Jo Adams ("a Chuck Berry type," Sonny recalled, a flamboyant dresser, "who had this knock-kneed dance that he would do," and "who performed X-rated blues in top hat and tails"), and dancers like the Four Step Brothers or Cozy Cole's Drum Dancers.

Henderson for his part showed little interest in the shows, spending much of his time at the race track or socializing with friends like Dorothy Donegan, a classically trained pianist out of the Art Tatum–Earl Hines tradition, famed for jazzing up classical music with virtuosity and flash. When Henderson's contract was up on May 18, 1947, he left without the band and headed west, playing one or two engagements on the way, and ending up in California. And with the exception of a brief tour as Ethel Waters's accompanist, some guest spots, and a few band jobs, he remained largely inactive until his death in 1952. But Sonny held Henderson in the highest esteem for the rest of his life, praising him in almost every interview, lecturing his own band about what Henderson represented. Where others saw Henderson as a passive and uncommitted musician, Sonny saw him as unselfish, gentlemanly, virtuous, and, in later years, as quite literally a kindred spirit:

> Fletcher was really part of an angelic thing. I wouldn't say he was a man. I wouldn't say Coleman Hawkins was a man, because they did things men hadn't done, and hadn't done before. And they didn't learn it from any man. They just did it. So therefore it came from somewhere else. A lot of things that some men do...come from somewhere else, or they're inspired by something that's not of this planet. And jazz was most definitely inspired, because it wasn't here before. If it wasn't here before, where did it come from?...Something, some particular being, used them to do things, inspired them so much, worked them so much, they had to do it.

Henderson was replaced by the Red Saunders Band, the group which had been the DeLisa's house band until mid-1945. When the other musicians with Henderson were let go, Sonny remained on in his job as rehearsal pianist and copyist for the next five years; and in addition he began rehearsing the band for Saunders and playing in the relief band that filled in when Saunders was off. Every week Saunders handed him new arrangements for the floor show, but during rehearsals Sonny began to make small changes—a note here and there, an alteration in a chord—but as time went on the changes became increasingly dramatic. During rehearsal one day Saunders walked in, looked over an arrangement, and shook his head when he saw the crossed-out notes and inserted harmonies: "I give you these nice, clean arrangements each week, and look at what you do with them!...But, damn, they sure sound good, though." Sonny was now rewriting arrangements used to accompany singers like B. B. King, Laverne Baker, Dakota Staton, Joe Williams, Johnny Guitar Watson, Sarah Vaughan, and Lorez Alexandria.

In spite of his obvious abilities and his importance to the DeLisa shows, Sonny was never close to the other performers at the club. A nightclub musician who didn't drink or smoke was anomaly enough, but one who lectured other musicians on morality like a country preacher, endlessly pronounced on astronomy, physics, and space travel, and told tales of a future when science would become one with music was something else. His reputation for weirdness grew daily, and even the chorus line took to ribbing him about his obsessions. One day Sonny saw a cartoon in a newspaper which depicted the sun saying something witty, so he pinned it to the club bulletin board. The dancers saw it on the way upstairs to change, and while they were laughing and joking about him in the dressing room, a voice—seemingly coming from nowhere—filled the room:

> "Yes, he had that [cartoon] down there. And what he's talkin' about is true. And besides that, he's gonna do everything he say he's gonna do. And nothing will stop him."
>
> One of the girls ran down, asking, "Did [Sonny] come upstairs?" A fellow named Don told her that he had not been anywhere else but downstairs, playing the piano for a considerable time, and that he still was playing. She told the other girls, and they became frightened. The next night the producer of the show went to the dressing room and sprinkled a powder to keep away whatever it was that had spoken.

One of the first people Sonny got to know in Chicago was Tommy "Buggs" Hunter, a student at the Midwestern Conservatory of Music and the drummer he had met with the Lil Green Band. In 1947 Hunter put together a trio with Sonny and tenor saxophonist Red Holloway to play at the Peacock, one of the strip clubs in Calumet City, a town just to the south called "Sin City" by Chicagoans. These clubs were big sources of income for Chicago musicians, but they were tied to the mob, and the schedules were grueling. The shows required continuous music for eight to twelve hours a night, so Hunter also hired Jimmy Boyd, a trumpet player and pianist who worked at a club next door, to join them during his breaks to spell one member of the trio at a time. The clubs were Jim Crow, and the musicians were treated like kitchen mechanics.

Birmingham was just as bad, Sonny thought, but at least there he had never had to play in such wretched settings, where music was reduced to such a base function. The whole experience was emblematized for him by a divider—he called it the "Iron Curtain"—that hung between the musicians and the dancers at the Peacock Club to prevent black men from seeing the naked bodies of white women. Still, he took his job as musician seriously and tried to make the best of it. It was an opportunity to learn hundreds of pop songs and standards. "He played straight music when the girls were dancing," Hunter recalled, "but when the dancers were offstage, he played 'out,' " using rhythms and chords alien to both pop music and jazz. Red Holloway remembered that "when Sun Ra was on it, it was a mysterious gig, trying to figure out what the chords were! But he was always correct in his playing, it was just the way he would voice his chords. He was something more or less like Thelonious Monk—in a way—but he had his definite own style."

By the end of the 1940s Chicago was possibly the best city in America for jazz musicians; there were at least seventy-five clubs on the South Side of Chicago alone—places like the Roberts Show Lounge on South Parkway, where Herman Roberts had turned the garage for his fleet of cabs into a 1,000-seat dance hall he leased to private social clubs (of which there were said to be at least 2,000 in Chicago); the Regal Theater; the Savoy Ballroom, also on South Parkway, a copy of the New York ballroom of the same name, which held 6,000 people and was the center of both boxing and black big-band activity in Chicago; the Pershing Hotel, which had a ballroom, a lounge, and in the basement, Birdland, a modern jazz club which had once been called the Beige Room. With a little luck and the Union's help, a decent musician could stay busy every night of the week.

The American Federation of Musicians Local No. 208 (the Negro musicians' local) was enormously powerful in Chicago, and like Chicago itself, it was run by its own unique politics, some of which was said to be enforced with pistols. It was believed that if a musician wanted to get jobs through the Union, it was necessary to hang out at the Union hall, play cards with Vice President Charles Elgar, and, so they said, let him win once in a while. Elgar was a shrewd and sophisticated musician of the old school who had come up through the worst years of mob control of show business, and socially and musically he was an accommodation-ist. But Sonny had never accommodated anyone. He curried no favors, seemed oblivious to practical problems of musical organization, and, worse, was socially and musically too strange for the Union. Not only did they refuse to help him, they openly discouraged other players from working with him, just as they warned young musicians against working with junkies.

Toward the end of 1947 Sonny began playing in the house rhythm section at the Congo Club, an after-hours place next to the Regal Theater. Off and on over the next three years he accompanied local stars like tenor saxophonist Gene Ammons and even big-name performers like Billie Holiday. It was at the Congo where Eugene Wright (later famous as the bassist with the Dave Brubeck Quartet) first heard Sonny and asked him to play and write arrangements for his band, the Dukes of Swing. With Wright's band he played the Congo and then the Pershing Hotel over the next year and a half. At times Wright had two bands playing at once in the Pershing, a twenty-piece group upstairs in the ballroom and the ten-piece Dukes of Swing band downstairs in Birdland. The big feature number was the chorus line's dance to Sonny's up-tempo arrangement of the theme from the 1945 movie *Spellbound*, which in the film had introduced the eerie, voicelike sounds of the theremin (one of the first electronic musical instruments) to evoke the psychological state of one of the characters. Wright wanted Sonny to direct the downstairs band while he was busy upstairs, but Sonny resisted the role of leader, and wouldn't even set the tempo for a song. But Wright kept him on, and in October of 1948 he used him on several recordings for the new Aristocrat label which would shortly turn into Chess Records. The Dukes of Swing recorded "Pork 'n' Beans" and "Dawn Mist," pieces credited to Leonard Chess and someone named "Crawfish," though both possibly were written by Sonny. At the same session they accompanied a popular vocal quartet called the Dozier Boys on four songs, "St Louis Blues," "Music Goes Round and Round," "She Only Fools with Me," and "Big Time Baby," the latter two composed by Sonny.

A month later Wright broke up the Dukes of Swing when he got an offer from the Count Basie Band. He remembered Sonny as "the most advanced musician in Chicago, but in his own space...that is, he was always reading or writing, keeping to himself." Saxophonist Yusef Lateef (then known as Bill Evans), who also worked in Wright's band, recalls Sonny's theories about music—that he was talking about using quarter tones and micro-tones in jazz, and that he had discovered a bass player who could play in quarter tones, the notes between the usual half tones which make up the scales of Western music.

At the end of October Sonny briefly played with Coleman Hawkins, the first great saxophonist in jazz. Over the years Sonny often mentioned his Henderson gig and his short stay with Hawkins to legitimate his connections to the history of jazz for those who doubted him. Years later in New York, Baroness Pannonica de Koenigswarter, the fabled jazz patroness, was just such a skeptic. She went so far as to ask Coleman Hawkins in front of Sonny if he had ever played with him. Hawkins laughed, "Yes, that's the only person who wrote a song [an arrangement to "I'll Remember April"] I couldn't play."

As in Birmingham, Sonny was willing to take any musical work available to him. In 1949 he was playing in an orchestra at the St. Biarritz House; he occasionally worked with trumpeter Jesse Miller's band or with a band headed by Al Smith, a pioneering figure in rhythm-and-blues recording; he filled in as a keyboardist at various churches; and for a year he rehearsed with the Co-ops, a dance troupe and their band, a project which came to a bad end:

Their first night, their debut, I wasn't there. The drummer couldn't read and he was the bandleader. Well, there was a place where they walked across the stage that was in 5/4 time, because they made five steps, and I wrote it like that. Opening night the drummer missed it, and the trumpet player started talkin' about it. So the drummer shot the piano player.

...the white man thinks in a written language and the Negro thinks in hieroglyphics.

ZORA NEALE HURSTON,
"Characteristics of Negro Expression"

If these [American tourists to Cairo] were to relate what
they saw to their own experience, they would notice that
the pharaoh was the same type of man who today walks
the streets of Kingston, Harlem, Birmingham, and the
South Side of Chicago.

ST. CLAIR DRAKE,
Black Folk Here and There

If Moses was an Egyptian...

SIGMUND FREUD,
Moses and Monotheism

You might say jazz came from the sun priests of Egypt.

SUN RA

Sonny's apartment was one flight up, with a piano and a moon-shaped
shade over the ceiling light. In his off-hours he lived the life he had led
in Birmingham, practicing, composing, strolling through the streets,
writing, reading. He had discovered W.E.B. DuBois and saw that, unlike
Booker T. Washington, DuBois thought that Negroes should be edu-
cated in the classics, in Greek and Latin, in the arts, and that it was possible for them to approach a state of universality where the spiritual
would reign over the mundane. It occurred to him that perhaps Booker
T. Washington and W.E.B. DuBois were *both* right: that it was possible for
the race to develop precision and discipline through the study of the sciences and mathematics, but also through the knowledge of languages
and books, both classic and obscure. And if the objectivity of science offered the means by which the evils of racism could be overcome, the
tools of scholarship and the arts could also be turned to discovering hidden truths and decoding the texts. Discipline and precision were nature's ways, the ways in which the planets spun through space, by which
birds flew; and precision rather than confusion was the answer, discipline
rather than freedom. The only truly free people were dead people.

The more he read the more he understood his mission. The confusion
and sadness he saw all around him focused his efforts, and a terrible urgency gripped him. He had to know more, to become a scholar, to go to

the limits of knowledge. He would have to increase his reading, find the books he needed, maybe read everything. If necessary, he would rebuild the Library of Alexandria on the South Side.

Visitors were astonished to see his books, so many that the walls had disappeared behind the stacks piled on the floor. Sonny haunted Chicago's used bookstores, and some remember seeing him carry home as many as three large bags of books at once. But he said that he didn't have to look for books: they appeared to him miraculously; they'd be left on the piano at the end of a gig; or would wind up on his pillow—rare antique books with gold edges and incomprehensible titles which you could never buy in a bookstore somehow would find their way to him.

Few people ever actually saw him with a book in his hands, so they assumed he was reading in the middle of the night. He read quickly, purposefully, sometimes by opening a book somewhere in the middle, landing on passages which would activate what was already in his mind; or he might read from the back to the front of the book, using what he called the "Oriental" approach. He marked up his books in copious notes of red, green, and yellow ink, circling, underlining, arrowing, echoing what he read with comments and cross-references, sometimes with arcane symbols from the world's religions.

Much of his reading emerged from the Bible, where more and more it seemed to him that what he was looking for could be found. But as he went deeper into the Bible he began to understand the meaning of "revised": it had been edited, and some books removed, maybe first at the Council of Bishops at Nicene, where it was said that certain important books which connected Egypt to the Bible had been suppressed. Now, as he read, some of the most critical passages appeared either suspiciously transparent or hopelessly impenetrable. Like Milton, he thought that much of the Bible seemed to be badly translated—perhaps intentionally so—from some unknown original. Soon he began to suspect that it had been put together wrong and was being read wrong. But nonetheless clues to correct reading seemed to be buried in the Bible itself—"the first will be last," "Alpha and Omega"—perhaps it, too, should be read backwards. What if Revelations was the first book of the Bible, Genesis the last? He also saw that the roles played by black people in the Bible were confused, distorted, ignored: Nimrod, Melchizedek, and all the sons of Cush and Ham for that matter were treated disrespectfully or pushed to the margins of the story. He saw that to decipher the true meaning of the Bible, to make it whole again, would take knowledge of ancient languages and histories as well as of esoteric texts that reached beyond the canonic boundaries established by Protestant churches. He would have to undertake hermeneutics in the most literal sense.

When Sonny was eight years old the tomb of King Tutankhamen was opened at Luxor, and like most of the world, he had heard the daily details of the slow progress of discovery which led up to it, the tribulations of Lord Carnarvon and his archaeologist Howard Carter. Sonny studied the magazine photographs of the riches of the tomb, and pondered the curse of the mummy and the peculiar circumstances of the death of Lord Carnarvon, after which the lights went out all over Cairo.

He fell under Egypt's spell—became obsessed, some might say. But it was an honorable obsession, one shared by Napoleon, Hegel, Poe, Derrida; European musicians like Rameau, Debussy, Verdi, Mozart, Euro-American musicians like Joseph Lamb, the California Ramblers, and the Louisiana Rhythm Kings, and African Americans Sidney Bechet, Clarence Jones, Duke Ellington, Miles Davis, and Pharoah Sanders; occultists such as Madame Blavatsky, Aleister Crowley, Rudolph Steiner, and Edgar Cayce; secret societies like the Freemasons; and by those whom the uncharitable simply call "kooks"—Uriel (Ruth Norman), the space lady of California, who spent her life preparing her followers for the ultimate day of Contact, or Omm Sety (Dorothy Eady), the London woman who believed she was the reincarnation of the tragic lover of Pharaoh Sety. But then Egypt had been the obsession of whole countries, and had served as a symbol for antiquity, cultural origin, beauty, esotericism, eternal life, power, the idea of the nation state, and social order. It was the source of art styles and periods in which Europe reimagined its own past: Egyptomania, Pharaonism, the Egyptian Revival, Nile Style, Egyptophilia, Neo-Egyptian Style—movements which reinterpreted, reworked, "Egyptianized" ancient Egypt in order to make it resonate with contemporary reality. Yet it was not an obsession limited to the West. People in far-flung places like Indonesia, Peru, and Africa had also been fixated by Egypt's secrets, and had also sought their beginnings there as well.

In Chicago intimations of Egypt were everywhere: in exhibits in the Field Museum, in the Oriental Institute, the libraries, the books sold by the street-corner Egyptologists on the South Side. He discovered the popular books by Sir E. A. Wallis Budge first, the three-volume translation of *The Egyptian Book of the Dead* which only a few years before had fired the imagination of James Joyce. In Budge's *Osiris and the Egyptian Resurrection*, Sonny read that just as Osiris had been raised back to life from death by the ritual taught to Isis by the god of death, Thoth, so the Egyptians thought that the dead could be led down the path of Osiris and the rising sun to eternity. Then with Budge's *Egyptian Hieroglyphic Dictionary* he began to teach himself to read the inscriptions on the tombs and the pyramids. He believed that hieroglyphics, like the pyramids and monuments, held secrets, and were part of the system of Egyptian science.

He learned the power and the rank order of the gods, feeling special affinity for Ra (or Re) of Heliopolis, the Egyptian sun god, elevated to highest of deities in the Fifth Dynasty; and to Thoth, who was also god of the moon as well as the inventor of writing. He saw that to the ancient Egyptians death was nothing like the beliefs that so disturbed him in Christianity: they knew secrets which had long been forgotten. "Resurrection" seemed the wrong word for what Egyptians believed. Even "death" seemed wrong. They were never dead, only asleep. *The Egyptian Book of the Dead* might better have been titled *The Book of the Awakening*.

One day a man he barely knew gave him a dark blue book with a strange image of the crucifixion on the cover—*God Wills the Negro* by Theodore P. Ford (who someone later hinted might have been the Honorable Wallace D. Fard himself in yet another guise), a book published in Chicago in 1939 with a subtitle like some eighteenth-century tome: *An Anthropological and Geographical Restoration of the Lost History of the American Negro People, Being in Part a Theological Interpretation of Egyptian and Ethiopian Backgrounds.* Ford began his book by saying that slavery in America had created a burden of shame that weighed down both whites and blacks, and that the Negro had been "frozen into inactivity by the wall of ignorance that surrounds him." It was this inactivity that he proposed to thaw by discoveries he had made in modern anthropology and ancient texts. As Sonny read on he learned that the black-skinned inhabitants of Ancient Ethiopia were the source of all peoples and nations, that from this single center all races and cultures had diffused out to the world. He read that the ancient peoples of Egypt had disappeared when their culture had fallen—possibly at the same time as the black peoples of America were enslaved.

Ford said that anthropologists had unconsciously incorporated into their scientific study of races the method by which American blacks could spot persons passing as white; that by this method blacks could even detect those racial features in the sculptures or monuments being claimed as European. By such means it was possible to assume the true origins of Negro Americans.

The ancient Egyptians, he said, were driven from Egypt by a series of invasions, and some were forced south, to Central Africa, where they were sold into slavery by less developed peoples with whom they are usually confused, and thus became known as so-called Negroes. Not all American blacks were Egyptians, however, for a small number of them were "undesirable" people who had been sold into slavery by their own African forebearers and did not fit into American society because of their "lack of ancestral ideals and folk background."

In another chapter called "Psychoanalytical Ethnology," Ford looked to black folk tradition for evidence, not of Africanisms, but Egyptianisms and Ethiopianisms. Like an ethnographer, he had done fieldwork in the old second ward of Chicago, posing as a hoodoo man. Working in his storefront sanctuary he saw these Chicago children of Egypt wearing head cloths of Sudanic derivation, heard their "superstitions of Egyptian origin"—beliefs concerning cats, dogs, cows, birds, snakes, and rabbits; observed charms and amulets, two-headed men, numbers, the evil eye; he noted that like Marcus Garvey they said that their ancestors had come from "God's country"; he observed their distance from mainstream Christianity and their belief in the "old-time religion," their religion before Christianity had been imposed upon them. Ford saw it all—speech practices, burial customs, beliefs in the spirit, the power and spirituality of rivers—and jotted it down in his notebooks.

From childhood Sonny had heard of black folks who believed that their ancestors had been the real Jews, the Jews of biblical prophecy and scripture, and that those who called themselves "Jews" were usurpers whose Talmudic scholars had fabricated a curse which condemned them forever, a belief which Christians all too eagerly embraced as their own. The understanding that blacks were the chosen people had carried many through slavery, given them hope, even while explaining their present condition as the punishment for having authorized the killing of Christ. The spirituals confirmed these legends, as well as countless sermons, for it was "ole' Pharaoh" and his army that those ancient Negroes feared and sought to escape. But what if they had it wrong? What if they were Egyptians? Was that the message being communicated all along to those who knew? It was an argument that he would discover had a long history which stretched back to Frederick Douglass's "The Claim of the Negro Ethnologist" and even before that to *David Walker's Appeal* in 1829.

From a street merchant Sonny bought a book, a pamphlet really, called *The Children of the Sun* by George Wells Parker, printed in Omaha in 1918 by the Hamitic League of the World. Again he read that human life had first appeared in Africa and that civilization had begun in Egypt, and even white people were descended from so-called Negroes. Parker suggested that there was reason to believe that the true story of mankind had been rewritten late in history to conceal the role of African peoples, and that you need only read the Egyptologist William Flinders Petrie (Howard Carter's mentor), the social theorist Frederick Ratzel, or the *philosophe* Count Augustine Volney to see for yourself.

It was Volney's 1791 essay, *The Ruins, or, Meditation on the Revolutions of Empires: and the Law of Nature* that he found next, a book which had been read by William Blake, Thomas Jefferson, Percy Shelley, Tom Paine, Walt Whitman—and it was the first book read by Frankenstein's monster. Shortly after Napoleon's triumphant entry into Egypt, Volney traveled there himself, then stayed for four years in the Middle East, learning Coptic and Arabic and writing books. Meditating in the ruins of Palmyra, he wrote that a phantom appeared to him in a vision and revealed to him the history of past civilizations, offered him the evidence for a deist argument that the source of all religions was in nature and natural experiences, and showed him a glimpse of a "New Age" in which all people would shed their religious and class differences and be one together in self-knowledge. The phantom then avowed to Volney that the very people who had given birth to civilization, religion, law, literature, science, and art were the same people now "rejected from society, for their sable skin and frizzled hair." In other books Volney went even further and argued that the face of the sphinx should be evidence enough of the black origins of Egyptian civilization, and then, perhaps aiming at Jefferson himself, Volney wrote:

> Just imagine, finally, that it is in the midst of peoples who call themselves the greatest friends of liberty and humanity that one has approved the most barbarous slavery and questioned whether black men have the same kind of intelligence as Whites!

Sonny discovered that there were several editions of *The Ruins,* and in the first American translation all references to the Negro origins of civilization had been eliminated. He learned that Volney was furious over this censorship and made certain those passages were restored to the next edition. On a tour of the United States, Volney had made the same points in lectures, for which his reviewers accused him of "Hottentotism," the blind worship of black people. Sonny now knew that he would have to read more carefully, for what was written—even by those acknowledged to be the greatest minds of all time—may have been deliberately altered. And if the history we received was so defective, so incomplete . . . mustn't there be another history that corrects it? Perhaps a secret history, known only in part by a few, but one which could be pieced together and reconstructed?

In another pamphlet, John G. Jackson's *Ethiopia and the Origin of Civilization,* names such as Volney, Flinders, and Ratzel appeared again, and more such as Herodotus and the anthropologist Franz Boas, who with the encouragement of W.E.B. DuBois pointed out the cultural developments which ancient Africa had made long before the Europeans. Nor had the accomplishments of Africa disappeared as some would say. Sonny found proof in the most unlikely of places, in David Livingston's *Missionary Travels and Researches in South Africa,* for example, where there were descriptions of African villages which were complete unto themselves—a census which listed barbers, doctors, weavers, blacksmiths, priests, carpenters. It was the sheer ordinariness of it that struck him; black people living complete, normal lives without white people. Livingston also went to great pains to draw parallels between Central Africa and ancient Egypt, even borrowing illustrations from books on Egypt for his own. Further proof was in *God's Children*, where he saw that Archibald Rutledge, a slaveholder's son, could say that the descendants of slaves on his plantation in coastal South Carolina were Nubians, with the "blood of Egyptians, Moors and Arabs in their veins"; and in *Home By the River* Rutledge called black people "orientals." (Even so, Rutledge was not about to surrender Egypt so completely: in a pastoral idyll set in a flat-bottomed boat along the reedy streams of the Carolina Low Country, Rutledge said: "My dusky oarsman might well have been a Nubian; I certainly felt like Marc Antony, and the girl within looked, I thought, like Cleopatra.")

When Sonny found Godfrey Higgins, in *The Anacalypsis, an Attempt to Draw Aside the Veil of the Saitic Isis; or an Inquiry Into the Origin of Languages, Nations and Religions,* scattered pieces of his thoughts and reading began to connect. Higgins also argued that all the world's religions had the same source, but he came to his conclusions through a mixture of etymology, numerology, and occult interpretation. Sonny read that the sun was the first worshipped deity, that "El" meant the sun deity in some languages, and that there were many other names for the sun, such as Mithra and ... Ham. He learned of the greatness of Ethiopia, that the Cushites were a great nation, that not just the Egyptians, but also the Indians and the Celts were black, that even Buddha is considered black in some parts of the world.

The trail ran from these books to the grand diffusionists, those turn-of-the-century writers who later anthropologists would come to call "extremists" for rooting all civilization in Egypt and Ethiopia—what some called Heliolithic culture—and who found vestiges of this original civilization not only in the north of Africa, but also in Greece, India, South America, Central America, and Mexico, maybe even the United States. There was Grafton Elliot Smith, the anatomist who spent thirty years in Cairo spinning out books like *The Ancient Egyptians and Their Influence Upon the Civilization of Europe;* and W. J. Perry, who in the same year had written his own *Children of the Sun;* and Albert Churchward, who wrote *Origin and Evolution of the Human Race* in 1921.

But Sonny noted that as painstakingly as these scholars worked to trace the influence of Egypt, they labored just as hard to show that Egyptians were brown-skinned Caucasians, not "true Negroes." Wherever else the evidence led them, they were not about to make room for contemporary black people. He was amazed that Godfrey Higgins could claim that the origins of civilization could be located within a *different* black people, the "Cristna type of black" whom he traced from India to the Middle East. Even in the best of books on Egypt, like Wilhelm Worringer's *Egyptian Art*, the first page could open with a discussion of Egypt's "Negro question."

Yet there were white scholars who did not seek to deceive readers. Gerald Massey, for instance, the working-class Chartist poet whom George Eliot had used as a model for her novel *Felix Holt—the Radical*: after a period of writing and lecturing on Christian socialism, in his later years Massey turned first to psychic phenomena and then finally to Egypt and its links to the occult. In *A Book of the Beginnings* he considered linguistic parallels across the world and concluded that ancient civilization must have spread from the interior of Africa to Egypt, then on to the rest of the world. Lengthy word lists compared English and Egyptian words to show the connection. Then in the twelve volumes of *Ancient Egypt the Light of the World* he went on to locate the roots of Christianity, Islam, and Judaism—all the major religions of the Western world—in the Nile Valley.

Sonny returned to bookstores and libraries in a frenzy of discovery, rifling through books to their indices, tracing key words across history, finding those words in dictionaries whose languages he didn't know, where without history or context, all meanings became infinite and possible. The books seemed to be waiting for him, peculiar but crucial books, like the Haldeman-Julius Little Blue Books published in Girard, Kansas; Leo Weiner's *Africa and the Discovery of America;* books on Atlantis, the bridge between Ethiopia and the Americas.

There was R. A. Schwaller de Lubicz, the Alsatian philosopher and mathematician, who worked at the Luxor site for fifteen years and wrote dozens of books. Schwaller de Lubicz believed that there was another Egypt before the civilization we know—perhaps Atlantis, perhaps not— an Egypt which was even more advanced spiritually and scientifically than we have been willing to admit. These first Egyptians had invented science, invented it as the other side of mysticism, so what to modern people looks like magic and superstition was once practical knowledge.

The wisdom of this other "Egypt" was stored materially and symbolically in its architecture, most of which was lost when a later decadent civilization deliberately effaced and dismantled it. If there was more than one Egypt, Sonny thought, and "Egypt" had been occupied by others, its original inhabitants might have been scattered across the world or sold into slavery as Ford had said. And its invaders had almost succeeded in completely concealing the race of the true Egyptians.

By the time he found the African-American author George G. M. James's *Stolen Legacy, the Greeks Were Not the Authors of Greek Philosophy, but the People of North Africa, Commonly Called the Egyptians* he was not surprised to see that the Greeks had been given credit for scientific and religious ideas they had learned from the Egyptians. It was the kind of thing which drives white people crazy when they hear it from black folks; but he had already read it in European writings from before the eighteenth century.

This was strange territory that Sonny found himself in. The ancient world, he was learning, was less a place than a myth. White people who made claims on it for themselves often did so in the same terms as black people. And though they wrapped their self-serving myths in science and scholarship and made "race" do their bidding, when Sonny looked closely it seemed nothing more than testifying, as in church. The British, for instance, long fancying themselves somehow or other linked to the Jews, found their first justification in *Lectures on Our Israelitish Origin* by John Wilson, a self-taught Irishman, who convinced many that the "Anglo-Saxon-Celtic" people of northern Europe were the lost tribes. This he had proved by his study of the languages of the world, listening for words that sounded alike, and concluding that the most common words in the "Teutonic languages" were pure Hebrew. Wilson's later followers narrowed his argument so that only the British and the Americans qualified as Jews.

When interest in Egyptian pyramids emerged in the mid-nineteenth century and speculation began to suggest that the pyramids might be divinely inspired monuments whose very form and dimensions could be used to prophesy the future, there were those who argued that it was not the Egyptians who could have been given the responsibility of building them, that they must have been the work of a superior people, the chosen people, the Jews, the ancestors of the Anglo-Americans. In the United States the lost tribes were further delimited to America, the word spread through the early white converts to black Pentecostalism in Southern California at the beginning of the twentieth century. Now, having gotten rid of the Egyptians, it was necessary to dismiss as impostors the people who had called themselves Jews for centuries, to treat them not as children of Jacob, but of Esau, who had intermarried with the Canaanites and the Edomites. Or maybe they should be cast as Khazars from the Black Sea area, bastard children of Jews, Mongols, and Turks who had migrated to Europe. Or again perhaps as the product of matings between Cain and the Pre-Adamites of Babylon, people of color who had been created separately, before Adam, all of whom became part of Satan's plan of revenge against God and the source of all evil.

Evil had a different source in Alexander Hislip's *The Two Babylons, or Papal Worship Proved to be the Worship of Nimrod and his Wife*, and even after all he had read, it was still shocking to Sonny. Hislip said that it was not Cain who had founded Babylon, but Nimrod, the son of Cush (who was a son of Ham), and after the slaying of Nimrod by Noah's son Shem, Nimrod became a deity in a cult of idolatry, prostitution, and human sacrifice. This cult ultimately went underground and now survives as the Catholic church, the Beast spoken of in Revelations, with Satan as its invisible head.

Anglo-Israelites, Pyramidologists, Edomites, Pre-Adamites, Khazars, Pentecostalists—it was a maelstrom of rival ideologies like out of William Blake's time. What had started out as idle conjecture and curiosity often wound up as movements whose sole reason for being was to eliminate the Jews, expose the Catholics, and crush the Negroes. These were ideas that some 150 years after their origins would resurface in the United States as the Christian Identity Movement, and fuel weekend militia warriors, closet anti-Semites, bomb-crazed crackers, and those who had the audacity to call themselves "freemen."

But through it all Sonny saw a bigger point: that Negroes had long been a threatening force, their race a cipher that needed to be explained away in order to sustain white people's claims to the ancient world. It was a competing mythology which white people had to at once suppress and demonize. It was another history of the world, history of the universe really, that needed to be discovered, and one which the right person might discover, a person whose heart was pure and whose sincerity was unquestioned.

There were many sides to Sonny. The musicians who played with him were surprised to find that he was exceptionally knowledgeable about microphone placement and recording technology, something very unusual among musicians at the time. When he heard about a new kind of tape recorder, one which recorded on paper-backed tape for a half hour at a stretch, he bought one, an Ampex. He began recording everything he could, rehearsals, performances, even the Calumet City gigs. In fact, he sometimes played all twelve hours of the strip shows without a break so that he could play and record every piece they did. His habit of documenting all his work became legendary among musicians in Chicago. Those who played with him later said that "if you worked for him for three years, you could say that you made 700 records." "Deep Purple," one of the earliest of those recordings to survive, comes from a period when Tommy Hunter was performing with groups led by violinists Stuff Smith and Eddie South at the Blue Note during weekend gigs the Union had gotten for him. It was Hunter who introduced Sonny to Stuff Smith, and the three of them went back to Sonny's apartment to play, Hunter using brushes on a telephone book, Sonny playing piano and Solovox. They played long into the afternoon until they ran out of tape.

Sonny meanwhile continued to compose his own music, and was looking for musicians who were right to play it. They were not always easy to find, because established musicians did not take to being lectured on nonmusical matters, and his demand that his musicians approach music as a way of life ("you eat it, breathe it, live it!") was too much for most. On top of this he was increasingly breaking with conventional jazz wisdom. Pianist Junior Mance said that during those years Sonny was often scorned for playing "all that Bud Powell stuff," which is to say a bebop piano style rich with long and relentlessly fast single-note melodies, with percussively jabbed altered harmonies in the left hand. But Sonny vehemently objected to being called a bopper: his was music of the future. Musicians who played with Sonny were warned not to become simple imitators of the popular bop stars. When Tommy Hunter began to snap his hi-hat cymbals closed together on the second and fourth beats of the bar like Max Roach, Sonny told him that he should be himself when he played and not copy anyone else: "Sonny didn't want to be limited to one style." And when Hunter was working with the old-time blues pianist Roosevelt Sykes and told Sonny that he was embarrassed by what Sykes was playing, Sonny said he should listen more closely, that Sykes had something to teach him.

As in Birmingham, he began to find a few young musicians—like drummer Robert Barry and saxophonist Yusef Lateef—who wanted to understand his music. But in order to underwrite a new band of his own, Sonny was forced to continue playing the strip clubs in Calumet City throughout 1949. But in spite of the long hours, he wrote music and rehearsed with whoever he could get to play it. By 1950 he had a loosely organized twelve-piece group which included Harold Ousley, Earl Ezell, John Jenkins, Von Freeman, Buggs McDonald, Sax Crowder, Wilber Ware, Vernel Fournier, and a variety of musicians who drifted in and out of the band. Vernon Davis, for example—Miles Davis's brother—played trumpet with him for two or three gigs, then sang on a few more, with a voice which reminded Sonny of Billie Holiday's. Saxophonist Von Freeman recalls that a few of Sonny's original compositions for that band—like their theme, "New Horizons"—had "space titles"; but the book of arrangements was largely made up of older standards and blues. They eked out two or three gigs a year, mainly at the South Park Ballroom and a club on 39th Street, and rehearsed only a few weeks before each engagement. Out of this band Sonny made up a smaller group, which included saxophonist Ousley, drummer Vernel Fournier, and bassist Wilber Ware, which played originals only, most of which had no titles, and were modal in character, the melody based on a single chord or vamp, an approach to jazz which would not be understood or popular for another ten years.

In 1951 Sonny was introduced to Alton Abraham, a precocious fourteen-year-old minister's son who lived nearby. Abraham had some relatives named Blount, so he at first thought that they might be related, but

Sonny insisted he had no family. Over the years they were drawn together by a common interest in thinking systematically about the future—making "projections" as they called it. Like Sonny, Abraham was philosophical by nature, serious and scholarly, with a deep interest in science, metaphysics, and Bible scholarship, and both loved to talk; but unlike Sonny he was practical, careful, a conservative dresser. At first Abraham found Sonny's music too strange, but he soon became devoted to it. While working part-time at Provident Hospital and still going to school, Abraham began to assume the role of Sonny's patron, fundraiser, and all-around booster. He talked his family into helping financially, and he assisted in getting the band engagements, sometimes even sponsoring dances himself. As he grew older he was a steadying influence for Sonny, and generally encouraged him to believe that he had a destiny even greater than music. He took the burden of finance off Sonny, and began to steer him toward the public. Sonny "was an introvert, he was turned in on himself," Abraham said. "He fantasized a lot, but he didn't mix with people much. Bad things had happened to him in Birmingham. They had locked him up to try and break his spirit. I acted because Sonny was afraid to come out of himself. Sometimes it was even necessary to trick him into appearing in public."

In time, a group of nonmusicians began to gather around Sonny and Alton Abraham: among them was Luis T. Clarin, Lawrence M. Allen, the man who first introduced Sonny and Alton, and James W. Bryant, who met Sonny in 1953 and who owned a bar where Sonny played. Eventually, they formed a discussion group which also helped Sonny out financially and practically. This was the group which would eventually incorporate itself as Ihnfinity, Inc.

The group undertook their own research into ancient history and the origin of the races; they studied astrology, and sought an alternative to Darwinian evolutionary theory. They searched for books which many said did not exist, on music, the Bible, and science. "The main purpose of this organization," according to Abraham, "was to do some things to prove to the world that black people could do something worthwhile, that they could create things, they could do things that other nations would take notice of. It was not for everyone, but for those who know why they're here, not just living blindly and routinely.... It was for those who 'know,' (not those who say 'no'). We loved the United States and believed the Creator wanted the United States to lead the world. We wanted to save the United States, and in order to do that, we needed to drop the old ways and seek new ones which worked. Southern blacks were still living in the past, because the future was hard on them: blacks would have to become disciplined and prepare for the Space Age to come, for the U.S. had a role to play in Space. Sonny wanted to do things not the right way, but *another* way, a *better* way. The possible had been tried, and had failed; now it was time to try the impossible." It was a vision of the role of black people rooted in Booker T. Washington, extended by the progressive thinking of the *Chicago Defender* editorialists into the technological future, but carried far beyond the wildest dreams of any Race Men.

The group studied prophecies of all ages and peoples, and saw that the Prophecies of the Pyramid had predicted the end of this world in the 1930s, and so they understood that we were living after the end of the world, on borrowed time, and now faced the prophecies of Nostradamus for the next millennium. At first their efforts were private, for their own edification. But as their work developed their certainty grew, and they began to publish some of their research and spiritual findings in the form of leaflets which were passed out free, especially to musicians.

Few of these sheets survive, but one of them, which Sonny later gave to saxophonist John Coltrane, was widely circulated.

SOLARISTIC PRECEPTS

To those who seek true wisdom, the bible should be considered as Code (Cod) word instead of the Good Word or God Word. If you regard the bible as the "Code Word," you will be able to gain its hidden secrets. The hidden secrets of the bible are revealed visibly in its outer manifestations. The fabulous ramifications of the vibrations of sound in the outer sense which is the center and middle of the solaristic Eternal Thought can easily result in the creation of a Phi Beta sequence of life, which is twofold. The Divisions of Two: First Two: The sequence of life is the thorough consideration of the patterns of the past because coming events cast their shadow before, therefore the keys to wisdom are revealed in the unfolding of Hebraic SHD-ology in the life-giving form and the principles of ancient Sinology plus the sealed and hidden books of the angels of God, namely the Teutonic race of angels which are the visible host of the Eternal God according to the earth grammatical conception but according to our conception for every angel who is for US because you are either for US or against US. Us IS, US ARE, US BE, US AM (RE AM). Second 2: The sequence of life is sound diminished to its smallest point, the we of the Time to Live which is not recorded in the bible and therefore is in opposition to those who do not have a sine and since they are without the proper certification as those who are sine-conscious they are not aware of the diminished part of the Kingdom, as it is written "only the Few are eligible."

It is lamentable that NOT many people will understand this treatise which could well be a treaty via the Akhneaton version of sound (tone), if the many were not bound to the Christ-covenant which states that only the Few are eligible for life so in order not to antagonize the Kirk, only those who have shall get. The decree is that those who have knowledge shall understand our words which are a passport to Life.

Secret Keys To Biblical Interpretation Leading To The Eternal Being—

THE NUMBER 9

1	10	19	28	37	46	55	64	73	82	91
2	11	20	29	38	47	56	65	74	83	92
3	12	21	30	39	48	57	66	75	84	93
4	13	22	31	40	49	58	67	76	85	94
5	14	23	32	41	50	59	68	77	86	95
6	15	24	33	42	51	60	69	78	87	96
7	16	25	34	43	52	61	70	79	88	97
8	17	26	35	44	53	62	71	80	89	98
9	18	27	36	45	54	63	72	81	90	99

AKHNATON
"RA"

Warning: This treatise is only for Thinking "Beings" who are able to conceive of the Negative reminiscences of Space—Time, as is expressed in Is,

Are, Be and reconcepted "AM" which to the initiate is—, a symbol of Not or Non: Of course the idea is The Time To Live because if you are, you be, you is and Re—Am is more appropriate than I AM (which according to the bible is A Dead Dog).

Many of Sonny's concerns and methods are already recognizable in this early publication: close examination of language through wordplay and the scrutiny of homophones or near homophones (God/good/cod/code; Phi Beta/far better; sine/sign/sin/[Latin] without; Teutonic/two-tonic; Akhneaton/a-not-tone) and etymology (treatise/treaty), especially as those words relate to music; the effects of the *sounds* of words (beyond their meaning); Biblical exegesis combined with a skeptical eye to Christianity as it is popularly understood; the cross-referencing of folk and pop culture ("only those who have shall get"); the mysteries and transcendent orderliness of numbers; and the importance of duality, secret knowledge, and authority (certification, passport) and the affirmation of life over death.

Sonny often went to Washington Park, a center for black public discourse and political and religious recruiting, the same park where Richard Wright had received part of his education a few years earlier:

When I was in Chicago I would always listen to black people talk different things. I was in the park when the Black Muslims were talking. Everything would be in that park. It was really wonderful in Chicago. Everybody was expressing their opinions. A true democracy in the black community.

There he talked to whoever would listen, and argued over matters of ultimate concern with other groups who met there—Garveyites, Communists, fundamentalist religious groups of every stripe, all of whom had their regular spots in the park. Sonny often outdrew the others because he offered to answer all biblical questions. But the answers he gave were so threatening that discussions sometimes became fierce, so Abraham and the research group came along to participate and protect him. "Some people got upset," said Abraham, "and protested Sonny's views, saying, 'Next you'll be saying you're gods!' We replied we were, gods-in-the-making." (Later, to their delight, they discovered a two-volume work entitled *God in the Becoming.*) "We talked of space and science, of man's ability to be anything and to do anything he wants to do. But we said that man was out of tune with Nature, and has no respect for himself and no belief in himself."

In this group Sonny had at last found individuals who recognized his seriousness, who understood the tasks he had set for himself and who might yet understand who he really was.

For Ra had many names, but the great name which gave him all power over gods and men was known to none but himself.

SIR JAMES FRAZIER,
The Golden Bough

I can hear my black name ringing up and down the line.

LIGHTNIN' HOPKINS

For years Sonny had been attempting to deny his given name. Like another Alabaman, pitcher Satchel Paige, whose whole family changed the spelling of their name from "Page" to separate themselves from their father, Sonny attempted to erase his alleged kinship in order to free himself from his past life. Like the Paiges, he made a modest change in the spelling of his last name to "Bhlount" when he came to Chicago because it distanced himself from the name associated with him and because it seemed to approximate ancient Egyptian spellings; it was also a spelling of "Blount" known in Alabama. And when he began signing his compositions he sometimes used "H. Sonne Bhlount": "Sonne" because it punned on "Sonny" and *son,* the French word for "sound" (thus, he said, "the 'son of God' is the 'sound of God' "; and "H." added a certain decorum and an element of secrecy. ("That's the way Fletcher Henderson did. He would be doing some things under another name.") What others insisted on calling his "real" name was to him a curse. Like physicians who give Latinate names and chromosomal codes to physical conditions which the public labels as freakish, he began to bury his name. At one point he wrote to Birmingham for a copy of his birth certificate and was overjoyed when he heard back that none existed.

The changing of names is not unusual among black Americans; there is a tradition which on one hand draws from African precedents for giving sets of multiple names at birth, and on the other is part of a process of earning, inventing, or discovering new names throughout life. This tradition emerges in part from complex kinship arrangements, and is also fueled by the same impulse that leads new immigrants—whether to the United States, Israel, wherever—to change their names with their shifting circumstances; but an extra layer of complexity was added when enslaved African Americans took or were given the names of their former owners. And in the South names of both blacks and whites convey a great deal of information, not just about to whom you are directly related, but also your more distant relations, where you come from, and sometimes even your religion.

Over the years this tradition of renaming was addressed by figures as different as Frederick Douglass, Booker T. Washington, Jean Toomer, Elijah Muhammad, Ralph Ellison, James Baldwin, and Malcolm X, each of whom pointed to the communal consequences of a name—or the costs of the lack of one. Frederick Douglass, writing to a primarily white audience, made the knowledge of his true family and name a political matter, manipulating his name in his autobiography as if it were a work of fiction. Booker T. Washington began *Up From Slavery* by declaring that he had no knowledge of his birthplace and name, only that he was "born somewhere and at some time"; and proudly declared that he had named himself (only to add that he found that his mother had named him Booker Taliaferro when he was born). A later writer, Jean Toomer, was named by his mother, but changed his name many times, sometimes to acknowledge his relationship to his grandfather, Pinckney B. S. Pinchback (Governor of Louisiana during Reconstruction), at others to deny it, to create a new self, or to return to an older one. Elijah Muhammad addressed a black audience when he wrote: "My poor blind, deaf, and dumb people are going by the wrong names and until you accept the truth of your identity and accept the names of your people and nation we will never be respected because of this alone."

Common as it is, African-American renaming has a ritual element to it, a communally recognized sense that the individual has changed, that internal conflicts have been unified, that a new status has been attained. Sometimes a name is changed at conversion, as was Sojourner Truth's or Father Divine's, and the new name expresses the burden of spirituality. But even in such renamings the change may be more figurative and allusional than based in religion. Before he changed his name, Malcolm X's last name was Little. By becoming X he was at once signaling a break with Euro-Americans (a biological and social heritage that he wished to reject), and announcing that his real name—like that of all African Americans—was an unknown quantity, and that he was an "ex-", an ex-slave and an ex-Negro. Perhaps Muslim renaming even obliquely revises early Christian symbolism for the name of Christ. In any case, Malcolm was no longer Little.

Ritual renaming—whether inventing or discovering names—is a commonplace in African-American fiction, a metaphor which often grows so important as to consume the novel. The *Invisible Man* of Ralph Ellison's novel loses his name and has it replaced by the Brotherhood, a political group, only to have it destroyed. James Baldwin's preoccupation with his illegitimacy led him to metaphorically extend it to all African Americans through a nameless persona he created in his writing (*No Name in the Street, Nobody Knows My Name,* "Stranger in the Village"), and which he used as part of what he saw as his role to prophesy. *Song of Solomon* by Toni Morrison is a virtual book of names: "Names they got from yearnings, gestures, flaws, events, mistakes, weaknesses. Names that bore witness." And like a character from her own novels, Morrison (Chloe Anthony Wofford) herself even became known by the wrong name: "I write all the time about being misnamed."

Stage names add another level of complexity to African-American naming. But black stage names operate on different principles from those of whites, who choose names with simplicity and memorability as paramount concerns: thus it was that Thelious Junior Monk could change his name to Thelonious Sphere Monk. Images of power and respect are also common among the stage names of African-American musicians in the United States and the Caribbean, where they signify nobility (Sir Charles Thompson, Duke Ellington, Count Basie, Queen Ida, King Pleasure), reverence (Earl "Fatha" Hines, Louis "Pops" Armstrong), strength, and dominance (Mighty Tiger) or mystery and horror (H-Bomb Ferguson, Screaming Jay Hawkins). Sometimes black stage names may reflect excess and lavishness: Ferdinand La Menthe ultimately became known as Jelly Roll Morton, but in between he was also known as the Winin' Boy, yet another name broadly connoting indecency. And even where dignity and respect are the focus, humor and playful interpretation are usually at work. On his thirty-fifth birthday the pop star formerly known as Prince announced that he had changed his name to an unpronounceable glyph which combined and elaborated the symbols for male and female. Asked about the change, he said, "I followed the advice of my spirit."

The man born Prince Rogers Nelson goes on to explain, "I'm not the son of Nell. I don't know who that is, 'Nell's son,' and that's my last name.... I started thinking about that, and I would wake up nights thinking, 'Who am I? What am I?' ".... Later, at the Sporting Club, he'll add that "it's fun to draw a line in the sand and say, 'Things change here.' I don't mind if people are cynical or make jokes—that's part of it, but this is what I chose to be called. You find out quickly who respects you and who disrespects you. It took Muhammad Ali years before people stopped calling him Cassius Clay."

It was within this tradition that Sonny began to play with various possibilities, using different names from time to time to test their effect. The moon was a plausible goal for space travel in the early 1950s, and Sonny was fascinated by the subject, reading everything he could find; he talked about it so much that some musicians took to calling him "the moon man." He had come to believe that "Re" was the name of the Egyptian moon god, and when Sammy Dyer suggested he change his name to

"Sonny Re" the idea appealed to him, since he thought " 'R' is the same as 'L' in ancient languages." By this means he could secretly be Sonny Lee. But he went further. He prefixed "Sonny Re" with "le," which allowed him to simultaneously use the French grammatical article and an inversion of "El," the name of the high god, the creator god of the Caananites, as well as "Lee." L is pronounced "El," and in the same way R is pronounced "are" ("Re" is also a musical sound, the second note of the scale).

When someone told him that "Re" was a feminine form of "Ra," the name of the sun god of ancient Egypt, a name which would connect with "cosmology and planets and stars" and was "related to immortality and the universe," he began calling himself Sonny Ra ("ra" also being the flattened form of the second note of the scale). Then, with "Le" as the equivalent of "Re" at the front, he had "Ra" at the end. "I have many names. Some call me Mr. Ra. Some call me Mr. Re. Some call me Mr. Mystery." Re–Ra, Mr.–Mys. [Ms.], it was a duality a Gemini could revel in.

When he first told Alton Abraham that the Creator had ordered him to change his name, he was afraid even to say the name aloud, and wrote it out for him: either it should be "La Sun Ra" or "Le Sun Ra." Then, for reasons which remain secret, he settled on the form "Le Sony'a Ra," but again changed it to "Le Sony'r Ra." Alton encouraged him to make it legal, and on October 20, 1952, he changed his name to Le Sony'r Ra in the Circuit Court of Cooke County, Illinois. Sun Ra would be the abbreviated form for practical purposes, the *nom des affaires* under which he later incorporated:

> You see, on this planet everybody who came here tryin' to help the planet, they couldn't do it because they didn't have the authority to do it. So what I did, I went and registered Sun Ra as a business. So then I put down what my business is. So if I want to go out and help people, it ain't nobody's business if I do!

"Ain't nobody's business if I do" plays on an old song title, but his point about the corporate nature of his name was serious, and the implications were forever:

Sun Ra is not a person, it's a business name..., it's a certificate which was gotten in New York City; they didn't notice that I didn't have down there what my business was. They stamped it, notarized it, and they filed it. So therefore, it's a business name, and my business is changing the planet. If Jesus had done that, gone and gotten himself a business certificate, he'd have had the right and he wouldn't have had to go up there on the cross. But then, he didn't have no legality, and he didn't have any authority behind him whatsoever.... So Sun Ra is a business name.... And business is not family, nothing. They just happen. A business just happens, it's not born.... And corporations are like that, they just happen. And they're eternal, too.

So Sun Ra was a stage name, in the tradition of jazz royalty, but no one, not even the most desperately ambitious entertainer, had ever assumed the name of a god, and defied mortality.

He was well aware of the implications of his choice, and the African-American tradition of naming which lay behind it. Once, while speculating on why black people were treated as property in the United States, why they entered, so to speak, through the Department of Commerce rather than through the Department of State, he saw that they were considered *goods*, a word he in turn traced to the Middle English "god." And as gods (as with kings and queens) they had no last names. When these names became necessary they were given or took those of their white owners.

That's why I don't use no name except Ra because I saw that, and I'm not going to go and take somebody else's name; I'm not going to do that. I got my name, the Creator gave me my name.... I did it scientifically, and according to the book, which does say, "God is the father of the fatherless" [Psalms 68:5].... Well, if you go all the way back to ancient Egypt, it does say that Ra is the father of the gods, not man; he had nothing to do with him.

Once in place, his name provoked an endless stream of doubters. He was constantly challenged to reveal his "real" name, but to him this *was* the real name that had been revealed to him. To some journalists he gave answers of the highest seriousness:

Q: How did you get the name Sun Ra?

Sun Ra: Well, first you have an everyday name which is given to you by others. But then you need a name which expresses what you want to do and what you are doing. "Ra" comes from the Egyptian and has many meanings. For example, "eagle" and "weakness," but also "life" and "sun," and all this is found in myself. And "Ra" also has something to do with the mythical god. The name corresponds exactly to how I'm living here in the United States. It also expresses that I don't feel at home here. Ra also means "fire." "Arson" is the anagram of Sun Ra. My name also has something to do with the holy ghost.

Ra is my spirit name. You receive an everyday name from your parents, a materialistic name; but you also have a spirit name. Ra [Reh?] means evil in Hebrew. It also means god. So you got a problem there.

Though the source of his name was occult, he went to some pains to root it in family tradition, one of the few times he ever did mention his family:

When I moved to Chicago I used symbols of my own names, in fact, the name of my great-grandfather. His name was Alexandra. And if you say that as El-as-sun-dra it is Sun Ra. That is as far back as I could go, to my great-grandfather.

Sonny's explanations were never easy to follow, and Len Lyons understood him to say in an interview that his great-grandfather's name was "Alexanra" (Wesley Alexander, a violin player, who died when Sonny was twelve), and that he had separated the syllables to A-le-xan-ra:

... the x pronounced like z or s, and the words sound the same regardless of its vowel: "xan," "xen," "xin," "xan," "xun" all are pronounced like *sun.* The *le* of Alexanra worked its way into Sonny's legal name. Le Sony'ra Ra.... And the *A?* I forgot to pin him down on that.

In a lecture Sonny once pointed out that Sun Ra "permutates" into "earth," then into "thera": "the Ra." "God said he'd send a New Jerusalem, a new earth. That's the Ra."

But then, "in a sense," he suggested, he was always Sun Ra. " 'Herman' reversed is 'nam(e) reh' " ("Reh" with a silent h is one of the variant spellings of the name of the god Ra). "Herman" is also "Armand" in French; "Armand" (silent d) reversed is "nam(e) ra," or "permutated," "Man Ra" (which also suggests Amon-Ra, the patron god of Thebes), and in fact for a while he considered calling himself "Armand Ra."

Sometimes his discourses on his name turned into broad comedy. When some nonbelievers doubted his name he replied, "My mama always called me 'son.' " On his first trip to London he said that "I always called myself Sun Ra. I can't remember having any other name. At football games they holler my name: Ra, Ra, Ra, because they want victory." He told dadaist musician and neon sculptor Anson Kenny that religion is

on my side ... I mean aside from the fact that the creator is a music lover ... 'cause look, the letters R-E, why that's just another way of saying RA, my last name.... So you see that religion is just the legion of RA ... it's a peaceful thought.

Once, while he was in Paris jazz critic Philippe Carles asked him what "Sun Ra" meant to him:

I'm very interested in names, and "Ra" is older than history itself. It's the oldest name known by man to signify an extra-terrestrial being. It's very interesting to note that there is "ra" in the middle of "Israel": Is-ra-el. Take away the "ra" there is no more Israel. It's very interesting. And there is "ra" in "France" as well.

Though his name became a curiosity, a joke to some who called him "Sun Ray," after the drugstore chain (Lionel Hampton called him "Sunrise"), there was no question that Sonny was serious. Years later, when playing in Egypt, a TV journalist asked him about his name, marveling that with "Sun Ra," he seemed to have taken the name of the deity twice: he answered simply, "It's my vibrational name." On the same tour Tommy Hunter suggested that since they had gotten that far, they should go on to Israel to visit a friend of Hunter's in Haifa. "Israel!" Sun Ra shouted, "What are you trying to do to me? I can't go there. If I do, they can kill me. The name Ra is blasphemy in Hebrew. I'd be killed.

Christ was killed for saying he was God." "But Sonny," Hunter objected, "it was the Italians who killed Christ." "Yes, it was the Italians," said Sun Ra, "but the Jewish people decreed it."

When he returned to Birmingham many years later and came face to face with those who knew him from childhood during an interview for MTV, his old schoolmates reminded him that his name had been Herman Poole Blount back then. He weakly assented, adding that his initials were H.P.B., the same initials by which Madame Helena Petrovna Blavatsky, the most famous figure of theosophy, was known.

In spite of all his efforts most Chicago musicians continued to call him Sonny Blount. And in fact when he sought to copyright a group of compositions in 1956 he wrote the Library of Congress that his real name was Le Sony'r Ra and that he had two pseudonyms, le Sun Ra and Herman S. Blount (though the copyright card notes that in the 1956 Chicago telephone directory he was still listed as Herman S. Blount). It was not until he reached New York City that he was able to became Sun Ra.

THE SPACE TRIO

In Chicago 'Fess Whatley's equivalent was Captain Walter Dyett, band master at DuSable High School. A figure of enormous respect, a strict disciplinarian and perfectionist, a music teacher of almost heroic aura, his students over the years included Dinah Washington, Nat Cole, Bo Diddley, Gene Ammons, Redd Foxx, Dorothy Donegan, and many of the key players in the Association for the Advancement of Creative Musicians. Like Whatley, he put together society bands which played in the community and gave professional training to young musicians. And by means of various musical activities—especially an annual four-to-five-day review called the High Jinks—he financed the DuSable music program. It was impossible to be active in black music circles in Chicago and not feel his presence. It was out of his students that in 1952 Sonny set about assembling a new band, beginning with drummer Robert Barry, who had been studying informally with him for a year or so.

The next was Pat Patrick, a baritone saxophonist of enormous resources, a prodigy; a humorous but highly organized person, whose playing reflected both qualities. "He'd be playing and suddenly this note would come from nowhere, and sound wrong," said bassoonist James Jacson, who played with Sonny many years later; "but as he went on you'd see how it was deceptive...it fit perfectly." When he was in high school in East Moline, Illinois, Patrick and his mother had moved to Boston so that he could have hip surgery, and afterwards his mother relocated them in Chicago so that Pat could attend DuSable and study with Captain Dyett. Even while in high school he had played baritone saxophone in the house band at the Regal Theater, backing touring singers like Nat King Cole, Eartha Kitt, Sammy Davis, Jr., and Pearl Bailey. When he graduated from high school in 1949, he was awarded a scholarship to Florida A & M, but had returned to Chicago to enroll in Wilson Junior College.

Patrick was something special, a musician of the right spirit, intelligent, honest, serious. He saw to it that Sonny was protected, and was quick to help any other members of the band in trouble. Patrick was the best musician Sonny had ever had in any of his bands. He got the point of ideas and music immediately ("You got it down, Pat," Sonny always said). He had great hopes for him, and felt that with Pat he had the basis for a band capable of executing the music he had been working on for over ten years. The first step was to form the Space Trio with Barry on drums and Patrick on saxophones, a group which he saw as a vehicle to express his own relationship to the world he knew and distrusted:

> It was for my own edification and pleasure because I didn't find being black in America a very pleasant experience, but I had to have something, and that something was creating something that nobody owned but us...I have a treasure house of music that no one else has.

Sonny had a friend who let him use a small studio on 63rd Street, not far from the Pershing Hotel, where they held daily rehearsals; but the only regular work he could get for the Space Trio was back in the strip clubs of Calumet City.

On January 15, 1953, Sonny was playing a gig at the DeLisa with a band put together by Tommy Hunter. It was Hunter's birthday, and when the other performers heard about it they threw him an impromptu party. Tommy had never had a drink before, but when they toasted him with champagne, he joined in, and soon became drunk. Before the evening was over he became involved with one of the chorus girls and left with her, breaking the first rule of the club. When he came to work the next night, the manager told Tommy that he had heard about it, and that if it wasn't for the fact that he liked him, he would be dead by now. This was not an idle threat, since everyone had heard about the black musician who had become involved with a white club dancer and had later been found in front of one of the clubs castrated, with his tongue and ears cut off. When Sonny heard about Hunter he warned him that the mob might kill him anyway, and that he should keep hidden until he could get out of town. Then Sonny picked up Tommy's airline ticket and saw him to the plane back to New York City.

With Hunter gone he had lost one of his closest friends in Chicago. Next, a mortal blow was struck against his plans for a new band: Patrick announced that he was going to leave the trio to go to Florida to get married. Sonny was hurt, then enraged, and saw it as a personal betrayal. He attempted to argue Patrick out of going. He worked on him at every chance, alternatively threatening him, then promising him a future he would never find anywhere else. Patrick was torn, and explained that Sonny had inspired him, helped him understand his roots, his identity, helped him with spiritual matters; he talked about how being black could drive a person mad, and how that could be resisted. "Sun Ra was another kind of being. He was educational, he helped you to grow and develop. He was a black self-help organization run on a shoestring. Blacks don't have many people like him. If he could've had the resources, the planet would be a better place. That's all he's done: tried to make life better."

Patrick finally left, and Sonny replaced him briefly with tenor saxophonist John Tinsley, and next with Swing Lee O'Neil, and then turned the trio into Le Sony'r Ra & His Combo by adding bassist Earl Demus. O'Neil was in turn replaced by John Gilmore, another Dyett student who had known Patrick in high school. Gilmore had recently come out of the air force where he had played in a base orchestra at Kelly Field in San Antonio. Back in Chicago he played in some local groups and had gone on the road with Earl Hines's Band. He was a gentle man, scrupulously honest ("Honest John" was Sonny's name for him), an intensely dedicated musician with a single-minded devotion to his craft and a willingness to make the sacrifices and changes that Sonny called for. His personal practice habits were myth among musicians. Each morning he played on the mouthpiece alone for hours, then after a lunch break worked for three or four more hours on the horn, often playing along with birds outside his window. Like an Eric Dolphy or an Olivier Messiaen, he heard a superior music in their song, and a spirituality and innocence no longer available to most musicians. Gilmore aimed at perfection, and he was intolerant of sloppiness and ineptitude: he could not understand, for example, how it was possible for anyone to play out of tune. And Sonny's habit of taking on lesser musicians strictly on the basis of their potential was a constant source of irritation to him, and one that drove him to leave the band from time to time, joining Art Blakey, Freddie Hubbard, Elmo Hope, and other hard bop bands.

Alton Abraham now became involved with Sonny and his band, acting as their agent, and he quickly found them work at Shepp's Playhouse and Duke Slater's Vincennes Lounge. Sonny and Alton meanwhile got the idea of rehearsing and recording some vocal groups. At that time black groups were characterized either by their jazz influences (like the Ravens) or rhythm and blues (like the Dominoes). This music was sweetly harmonized, community-based, full of local values; but it was also a music widely admired and approved, since it was seen as a sentimental and romantic strain of black culture. In Chicago, small independent record companies were thriving on the sales of local artists' recordings, and some groups, such as the Spaniels, the Moonglows, and the El-Dorados, were just on the verge of becoming nationally known. Sonny's many years of hearing gospel quartet singing in Birmingham made writing for these singers easy.

One such group, the Rhythm Aces, had recently moved to Chicago after having been formed on an American military base in Germany, and began to rehearse with Sonny. When Jimmy Davis, the owner of Club 51 Records, heard them, he hired Sonny to coach one of his groups, the Four Buddies, to get them into the better clubs. Ularsee Manor of the Four Buddies remembered rehearsals at Sonny's apartment:

He taught us standards. We did "A Foggy Day," which I remember we sang at parties for some rich white people on the North Shore. He also taught us "Deep Purple," "My Future Just Passed," and "Summertime."... We didn't do any space songs, but Sun Ra did teach us this one song that imitated the sounds of the traffic and the el.

They didn't call him Sonny Blount or Sun Ra, but

Lucifer! That was the only name he would have us call him. Even after a year when he changed to Sun Ra we still called him Lucifer.

Sonny's rehearsals with singing groups went on for hours, and he recorded everything. Out of these tapes they began to issue records. There were the Nu Sounds, a group led by Roland Williams which Sonny recorded in 1954 at the Club Evergreen singing a straightforward version of "A Foggy Day," which they released years later on a Saturn single backed by a rehearsal take of the Cosmic Rays' a capella "Daddy's Gonna Tell You No Lie"; other groups they rehearsed were the Clock Stoppers, the Cosmic Echoes, and the Qualities, who Sonny recorded in 1956 doing two of his own holiday songs—"Happy New Year to You!" and "It's Christmas Time." The Cosmic Rays did two more singles, "Bye-Bye"/"Somebody's in Love," around 1956, and an instrumentally backed "Daddy's Gonna Tell You No Lie" coupled with "Dreaming":

> Dreaming, dreaming
> Here I am dreaming again
> Dreaming, dreaming
> I'm in a daydream again
> Sleeping, sleeping
> It's time for me to wake up
> For no matter how I dream
> It always makes me cry
> If you live in fables
> Then you'll know what I mean
> For that is a world
> Where things aren't what they seem
> Dreaming, dreaming, etc.

These were lyrics which could pass for a teenage lover's musings, but they were the first in a series of meditations on dreams which Sonny recorded over the years, including his own "Dreams Come True" and "Strange Dreams," as well as "Street of Dreams," "Daydream," and "I Dream Too Much," written by others. Accompaniment on these singing group recordings was rudimentary, often just some percussion to keep time, giving most of them the feel of rehearsal recordings (which by and large they were). But Sonny approached these sessions as seriously as any of his other projects. In fact, he wrote a whole book of songs and arrangements for the Cosmic Rays, including a stripped-down version of Walter Schumann's 1951 choral recording of the instrumental "Holiday for Strings." He also wrote the quartet "Chicago, USA," a cycle of songs which in the spirit of James Joyce's *Ulysses* was intended to represent an exact portrait of Chicago as experienced by a midcentury resident. No recordings of the songs survive, but John Gilmore recalled that "When you would hear the songs, they would depict Chicago perfectly.... The words would make you feel it ... "Take the Outer Drive / To the South Side..."

Later in 1958–59 Sonny appeared at least once again as pianist on a single for the Pink Clouds label, a recording company devoted mostly to gospel songs. On "Teenager's Letter" and "I'm So Glad You Love Me," he played behind Juanita Rogers and Lynn Hollings with Mister V's Five Joys singing backup.

During the same period, Alton Abraham arranged through his medical contacts for Sonny to play for a group of patients at a Chicago mental hospital. Abraham had an early interest in alternative medicine, having read about scalpel-free surgery in the Philippines and Brazil. The group of patients assembled for this early experiment in musical therapy included catatonics and severe schizophrenics, but Sonny approached the job like any other, making no concessions in his music. While he was playing, a woman who it was said had not moved or spoken for years got up from the floor, walked directly to his piano, and cried out, "Do you call that *music?*" Sonny was delighted with her response, and told the story for years afterwards as evidence of the healing powers of music. "Advice For Medics," a song from this period, commemorates this experience.

Slowly, with Abraham's encouragement and a few successes, Sun Ra the charismatic figure was beginning to emerge in the public. But if leaders are born and not made—and Sonny was not one to let a proverbial saying or a cliché pass unexamined—it follows that leaders would die. So teacher, scholar, another kind of being, agent of the Creator, messenger, he might admit to being; but a leader never.

THE ARKESTRA ARRIVES

When Pat Patrick returned to Chicago Sonny hired him back, but also kept Gilmore, turning the trio into a quartet. It was the beginning of many comings and goings for Patrick, but over the years he was one of Sonny's most important musicians. Now Abraham urged Sonny to assemble a larger band, surprisingly at a time when rhythm and blues and rock music were beginning to take their toll on jazz, and big bands were on the skids. And getting musicians to play with him was not easy. The arrangements were difficult, the music too strange for some, and Sonny's lectures at rehearsals were getting longer and more taxing. But he was able to recruit Richard Evans, a studio bassist for Chess Records, and trombonist Julian Priester, both of whom had been working in blues bands. Added to the quartet, this was the nucleus of a band that he would enlarge when work was available. Jim Hernden, a tympanist with the Chicago Civic Orchestra, was the next; then came Dave Young on trumpet, and later Wilburn Green (one of the first musicians to play electric bass), who sometimes replaced Evans; and bassist Victor Sproles, so two basses were sometimes used at rehearsals and on recordings. And from time to time Von Freeman rejoined them on alto saxophone, as did tenorist Johnny Thompson.

Sonny loved the bottom sounds of an orchestra, the baritone saxophone, the string bass, and the timpani, drums which were capable of playing bass lines, of changing pitch midbeat, and even of playing simple melodies. And Patrick was a powerful and experienced baritone saxophonist who could moor the band with stage-rattling resonance or sail above it in thin, vaporous tones. But when Sonny heard the playing of tenor and baritone saxophonist Charles Davis, another Dyett student, he asked him to join, so that he would use two baritone saxes as he had heard Erskine Hawkins do a few years before. Later he added alto saxophonist James Scales, who had played with Sonny in the Henderson band and who was now extending his playing in new directions beyond bebop; then came Art Hoyle on trumpet. With four to six horns and a rhythm section, the music was beginning to take on a special character, partially based on the blues, but much of it also intensely percussive.

During an engagement at the Summit Club, Alton Abraham organized a Sunday matinee concert for them at the Grand Terrace, the ballroom once run by Al Capone which had become famous while musical director Earl Hines's band was broadcasting weekly from there. This concert, Sonny said, was to be something else, an "outer space concert": "Our enemies were always saying that we were a bop band, trying to get us fired, but we were playing everything." The crowd they drew that Sunday was large and attentive, and for the first time included many University of Chicago students.

The band changed names several times. It was briefly known as the Modern Jazz Band, and then as the 8 Rays of Jazz. But now Sonny named it the Arkestra, a name which alluded both to the Egyptian god Ra's ark, his solar boat, and to the ark—literally a box—which held the covenant. " 'A covenant of Arkestra': it's like a selective service of God. Picking out some people. Arkestra has a 'ra' at the beginning and the end," Sonny said. "Ra can be written as 'Ar' or 'Ra,' and on both ends of the word it is an equation: the first and the last are equal. . . . That's phonetic balance." In the middle there is " 'kest,' which equals 'kist,' as in 'Sunkist,' and at first he spelled it 'Arkistra.' I read that in Sanskrit 'kist' means 'sun's gleam.' This is why I call my orchestra 'Arkestra.' " "Besides," he once told road manager Spencer Weston, "that's the way black people say 'orchestra.' "

Over the years Sonny changed the name of the Arkestra, sometimes even from gig to gig, adjusting it to the spirit of the occasion and the different feelings he wished to express. Put in a list, they form a concrete poem of names: the Cosmic Space Jazz Group, the Myth Science Arkestra, the Solar Arkestra, the Solar Myth Arkestra, the Intergalactic Arkestra, the Intergalactic Research Arkestra, the Power of Astro-

Infinity Arkestra, the Solar-Hieroglyphics Arkestra, the Nature-Immortality Arkestra, the Solar-Science Arkestra, the Solar-Nature Arkestra, the Intergalactic Research Arkestra, the Humanitarian Arkestra, the Transmolecular Arkestra, the American-Spirit Arkestra, the Blue Universe Arkestra, the Intergalactic Cosmo Arkestra, the Cosmo Drama Arkestra, the Cosmo Discipline Arkestra, the Cosmo Jet Set Arkestra, the Omniverse Arkestra, the Outer Space Arkestra, the Cosmic Stellar Arkestra, the Disney Odyssey Arkestra, the Spaceage Jet-set Arkestra, the Atlantis Odyssey Arkestra, the Astro-Solar Arkestra, the Solar-Infinity Space Arkestra, the Intergalactic Cosmo Arkestra, the 21st Century Echoes Arkestra, the Intergalactic Infinity Arkestra, the Inter-galactic Astro-Solar Infinity Arkestra, the Intergalactic Splendors of Love Arkestra, the Outergalactic Discipline Arkestra, the Year 2000 Myth Science Arkestra, the Astro Intergalactic Infinity Arkestra, the Transgalactic Astro Infinity Arkestra, the Omniverse Ultra 21st Century Arkestra, the Intergalactic Myth-Science Solar Arkestra, the Alter Des-tiny 21st Century Omniverse Arkestra, the Astro Infinity Micro-Ensemble Unit, the Love Adventure Arkestra, the All-Star Inventions, the All-Star Originals Arkestra, the Omniverse Ultra 21st Century Arkestra, the Chicago Reminiscence Arkestra, among others....

Once asked by a journalist why he had recently changed the name of the band to the Intergalactic Arkestra, he said,

> That's the dimension I'm currently involved in. Six months from now I might change it into something else. It all depends on what I write and what I'm thinking about. "Intergalactic" is about the things outside our galaxy. It's about the unity of all galaxies together. That's unmeasurable and, because of that, also eternal. In the old days I talked about being "interplanetary"; that was hip, too, but not immeasurable or eternal.

There was an element of secret knowledge about the unpredictability of the name of the band, as there was about the names Sonny gave to some of the instruments they used. A few of them were homemade, more were foreign, picked up on travels about the country, and some were not that unusual. But again like Satchel Paige, who gave dozens of strange names to the same three common pitches, Sonny was creating an instrumental mythos. There was the flying saucer, lightning drum, space gong, space harp, space-dimension mellophone, space drum, space bells, space flute, space master piano, intergalactic space organ, solar bells, solar drum, sunhorn, sunharp, Egyptian sun bells, ancient-Egyptian infinity drum, boom-bam, mistro clarinet, morrow, alto sax, spiral percussion gong, cosmic tone organ, dragon drum, cosmic side drum, and tiger organ.

SPACE LONELINESS

Loneliness was a leitmotiv in Sonny's life, and he performed it publicly with a thousand variations, weaving it through his conversations and his music. He reckoned it as the cost of being perceived as a leader and a scholar. And while he said he distrusted man, he would happily start a conversation with anyone on the street—children, old folks, winos, shopkeepers—and once started he could talk with the ardor of one who has spent too much time alone. Anything could animate him: a question, a word, something he read or heard on the radio or saw in a store window. You could say anything to him, ask him anything, and he would respond at length—though not necessarily to what you had said—in a soft hypnotic monotone which betrayed him and pointed south to Alabama. He seemed forgetful about dates, places, names, specifics, or maybe was simply evasive. The past, he said, was dead, passed, so he thought about it in a "futuristic" way. He appeared to think out loud, letting his ideas float loose, not in the style of the preacher or the lecturer, but as casual asides, lightly articulated. He might even fall asleep for a moment while talking, but would wake if you started to leave, and scold you, saying he wasn't asleep, just "cogitating."

For a man identified with outer space, he was markedly down to earth. His face was a mask, except when he laughed, and he would laugh at anyone, especially himself. Yet he was eager to meet everyone. Even years later when he was world famous, he'd welcome anyone backstage or into the dressing room. And if he had to, he'd sit on the floor or stand for hours to talk with someone, while the band waited in the hall or the bus. He'd rather talk than play, they said. Often in the middle of the night he got on the phone and woke up other musicians to play a composition he had just written or to talk about an idea which preoccupied him. The word soon spread that time meant nothing to him, that he never slept, that he had found a way to do without it, abolished it from his "so-called life," just as he had come to do without the distractions of drugs, alcohol, tobacco, women.

Those who live the jazz life, those who dwell and create on the margins of society and art, who toil on the real graveyard shift of life, whose art is rewarded less with fame than notoriety, develop means for dealing with it: brilliance, madness, hip talk, worldly polish, simple withdrawal, disdain, obsessions, addiction, a whole panoply of defenses, evasions, and shields. For a Thelonious Monk or a Bud Powell the technique was mute indifference; for a Charles Mingus it was irascibility and verbal barrage; for Duke Ellington a velvet wall of savoir-faire and sophistication. In some cases it was family that sustained these people, that made sleep in the middle of the day and sporadic employment seem normal. And for most, life with other musicians was limited to the bandstand, coworkers who didn't have to like each other; and when they did hang out they were like policemen who picnicked and drank together on weekends for the want of friends in the real world. But Sonny sought to make his musicians his friends, his community, a community he would recruit and train, who would live together and devote themselves entirely to his music and teaching, musician-scholars who he would tear free from outside interests and worldly distractions to be on twenty-four-hour musical and spiritual call. Though he never used the word "family"—except to deny that he had one—it was nonetheless the model which underlay his plans. The Arkestra would be family, with all the African-American resonance of the word for unity and survival and resistance; a family over which he would preside, paternalistically but benignly, with the discipline and precision that nature demands. They would be an example to the world of what a group of black men could achieve together, an echo of what the great dance bands had achieved under strict, intelligent leadership.

Though it was not easy to realize this dream in Chicago, he did what he could. They rehearsed every day in Pat Patrick's mother's house, or in the clubs where they were working, or in any space they could borrow. Rehearsals were exhausting but exhilarating ordeals, half musical instruction, the other half teaching, prognostication, and spiritual and practical advice. Although he did not insist on every musician believing him, or even understanding him, he nonetheless lectured them on personal discipline; on the history of black people and their role in the creation of civilization; on the use of music in changing the world; and on etymology and numerology, on astronomy and astrology . . . all of it interspersed throughout the rehearsal, spiked with jokes, wordplay, biblical interpretation, and anecdotes about famous jazz musicians.

He maintained that everyone should be vegetarian and eat natural foods and large quantities of fruit and fiber. It was a view that was strange enough for the time that it could make Eden Ahbez, the composer of the 1948 hit song "Nature Boy," the subject of newsreels and magazine spreads. But Sonny's own eating habits seemed stranger to the musicians. Even when they played in clubs which served good food and where the band could eat what they wanted for free, Sonny would bring his own food—an apple and bread, or peanuts and a special honey.

His lecturing style at rehearsals was not especially dialogic, nor did he encourage the musicians to play with ideas and words in the same way as he did. Once when he was discoursing on music as an example of how harmony, unity, and beauty could be created from the totality of a work—even while individual notes seemed to be in disarray—a musician who thought he had gotten the message asked him if "disarray" was something like a "sun ray." Sonny was not amused.

At a rehearsal he might begin (as he did at one in later years) by joking about something which had happened during his recent trip to Robert Moog's laboratories to look at the new synthesizers. One of the technicians showed him a theremin which was activated by touching a band of steel. But it wouldn't work for Sonny. "The man said, 'For some people there is a kind of skin resistance.' " "In other words," Sonny said, "for black people, it ain't gonna play!" Then, like a Booker T. Washington, he turned the joke into a serious discussion of the progress being made on electric instruments and how he had seen only white people playing at Moog's studios. "Black people are behind on these things, and they've got to catch up." Next he talked about his own preproduction model synthesizer and its uniqueness ("Sometimes it'll just start up . . . it acts like it's got a mind of it's own."). Then he interrupted himself to tell someone who had just arrived to get something to eat. Sonny then remembered that they had to visit the place they were going to play the next day in order to assess the acoustics, to decide on what they should wear, and to generally determine what effect they would have on the audience ("Sometimes an audience is afraid of me. They be like a bunch of zombies out there—*I'm* the one who ought to be afraid of them!"). A phone call interrupted him.

Then they began to work on a few bars of "Friendly Galaxy," after which he criticized the drummers' lack of energy ("You up in that Baptist snug-as-a-bug thing") which he contrasted to their extreme opposite: his sometime-drummer Clifford Jarvis's inability to control his playing and his temper. Back to the music. He cautioned the saxophone section that they were phrasing on the beat: "You got to anticipate the beat. It may sound out of rhythm, but it's not—it's an energy thing. Anticipate every beat—it was designed like that." They started again: "Don't worry about what's written, most of the world plays music without writing: your eyes and your spirit will have to come to terms. Don't count, don't even think." They tried again.

Listen to me. When I talk I don't count. When I want to emphasize a word I h-o-l-d it longer. Preachers reiterate and reiterate and reiterate (and meanwhile they're saying, "You're going to heaven, now give me money"). You got to reiterate, too. People can relate to that. Most people live like that. They do the same things over and over. Don't worry about sounding wrong. If you sound like you're wrong people will be interested. You don't ever hear people say, "Let's go hear that band: they play everything right." But if you play some things wrong, they say, "That band plays wrong: let's go see them." Sometimes we should even look like we don't know what we're doing. I knew a man in Chicago came to see me with his friends. He said, "I told them I wanted them to see you 'cause you *abuse* the piano." He wanted to see a piano *abused*.

They played the passage again.

That last phrase was off because you played it correctly. You should play it wrong—a little ahead of the beat. It's very effective. That's the way the older jazz musicians played it. They played a little bit ahead, then later, Chicago musicians decided to play a little bit behind the beat and that's

not easy to do. It's a little ahead or behind. Then there's music that's right
on the beat. Well, white people can do that. If it's on the beat they got you,
and say, "That's *my* stuff!" If you get ahead of the beat or behind the beat
they be talking about you and say it ain't even music, 'cause they can't
play it. If you play on the beat you can forget it, you won't have a job. So
stay ahead of the beat, something you can't count. Now, Lex Humphies
[the drummer] is passive. He's thinking, "Everything is beautiful, 'cause
I'm going to heaven when I die." So he's happy. But you don't believe that,
you're restless. You look out at the world and you say, "Something's
wrong with this stuff." Then you get so mad you can play it on your instrument. Play some fire on it. If you're not mad at the world you don't
have what it takes. The world lacks for warriors. You have to prepare
yourself accordingly.

They start the same passage one more time:

In your solos you can do that: play ahead of the beat . . . then you got three
things to work with. Because it's war in music. Black and white. You got to
be where you can win. You can't win over there with a symphony band,
cause you ain't got no symphony band or nothing. Without unity you
can't win. The white race is together. Don't be fooled, talking about revo-
lutin' . . . what the white race got to revolute against? They got everything.
That's not for you. Not no revoluting for black people, no freedom, no
peace. They need unity, precision, and discipline. That's what jazz is.
They say jazz is dead. No, the musicians are dead, jazz will never die.
They make the music dead 'cause a dead man can't play live music. He
can only be dead.

But by the time he returned to the music they were rehearsing, they
often forgot what it was he had wanted them to play. He could easily fall
asleep at the keyboard in the middle of rehearsal for a minute or two, but
seemed to always hear what was going on—especially badly played
music. It was not hard to see that he wanted to keep them around him as
long as possible, to avoid being alone. But nonetheless there was always
a serious purpose behind his talk.

I wanted them to be able to interpret things and I wanted them to expand
their minds, so they could play every kind of music, African, American,

or classical, and could make it sound natural. Everything we did had to be natural. For instance, if I write an orchestration, I want the solos to sound as if I'd written them, too, as if it were a continuum. I'd heard pieces written by an orchestrator and when the soloists started, something completely different happened, without continuity. To prevent this I had to give my musicians some understanding of the things I was talking about. Not that they had to believe in it, but they needed to know how I was thinking. I also knew how they thought and in that way I could write something that fit their personalities and capabilities.

> Some folks is born with they feet on de
> sun and they kin seek out de inside
> meanin' of words.
>
> ZORA NEALE HURSTON,
> *Mules and Men*

> Everything is here.
>
> SUN RA

Chicago in the late 1940s was fading from its early promise, its industrial base slipping away to expose the crime, political corruption, overcrowding, and ghettoization which lay beneath. It had become an October sort of city even in spring, someone said. But for Sonny it was another kind of magic city. You could see Frank Lloyd Wright and Carl Sandburg chatting and joking together on television; or go to Wrigley Field to see the Cubs and watch Ernie Banks, fresh from the Negro Leagues, becoming MVP twice and reminding everyone what a big mistake segregated sports had been. It was from Chicago that James C. Petrillo had demonstrated just how powerful unions could be by bringing recorded music to a stop in a nationwide musicians' strike; it was a city where an Alfred Korzybski could stride back and forth in front of a class, riding crop in hand like a Polish nobleman, propounding general semantics, a vision of language focused on the meaning of words as autonomous entities; a city whose main post office was fabled for being staffed by novelist Richard Wright, George Mitchell, the trumpet player from Jelly Roll Morton's Red Hot Chili Peppers, and—it was said— many of the black Ph.D.s in America. A city where an Elijah Muhammad could construct an empire out of an epiphanic meeting with a remarkable man and what he saw as the ruination of a great race; where a publisher named de Laurence produced books and pamphlets which revealed the magical Sixth and Seventh Books of Moses to people of color, books so threatening that they were banned in certain Caribbean countries; just over the city line in Evanston, anthropologist Melville Herskovits was dismantling the myth of the Negro past. And as Sonny would always remind folks, it was the city where the atomic bomb was developed.

Days, you could see him walking, now on the streets of the neighborhoods of Hyde Park and Washington Park. And though those sections of the city were suffering from a loss of affluent residents and were becoming overcrowded with southern workers moving north, they were vital and full of spirit, and they also contained Chicago's bohemia and the University of Chicago. Unlike Birmingham, all of the city's cultural institutions were open to people of color: there was the Museum of Science and Industry, the Oriental Institute, the Field Museum, the Art Institute, the public libraries, the bookstores on 57th Street, the Adler Planetarium. And there were parks, like Washington Park, where hundreds of acres left from the 1893 World's Colombian Exposition had been kept intact; or the Promontory Point, a park reaching out into Lake Michigan, where concerts and religious activities were often held. On Sundays there was the Maxwell Street Market on the West Side, which in another ethnic manifestation had been known as Jew Town, with its blocks of clothing stores, soul-food spots, and street vendors specializing in books, auto parts, Polish sausage, or nothing at all. There was Goldstein's music store, and Leavett's, a bar favored by musicians. And Smokey Joe's, the primary purveyor of hip male clothing in the city. In good weather the streets drew together jug bands, the Church of God in Christ singers, blues singer Daddy Stovepipe up from Birmingham, and Arvella Gray, who played an old National guitar and sang folk songs from the South. Between Maxwell and 14th Street on Newberry there was an empty lot where crowds gathered to talk and listen to the music under the boughs of a huge cottonwood tree. In front of them there was dancing in the streets.

Many nights he read straight through to dawn, and often in the cold of morning, just before light, he saw things most clearly. He found others who had been there before him, opened the same doors—holy men, cranks, scholars, eccentrics, self-ordained agents of the absurd.

The Bible was the thing he still had to wrestle with, what they call the "Good Book," but a book filled with the worst things imaginable, every form of death and suffering. When terrible things happened, people said they were "acts of God"; but why were God's acts so awful? What was the book meant to tell us? Why was fear of death the force which lay behind it? How could God allow his own son to die?

The babble of languages that filled the world since the Tower was built had to be decoded, reworked so that the original language of the Creator could be restored to its pure form. Some said that the Creator's original language had been broken into seventy-two fragments. Some said that the answer lay in scrutinizing the elements of existing languages, inverting letter and syllable order, reversing words; others insisted that writing was the root of the problem, that it was necessary to understand the true sounds which lay behind the misleading unity of the alphabet.

One approach was to learn Hebrew, the language that the Jews said was the closest to the Creator's. But the Kabbalists said that knowing Hebrew was not enough, that every character in the Hebrew alphabet would have to be pored over, investigated, understood as an element of the design of creation itself. In this way, they said, it was possible for the adept to meditate over these letters in a self-hypnotized state and glimpse, if only for a second, the true name of God. These letters could be weighed, given numerical values, and their meaning could be determined mathematically, by comparison with other words.

Some others said it was the word which contained the truth, not the letter. So powerful was the word, the Talmud said, that one letter too many or too few, one word out of order could destroy the world. And was it not just such human errors which created the obscurity of the Bible and set ignorance and disorder loose in the world to begin with?

He bought several Bibles, including one in Hebrew, and dictionaries in French, Italian, German, and Hebrew, *Strong's Exhaustive Concordance of the Bible, Blackie's Etymology,* Frederick Bodmer's *The Loom of Language,* and launched himself into the study of etymology, the search for the true meaning of words by comparison between languages and by tracing their roots. Etymology books could be read like histories, with their own story to tell of the paths taken by peoples and nations. A different word might flash in front of him every day for him to investigate. Single words could be studied, sounded out to release the meaning hidden behind the letters, to connect hidden meanings across different words and languages.

Even mistakes yielded meaning. Sonny told the Arkestra that if you listened closely to people mispronouncing English words, you could hear the way that they said them made them sound like words in other languages. It was also possible to find phonetic similarities hidden behind the letters of the alphabet, to find words within words, to find contradictions within single words. The written and the spoken word often existed in an antagonistic relationship. Only when the word had been activated by speech, and sounded out (what Rastafarians call "word-sound-power"), could the true meaning be known. It was something those Baptist preachers had known when they began by reading from the Bible in front of their congregations, and then went on, through chant and song and improvisation, to activate the text and transform the Bible's meaning.

This was dizzying business, endless, where even the simplest of words might have another meaning, and even the spoken word could conceal other words and meanings. The most innocuous of exchanges had to be scrutinized: he might respond to a simple greeting of "good morning" by asking whether it was "morning" or "mourning" that you meant. One word bled into another, sometimes leading you in one direction, sometimes in loops. After hours of close study you might even find your own name buried in an everyday word. Etymology was the path to wordplay, to puns and jokes, but also to the truth and beauty available only through poetry.

> Islam is mathematics.
> ELIJAH MUHAMMAD

Not many blocks away at the headquarters of the Nation of Islam, Elijah Muhammad was leading his own quest for knowledge and seeking the truths about African or "Asiatic" man as a means of liberating Negroes in America. Muhammad, the son of a preacher, had moved north and first joined the Moorish Science Temple of America in Detroit, a group which combined New Age Christianity with elements of Masonry and the Islamic tenets of a group of Moors who were said to have been part of America since the colonial days. But soon Muhammad encountered Wallace D. Fard, a Detroit silk merchant, who he came to recognize as the reincarnation of Allah, and he became his principle disciple. When Fard mysteriously disappeared, Muhammad moved on to Chicago where he founded the Nation of Islam.

At first glance Sonny and Elijah Muhammad seem to have much in common. Both had been raised Baptist and had been imprisoned during World War II for refusing the draft. And many of their beliefs seemed quite similar. They both perceived history as only one history among many, as a "white history," a history which robbed black people of their past and their true individual and collective names. They shared the idea that Negroes were spiritually dead and needed to be shocked awake (though the Black Muslims saw the answer in stripping "Negroes" of the materialism of the white world and returning to the message of their own version of the Koran and the Bible). And like Sonny, Muhammad believed the Bible (the "poisoned book") had been tampered with, and that it was necessary to reverse many of its symbols and meanings. They both believed in the power of secret and esoteric knowledge, and the importance of certain books in revealing the truth (Fard himself had a syllabus of 104 books which included Higgins's *Anacalypsis*, Churchward's *Signs and Symbols of Primordial Man*, and Massey's *Egypt the Light of the World*). There was their mutual identification with Ethiopia, Egypt, and the Sudan rather than with Sub-Saharan Africa; their belief that the

Negro had fallen from grace, and that existence in the United States was a discontinuity in a history of a great people; that black people must learn to restore their former glory and walk as kings and queens; and that apocalypse might be the eventual outcome for the peoples of Earth.

Sonny and his friends heard the Muslims talk in the park, argued with them, and they believed that they had come to influence the Nation of Islam with ideas such as questioning the name which had been given to African peoples in the United States ("so-called Negroes"). Muhammad's idea that "Negro" = "death" Sonny felt was his own. He had discovered that Roger Bacon's book on ceremonial magic was called *De Nigromancia*, and he found in etymology books that the Middle English "nigromancie" had been formed by folk etymology from the Latin "nigro" and had been substituted in Middle Latin for "necro" (dead). He also noted that the Muslims got the idea for starting their newspaper, *Muhammad Speaks*, after he had begun distributing his own leaflets, which they had read.

Nevertheless, Sonny and his research group were opposed to the teachings of the Nation of Islam overall: they could not accept that white people were devils ("black people could be devils, too"), nor did they believe in separatism. They felt that the Creator had a purpose for this planet, and the purpose included blacks and whites. Indeed, one race requires the other, and both are part of the equation of life. Further, it seemed wrong to them to deny many of the achievements of black American culture as Elijah Muhammad had done: for in that culture there were truths to be found, models to be emulated, even in the blues, in dance, and in jazz. Where Elijah favored a controlled, cautious approach to belief, putting behind him any sense of Christian ecstasy, Sonny reveled in a Dionysian display of joy. And though Sonny shared Muslim views on avoiding liquor and alcohol and minimizing the distractions of sex, the Nation's concern with modest, conservative dress made no sense to him as a performer.

At meetings with Alton Abraham and his friends he continued to discover new texts and pore over them for hours. Through Egyptian readings he learned of Hermes Trismegistus, whose writings had first appeared in the 1400s when a Greek monk brought them to Florence.

This Hermes was not the Greek god who had been syncretized with the Egyptian Thoth, but a man who was said to have lived before Plato's time. His ideas appeared Pythagorean, Platonic, and even vaguely Christian, and seemed to connect loose threads of Western thought, like those which ran between Greece and Egypt, and between magic, science, and religion. But Hermes, it turned out, was not ancient or even Egyptian: he was a Greek from the second or third century A.D. and was part of a Gnostic cult. But many—like the Freemasons, the Rosicrucians, and the founders of America—went on believing in the antiquity of his ideas, as he epitomized the nature of hermetic knowledge as they conceived it, the lost secret wisdom of Egypt as mystical tradition. Modern science had made this kind of knowledge appear strange and irrelevant, maybe even malign in intent. But its purposes were neither good nor evil, merely an effort to know the truth. And though it seemed lost and dead, bits and pieces of it still remained sealed in books and in the wisdom of a few, waiting to be shared.

Through his reading in science, Egypt, and spirituality he learned of the late-nineteenth-century visionaries and cultural revolutionaries loosely known as theosophists. First there was Madame Helena P. Blavatsky, the Russian-born mystic who spread her own version of Egyptian, Indian, and Gnostic occult ideas throughout the West, promoting a higher reality, reinventing herself as she went along. She had been, so it was said, an initiate of the Druzes, had studied hoodoo rituals in New Orleans, watched Dervish rituals, crawled over the ruins of the Yucatán, slept in the pyramid of Cheops, explored the beliefs of the Yamabushi in Japan, consulted Coptic magicians, and finally spent seven years with a group of mahatmas in a valley in Tibet who became her spirit-guides to the mysteries of the universe. Blavatsky had incredible influence at the turn of the century, inspiring Edison to consider the theosophic implications of the phonograph; focusing the mysticism of the Russian composer Scriabin to go on to experiment with synthesthesic composition and light organs. Theosophy was the force behind *Prometheus,* "The Poem of Fire," Scriabin's fifth symphony, with a chorus (and audience) dressed in white, and an organ which played lights and colors; and the source of what the composer planned as his ultimate work, *The Mysterium,* a week-long piece that would literally destroy the world and raise the human race to a higher plane at its finale.

Through Blavatsky's writings Sonny learned of all the secret societies, real and imagined, that were theosophy's precursors—the Rosicrucians, the gymnosophists, the Priests of Isis, the Pythagoreans, the Chaldean Brotherhood, the Keepers of the Orphic Mysteries, the Great White Brotherhood of Masters in Luxor. He read HPB's commentary on Darwin in *The Secret Doctrine,* where she asserted that "root races" were formed on earth from beings from the moon, as a part of a move of spirits from planet to planet in various stages of cosmic evolution.

In the work of one of her offshoots, Rudolph Steiner, he read of a German who attempted to bridge the everyday and the spirit worlds by means of scientific methods. Even though he was a scientist, more than any other theosophist Steiner knew the arts and treated them as central to his spiritual project. He had studied architecture extensively, extended Goethe's theory of color, and drawing from Wagner's notion of *Gesamtkunstwerk*—in which all arts would be incorporated into drama— he developed Mystery Plays which traced the spiritual development of characters through the use of music, color, speech, movement, and stage design. Through eurythmy—"visible speech & song"—he recognized that dance rhythms had been involved in the creation of the cosmos, and saw the need to restore rhythm to modern life as a means of communicating with the spirit world.

Then through Pyotr Demianovitch Ouspensky's writings Sonny uncovered the strange Greek-Armenian mystic Georgei Ivanovitch Gurdjieff. By means of a synthesis of number symbolism, Pythagorian musicology, cabbala, physics, esoteric Christianity, theosophy, and an interest in theater and music, Gurdjieff saw that man lives by habit, that he is asleep and must be wakened from this sleep, that there were other possibilities as yet unthought of in human life. It was necessary to shock people from their sleeping state, and music and dance were means of awakening emotional spontaneity. By assuming the role of jokester-guru to a group of intellectuals and artists who off and on lived with him communally, he had enormous influence in his life, even on those who had never met him.

Sonny was particularly impressed by Ouspensky's *A New Model of the Universe,* and took seriously his concern with the limits of scientific reasoning, especially in matters as important as the theory of evolution, and the need to reach beyond the limits of what are called objectivity and subjectivity to answer questions which otherwise appear unanswerable.

The key ideas he received from his readings in theosophy were those which reinforced ideas he already held: that the Bible must be de-mythologized, decoded, and brought in tune with modern life; that it was possible to unify all knowledge; that the universe was organized hierarchically, with forces or spirits which moved between the levels and affected life on earth; and that there were charismatic leaders who had the means to come to know these secrets.

Now everything flowed towards him, one idea leading to another, connecting unpredictably ... strange ideas, bizarre associations. Sometimes only a single word he read had meaning to him, but sooner or later it connected to others, so that everything was eventually related ... relativity, synchronicity, telepathy, clairvoyance, levitation ... all parts of the whole. After all the years of wandering he had done, all the blind spots and dead ends in which he had wound up, his reading was pointing him to the way; a golden road was opening up before him, leading him through the rubble of life, concentrating his dreams and fantasies, making clear what he must have always known, that there was something greater than Birmingham, than Chicago, greater even than the earth itself, and in it all he had an ordained role: he was a secret agent of the Creator. With music he would reach across the border of reality into myth; with music he could build a bridge to another dimension, to something better; dance halls, clubs, and theaters could be turned into sacred shrines, the sites of dramas and rituals, and though people would be drawn to hear the music, it was they who would become the instrument on which it would resonate, on which he would create the sound of silhouettes, the images and forecasts of tomorrow ... all of it disguised as jazz.

CHAPTER THREE

The rehearsals were the stuff of musicians' legends. Though Sonny said they were preparation for performing in public, music often seemed to be the subtext of some grander plan, one not always clear to the musicians. His teaching and orchestral directions were seamlessly connected, communicated by methods which were unorthodox, even within a musical tradition which self-consciously skirted the normal. He painstakingly demonstrated and modeled and described what he wanted from them in both musical and metaphorical terms. He wanted them to draw on spiritual resources that went beyond intelligence and knowledge: "If you can't involve your spirit in the creative process, you can't defeat the destructive elements on earth." Marshall Allen said that "Sun Ra taught me to translate spirit into music. The spirit makes no mistakes." This meant forgetting fundamentals, technique, method, style—forgetting "music." But to accede to these demands would leave musicians feeling ignorant and exposed. Which was exactly his intention: "Ignorance is the voice of the spirit." There were even drills and exercises for spiritual discipline. When they were on the road, and the musicians were becoming concerned that the bus might leave without them, Sonny would order them to take time to unpack and repack their bags. "The spirit will not lead you wrong." And most times, they said, the bus would be delayed or something would happen so that they would still catch it. But many musicians would leave the band at this point, especially those well trained in music and resistant to regimentation.

He did not tell you how to play your instrument, but what sounds should be gotten out of it and how and what they would affect, a differ-

■ 111

ent level of creativity. In order to activate this other level Sonny resorted
to paradoxical forms of communication. "He could *confuse* you into
playing what was necessary," said bassoonist James Jacson:

> He once said to me, "Jacson, play all the things you *don't* know! You'll be
> surprised by what you *don't* know. There's an infinity of what you *don't*
> know." Another time he said, "You know how many notes there are be-
> tween C and D? If you deal with those tones you can play *nature,* and na-
> ture doesn't know notes. That's why religions have bells, which sound all
> the transient tones. You're not musicians, you're *tone scientists.*"

Tone scientists. Not musicians. This was the crucial distinction for
Sonny. They were exploring sound, experimenting, not re-creating what
already existed. Tones. Not notes. Every C note had to be sounded differently from every other C, with a distinct timbre and volume. If you
worry about notes, you're stuck with certain rules and systems; but once
you hear music as tones you can make any tone fit any other tone. And
"you can hear what Billy Strayhorn heard on that subway which led him
to write 'Take the A Train.' "

Sometimes Sonny would try to disrupt the thought processes of a
musician by shaking a pair of maracas in his face, or by playing something on the piano which would break the flow of his playing. Sometimes he would ask them to try and remember what it felt like before
they knew how to play their instruments: "Remember how heavy that
horn was, how strange your fingers felt on those keys, how you never
knew what would come out when you blew on it? I want you to play like
that, to get that spirit."

He told them they needed to project their music: not to play louder,
but to put their sound in a particular place, "over there in the corner, for
instance." Horns should sing, not play—just as Billie Holiday sang like a
horn. They were to play with absolute individuality, but at the same time
be able to come together and sound with one voice when necessary.

His directions were often as metaphorical as were the goals of the
music. And with goals such as this it was difficult to know if they had
succeeded in a performance. Some instruments were told "to dig
ditches" on some pieces, or be more melodic and "touch someone" on

the next. He told Wendell Harrison, a Detroit saxophonist who rehearsed with the Arkestra in the 1960s,

"Play that apple." Or "play the warmth of the sun." Or "how does water feel? Play that." He said forget about form and play what you feel. He told me I'd have to learn to feel all over again.

He demanded precision and discipline, but the kind which comes from a natural affinity for music rather than from an impulse to suppress individuality.

It's probably this precision and discipline that are most difficult when working with me. Once during the recording of "Island in the Sun" the drummer, who had been playing with me quite a long time, just couldn't play the rhythm that I wrote for him. He still hadn't gotten it after a few hours and he was quite upset because he just couldn't understand. And he came back with his friend. I asked the companion to try and play the rhythm. She got it immediately. She was a dancer and could feel intimately this type of thing. On another occasion, another drummer was in the same situation. So I called some kid going down the street who didn't even know what a bass drum was. I told him to play it and he got it immediately. I suppose it's natural. I don't know what it's really all about, but it means that it's not necessary to really know music. Thus, when the concert was given in New York, the Arkestra started to parade around in the room, singing a tune that I had never given them, the audience was singing, too. We had to come back and sing it again. The public had learned all the words, the rhythms, and the harmony.

Sonny charged his music with Neoplatonism—the philosophical-mystical tradition in which music is seen as both a model of the universe and a part of its makeup, and where it has the power to bring human beings in line with the cosmos. These ideas could be found in Plato, or even before that in Damon of Athens or Pythagoras of Samos; and after Plato, in Anselmi, Ficino, and Agrippa, all the magical musicologists of the fifteenth and sixteenth centuries. But black musicians have kept alive their own version of this common heritage: one in which communal order and survival are modeled in musical performance, but also where the universe can be constituted from the interaction of the musicians, and in which aesthetics takes a back seat to the ethics displayed in the interplay and representation of the music. Sonny, along with Schopenhauer, thought that music is the purest form of expression, a universal language which reaches the emotions directly. Then again, unlike language, music is neither arbitrary nor a creation of human beings. Music preceded the human world, and could continue to exist without humans.

By erasing the line between rehearsal and performance, by tape-recording both, he put incredible responsibility on the players. He warned them that a single wrong note could cause incalculable harm to the universe. But what was a wrong note? Playing out of tune? "Anyone can make sense playing in tune. But can you make sense playing *out* of tune?" he asked. A mistake? "There *are* no mistakes. If someone's playing off-key or it sounds bad, the rest of us will do the same. And then it will sound right." The lesson was that it was a common enterprise, and that solutions to problems were a collective matter. Was a wrong note one that was unplanned for, one that was unexpected? This band thrived on the unexpected. And just in case nothing unexpected happened, Sonny built in surprises. Sometimes he raised or lowered given notes (changing the *accidentals*, the sharps and flats) on popular standards to give them a dissonant edge and wake up the audience. Or he might call on a single player to play sharp for the whole evening.

Sonny said, "If music is in your heart, you can't do anything wrong." A player struggling with one of Sonny's melodies would be told to "play it like you feel it." He would try again, and when he apologized for missing notes, Sonny would say that as long as he had the feeling, he didn't care about wrong notes. "Let it stay in the air. It'll be resolved." Or he might say, "Why don't you make a mistake and do something right" (that is, if you don't make mistakes you won't ever be creative). Or again, "If you can't play it perfectly right, then play it perfectly wrong."

"Sonny gave you a form, but freedom to do what you wanted to do with that form. He didn't want his music to be perfect," trumpeter Lucious Randolph—the son of Zilma Randolph—said. "He continued to turn a new page; one thing at rehearsal, another at the gig." It was part of Sonny's definition of discipline.

In the army you have to go through disciplined training. After that, in battle, you are confronted with something different from what you learned,
so it's necessary to invent on the spot. If you're not capable of finding
something else you're not a good soldier. Discipline ought to permit people to find the most natural things. Without the base, total freedom is impossible. Everything needs roots.

Now, in rehearsal we do just like a football team. I give them their little exercises, strict, disciplined rhythms. But when you get on the field
you don't do exercises. Then it's part of the game, and you do what you
have to do.

His compulsion for change put the musicians on edge: According to
Randolph, "We rehearsed one way on paper and then played another
way on the gig. It was frustrating. When you complained, Sun Ra said, 'If
you're a musician you'll follow me.' He was obsessed with change. He
wouldn't eat the same thing at a restaurant two times in a row, even coffee... he'd order water with sugar."

As the years passed a more or less stable group of musicians developed around him, and his rehearsals become increasingly enigmatic and
complex. For one piece he would tell a musician, "You start a four [four-
bar solo]"; then tell another, "You start on the second measure of the first
guy's four." "It got real mixed up. Sometimes Sun Ra had the whole band
soloing; he'd tell the whole band to take four, then there would be two
written bars, then the whole band would take four again."

JAZZ MAGAZINE: How would you define your rapport within the Arkestra? Strictly professionals, quasi-family, or scholars?

JOHN GILMORE: With Sun Ra we're like pupils with the master.

PAT PATRICK: You could even say that we are less than his pupils: we're nobodies with the master.

When a musician approached Sonny and asked if he could join his band, he often answered that it wasn't his, it was the Creator's, and he was only carrying out orders. Part of his orders seemed to be to welcome into the band a few musicians with emotional and drug-dependency problems and make them a special part of his plan. Sometimes these were people who were not especially good musicians and could not succeed in other efforts in life and might even be destructive if left on their own. He would complain ("Why does the Creator send me such knuckleheads?"), but he knew they had something to offer, a vision to express; even the illiterate or the child knows something unique and important, he said, and we could know what that was if only the right discipline could be brought to bear. And discipline and control were required to create a band which could at once include musicians from the very best music schools and amateurs; intellectuals and comedians; those who had given up otherwise lucrative careers and those who had never held a job; and sociopaths whom only their mothers, the army, or prison might be able to restrain.

"He sometimes brought people into the band who we couldn't understand what he saw in them," James Jacson said.

We'd complain that they were drinking too much, using drugs, and going after women—not realizing that we had all been like that before we managed to discipline ourselves. Sun Ra sensed who would have the will power to give up everything and start a new life. He knew who would be able to subordinate himself to him in order to play his music. He was almost always right.

Sonny's business relations with individual Arkestra members were perhaps no more paternalistic than those of other big bandleaders of his generation, but unlike most, he handled business himself; and since most of the musicians depended on him at least some of the time for a place to stay and for something to eat, his involvement in their lives was more complex. In later years he insisted on a level of moral adherence which was at odds with the lives led by many jazz musicians, even when it was not always clear what he wanted. Drugs were forbidden, certainly, as was drunkenness; and involvement with women was discouraged, especially across race lines. This meant that some of the band had to go out to drink, sneak a joint on the gig, or see women on the sly, like athletes tricking the coach.

Punishment was usually verbal, couched in jokes and wordplay, and, like the music's parts, suited to the individual. Some he would cajole and compliment; others he would curse, insult, use the dozens on them. He might put the "fire" on them, in both a physical and a psychological sense, where everything might go wrong for you—but you alone. What might be negligible to another would be hell to you. It was your own personal hell. Or he might give you the "royal treatment," put you in the best room in the best hotel in town, make sure you had the best meals and transportation and were well paid, but always separate from the band, and not allowed to perform.

Sometimes Sonny's sense of discipline demanded a witnessing: a member of the Arkestra might give a brief account of his progress and testify as to what Sun Ra had done for him. Or an errant musician might make a short confession of what he had done wrong and how he was being corrected.

Those who broke the rules were punished subtly. You'd be allowed to sit on the stage with the Arkestra, but forbidden to touch an instrument. He might even inform the audience about the punishment being meted out. He called me up front and told the people: "This is James Jacson. Two months ago he missed three of four rehearsals and that's why he's not allowed to participate tonight." You'd be put in your place like a child. It was one of the sacrifices you had to make in order to work with Sun Ra.

For those who were otherwise incorrigible the discipline could sometimes amount to house arrest. This was the scene that Jacson encountered at the first rehearsal he attended:

> When I sat down in the back of the band I noticed there was someone be-
> hind me in the closet. Every once in a while I'd look back and he'd still be
> in there. At one point he asked Sonny if he could get something to eat.
> Sonny sent him into the kitchen to get some food off the stove, and once
> he'd eaten, he told him to get back into "jail." After a while Sonny told
> him to come out, and he started playing drums. He was a hell of a drum-
> mer! And I thought, what kind of band is *this*!
>
> Later when I got a chance I asked Sonny why he was in the closet, and
> he said, "For being disobedient. I told him to leave Sweet Lucy alone." I
> thought he meant women, but he was talking about wine.

Other members of the band usually enforced the discipline, but on
rare occasions if he was angered, Sonny was capable of physical force as
well. He said he never fired anyone (it was the Creator's band, after all),
so you would have to fire yourself. There were other jails you could live
in, he would add, but make no mistake, you have to live in one jail or another. And Ra's was the best.

As the press became curious about the mysterious workings of the
band, he forbade the musicians from speaking to them without his permission or without him being present. And by and large his wish was
kept. His domination of the band set them apart from all other musicians of the time, and made them the subject of joking and cruel re-
marks. But there was respect for them as well, especially as it became
obvious that they were achieving something unique. Even enemies
would grudgingly grant that Sun Ra knew how to keep an orchestra together.

It was not money which kept them together, however, for they seldom
made much money as a band. And Sonny administered their individual
pay by a logic which was not always apparent—by how well they were
playing, how many rehearsals they attended, how long they had been
with him, how well they obeyed his instructions: "You never knew what
you'd get paid—$5, $15. But you always got something." In any case he
never tolerated questions or arguments about money.

Occasionally, the problem could come from one of the regulars in the band, as when Ronnie Boykins's complaints about pay and not receiving credit for his compositions led him to leave the band, a loss that Sonny never quite recovered from, and sometimes had him playing with no bassist at all rather than accept a player inferior to Boykins.

When new members were added for a performance his financial practices could provoke some weird scenes. Once after a gig at Alice Tully Hall, an out-of-town trumpet player hired for the night approached Sonny as he sat on the steps of the hall and asked for his pay: "It's getting about that time, Sonny." But Sonny suggested that he not be so impatient and that he sit down with him and talk about more important things... the stars, for instance. "I know what you're saying, my brother, but I'm tired, I'm hungry, I got a train to catch, and I want my money!" When Sonny told him that if that was his attitude he could forget about the money, the trumpeter pulled a gun on him, and had to be wrestled to the ground by half the saxophone section. Meanwhile, New Yorkers strolling by on Broadway, enjoying the balmy evening, scarcely noticed a group of golden-robed musicians rolling around on the steps with a pistol. "Some people have no discipline," Sonny said.

"Guys like Monk and Sonny thought music twenty-four hours a day; they were like scientists... like Einstein. We'd rehearse all day and right up till you performed, get off at 4 A.M., rehearse at 12 until 4, then back again." "Sonny felt that the spirit of God was there. He couldn't stop rehearsing until it left." The long rehearsals were part of his plan, a way of building up stamina and testing commitment. One of the musicians estimated that they practiced 180 hours for every hour that they played in public. It was not unusual for them to rehearse for hours before a gig, pack up their instruments, and proceed right to the performance. Those who joined the band and complained about money were told "If you can't stand the snow, you shouldn't go live at the North Pole." Or, "The Creator doesn't charge you anything for the water, the sun, life. What gives you the right to nag about payment for music that you make?" At times he tested new players' commitment by refusing to tell them where their first gig was: "Use your intuition," he would say. And by whatever means they used, they usually found it.

Once when he was talking to Dutch interviewer Bert Vuijsje about the resistance that musicians could show to his teachings at rehearsals, he said,

> I realized that it would be very difficult. It had something to do with what you could call philosophy. In the beginning they showed lots of resistance, although they liked my music, because I was working with all those new chords. They also knew that I could teach them something because I knew music theory. That's why a lot of musicians came to me.
>
> BV: But you wanted to teach them more than just music.
>
> SR: Right. I wanted them to be able to interpret things and I wanted them to expand their minds, so that they could play every kind of music, African, American, or classical, and could make it sound natural. Everything we did had to be natural. For instance, if I write an orchestration, I want the solos to sound as if I'd written them too, as if it is a continuum. I'd heard pieces written by an orchestrator and when the soloists started, something completely different happened, without continuity. To prevent this I had to give my musicians some understanding of the things I was talking about. Not that they had to believe in it, but they only needed to know how I was thinking. I also knew how they thought and in that way I could write something that fit their personalities and capabilities.

"At the beginning of each rehearsal," Jacson said, "Sonny talked about [his cosmic philosophies], sometimes for many hours."

> But nobody was obliged to agree with him. He forced us to understand his philosophies, but that too was a training in discipline, and after all, they weren't that strange. Almost all jazz compositions and songs were about love, but Sun Ra wanted to communicate an emotion that people don't know. That's what he chose the cosmos for. Music is the language of the universe. Imagine you meet a creature from another planet. You won't be able to communicate in language, but you will be able to tell something in music. That's what Sun Ra meant when he said his music came from "outer space."

Like punishments, every part of any arrangement he wrote was suited to a specific individual, "according to his vibrations, capabilities, and potentials," because he sensed that each person, musician or not, gave off a different vibration, and each vibration had a different color.

> Can't nobody else in the world play it. It's just like a suit made for you. It might fit somebody else who looks like you but it'll fit you [better] because it's made for you.

He needed a permanent body of musicians to play what he wrote, but without steady work for them it was tough. He resented his musicians playing with other bands, but there was little he could do, and he said nothing about it to most of them. Though he wrote out each instrument's part in a hand that was so large and clear that it seemed like something out of a school exercise book, his music was too complex to sight-read, too full of unusual intervals and unexpected rhythms, so long rehearsals were necessary even in periods when they were working regularly.

With such individualized music a great deal of work was necessary to pull a piece together, especially if new players turned up at rehearsals, or if any players were missing or left the band. When one of their best drummers turned out to be unreliable, Sonny talked John Gilmore into playing drums and for years he kept a small set beside his seat in the saxophone section so that he could double on them. And since Sonny could not count on every musician being at rehearsals—or even at paying engagements—he tried to write pieces which were adaptable for any size group, from trio to twenty players, but sometimes wrote pieces to be played only at a single rehearsal:

> First I need to know who's coming to practice. If seven musicians show up I write a septet, and then nobody else can join that piece. Everything I write is compact. If it's written for two instruments it's so compact that nobody else can join. It's the same with one instrument. If I write a piece in which I have no part, then I can't play in it. Then I don't belong in it. I sometimes do that—writing something in which my only contribution is my being there.

But regardless of how few instruments he had, his harmonies always seemed full and rich to the musicians.

When musicians left the band they often took their parts with them—
Sonny encouraged them to do so—they'd need them sooner or later, he
said. So when new players joined the band he had to write out fresh parts
for them and gradually the old arrangements would be transformed into
new ones. But he continued to hear certain musicians in certain pieces,
even if they had left him years ago. When saxophonist Ronald Wilson
turned up by surprise at an Arkestra performance after having been gone
for twenty years or so, Sonny handed him a part for "The Mystery of
Two" with his name on it: "I just wrote a part for you."

...in my music, there's a lot of little melodies going on. It's like
an ocean of sound. The ocean comes up, it goes back, it rolls.
My music always rolls. It might go over people's heads, wash
part of them away, reenergize them, go through them, and then
go back out to the cosmos and come back to them again. If they
keep listening to my music, they'll be energized. They go home
and maybe 15 years later they'll say, "Whoa, that music I heard
15 years ago in the park... it was beautiful!"

SUN RA

Composing for him was not a matter of commerce, not a means to
material success; it was not even music necessarily intended for a human
audience. His compositions were all dedicated to the Creator, and
formed what he called "the private library of God":

It was really not to be part of the world.... I felt that every innovator on
this planet was never accepted, whether they were classical composers or
otherwise.... I did not want to fight to get people to listen to it. They
needed me. I didn't need them. So, therefore I went the way anybody with
wisdom would go: you just disconnect yourself spiritually.... Some people develop their minds. I developed my spirit and I went in another direction.

Therefore I went places, I saw things and I heard things that possibly no one else on this planet had heard before and I recorded it so that I remembered some of it when I played it back; because it is like in code, you see, and by me listening...I can recall something that I may have forgotten about.

Few people recall seeing Sonny composing or writing arrangements, since he worked alone, usually in the middle of the night. He wrote out parts quickly, instrument by instrument, as fast as he thought them up. It was all laid out in his head. Sometimes the musicians' parts would be two or three pages long, while Sonny's own part would be only a scrap, or something written on a matchbook. But since arrangements were corrected, embellished, and improved at rehearsals and each player was expected to make corrections in his own parts, every musician in the band was part of the composition process. Often arrangements were developed on the spot, Sonny calling out the musical line for every player so they could write them down. And while the band played the melody he would improvise a counter-melody on the piano and give that to another part of the group. This way he could arrive at a rehearsal with two or three compositions and leave with five or six.

Sun Ra writes his compositions the way plants grow. It starts with the seed of a few lines he'll write to be played by one of the Arkestra. Sun Ra thinks in terms of a specified soloist; say, for instance, oboist–alto saxophonist Marshall Allen. Sun Ra has come up with a particularly exotic line for Allen's oboe. Just a few bars. This takes root and grows into a full melody. And then the branches form: a harmonic line for one of the trombones, another line against that for trumpet, and so on, until the whole thing is complete, and there's a part for everyplace.

It was a process of composition comparable to Duke Ellington's, with the band serving as the leader's instrument. Over the years, he adopted this collective compositional method as his means of working, "according to the day, the minute, and what's going on in the cosmos. And actually each one of my numbers is just like a news item, only it's like a cosmic newspaper."

He composed and arranged without concern for the difficulty of performance or the limitations of specific instruments. "He would throw you. The writing would go out of range, or get into a range that a musician wasn't comfortable with. His writing would ask for falsetto tones or go below your range." Each part was built up from the melodic line, with extraordinary attention given to individual notes, their articulation, dynamics, and the quality of sound.

Yet despite the rigorous rehearsals and the meticulously notated music, it was never played as written. "Sun Ra was an enigma for me," said trombonist Julian Priester.

> ...I mean he would write something out, it would only be a sketch of what he really wants and then he would go through a process of changing that original idea around, so that by the third or fourth rehearsal there was nothing familiar on that paper. Everything was committed to memory and it started to grow from that and he would still add ideas to what he was directing every day. Sun Ra was a genius at it, he sort of directed us and kept us in the dark at the same time.

But Sonny explained why he wanted the musicians to play everything from memory: to keep the music open.

> ...that way they gotta rely more on their feelings, their intuition. They gotta work harder, put more of themselves into it. That way, even the written ensembles sound like solos. That way, the band never sounds complacent. Something that's perfect is something that's finished, and if it sounds finished, it doesn't have any spontaneity left, and then it isn't jazz. That's how I keep that feeling of swing in there—the true feeling of jazz.

When he began a new composition he sometimes started by imagining a title. Some titles became music, others remained cryptic notes on scraps of paper: "One day he started talking about Chicago blues," Lucious Randolph remembered, "the blue of the sky, policemen's uniforms, bus driver's uniforms. 'I'll call it the "Land of the Blue." ' But he never wrote the tune." The titles were meant to serve as guides to the musicians as to what should be played, but he seldom elaborated on the meaning or gave the musicians more specific instructions. "Each song and album title had a message in it," Alton Abraham said, "a coded message to improve the lot of the people of the earth. 'Call for All Demons,' for example, was a warning about the future." But often that was enough. Baritone saxophonist Danny Thompson said that once in Detroit they were playing "Sun Procession" which had a long baritone line:

> I could feel the heat rising through my feet and into my head. It felt like the sun. Another time we were rehearsing "Along Came Ra": All the lights on the block went out for five minutes. Sun Ra said, "You got it right!"

Yet sometimes the musicians weren't even told the titles of the pieces, and records were known to appear with black labels and no titles at all. This was the music that Sonny called particularly "primitive, natural, and pure." At other times the same title would be given to two totally different pieces, as in the 1956 and 1986 recorded compositions "Reflections in Blue," the 1958 and 1986 "Hours After," or the 1960 and late 1970s "The Others in Their World." Still other compositions were titled only by the dates on which they were written, sometimes several on one day, such as "December 16, 1984A" and "December 16, 1984B"; and there was also a series in his book called "No Name #1," "No Name #2," etc.

But by and large Sonny's titles were programmatic in the grand sense of the word, and his compositions which referred to Egypt, Africa, and the ancient world sought an exotic change of place (just as did Duke Ellington's in his "jungle" phase): "Africa," "Aiethopia," "Along the Tiber," "Ancient Aiethopia," "Ankh," "Ankhnaton," "Atlantis," "Bimini," "Dawn Over Israel," "Egyptian Fantasy," "The Nile," "Nubia," "Pharaoh's Den," "Pre-Egyptian March," "Pyramids," "Solar Boats," "Starships and Solar Boats," "Sunset on the Nile," "Tiny Pyramids," and so on. Later his titles shifted to a kind of exotic futurism: there was the Cosmic and Cosmos series ("Cosmic Chaos," "The Cosmic Explorer," "Cosmic Forces," "Cosmic of Africa," "Cosmo Approach Prelude," "Cosmo Dance," "Cosmo Energy"); a series on the planets ("Blues on Planet Mars," "Earth Primitive Earth," "Jazz from an Unknown Planet," "Jupiter Festival," "Neptune," "Next Stop Mars," "On Jupiter"); on the sun ("Children of the Sun," "Dancing in the Sun," "Face the Sun," "For the Sunrise," "The Sun Myth," "Sun Procession," "Sun Song"); on outer space ("Celestial Love," "Celestial Realms," "Celestial Roads," "Cluster of Galaxies," "Distant Stars," "Friendly Galaxy"); on space travel ("As Spaceships Approach," "Cosmonaut-Astronaut Rendezvous," "Journey among the Stars," "Journey Outward," "Journey Stars Beyond," "Journey through the Outer Darkness"); and on the future ("Future," "Music from the World Tomorrow," "New Horizons," "Where Is Tomorrow"). In an earlier phase he had taken people to what Amiri Baraka called a spiritual past; next he sought to take them to a spiritual future.

As recondite as these titles might be, a black tradition already existed for this kind of labeling in jazz. The earliest jazz musicians often gave their pieces obscure or extremely local names (based on the names of friends, local characters, places, trains, towns, and streets; dance crazes; or obscene expressions); by the 1950s jazz titles were sometimes simply based on sounds ("Klactoveesedtene," for example, a word which Charlie Parker felt had a "Swedish" sound to it); rhythms (Thelonious Monk's "Let's Call This," the first and third words perhaps suggesting quarter notes, the middle word a half note); or speech-inflected instrumental figures (Miles Davis's "So What" with its falling pitch).

The point was to expand possibilities, to reach beyond the limitations placed on them by circumstances:

> The music up till recent years was always about "Sweet Sue" and "Mary Joe," it was always about love. Very seldom did they branch over into anything else unless maybe it was about the blues. It was always about human emotions that everybody could feel, but it was just a repeat thing. It wasn't bringing people any new emotions, you see, although they got a wide range of emotions that they never used, a lot of feelings they never felt.

Inspiration for compositions was not strictly a matter of chance for Sonny, if for no other reason than he didn't believe in pure chance; but he did take advantage of moments of sudden inspiration created by the convergence of various elements. So while playing a piano exercise one day, it struck him that if he merely changed the accents it might swing, and turn into a different piece. Like many pianists-composers-orchestrators, he thought orchestrally even when playing piano:

I have always thought orchestra. I play that anyway, even when playing the piano. I'll be doing these things without thinking about it because the mind can't handle it...Today I was humming something and analyzing how I was going to write it for the band. It was imagination. It wasn't 3/4, wasn't 4/4, wasn't 5/4. It was none of the times. It could be something like 3 1/2 time. A little hesitation, a slice of a beat in there and you really can't count that, you play it.

He might also be led into a composition by the peculiarities of one or another type of keyboard—celeste, piano, organ, Solovox—which produced a specific feeling that he could use. In the same spirit he encouraged his musicians to bring different types of instruments to rehearsal, and if he liked what they'd brought, he'd work them into his compositions.

[When I compose] I pay most attention to the brasses, but I can orchestrate or compose for the voice or just about anything else. It's a lot of work to organize all of it. When a composition comes to me, I find melody, harmony, and rhythm all at the same time. It means that in practice, for example, I may end up giving a piece of music to the drummers, too, because if what they play doesn't please me, if it doesn't correspond to that very thing among the "multi-beings" that exist in the universe and that I have in my head, if they play the rhythm just right you have to also be on the right tone or on the right drum. It's necessary that they find the appropriate instrument somewhere in the world. It won't be right unless they use just that instrument.

He began to write pieces in what he called the "space key"—using a drone or a pedal point to anchor the composition since keys had begun to disappear in his music—allowing the musicians an unusual amount of choice in improvisation; in other pieces he accomplished the same thing by superimposing one chord over another. (Trumpeter Art Hoyle recalls Miles Davis hanging around to talk to Sonny about this technique when they were backing former Stan Kenton vocalist Jerri Winters at Chicago's Birdland in the mid-1950s.) All these techniques he saw as deriving from nonhuman sources which black musicians might be attuned to:

If the harmony is just what they teach you in schools, then it wouldn't be any other than what we've been hearing all along, but when the harmony's moved the rest is not supposed to move and still fit, then you've got another message from another realm, from somebody else. Superior beings definitely speak in other harmonic ways than the earth way because they're talking something different, and you have to have chord against chord, melody against melody, and rhythm against rhythm; if you've got that, you're expressing something else.

Occasionally they played with no apparent harmonic structure at all. He'd say "let's start here and see what happens." "He wanted as much as possible added to what he had written," said drummer Jim Herndon, and "he believed that if you wanted to, you could do anything."

> We're not concerned with the world. Other music has been started over in dope dens. This music is started another way. It's started from an intellectual point of view and a spiritual point of view. It's being developed without any white person sponsoring it. It's another kind of music. I want it like this to purify our own music. We have to do it this way.

Distancing themselves from whites was not simple Crow Jim or reverse racism for Sonny. He had seen black bands in the South develop entirely within the black community and knew what they were capable of on their own. But Chicago was not Birmingham, and by 1950 most black entertainment was under the control and direction of white entrepreneurs, and conventions of performance and cultural expectations alien to the black community were being imposed from outside. At the worst of this development, black musicians were expected to conform to white stereotypes; at the very least they were handed incongruous models of performance developed in the white community. Virtually every black innovation in the north—whether blues, jazz, rhythm and blues, the novel, musicals, or sepia films—were mediated, controlled, and adjudicated to some degree by whites. And the day-to-day production of black-created entertainment was now being realized within conditions beset with racial anxiety—arguments with club owners and bookers, the tension which came on the road in hotels and transportation, in the hassles of the studio. The modern history of black music was strewn with such incidents: Aretha Franklin's first recording session at Muscle Shoals was disrupted by racial epithets and pistol-whipping; film of Thelonious Monk's recording sessions shows them as fraught with misunderstandings and sullen disagreement; and the friction in Miles Davis's recordings for Prestige show up on records in bits of acrid verbal byplay. Despite the smooth surface of public performance, the racial animus of rehearsal and recording was received secondhand by the audience, and perhaps even experienced unconsciously or consciously by them as a subtext. Black performances could no longer be seen—if they ever had been—as innocent of racial politics.

As we staggered out into the Sunday afternoon sunlight, somehow the subject of space flight came up. Bill [Broonzy] and his buddies began to sound off about what the people on the moon would look like. "Man," said Bill, "they gonna be so ugly, if you threw 'em into the Mississippi River, you'd skim ugly for six months!" "That's right," said Sonny Boy [Williamson], "they got feet comin' out of their ears and eyes comin' out of their toes, and their mother would cry if she looked at 'em!"

ALAN LOMAX, Notes to *Blues in the Mississippi Night*,
Rykodisc 90155 [1990]

Little Sally Walker, sitting in a flying saucer

Arkestra chant at Slug's, c. 1967

So I found myself talking on street corners to black people—I felt they needed it. No white people—I was talking about computers, I was talking about spaceships, I was talking about flying into outer space. I was talking about everything—satellites!—to black people. A black minister told me, "Hey, well, you know, it ain't in the Bible." I'd say, "They're going to the moon, they're going to go further, I don't care what it says in the Bible—that's what's going to happen." And it happened.

SUN RA

Space: the limitless three-dimensional expanse in which all material reality is located, the region beyond the planet Earth, the site of the rest of the universe. Space was yet another of Sonny's efforts to relocate himself so as to embody all time and nature and to escape the confines and limits of life on earth. Space to him was not empty, cold, and lifeless, but the container of the cosmos, and his true home, the greater reality, rich with potential, alternative, and promise. His sense of the cosmos was closer to that known in the nineteenth century—as when the Prussian naturalist Alexander von Humboldt had declared the cosmos one "harmoniously ordered whole" containing all created things. Space for Sonny was profoundly personalized, an individual reflection of the bigger picture, the "kosmos" which Walt Whitman declared was a "noun masculine and feminine, a person who[se] scope of mind, or whose range in a particular science, includes all, the whole known universe," part of a vision which unified science and art, astronomy and poetry, the rational and the mystical. In Whitman's vision it was a person

> Who believes not only in our globe with its sun and moon, but in
>   other globes with their suns and moons,
> Who, constructing the house of himself or herself, not for a day but
>   for all times, sees races, eras, dates, generations,
> The past, the future, dwelling there, like space, inseparable together.

Edgar Allan Poe also read von Humboldt, and had spun his reading notes into *Eureka*, in which he suggested that the Earth had fallen away from God and that a reunification was now necessary. It was a large prose poem thinly disguised as a scientific essay:

> It will now be understood that, in using the phrase, "Infinity of Space," I make no call upon the reader to entertain the impossible conception of an *absolute* infinity. I refer simply to the "*utmost conceivable expanse*" of space—a shadowy and fluctuating domain, now shrinking, now swelling, in accordance with the vacillating energies of the imagination.

Sonny knew Poe's works, quoted him often, and at rehearsals he sometimes told recalcitrant musicians, "Y'all don't know; but Poe know."

Sonny's own sensibilities gave him an odd affinity with other related forms of nineteenth-century thought—the various branches of "spiritual science" which merged Swedenborgianism, Mesmerism, and spiritualism. There are hints in him of Mary Baker Eddy and Christian Science (the belief that illness and death were errors, that evil is a kind of mistake, that the material world is an illusion, that the evidence given by the senses leads only to death), and of Emmanuel Swedenborg (that science and religion need not be opposed, that the Fall could be reversed by a combination of imagination and intuition). He also suggests the post-Swedenborgian Harmonialists, those Christian out-visionaries, like Thomas Lake Harris, the trance-based poet of space travel; or Andrew Jackson Davis, who mixed science, Mesmerism, and Christianity in an effort to be one with the infinite, the universe, to travel in time and space through divine trance, and to describe life on other planets for his followers. But Sonny thought of his own conceptions not as a matter of religion, philosophy, or politics, for they were not about belief, but a kind of science.

[This is] not science as we know it, but another kind. I've been looking for a solution which goes back to Egypt, and to the whole universe. I think musicians are on a superior level, but unlike scientists, they haven't been accepted for their abilities.

He followed the rise of science fiction as a child, reading early comic books and seeing the movie serials of Buck Rogers and Flash Gordon; learning its language, incorporating its themes and motifs into his performances. Even in later years he continued to take a serious, almost professional interest in sci-fi films, though more often than not he was distressed by what he saw:

They make strange and horrible ones, and I don't see any reason why space is horrible. I believe, rather, that people who make these movies show a sort of portrait of the Earth. Moreover, in these movies you often see people from space who after doing something worthwhile, are conquered by Earthlings. I believe that someday Earth will be invaded by beings from outer space. It will be necessary that people from space and Earthlings teach each other, or else it will be general destruction for us all.

For Sonny "science" was somewhere between or beyond science fiction and science. More than a method of reasoning and a set of laboratory practices, it was also a mystical process, and (as the rappers imply by "dropping science") a kind of secret or suppressed knowledge which had the power to create new myths, erase old ones, altering our ratio to each other and the rest of the universe. His thinking stemmed from an age when science, Hermetic philosophy, and magic were not so distinct, as well as from an earlier African-American understanding of "science" which meant a magic based on writing, and where science might include "conjure" or even "blackness" itself.

"Science" was also important to the thinking of the Nation of Islam teachings, and though Sonny could not share their conclusions, he followed their development. He had heard that the Honorable Fard himself taught that the universe was under the control of a single Creator who had in turn entrusted creation to twenty-four Imams or scientists, each of whom was given 25,000 years to carry out his own part of work on this planet and the others. It was Yacub, a dissident among those scientists, who was exiled in the current 25,000-year cycle to the Greek island of Patmos (the same Patmos on which John had received the Book of Revelations from an angel), where left alone in his madness he had created the mongrel white race which turned evil loose in the world and ultimately dominated all mankind. But, Fard said, the era of white dominion was coming to a close, and he had come to earth to oversee the end of the world. It would be ended by means of the Mother Ship, an enormous aircraft which had been built by the originating Black Scientists, a ship which, though it remains invisible to most, the prophet Ezekiel had seen as a great wheel in the sky. The ship produces its own power and takes in earthly oxygen and can stay in space for up to a year, carrying 1500 wheel-shaped warplanes with bombs so powerful they could drill into the earth before they explode, as indeed they had once done, creating the mountains of the earth. Now the ship would be used to obliterate the enemies of Allah.

Sonny read Elijah Muhammad's *The Theology of Time*, where nothingness was equated with blackness, and with God and darkness, a darkness which

> ...speaks of the force in the blackness of space producing life, the force of space which seemingly looks as though it is nothing, has the power to bring up objects that are hidden in it to our point of view.... The One was already in the darkness but could not be given to us until the Time brought it about.... If One emerged out of this Black darkness and started the Black darkness moving, with power that the Black darkness can use itself in calculating Time, this is a wise God.

He saw that in some Muslim teachings the facts of science and mathematics assumed such force that they broke loose from their bounds and assumed a life of their own. Numbers seemed to escape their limits and form a poetic surface, a skein against which an obsessional scientific poetry could be written. Khalid Alif Muhammad, for instance, in responding to the Honorable Fard's teachings, might write:

> One atom of Oxygen weighs Cipher point 21 ciphers—written out in integers it would be (0.00000000000000000000) equal to 026,57 gram. One gram is a metric unit of mass & weight equal to 1/1000 Kilogram & circa One cubic centimeter of water at its ultimate density. There are 1/100th of a Cubic inch possessing 200,000,000 Atoms. The Atmosphere in the original language is Al Jaww and is six miles high equal to 31,680 feet or 380,160 inches. Al Jaww covers all of Asiya (196,940,000 square miles). Thus her extracted weight is 11,666,666,666,666,666,666 pounds. Approximately 12 Quintillion pounds. And is 78% Nitrogen, 21% Oxygen, 0.93% Argon & 0.07 Carbon Dioxide and minor gases.

Like a preacher who could sermonize on the chemical nature of the body, only to show the inadequacy of science to explain Man, the Muslims could make the facts of science work within a mystical process to unify their own beliefs with the world around them and to redefine their place in it.

African Americans have always talked cosmology with a premodern ease, a discourse distantly rooted in African conceptions of the cosmos, but yet also shaped by modern science and tempered by a wariness of how that science had sometimes been used against them. In Afro-Baptist discourse, for example, in their hymns and sermons, there is a consciousness and almost matter-of-fact perception of their place in the cosmos and the possibility of spiritual travel within it. "The White Flyer to Heaven," a 1927 commercially recorded sermon by Reverend A. W. Nix, a Baptist preacher from Birmingham, turns the familiar gospel-train motif into a journey by spaceship through a finely etched solar system:

> Higher and higher! and higher!
> We'll pass on to the Second Heaven
> The starry big Heaven, and view the flying stars
> > and dashing meteors
> And then pass on by Mars and Mercury, and Jupiter and Venus
> And Saturn and Uranus, and Neptune with her four glittering
> > moons.

Within this cosmology they are free to be transported out of the South, out of the country, out of this world. There is no necessary orthodoxy in black cosmological views, no agreed-upon astrophysics of faith, so within the same tradition it is possible for John Jasper, the late nineteenth-century Virginia preacher, to became famous for his "The Sun Do Move" sermon, a sermon which tested faith by using the Bible to prove that the earth was flat, and that the sun moved around it. Or for quilter Harriet Powers to adorn her religious-inspired apron and quilts with an ambiguous astronomical symbolism. And for artist Houston Conwill to construct maps which project South Carolina as a model for the universe. They are part of a shared vision of a black sacred cosmos, a spiritualized vision of the universe, where the pilgrim is comfortable wherever he or she may travel, but not as doomed wanderers in the endless cosmological emptiness of some other religions. This black cosmic vision is easily seen as part of the theme of travel, of journey, of exodus, of escape which dominates African-American narratives: of people who could fly back to Africa, travel in the spirit, visit or be visited by the dead; of chariots and trains to heaven, the Underground Railroad, Marcus Garvey's steamship line, Rosa Parks on the Mobile bus, freedom riders. It was also a vision which lurked distantly but stubbornly behind blues songs which praised the technology of motion and travel, where trains, cars, airplanes, buses—even transmission systems ("Dynaflow")—were celebrated as part of African-American postagricultural mobility within a Booker T. Washington/*Popular Science* optimism about the future.

Sonny's Baptist childhood fused with his reading of the theosophists, who had also kept alive ancient notions of the cosmos. Aristotle's idea of a series of crystal spheres around the earth, for instance, was picked up by Hermes Trismegistus (who said it was possible to ascend and pass through the seven spheres if you knew the secret word that would placate the demons who rule the spheres, until you reach the seventh sphere, the ogdoadic sphere, and the soul is released into infinity), and passed on by the fifteenth- and sixteenth-century Neoplatonists and in turn incorporated by Blavatsky and fellow travelers, like Gurdjieff.

One of Gurdjieff's strangest and most unreadable books is *Beelzebub's Tales to His Grandson*—a neologistically multilingual account of Beelzebub, a being from the planet Karatas, and his travels across the universe in a spaceship with his grandson Hassein. During their long journey Beelzebub answers the youth's questions about the cosmos, especially about Earth, which he explains has become disordered through a mistake made by those in charge of the cosmos. Throughout this narrative everyday elements of life on Earth are treated ironically, as if they were strange and exotic, being observed by an anthropologist from Karatas; and even the most fundamental behaviors are treated relativistically as just one of many possible in the universe. Gurdjieff's students understood the book as a case study in his method of "self-remembering," whereby it might be possible to observe oneself objectively and thus awaken from the sleep which afflicted humans, the creatures of habit. Jean Toomer, for example (who had dreamed and sketched about traveling in space in his youth), incited by the book, wrote in his notes:

I have an intimation that this earth, instead of being my home planet—as Toomer assumes and feels that it is—will become strange, foreign and remote, while at the same time I will increasingly feel Karatas or the Sun-Absolute to be my home. This, in the reality of fact, knowledge, attitude, realization; not in mere words or fancy....

Let me observe where *this* remote being Toomer dwells, what he does, where he goes, what things he uses, and how he lives, in general. Let me likewise observe the life of these other remote beings, bipeds, quadrupeds, insects, etc., seeing them all as *remote,* distant from my native planet, friends, associates and surroundings. If I can hold this state, wherein this Earth—all of it, New York and Toomer's room and friends in New York included—is *really* the remote place, whereas Karatas is *really* home, the chief feature will then at once wish to leave this place and will become nostalgic, will wish to reach Karatas. And in this way, it can be used to aid my return.

But this kind of radical alienation was something that some black folks did not need a theosophist to discover. Tenor saxophonist Johnny Griffin, in an interview with drummer Art Taylor, said,

The main thing is I'm here because I did something wrong on my planet. I'm not really from this planet. I did something wrong on my planet and they sent me here to pay my dues. I figure pretty soon my dues will be paid, and they're going to call me home so I can rest in peace.

When Taylor asked him if he was serious, Griffin answered,

I can't be from this place, Arthur. There is no love here, and I love people. All I see is hate around me.... That's what's wrong with the earth today. Black and white on this planet, there is no love, there is only hate. I was thinking about reading some books on anarchy, because all this government stuff is b.s. anyway. These governments drawing lines between men, between tribes. Yellow people against brown people, against black people against Muslims against Christians against Hindus. What is all that?

I know I'm not from this planet; I can't be. I must be from someplace else in the universe because I'm a total misfit. I can't get with none of this.

Jazz vocalist King Pleasure in his liner notes for his 1960 album *Golden Days* prefaced his comments on songs such as "Moody's Mood for Love" and "Parker's Mood" by explaining that as a six-year-old named Clarence Beeks living in Oakdale, Tennessee, he awoke from a dream with the revelation that he was the "real saviour of the universe," and that he was a "baby planet nucleus"; in a similar revelation he learned that his name should be changed to King Pleasure. In the remaining few paragraphs he sketched out a new philosophy, "Planetism," wherein

> Space is perfect (one, same, complete, throughout, etc.).
> Space is everywhere (omnipresent).
> Space is nucleus around which all "matter" gathers.
> All things come from "nothing" (space).

> It is this medium of differentiation and distinction between all things. Space comprehends and opposes all things. It is reflection (mind, wisdom, etc.).
> ALL things exist, live and react in relation to space.

Having implied that God is space, he goes on to question the inevitability of death, and to say that selfishness is the source of all illness, and to promise to reveal more at a later date.

This discourse of science, of space, of mysticism, of nationhood, of spirituality, meets at a strange intersection where the passivity of New Age, the aggressiveness of science fiction, the coolness of mathematics, the oppositionality of mysticism, and echoes of the mythos of the Nation of Islam all come together. Some might call this black science fiction, focusing on the interplay of the themes of freedom, apocalypse, and survival; or maybe "Afrofuturism," where the material culture of Afro-American folk religions are used as sacred technologies to control virtual realities. Those less charitable would say that it is nothing more than a deliberate attempt to obfuscate and mystify the art in order to control access and advance individual careers. But surely something more than personal expediency and privacy are involved here.

Artistic creation involves a search for a zone, a space, in which to create, an area open to imagination and revelation. In this quest African-American artists find many spaces already occupied, closed down to them, and those still open restricted, tarnished, already interpreted—as when black artists find their work treated as merely "social," as nothing more than "functional" or "political" art. One liberatory space still left to them is ancient Egypt, since a partially understood and sketchily drawn history of the ancient world helps to keep it open. Nor has the ease with which scholars have projected contemporary racial thinking backwards onto the ancients escaped African-American scrutiny, and so provides African Americans with a basis on which to attempt a recovery of Egypt, and at the same time this effort paradoxically reconnects them to Western history and culture.

But Sonny did not limit himself to Afrocentric canonic thought. Egypt, he discovered, had already been connected to the galaxies by Edgar Cayce, Gurdjieff, and others of theosophic bent, following the lead of Pythagoras and the Hermeticists. And speculative space observers like von Daniken had made another kind of case for contact between space aliens and ancient Egyptians. By the 1960s and early 1970s popular imagination had absorbed it all. It was even common for the covers of albums by black artists—especially Earth, Wind and Fire—to celebrate ancient Egypt as a technologically advanced civilization with roots in outer space.

Sonny's own comment on his shift from a focus on Egypt towards space showed that it was deliberate, and not—as critic Greg Tate once said of some black sci-fi observers—a mistake of "putting the interstellar carriage before the Egyptian horse":

> I think that man has not reached his best because he has been hindered by many things, and some of those obstacles are not even human, and they don't even belong to this planet. This is the reason why I've been looking for answers to these problems, and I've been looking for a solution going back to ancient Egypt, and now I'm looking for answers in the entire universe because I want to know the real potential of man. Beyond music, I try to find another meaning, another reason. This is why now I'm dealing with the potential of humanity. But not with what has been done, because that doesn't leave much space for what I want to do.

The success of the USSR in launching *Sputnik*, the first satellite into space, in October of 1957 drove the United States to a peak of Cold War hysteria and induced an overheated response in which massive resources were thrown into what soon became known as the "space race." And though it ostensibly had nothing to do with questions of social justice, it occurred only days after the governor of Arkansas had provoked riots by stopping nine black schoolchildren from entering Central High School, and forced President Eisenhower to call in federal troops. Ray Bradbury had already brought America's racial anxiety to bear on space in one of his stories in *The Martian Chronicles,* " 'Way Up in the Middle of the Air," where all the black people of earth leave in rocket ships for another planet. Then shortly after *Sputnik's* launch, Duke Ellington wrote an essay called "The Race for Space," which for one reason or other was never published. It begins as a meditation on creativity and the common roots of music and science, reflecting on the tendency to recognize achievements such as *Sputnik* and the pyramids as great works of art even in the face of the human sacrifice involved in their creation. But Ellington quickly warmed to his real subject, space *and* race, and proceeded to calculate the cost of racial prejudice in terms of a loss of creativity which ultimately resulted in the United States' failure to get a satellite into space first. In his conclusion he offered up jazz bands as microcosmic utopias, and literalized the idea of harmony:

So, this is my view on the race for space. We'll never get it until we Americans, collectively and individually, get us a new sound. A new sound of harmony, brotherly love, common respect and consideration for the dignity and freedom of men.

Space and race would continue to be linked in the American imagination, and would creep to the surface for years. Following the successful moon landing of *Apollo 11,* Norman Mailer, in *Of a Fire on the Moon,* projected himself into what he considered black America's resentment over the manned space program, and fantasized that, since in their cosmology magic predominated over technology, they had been left embittered and out of the celebration. Mailer, like most white Americans, viewed the space program as the reopening of the frontier, the West now extended to the heavens. However, for Sonny, technology was not opposed to magic, and if anything, the space age meant a final chance to go Home, to climb to the ultimate mountaintop. Or it could merely be a diversion from the social evils of the Earth. In a 1968 interview Sonny was asked about the "race for space":

According to my research, the governments of this world have conspired to destroy the nations of black people. Those were Europe, Asia and Africa, and especially Ethiopia, India and South Africa. And all other nations have helped with it; some by just holding off and doing nothing. The consequence though has been that there now exists a separate kind of human being, the American Black man. And I should say that he doesn't belong on this Earth. Some of them have assimilated themselves to the white race, or pretended to do so. You could call them the people of the earth from the point of view that they have given up everything in favor of materialistic comforts. But here in America there are also Black people who have given up nothing, who couldn't give up anything because they live in harmony with the Creator of the cosmos. And they will always be a source of difficulty for every nation on this planet, because they've no other ruler than the Creator of the cosmos and they're faithful only to him. The Bible speaks about that too. They're the only people who stand apart. Nobody can say that Israel is that people, because Israel is counted as one of the nations of this world, at least in the United Nations, but not the American Black people.

Here, as elsewhere with Sonny, space was both a metaphor of exclusion and of reterritorialization, of claiming the "outside" as one's own, of tying a revised and corrected past to a claimed future. Space was also a metaphor which transvalues the dominant terms so that they become aberrant, a minority position, while the terms of the outside, the beyond, the margins, become the standard.

After the Arkestra's first appearance on the West Coast, reviewer Joe Gonçalves shared his understanding of Sonny's "space":

It's us in outer-space, sitting down, tired, with Universe charts, not clear where we are but sure of getting there. It's pyramid-building, world-construction, Universe revision. But all these names are small, because it gets beyond barb-wire frontiers, ghettos, bloated categories, things like that. It's outer space. Comes outside the stage. Into you. These gemini players. Players. Space-players. Spacers. Space-makers. For us:

What we never had for so long, space, outer space. Or no space at all. Squeezes so tight. From the slaveship to the shack to the tenement. No space to really move. No space to really function. Sun Ra & Co. herald Space to Come, Freedom, to move, to live again as ourselves. Expansion.

And future talk is ordering talk. Getting pretty much what we order and ordering pretty much what we get, future has to be incorporated into today as surely as history. When we hear a brother say, "A nigger ain't never *been* shit, a nigger ain't never *going* to be shit," we know he has no knowledge of his past, and no past = no future. Sun Ra is future/ ALTER/ what's coming. Tomorrow's breath, breathing. Getting Ready.

Space was a metaphor which Sonny could express in words or in music. "Sonny didn't like being called 'avant garde,'" said Tommy Hunter. "He thought of the band as a 'space orchestra'; space was the central idea. He began with the idea that the earth was traveling in space, so that the planet was like a spaceship. What he had in mind was an orchestra that was traveling together in space.... And, really, anyone can travel in space in their dreams and their imagination." Sonny addressed this dream in a song, "Imagination":

Imagination is a magic carpet/Upon which we may soar
To distant lands and climes/And even go
beyond the moon
To any planet in the sky/If we came from
nowhere here
Why can't we go somewhere there?

"Space was Sonny's medium, so it was space music," trumpeter Phil Cohran recalls. "Only a few modal things. Much of it was 'vertical sound.' It was a question of attitude. You had to think space. Had to expand beyond the earth plane.... We didn't have any models, so we had to create our own language. It was based on sound. It wasn't just something you could pick up and physically deal with. *Space is a place,* and you had to think space, to expand beyond the earthly plane—that's why everyone was so creative."

One night, many years later, the Arkestra arrived at a bar in which they had never played, and found that the tiny bandstand was only large enough to hold a piano trio. When drummer Craig Haynes complained that there wasn't enough room for him to set up, Sonny chided him, "Remember, this is a *space* arkestra."

ARS GRATIA ARTIS

Sonny began to organize a band in 1954, an octet, which he said would be different. He told the musicians this band would not make money; they might have to rehearse five, maybe ten years before they would be ready to play in public; so if they wanted to join they would have to make their living by playing in other groups. Like a space-age Noah, he told them that he wanted them to help him prepare for what was coming.

> [There are] many different musicians all over the planet who are experimenting, particularly the white musicians who are trying to do something to change their race over another way, 'cause they knew something was going to happen to them if they don't change.... In the black race, it hasn't been like that. Musicians weren't planning nothing for their people as far as change is concerned. I had dedicated a so-called lifetime to doin' exactly that 'cause I knew we was gonna need it.

They were to devote themselves to saving the whole planet by keeping to their own people and avoiding social distractions. They would become what musicians call a rehearsal band, an art-for-its-own-sake scholarly ensemble. Only this would be art for the Creator's sake.

> So that's what we did. Then some entertainers and singers started comin' to our rehearsals, and one fellow came up and said, "This band is too good not to play for anyone. A band like this should be in Birdland." Which was a Chicago club. He went and arranged an audition for us. Since we didn't want a job there, we played the furthest out things that we had. The owner [Cadillac Bob] listened and said, "Play that number again." We played it, and he hired us.
>
> I was frustrated. I had my thing about the 10 years of rehearsal, but the band wanted to work. So we stayed at Birdland two years. At one point there was some trouble: the Birdland in New York complained, and were

going to sue. So I told the owner to change the name to Budland. He did, and we kept playing. The [Pershing] Lounge was upstairs, and by the time we left Chicago, we had also been playing there.

For over a year Sonny's octet played for five to seven nights a week at Birdland/Budland (which for a brief time in 1956 had no name at all), and were kept on for Monday night jazz sessions the following year. Budland had a Las Vegas–type review which required them to accompany featured performers like Della Reese, the 5 Echoes, Lowell Fulson, Lorez Alexandria, Dakota Staton, Johnny Guitar Watson, The Sweet Teens, and a wide assortment of blues singers, comedians, and dancers. The arrival of the mambo at the beginning of the 1950s had set off a series of Latin dance crazes which seemed to arrive on time every year, so several nights a week they also played for dancers who demonstrated and then taught the steps of the rhumba, mambo, merengue, and cha-cha to the audience.

It was at this club that Sonny's band began to wear a variety of uniforms, including one with green sport shirts, rust-colored pants, and red fezzes such as were worn by black religious sects like the Moors, and even briefly by the Nation of Islam. This was the uniform they were wearing one night at the club when three men stood in the back watching the band closely; at the break they walked up to the bandstand and, without identifying themselves, warned them to never wear the fezzes again.

If you had wandered into a club where Sonny was playing in the mid-1950s maybe the first thing you would have noticed were the drummers: there were two, three of them, as many as he could get (he once took a band into the Jazz Showcase with five drummers). He wanted as many different percussion instruments as possible in the band, so he divided them up among the drummers: there were bells, timbales, congas, timpani, and there were other rhythm instruments distributed among the horn players. Though the drum parts were sometimes written out, much of what they played was memorized during rehearsals. He taught the drummers "every beat, all the nuances and everything. They played exactly what I wanted them to play." He wanted a distinctively rhythmic band, but Tommy Hunter believed that Sonny also used so many drummers to cover weaknesses in individual musicians. "Because he wanted a big band, he sometimes had to accept musicians who lacked some basic skills, and had to work around them."

Long before minimalism, "Sonny gave his drummers long solos," said Lucious Randolph, "and sometimes asked them to play the same thing over and over until you could hear something else in it. You'd ask him, 'How long is this going to go on?' and Sonny would answer, 'I'm trying to tell you something else...like, if you keep eating peach pie every day, [sooner or later] it's going to taste like something else.' "

Sonny told Hunter that he wanted the "burlesque sound" from his drummers, that "Calumet City sound," a sensuous beat played mostly on the snare instead of the cymbals. Yet when Mississippian Alvin Fielder was hired as a drummer with the band, Sonny told him he wanted "a Mississippi drummer with a Mississippi feel." Fielder thought this was odd, since he had been working to get a New York feel in his drumming. "Sonny wanted the drummers to play loose and let the music flow through us, but we weren't playing loose.... He was looking for a different kind of rhythm.... When I later heard Beaver Harris play with Archie Shepp in the 1960s I finally knew what Sonny wanted from his drummers and what playing loose meant."

Lucious Randolph said that on a typical gig in the late 1950s they mostly played Sonny's compositions; maybe some classic swing tunes which Sonny had transcribed from records by Jimmy Lunceford, Fletcher Henderson, or Duke Ellington; or they played arrangements written by members of the band, especially those of Richard Evans, Pat Patrick, and Julian Priester. And when they *did* play standard pop songs, they functioned like an intermission, an *entracte* "so they could rest people's minds, they could go to the bathroom, get a drink; but the standards would be way out, not on the chord changes musicians would be familiar with." Sonny believed that he had developed to the point where he might even be able to improve the playing of the great swing bands. But he had passed that point: once when Count Basie's band was playing at the Regal Theater, Sonny was asked to write an arrangement for Basie's group to accompany some dancers, and he wrote up a treatment of Kurt Weill's "Speak Low." John Gilmore later said "Basie had to lay it aside.... He just couldn't play it because of the way it was written.... It was sim-

ple, not difficult at all. But for them, it was the way it was written....
They just couldn't play it."

The Arkestra's performances became more physical and synesthesic,
but not just the conventional swing band choreography, the rocking back
and forth and the swaying of horns in rhythm:

> Sun Ra was going through a change: we started jumping around...not
> like jumping jacks, straight up and down; and it had to be in a specific
> place.... It seemed to have a special significance for Sun Ra. We started
> wearing beanies with propellers that lit up. Sun Ra wore a space hat with
> a light on it.... And [we were] marching and dancing through the audi-
> ence—a kind of cosmic ring shout.
>
> Halfway through the night, he'd start going out of his mind. He would
> put excerpts of the next tune in his right hand or in his left hand (while
> they were still playing the previous tune). We did space chants such as
> "We Travel the Spaceways," and we'd cry out things like "Get off, get off!"
> or "What Stop?" "Where"? "Venus!"

They jumped up and down for sixteen bars, but never too far from the
music stands, because "it was hard to read the charts. The lighting was
bad in those little dives we were playing."

The performances were growing more and more complex, and Sonny
had to develop new devices to communicate what they were to play
next. This was not just a matter of identifying the tunes, for he was now
using a variety of backgrounds for each of these tunes, and he made
choices on the spot that would have to be identified for the band. Sometimes they played a five- or ten-minute piece with only two pages of
music, the development worked out by hand signals. He also encouraged
the band to respond to what was happening verbally as well as musically,
to shout out encouragement and show some pleasure in what they were
hearing ("Don't just be gentlemen up there"). As he expressed in an interview, his model for these performances had become dialogical:

> When we play concerts my musicians never know when I'm going to fin-
> ish or when they'll have to go home. It's like a conversation when you try
> and express something important: when you think that you've really ex-
> pressed something, you don't feel the need to add anything more. At

other times you need to keep adding explanations. So sometimes while playing I say all I need to, and there is nothing else that I have for the musicians to do, and I just stop. And then I take off in another direction. At other times they have the sense of what I'm hoping for. Sometimes I arrange to give them a signal. At other times I just content myself with looking at them and they regroup.

Sometimes they stop at the wrong time, and then I just change and go in a different direction and everything goes really well. It's not exactly what I would've wanted to do, but the continuity of the music has been protected. We've simply changed directions.

Every evening I move, so to speak, along with the cosmos. It's like reading a newspaper; somewhere in the world and somewhere in the universe something is happening and I then paint a picture of what I feel from nature and from the universe. And whatever that may be, that's what we are talking about, because it's actually a conversation. I play something and they hear what I play and then John, for instance, wants to say something, so then he talks for about fifteen minutes while all of us are listening. And then somebody else. If I get the feeling that somebody has something to say, so then he talks for about fifteen minutes while all of us are listening. And then again someone else. If I get the feeling that somebody has to say something, I just point at him and see what develops. Just like a teacher in front of a classroom. You talk and questions are asked. It actually looks more like that than music per se.

Then something happens, something that surprises me. Marshall [Allen], for instance, got a big drum, and all of a sudden he started to bang on it in a number where he wasn't supposed to. At first, it looked as if the rhythms we played would be broken up by that, but that didn't happen. It sounded good and he kept banging on that drum. I think he tried to bring Clifford Jarvis [the drummer] more into the action or maybe to confuse him.

The audience, from his point of view, was also a part of the dialogue:

I always know what's going to happen when I come in, but it also depends on the people there. I change something every time someone else comes in, I change directions. Because the public is a part of the music too; if somebody comes in, then the acoustic changes. The music goes all the way around them and then comes back, so I can hear it. If I play in an empty hall I need to have other arrangements and a different presentation than when the hall is full of people.

And when they were recording, the engineer also became part of the performance:

What I play is influenced by what kind of technician he is. When, for instance, we were recording for ESP, Dick Alderson happened to be the technician and he happens to like avant-garde music. He happens to like to do things that make the music sound real, gets it across better. He's very precise in those things and in that case we had an audience. If there had been another technician who didn't like that kind of music, I would have had to play something different...If I listen back to the first part of the tape, I know what direction I have to take. Then I know what kind of mood he's in and how he'll punch the buttons and everything. And then I make sure that whatever he does, the music comes through one of those dimensions. If it doesn't happen in the dimension I have in mind it will happen in another dimension. And it will still reach some people; maybe not many, but everything we do happens in a sphere of slow motion. If we can't reach them this year, it will happen next year.

He sought spontaneity in the studio as well as in the club, and nearly always used the first take of a piece: "The first take is the pure expression, the second take is only an imitation of the expression." It was a belief shared by many musicians, but few would risk putting out an imperfect take in order to get the freshness of the first performance.

When Sonny heard in 1955 that a local music store was demonstrating an electric piano, he bought one of the first ones they received, because this was just the kind of instrument he had imagined in Birmingham years before. He was now billed at clubs as Sun Ra and His Electric Piano and Band. He and Ray Charles became the first musicians to record with the electronic piano: "I liked the Wurlitzer because it had a tender, lyrical kind of sound because of the reeds they had on it. It had the sound of a guitar or lute to me." The Hammond B-3—one of the first quality portable electric organs—had been introduced the year before, and almost immediately found its way into storefront churches and neighborhood bars. As other companies raced to get their own models out, Sonny bought a new portable Wurlitzer organ to extend his palette of electronic sounds.

He found gigs in a number of smaller clubs like the Rhumboogie, and some of the larger ones, such as the Parkway Ballroom or—backing floor shows—in the Grand Terrace during October and November of 1955. They rehearsed anywhere they could—at Pat Patrick's house, at a club called the Circle, and in smaller groups, or individually, at Sonny's apartment. Though they were getting more work now, the band sometimes took engagements with only the shakiest of understandings. They once played at a club for eleven weeks but when the owner came up short they were only paid for seven. At other times the gigs turned out to be nonpaying altogether. At the end of 1955 a promoter offered them a Christmas performance with a promise of a European tour to follow. Sonny and Abraham assembled an elaborate show with dancers and singers, and they rehearsed for weeks. When the date for the performance came and the engagement fell through, they faced the Christmas season with no money.

Throughout the first third of 1956, Sonny's band continued working at Birdland, and ended their stay on the week of March 7 by opening for a new Miles Davis group which included John Coltrane. Pat Patrick had urged Coltrane to meet with Sonny and had given him a copy of the "Solaristic Precepts" leaflet. In July of the next year, they met and talked for four hours, and whenever Coltrane was in town they met again, and talked of playing together.

Despite his strictures against playing for whites, in the summer of 1956 Sonny took a job with a quintet of Hoyle, Gilmore, Sproles, and Cohran playing alternating thirty- to forty-minute sets with the actors at the Compass Theater. The Compass Players were a six-actor improvisational group which included Mike Nichols, Elaine May, and Shelley Berman, and which had been formed the year before and had been performing in a storefront near the University of Chicago. They had just relocated to the Argo Off-Beat Room on North Broadway on the North Side of Chicago in May when Sonny's group was brought in to replace pianist Bill Mathieu, who went on to write arrangements for the Stan Kenton Orchestra. Now Sonny was not only playing for white audiences, but for the first time he was also working outside of the constraints of nightclubs and strip joints, and was free of the demand for strictly functional music. The actors at the Compass were performing sophisticated material like parodies of Gian Carlo Menotti operas, or a *Hamlet* set in a delicatessen ("Mrs. Rosencrantz and Mrs. Guildenstern, *their* sons don't act like this"), much of it improvised and full of risk. The nightly excitement of the chances taken by the actors inspired Sonny to think about increasing the collective improvisation within his compositions. Asked about the change in his music years later, he said, "Sometimes we do that."

> I play the piano and give the general spirit and feeling in the introduction, and then the Arkestra plays. I get a complete piece just as if I'd written it. But I'm only able to get that because certain of my musicians have been playing with me for nine years. They feel what I want them to say.

Word now began to get out about them beyond the South Side, and jobs at Northwestern University and at Mandel Hall at the University of Chicago followed. But the mainstay of the Arkestra's work was still the black community. On Sunday afternoons they played at Roberts Lounge, where the band was sponsored by a large social club, the Rounders (whose motto was "No squares allowed"). And though the music was for dancing, the Rounders were a progressive group, and Sonny played some of his most advanced compositions there. The shows were not advertised, but the audiences the Rounders drew were large and receptive. The band was also finding jobs at places like the Workers Hall, the Kitty Kat Club, Saurer's on E. 23rd and Wabash, Strand Hall, the CC Club on South Cody, the Appomattox Club, the Palladium, the Mystic Ballroom, and Princeton Hall.

The nervous energy of bebop may have seemed a scandal in the mid-1940s, but soon it began to make swing seem tired, prewar, symmetrical, a thinly veiled pop form suddenly laid bare. But as far as Sonny was concerned bop was also a limited form, merely a style, and one which aimed too low; and for all the boppers' changing identities—now revolutionaries, now *artistes*—they could not conceal their limitations as composers. After all their harmonic tricks were counted, their instrumental pyrotechnics, their sly polyrhythms, for him they were pop-song revisionists more than composers, and their formula of melody-variations-melody if anything was more mundane than their swing predecessors'. It was just such limitations which drove Charlie Parker to seek lessons from Edgar Varese, and Dizzy Gillespie to recruit a whole slate of arrangers to create musical structures which could spark up his music.

If Sonny disparaged the boppers' contribution as merely a product of its time and thus instantly dated, he did not do so from the bitter perspective of a swing-band professional watching his era erased by young usurpers. He knew how to use bebop conventions, and used them effectively—some of his recordings from the late fifties compare favorably with Tadd Dameron's efforts to orchestrate bop lines for big bands. He appreciated the ways in which Thelonious Monk rigorously reexamined the materials of jazz and produced compositions which made both swing and bebop seem strange. But the sources for the dreams of music he had were Fletcher Henderson's "Soft Winds," "Moonrise on the Lowlands," or "Shanghai Shuffle," or Duke Ellington's "Dust in the Desert," "Pyramid," "Moon Mist," "Perfume Suite," or "Magenta Haze," those compositions which transported dancers and listeners into different times and cultures within the compass of an Afro-modernist stance. Yet Sonny thought of music in terms of even bigger intentions, of music with the power to change the listener with the aid of myth and folklore.

In fact, he was a romantic in the strict sense of the term, one who believed that music should be composed and played through the "addition of strangeness to beauty." Wagner's agenda for remaking all of the arts into ritual in order to redeem humanity fascinated him, and so did Tchaikovsky, whose grandly programmatic concepts coexisted with a love of beautiful melodies. But above all he was drawn to composers like Scriabin—poised between romanticism and modernism—who pushed Wagner's ideas to the breaking point, putting color, cabalistics, and Eastern wisdom in service to the instant and radical destruction of the consciousness of the everyday world; or Debussy, shocked into enlightenment by mysticism and the music of Bali and Vietnam, who heard the history of music in Europe as if it were underwater. Against this scale, the skirmishes of bebop were only local color.

The big postwar jazz bands held little interest for Sonny, as most were either recycling past successes or shoving singers to the front; or else attempting to paste the innovations of Charlie Parker and Dizzy Gillespie onto older formulas. Sonny was now listening to the Hollywood-inspired music being made by people like David Rose, whose lush, massed string writing could be heard as theme songs on several popular radio programs; or Walter Schumann, who brought classical choral methods to pop songs; or to the exotica of people like Martin Denny, who recorded in Honolulu under Henry Kaiser's Aluminum Dome accompanied by animal noises, natural accoustic delay, and reverberation; and especially to the arrangements of Les Baxter, the premier figure in what was being called mood music.

Baxter was a big-band saxophonist and singer who developed a post-swing style in the late forties and early fifties of spectacular orchestral writing, full of timpani and hand drums, tumbling violin lines, harps, flutes, marimbas, celesta, Latin rhythm vamps, the cries of animals, choral moans, and flamboyant singers, creating imaginary soundscapes which he helped evoke with titles like "Saturday Night on Saturn," "Atlantis," "Voodoo Dreams," and "Pyramid of the Sun." Sonny first heard Baxter on *Perfume Set to Music* (1946) and *Music Out of the Moon* (1947), two albums built around melodies for theremin performed by Dr. Samuel Hoffman, a Los Angeles podiatrist who had played on the soundtracks of *Spellbound* and *The Lost Weekend*. Baxter went on to produce records which celebrated the Aztecs (*The Sacred Idol* in 1959), South Asia (*Ports of Pleasure* in 1957), Africa and the Middle East (*Tamboo!* in 1955), and the Caribbean (*Caribbean Moonlight* in 1956), all of which used Latin rhythms generically, as did his two big band records, *African Jazz* (1958) and *Jungle Jazz* (1959). Though later generations would understand this music in strictly utilitarian terms, and hear in it the sounds of air conditioning and the clink of ice in cocktail shakers, for Sonny it was music rich with imagination and suggestion, and free of material constraints. His genius was to take as raw material what others in the 1950s thought of as "easy listening" and turn it into what in the late 1960s would be heard as "Third World music" by some and as "uneasy listening music" by others.

EL SATURN RESEARCH

The music Sonny wrote grew wilder, and the musicians were astonished by what they heard. Each rehearsal was a revelation. Sounds emerged from the ensemble that no one was playing. One of the pieces he brought in sounded to them like children on a playground—they said you could hear voices on the swings and in the sandbox. At performances and rehearsals Alton Abraham often ran the tape recorder and sometimes sent a professional to do it. A pile of tapes began to grow, and Abraham suggested that they ought to be putting out records, in fact, ought to have their own record company. The recent success of Vee-Jay Records, a black-owned company in Chicago, was on their minds, especially as the Vee-Jay house band included many of Sonny's former musicians, like Vernel Fournier, Red Holloway, Von Freeman, and Al Smith, who had also become the label's musical director. So Sonny and Abraham decided on the name that suggested the seriousness of their purpose—El Saturn Research—and registered it as a record company with the Musicians Union in 1956; the tapes they had recently made of the singing group The Cosmic Rays became the first Saturn records, two 45-rpm singles. Ownership of his own company seemed a necessity for Sonny because "I didn't want to go through all the starving in the attic and all that foolishness.... I wanted to bypass that particular trauma they put on artists today." But the idea of any musician, black or white, being able to produce and sell his own records was so daring, so unprecedented, as to be heroic in the music business.

Next Abraham and Sonny rented the RCA Studios in Chicago and began work on three singles under the name of le Sun Ra: "Medicine for a Nightmare" backed with "Urnack"; "A Call for All Demons"/ "Demon's Lullaby"; and "Saturn"/"Supersonic Jazz." All six compositions have some family resemblance to the music of the era—clipped post-bop touches, funk gestures, Latin affectations. But with the exception of "Urnack" (written and arranged by trombonist Julian Priester) none of them fit easily into the mold of the times. The presence of an electric bass, acoustic piano and electric piano alternating within the same solo, otherwise evocative melodies decentered by unexpected accents and intervals, swing with an unusually heavy rhythm created by timpani drums—all are characteristics which seemed alien to swing, bebop, or the new, more soulful and hard-edged music which was coming to be called hard bop by some.

Another single they recorded, "Super Blonde"/"Soft Talk," became part of what was to be their first Saturn long-playing record, *Super-Sonic Jazz.* On its cover a pale red piano keyboard burned, smoke and fire seeping from between the keys, and in the background two piano lids raised up like mountains, drawing lightning from a pale yellow sky. A conga drum hanging in the air gave off thunder, its side painted with ancient Dahomean markings.

On the record were "India" and the two-part "Sunology," segments of a larger suite he had written. "India" was built on a single chord, and loaded with percussion; and "Sunology" was rightly described by Sonny as "a different kind of blues." Some of the titles are wordplays: "Sunology" ("Sun-knowledge-y") and "Kingdom of Not"—"a piece," Sonny wrote in the record's liner notes, "which does not evoke a former kingdom, but a kingdom which although it doesn't exist, exists nonetheless." Chicago was a source of inspiration, as some of the titles reflect, though the connection was never simple and direct. "El is the Sound of Joy," for instance, honors the Caananite God, but also signifies on Fletcher Henderson's 1934 recording, "Hotter Than 'Ell," as well as being a praise song for the elevated trains which connect all of Chicago. This was part of a "Chicago Suite," never completely recorded, which also included "Springtime in Chicago" and "Street Named Hell." On "Springtime in Chicago" Sonny played a piano so out of tune it sounded "prepared," altered for percussive effects. And the electronic delay used on this cut was so extreme that it reverberates like Jamaican dub music which would not be heard until the 1960s.

His first review came from Don Gold in the Chicago jazz magazine *Down Beat.* With a rating of three stars (out of a possible five), Gold said that *Super-Sonic Jazz* "represents the eclectic meandering of a Chicago jazz cult" and "was an attempt to blend the music of East and West," an attempt, he added, which failed. "India" was a valid effort at portraying Eastern percussion, he thought, but "Sunology" pointlessly tried to connect the blues to "Indian music." He thought the musicians were only adequate, and he singled out James Scales's solo on "Springtime" as particularly awful. Yet sensing that something special was going on here, Gold hedged a bit, adding, "There is a philosophy allied to the music itself, a philosophy somewhat comparable to that of William Saroyan in a particularly giddy mood," though he could see no relation to the music except in the titles. Here, at the beginning of Sonny's recording career, Gold was clearly laying out the agenda of jazz critics that the Arkestra would face for years: nothing should distract from the music, not costumes, lights, or ideology (civil rights being a possible exception among liberal critics). Whatever message Sonny might have would be scorned or ignored.

But Chicago was beginning to pay attention to the band. An odd assortment of acolytes, neighborhood folks, curious musicians, and tourist intellectuals attended their open rehearsals. One out-of-town visitor was Norman Mailer, who heard them in rehearsal one night in 1956:

> Once, years ago in Chicago, I was coming down with a bad cold. By accident, a friend took me to hear a jazz musician named Sun Ra who played "space music." The music was a little like the sound of Ornette Coleman, but further out, outer space music, close to the EEEE of an electric drill at the center of a harsh trumpet. My cold cleared up in five minutes, I swear it. The anger of the sound penetrated into some sprung-up rage which was burning fuel for the cold.

Mailer later said that he thought this music was "strangely horrible," but at the same time he was deeply impressed by the dedication with which Sonny's musicians toiled on in semiobscurity.

The first commercial interest in recording the Arkestra occurred when Tom Wilson came to Chicago. Wilson was an African-American producer from Waco, Texas, who after graduating from Harvard in 1954 borrowed $900 to start a recording company called Transition which he ran from his apartment in Cambridge. Wilson's plan was to document the most advanced jazz musicians of his time, and he largely succeeded, becoming the first to record Cecil Taylor, John Coltrane, Curtis Fuller, and others as leaders of their own groups. Meantime, he underwrote his company by teaching courses on jazz at several colleges in the Boston area. On July 12, 1956, Wilson took Sonny and ten musicians into Universal Recording Studio, the best facility in Chicago, and recorded *Jazz by Sun Ra, Vol. 1,* which was released in 1957.

The cover of *Jazz by Sun Ra* bore a painting with smudges of gold against black, like an early Mondrian. The record included some pieces which looked back to earlier times, like the "New Horizons" theme which he had written for his first Chicago big band; "Fall off the Log," which recalled a chorus-line dance step from the DeLisa; and "Possession," a waltz written by Harry Revel for Les Baxter's *Perfume Set to Music,* a suite of tunes associated with fragrances from the French perfume company Corday. Sonny was struck by the lush string writing, the mysterious sound of the theremin, the interpenetrations of senses the arrangement provoked. "Jet" was the big number from the album—it was a hit, in fact, for Nat Cole—but it was the strings, harp, oboe, theremin, and Novachord organ on the original recording of "Possession" that led him to request an arrangement of it from pianist-trombonist Prince Shell, who turned it into a 4/4 ballad which nonetheless hewed close to the original in spirit.

Wilson proposed that a booklet of Sonny's notes be included with the record—a very unusual practice then or now, as musicians are seldom trusted to explain their own work—and he took full advantage of it, filling it with his poetry and various musings. Yet when Sonny suggested the notes be titled "Preparation for Outer Space," Wilson thought he was going too far and refused. Still, it was to be the most complete statement on a specific body of work he would ever make.

THE AIM OF MY COMPOSITIONS:

All of my compositions are meant to depict happiness combined with beauty in a free manner. Happiness, as well as pleasure and beauty, has many degrees of existence; my aim is to express these degrees in sounds which can be understood by the entire world. All of my music is tested for effect. By effect I mean mental impression. The mental impression I intend to convey is that of being alive, vitally alive. The real aim of this music is to co-ordinate the minds of peoples into an intelligent reach for a better world, and an intelligent approach to the living future. By peoples I mean all of the people of different nations who are living today.

THE TECHNIQUES I EMPLOY:

I always strive to write the sounds I hear both inwardly and outwardly. I use the simple rules of harmony as a basis but I employ my own rule as well. My rule is that every note played must be a living note. In order to achieve this, I use notes like words in a sentence, making each series of sounds a separate thought. My watchword is precision. I never forget that a "sound" is just as important as a sound doctrine in a nonmusical field.

We rehearse every day on new sounds and new approaches to projection. Projection is very important. Dynamics, melodies that have a story to tell, chords that alert the ear, contrapuntal rhythms, all combine in my creations to make a new form of modern jazz.

THE SONGS I PLAY:

Most of my compositions speak of the future. For instance, in this album we present *Future...New Horizons...Transition...Sun Song... Brainville*. In all these songs I am deliberately attempting to tempt people to like higher forms of music. Eventually I will succeed.

Elements of Sonny's later thought are already in place here: an emphasis on discipline and rules, puns ("sound," "tempt"), the new and the modern, but also a concern with music tradition (the linear, narrative vision of music as expressed in the analogy to language). After a brief account of his musicians' skills, the notes go on:

POEMS ARE MUSIC:

Some of the songs I write are based on my poems; for this reason, I am including some of them with this album in order that those who are interested may understand that poems are music, and that music is only another form of poetry. I consider every creative musical composition as being a tone poem.

In calling his works tone poems he further aligned himself with the romantic tradition of programmatic music, as narrative, the storytelling of Debussy's *Prelude to the Afternoon of a Faun* or Tchaikovsky's *Romeo and Juliet*. The text to "New Horizons" was typical:

Music pulsing like a living heartbeat,
Pleasant intuition of better things to come...
The sight of boundless space
Reaching ever outward as if in search of itself.
Music spontaneous rapture,
Feet rushing with the wind on a new world
Of sounds:
Invisible words...vibrations...tone pictures
A new world for every self
Seeking a better self and a better world.

Music akin to thought........
Imagination...!
With wings unhampered,
Unafraid.......
Soaring like a bird
Through the threads and fringes of today
Straight to the heart of tomorrow,
Music rushing forth like a fiery law
Loosening the chains that bind,
Ennobling the mind
With all the many greater dimensions
Of a living tomorrow.

The music for "New Horizons" has the slightly portentous feel of other swing band theme songs used to introduce groups at the beginning of an evening's performance, but also shows some affinity for some of Ellington's ballads. In his notes Sonny says that this piece is "A sketch of a new and better day dawning. It is meditative, an expecting mood. What is it expecting?...Excitement in an enjoyable form, beauty, and superior love."

The music of "Sun Song" is described as "The reach for new sounds, a spacite picture of the Atonal tomorrow...broad in scope, unafraid in rendition...a real example of freedom in melody, harmony, and rhythm. This is one of the songs which they say people will not be able to understand...." It is dedicated to Art Tatum. Sonny plays both organ and piano on "Sun Song," with a counter-melody on chimes and a trumpet solo. Temple blocks, tambourine, and slightly out-of-phase tom-tom and timpani sounds are the rhythm base over which its quasi-modal harmonic form moves.

SUN SONG

In my nest..... in my nest;
I do have a nest, a beautiful golden nest
Soft and shimmering with many colors....
Radiant like the Sun.
Yes, I have a nest;
Out in outer space on the tip of the worlds.
There dwell I.
Come my love:
My many peoples, my sundry nations
That I adore,
Fly with me
Away to my nest.
High beyond the highest mountain,
Far away beyond the earth
Surrounded by fire and flame
Is my nest.

You there!
Thou bird of the golden wing:
How happily would you fit into my nest.
You there!... You there!...
You people of the planet earth
Forget yesterday and sorrow
Fly away with me to my ever Living
World of Tomorrow,
And dwell with me in my nest,
My fiery nest of many mansions,
Of kaleidoscopic vision and beauty...
A real world... a rare world of being alive.

Again, they received only one review, this time from Nat Hentoff in *Down Beat*. And again, the reviewer expressed his doubts with a three-star rating and patronizing advice. Rather than philosophizing, he said, Sun Ra might better spend his energy "on the here and now of his own writing equipment." The music was too repetitious, built merely on riffs with little development. Yet Hentoff found the musicians up to the task, even if the solos were too short: "I'd like to hear them in a blowing date without the need for Hegel." He praised the booklet, but criticized it for having no biographical information on the musicians, failing to tell even where they came from. Instead they wasted the space on Sun Ra's "re-markably bad 'poems.' " Hentoff admired the goals expressed in Sun Ra's "credo," but said that he had a long way to go to "start fulfilling them. . . . He has, though, some potential."

Enough material was recorded that there was to be a second volume of *Jazz by Sun Ra,* but Wilson's success with Transition got him a job at United Artists Records in 1957, and he soon gave up his own projects. He then went on to do stints as a producer for Savoy, Audiofidelity, Columbia, Verve, and MGM, and had a remarkable career, recording the Blues Project, Frank Zappa, Eric Burden and the Animals, Simon and Garfunkel, Country Joe and the Fish, Richie Havens, Nico, Bob Dylan's first electric band, the Clancy Brothers, Pete Seeger, the Velvet Underground, Herbie Mann, Cannonball Adderley, and Hugh Masekela. He would record Sonny again several times. But by 1968, Wilson had given up on jazz, claiming that rock now best represented the excitement that jazz had once produced, and sold the original tapes of *Jazz by Sun Ra* to Delmark Records of Chicago, who reissued it. The record then reached an even wider audience under the title of *Sun Song,* but it fared no better critically. Reviewer Martin Williams in the *Saturday Review* would call it "professional," but "conservative," "glib," "shallow," and "dull." Years later when Miles Davis heard it in a "Blindfold Test" in *Down Beat* he would dismiss it as a sad "European" band, something like Raymond Scott might have done; and even later, Wynton Marsalis would say that Sun Ra in this period was imitating early European avant-garde music.

But in a French reassessment in 1968, critic Philippe Carles heard it all quite differently:

It is a music derived from bebop, of course, which seems normal and re-assuring, yet something has moved, something is in the process of chang-ing. Barely perceptible slippages in the structures and development of themes, and unexpected accentuation of certain sounds, sudden dimin-ishing of intensity and volume, the softening or the metamorphosis of rhythms, the transformation of acoustic relationships (echoes, reverbera-tion, amplification, and other procedures which allow space to be modi-fied), or a dramatization of the ensemble through certain somber sounds which become more and more insistent (on the baritone, the timpani, the bass, or the Hammond organ), cause a sense of anxiety to be added by moments. Everything happens as if the orchestra were sending to the au-dience a musical image identical to the musical object, which it is charged with reflecting. But at the same time it is perfectly inverse or out-of-sync relative to this. The known elements become in this way so many sources of a feeling of malaise. They're different, they're no longer where we ex-pected to hear them. They are no longer lighted as they were before. Their sound or their shadow is at the same time unrecognizable and fa-miliar. This allows for a third goal to be obtained: it bothers, surprises, and awakens attention. "Today is the shadow of tomorrow/today is the future present of yesterday/yesterday is the shadow of today/" (Sun Ra, "Se-crets of the Sun"). That is to say that one can still see the evolutionary character of mutations, for even the revolutions just continue what pro-ceeded them.

In 1968 Delmark issued Volume 2 of *Jazz by Sun Ra* under the title of *Sound of Joy*. Several pieces ("Two Tones," "Ankh," "Reflections in Blue") use two baritone saxophones, which combine with bass and tim-pani to give the band a powerful bottom sound. "Overtones of China" extends the orientalism of early jazz with gongs and wood blocks, asym-metrical themes, and the feel of shifting time; two pieces ("Paradise" and "Planet Earth") are given Latin rhythms; and "Reflections in Blue" and "El Viktor" make full use of timpani with solos or a heavy back beat. Throughout, there are unusually conceived background riffs, surprising counter-melodies, and multiple themes (each with a different rhythm and in a different key). Two ballads written by Sonny and sung by Clyde Williams in a full, baritone voice ("As You Once Were" and "Dreams Come True") were left off the LP since Delmark's president Bob

Koester felt they didn't fit with the other pieces on the session. But this sequence of tunes, like those on some of Sonny's other early records, approximates what he played at clubs at the time.

This time the only reviews came from England, and all were positive. For example, in *Jazz Monthly*, Jack Cooke accurately noted Sonny's sources as being "big swing bands, the smaller, James Moody type off-shoots of the early 1950's, various forms of Hollywoodish exotica, a touch of Broadway" and then went on to offer a shrewd reading of Sonny's place in the music of that time:

> One of the things that's noticeable here is the lack of contemporary relevance in Ra's music at this stage; when one considers what else was going on in November 1957—Silver, the Messengers, Rollins, Roach, Monk, Miles and Coltrane: the high tide of the hard bop era in fact—it's remarkable not to find any response in the music, except for the work of some of the individual soloists. It sounds ahead of, or just as often behind, but never of its time; its occasional gaucheness is offset by flashes of real complexity, but it never tries to be even remotely fashionable. This perhaps suggests another point to bear in mind about Ra's development and the extreme originality of his later music; the sense of being cut off, musically, maybe to some extent geographically, certainly intellectually, is very strong here: whether by accident or design is hard to say.

This *was* unusual music, evoking its sources, but never surrendering to them. It was a music that could drift past without surprise, that could bring dancers to the floor, but nonetheless could leave the listener feeling vaguely uneasy. Nothing was quite what it seemed. American jazz fans, however, were in no mood at this point for ambiguity.

Edward O. Bland was a young jazz disc jockey in Chicago who regularly played Sonny's records on the air. When he and Sonny met, Bland told him that he was working on an experimental film about the nature of jazz and its relation to the lives of blacks in the United States, and Bland asked him to appear in the film and let him use his music in it in exchange for the publicity Sonny would get on the film's release. He agreed, and in 1956 Bland began following the band around and filming them at the Gate of Horn and several other clubs around 63rd Street. The film that resulted—the thirty-three-minute black-and-white *The Cry of Jazz*—was based in part on an unpublished book by Bland entitled *The Fruits of the Death of Jazz*.

The film opens just as a meeting of the "Parkwood Jazz Club," a young, politely dressed, interracial gathering, is breaking up. When a white woman asks what jazz is, one of the young black men answers that "jazz is the cry of the Negro's joy and suffering," and consequently only the American Negro could have invented jazz. Arguments follow over the universality of suffering and just how "American" jazz is. Against scenes of ghetto street life, pool halls, of "the hazards of being Negro," a narrator explains that jazz is an expression of the triumph of the Negro's spirit. Yet that music is also built on a contradiction between restriction and freedom: improvisation of melody occurs against two restraining features: song form, which repeats itself endlessly without going anywhere (and is a reflection of the Negro's condition—"a future-less future"), and harmonic changes, and is a pattern which repeats itself over and over again. Rhythm and melodic improvisation represent joy, while form and harmony represent suffering. This is the "worship of the present" in the face of having no future, life as it should be versus what it is.

The narrator continues against images of black religious life, from storefronts to large churches: like jazz improvisation, there are many individual solutions by which Negroes transform their condition. Scenes of affluent whites accompany examples of cool jazz. Back at the meeting again, more controversy surfaces when one man insists that "the Negro is the only human American," because "you have to have a soul to be human." There follows a brief history of jazz styles, concluding with Sun Ra, who the narrator says combines "bebop melody, Duke Ellington, and Thelonious Monk." But then he adds that "jazz is dead because the Negro needs more room to tell his story," and it "cannot grow, but only repeat itself": "change cannot occur and still have form; form cannot change and still have swing"; and form and harmonic change cannot exist simultaneously and still have jazz." "Jazz was not supposed to grow ... it was supposed to die like the Negro, for a futureless future has made the Negro dead." Jazz is a "period music," it is "genteel slavery." Someone at the party then asks, "Can whites play jazz?" For whites to play jazz well they will have to pay the price of suffering, by learning to be humble and accepting the Negro; in order to become human, whites need jazz to understand the Negroes' suffering. For the Negro is America's conscience.

The Arkestra is heard behind most of the film and is seen in several clubs, in several forms, including quintet and full band, dressed in suits or tuxedos. They appear in shadows or are shot at oblique angles, in part so they could appear to be different musicians representing different eras and in part to avoid problems with the Musicians Union for working without pay. They play "Demon's Lullaby," "Urnack," "Super Blonde," "A Call for All Demons," and Sonny improvises on piano to illustrate the film's point about the restraint imposed by harmony.

The film premiered at Roosevelt University in Chicago in early 1959, and drew considerable attention in early underground film circles. It had a second life when it was widely shown in black studies courses in the 1960s and 1970s. In the summer issue of *Film Culture* in 1960 Edward Bland wrote that "jazz was the Negro's act of transcendence; without this act the Negro would have been a sub-human animal or dead." It was a "holding action," as jazz provides a portrait of the Negro, and "is a musical expression of the Negro's eternal re-creation in the eternal present." In the last ten years jazz has "become a cult of romantic and futuristic pretensions." No future for jazz; jazz is dead. He concludes that in his next film the viewer will not even be able to use jazz as an escape.

Sun Ra seldom mentioned *The Cry of Jazz*, though once in an interview in which Bland's thesis was raised, he softly remarked without elaborating that "he was wrong."

In spite of increased attention and more work, most of the Arkestra's engagements did not pay much, especially as rock and roll was becoming stronger by the day, and many clubs were shifting their entertainment policies to follow the crowds. Sonny still used a smaller group when it was called for, and when he needed money badly enough he'd return to the strip joints for work. Most of the band's musicians had day jobs and so were able to manage on their own. They were young and full of the energy needed to keep up with their forty-two-year-old leader. Trombonist Nate Pryor, for example, worked days at the post office, and after work he'd eat, go to rehearsal, run home to change, and go right to the gig. When they were working at Budland that meant that they would play until 2 A.M., but they often stayed until 4 or 5 A.M.—since they didn't get paid until the entire show was over and the receipts from the door were counted—and then home for a couple of hours sleep and then back to work at 8.

Sonny's band had become more solid with the addition of some first-rate musicians: Lucious Randolph on trumpet, his sister Hattie as a singer, and alto saxophonist James Spaulding, an accomplished bebopper with experience recording with Jerry Butler and Curtis Mayfield. The bassist was now Ronnie Boykins, a player with a wide range of experience in blues and jazz groups, and especially strong using the bow.

But the band was also a magnet for the strange, drawing all sorts of people off the streets to rehearsals and performances. One of the most bizarre of those who turned up was Yochannan, one of many eccentric blues singers (like Dr. Jo Jo Adams and The Sandman) who could be seen on weekends on Maxwell Street and at local blues clubs like the Green Door. Yochannan had many stage names, including the Man from Outer Space, the Man from Mars, and the Muck Muck Man, and declared himself a descendant of the sun. Dressed in turban, sandals, and red, orange, and yellow "Asiatic" robes, he was always quick to hold forth to anyone on his private philosophy. And when he performed he was unpredictable and crude, often working bawdy material into the last song he sang at club appearances. His performance was wild, and Hattie Randolph remembers a gig with Yochannan in Kokomo, Indiana. "It was a big package thing. There was a band for dancing, a comic, a blues singers... and Yochannan was on the show." When he started his act and began leaping over tables, one woman jumped up and shouted, "He's possessed! He's possessed!" and ran out of the club."

Sonny put out a single featuring Yochannan on "Muck Muck"/"Hot Skillet Mama," songs vaguely reminiscent of two previous rhythm-and-blues hits, "Rag Mop" and "Open the Door, Richard" respectively, though slightly naughtier, with hints at the dozens Yochannan used in performances at clubs. Two years later Sonny recorded several more Yochannan singles: "The Sun One"—which was originally titled "The

Man Who Flew in from the Sun"—was a boasting riff tune with cosmological overtones ("I'm the one from the sun")—in effect, the Sun King
as Mack man; the B-side, "Message to Earthman," was a short sci-fi narrative of an alien invasion set against swirling horns. And in 1968 an alternate take of "The Sun One" was issued under the title "The Sun Man
Speaks," now including a monologue with quasibiblical allusions to
Yochannan's own death and resurrection.

In late 1957 jazz was about to undergo a major shift, a change that
would take it in several directions at once, opening up a future history of
permanent diversity. But for the moment the music was dominated by a
group of well-known figures who spanned the whole history of the
music: traditionalists and mainstreamers like Louis Armstrong, Red
Allen, and Coleman Hawkins; swing bands like Basie's and Ellington's;
beboppers and post-boppers like Art Blakey; and cool icons such as Chet
Baker and Dave Brubeck. Miles Davis's recording of *Miles Ahead* with
Gil Evans's arrangements had set a new standard for urbane jazz; Bill
Evans was bringing a fresh lyricism and harmonic sophistication to the
piano, and Ray Charles was making funk and rhythm and blues safe for
jazz listeners. But more often than not the public thought jazz meant
records like *Sonny Criss Plays Cole Porter*, *The Jazz Messengers Play Loerner
& Lowe*, or *Shorty Rogers Plays Richard Rodgers*, jazz translations of well-
known Broadway show tunes.

Sonny recorded *Sun Ra Visits Planet Earth* in this year, though it was
not released until 1966. And by the time it finally appeared on a Saturn
record, its cover made it seem even further out of its time: a tropical
bandstand sits in grass, out of which instruments grow; down below
drums are literally cooking; the whole sitting on a layered, terraced
topographic landscape which anticipates the graphics of video games.
Four of the pieces recorded for Tom Wilson were again included, and
two new versions of compositions which had also been recorded for
Transition. "Eve" was the only completely new piece, heavy with percussion and with a strange, unresolved melody; in spite of being only
five and a half minutes long, it seemed as if it could go on forever.

Times were tough in Chicago in the late 1950s with the bite of reces-
sion especially hurting the entertainment business, but the Arkestra took
work where it could, locally and in nearby states. They traveled as far as
Indianapolis, where Hoosier stars-to-be Freddie Hubbard and Wes

Montgomery sat in with the band at a dance at the YMCA gymnasium. Most often Sonny used an octet—a stripped-down version of a full band with trumpet and trombone, saxes, bass, piano, drums, and timpani. Though they worked almost every night the pay was low. But whenever they worked somewhere, Sonny made the use of the club or the hall for rehearsals a part of the deal.

New people were now continually drifting in and out of the Arkestra. One of the new ones was Marshall Allen, an alto saxophonist from Louisville who had settled in Chicago in 1951 after returning from Paris where he had studied at the Paris Conservatoire on the GI Bill and played and recorded with James Moody. Since James Spaulding was the alto player that Sun Ra had been using, he encouraged Allen to play other instruments, especially as he was already strong on the flute. Yet Allen stayed with the alto, and developed into one of the most individual voices on the instrument. His taste in alto saxophonists ran to some of the greats of the swing era, like Johnny Hodges or Earl Bostic, and he evoked them night after night as leader of the saxophone section. But Sun Ra also pushed him towards expressing other dimensions of his spirit, and he found ways to draw howls, screams, and bird songs from the horn, sluring and fluttering tones by strumming and flailing the keys like a guitar, violently jerking it around in his mouth and producing explosions of sound. He was able to play "in" and "out" on the same piece—to follow the melody line and chord structure and simultaneously suggest that he was free of them to play what he wanted. Sun Ra came to count on him to try anything, no matter how outrageous. When Sonny began to explore Scriabin's work he discovered the Russian composer's "mystic chord," which was the basis of *Prometheus* and the last five of the Russian composer's piano concertos. When the chord was played in scalar form it produced a modified whole tone scale. When Sonny asked Marshall to learn it, he began to use it in all of his solos. Allen was to become perhaps the most devoted musician that Sun Ra would ever have, and from then on he played with no other bands unless Sonny encouraged him to do so.

The band's book had grown to three or four inches in thickness, with 200 to 300 compositions, so many that they seldom played the same piece twice on the gig. They were now playing breakfast dances at Budland every Sunday with seventeen pieces. They became a regular stop for visiting musicians after hours, people like Frank Foster and Miles Davis. The Arkestra continued to record, even when they couldn't afford to put records out, and their backlog continued to grow. Never once did Sonny doubt that this music would be issued; time and history and the Creator were on his side. And right on cue on January 31, 1958, the United States launched its first satellite, *Explorer I,* which Wernher von Braun's group had been developing in Huntsville, Alabama. Sonny was vindicated for his predictions—the space age had arrived and synchronicity or something had put him in the picture.

Later in the year *Jazz in Silhouette* was recorded and released as the second Saturn album, its cover offering virtually naked space nymphs sailing over the pitted surface of a red moon of Saturn as seen from approximately 300 miles up. The record notes suggest: "In tomorrow's world, men will not need artificial instruments such as jets and space ships. In the world of tomorrow, the new man will 'think' the place he wants to go, then his mind will take him there."

Elsewhere, the cover proclaims: "This is the sound of silhouettes, images and forecasts of tomorrow disguised as jazz." "The Shadow of Tomorrow," a poem included on the back cover, expands on the meaning:

Today is the shadow of tomorrow
Today is the present future of yesterday
Yesterday is the shadow of today.
The darkness of the past is yesterday.
And the light of the past is yesterday.
The days of yesterday are all numbered and summed
in the word "once";
Because "once upon a time there was a yesterday."
Yesterday belongs to the dead,
Because the dead belongs to the past
The past is yesterday.

Jazz in Silhouette was a major statement by the Arkestra, helped by Hobart Dotson, an exceptional trumpet player who later worked with Lionel Hampton and Charles Mingus. Dotson immediately brightened the ensemble sound. "Enlightenment," a space march he cowrote with Sonny, announced the band, first with loping figures like some Disney cartoon theme, and then quickly transformed itself by turns into a hard bop anthem and a rhapsodic theme, cut by cha-cha, march, and 4/4 swing rhythms, all of it accomplished without the melody repeating itself. "Enlightenment" became a nightly staple with the Arkestra for the next thirty-six years, a vehicle on which the whole Arkestra stood or marched and sang in unison, in the style of old Doc Wheeler's Royal Sunset Serenaders:

> The sound of joy
> Is enlightenment
> Space, fire, truth
> Is enlightenment
> Space fire,
> Sometimes it's music
> Strange mathematics,
> Rhythmic equations
>
> The sound of thought
> Is enlightenment
> The magic light
> Of tomorrow
> Backwards are those
> Of sadness
> Forward and onward
> Are those of gladness
>
> Enlightenment
> Is my tomorrow
> It has no planes
> Of sorrow
> Hereby, my invitation
> I do invite you
> To be of my space world
>
> This song is sound
> Of enlightenment

The fiery truth
Of enlightenment
Vibrations come
From the space world
Is of the cosmic
Starry dimension

Enlightenment
Is my tomorrow
It has no planes
Of sorrow
Hereby, our invitation
We do invite you
To be of our space world

"Ancient Aiethopia" calls up the spirit of Ellington's programmatic statements on Africa like "Pyramid" or "Menelik." But what Sonny achieved with this piece was unprecedented in jazz (though Ravel's "Bolero" might be claimed as a distant relative): by means of the simplest of structures (a single chord and a crisp but subtly shifting "Latin tinge" rhythm of bass, tom-toms, and timpani) the Arkestra is set free from the conventions of the pop song and its grip on the swing era, but also free from the harmonic residue of the same songs left from the beboppers. Once the ensemble states the melody, two flutes begin to improvise collectively; a poised trumpet solo by Dotson takes full advantage of the harmonic freedom which in a few years would be called modality; the piano solos with the bass tones allowed to ring out rhythmically against the drums; musicians blow through mouthpieces without their horns; and two singers intone words so softly and independently of each other that their parts cancel each other out. Though there had been efforts at opening up jazz before, setting it free of its conventional and recurring structures, what made this composition so startling is the ease and assuredness with which it was achieved. As improvised and open as it is, there is an inexorable sense of direction, a destiny about the piece. But as with most of Sonny's records, pieces as prophetic as these peculiarly coexist on the same record with slight compositions like "Hours After," with a two-beat feel which alludes to the Erskine Hawkins band ("After Hours") of more than a decade before.

After *Jazz in Silhouette,* no other Saturn LP was issued for seven years, though Sonny and Alton continued to record the band and to produce 45-rpm singles. The process by which individual Saturn records came into existence and were distributed was as mysterious as the rest of Sonny's life. The musicians never knew what would appear on which records, or what the titles would be. The albums were assembled and sequenced with no obvious order, often mixing together recordings done on different occasions, in rehearsals and in the studio, then labeling them with the same date, sometimes the wrong one, or with the wrong personnel, so the Arkestra might seem to be playing in widely divergent styles on a single record; 45-rpm singles of a given composition might or might not contain the version which appeared on the LP which followed; or the same composition might turn up on different LPs with no mention that they had been issued before. Many of the records had hand-drawn covers and labels, the wrong titles, or no titles at all. Sometimes they were labeled as being in "Solar High Fidelity" or were registered with "Interplanetary BMI." Sonny called the Saturn releases his "avant-garde" records: "Whatever I think people are not going to listen to, I've always recorded it. When it'll take them some time—maybe twenty years, thirty years—to really hear it."

El Saturn Records purchased no advertising, gave out no promotional copies for review, and had no distribution channels except mail order, hand delivery to the record shops, and, in the southern tradition, sales from the bandstand after performances. An order to the El Saturn address might or might not get a response, and when a record came it might be a different one than ordered (a 1971 Saturn price list asked orderers to list five alternates), or arrive months later.

The pieces that made up the album *Sound Sun Pleasure!!* were recorded late in the year, and all were selections which appear to have been a rather conventional dance-band set—songs like "I Could Have Danced All Night," "Hour of Parting," and "Back in Your Own Backyard." A similar album, *Holiday for Soul Dance*, was recorded the next year, but both it and *Sound Sun Pleasure!!* were not released for another ten years or so.

Yet in 1959 Sonny recorded a number of compositions which would make up *Lady with the Golden Stockings* in 1966 (and which would be reissued in 1967 with the title *The Nubians of Plutonia*, linking Africa and space); but it was first sold in what was to later become a generic Saturn cover used for many records, with the title *Tonal View of Times Tomorrow*. With this record Sonny showed his response to the burst of interest in Latin rhythms set off by the mambo in the mid-1950s and the calypso craze of 1957–58. And like many big bands, the Arkestra's take on these rhythms was less specifically Latin than a North American impression of these rhythms within dance-band conventions. The Arkestra was in effect reinventing these rhythms. Where Cuban musicians might layer a few discrete rhythms together to interlock and form an emergent new rhythm, North American musicians often heaped a number of percussion instruments together, all playing the same rhythm. Despite the comparative complexity of many of these pieces there is a tendency for them to simplify as the solos begin—to turn into the blues or a rhythm jam with no chordal accompaniment. A new version of "Aiethopia" on this album shows just how many Arkestra members had begun to double on percussion in just one year, though their use of them is relatively simple. "The Golden Lady" resolves quickly into a series of solos fit to the accompaniment of a half a dozen rhythm instruments. "Africa" opens up a bit more: drums hold the piece together, while a flute plays, and four male singers softly and wordlessly sing along. "Watusa" (credited to Sun Ra, but copyrighted by Andre Pitts and Terri Vanne Sherrill) suggests South African pop music, and responds to the 1959 film *Watusa*, MGM's sequel to *King Solomon's Mines*.

The implication of these recordings is that a piece of music could be built out of the simplest of elements: a continuing string of drum rhythms and a series of melodies based on a chord or even a single note. Or nothing. On one hand it was a primitivist gesture, but it was also a stripping away of the previous generation's obsession with harmonic complexity.

His wrists and arms were encircled by copper wire strung with
good luck charms; his fingers were covered with several large
plain rings. A copper wire was bound around his head and
attached to this wire were two broken bits of mirror, which
lying flat against his temples with the reflecting side out,
flashed and glittered when he moved his head.

> GEORGE BODDISON, "mayor" of Tin City,
> a shantytown outside of Savannah, Georgia,
> as described in *Drums and Shadows* (1940)

When the Arkestra was booked into the Wonder Inn on 75th & Cot-
tage Grove for five nights a week, Abraham bought them an old ward-
robe from an opera company, one heavily stocked with capes, puffed
sleeves, and doublets, and they began to dress for "space," though it
might have seemed a space closer to *William Tell* than to Mars. "We had
a basement full of opera clothes," Sonny said. "We'd come out in opera
clothes and they thought that was weird but they used the costumes in
the opera, so why couldn't we use it?"

The traditional uniform of the swing-band musician of the twenties
and thirties was the dress of the gentleman—modified evening wear or
matching dark suits. It was one of the marks of the black musician's relative freedom from segregation and discrimination. Young musicians aspired to wear the clothes of the bands almost as much as they did to play.
But in the late forties and fifties the same younger musicians began to
break with the established look of the stage band with its faint echoes of
servants' uniforms. Some musicians of this period, like Billy Eckstine,
were even regarded as fashion trendsetters. Miles Davis's clothing on the
front of his album covers sent young men racing to their favorite men's
store. The green shirt he wore on the cover of *Milestones* was famous for
its cool statement. So in 1958 when Sonny decided to dress his band with
high theatricality, he stepped far outside the limits of the tradition.

He had been reading into the lore of color among the Egyptians,
Greeks, and Tibetans, and he knew something of color therapy, so as he
thought through the possible scenarios of the band's productions he

began coordinating the costume colors by mystical principles. "Some-times," Lucious Randolph recalled, "the musicians would have to change their shirts because of the colors they were wearing, even change them in front of people in the audience. Sun Ra said some colors disturbed him, made him feel uncomfortable. He really seemed uncomfortable. He'd say, 'Don't wear that color, it's the devil's color!' Sometimes you'd have to change to a different color just to be able to talk to him." His sense of the power of color extended far beyond clothing—to food (purple was his color of choice at the time, and when he bought some hard candy he'd pick out only the purple ones to eat and leave the rest) and hotel rooms. He became notorious when they were on tour for insisting on seeing the color of each room before he assigned individual players to them.

Soon Sonny was designing their clothes, shopping for fabric, and organizing the band to sew their own outfits. The vests, crocheted hats, and oversized T-shirts that they wore were to become so common with them that some began to wear parts of them on the streets. Although Sonny was practical enough that they continued to wear suits for formal dances, he also worked out a rationale for space outfits and calculated the ambiguity of their designs:

> We started [wearing space costumes] back in Chicago. In those days I tried to make the black people, the so-called Negroes, conscious of the fact that they live in a changing world. And because I thought that they were left out of everything culturally, that nobody had thought about bringing them in contact with the culture, none of the black leaders did that . . . that's why I thought I could make it clear to them that there are other things outside their closed environment. That's what I tried with those clothes. I designed some of them myself. I did it because just by seeing those clothes the people could get an idea of what I meant. Some people may not be able to accept this music or know what it is, but in fact they don't need to listen to the music; they just need to look at our clothes because I have incorporated music in them too. What's more, I had the idea that the musicians would feel more relaxed if they played in something that was not restricted to the normal kinds of clothes that the people are wearing now. If, for instance, you would go back to the Roman empire and would wear the clothes I am wearing now, you would be dressed completely in style. And the same is true if I would go to Africa

or Asia. It's like some of the songs that are accepted in every country by people because of the timeless element in it. With these clothes we wear I have also tried to create a timeless element.

He thought "something had been destroyed in humanity when men gave up flowing garments to women," and like D. H. Lawrence, he also bemoaned the surrender of color to women.

While they were playing at the Wonder Inn, Sonny began to escalate the staging of his performances. The choreographed routines of the band became more elaborate, the costumes more outrageous. Some nights he would change his costume for every piece. Once the curtain rose to an Arkestra playing under mosquito netting. And when the club was having trouble meeting bills and had their electricity cut off, Sonny brought some wind-up spaceships and set them crawling and whirred around the dark stage, lights blinking, bumping into things and reversing direction (their whirring can be heard at the end of "We Travel the Spaceways").

Sonny's own costume was constantly in the making, reconfigured by a larger set of principles than "entertainment" allowed:

I had a special space hat with a light on top and people said to me, "Why you got to have a blue light on the top of your head?" I said, " 'Cause I feel like it!" They were worried about that light you see. Some people said I was hypnotizing people, but it wasn't that. Astronauts are wearing hats like that. They could wear tuxedos in outer space but they wear space suits 'cause it's more suitable. So if I'm playin' space music, why can't I wear my celestial hats and things like that. But they want to chain a musician, where he just got to wear black all the time.

Sonny's hats were particularly important to him—especially after he began to develop a bald spot—and over the years they became increasingly complex—miniaturized solar systems made of wire, pyramid-shaped cushions, exploding crowns of solar flares.

A costume *is* music. If the musicians dress creative, instead of wearing overalls and jeans, people can appreciate that. The average person, you see, they have a hard time working, they wear their work clothes. But musicians don't need to be in competition to the working man. They need something else, so the working man will say, "That's beautiful."

Marcus Garvey, the early black nationalist leader (who appeared publicly in a variety of academic gowns and military uniforms, and used Egyptian symbols on his followers' caps), once said, you have to "*show* Negroes, cannot *tell* them." It was necessary "to make noise, beat the drum to have arguments." And when observers mocked the costumed members of Garvey's organization by calling them characters in a musical or an opera, Garvey defended this dress by reminding them of the pomp and circumstance of European culture. Similarly, Sonny said:

> [I]n the early days in every nation, everyone had their costume. 'Cause they identified the nation. Like everyone got their flags and things. That represents the nation. And that's the colors. If you're out fighting a battle, they say, "Fly your colors. You got to have your colors." And so every night I'm fighting a different kind of battle, so I have to change according to that night.... Costumes are music. Colors throw out musical sounds, too. Every color throws out vibrations of life.

"All police, all militaries have uniforms, but musicians have been wearing whatever they want. It doesn't show any unity, any image. If we wear uniforms we'll get applause just for the image." The Arkestra was conceived in martial terms: "Sun Ra used to compare the Arkestra to a disciplined army," James Jacson said. "Soldiers can only win the war if they believe in what they do. We weren't trained in killing the enemy, but in the spirit of humanity."

> We're like space warriors. Music can be used as a weapon, as energy. The right note or chord can transport you into space using music and energy flow. And the listeners can travel along with you.

They were—some might have said—soldiers of the Lord.

But for Sonny unity and discipline did not have to be expressed in terms of military conformity and rigidity. In fact, his musicians' performances were like parties which they gave for themselves as well as the audience. He said that they should seem childlike in their presentations.

There were often two or three changes of costume in an evening—from Spanish to rock and roll to space clothes—as if they were a different band every time. And each of them was given the chance to develop their own costumes, roles, and dances. "You could be something by dressing up, by taking a role," said Jacson. "You could be a myth. And yet we became uniform in the abstractness of what we were.... And later this idea fed back to the flower children in the 1960s."

Younger musicians were often in Sonny's audiences now, especially future members of the Associated Artists of Creative Music like Muhal Richard Abrams and Joseph Jarman, or Jack De Johnette and Andrew Hill. Even some of the more established, conservative Chicago musicians had developed respect for Sonny's musicianship, and some, such as Gene Ammons, used him as a pianist from time to time. Others, like Sonny Rollins, knew of Sonny's music, and generally admired his intentions, if not his methods. Arkestra members regularly invited outside musicians to rehearsals; Pat Patrick, for one, encouraged John Coltrane to play with them, and passed some of Sonny's writings on to him. And when he didn't come, Sonny visited him when the Miles Davis Quintet was in Chicago, and played him some of his own tapes.

By the end of 1959 the band's book began to carry more pieces with space titles, and records from that period showed fewer references to Egypt. A new recruit to the band was trumpeter Phil Cohran, who was asked to a rehearsal by John Gilmore. Cohran was a serious student of world musics who had done research in Irish and African music, and was interested in the religions of the world. Fascinated by Sonny's dress and his musical range ("He could play both Tchaikovsky's and Rachmaninoff's piano concertos"), he joined immediately, and even offered some of his own compositions to the Arkestra. Though Cohran stayed only a year (being replaced by George Hudson on trumpet), Sun Ra helped him find a distinctive voice in his playing, and he was featured on several records, bringing a number of unusual instruments and musical textures into the band. He later became a founding member of the Association for the Advancement of Creative Musicians, and influenced many Chicago musicians through his teaching and the Afro-Arts Theater he founded. (One of his students was Maurice White of Earth, Wind and Fire, a group which borrowed many ideas from Cohran, including the use of the thumb piano.)

Stereo had now become the standard format, and percussion recordings were popular: Max Roach, Art Blakey, Gene Krupa, and Buddy Rich made records which sometimes featured nothing but drums; and Sonny, like Stan Kenton, Pete Ruggolo, and other composer-arrangers, took full advantage of the stereo process to give shape to his work. Though they were not to appear for another five or six years, the bulk of the music on a series of four Saturn LPs was recorded between 1959 and 1960, and represents the next stage of Sonny's thinking: *Angels and Demons at Play, Rocket Number Nine Take off for the Planet Venus* (later reissued as *Interstellar Low Ways*), *We Travel the Spaceways*, and *Fate in a Pleasant Mood*. The bulk of the material for these albums came from one all-day session at Hall Studios on June 17, 1960, where thirty to forty compositions were recorded with a septet including Sonny, Phil Cohran on cornet and violin uke (a zither-type instrument which is bowed and picked at the same time), Nate Pryor on trombone, drummer Jon Hardy, and Gilmore, Allen, and Boykins.

When *Angels and Demons at Play* was issued in 1965, it came with a dark yellow cover with the simplest of ghost images outlined in black. It included four compositions recorded in 1959–60 credited to Sonny, though Boykins later claimed that he wrote the title piece and "Tiny Pyramids." "Music from the World Tomorrow" was the signal piece: played only by bowed bass, the violin uke, organ, and percussion. Lasting barely over two minutes, it was a "sound" piece, less melody than sonority and texture, and marked a new freer, more open direction for the band. The rest of the LP consisted of two repackaged singles from 1956, which though hardly dated, jarringly showed how much the 1960 version the Arkestra had changed.

Rocket Number Nine Take off for the Planet Venus, not released until around 1966, contains "Somewhere in Space," a piece which harmonically rocks back and forth between two chords, suggesting "Flamenco Sketches" from *Kind of Blue* which Miles Davis also recorded in 1959. The melody of "Interstellar Low Ways" is stated by two flutes and tenor saxophones, and is followed by Marshall Allen's solo flute, and piano and bowed bass against a bolero beat, with several stretches empty except for minimal percussion. "Rocket Number Nine" begins in a fast tempo with the band chanting the title, and superficially recalls Dizzy Gillespie's "Salt Peanuts." But none of this prepares the listener for what was to come next: the start-and-stop passages and three exceptional solos: John Gilmore's tenor, Boykins's unaccompanied bowed bass, and Sonny's pedal-down blur of notes, ending with the band's repeated chant, "Second stop is Jupiter," and their final announcement, "All out for Jupiter."

We Travel the Spaceways, again not issued until 1966, came in a cover over which pale blue waves wash, while blue keyboards (still on fire, as on *Super-Sonic Jazz*) float overhead, and notes emerge from pieces of musical instruments on which disembodied hands play. A red flying saucer streaks past overhead. "Interplanetary Music" continues the same conception as "Music from the World Tomorrow," but with the band incrementally chanting

> Interplanetary
> Interplanetary
> Interplanetary music
>
> Interplanetary melody
> Interplanetary harmony
>
> Interplanetary
> Interplanetary
> Interplanetary music

The words to "We Travel the Spaceways" are simply "We travel the spaceways/from planet to planet," sung and hummed in straightforward harmony by three singers, but the stepwise descending melody is oddly affecting, especially since it is accompanied near the end by toy-robotic noise. The stress in the rhythm (as in "Space Loneliness") is on the fourth beat of the bar, a practice then popular with groups like Miles Davis's; but when the Arkestra used it to accompany their marches through the audience it marked the place for a "bunny-hop" step.

Fate in a Pleasant Mood (not issued until 1965) came with a black-and-white photo of Sonny on the cover, the Arkestra out of focus behind him. This would be the last record of Sun Ra's band from Chicago, and it includes "Space Mates," a ballad for flute, piano, and drums which moves from free tempo to a slow ballad tempo and then back to free time; "Lights of a Satellite" with its Ellingtonish voicings; and "Distant Stars," bebop with a startling harmonic configuration. But Chicago composer William Russo reviewed the record in *Down Beat* and dismissed it as full of underdeveloped themes and "thick-fingered piano."

Most of the compositions in these albums recorded at the end of the 1950s follow conventional pop-song form (AABA), twelve-bar blues, or some variation of them. But they never sound conventional, either because the harmonic structure or rhythms of a particular sequence are unexpected, or because of the freedom of their interpretation, which might leave out a bridge (B) section or reduce the harmonic structure of one section to an absolute minimum. To a seasoned jazz listener at the time they might seem either slightly out of kilter or evidence of a band with a hidden agenda.

Work had become tougher to find with the rise of rock and roll, and Sonny was losing some of his best musicians: Dotson, Priester, and Davis had left for New York, Art Hoyle went on the road with Lionel Hampton, Pat Patrick was playing from time to time with Latin bands, James Spaulding returned to Indianapolis, and Lucious Randolph married and took a job in the post office. Alton Abraham suggested that Sonny reach out beyond Chicago, "because nobody was listening to him there...the Chicago newspapers ignored him except for an occasional brief mention in the club listings." So when a booker who had heard of these "outer-space men" offered them two weeks at the Mocambo in the fall of 1960, a rock-and-roll club on St. Catherine Street in Montreal, they accepted. Sonny took a small group with him: Billy Mitchell on drums, vocalist Ricky Murray, Walter Strickland on trumpet, Ronnie Boykins, John Gilmore, and Marshall Allen. Part of the band went ahead on the train, and the rest headed north with the equipment in Ronnie Boykins's father's '54 Chevy. Boykins, already tired from a late night out, had to drive eighteen hours straight, as he was the only one with a license. When they arrived at the hotel he opened the car door and fell out into the street in a faint. When he was taken to the hospital he was diagnosed as suffering from exhaustion. (When the nurse asked Boykins his religion, he answered, "Cosmic philosophy.") The band nonetheless went on to the club, set up, and donned their costumes of sequined robes and vests, helmets, and turbans (Ra's own turban studded with tiny lights), and launched into "I Struck a Match on the Moon" (a gentle parody of Count Basie's record, "I Struck a Match in the Dark"), and followed it with "Saturn." But something was wrong here: the club owner had been assured by the booker that he was getting a rock show. After a couple of other pieces he asked them when they were going to get into their specialty. Then Sonny let the band loose, and a crushing roar of sound filled the club. When some customers fled for the door, the owner screamed at the band that this was wrong, that what they were playing was "God's music": "That's what I hear," smiled Sonny, and urged the band on. Whatever they were playing, the club owner said, he didn't want it in his place. He called the Musicians Union, and a representative came over and asked them to change their style. They made an effort, and pulled out "China Gate," the theme music to Sam Fuller's 1957 movie which Nat Cole had sung behind the credits. But it was too late; the owner paid them for two nights and told them not to come back. Yet by the night after, the word had spread among university students, and a large crowd gathered at the club only to be disappointed.

Just as in the South years before, the band was broke and stranded on the road. Sonny put the band under John Gilmore's name to give them a fresh start, and located them a job at a resort on a lake in St. Gabriel in the Brandon Mountains a few miles north of Montreal. They were hired for four weeks to play for teenagers, playing resort favorites like "When the Saints Go Marching In." They were such a success that on their last night the management threw a party for them and gave them each a bonus.

Back in Montreal, the manager of The Place, a coffee house across the street from McGill University, had also heard about them and asked them if they would be willing to play for a little money and food and housing for at least part of the band upstairs. After a few nights there, large lines began to form outside each night, and a steady following of college students developed as the weeks went by. Musicians like guitarist Sonny Greenwich sat in regularly. The music became freer and the costumes wilder, and the band settled in for a winter's stay. Ronnie Boykins meanwhile met a lady who picked up the rent for himself and Marshall

Allen. It was at that apartment that Marshall became friends with a girl who was underage; and when her parents heard about her seeing a musician they became irate and talked about calling the law. The band heard that the punishment might be public caning. So when the parents came looking for Marshall, he escaped in a bass drum case that the band carried out to the car with some other instruments.

Sonny seemed remarkably at ease in this new city, and he became a familiar sight on the streets. He created something of a smash when he turned up for a prizefight at the Forum wearing his stage costume. But after a few months the police and fire departments responded to complaints about overcrowding and traffic being blocked at The Place, and Sonny was interviewed for the evening news. "They said I was playing God's music... [but Canada is] supposed to be God's country. And even if it's God's music, why couldn't I play it?" But in the end the authorities terminated their stay. There was some talk about the band doing a series of performances around the province, but Sonny began to fear that if they didn't go now they might never be able to leave. In any case, in January 1961, the government refused to renew their work permits.

Despite the mixed success of their tour to Canada, it was enough to show them that it was possible for them to survive on the road. Even so, they had no money. So Sonny got on the phone to Ed Bland, who was now doing arrangements for rock and pop recording sessions in New York City, and asked him for help in getting work. Bland was encouraging enough that they decided to give it a try.

So in the dead of Canadian winter, the Children of the Sun packed up their instruments and set off for New York City, taking the same route through rural Quebec and New Hampshire where only six months later Betty and Barney Hill would claim that *they* were the first people ever abducted by a flying saucer.

CHAPTER FOUR

ew York City, 1961. The idea was just to play a few gigs, maybe some studio work, and then go back to Chicago and work at the Pershing again. But as soon as they crossed the George Washington Bridge they collided with a taxi and bent one of the wheels on Ronnie Boykins's father's car. With no money to have it fixed they were stranded again. Sonny went to a phone booth and called Ed Bland and Tom Wilson to tell them they were in town, and the band moved into a couple of hotel rooms over the Peppermint Lounge on 45th Street. But after a few days of waiting, Strickland and Mitchell got anxious, called home for money, and left. The five who remained then moved to a room on 81st Street between West End Avenue and Riverside Drive, and after a few days found a cheaper place farther downtown in the seventies.

New York City in the early 1960s had the air, as it always does, of something about to happen. Though Sonny was now forty-seven, and still unknown to most musicians in New York, the energy of the city revitalized him, and he started making big plans and calling musicians in Chicago to talk them into joining him. But most of them didn't want to leave home, either because they had regular jobs, or, like Lucious Randolph, because they now had families. But Pat Patrick's marriage had become shaky, so he agreed to give it a try and caught a train to New York within a day or so.

History doesn't record how New York City reacted to Sonny that summer, but he began to wear his stage clothes on the street, and he could be seen dressed in a short, loose robe and a skullcap emblazoned with occult symbols. The five bandmembers strolled through the streets of Manhattan, Sonny usually in front, the others following. If anyone would have wondered what it was all about, he would have introduced himself as Sun Ra, and told them that he was a descendant of the ancient Egyptians. Then again, he might have said that he was from Saturn, the planet of discipline and sacrifice...

Trumpeter Art Hoyle had just left the Lloyd Price Band and was staying at a hotel near Times Square when Sun Ra brought six of the band around to visit him one night at 2 A.M. in full regalia.

> Sun Ra had this big sunburst on his chest. They freaked out the lady across the hall. She opened her door a crack and peeked at them, then backed into her room. She must have thought they were space aliens!

They had come to try and talk Hoyle into joining the band for an audition at Basin Street East, and they talked well into the night, with Sun Ra promising him that if he stayed they would be successful in New York as they never were in Chicago. But more than that, he showed Hoyle one of his pamphlets which claimed that death need not be the natural outcome of human life. The core of his understanding was built on a single line from John I (5:16–17), "There is a sin for which there is no death," a line for which there was no standard Bible concordance. It was just the kind of cloudy passage that fascinated Sun Ra and drove his scholarship. What was this sin that a person could commit and by so doing defy death? "Sonny showed me his pamphlet with the equation for eternal life, but it was difficult to understand." So Hoyle chose to return home to Gary, Indiana.

Sun Ra was fascinated by the street life of New York. It was more haphazard than Chicago's, less focused—the city changed from block to block. He took long walks, sometimes from one end of the city to the other, from Harlem to downtown. He fast became an acknowledged New York character, a public fixture like Moondog, the monkishly dressed street musician who could be seen on 52nd Street, or Joe Gould, the legendary Bowery barfly who told everyone that he was writing the history of the world. If you stopped to talk to Sun Ra long enough, maybe have a glass of fruit juice or a cup of coffee with him, he'd start to write on napkins, show you equations of words, verbal formulas; there'd be talk of mystical things, the numerological weight of the letters of the alphabet, or the hierarchy of the universe.

Sun Ra dropped into clubs downtown, poked around the stores on Canal Street on Saturdays, and got into animated conversations on corners with other characters. One day he ran into God on the Bowery, and then saw him again on 125th Street a few days later. A skinny black teenager greeted him, "Yo, Sun Ra!" Sonny stopped and asked him who he was. "I'm God." "Nice to meet you, God," Sonny said. When he saw him again, God said, "I like you, Sun Ra, because if I had told anybody else I was God they would have denied me."

When Hunter heard they were in town he rejoined the band. He and Sun Ra spent many days together talking, and on Sundays Hunter would take him home to his parents' house in Bayside where he'd play piano or sit quietly and respectfully. Some days Sonny went to the movie theaters on 42nd Street where second-run and B-films were shown continuously for twenty-four hours. He'd sit through three or four films at a clip, often falling asleep, doggedly staying on until the part he had missed showed again, then sometimes move on to another theater. And when the first Hong Kong action films reached New York—*Come Drink with Me, One-Armed Swordsman, Dead End*—he became a devotee and tried to see them all.

In April Sonny saw on television that Soviet cosmonaut Yuri Gagarin had become the first man to orbit the earth in a spaceship, and he felt vindicated, and boasted of having been right about the space age for almost thirty years. But less than a month later the evening news also showed that the Freedom Riders from Birmingham had been violently attacked in Montgomery, Alabama. Like hundreds of thousands of others, he felt the life he had hoped to escape had followed him north.

Though the band had no luck at finding places to play, Tom Wilson came up with a recording session for them with Savoy Records. On October 10 they crossed the river to the Medallion Studio in Newark with a few musicians they added for the date—Detroit euphonium and trombone player Bernard McKinney, drummer Willie Jones, and Leah Ananda, a conga drummer from Kashmir. Sun Ra had the octet plus vocalist format he often used in Chicago, and they produced a record which could have easily represented their repertoire during an evening at a club there: included were some especially angular and contrapuntally played bebop tunes like "Jet Flight," Latin vamps, ballads such as "China Gate" (sung by Ricky Murray in a Billy Eckstine baritone against bells and gongs), and modal pieces like "Where Is Tomorrow," with two flutes and a bass clarinet improvising collectively over a lower-register single-chord figure on the piano against a tambourine backbeat. But there was also something new: in "The Beginning," wood blocks, maracas, claves, and conga drum established a fast pulse over which a long, languorous exchange was set up between bass clarinet and trombone free of any harmonic structure or song form; and in "New Day," the same open form allowed Gilmore's bass clarinet and Marshall Allen's homemade morrow (a Japanese shakuhachi with a Bb clarinet mouthpiece) to intertwine freely, yet play with a beat and atmospherics which could have come straight from Martin Denny's exotic workshop in Hawaii, all of it buoyantly danceable.

Despite a heavy title—*The Futuristic Sounds of Sun Ra*—and a cover painting of a conga drum swirling like a tornado through a valley of piano keys against an orange sky, the record was plagued from the start. Tom Wilson's liner notes were filled with inaccuracies: several titles were wrong ("Of Wounds [Sounds] and Something Else" and "China Gates [Gate]"); Sun Ra's birth date was off by at least seven years; he was wrongly given credit (though no doubt at his suggestion) for inspiring the spare, modal piano style of Ahmad Jamal; the name of his college was wrong; and the Erskine Hawkins Band was called the "Erskine Caldwell 'Tuxedo Junction' Band" (in which case the "Tobacco Road Band" would have been more appropriate). Distribution was almost as poor as it was with the Saturn records, and there were no reviews for twenty-three years, when it was reissued in 1984 as *We Are in the Future.*

Tommy Hunter found them free rehearsal space in the Columbus Rehearsal Studio where he was working on 8th Avenue between 57th and 58th Streets. Sun Ra picked up work there accompanying singers like

Brock Peters and playing for rehearsals of dance groups. When the building was sold, Hunter got a job at the Choreographers' Workshop, a dancers' rehearsal space at 414 West 51st Street. For the next three years this was to be the band's studio for rehearsal and recording at nights and on weekends. When it was available they used the basement because it had a good piano and better acoustics, but they took what they could get. Hunter was now the second drummer with the band, but he also began to record all of their rehearsals with an Ampex 601 tape recorder he had bought for $800 at a pawnshop, and then to edit them with Sun Ra.

A month later Sun Ra sent some of their tapes back to Alton Abraham in Chicago, although they were not released until 1972, when *Bad and Beautiful* became the first of eleven Saturn records which was recorded at Choreographers' Workshop. Its stark black-and-white cover photo of Sun Ra in the middle of the Arkestra belies what was a surprisingly conventional record done with a sextet. With theme music from the film *The Bad and the Beautiful* and Broadway show tunes like "And This Is My Beloved" and "Just in Time," Sun Ra announced that he was now in New York. Yet other pieces recorded at rehearsals during the same year show the band was changing rapidly throughout this period, and only two pop tunes appeared on any of their recordings over the next four years.

Another Saturn album called *Art Forms of Dimensions Tomorrow* was recorded at almost the same time (though not released until 1965), and shows them beginning to make musical leaps forward. With a cover designed by Sun Ra—his name in large, blue spidery letters with a sharply detailed pterodactyl-like figure hovering overhead—it contained "Cluster of Galaxies" and "Solar Drums," two rhythm section exercises with the sound treated with such strange reverberations that they threatened to obliterate the instruments' identity and turn the music into low-budget *musique concrète*. While testing the tape recorder when the musicians were tuning up one day, Hunter had discovered that if he recorded with the earphones on, he could run a cable from the output jack back into the input on the recorder and produce massive reverberation:

> I wasn't sure what Sun Ra would think of it.... I thought he might be mad—but he loved it. It blew his mind! By working the volume of the output on the playback I could control the effect, make it fast or slow, drop it out, or whatever.

When Hunter asked to be credited as the engineer on the records, Sun Ra told him that they would have to keep that a secret for fear that people would try and discover his recording tricks.

On "The Outer Heavens" Sun Ra used no rhythm section at all, just a chamber group of Ra's piano and a quartet of reeds and a trumpet, and each player developed his own lines with relative independence of the others. But then "Infinity of the Universe" was nearly all rhythm section, built around a center which was established by a repeated rumbling figure deep in the bass of the piano, with trumpet and bass clarinet joining only at the end. From the very first, the New York Saturns suggested that every record would be idiosyncratic, as if they had been recorded by different bands.

By the 1950s commercial recording companies had developed a classical style of recording which assured that the recording process itself would be invisible, the machinery of recording being used like a picture window through which an illusion was created of "being there" with the musicians. But Sun Ra began to regularly violate this convention on the Saturn releases by recording live at strange sites, by using feedback, distortion, high delay or reverb, unusual microphone placement, abrupt fades or edits, and any number of other effects or noises which called attention to the recording process. On some recordings you could hear a phone ringing, or someone walking near the microphone. It was a rough style of production, an antistyle, a self-reflexive approach which anticipated both free jazz recording conventions and punk production to come.

GILMORE

Without any work some of the musicians grew restless. Pat Patrick began working with Ted Curson's band, various Latin groups, and in 1963 became the musical director of Mongo Santamaria's Cuban pop/jazz group, and even wrote their hit song "Yeh Yeh." John Gilmore began to take his tenor to Birdland every Monday, the night when groups appearing there allowed some musicians to sit in. But he was unknown to New York musicians, and it was four months before he got a chance to play. Willie Bobo's Latin jazz group was appearing there with

Patrick on saxophone, and Pat interceded to get Gilmore on the stage after closing time. But as soon as John started to play he was in trouble, for the New York rhythm section was different from what he was used to, and unyielding. He told writer Val Wilmer,

> "I couldn't get my thing going. I started getting nervous because, you know, the impressions that you make in a place like Birdland, they mean a lot. They mean whether you work or not. I said, 'I'd better get *something* together quick!' "

Unable to play *with* the musicians, Gilmore decided to play against them. "I played contrapuntal to what they were doing rather than trying to get into the same groove. Anyway, it worked out. It worked out so good that they didn't know whether I was playing anything or not!"

Musicians and audience alike were confused at the totally new direction the music had taken. One person was not. John Coltrane was sitting at the back of the club and the impact on him was amazing. He ran right up to the stage shouting, "John Gilmore, John Gilmore, you mother-fucker. You got it, you got the concept!" "All the other cats was standing around me doing, 'I don't know 'bout this cat, man—whether he's playin' something'. But when they heard Trane say that, they said, 'Aw this cat, he *must* be playin'!' "

Saxophones, especially tenor saxophones, by the 1940s had begun to assume the leadership role that brass had played in earlier jazz. In spite of being relatively late inventions in the history of music, they offered the potential for an enormous variety of tones, many of which lay out-side the Western aesthetic: overblowing, new extremes of vibrato, alternate ways of producing the same note, extreme vocalized articulation, and the so-called false upper register (which the bar-walking rhythm-and-blues saxophonists knew as the true register of the horn). With these horns it was possible to honk, scream, cry, growl, pop, and slap tones, and generally explore the mechanical and human limits of beauty and sheer nastiness of sound. And Gilmore, pushed by Sun Ra, pursued these techniques perhaps more rigorously than anyone before or since, with almost religious zeal. And though his commitment to Sonny's music kept him from being better known by the public, his influence on

other saxophonists like John Coltrane was profound. As Gilmore's reputation spread, he moved out of the Arkestra from time to time (sometimes against Sonny's wishes and sometimes with them) to play and
record with drummer Pete LaRoca, and then with Freddie Hubbard,
Elmo Hope, McCoy Tyner, Paul Bley, and Andrew Hill. It was often a
source of tension, but John always came back, and Sonny counted on
him to do so. Once in a while, when Sonny was raging about some musician's failures, Gilmore would ask him, "You'd even fire ME, wouldn't
you?" And Sonny would always answer yes.

In January of 1962 the Arkestra finally located a place to perform, the
Cafe Bizarre on 3rd Street, a long, narrow room with sawdust floors, a
pot-bellied stove, and cinnamon sticks in the tea, a self-consciously Beat
place which drew aspiring poets and artists, and later, bands like the Velvet Underground. Billed as The Outer Spacemen, Sun Ra's musicians
made only two dollars a night plus hamburgers and tea, but their music
began to be heard by other musicians, some of whom asked to rehearse
with them, while some others dismissed them as a one-joke band.
Charles Mingus, for example, heard them there and became an early defender of their music, even introducing Sun Ra to choreographer
Katherine Dunham and setting up an audition for him. Dunham was in
New York for a revue called *Bambouche,* with African dancers, and to
choreograph *Aïda* for the Met using West African and Haitian dances.
And though nothing came of the audition, Sun Ra was delighted when
she asked her own drummers why they couldn't play rhythms like those
he was giving her. A short time later when Sun Ra went downtown to see
Mingus play at the Five Spot, Charles saw him, and asked him what he
was doing down here. "I come down to the Village a lot," he answered.
"No,' said Mingus, "I mean what are you doing down here on *Earth?*"

The time at Cafe Bizarre paid off: Sun Ra was asked to give a concert
in the "Jazz & Java" series which followed film showings at the Charles
Theater on 12th Street and Avenue B. The Charles was the center of
avant-garde film activity in the Village, the theater where Jonas Mekas
was programming new American underground filmmakers like Stan
Brakhage for midnight showings and running a nightly series of films by

auteurs like Fritz Lang and Sam Fuller. Mekas had met Sonny when he was with Ed Bland at a film festival in Chicago, and thought that he would be perfect for adding music to their programs. So on February 18, at 2 P.M. (an ad in the *Village Voice* announced) Le Sun Ra and his Cosmic Jazz Space Patrol gave an "Outer Space Jazz" concert, a "combination of Monk, Ellington and Ornette Coleman. HARD SWINGING JAZZ plus the NEW SOUNDS of the Zebra Drums—Japanese Flute—Fireplace—and the Tomorrow." Two dollars admission included the concert, coffee, and the feature film.

The night before the concert Tommy Hunter left his drums in his car and when he got back the car was gone. A last-minute drummer who didn't know the music was hired to fill in, which caused them to have to make changes in the music to indulge his neo-African style. But the audience could hardly have known the difference, or cared. For when the curtain rose they saw Sun Ra dressed in a gold headband and black-and-gold-spangled cape, the stage overflowing with domestic, exotic, and homemade instruments like the fireplace (tuned logs), the sun harp (Ukrainian *bandura*), and the flying saucer (which turned out to be a silent-running version, with flashing red, green, and white lights). When they began to play there were recitations and chanted songs, a chorus of rhythm instruments surfacing under piercing flute solos, a furiously bowed bass, threatening bottom-heavy ensembles of horns, and weaving through it all, Sun Ra, moving about the stage conducting, carrying the flying saucer, or using his cape as a prop.

This performance was enough to give the band their first national notice (an amused mention in *Down Beat* under the title, "The Sun Also Rises") and their first review in the *New York Times*. John S. Wilson limply welcomed them to New York City with the headline, " 'Space Age Jazz' Lacks Boosters: Cosmic Group Fails to Orbit with Rhythmic Propulsion." Distracted by the cosmic flash and the glitter of the occasion, Wilson found the music rhythmically strong but full of "keening dissonances varied by thick, heavy ensembles, by three saxophones and a euphonium." Yet, "If nothing else," he concluded, "Mr. Ra's music keeps an audience on the alert."

■ ■ ■

Many of the recordings they were making at rehearsals appeared on records years later, sometimes, as with *What's New?* issued in 1975, confusingly mixed with recordings from much later sessions. But *Secrets of the Sun* was recorded entirely in 1962 (though not released until 1965, in a violet cover, with a drawing of Sun Ra, his eyes covered by a turban, a beam of sunlight striking a nine-pointed star, a "third eye," on his forehead). The notes contain a short optimistic statement by Sun Ra:

> Here's a music which announces the presence of another age. At a time when so many voices speak to the people of earth, I hesitate to add my voice to the tumult. But what I have to say I must say now, and as I feel that I can say things more quickly through music, I have chosen to speak. I need say no more but that we are driving ourselves rapidly and splendidly towards a meeting we have with a better destiny, with a better and more important life.

Secrets of the Sun introduced two pieces which would become part of the Arkestra book for years to come: "Friendly Galaxy," which began as a chamber piece, with an ensemble of flutes, bass clarinet, and fluegelhorn; and "Love in Outer Space," a strangely familiar-sounding ballad. Tommy Hunter was now the band's full-time recordist and C. Scoby Stroman was more often heard on drums; and on "Solar Symbols," a duo for percussion, Hunter used the reverberation technique he had discovered to produce what later would come to be called pure ambient music.

"Solar Differentials" introduced Art Jenkins, a new "space vocalist" ("Ahrt Jnkins" on the cover, following Sun Ra's Egypto-mystical spelling). Jenkins had sought an audition with Sun Ra a few months before the recording, and sang some rhythm-and-blues tunes for him. Sonny told him that he had a nice voice, but what he was looking for was a singer who could do the impossible ("The possible has been tried and failed; now I want to try the impossible"). Art came back one day when they were recording at the Choreographers' Workshop, and dead set on getting on a record somehow, rummaged through a bag of miscellaneous instruments looking for something he could play. But every time he picked up something, someone in the band would tell him to leave it alone. When no one objected when he pulled a ram's horn from the bottom of the bag he began to sing into it, but backwards, with his mouth to the large opening, so that it gave out a weird sound which he made weirder by moving his hand over the small opening to alter the tone. Sonny broke out laughing, "Now *that's* impossible!" and asked him to improvise wordlessly on the record:

> Sun Ra asked me to sing from my African side—not just a color, and black and white are just colors. My spirit took me back to Africa and my African village with its singers—it was like in a dream. Since the universal voice is a singing voice, I could connect with it.

He later recalled that as a child he stammered badly, and neighbors suggested that he could be cured by having him drink honey with herbs out of a ram's horn. It didn't cure him then, but he now understood their suggestion was prophetic.

THE EAST VILLAGE

Other jobs materialized downtown: first, four weeks at Les Deux Mégots at 64 East 7th Street, another haunt of the poets and writers, where the ads read "Jazz from Other Planets" and "Jazz Tone Poems"; then they began to find work at the Cafe Wha? and other coffeehouses and eateries. But no orthodox jazz club would touch them. So Sun Ra found himself a bellwether of the new bohemia by default, a familiar figure in the venues where the new hipsters of the Village were moving to distance themselves from the glitz, booze, and tourists of the traditional jazz clubs which still represented the fifties to them.

A new wave of Village bohemians had been moving into the Lower East Side, magically transforming it overnight into the "East Village," an area which had once been the most crowded slum in America, a neighborhood still imprinted with the Jewish, Italian, Puerto Rican, and Ukrainian waves of immigrants who had settled in the five-story tenements there, and an area where many of them still remained and put up with the newcomers because they were good for business. The new settlers' way was made easier by the city's destruction of certain areas it labeled slums (which sometimes included legendary sites like the first Five Spot). An extraordinary number of black artists, writers, and performers were among the group which gravitated to the East Village at the beginning of the sixties and quickly formed their own institutions, music, theaters, and journals. Within a few years, there was La MaMa Experimental Theatre, the Negro Ensemble Company, the New Federal Theater, the Nuyorican Poets Cafe, and the Umbra poets group, run by people like Ellen Stewart, Steve Cannon, Ishmael Reed, David Henderson, Emilio Cruz, Robert Thompson, Moses Gunn, Lou Gossett, Roscoe Lee Brown, Bill Dixon, and LeRoi Jones. It quickly became what should be known as the second Harlem Renaissance, though some still refuse to recognize downtown as a center of black arts. It was an island of creativity and excitement, and the closest thing to an integrated community that America could produce at the time. Though it would soon be shadowed by war, heightened racial tension, and chaos, it existed dreamlike for a few years as an urban pastoral... with cheap rents.

Sun Ra was drawn by the heat of this East Village expansion, and in 1962 he moved the nucleus of the Arkestra into a house at 48 East 3rd Street, in the heart of what playwright Miguel Pinero would later call Alphabet City. Sonny lived in the back of an apartment on the second floor which had two rooms connected by an alcove and a large kitchen. He brightened up the walls by spray-painting them in orange, silver, and gold, and then drew black figures on them. A red plastic canopy illuminated from above threw a crimson light over the room. The closets and floors were heaped with boxes, drums, costumes, instruments, phonographs, paintings, music, magazines, papers, tapes, records, and a collection of strange lamps. And on the back of a door were clippings of articles on space aliens with headlines like "World's First UFO Murder" and "Russians Concerned About UFOs."

The front room on the second floor was used for rehearsals and as a place for musicians to hang out and stay overnight. There was a pay phone in the front room, and several musicians had their mail delivered there to their own mailboxes. The rooms on the third floor were occupied by John Gilmore and Pat Patrick. The house would become known as the Sun Palace.

As it changed, this East Village neighborhood rapidly became a kind of extended family. Fences were torn down between houses so that chil-

dren could safely roam from yard to yard; mutual babysitting arrangements were worked out between families, and meals were shared. It was
a neighborhood in which poets, painters, dancers, and musicians gravitated, and the musicians soon found each other. On 3rd Street or within
a block or two lived the A-list of what was about to become the new jazz
avant-garde: Archie Shepp, Ornette Coleman, Giuseppi Logan, Sonny
Simmons, Burton Greene, Henry Grimes, Charles Tyler, Charles Mof-
fett, Sonny Murray, James Jacson, and Cecil Taylor. Mingus lived
nearby, as did the Ayler brothers, Danny Davis, Sonny and Linda Sharrock, Byard Lancaster, Dave Burrell, Pharoah Sanders, and Marion
Brown. And a few blocks away, Sonny Rollins could be found practicing
on the Williamsburg Bridge at night. Sun Ra was in position to influence
another city of musicians at a critical moment, and among his first students and fellow travelers were Dewey Johnson, Rashied Ali, Sonny
Sharrock, and Marion Brown. John Coltrane dropped in on several rehearsals to listen, and he and Sun Ra talked on the phone, Sonny offering him musical and spiritual advice, and playing him selections from
rehearsal tapes. They were all stalwarts of what was being tentatively
called "the new thing."

Though Sonny at last had a house where the Arkestra could practice
and where some of them could live, holding the band together was more
difficult than he had imagined. Rehearsals were not always easy to call
on short notice when everyone did not live in the same place. And there
were all of the distractions of the city. He was in effect the father of a
motherless family, forced to play both parental roles. Though he pre-
ferred the high road, the deeper agenda, he often found himself giving
financial advice, housing the destitute, and in some cases struggling to
keep some musicians alive and free of their excesses. They seemed to
some like a band of codependents, the Sun Palace a haven against the
storm of the chaos of New York and the sixties.

Sometimes when they were short of money for food he took over the
cooking, and his cooking was like the music, individualized, spiritually
guided, mysteriously concocted. Moon Stew was his chief dish, a mix of
green peppers, onion, garlic, potatoes, okra, tomatoes, and ears of corn.
And when it was done right, he said you could taste each ingredient individually. Once when he was asked to share the recipe for a musicians'
cookbook, he warned the authors that there were no fixed proportions to

it, and that it required the ingredients of sincerity and love, to say nothing of the ability to make the fire burn with psychic intensity:

> You can't say, "One teaspoon of this, or one teaspoon of that." Like a musician, you improvise. It's like being on a spirit plane; you put the proper things in without knowing why. It comes out wonderful when it's done like that. If you plan it, it doesn't work.

When Arkestra members brought their girlfriends around he could be insulting, for he feared it would lead to them leaving the band. He wanted the musicians to follow his example in breaking their ties with their families as well, or at least in weakening their sentimental attachment. And death only complicated it, because just as he did not want them to recognize birth, he wanted them to deny death. So when John Gilmore's mother died he tried to talk him out of going to the funeral; and even when one of his saxophonists died he managed to keep the band from going.

He could be vengeful in these matters. If they were among his older players, and perhaps beyond the usual punishments, he literally blue-penciled them out of publicity photos or cut their solos from records as a form of punishment. Or he might not announce a solo as a means of reminding a player of something done wrong.

Most American music critics had written off Sun Ra from the beginning, and his perseverance and slow ascendancy was all the more annoying. A group of men who lived together and wore strange outfits was not good for jazz. And Martin Williams, the dean of jazz critics and one who had worked mightily to make jazz safe for democracy, said that someone ought to debunk them. Even many musicians in New York were wary of Sun Ra and his methods. "Everyone on the Lower East Side in the sixties was strange," said James Jacson. "Even the cops were strange. But the Arkestra was stranger than strange." To some musicians Sun Ra was the father they had escaped; others said he reminded then of their time in the army. Yet even though old-time southern male-dominated families were out of fashion, patriarchy was beginning to creep back in with black cultural nationalism, and Sun Ra was strangely coming into style.

Some other musicians complained that the Arkestra played too long without breaks, that they worked too cheap, that they were setting a bad precedent. But slowly, Sun Ra began to gain respect, a respect which often gave way to astonishment. "They called us Sun Ra and his Supermen," said Jacson, "because of the demands put on us by the music. They saw us able to do things like drive across the country, play a gig, turn around, drive back, and as soon as we got in the house, start rehearsing again." Musicians dropped in just to watch at rehearsals, to see if what they'd heard was true, or, like Rahsan Roland Kirk or Charles Lloyd, came over to buy records. Then others started to come by—dancers, poets, actors. What was surprising to them all was Sun Ra's willingness to accept even beginners and nonmusicians into his rehearsals. Antonio Fargas, an actor who later became a fixture in black-oriented films such as *The Cool World*, *Putney Swope*, and *Across 110th Street*, was one such visitor:

Sun Ra had this loft in the Village and he would invite people to come in and bang on a pot or somethin'. And I went. I remember being in his presence. He was the kind of guy who could find the music without the music. Not knowing anything about music but having feelings, I felt like I was really playing when I was giving to the group. Maybe this was the world I was looking for—the whole idea of an *eclectic life*, I think, is where the artist has to stay.

Off and on for the next year the Arkestra found work at pianist Gene Harris's Playhouse, a MacDougal Street coffeehouse where they often played to an empty room. It was there that Sonny first met Farrell "Little Rock" Sanders, who sometimes was working as a waiter. Sanders was a tenor saxophonist with a rhythm-and-blues background who played with startling volume and with a buzzing, incandescent edge. He had come in from San Francisco, and was barely surviving in New York City; he was often living on the streets, under stairs, wherever he could find to get through the night, his clothes in tatters. Sun Ra gave him a place to stay, bought him a new pair of green pants with yellow stripes (which Sanders hated but had to have), encouraged him to use the name "Pharoah," and gradually worked him into the band. Sanders recalled his first night at the house as auguring what you could come to expect of Sun Ra. With no bed, he had to sit up in a chair all night. Shortly after he fell asleep he woke up, and unable to get back to sleep began to walk around the living room. A few minutes later the ceiling fell in on exactly the spot where he had been sleeping.

Recordings from rehearsals in 1963 yielded up enough material for three records, but only one, *When Sun Comes Out*, came out that year, in blank or handwritten covers. There were still atmospheric flute solos and bolero-like drums, and "Circe" had a wordless vocal which looked backward to the Duke Ellington tradition of "Creole Love Song." But hints of the future were everywhere else on the record: three years after the first version, a new treatment of "We Travel the Spaceways" shows Sun Ra's piano becoming increasingly atonal, suddenly erupting into double-double time figures; on "Calling Planet Earth" Pat Patrick tests the physical limits of the baritone saxophone and strays freely from Sun Ra's persistent mining of a single tonal center on the piano; and behind them, breaking up the beat, is the most tempestuous and sophisticated drummer that Sun Ra would ever have—Clifford Jarvis, son of Malcolm Jarvis, the "Shorty" of Malcolm X's prison days, and who was often seen in the company of the daughter of Baroness Pannonica de Koenigswarter.

The title song introduced a second alto saxophonist into the band, Danny Davis, a seventeen-year-old from downtown, who was a natural foil for Marshall Allen's radical revision of the alto, and this was the first of the saxophone duels which would become a nightly showpiece for the Arkestra: "He and Marshall were so tightly connected it was impossible to tell them apart," said Jacson.

> They could start and stop on the same note, with the same impossibly convoluted rhythms. They would sit down at the same time, pull their horns out of their mouths at the same time. The whole audience would burst out laughing.

Saxophone battles were an established part of 1940s jazz, but Sun Ra pushed the idea further, having the players mime the battles physically, jumping at each other or rolling with each other on the floor. And sometimes four saxophonists took up altos for a battle royal.

When Angels Speak of Love, a second record from 1963, was issued in 1966 in a red-on-white cover with a photo of Sun Ra pulled sideways to create streaks. It was considered a bizarre record when it was heard even three years later, made more bizarre by extreme echo, horns straining for the shrillest notes possible, rhythms layered, their polyrhythmic effect exaggerated by massive reverberation (which was abruptly turned off and on). "Next Stop Mars" is the centerpiece of the album, a very long work which opens with a space chant, followed by Allen and Gilmore taking chances on their horns beyond what almost any other musician would dare at that time. Sun Ra played behind them, again relentlessly spinning around a single tonal center with two-handed independence, then rumbling thunderously at the bottom of the keyboard against Boykins's bass, a clangor made heavier by electronic enhancement.

The record jacket carried a poem by Sun Ra which for the first time identified himself with angels, angels conceived of as cosmic musicians, as creators, like Lucifer, of light out of darkness:

WHEN ANGELS SPEAK

When Angels speak
They speak of cosmic waves of sound
Wavelength infinity
Always touching planets
In opposition outward bound

When Angels speak
They speak on wavelength infinity
Beam cosmos
Synchronizing the rays of darkness
Into visible being
Blackout!
Dark Living Myth-world of being

Cosmic Tones for Mental Therapy, the third of the records recorded in 1963 (this one not issued until 1967), was equally startling. "And Other-ness" is a small group study of the lower tones—bass, bass clarinet, bass trombone, baritone sax, the chamberlike quality of the piece bolstered by Boykins's rich, bowed passages; in "Thither and Yon," oboe, bowed bass, and drums are overwhelmed by such reverberation and tonal processing that it seems to anticipate psychedelia two years before the hippies discovered it in San Francisco. Other pieces on this record were recorded live at ten in the morning at the Tip Top Club in Brooklyn where it was possible to use a Hammond B-3 organ while Tommy Hunter was playing there with Sarah McLawler's trio. (Hunter remembered that during the recording some neighborhood kids stuck their heads in the door and cried out to the breakfast drinkers, "These guys don't know how to play!") This was one of the few times when Sun Ra played the Hammond, the organ of choice in the sixties, but instead of using it for obvious funk purposes he employed it primarily for tonal color.

Later in the day a scene occurred at a nearby restaurant in Brooklyn when Sun Ra refused the manager's request to remove his hat while eating ("This is a family place!"). The manager then ordered them out of the restaurant, but also insisted they had to pay for what they had already eaten. The police were called, and a lengthy discussion followed, with the police deciding that the manager should have told them to leave before they had eaten, and dismissed the incident. Hats were a sensitive point with Sun Ra, and he was never seen in public without one, especially after he had begun to develop a bald spot. Around the same period he had a nasty confrontation with a priest and was ordered out of a Catholic church on 3rd Street for wearing a hat.

Early in the 1960s Sun Ra was in Audiosonic, an independent recording studio in the Brill Building near Times Square, when he ran into one of their engineers, Fred Vargas. Vargas was a Costa Rican who had worked his way up from the garment district to a job in the REL labs with General Edwin Howard Armstrong, the inventor of FM radio, and then on to becoming a recording engineer. Shortly after, Audiosonic was turned into Variety Recording Studio on 225 West 46th Street when it was bought out by Vargas and Warren Smith, an English teacher in Connecticut. Vargas and Smith were intrigued by Sun Ra's music, and they began to record his small groups; and when the studio burned in 1968 and they had to move to West 42nd Street, their new studios were large enough to record Sun Ra's whole band (sometimes with as many as thirty musicians). They extended him long-term credit, living with occasional bounced checks, and helped him cut costs (Sonny often saved fifty dollars by sticking his own blank labels on the records, keeping his cost for a 12-inch LP to ninety-nine cents). Vargas and Smith allowed Sonny to press as few as 100 copies of a record at a time, when most recording companies had a minimum of 500. By handprinting the covers, they could avoid printing costs altogether. Often the covers carried only a simple title, or only the location of the recording in black ink; but at times they became more elaborate, with multicolored grids, rainbows, or astral scenes; or there might be photos of Sun Ra pasted on, hand-tinted, the whole cover laminated with a piece of textured plastic shower curtain. Sometimes every cover of a single record was different.

For the next thirty years Vargas recorded much of Sonny's music, editing the tapes with him, mastering them, and helping him get his records pressed. He introduced Sonny to people in show business, like Gershon Kingsley, an early synthesizer enthusiast, who later helped Sonny program his first Moog. The Arkestra was usually recorded in stereo with two overhead microphones, but occasionally by laying down tracks, then later overdubbing whatever parts Sonny decided to add. The whole recording process was open to discovery. Smith tells the story of when Vargas and Sonny were editing at three in the morning, and Fred accidentally played a tape backwards. "Galactic!" cried Sonny, and insisted that the sound be dubbed into the final version just as it was.

Warren Smith took care of business matters at Variety and had long conversations with Sonny about philosophical, personal, and financial matters when he was in the studio. Sonny began to have disagreements with Alton Abraham and feared that he was being cheated by other producers. So Smith created a fictive corporation by having "Enterplanetary Koncepts" stationery printed up, and he sent out inquiries to producers and record companies requesting accountings of money owed to Le Son'y Ra, Sun Ra and His Arkestra, and El Saturn Records. No money was ever collected, but Sonny treated Vargas and Smith as his colleagues: Arkestra members often slept overnight at the studio after recording sessions; they mailed press clips from their tours back to Smith, who stored them for them; and Sonny frequently sent them cheery postcards from his travels, which typically read "Having a wonderful time. Ciao, Sun Ra."

Sun Ra now denied that his name had ever been Herman Blount, but once in a while a musician from Birmingham like Walter Miller would come to town, and he might obliquely admit to it, but nonetheless insist that he simply arrived in Birmingham from somewhere else, and that he had no family there. Or anywhere. And in fact he had had no contact with his family since he left. Yet, like the rest of America, Birmingham was painfully brought home to him now almost every night on television as it became the focus of the civil rights movement. Then Martin Luther King was arrested in Birmingham, and wrote his "Letter from the Birmingham Jail" ("I am in Birmingham because injustice is here..."). And when the 16th Street Baptist Church in Birmingham was bombed and the daughter of a musician friend was one of the children killed (an incident which is sometimes said to have been the inspiration for John Coltrane's "Alabama") Sonny's past began catching up with him.

Olatunji was from Nigeria, a Yoruba who had come to the United States on a Rotary scholarship to study at Morehouse College, where he was something of a sensation—playing football, becoming student-body president, forming a troupe of African dancers and musicians. And when he graduated in 1954 he came to New York City to study for a Ph.D. in public administration at New York University. He began performing in New York in 1956, just as Harry Belafonte had broken into the pop charts and launched the calypso craze. In 1959 Olatunji recorded *Drums of Passion*, the first record to widely introduce African music to Americans. By the early 1960s he had done a number of TV appearances, played at the New York World's Fair, written a score for *Raisin in the Sun*, and become a club act popular among Jack Kerouac and the Beats. By 1961 he recorded his second record, *Zungo*, now with jazz musicians like Yusef Lateef, Clark Terry, and George Duvivier, which eased his way into playing clubs like Birdland and the Village Gate. It was then that he met Sun Ra, and Sonny was impressed by his music, as it paralleled some of the things he had been doing. But he was struck even more by Olatunji's total performance: on a typical night the whole company entered slowly and regally through the audience, one by one, playing and dancing, building up the rhythms and the volume—five dancers, three drummers, maybe three other musicians playing African and Western instruments, all dressed in brightly flowing robes and headgear. Olatunji himself played two wooden drums with carved sides as tall as he was. By the end of the evening they had run through music from all parts of Africa, as well as African-American musics, a virtual history of Afro-derived music and dance. And at the end they marched out, still playing and dancing. Within only a few years reviewers would speak of his performances in LSD-color terms, as total experiences, as freak-outs.

Sonny and Olatunji met a number of times, exchanging ideas and plans. Olatunji saw a need among black Americans to be in touch with their roots, and he began to take on students in dance, drumming, language, and culture. And by 1967 he had set up his own Center of African Culture at 125th Street and Lexington Avenue, using a part-time faculty of African academics and theater people resident in New York City, a program which soon became a model for many black culture programs.

Jazz musicians like John Coltrane came by the center and played, and Sun Ra recorded *Atlantis* there live in a concert in 1967. Olatunji and Sun Ra soon began exchanging musicians and Olatunji sometimes used the members of the Arkestra in his performances and on records (such as on the 1964 recording *Drums! Drums! Drums!*). Guitarist Sonny Sharrock recalled running into Sun Ra in the early sixties and asking him if he could play with him. Sonny told him to come to a rehearsal, and when he arrived he put him in another room while the band rehearsed, leaving him to look at *The Cry of Jazz* and another film called *Unheard Melodies,* which showed how wind caused statues to give off distinct sounds, "so that people who are worshipping some kind of statue, they are being frequencized you might say. They keep on standing in front of that statue and the vibrations are coming at them, and they're being made into the frequencies of their statue, whether it's Buddha, Jesus Christ, whatsoever." After the rehearsal was over and Sharrock had seen the films, Sun Ra received a call from Olatunji asking if he had a guitarist, and he recommended him, without ever hearing him play.

The music for the Saturn LP *Other Planes of There* was recorded in early 1964 but not issued until around 1966 when it appeared in a cover with light blue letters swirling against a fuchsia background. Once again, Sun Ra was shifting his methods and taking the Arkestra in new directions. The title piece is one of his major works, and a departure from everything he had done before. At twenty-two minutes, it takes up a whole side of the LP, and was one of the longest pieces ever recorded by a jazz group at the time; and despite being collectively improvised it was arguably one of the most coherent and organic. There are twelve instruments in this piece, but very few appear at the same time: soloists appear and disappear quickly; a trombone trio seems to rise from nowhere and lay a foundation for the other horns to enter; the piece threatens at times to become conventionally rhythmic in jazz sense, but never does, as the drums continue to play textually, almost melodically; Sun Ra's piano weaves throughout it all, threading through the parts, until at the end they all rise together.

As some of the musicians began to get a taste of the opportunities New York offered they began to feel restless and ignored. Rehearsals were not enough. John Gilmore spent hours every day practicing, then going out at night to hear lesser saxophonists making money: "I'd been walkin' around New York and I wasn't working anywhere, and half the cats were out there playin' my ideas," he told *Down Beat*. "I said, what is this? Here I am not workin', and they're workin', and they're stealing my ideas." When Lee Morgan recommended him to Art Blakey as the Jazz Messengers were leaving for a tour of Japan and Europe, he accepted the offer and left the Arkestra. But his bitterness even carried over into the Blakey band, and annoyed Blakey to the point where he let him go:

I criticized him because he'd be talking the way he was thinking. The way he thought about life and what he believed in and why he would put down other people. I didn't think it was right. He was young and running off the top of his head, don't tell me that Lester Young steals from him, or Coltrane steals from him—that's not true. He's off.... I wasn't concerned about his playing, he'd be telling me about his fans on Mars or Jupiter, but I said it's the fans on this planet we're concerned with, not back there.

In mid-1964 fluegelhornist/painter Bill Dixon and filmmaker Peter Sabino were presenting musical performances at an unlikely location in New York City, the Cellar Cafe, a coffeehouse on West 91st Street. On June 15 he booked Sun Ra, who brought in a fifteen-piece band, the largest he had had since years before in Chicago. Pharoah Sanders had now replaced John Gilmore, Black Harold (Harold Murray) from Birmingham was on flute and hand drums, Robert Northern was added on French horn, and Clifford Jarvis was the drummer.

The crowd which turned out for this concert and one by Archie Shepp encouraged Dixon to stage a four-night festival of the "new thing," a music still too new to be named or defined, but which was audaciously emerging in the face of a resistant jazz mainstream. Having himself been closed out of conventional jazz clubs and concert halls and told by record companies that there was no interest in this music, Dixon intended to show that there was an audience for new forms of jazz and to demonstrate what musicians could do to further their cause. He called those four nights the October Revolution in Jazz.

Without advertising—or electricity, since Con Ed had cut off the power in the coffeehouse—Dixon organized over forty musical events as well as panel discussions on the state of the music, and hundreds of people packed the cafe every day from four o'clock in the afternoon to three o'clock in the morning. Some of those musicians who performed still continue to represent the excitement of that moment—Paul Bley, Jimmy Giuffre, Cecil Taylor, Steve Lacy, Andrew Hill, Milford Graves, Sheila Jordan, John Tchicai, and Roswell Rudd—while others have gone on to "even greater obscurity," as Dixon once wryly put it.

Though there were no reviews in the New York press, word slowly filtered out that jazz had announced the arrival of its modernism, what was to become its seemingly permanent avant-garde. A few days afterwards Cecil Taylor and Bill Dixon called a meeting proposing to form some sort of cooperative group to bring the new jazz to the public. The Jazz Composers Guild was the outcome, and Sun Ra and the Arkestra were some of the first to sign on; and only two months later the guild staged "Four Nights in December" at the Judson Church, which in some ways was an even grander enunciation of the new music. From December 28 through 31 the guild presented concerts with groups led by Bill Dixon, Cecil Taylor, Paul Bley, and Archie Shepp; the Jazz Composer's Guild Orchestra played compositions by Carla Bley and Mike Mantler, followed by the Free Form Improvisation Ensemble.

On the last night, New Year's Eve, 1964, Sun Ra and the Arkestra and the John Tchicai-Roswell Rudd Quartet performed. In a review in *The Nation*, A. B. Spellman struggled to convey to readers what he had seen. "They present a reviewer with a difficult problem," he said,

> how to render a sympathetic appraisal for what was one of the more exciting series without making this group seem either utterly insane or sickeningly corny?... [Sun Ra's philosophy] leads him to some really wild and original effects in his music, though it sometimes gets in the way, as when the musicians start talking in the middle of the piece about getting off at Jupiter and about Martian water lilies. Yet, in these instances the spoken word itself will have a musical value, as Sun Ra's concept is well worked out, though the words will have no literary value to anyone except Sun Ra's people. His musicians were in African costumes, and they did a good deal of walking around under blinking, multi-colored lights.... Yet, yet... well, you had to be there.

On March 6 and 7 the Jazz Composers Guild staged "Sun Ra and his Solar-Jazz Arkestra Featuring Clifford Jarvis and Pharoah Sanders" at the Contemporary Center on 7th Avenue at West 11th Street, and again a week later, "Sun Ra and his Myth-Science Jazz" ("a space age presentation of hieroglyphics in sound" featuring Jimhmi Johnson, Roger Blank, Eddie Gale, Pharoah Sanders, Danny Davis, Marion Brown, Marshall Allen, Pat Patrick," with "abstract paintings by George Abend"), along with the New York Art Quartet with Roswell Rudd and John Tchicai.

But a few months later Sun Ra lost interest in the Jazz Composers Guild because he felt that the Arkestra was doing most of the work of

The terminal station in Birmingham, Alabama, near the home of Herman P. Blount and his great-aunt Ida Howard. *(Photograph Collections of the Birmingham Public Library)*

Above: Robert Blount, Sun Ra's older brother, in the mid-1930s.

Left: Sonny Blount at the piano and Solovox, circa 1941.

The Sun Ra Arkestra at the Parkway Ballroom in Chicago in 1955.
Left to right: Pat Patrick, Julian Priester, John Thompson, Sun Ra,
John Gilmore, Dave Young, Robert Barry, Richard Evans,
and Jim Herndon. *(Robert Pruter)*

Sun Ra in New York City
in 1961, having just
arrived from Montreal.
(Thomas Hunter)

Rehearsing and recording at the Choreographers' Workshop in New York City in 1962. *Left to right*: Pat Patrick, Sun Ra, Marshall Allen, John Gilmore, and Ronnie Boykins. *(Thomas Hunter)*

Left: Pat Patrick at
the Café Bazaar in
New York City in 1962.
(Thomas Hunter)

Above: Sun Ra in
the 1960s. *(Thomas Hunter)*

Sun Ra and Earl Hines at Hines's seventieth birthday party at the
Biltmore Hotel in New York City in 1975. *(Thomas Hunter)*

Top: Sun Ra in a promotional still for *Space Is the Place* in 1973. *(© 1973 Jim Newman) Bottom*: Sun Ra as "Sunny Ray" with the "Ebony Steppers" in a scene from *Space Is the Place*.

(© 1973 Edmund Shea)

Sun Ra's Kabbalistic equations, as he wrote them down in 1970. *(Victor Schonfield)*

Above: Sun Ra in the early 1970s. *(Thomas Hunter)*

Right: The Arkestra with the Spacescape light organ at the Modern Theater in Boston in 1978. *(© Alan Nahigian)*

Right: Sun Ra performing at the Modern Theater in 1978. *(© Alan Nahigian)*

Below: June Tyson with the Arkestra at Roger Williams Park in Providence, Rhode Island, on August 11, 1985. *(© Alan Nahigian)*

Above: The Arkestra at the
WHYY television station studios
in Philadelphia, 1990.
(© R. Andrew Lepley)

Left: *A Fireside Chat with Lucifer*,
the album cover painted by Sun Ra.
(© Alan Nahigian) Above: The album
cover for *Somewhere Over the Rainbow*.
(© Alan Nahigian)

promotion of concerts and that the other members weren't sincere. He also disagreed with the organizing principle of the group: for them to be successful, he thought, someone should be serving as the leader. As disagreements on how to handle business matters increased, Dixon himself was one of the first to quit the guild.

Yet these few months of collective activity had lasting results. One person in the audience at the Cellar Cafe sessions was Bernard Stollman, a young lawyer who had been representing jazz musicians. Stollman was so overwhelmed by the music he heard during those nights he dreamed up a plan to record every one of them. In a sense he already had the record company to do it: in 1960 he had issued an instructional record for another of his passions, the universal language Esperanto—*Ni Kantu en Esperato,* or songs in Esperanto. The company's name was ESP, and when he began to issue the new jazz records under that name most read it to mean extrasensory perception (even though every record carried instructions on the back to "Mendu tiun diskon ce via loka diskvendejo au rekte de ESP" ("Order this disk at your local record store or directly from ESP"). The company was modeled in part on Folkways, another independent record company on the margins and run on a shoestring. Most of Stollman's recordings were done in RLA-Impact Sound Studio, owned by Richard Alderson, who also did most of the engineering. The details of recording were left up to the artists, though they typically had no more than two to three hours of production time and none for remixing later. The musicians also had the option of doing their own cover art. Under the slogan "You Never Heard Such Sounds in Your Life," ESP inaugurated its jazz series in 1964 by releasing Albert Ayler's *Spiritual Unity,* and by the time nine records were produced in the mid-1970s they had recorded Ornette Coleman, Pharoah Sanders, the Fugs, Timothy Leary, William Burroughs, the Holy Modal Rounders, and Charles Manson, a catalog with a remarkable representation of the range of 1960s culture on record.

The guild's brief success also inspired other musicians to use every conceivable New York City space for staging their own concerts—coffeehouses, churches, museums, basements, lofts, the streets.... And many New York artists outside of music—especially those in theater and dance—were encouraged by these daring acts of independence and the declaration of freedom which lay behind it.

The Village was awash with all kinds of music in 1965. The folk revival was booming, the "new thing" was threatening to dominate the jazz
scene, and the British invasion had sent a shiver through the complacency of early rock and roll. New clubs and coffeehouses like the Cafe
Wha?, the Cafe Au Go Go, and the Dom (the Domska Polska Nationalna
which would turn into the Exploding Plastic Inevitable under Andy
Warhol, then into the Electric Circus) were drawing together programs
which might present the Blues Project one night, Cecil Taylor the next,
and Jimi Hendrix on the third. Audiences often found themselves listening to music totally unfamiliar to them, but in settings which were cool
enough to make it seem all right. Much of the music was still happening
away from the eyes of the media, so musicians were free to borrow from
each other across the usual lines, and eclectic groups such as the Fugs
and the Velvet Underground were coming up from the cracks. On weekends downtown streets were so jammed with club hoppers and tourists
that the police blocked off traffic.

Sun Ra was incited by the weird mixture of glory and vulgarity which
surrounded music in the Village in the mid-1960s, and a band which had
once strictly limited itself to small black clubs and dances was now finding itself beginning to become a musical institution. They worked wherever they could, and when there was no work they offered free concerts
in the parks or played at poetry readings such as one they joined on the
13th Street Pier, where wine and sardines were served by candlelight.
Another free performance on a pier on the East River was sponsored by
ESP Records, with food provided by a 7th Street macrobiotic restaurant
which had just gone out of business that day and sent over all of its left-
overs. A Portuguese sailing ship was tied up at the pier, and its crew, who
had been denied shore leave, watched from the deck. When the Arkestra
began to play, the captain relented and they came ashore dancing.

Following Patrick's and Gilmore's lead, some of the Arkestra were
taking gigs with other bands, or occasionally backing up pop or blues
artists on recordings. Even Sun Ra took some gigs out of town with vi-
braphonist Walt Dickerson's Quartet, always dressed respectfully for the
other musicians, usually in a dark suit or a sport coat and tie. He also was
writing more poetry and published a few of his new poems in *Umbra An-
thology 1967–1968,* put out by a group which included Calvin Hernton,
Tom Dent, David Henderson, and Ishmael Reed.

THE BLACK ARTS

LeRoi Jones first ran into Sun Ra on the streets or maybe in a coffee-house "early in the sixties, when Sun Ra was getting socialized to Village life." Jones had been living in the Village for seven years, had become one of the key figures of the downtown literary and political scene, and had just won an Obie Award for his play *Dutchman*. He was an early defender and interpreter of the new jazz and like most was initially suspicious of Sun Ra, and saw him as a " 'modernist' faddist," but became an early admirer of his grasp of the history and accomplishments of black civilizations, as well as his music. "Ra was so far out because he had the true self consciousness of the Afro American intellectual artist revolutionary. . . ."

Jones's poetry is always discussed in terms of its relationship to the Beats and the New York poets of the 1950s, of his having later rejected them in favor of Césaire and Langston Hughes. But Sun Ra was also a silent partner. He is there in Jones's historical allusions, in the tone and pitches of his reading, in his sense of the importance of language, and in his consciousness of the possibilities of playing the spoken word against the written, unleashing the phonetics buried within the printed word. This influence could be seen early in "Black Dada Nihilismus," where Neoplatonism is evoked (and punned on) to lay the basis for the black arts; in the romantic turn of his poetry where black men and women are understood as a race with limitless possibilities. In "Meanings of Nationalism," an essay in *Raise Race Rays Raze* (a book whose title alone shows Sun Ra's influence), Jones makes reference to books loaned him by Sun Ra:

> Study the history of ancient Egypt. The move from Black to white. Reversed is the story of America. America who always (secretly) patterned her self after Egypt. Because she was so influenced by the sons and daughters of the ancient Egyptians. (See *Astrology Space Age Science* re: American Money and its symbolism. See *God Wills the Negro* . . . & more). The ancient race of Black giants come to life again.

After Malcolm X was shot on February 21, Jones changed his name to Imamu Amiri Baraka and moved up to Harlem to establish the Black Arts Repertory Theater/School, in part with money he had raised with a benefit he put on at the Village Gate on March 28, at which John Coltrane, Albert Ayler, Grachan Moncur III, Archie Shepp, Charles Tolliver, Cecil McBee, and Sun Ra played; and in part through the arts and culture program of Operation Bootstrap, a division of HARYOU ACT, the first War on Poverty program set up by Lyndon Johnson in an effort to stop violence and rioting after the "long hot summer" of 1964.

Black Arts announced its arrival in Harlem with a parade across 125th Street of the Arkestra in full regalia, the Ayler Brothers, Milford Graves, and the Yoruba Temple people led by Baba Oserjeman, another down-town hipster who had appeared uptown in a new manifestation. And though Sun Ra remained downtown, he came up to the Black Arts office almost daily and held forth to whoever would listen. Like Chicago's South Side, Harlem was filled with competing philosophies, religions, and politics: the Garveyites, the Nation of Islam, the Communists, the Christians, of course, but also the Yoruba Temple and the Egyptian Coptics, all of whom debated in front of the Hotel Theresa or in front of Michaux's Afrocentric bookstore. Once again Sun Ra was there in the middle of it all.

For the next three months the Black Arts sent trucks out into the community presenting music, dance, drama, paintings, and poetry in va-cant lots, playgrounds, parks, anywhere they could find to reach the community. The Arkestra was able to add musicians with funds from the Black Arts, and on weeknights the new expanded Arkestra appeared, often with Sun Ra playing his new sun organ (which played colors as well as sound, the low notes deep blues and dark hues, the high notes or-anges and yellows). Baraka saw, as no one else, the spiritual or visionary nature of Ra's music as inherently political:

What Trane spoke of, speaks of, what Ra means, where Pharoah wd like to go, is clearly another world. In (w)hich we are literally (and further) "free."

"Even though we were entering a deep nationalist phase," Baraka re-called, "Sun Ra understood it in terms of his idea of angels and demons at play—that is, if being good means being in tune with this planet that was no good—so he insisted on being a demon. Sun Ra had a larger agenda."

But the OEO withdrew the funds from Black Arts once they saw the shape the program was taking, and the police closed them down after a cache of weapons was found stored in their building. In the turmoil that followed, Baraka moved back to his hometown, Newark, where he established Spirit House, a black cultural center which he soon developed into a theater, a bookstore, and Jihad, a book and record company through which he edited several publications including *The Cricket,* a jazz magazine which was given away free to musicians. Baraka brought the Arkestra to a vacant lot up the street from Spirit House to play in the summer, then for a Mardi Gras festival at Kimako's Blues People, Baraka's basement theater, which turned into a block party:

> Ra held court, in front of a spectacular spread of classic Afro American cuisine Amina had prepared. A bottle of Courvoisier, diverse friends... like the grand salons of advanced civilizations, where philosophers and intellectuals and artists could hold forth in open, pleasurable, serious discussion about the whole world and profound reality.

When Baraka's play *A Black Mass* was first performed at Procter's Theater in Newark in May of 1966, the Arkestra supplied music. The play roughly follows Elijah Muhammad's story of Yacub, the mad black scientist who created the white race in an act of hubris. But in Baraka's retelling, it is the aesthetic impulse gone astray which is at center, leading not only to the creation of evil and the destruction of the holy place of the black magicians, but also to a violation of the spirit of the black aesthetic. The white beasts are exiled to the cold north, and at the end of the play charge out into the audience, "kissing and licking people," and screaming "Me, white!" while a voice offstage is heard calling for the Jihad to begin. The Arkestra, seated on the stage throughout the performance, improvised the music, following cues written in the script such as "Music can fill the entire room, swelling, making sudden downward swoops, screeching," or "Sun-Ra music of shattering dimension." The instrumentalists worked their music in among the actors' lines, calling and responding to them, phrasing and inflecting their parts like human voices. At one point the actors and musicians joined together to hum "The Satellites Are Spinning." The play mixed science fiction and Muslim mythology, and as Larry Neal (echoing Sun Ra) suggested, it led the audience to "understand that all history is someone's version of mythology."

When Walter Miller first came to New York from Birmingham he was surprised that Sonny had gotten into "racial issues," and thought Baraka had talked him into it. "Sonny seemed angrier: like, when one night after a gig at a club he took his time dressing, and they turned the lights out on him. Sonny hit the guy. I couldn't believe it." And while Ra thought that many of Baraka's efforts were wrong—that he should not push blacks into conflict with whites, that his nationalism was too earthly and materialistic—he was nonetheless influenced by him and encouraged by the audience at the Black Arts to take his music further out.

Sun Ra had turned a few heads around since he first came to New York, but now something truly radical was happening in his music. The performances were growing longer, the rhythms wilder and more complex, and the soloists were being encouraged to go even further beyond their means. Tommy Hunter returned from Sweden after nine months where he had been in film school and was stunned to see how much the Arkestra had changed: "It was like a fire storm coming off the bandstand." Whatever one hears in Sun Ra's music before or after this period, it's clear that 1965 was a turning point, and that the recording of *The Magic City* was the clearest signal of the change.

"The Magic City" was a promotional slogan for Birmingham, a boast about its quick rise and development after minerals were first discovered there, and the words on the huge sign in front of the train station which greeted Sun Ra every day as he left the house. Despite his bitterness about Birmingham he still had affection for the town, and, just as he had done for Chicago, he wrote a number of compositions which memorialized the city and the state of Alabama ("Magic City Blues," "The Place of Five Points," "West End Side of Magic City") or played Alabama praise songs by others, such as Parish and Perkins's "Stars Fell on Alabama" or Jothan Callins's "Alabama." But as the drawing on the original cover of the album suggests, *The Magic City* was also a city of fantasy, "a city without evil, a city of possibilities and beauty," as Alton Abraham put it. And in a poem, Ra described the Magic City as "the universe of the Magi."

THE MAGIC CITY

This city is the Universe
Because it is that city of all natural creation
It is surrounded by the wilderness
The encircling forest of the edge of itself
All that is endlessly beyond
This city is the Magi's thought
This city is the magic of the Magi's thought.
The idea, the calculated knowledge of it
Eternally balanced by the uncalculated presence of
The intuition potential intruder/the beam
Harmonic precision celestial being
Chromatic rays race.

Walter Miller suggested that being a Gemini, Sonny always consciously expressed doubleness in his work, especially in the pairing of "outer space with earthly matters."

"The Magic City" was collectively improvised and lacks a fixed theme as such, though individual statements and isolated notes flow together to form an incremental melody. Sun Ra simultaneously plays piano and Selmer Clavioline ("the purest sound I ever got from an electric instrument"), usually in conjunction with Ronnie Boykins's bowed bass, but also at times with Roger Blank's reverbed drums, Robert Cummings's bass clarinet, or Marshall Allen's piccolo. The piece ebbs and flows, with duos and trios appearing and disappearing, yet always returning to Ra's quietly gyrating keyboards and Boykins's singing bass lines. Almost three-quarters of the way through, saxophones begin to enter in various configurations: Danny Davis's alto first, then John Gilmore's tenor, Pat Patrick's baritone, and finally the altos of Marshall Allen and Harry

Spencer. There is a sudden ensemble cry at the end, and then a quiet return to Ra and Boykins.

Programmatic statements in music have been common in the history of jazz. Duke Ellington is the obvious case, with his many compositions addressing life in Harlem or the South. The subject of these works was outlined by the ensembles, but the soloists were usually left to play whatever they wanted, constrained only by the riffs and counter-melodies introduced behind them. Sun Ra's music often attempts to completely integrate the soloists with the ensemble to make a single statement, even when his programs are more in the realm of feelings and emotions. When he sensed that the piece needed an introduction or an ending, a new direction or fresh material, he would call for a space chord, a collectively improvised tone cluster at high volume which "would suggest a new melody, maybe a rhythm." It was a pianistically conceived device which created another context for the music, a new mood, opening up fresh tonal areas. "The Magic City," like many of his compositions from this period, was sketched out with only a rough sequence of solos and a mutual understanding which came from grueling daily rehearsals. Sun Ra gave it order by pointing to players, and by signaling with numbers which referred to prepared themes and effects, and with hand gestures that directed the musicians what to play during collective improvisation—what composer Butch Morris would later call "conduction." Ornette Coleman's earlier *Free Jazz* and John Coltrane's contemporaneous *Ascension* were also collective improvisation but neither had the seamless quality of "The Magic City," nor its secret formalism. It was not played at concerts, John Gilmore said, because it was "unreproducible, a tapestry of sound."

The conventions (or the relative lack of them) in the new jazz made length an increasing problem for recording as the music developed, and Sun Ra was one of the first to confront it. Since "The Magic City" was recorded at a rehearsal, time was not a concern: but on the issued record there are hints of editing at several points. He soon began to edit routinely, shaping album-sized works out of hours of rehearsal recordings, making the studio a part of the performance.

"Shadow World" was recorded in Olatunji's center earlier in 1965, possibly before an audience. "It's really saying that this whole world here is nothing but shadows and images, that's what it is, it's not a reality, and people have come to find out where there's going to be the reality . . . that they would be 'made'; by that I mean initiated, because in secret orders the word 'made' means 'initiate.' " For this work, he set a complex, composed melody for unison saxophones against a 7/4 cymbal, bass, and marimba beat and his own piano counter-melody. Following brief solo moments of Gilmore's tenor, piano and electric celeste, drums, and Chris Capers's trumpet, the saxophone melody returns with a trumpet counter-melody which the piano has hinted at throughout. John Gilmore remarked that many have tried to play the intervals of this difficult melody and failed. And Sun Ra said that "it quits in strange places. I wrote it with the idea of a twelve-tone series which I had. It doesn't sound like it, but in fact I used it, with one chord against the other." Sun Ra took considerable pleasure from the agitated difficulty of the piece, and noted that once during a rehearsal for a French TV show the producer was so disturbed by it that he threatened to cancel the show if they insisted on playing it. "Shadow World" was to become a standard with the band, and they recorded it three or four times, usually at even faster paces.

"Abstract Eye" and "Abstract 'I' " are two versions of the same piece. "Eye" refers to the Egyptian hieroglyph, which in turn means many things—the eye of Horus, the Egyptian god of the skies; or the all-seeing eye, or again, the mind's eye. (A note on the back of the original Saturn album seems to suggest that the title may have once been "Cosmic Eye.") In contrast, "Abstract 'I' " is the person, the beholder. Both performances begin with an ominous conversation of bass marimba, bowed bass, two trombones, piccolo, bongos, and timpani, and the second and longer version adds brief moments of cymbals, tenor saxophone, and trumpet to the second half. *The Magic City* was issued in 1966 on Saturn and reissued on Thoth Intergalactic, a new Saturn subsidiary label in 1969, and again on El Saturn sometime in the 1970s. (Two other compositions, "Cosmic Machine" and "Flying Saucer," were recorded at Variety Studios during the same sessions, but neither was ever issued.)

After meeting Bernard Stollman during the October Revolution, Sun Ra asked him to come and hear the Arkestra at a loft in Newark, and once he did, Stollman quickly agreed to record them. The Arkestra went into

Richard Alderson's studios on April 20 and began work on *The Heliocentric Worlds of Sun Ra, Vol. I,* the second in an extraordinary series of recordings in 1965. "Heliocentric," like all of the works on these mid-sixties albums, builds its melody cumulatively, additively, through collective improvisation. Discussing the *Heliocentric* recording sessions, Marshall Allen described how Sun Ra directed improvisation:

> Sun Ra would go to the studio and he would play something, the bass would come in, and if he didn't like it he'd stop it, and he'd give the drummer a particular rhythm, tell the bass he wanted not a "boom boom boom," but something else, and then he'd begin to try out the horns, we're all standing there wondering what's next. . . .
>
> I just picked up the piccolo and worked with what was going on, what mood they set, or what feeling they had. A lot of things we'd be rehearsing and we did the wrong things and Sun Ra stopped the arrangement and changed it. Or he would change the person who was playing the particular solo, so that changes the arrangement. So the one that was soloing would get another part given to him personally. 'Cos he knew people. He could understand what you could do better so he would fit that with what he would tell you.

If "Heliocentric" lacks a melody, it nonetheless has motives, like the staggered entry of three trombones (which oddly suggests the "Kane" motif at the opening of *Citizen Kane*), which also occurs in "Outer Nothingness" and "Of Heavenly Things." It maintains interest by contrast of register, texture, piccolo against bass, timpani, trombones, and bass marimba. "Outer Nothingness" follows a similar pattern, and seems to be another take of "Heliocentric." "Other Worlds" pits Sun Ra's furiously atonal piano (sometimes played simultaneously with celeste) against the rest of the Arkestra. The Arkestra at this point had such confidence in what they were doing that the rest of the group could suddenly drop away in the moment to reveal a cymbal solo or a bass and timpani duo. And even where there is no contrast in the music, as on Sun Ra's celeste and piano solo piece "Nebulae," there is such independence of movement and free rhythm of right and left hand that interest is still maintained. The album ends with less than two minutes of free collective improvisation over a fixed "swing" beat, as if to say, we can do *that*, too.

Back in the studios with a smaller group for ESP on November 16, they recorded three extended pieces for *The Heliocentric Worlds of Sun Ra, II.* "The Sun Myth," the longest, is something of a double concerto for Boykins's bowed bass and Ra's piano and Clavioline which hold together the instrumental bursts of free improvisation from the rest of the Arkestra. The piccolo and nasal Clavioline opening of "A House of Beauty" gestures towards Stravinsky's "The Rite of Spring," but soon adds arco bass for an exercise of counterpoint between the three instrumental voices. And "Cosmic Chaos" hangs a series of solos on an arhythmic thread created by tuned drums and other percussion. Through these three pieces the combination of timbres and textures is constantly shifting in spite of the presence of only eight instruments in the group. Sun Ra orders the proceedings either from keyboard or tuned drums, and directs the construction as they go forward. Again, some have tried to read the titles of Sun Ra's compositions as pure programmatic statements, but by this point the changing textures make it virtually impossible to hear even a fixed musical metaphor within a single composition.

This time the record cover is an early German illustration of the solar system above a gallery of portraits of scientists chiefly from the sixteenth century, the period in which belief in the solar system was established—Leonardo da Vinci, Nicolas Copernicus, Galileo Galilei, and Tycho Brahe. But square in the middle of the row of portraits are pictures of Pythagoras and Sun Ra, calling attention to Sun Ra's links to the Greek astronomer-mathematician-musician who studied in Egypt, and who formed a brotherhood which attempted to purify their souls to allow the initiates to escape the "wheel of birth" and to aid them in the transmigration of the soul after the death of the body.

As soon as the ESPs were issued, Willis Conover, a Voice of America disc jockey, bravely began to play them nightly on his jazz show aimed at Europe, where an intensely loyal following began to develop. But while Sun Ra was becoming a weapon in the Cold War, most Americans remained ignorant of him. And then out of the blue Alton Abraham suddenly released a flood of Saturn records which had been recorded over the last few years—*Angels and Demons at Play, Fate in a Pleasant Mood, Art Forms of Dimensions Tomorrow,* and *Secrets of the Sun.*

Tom Wilson used Sun Ra on an MGM recording date with Walt Dickerson for *Impressions of a Patch of Blue* (the Sidney Poitier, Shelley Winters, Elizabeth Hartman film on race relations) in 1965, producing a quiet, subtle film score which owed something to the cool sonority of the vibraphone-piano groups of George Shearing and Cal Tjader.

Ed Bland continued to hire the Arkestra's people whenever he could. He called them for a limbo record he was doing for Audiofidelity, used them for some singles for Epic Records with soul singer Popcorn Wylie, and on blues guitarist Phil Upchurch's *Feeling Blue.* Their flexibility allowed him to use them on projects other musicians might fumble, like the non-Union session he hired them for in Newark in January 1966, to record a children's record of *Batman and Robin* for Tifton Record Company. Under the name of "The Sensational Guitars of Dan and Dale," and with Tom Wilson as producer, they pieced together a band of Sun Ra on organ, Jimmy Owens on trumpet, Tom McIntosh on trombone, Al Kooper (on organ when Sun Ra wasn't playing), Danny Kalb on guitar, and the rest of the members of the early rock band The Blues Project. Though the *Batman* theme does appear on the record, most of the rest of it was made up of rearrangements of music in public domain (such as a theme by Tchaikovsky), all played in rhythm-and-blues style with prominent twangy guitars.

Wilson used members of the Arkestra again for a record date for MGM with African drummer Chief Bey which included James Moody and Tommy Flanagan, but it was never released. In any case, Wilson soon lost interest in Sun Ra—just as he was beginning to be noticed internationally.

SLUG'S SALOON IN THE FAR EAST

Down 3rd Street from The Sun Palace, at No. 242, between Avenues C and D, a new bar opened up called Slug's, replacing a Ukrainian bar and restaurant on the same site. It was a long, dark room with bare brick walls and antique iron window grates, and with nylon parachutes draped from the ceiling. Slug's location was enough to guarantee its furtive exclusiveness, being nowhere near a subway line and well off the cab track in an area largely unknown to tourists and those uptown. Getting there meant walking east from the Bowery, or past the projects and the bombed-out zone, and past the Hell's Angels of New York City headquarters where Hogs lined the street, Christmas lights hung perpetually, and a huge Angel security guard seemed always to be lounging in the doorway.

From the first night, Slug's drew a steady, though strange crowd: serious, rakishly dressed men packing what they called heat—drug dealers, frankly, from all over lower Manhattan carrying on stylized negotiations while their bodyguards fanned out across the room. The dealers' presence guaranteed that some musicians would turn up, and a few began to play there with the owner's encouragement. Night by night, musicians came to replace dealers, until it was essentially a musicians' club, for in this time, a few years before mass bohemia gripped America, it was still possible for artists to have spaces all their own.

Slug's seemed like a gift from the Creator. Sun Ra suggested to the owner that the Arkestra be allowed to work there every Monday night, the traditional night when musicians were off and the clubs were dark. He reasoned that since they were off, it would be the only place they could go to hear music. The owner agreed, and Slug's became the Arkestra's home down the street and concert hall every Monday night from March 1966 for the next eighteen months, and a regular venue for them off and on over the next six years (or at least until shortly after Lee Morgan was shot to death there by a woman on February 19, 1972, a performance transgression whose memory still gives musicians the shivers).

And the musicians came. Cannonball Adderley, Jimmy Heath, Philly Joe Jones, and Art Blakey showed up. Dizzy Gillespie came (and as Sun Ra walked past, Dizzy leaned towards him and was heard to say, "Keep it up, Sonny, they tried to do the same shit to me"). One night Art Farmer, Mingus, Coltrane, and Monk all showed up. In fact Monk came a number of times, sometimes in the company of the Baroness Nica, who continued to be a doubter. (Once the baroness took Sonny to Monk's house and played one of the Saturn records for Monk and his wife Nellie: "That's too far out," Nellie exclaimed. "Yeah," Monk said, "but it *swings."*) From 9 to 4 in the morning, with no breaks, they played on and on, so long that by the end of the night some of the customers had nodded off on top of the tables. And in spite of the long hours, rehearsals continued at the same brutal pace, even on Mondays. Often they started rehearsing hours before the gig and then walked down the street with their instruments: by the time the night was over they had played ten to fifteen hours straight. But then rehearsals were held anytime, during costume fittings, even on the way to gigs, and in a sense all of the time, since Sun Ra was constantly talking about music.

The band began to grow with the steady Slug's gig, with some musicians sitting in only for the night, others coming to rehearsals and staying. Some—like Tommy Hunter—drifted away, but came back from time to time. But Gilmore was back; Black Harold was now playing the flute, or a drum so long that it stuck out into the tables. Some musicians, like Danny Davis and trombonists Teddy Nance and Bernard Pettiway, were added with the help of Baraka, through HARYOU ACT. Others, like James Jacson, he found in the neighborhood.

Jacson was an oboist and bassoonist from New Haven who had been recruited to the Yale School of Music by Paul Hindemith, and who now was living with his family on 3rd Street where he ran jewelry and crafts shops and worked at a nearby musical-instrument repair shop. One of Jacson's stores was called Charms and Amulets, and had a scale model of the Giza pyramid complex in the store window. His art specialties included large industrial light bulbs filled with tableaus with HO-gauge model railroad figures of a ghetto high-rise with a wino out front on the curb or Buddha under a tree. He also ran an "antique" store where he made distressed Spanish provincial furniture, very popular at the time.

Jacson had joined with some other neighborhood men to negotiate with the Nunchaku Brotherhood, a gang that terrorized the Lower East Side. They sold them on the idea of improving the neighborhood, and one of their projects together was an "igloo" made of old car hoods constructed under the Brooklyn Bridge in which the homeless could live. It was that multicolored igloo that Buckminster Fuller (the popularizer of the "spaceship Earth idea") saw from the bridge while he was commuting back from Brooklyn. He came down to the Lower East Side and asked around about who had built it, and ended up becoming involved with Jacson and other neighborhood groups and returned every week for the next eighteen months to teach them his architectural theories.

Jacson came to Sun Ra's attention when he began making what he called "rhythm logs," wooden boxes which were tuned and made a deep, rich sound when struck. Jacson had also made the sign at Slug's, as well as the carved door for the bar, to which he gave an ominous squeak through an ingenious combination of the cut of the wood and its treatment by soaking in salt water. For a long while he came to rehearsals, but was not asked to play with the band. Then, when Sun Ra felt he was ready, he wrote him some parts for his oboe and suggested he spell his name "Jacson," without the "k" so as to more accurately reflect its pronounciation. Later Jacson took up the big drum which had been played by Black Harold, and more often than not was the first musician seen on stage at performances.

By the end of their stay at Slug's in the early seventies Sun Ra had added singers and dancers to the mix. And since so many musicians sat in or drifted through the band, it was never clear who would be playing with him on a given night. "I look for the incorrigibles," he explained to a *Newsweek* reporter. "If they don't fit in with somebody else, they're gonna come back to me. That way I don't have to worry about keeping a band together."

The Arkestra made Monday nights at Slug's seem like testing grounds for new forms, new identities. One night a man dressed as a ninja warrior crashed through the door, and when some people began to laugh, he jumped on the bar and took the tops of the bottles off with a sweep of his sword. Another night a man from India approached Sun Ra at Slug's and warned him, "You just played the forbidden sacred music!" Sonny replied, "That's what I hear."

The painters were among the first to come to Slug's: Larry Rivers, who played jazz himself; James McCoy, whose paintings were wild explosions of color miming the Arkestra's music; or Robert Thompson, a figurative expressionist who worked the new music into his art, quoting the Old Masters' works in his paintings like a bebopper interpolating snatches of pop songs in solos, who sat and sketched at the tables, and gave Sun Ra his painting of the Arkestra peeking out of jungle foliage, like it might have been imagined by some crazed Henri Rousseau; and even Salvador Dali came, with his acolytes following him carrying candles.

Then there were the poets. Amiri Baraka spoke of wherever Sun Ra was as a "salon," a gathering place of minds and a site of creativity. And the forces Sun Ra unleashed were of a magnitude that beg for words like "salon" or "atelier." Wherever he went he was followed by musicians, artists, writers, visiting critics, tourists even, drawn to the incredible things they heard might be happening there. To young black poets he provided a means for releasing the words from the page, and for relocating them in the conventions of black instrumental and ritual performance. At Slug's on a Monday night you might have seen Amus Mor reading his poetry with the Arkestra, or Yusef Rahman, whose performances with the band A. B. Spellman observed:

Costumed and jeweled in a manner reminiscent of the Sudanese, preparing the room with incense, shaking chains of bells as he moved among the tables, Yusef danced and sang his poems. The lines as written were like chord changes for verbal improvisation. Taken literally, from the page, we might think the author of these lines to be a silly second-rate Surrealist:

A Gnostic frog-eyed owl / quilted by
bone yards bitter blacknight /

SOMEWHERE OVER A COSMIC RAINBOW . . .

But, in performance, the audience's mind straining to visualize the images from this whirling black man who played on every sense and backed by the empathetic Sun Ra band, the effect was strong indeed.

On another day you could have seen the young Ishmael Reed at Slug's. Though he was never a close follower of Sun Ra's, he was a musician, poet, and novelist who had come to know him at Slug's. And even though Sun Ra is not a character in *Mumbo Jumbo*, Reed's satirical history of the spread of black culture in the United States, the novel resonates with Sun Ra's discourse through its convergence of levels of history, science fiction, and Egyptology. But it is Reed's "I Am a Cowboy in the Boat of Ra" which is the most obvious point of contact with Sun Ra: though it is dense with allusions to Blake, Haitian vodun, gnosticism, and Yeats, it is the gospel of Sun Ra which gives it its focus.

And it is the ark which turns up in another young writer's work, Henry Dumas's "Ark of Bones," a tale in which some young men discover a river boat, an ark, which carried the bones of all their ancestors. Dumas hung out at Sun Ra's especially between 1965 and 1966, while he was employed as a social worker in New York City; and of all the young black writers of the time, he was closest to Sun Ra, and was inspired to draw on Egyptian and West African mythological material, as well as Deep South folksay and science fiction. "Outer Space Blues," for instance, cast Sun Ra's discourse into a vernacular form:

Hold it people, I see a flying saucer comin
      guess i wait and see
Yeah, a spaceship comin
      guess I wait and see
All I know they might look just like me

Hank (he sometimes spelled it "ankh") Dumas was a quiet young man, a little mysterious. "He seemed to be speaking from behind a curtain," someone said. Though extraordinarily rooted in everyday life, Dumas wrote what Baraka called "Afro-Surreal Expressionism," with no apparent limits on his source material. His poetry was richly layered and antiphonal, like black folk music, with a strong sense of the chromatic. And with Sun Ra he shared the Afro-Baptist affinity for imagery of birds, eagles, the wind, and other figures of escape, height, and majesty. After a year away working in Katherine Dunham's Performing Arts Training Center in East St. Louis in 1967, Dumas returned to New York City and was shot to death by a New York City Transit policeman on May 23, 1968. When Sun Ra heard about it, he became angrier than anyone had ever seen him before, and he raged on and on for days, cursing the city and its inhabitants, and reminding anyone who would listen that he had warned Dumas to be careful.

It took almost seven years for the *Village Voice* to notice Sun Ra, but in 1967 jazz critic Michael Zwerin dropped into Slug's to hear his band. Zwerin was no dilettante: he had played in Miles Davis's Birth of the Cool Nonet and with other innovative musicians of the time. Still, nothing he had ever heard prepared him for what he saw that night. There were four saxophones, three brass, three bass players, two drummers, two African percussionists, all dressed in peaked straw hats, polkadot shirts and ties, and African robes. Sun Ra was seated behind an old upright piano. John Gilmore was soloing when he walked in:

> He was Gene Ammons and Albert Ayler but also neither of them. Periodically, he became inaudible through the percussion. They swung harder and harder until quibbles about things like balance became totally irrelevant. Then an ensemble began with eerie precision. The notes were from the swing era, but the interpretation had an indefinable vigor.
>
> Next, at least a half hour of percussion.... The beat kept on, building intensity. Everyone in the band was playing a percussion instrument of some kind. One of them started to chant. The volume grew and spread. It built further. I was being altogether mauled and caressed at the same time. It was a loving grit, a soft racket. It wrapped itself around me. It ended.
>
> A few minutes of rest and silence. Without an apparent signal, the entire ensemble attacked up-tempo free collective improvisation. Simultaneous and tumultuous screeches, sheets of sound, honks and grunts filled the smoky room. It was both awful and wonderful, a kind of chaotic order. Continuing like that, the horn players happily filed up the aisle....
>
> I was wrung-out: Sun Ra's music is pagan, religious, simple, complex, and almost everything else at the same time. There is no pigeon-hole for it. It is ugly and beautiful and terribly interesting. It's new music, yet I've been hearing it for years.

One day while walking past a midtown Sam Goody's record store, Sun Ra saw a boxed set of records in the window with the title, *A Study in Frustration: The Fletcher Henderson Story*. Sun Ra was incensed: "He wasn't frustrated, that had nothing to do with it! He was a master, he got the job done!" He brooded about it the rest of the day and when he got back to 3rd Street he started transcribing Henderson's music from records, changing only a few notes to allow for contemporary tastes (changes which he said he knew were correct because he was attuned to Henderson's vibrations). Then he began to prepare the band for playing a music from before their own time by showing them a picture of the Henderson band immaculately dressed in sharp suits and black-and-white shoes (except for one member, who was trying to push his pants down to hide his brown shoes); he told them about Henderson's tastes, what he drank, where he had been and what he had done, his love of horse racing; while rehearsing "Limehouse Blues" he told them that work in the lime houses was so bad that only Chinese and blacks worked in them. They learned the words of the songs, talked about their meaning, heard about what was happening in 1934 when Henderson recorded it, what the popular dances were. He sent members of the Arkestra out to research individual players in the Henderson group in order to get the feeling right when playing their parts. Sun Ra told them they weren't copying those pieces, they were re-creating them, and with the proper information they could know the spirit behind the original. The improvised solos were written out note for note, even the mistakes, out of respect for the originators: "If you get the musicians' feelings right, you can feel the presence of them smiling." But when jazz historian Phil Schaap took the Henderson saxophonist and clarinetist Russell Procope with him to a Sun Ra tribute to Fletcher Henderson, Procope was visibly shaken when he heard John Gilmore reproduce the same mistake he had made on an original 1933 recording with the Henderson band.

Sun Ra's taste in swing ran towards the music of his youth, the music made by those bands in the first blush of the swing era—the 1932–34 compositions of Fletcher Henderson and Duke Ellington, like "King Porter Stomp," "Yeah Man!" "Queer Notions," "Can You Take It?" "Hocus Pocus," "Big John's Special," "Happy as the Day Is Long," "Shanghai Shuffle," and "Tidal Wave." These were the compositions he chose to transcribe, not the better known music of the mature bands of the late 1930s to early 1940s.

After the first six or so hours of rehearsal on Henderson's "Limehouse Blues" they went straight to Slug's, where West Coast critic Ralph Gleason was sitting at a front table with the Baroness, and even she was amazed by this change of repertoire. When Sun Ra was asked years later about this shift, he said, "America never heard the beauty of those bands. I don't believe in equality in creative things—it means sameness—I'm looking to play something eternal, that will be valid in 1,000 years."

A year later John Wilson of the *New York Times* made the trek to Slug's and he noticed the changes from the first concert the Arkestra had given five years before. For one thing, Sun Ra had moved from "space-age jazz" to "infinity," and a large banner hung behind the band proclaiming "Infinity—Sun Ra" over a great yellow sun:

> By infinity Mr. Ra means creating a jazz of the future, but also covering the past.
>
> As a result, a Sun Ra composition that offers twittering bird calls rubbed from a pair of Chinese tiddies, a vast percussive orchestral hullabaloo of grunts and squawks and a hot solo on a ram's horn will dissolve into Fletcher Henderson's arrangement of "King Porter's Stomp."

And out of the riffs of that arrangement came a Sun Ra piano solo

> in a completely different mood, a mixture of Art Tatum and Bud Powell—the tune has become "What's New"—until a piccolo goes sailing off over a fat ensemble sound and a hard, driving tenor saxophone rises up in solo. Suddenly the band is chanting "We'll take a trip to space—the next stop Mars!" and a frantic saxophone squeals its way through a blazingly discordant ensemble. Somewhere along the way, everybody in the band has been drumming on something, so that at times it turns into a complete drum ensemble.

The costumes for the night were "glittering, golden pullover blouses and soft yellow straw and cloth hats molded into jaunty shapes," bells, beads, African print shirts, scarves of polka dots of all sizes and hues, medallions of silver and gold around their necks. Sun Ra wore a "long golden robe, his head encircled by two golden bands." In addition to their usual instruments the Arkestra had an amplified koto, a Nigerian horn, a kora, Chinese violins, an oriental lute, and a number of Sun Columns—golden metal tubes with rubber bottoms which gave off a sound when they were struck—and a small, gold electronic box which played music. Musicians spilled out in the audience, instrument cases piled high around them. Lights might go off on some pieces, come back on, or blink off and on. Sometimes a motion picture with no obvious relation to what they were playing was projected behind them on the wall.

Seated in the back of the band at Slug's, hidden behind piano, Clavinet, and Spacemaster (an organ made for him by the Chicago Musical Instrument Company that sounded like a theremin or bagpipes),

Sun Ra could sometimes be seen picking up a one-stringed instrument he called a Chinese violin; occasionally he shyly conducted with a thin wand topped with a peacock feather. But then all of the members of the Arkestra were partially veiled by the lighting; and in a period in which individual musicians were as distinct and celebrated as sports stars, their anonymity was all the more striking.

During this same period, drama critic Stefan Brecht wrote about his visit to Slug's in the *Evergreen Review:* he thought the re-creations from the swing era mixed in with the more abstract music were in bad taste, but said he had noticed the same thing pervading the playing of Charlie Parker. "There is probably something there that I didn't get." At the end of the review he added a note:

> These piano solos during the three-hour sets introduce a historical sequence of jazz styles leading through the big-band sound of the forties, through cool jazz, to the shrieking-bird saxophone solos of the sixties up to the cosmic-reproduction in sound-matter of the "true Sun Ra," which is now and out of history—a spatial music. That is, they serve to get us from our historical place into absolute reality. That "bad taste" is our own. Whether Sun Ra shares it is another matter. He is not ironic.

The years at Slug's allowed Sun Ra to emerge as a leader and composer and for the Arkestra to develop its character. Audiences saw a group of black men in roles new to white people, new even to many blacks. No longer playing as an excuse for a bar's existence, not even playing for dancing, they abandoned all signs of the servitude of show business— the waiters' uniforms which created the atmosphere of class, the willingness to oblige customers by playing pop hits, the egregiously placatory smiles that signified "performance"; but they also disdained the chic icy surface of cool, the au courant disengagement of the rebel. In their strange costumes and dark glasses they were vaguely unsettling, even a bit frightening, to people going to a club for an evening of fun. They were reasserting black performance values which were completely alien to white experience, conventions drawn from the church, the black cabaret, bar life, and the community picnic; they were reclaiming the aesthetics of those Amiri Baraka called the Blues People: honking and shrieking saxophones, bar walking, guitar playing behind the head, eccentric dancers, capes and exotic costumes, weeping and pleading on bended knees, ecstatic states of speech and dance—the flash of the show, the elements which James Brown and Jimi Hendrix were startling whites with elsewhere: "They didn't know how to take us," Jacson said. "As a bunch of drunks? Some slightly crazy people? A bunch of addicts? But whatever we were, they knew we were not broken men."

Slug's was the heart of what was now being called underground culture in the United States, a culture that was in the process of rapidly being internationalized. (By the early 1970s a club in Paris called The Gibus tried to recreate the funky ambience of Slug's, but when the Arkestra played there in 1973, the musicians judged it "much too nice to be 'underground.' ") When someone finally got around to asking Sun Ra if he was part of the underground, he declared that he was in the sub-underground.

N O I S E A N D F R E E D O M

"Noise" was one of the first words which came to mind to many of those who heard Sun Ra's Arkestra in the 1960s. "Noise," in the abstract, is what scientists call phenomena which is unpredictable, out of control, beyond the system. In music, noise is a lack of defined pitch, the presence of disorganized sound, too much volume. But like the word "madness," it's easy to use, but hard to justify objectively. There is a long history of ambiguity around the word "noise" in English: to Shakespeare and the Elizabethans it meant an argument, a quarrel, but it was also used to describe a band of musicians, as well as "an agreeable or melodious sound." And likewise in practice what categorizes sound as "noise" or "music" is fiercely ambiguous and subjective.

The history of Western music might be rewritten as one in which noise gradually triumphs over what is perceived as pure sound, where "noise" in one era gradually transforms into "music" in the next—harmony grows more intense, the size of musical groups increase, new instruments appear, or new techniques for playing replace old ones; or the elements of noise which lie within pure sounds are exposed. It was thinking in terms like these which led the Italian futurists in the early 1900s to blandly acknowledge that noise had increased in modern life, but then to go on to claim that a hunger for noise had also increased, a hunger which music must address. Noise, they contended, was richer in harmonics than pure sound; and if audiences failed to understand that, they should be trained through concentrated listening to hear the musicality of noise and understand its emotional effect. New noise-creating instruments, *intonarumori*, could be invented to make entirely new sounds, musical noises. And seeing no adequate models for this kind of noise in nature, they sought them in modernity itself, in machinery, in transportation, and the sheer volume and scale of city life.

The futurists worked at a time when the invention of sound recording had increased demand for novelty and fresh musical ideas, a demand which continued to escalate over the years. But by the late 1940s innovations in electronics replaced the need for new noise instruments. Wire and magnetic recording tape, and the technology which followed—multitracking, speed variation, flanging, looping, and the like—opened up a world of new audio possibilities. But then came electrically amplified musical instruments, and with amplification came distortion, a phenomenon first thought of as "technical difficulties," something going wrong, technology doing something it shouldn't do. But distortion also made it possible for the simplest of sounds to take on completely new musical meanings: that something is out of hand, that the performer is either incompetent or too powerful for the instrument, or that a music is being produced which is more natural, primitive, unrehearsed, perhaps more dangerous.

As the twentieth century progressed and more music than ever became available and virtually omnipresent, the desire for unorganized sounds also increased, but also a need for sounds free of aesthetic intention, and for organized silence (a kind of noise in the absence of organized sound). And silence and noise both provided the raw materials for generating other kinds of music, even antimusics.

Yet another version of the history of Western music might be written, one which examines its evolution in terms of the increased presence of foreign and exotic musics (other kinds of noises) within the mainstream, appropriations which restarted the engines of creativity when restlessness or ennui set in and provided the shocks to the system which helped define modernism. And more often than not it was some form of black music—African, West Indian, Latin, jazz, or folk—that was appropriated. Black music represented for Western music a kind of preelectronic distortion, an irruption into the system, a breaking of the rules of musical order; later, electronic distortion itself became a technological emblem of the black component of Western art.

Beyond pop music, jazz, and the classical establishment was a group of composers who inherited both of these visions of music and noise: the experimentalists, as John Cage called himself, Pierre Schaeffer, Edgar Varese, Henry Cowell, and others who questioned the nature of music itself, and the social matrix into which it was set, and who sought to replace the logic which underlay Western classical music with one based on sound alone. Though there was not much agreement among them on what constituted music, what it should contain or how it should be assembled, most of these experimental composers took the view that sound (or noise) had to be organized *musically*. Then what was to be done with the composer: how much control should the composer retain in opening up the music? Only John Cage among the early experimentalists (and to a degree, followers like Morton Feldman and Earle Brown) deemphasized the composer's role, and even the performer's, by putting the weight of the musical experience on the listener, and by assuming that all sound is already musical and only needs to be allowed to enter the musical work by creating situations "in which any sound or noise at all can go with any other." It was the last step in the rejection of the expressive tradition of nineteenth-century music.

Openness to alien forms of music was one of the reasons students were drawn to the classes John Cage taught at the New School for Social Research in Greenwich Village from 1956 to 1960. Many of the students in that class (like Alan Kaprow, Red Grooms, or Claes Oldenburg) thought of music as a kind of visual art, or theater, or performance art, as it would later be known, and drew a straight line between music and European surrealism and dada. This synthesis in the early 1960s was the source of happenings—a new form of theater, often crude, rough, amateurish, performed in lofts, storefronts, and vacant lots, mixing visual, verbal, choreographic, and musical elements, but using none of them as they were traditionally understood in the theater. They were ambiguously staged and set in time and place, without narrative structure, and played by actors who renounced full artistic control or "craft."

Some of the Cage students (and those of Richard Maxfield, an electronic composer who took over his class in 1961) were responsible for the development of Fluxus, an antiart movement which pushed music in two different directions at once: either towards a concern with sonics for its own sake—the physical properties of sound and its effects on listeners and the world; or towards a preoccupation with the mechanics of the musical performance itself. Some of them incorporated incidental sound into "music" (squeaks, rattles, the premusical sound of air blowing through a horn), used instruments in unmusical ways, amplified the inaudible, or pushed musical repetition to the point where it revealed hidden features. Those who foregrounded performance worked to make music appear strange, exposing the tricks of the players, violating professional or traditional standards of behavior, or violently destroying instruments.

Fluxus was part of a reaction to the cult of personality which had sustained the previous generation of artists. These new Village artists were committed to a kind of nonprofessional art, to nonperformance and artlessness. Their new paradigms were being drawn from the folk and pop arts in the belief that they minimized the role of the artist, and were more egalitarian and antihierarchical. "Performance" was looked upon with suspicion, while the ordinary was celebrated. Freedom was everything, freedom from Art, and from the conventional expectations surrounding dress, family, race, class, and, to a more limited degree, gender.

It was into this world that Sun Ra came in 1962, and the Village was, as the art historians might say, in a state of cultural readiness for anyone who shared their views. And superficially he *did* share some of their concerns: he sought to erase some of the distinction which existed between audience and performance; he believed that performance can model, maybe even effect social change; and like most people in the Village art world at the time, he was happy to say that he came from nowhere and never mention his family. On the other hand Sun Ra also believed in the redemptive powers of art, in discipline, in tradition, in exposing the no-tion of freedom as a trick; and he tirelessly promoted absolute authority, the importance of leaders and the need to respect and follow them. And it was the expressivity of music and its effects on listeners which con-cerned him most of all. But the Village ignored all this in Sun Ra, or mis-understood it. Weirdness was given considerable respect, wildness a certain indulgence, and the privileging of blackness was viewed as an act of social rebellion. And if in the process the meaning of Sun Ra was dis-torted, that was at least in the tradition of modernist appropriation and racial stereotyping which underlies the history of popular music in the twentieth century.

Sun Ra entered this world from jazz, which had a different history. Before the 1960s jazz had been in a comfortable position. It was clearly marked off from classical and popular music and had an audience which had grown with the music over the last thirty years and knew what to ex-pect. There were informal rules as to what was acceptable, effective, and successful in improvisation, and there were objective standards of suc-cess, even if they were difficult to articulate. The evolution of jazz had minimized the decisions musicians had to make before the playing began. True, bebop had the cachet of radicalism because it had attacked the conventional symmetry of the pop songs which underlay older jazz, but it had also expanded the role of harmony, since bop musicians were retaining and expanding the chords of the pop melodies they were elim-inating. Bebop had subdivided and complicated the conventional rhythms of pop music, but it still had a linear pulse, along with a cycle of climaxes and repeats which organized harmony and melody and which helped listeners locate themselves corporally in the performance. Jazz had of course stretched and bent time, the variations within which were called swing, but nonetheless an overall tempo was kept within which the listeners still felt comfortable.

The harmonic limitations of bebop had been noted by the musicians of late-fifties modal jazz—Miles Davis, George Russell, Gil Evans, and Sun Ra himself, who had attempted to slow down and reduce harmonic change. John Coltrane, for example, had pursued a more static and open form of harmony with the use of minimal scales and drones (on "Naima," for instance), even while he was testing the limits of bebop harmony with "Giant Steps." But this was only a first step, and often meant that musicians would transfer modal procedures into the conventional pop song format.

In 1959, however, Ornette Coleman went one step further, liberating musicians from having to improvise on chordal patterns the structures which set up the cycles of repeats, returns, and cadences, and predetermined what would be played. Coleman often let the limits of his breath determine structure (like some contemporary poets); he was more interested in melody than harmony; and his melodies became more irregular and asymmetrical (made even more so by his wide-ranging and free tonality) than bebop had ever imagined. Yet even while he minimized harmony, his work was still strongly rhythmic in a conventional way, appealing to a physical sense of pulse or heartbeat, and his phrases were often predictable and even blueslike. As revolutionary as he was, he seemed to know how far out *not* to go.

Here the new jazz of the 1960s strangely found itself taking an evolutionary path parallel to the one taken by twentieth-century classical composers. Arnold Schoenberg's serial reorganization of pitch and Ornette Coleman's realignment of tonality and melody both kept rhythm and phrase structure, even while radically changing melody and harmony. The next step for both jazz and experimental music would seem to be a suspension of time. And post-Cage and post-Coleman, these new musics did began to make rhythm unreliable, giving listeners no sense of regularity. It became harder for listeners to find the center, being lost in time, with no recurrent cycles or endings. With a sense of inertia threatening to set in, both experimentalists and new jazz players were forced to use volume, texture, grain, tone color, and other variables to create variation and interest, and demanded of the listener a focus and appreciation of sound for its own sake. And at times the results of free jazz and experimental music seemed very similar: the improvised collectivity of Ornette Coleman's *Free Jazz* and John Coltrane's *Ascension* seemed to converge with Karlheinz Stockhausen's completely notated *Zeitmasse*.

As much as the development of free jazz may have been synchronous with experimental music, when it surfaced on the Lower East Side most people did not make the connection. Free jazz lacked the European art and laboratory trappings which would make it recognizable, if not necessarily appreciated. "What they saw was squeaking, howling music," James Jacson put it, "people looking and dressing strange—unkempt, raggedy, with bad hair and whacked-out talk; musicians were accused of having just bought their instruments in pawnshops and going right on-stage and pretending they could play them." These were players who demanded that jazz die to be born again. In the process they discovered parallels between the cut-and-paste montage aesthetics of postmodernism and those of African-American aesthetics; between surrealism and spirit possession; folk music and turn-of-the-century Viennese classical practices. It was a highly compressed, intense period of creativity, much of it occurring outside of the public's hearing.

Though collective memory now often fails us, there was an incredible amount of variety in free jazz: it could be loud and insistent, but also exceptionally soft and chamberlike; it was physical, but intensely emotional as well; some of the new musicians were barely amateurs, but many were among the most virtuosic of their time; and its openness to all alien musical codes frustrated easy characterization.

Within a few short years these musicians were to interrogate and then redefine most of the conventions of conventional jazz: they completed the erasure of the line between composer and improviser that earlier jazz had hinted at, and reinvented collective improvisation; they moved pitch away from the convention of playing in or out of "tune," and made tonality a conscious choice, just as time keeping or swing were turned into resources to be drawn on, rather than laws to be obeyed. New techniques were applied to conventional instruments—drummers might play with knitting needles or tree branches with the leaves still on them, or play the cymbals with a violin bow; pianists played inside the piano, bassists played above the bridge, horn players found ways to produce chords. New instruments appeared—plastic saxophones, Middle Eastern double-reed horns, African and Asian drums, bells, and whistles; and old ones, like the soprano saxophone, the cello, and the tuba, were revived. It was competitive, daring, and risky, but also spawned communalism and cooperative institutions. To grasp these developments new metaphors had to be introduced to explain the music, the most important of which were energy, spirituality, metaphysicality, and freedom. It was the idea of freedom as expressed within new definitions of improvisation that was echoed and adapted well beyond the bounds of music—in drama (The Living Theater, The Judson Poets Theater, Squat Theater, The Open Theater), in dance (Judith Dunn, Fred Herko, Molissa Fenley, Trisha Brown), film (Shirley Clarke, John Cassavetes), in classical and academic experimental music (John Adams, Terry Riley, La Monte Young, Steve Reich, Philip Glass), and even in rock (Captain Beefheart, Iggy Pop, the MC5, and Rip, Rig, and Panic).

Free jazz quickly expanded the vocabularies of musicians all over the world, but especially those in Russia and Eastern Europe, where "freedom" had special connotations, and where they saw within it the message of their own liberation. Free jazz had become a kind of new internationalism.

Sun Ra, on the other hand, did his best not to be identified too closely with free jazz:

> What I do is based on the natural, while what they do is probably based on what they learned in school.... Their composers write the melody and leave it to the rhythm section to put their own rhythm to the melody. That's not the way I work. For me, the note is in my mind at the same time as the rhythm. My music is the music of precision. I know exactly the rhythm that must animate my music, and only this rhythm is valid. I have in my mind a complete image of my work, on all the different levels: melody, harmony and rhythm.

Asked in 1970 by writer Bert Vuijsje about what he thought of the jazz avant-garde, he said:

> The musicians don't know how to connect with the people. They play music, and are very good at that, but what they're doing has nothing to do with the people. They have no sense of humor.... They look at things from their own ego and through their talent, and they say: "You need to praise me because I am wonderful." And it's true, they are wonderful, but everybody is wonderful in what he does. Because you happen to be a musician that doesn't mean that the people should worship you.

...There's humor in all my music. It always has rhythm. No matter how far out it may be, you can always dance to it. Actually I don't play free music, because there is no freedom in the universe. If you were to be free you could just play no matter what and it doesn't come back to you. But you see, it always does come back to you. That's why I warn my musicians: be careful about what you play ... every note, every beat, be aware that it comes back to you. And if you play something you yourself don't understand, then that's bad for you and for the people too.

Musicians often play wonderful things, bring together wonderful sounds, but it doesn't mean a thing. Not for themselves, not for other people, Everyone says: that's wonderful, that's the work of a great musician. Of course that's true, but what's the significance of it? People don't get better because of the music, even though they certainly need help. I believe that every artist should realize that. That his work has no meaning whatsoever unless he helps people with it.

When he was asked how his music helped people, he replied:

First of all I express sincerity. There's also that sense of humor, by which people sometimes learn to laugh about themselves. I mean, the situation is so serious that the people could go crazy because of it. They need to smile and realize how ridiculous everything is. A race without a sense of humor is in bad shape. A race needs clowns. In earlier days people knew that. Kings always had a court jester around. In that way he was always reminded how ridiculous things are. I believe that nations too should have jesters, in the congress, near the president, everywhere.... You could call me the jester of the Creator. The whole world, all the disease and misery, it's all ridiculous.

He also kept himself apart from currently popular musics like soul music and rock. "Soul music is body music; I want soul-force music." And though Sun Ra had promoted the electrification of music from as far back as Birmingham and used amplification in his band, he expected his musicians to be able to get their effects acoustically. He knew that most if not all of the electronic effects produced so far were rooted in African-American acoustic playing: the wah-wah sounds came from plungers used on horns; phasing and delay from call and response; fuzz tones and distortion from old-time "dirty" tones or mutes and hats; and multitonal effects from split tones. And even loudness itself was not a purely acoustic phenomenon, but socially constructed between the number of players, their organization, and who they were.

> There's not so much difference between nonelectrical instruments and electrical ones: it's like the difference between a horse and a car... you got to give maintenance to the machines, but you also got to take care of the horse. You might have an emotional connection to live animals, but even that gets transferred to machines. They always call machines "she."

In May the Arkestra went on a one-week package tour of New York State colleges sponsored by the ESP's Esperanto Foundation and supported by the New York State Council for the Arts. The other musicians on the tour were Ran Blake, Patty Waters, Giuseppi Logan, and Burton Greene. Each group was recorded at every concert, and Sun Ra's *Nothing Is* (released in 1969) offers a glimpse of the Arkestra live on that tour, suggesting that they were attempting to do as much as possible within a limited time; Sun Ra can be heard cuing the band as to what composition is coming next, moving from abstract piano openings to recognizable melodies, compressing both "Imagination" and "Rocket Number Nine" into one minute and forty-four seconds. But it also shows that they could improvise collectively live, even under pressure. (A live performance from two years later issued as *Pictures of Infinity* proves again that the Arkestra was capable of collective improvisation in the moment, but equally able to quickly switch to tightly arranged material.)

Strange Strings (issued in 1967) pushed further in the direction that Sun Ra had been heading in *The Magic City*. From a search of curio shops and music stores Sun Ra had assembled a number of stringed instruments—ukeleles, koto, mandolin, a "Chinese lute"—and passed them out to the reed and horn players. He thought that strings could touch people in a special way, different from other instruments; and though the Arkestra didn't know how to play them, that was the point: a study in ignorance, he called it. Next they prepared a number of homemade instruments, including a large piece of tempered sheet metal with an "X" chiseled on it. Then they miked the Sun Columns.

Marshall Allen said that when they began to record the musicians asked Sun Ra what they should play, and he answered only that he would point to them when he wanted them to start. The result is an astonishing achievement, a musical event which seems independent of all other musical traditions and histories. The music was recorded at high volume, laden with selectively applied echo, so that all of the instruments bleed together and the stringed instruments sound as if they, too, were made of sheet metal. The piece is all texture, with no sense of tonality except where Art Jenkins sings through a metal megaphone with a tunnel voice. But to say that the instruments seem out of tune misses the point, since there is no "tune," and in any case the Arkestra did not know how to tune most of the instruments. There is no structure per se to the piece, as it is built from layers of strings of varying thickness, at changing volume, the strings being bowed, struck, pulled, plucked, strummed, and rubbed, producing as many transients, overtones, and partials as possible. From time to time Clifford Jarvis enters briefly on the drum kit, or timpani, and Boykins begins a bass line. It is a piece of astonishing variety, and despite taking up one-and-a-half sides of an LP, speeds past quickly. This was not a scratch orchestra, like Gavin Bryars's Portsmouth Sinfonia, attempting to make well-known music appear strange by mixing skilled and incompetent musicians. Nor was it an aleatory exercise. Sun Ra here succeeds in creating perhaps the most completely improvised but organic piece in the history of jazz, with no prepared rhythmic, melodic, or harmonic material, performed by players on instruments foreign to them.

The album notes suggest that the record links East and West, the primitive and the modern, to create a balanced equation in the world. The writer was Tam Fiofori, a Nigerian poet-writer who had come to New York in 1965 by way of London, where he had been the London editor for the journal *Change;* and now he was a contributing editor to *Guerrilla* and was beginning to write about the Arkestra in underground or arts publications like *Arts Magazine, Liberator, Negro Digest,* the *Chicago Seed, IT, Friends, Evergreen Review, Artscanada, New York Free Press,* or jazz magazines like *Down Beat, Jazz and Pop, Melody Maker, Jazz Magazine* of Paris, and the *Orkester Journalen* of Sweden. He had attached himself to the Arkestra, and he could often be seen at work at the typewriter in The Sun Palace or traveling with the band. More than anyone else, Fiofori made Sun Ra known internationally. And he ambitiously drew Sun Ra deeper into the world of avant arts. In 1969 a new magazine called *Sun Arts: A Magazine of Presence, Be/ing & Motion To/wards Infinity* was announced, with Tam Fiofori, Sun Ra, James McCoy, and Charles Shabacon as editors, with Tenk Har Shentep, De Leon Harrison. Malcolm Morris, David Thomas, Jay Wright, Patrick Griffiths, and Babs Williams as contributing editors. But Sonny was not about to let Fiofori or anyone else be his interpreter: "For three years [Fiofori] wrote down everything I said, publishing it all over the world, but he didn't hear any of it."

Again a great number of records were released which had been previously recorded: *Sun Ra Visits Planet Earth, Rocket Number Nine, We Travel the Spaceways,* and *When Angels Speak of Love.* And with them two new records, *Monorails and Satellites, Vols. 1 and 2,* Sun Ra's first solo piano recordings. The covers of both albums show disembodied hands playing a keyboard that reaches through the solar system back to Jupiter, with Sun Ra's head appearing as an egg-shaped planet in the far end of space. Recorded in the year in which the film *2001* was released (and in which Erich von Daniken's *Chariots of the Gods* first appeared in English), the title may refer to the monolith of that film, which Sun Ra elsewhere seems to remember as a monorail, perhaps connecting it to his UFO experience. The first volume's "Space Towers" and "Cogitation" use the full range of the piano and could seemingly be directly transcribed to an orchestra, but at the same time suggests why his scores are so hard to play: eighth-note runs jumping between two octaves are no fun for horns. "Skylight" is a ballad, close enough to evoke the pop tune "Skylark." And a standard like "Easy Street," the only pop tune on the first record, is played simply, the left hand walking the bass line, hinting at a stripped-down Art Tatum. Sun Ra was a not a dazzling technician like a Bud Powell or an Art Tatum, nor did he possess a keyboard touch or harmonic sense so consistent that it was immediately identifiable. His sensitivity to subtle variations in tonality made a single "style" impossible for him. Once asked if he could hear quarter notes, the notes "between the cracks" on a piano, he answered

> Oh, yeah, I'm using these intervals. You see, the way you attack a note can create those effects. Depending on how hard you hit the key, you can hear the third or the fourth or the fifth—those sounds in the cracks—coming out. So the touch, the attack, is very important. When I hit a note, the undertones also sound. With the undertones and overtones blended, I can get quarter-tones. Not too many piano players have that touch. Earl Hines had it, Art Tatum had it, Duke Ellington had it.... I sing that way too, dividing the octave into 24 or 36 steps, just like the Indian singers do. I'm doing world music.

The second volume of *Monorails and Satellites* seems more a set of keyboard memos for compositions and arrangements with extreme contrasts. And even though it is perhaps less striking than the first volume, nothing on these two records is at all obvious.

As the Arkestra's reputation spread they became vaguely identified somewhere between the new rock and roll and free jazz of New York and were offered engagements at a few elite universities such as Swarthmore and Princeton. With full-sized stages to perform on, Sun Ra began to try out ideas he had never had room for or money enough to attempt before. At Princeton University, for example, they stunned students by bringing along ten painters who worked with canvases and sketch pads on stage throughout the performance, while the musicians climbed over the modern sets which were left on stage from a contemporary production of Shakespeare. Some who attended these concerts later said it was something like one's first exposure to Richard Foreman's plays.

Sun Ra continued his partnership with Alton Abraham in Chicago, and sent him recordings to issue on Saturn even though Abraham was still unhappy over the band's move to New York. In fact Abraham came up with the idea of incorporating their projects into a larger business arrangement. On April 10, 1967, Ihnfinity, Inc., was incorporated in the State of Illinois. Alton E. Abraham, Sun Ra, Almeter Hayden, and James Bryant were listed as incorporators in the corporation, with an address at 4115 S. Drexel Boulevard, the office from which Saturn Records was operating. Sun Ra was listed as still living in Chicago.

Ihnfinity, Inc., was to be an umbrella group for many projects: " 'Ihnfinity' is about everything," Sun Ra said.

> The idea of Ihnfinity, Inc., is that everyone on this planet should have a share in the universe. My friend Alton Abraham, who drew up the charter, wanted to make it a nonprofit. But I said, "Abraham, I don't think the state will stamp this if we said it was nonprofit. We'll have to make it a profit-making corporation to get it stamped. Let's make it profitable in a humanitarian way." So we made it a profit-making corporation and the state stamped it and gave us our charter. No one else has a charter to own space.

The purposes of the corporation were:

> To perform works of an humanitarian nature among all people of earth, to help stamp out (destroy) ignorance destroying its own major purpose, to changing ignorance to constructive live creativity, to own and operate all kinds of research laboratories, studios, electronic equipment, electro-chemical communicational devices of our own design and creativity, and electromechanical equipment, electronic equipment relating to audio and video devices and audio and video devices themselves including sound recordings and tapes as well as video recordings, tapes, teleportation, astral projection devices, mind cleansing sound devices, magnetic computers, electrical and electronic devices related to all phases of en-terplanatary space travel including magnetic energy producing ships with speeds greater than the speed of light (as presently known), including enterplanetary cosmonetic devices of an astro infinity nature, to own real estate including land, buildings, factories, water, including air space above same, to use these values for the greater advancement of all people of earth and creative live beings of this galaxy and other galaxies beyond the sun.

It was an extraordinary charter for a state to grant, and reflected Abraham's faith in electricity, and a part of the interest at the time in magnetic healing, orgone boxes, and the like.

In 1972 the corporation was dissolved by the state, and on January 16, 1974, it was registered again, this time as a nonprofit. Its statement of purpose now read:

> To perform spiritual-cosmic-intergalactic-infinity research works relative to worlds-dimensions-planes in galaxies and universes beyond the present now known used imagination of mankind, beyond the intergalactic central sun and works relative to spiritual and spiritual advancement of our presently known world. To awaken the spiritual conscious of mankind putting him back in contact with his "Creator." To make mankind aware that there are superior beings (Gods) on other planets in other galaxies. To make mankind aware that the "Creator" (God) is here now and that he is also present in other world-galaxies. To help stamp out (destroy) ignorance destroying its major purpose changing ignorance to constructive creative progress. To use these spiritual-cosmic values for the greater advancement of all people of earth and creative live beings of this galaxy and galaxies beyond the intergalactic central sun. To establish spiritual energy refilling houses (churches) where people can come to refill themselves with spiritual energy and to seek their "natural Creator" (God). To perform works as the "Creator" (God) wills us, "Ihnfinity," to perform.

"The period of duration of the corporation is perpetual," it noted. To celebrate their first incorporation, Sun Ra gave a mass concert in September dedicated to "Nature and Nature's God," in the band shell in Central Park with a hundred musicians, including six drummers, ten bass players, ten trumpets, ten trombones, and three French horns made up of his older musicians from Chicago and his New York players. But unlike the massive Central Park Be-In of the same year, when the Arkestra arrived the audience was mostly photographers and filmmakers. Then six police cars turned up, and the officers joined the audience. At one point during the concert the Arkestra hit a screaming space chord, and the large American flag stretched across the back wall of the band shell fell down. With that, Sonny abruptly ended the concert.

One hundred musicians was a kind of triumph, but he had wanted 1,000, and thought that even 10,000 might be necessary to realign the earth and "melt all the atomic bombs" and create peace. Almost ten years later in Philadelphia Sun Ra called WXPN disc jockey Jules Epstein and asked him if he could help him find money to get 144,000 musicians together for a sacred concert, obviously anticipating the end of the world (Revelations 7) and knowing even *that* would not be enough to get musicians to play without money. (A cynic suggested that they could play for the door like everybody else.)

Over the next few months they played the Fifth Annual Avant-Garde Festival of New York on the Staten Island Ferry, organized by the reigning queen of the avant, Charlotte Moorman; they made their first appearance in Boston at a rock ballroom, The Boston Tea Party; worked the Spirit House in Newark, the Meridian Park Festival in Washington, D.C., and did a concert for the Betterment League at the Lincoln Square Neighborhood Center in New York City. Another concert in Central Park, a part of the "African Stroll" series put on by the Parks Department, was announced to be performed from rowboats in the lake; but by the time they were afloat and ready to perform they were preempted by the Goldman Band concert going on nearby.

KICK OUT THE JAMS

As the protests against the Vietnam War developed alongside the civil rights movement and various branches of the student movement, they each adopted some form of music to identify themselves with—spirituals, folk songs, rock and roll—and each choice told a lot about the group's ideology and history. One of the most interesting was the White Panther Party, an offshoot of the yippies, which attempted to unify free jazz with the hardest forms of white rock and roll.

Their manifesto, the "Statement for the White Panther Arm of the Youth International Party," argued that their program derived and extended the Black Panther Party's program, "just as our music contains and extends the power and feeling of the black magic music that originally informed our bodies and told us we could be free" (they offered as models James Brown, John Coltrane, Archie Shepp, and Sun Ra). The central message of the White Panther Party was freedom—in every aspect of life, free sex, legalized drugs, freedom from wearing underwear, freedom in music—"Music is revolution." The statement ends, "Free all people from their leaders—leaders suck."

The WPP's founder was John Sinclair, a graduate student in American literature at Wayne State University in Detroit, who was also one of the cofounders and directors of the Detroit Artists' Workshop and the Artists' Workshop Press during the late 1960s. Sinclair had a scholarly devotion to jazz and the blues revival, and he wrote widely on them for *Down Beat*, *Vibrations*, and *Guerrilla: A Newspaper of Cultural Revolution*, which he coedited. But he widened his tastes as rock and roll developed and he became involved with the operation of the Detroit Rock & Roll Revival and the Grande Ballroom. And in the mid-sixties he became the manager of MC5, who along with Iggy and the Stooges, were the preeminent underground rock bands of Detroit.

In spite of Sun Ra's lack of interest in the new amplified music of rock, the staging, lights, and the sheer volume of the Arkestra alone caught the attention of the new rockers. His rap and costumes had anticipated the excesses of the late sixties. And in the meantime he had put on weight, and with his flowing robes he began to look like R. Crumb's cartoon character, Mr. Natural (and, some would say, act like him as well). But the MC5 and the Stooges also heard in the music of Sun Ra, John Coltrane, and Archie Shepp a sound which they thought they might be able to get from their amplifiers if they were overdriven. They also sought to loosen up the performances of white rockers and assume the visual and musical interaction of free jazz concerts. Under Sinclair's musical and political tutelage, the MC5 took rock and roll in directions it had only teased about before. They came on stage carrying rifles and guitars, their amps emblazoned with inverted American flags. They played thirty-minute songs, planned an album to be called *Live on Saturn*, tried to get ESP to record them, created versions of Archie Shepp's, Pharoah Sanders's and John Coltrane's compositions, and recorded "Starship" on their 1969 *Kick Out the Jams* Elektra album, using a poem from the back cover of *The Heliocentric Worlds of Sun Ra, Vol. II* ("There is a land/Whose being is almost unimaginable to the/Human mind...").

To Sinclair, Sun Ra, the Nation of Islam, and the Black Panther Party offered the only political alternatives which he saw as being non-Christian and nonwhite. Sun Ra's music seemed the essence of strangeness to many young people in the late 1960s and early 1970s, his message sufficiently ambiguous and their living arrangements close enough to a "commune," that contradictions in his beliefs and teaching were ignored by Sinclair and his followers: "We knew he was a dictator, but at least he was a benign dictator."

Sinclair's activities on behalf of legalizing drugs resulted in one police hassle after another in Detroit, so in 1967 the White Panthers moved to a house on Fraternity Row in Ann Arbor, where they continued their organizing and demonstrating. Sinclair had previously interviewed Sun Ra for *Guerrilla* and published Tam Fiofori's articles and poetry, and now he booked the Arkestra onto the same stage with the MC5 on June 18, 1967, at the Community Arts Auditorium at Wayne State University. MC5 guitarist Wayne Kramer said the audience became combative when they saw the Arkestra, and the band "thought there might be a riot until the audience figured Sun Ra out." (Shortly afterwards the MC5 were purged from the WPP after they signed with Atlantic Records and used their advance to buy Jaguars, Corvettes, and Rivieras. Sinclair said, "You guys wanted to be bigger than the Beatles, but I wanted you to be bigger than Chairman Mao.")

Sinclair brought Sun Ra and the Arkestra out to Ann Arbor for a month in May of 1969 for a series of concerts there and in Detroit, and moved them into the house next door. But Sun Ra was shocked by their hippie lifestyle—their language, drugs, their state of undress, and the police surveillance which followed them. And to make matters worse some of the Arkestra musicians were drifting over to hang out with the ladies in Sinclair's place.

Then late in 1969 Sinclair was arrested by a Detroit narcotics detective to whom he had given two marijuana cigarettes, and was sentenced to an unheard-of ten years in the State Prison of Southern Michigan at Jackson (and later the Marquette Branch Prison). He became an instant focus of international attention and a Committee to Free John Sinclair was formed which included people such as Allen Ginsberg, Jane Fonda, William Kunstler, and Mitch Ryder. On December 10, 1971, 15,000

people attended the John Sinclair Freedom Rally in the Arena in Ann
Arbor, along with John Lennon and Yoko Ono (John sang, "[It Ain't Fair]
John Sinclair"), Archie Shepp, Roswell Rudd, Allen Ginsberg, Dave
Dellinger, Bob Seger, Stevie Wonder, Bobby Seale, and Jerry Rubin.
After a federal court threw the case out and he was released in 1971, Sin-
clair continued as artistic director and coproducer of the Ann Arbor
Blues & Jazz Festival, and brought Sun Ra back for other concerts.

Talk shows were one of Sun Ra's nightly pleasures. He'd listen to any of
them long into the night, but especially to Long John Nebel, who specialized in guests who had strange stories to tell or were themselves
strange. On television Sonny regularly watched a shock talk show on
CBS run by Alan Burke, who invited the city's crackpots onto his program and viciously mocked them to the delight of his audience. One
night out of the blue Burke made a snide remark about avant-garde
artists in New York City. Later, when he received a letter from a viewer
named Sun Ra demanding equal time, he sensed it was made-to-order
Burke material, and he invited Sun Ra onto the show. On May 25, 1967,
there he was, seated among the rest of the quaint and the aberrant of
New York City that Burke counted on to be summoned before him to be
debased for a few laughs. This time, however, Burke seemed off guard,
and for him at least, almost chastened:

BURKE: What was it you wanted to say?
SUN RA: Well, the message is that the reason that America is in turmoil is because there's a nation missing among the nations, a nation from
an ancient world. And because that nation is missing and we have a void
among nations.
BURKE: What nation is that?
SR: The nation of ancient Egyptians.
BURKE: The ancient Egyptians?
SR: The Egypt that is there now is not the real Egypt, and these people have been displaced and some of the people down among the so-
called Negroes are ancient Egyptians, and the American people are mean
to these people and they're going to have to turn them loose in order to
have peace upon this planet.

BURKE: What is that, that you're playing with?

SR: Well, this is just a hat.

BURKE: It's a what?

SR: It's a hat.

BURKE: A hat? Would you put it on for us?

SR: I use it sometimes when I'm playing for a band, playing space music.

BURKE: Space music?

SR: Yeah.

BURKE: What are the instruments in this orchestra?

SR: Well, I use ordinary instruments, but actually I'm using them in a manner.... I'm using the fellows who are playing the instruments as the instrument.... It's just a matter of transforming certain ideas over into a language which the world can understand....

BURKE: Do you have a message for *us*?

SR: Yes, the message is that you must study and at least you should try and understand about the ancient Egyptians. We hear that the Negroes are in need of help and they aren't getting any and the Negroes are getting riled up and everybody is saying they're poor, and that they don't have anything, but the ancient Egyptians are never mentioned in the press or anywhere else. They've come to America from the Middle East....

BURKE: Do these ancient Egyptians that you speak of have a spokesman other than yourself?

SR: Well, who should be a better spokesman for the ancient Egyptians than I?

BURKE: Well...I, just don't know, Ra.

SR: That's the way it's written, and as it is written so it is.

BURKE: Well, I'll just have to take your word for it. I, uh, thank you for coming up and good luck in your pyramid.

SR: What I want to say is that I have this space music which has a message of its own which is that...

BURKE: I'd like to have you back sometime and hear your space music. Would you make arrangements?

SR: Quite so, it's time for America to hear it.

BURKE: I don't know if we're ready for it, but I'd be delighted to listen to it. Thank you so much.

At a concert at the newly opened Olatunji Center of African Culture *Atlantis* was recorded, a twenty-one-minute epic, with Sun Ra on Clavioline and "Solar Sound Organ" (a Gibson Kalamazoo Organ, a copy of the original Farfissa combo organ used by pop groups). The piece began ominously with sonar beeps from the organ, and as it developed, Sun Ra rolled his hands on the keys, pressing his forearm along the keyboard, played with his hands upside down, slashing and beating the keyboard, spinning around and around, his hands windmilling at the keys—a virtual sonic representation of the flooding of Atlantis; it was a great smear of a solo, Sun Ra's "Toccata and Fugue." Five minutes later the brass entered, and then a rather conventionally notated swing saxophone-section melody surfaced to be undercut first by brutal bursts from the organ and then by the brass and drums. The weight, the sheer gravity of the piece which developed was almost unbearable. And then suddenly the Arkestra shifted to the "Sun Ra and his Band from Outer Space are here to entertain you" chant, as if "Atlantis" had just been another pop song in an evening's dance band repertoire.

When word reached Sun Ra of John Coltrane's death, he was distraught. Even though they had only met a few times Sun Ra felt that Coltrane was truly remarkable, both as a man and a musician, and that he even had messianic qualities. At some moments he seemed to take the responsibility for his death on himself—claimed that he should have given him more warnings, or that the secret knowledge that he had told him was too much for him to handle; but at other times he said that Coltrane had been warned, that if he had joined the Arkestra it would never have happened, and it was his own fault. The Arkestra played at a memorial for Coltrane at the University of Pennsylvania shortly after his death, and for years afterwards Sun Ra would suddenly bring up Coltrane's passing in conversations as an object lesson—whether to himself or to others was not always clear.

■ ■ ■

It was a time in which black people were rebelling in city after city, with Detroit and Newark already in flames; there were demonstrations at the Pentagon, and Muhammad Ali had been arrested for draft resistance; the Democratic National Convention was beset with riots, Columbia University had been brought to a halt by its students, SNCC, yippies, Weathermen, every conceivable fissure and crack seemed to be opening. Then Martin Luther King, Jr., was assassinated. To many the country seemed to be on the edge of revolution. All of this had been predicted, of course, but it was becoming difficult for Sun Ra to keep apart from race, politics, religion, to maintain his low profile as messenger, and to dismiss it all as the rotten fruit of the tree of earth. His constant tirades against the planet were as always heard as condemnations of white Americans, or at least the United States. His spiritual message was being turned into a mere political posture. He had doubts about Martin Luther King, Jr.'s program from the beginning, because King had put his weight behind freedom and equality—a mistake, Sun Ra thought, since they were false idols. And King seemed to him too willing to placate his followers, to tell them what they wanted to hear. And revolution made even less sense: that was for white people to play at.

The Arkestra meanwhile had picked up a part-time manager, Lem Roebuck, who had gotten them concerts in the parks, sometimes with as many as thirty musicians, through Simon Bly, a man who staged musical events in Jackie Robinson Park on 145th Street and other parks in the city and who also ran an Afro-art gallery uptown. Roebuck had seen a dancer and singer in Bly's series of outdoor Broadway musicals who, he told Sun Ra, would broaden his appeal. So Roebuck talked June Tyson into coming to a rehearsal, telling her that Sun Ra was more knowledgeable than anyone she'd ever met, and that this was a great career opportunity for her. At the first rehearsal she worked on "Somebody Else's Idea" (a song also known as "Somebody Else's World"), which Sun Ra told her was a "space cha-cha." It wasn't clear to her where she should start singing and stop, so he pointed to her when she was to come in. At the end of rehearsal Sun Ra simply told her when the next gig was.

June Tyson became more than a singer and dancer with the Arkestra. Her blissful smile, guileless orations, and flowing movements introduced a new dimension into the show. She became Sun Ra's foil in front of the band—sometimes as his shadow, as his handmaiden, or as goddess of space. She helped liberate Sun Ra from the keyboards, and made it easier for him to come to the front of the band: first as leader and conductor, then as quasidancer himself, with her beside him, holding his hand, leading him around the stage, displaying his robes, crowns, and jewelry.

But June's presence in the band, not just at performances but at rehearsals on a day-to-day basis, presented a problem. Sun Ra viewed women as potentially dangerous, as distractions from the divine purpose. He resolved the problem by treating June as family, and since she was married to Richard Wilkinson, who he hired to handle sound-and-light shows, the familial relationship was doubled and extended. Over time she became very important to him, as a performer, but also as adviser on stage routines, clothing, and personal matters. On tours they went shopping together, took walks, and had long conversations. In later years Sun Ra bought her a violin, and even before she knew how to play it he worked her into the band. Yet it was still possible for him to sometimes ask her to leave the recording studio if things were not going well: "I can't create with women in my environment."

Just after June had joined the Arkestra, Sun Ra decided to add another dancer-singer, Verta Mae Grosvenor, an actress in the Village scene who lived just around the corner. She was tall and moved with a regal air, and he thought she would bring a certain tone to the productions:

One day Jacson knocked on my door with a stack of Saturn records and some poems and said, "Sun Ra said"—mind you, I'd never had a conversation with Sun Ra, I just lived near Slug's—"Sun Ra said for you to read these things over and listen to the music and the gig is going to be Wednesday at seven o'clock at such-and-such church." So I read the poems and listened to the music. And I wondered, what did the records mean? How did they fit together with the poems?

I sat there with my sheets of poems and Sun Ra said, "When I nod, you get up and read." And I said, which one? And he said, "You'll know." Since I can't sing sometimes I was allowed to carry the Sun sphere. I sometimes carried things I found, like silver beads...things I found and took to rehearsal. Sometimes he would be very specific about poems. Or he might give me a stack of them, since he was constantly writing new ones.

"June Tyson and I integrated the band," Grosvenor said, "and we had to develop roles which fit with the Arkestra. So we decided to be space goddesses," roles they played for all they were worth. Choreography, costuming, and poetry were all tightly related, and the two women began to add their own devices:

> June had developed her own moves, which were more dancelike, so we had to learn to move together. And we had to make our own costumes. We had these heavy capes, and I discovered I could enhance the walk by swirling them.
>
> I lived near Orchard Street, so I went down there to shop, and I found this metallic fabric... and since it was cheap, I asked for twenty yards of it. The owner was wondering, "What do they do with this stuff?" June and I took this fabric... and you know that old-fashioned way that people used to fold a sheet? We did that on stage and played around with it. It was very serious business: it became the metallic fabric of life!
>
> When we were rehearsing for Carnegie Hall I had to have something to do on the stage. I had no idea what to do, how to get from one place to another, and the stage at Carnegie Hall is *long*! I was scared! So I developed the space walk—the one that Michael Jackson did later and called it the "moon walk." Larry Neal saw me and said he thought, "What is she doing up there with Ra?" He told me, "I know you can't sing, you can't dance, you can't play an instrument... but, girl, you can *walk*!"

Like Isadora Duncan (who adopted Greek dress, posture, and motion for her dancers from Grecian urns) and Ruth St. Denis (who modeled her costumes and dances on Egyptian illustrations on Fatima cigarette packages), Sun Ra's dancers looked to Egyptian wall drawings for inspiration, while still seeking the same natural, easy flow of motion that modern dancers sought. Yet they also could assume postures reminiscent of the neoclassical photography of the 1930s where nudes held discs or balloons on their shoulders.

> There comes a point where musicians, being limited by man-made instruments, can't bend to a certain thing you want to express. The dancers have to bend, so they can express music the band can't. The dancers become a note by the way they stand or move, and the people can feel it.

Sun Ra gave the dancers little more than a sketch of what was going to happen and what they were to do. A later singer-dancer with the Arkestra, Rhoda Blount (who was not related to Sun Ra, though he enjoyed introducing her as his daughter), said that he cautioned her that she "sang too much in time...and did the same when she danced." And there were too many straight lines in her dancing. "You should dance 'out.' " Since he had been involved in coaching dancers in Chicago he had a conception of some of the things dancers were capable of. Later he hired Robert Johnson, director of the Pittsburgh Afro-American Dance Company, as a dancer-choreographer, and at times there were as many as six or seven dancers on the stage. And when they went on well-funded European tours, the dancers were a central part of the show, with their flowing earth-tone robes and scarab pins. "Butterflies of the night," one French journalist called them.

Once after a long night at Slug's, Verta Mae walked back to her apartment a couple blocks away on Houston and got into bed, only to realize that she had no milk for her children's cereal when they woke up. She slipped a coat on over her nightgown and went back out on the street to an all-night *bodega*, when a man approached her and cried out,

"Just hold it, space bitch! You're not going nowhere!" And it was the kind of thing where your mama always told you to wear clean underwear so if something happened...? So I ducked into the store, and this guy says to the two people working there, "She may be foolin' ya'll, but she's not foolin' me, 'cause she's not *from* here." And this guy is ranting and raving. The store owner warned me not to go outside, and he went in the back to call the police.

When the police arrived, the policeman said, "Ma'am, I don't know how to say this, but this guy says you're from outer space." "What do you think is going on with him?" he asked. I told the cop, "I have no idea. I need to get back for my children's breakfast." And then the cops walked me home. This poor guy had been at Slug's and was doped up, hung over, and everything else...and when he saw me as he walked past the store it just put him over the edge.

■ ■ ■

Early in 1968 George F. Schutz, a producer who had presented Mozart cycles at Lincoln Center and who had been associated with performers like the German jazz and classical pianist Friedrich Gulda, proposed two nights of concerts for the Arkestra at Carnegie Hall. Schutz wanted to announce Sun Ra's presence in a big way, bringing East Village culture uptown for the first time, and their press release announced "The Space Music of Sun Ra as a free-form excursion into the far reaches of sight and sound." In addition to the Arkestra there would be the Chuck Davis dancers, a light show designed by the Pablo Light Company (who had worked with Charles Lloyd's early efforts at bridging jazz and hippie culture), and Sun Ra's poetry read by Willis Conover, who would also be broadcasting the performance worldwide on Voice of America. A serious effort was made by everyone to promote the concert. Conover's wife even handed out promotional literature on the streets of Harlem. Sonny threw himself into the project, increasing the size of the Arkestra and writing new parts. He brought in Lucious Randolph from Chicago, Art Jenkins, and Bob Northern. And just before the concert he added saxophonist Danny Thompson (nicknamed "Pico" after the Los Angeles boulevard near where he was raised). As a child Thompson had been an actor and a musician and was encouraged by his mother to try out all the arts. When he came to New York he first played with Olatunji. Later, when he approached Sun Ra about playing with the Arkestra, Sonny assigned him to watching the house on Monday nights while the band was playing at Slug's; after a while he was moved to van driver, a job he continued to hold for years. Once he began playing in the Arkestra his first role was playing a bass line on the baritone to fill in for a missing bass player. Within a few years Thompson was to become one of the most trusted people in Sun Ra's entourage, and some even said, the heir apparent to the leader.

On April 12 and 13, the week after Martin Luther King was assassinated, the Arkestra played Carnegie Hall. The stage was in almost total darkness, while red and green lights flashed from the band and a light show played above the twenty musicians. Still shots of Sun Ra, the moon's surface, Saturn, and abstract images were projected on the ceiling and the

backdrops, along with two experimental films, the minimalist composer
Phill Niblock's "The Magic Sun" (close-ups of the Arkestra shot in
high-contrast black-and-white) and Maxine Haller's "The Forbidden
Playground," performed with the Edith Stephen Dance Theater.
Singing and poetry recitation went on offstage. The lights came up only
for a moment, just enough to show that the Arkestra was in red, green,
and orange robes, but then sank back to semidarkness. Players wandered
off and on stage, sometimes changing their costumes. Sun Ra strolled
about with one of the dancers on his arm, another behind him ringing
bells, and ended the concert by marching with the band through the audience. Scarcely 500 people attended each night, and Sun Ra was angry
that no sizable black audience turned out: "So what happened? They
killed Reverend King. They was so involved with him that they couldn't
see me."

Before the concert John S. Wilson gave Sun Ra the largest coverage he
had ever gotten, a preconcert piece spread over two pages in the *New
York Times*. But afterwards, Wilson was disappointed again, this time by
the staging. The lighting was so dark, he said, that the Arkestra was invisible and seemed to be accompanying the light show, films, and
dancers. A super-happening, the *New Yorker* sniffed, but "It wasn't a good
movie, and it wasn't a good concert, and it wasn't good Dadaism. It wasn't
even adept put-on."

The Arkestra continued to pick up work of all sorts, in part because they
could play anything but also because they would sometimes work for almost nothing. They did incidental music for a half-hour experimental
radio play, Maxine Haller's "The Stranger," for WBAI in New York,
which was in turn featured on Pacifica Radio stations as part of the
"Mind's Eye Theater" series. The Arkestra became regulars at The East,
a black cultural center in Brooklyn which had profound influence on the
development of Afrocentric thinking and politics in New York City
(though the few whites who even knew of its existence only knew it as a
place which would not admit them for jazz performances). Sun Ra was
honored there once for a whole day as a key figure in the black cultural
revolution.

From June through July the Arkestra played to small crowds ("we scared them away") at the 300-seat Garrick Theatre on Bleecker Street, where the year before Frank Zappa's Mothers of Invention had been ripping the heads off dolls two nights a week. Each show started in the dark, with a film projected on the wall of hands playing flutes and horns in close-up, followed by the musicians segueing into the live performance. There were fourteen musicians on the stage and along the sides and back of the theater, and slides were shown from a handheld projector.

They even played a couple of weddings, one for Latins downtown, and a Quaker ceremony for a couple who had first met at Slug's. Michael Zwerin of the *Voice* was in attendance, and said that the band played a quiet, Webernesque wedding march to start:

> After the vows, however, total energy beyond fortissisimo. Honking, sheets of sound, grunts, and screams; everybody playing as loud and fast as possible at the same time. A good half hour later, even though the Friends Meeting Hall is deserted, there is still full scale sound there.

In August they went to Washington, D.C., for the first time to play one of a series of black cultural events in the atrium of the Corcoran Gallery of Art arranged by Gaston Neal of D.C.'s New School of Afro-American Thought. Sun Ra brought his whole museum without walls with him—films, slides, paintings, twenty musicians in robes, leggings, and leopard skins, along with various exotic drums, gongs, bells, harps, and amplified cello, and six dancers and three singers. Reviewer Paul Richard of the *Washington Post* said that this was the first time that the Corcoran had been able to draw a black audience, though they had no idea what was going on. "Sun Ra was a kind of black John Cage," but his "happenings" were not "pitiful and dull" like most. The words they sang and chanted "sound vapid, slogan-vague," but they took on weight in the context of the ritual atmosphere. And at the end of the performance Sun Ra bestowed names on the musicians for the rest of the evening by touching their shoulders and calling them "Saturn," "Neptune," "Yesterday and Beyond."

■ ■ ■

The Arkestra's performances were structured into what Sun Ra called the "cosmo drama," or the "myth-ritual," a program which expressed his beliefs and which he sought to offer as a model for changing the people of Earth. He said it was like a passion play; it dealt in myth because truth was ugly, evil, and too threatening to be expressed openly in words. He originally conceived of this musical drama for black people only, for he saw them as literally prehistoric, not part of history, not taken to be real within the society in which they live. "If you are not a reality, whose myth are you?" Astro-Black mythology was the idea at first:

> ...something that's greater than the truth.... Myth was here before history. That's what everybody was dealing with before history. They was dealing with myth...but they were more pliable, you see. But when they started with history, the truth, it could move, and they put a lot of lies in there. [With "Astro-"] I'm talking about space; I'm talking about not being part of this planet, because it's not proper. The big experimental thing, the people doing all kind of things that's terribly improper—they got the planet on the edge of chaos and destruction with what they call "the truth" and what they call "God." Everything they got here is improper; it doesn't fit with the universe and is selfish and egotistical.

Astro-Black mythology was a way of expressing the unity of Egypt and outer space, of bringing a black reading of the Bible together with elements of ancient history and science to update the black sacred cosmos.

But as his music began to find more favor with whites than blacks he changed direction. He spoke of creating myths of the future. Myths have always been about the past, to explain what happened. He proposed myths to tell us what we should do. The future that people talk about is no good; we need to do the impossible, for everything possible has been tried and has failed. Truth (the possible) equals death; but myth (the impossible) equals immortality.

Music could be a bridge to potential, to the future; it's possible to paint pictures of infinity with music. "The bridge" was a metaphor for another reality, a break with the cyclic order of birth and death. Music could be used to coordinate minds. It could touch the unknown part of the person, awaken the part of them that we're not able to talk to, the spirit.

The order of the cosmo drama is simple enough to describe: stage performances might be opened by the thunder drum alone, which was then joined by a wind instrument, perhaps the bass clarinet or bassoon; or the kora, an African harp, might be the first heard; or a trombone, played furiously, the slide menacing those seated near the stage. Other musicians came on stage playing on percussion instruments of various sorts, then picked up other instruments and improvised together (Sun Ra said that when you walked on stage, the audience should hear music from the way you walk). Though the opening appeared unique, it was yet another version of staggered entry, one instrument added to another, often in different rhythms or meters, until all were playing together—a formula as old as Africa and as new as rhythm and blues. Then suddenly they stopped, as June Tyson entered, singing "Along Came Ra," with Sun Ra brought out by the dancers; "Discipline 27" would be next, then a series of complex group improvisations directed by Sun Ra through hand signals; there might also be mimed battles between duos or quartets of horns, with the whole band joined in, the music building in intensity and volume to the point of chaos; interspersed throughout Sun Ra might offer variations on popular maxims or homilies, like "To be or not to be. That's the question?" Or he might ask the audience to join hands to help conquer death. Or he'd chant or sermonize, with the Arkestra repeating back every sentence: "This world is not my home. My home is out there," or "The truth about mankind is a bad truth." He might then introduce a soloist by saying, "Here is Marshall Allen. He's going to tell you about Saturn." Or he might ask June to cry for the people of earth, and she and the band would begin to cry, and then the audience. An electric keyboard solo could come next, rising from a few strange sounds to a storm of flailed and crushed keys. The drummer might lean over, strike, and then scream into his cymbals. Then a calmer series of older pop songs or swing arrangements followed, possibly with a vocal or two, leading to a number of space hymns or anthems like "Love in Outer Space" or "The Satellites Are Spinning." Meanwhile, there were dances of various sorts, light shows and slides, art displays, films, and even juggling, tumbling, or fire eating. Finally the Arkestra would circle about the stage, making eye contact with the audience, talking to them, maybe surrounding one unlucky person, the horns howling all the while, as Sun Ra shouted in his or her face, "If you're willing to give up your life for your country, will you give up your death for me?" One such initiate, George Mostoller, recalls his experience in the Squat Theater in 1978:

> As the song rose in intensity with the combined voices of the Arkestra and the band began to snake its way again and again around the two aisles of the Squat, I sat there in utter amazement, awestruck at what I heard and the idea that all forms of music could be played at once and that the man who had just done this was now snaking his way towards me in an absurdly beautiful Cosmic Robe.
>
> And then suddenly I was awe*stricken,* even terrified, as Sun Ra, bigger than seemed possible, with eyes that seemed to be two blood red slits, reached down and grabbed me up out of my seat and held me to his side with some combination of compassion for my terror and sheer ferocity, as he forced me to kick-step my way around the Squat Theater with him. Unfortunately at the time I had never done much dancing—only what was required in four weeks of eighth grade gym class—and my sorry ass could not get in step. As we completed the first circle the two friends I had come with were chuckling. By the second, they were turning purple, and by the third, the entire audience was in tears. I was hopelessly mortified as I had been on only one or two occasions of public foolishness, but I will never forget the look Sun Ra gave me that told me it just didn't matter. Transcend. I couldn't quite then, not in those circumstances, but the concept was planted and I have never heard music the same way since.

Then they would leave the room dancing to something like "We Travel the Spaceways."

What is not so easy to convey about the cosmo drama is that every performance had a distinctive texture, a feel to it that set it apart. Sun Ra assayed the audience and the venue and made adjustments. But Verta Mae Grosvenor also says that some of the variations depended on what they had been rehearsing just before the performance:

> If we had just rehearsed a new song we did it that night. But Sun Ra directed it. You might not know the specific time, but if it was of a certain type, you knew it would be one of fifteen chaotic pieces to be played at a point where there was supposed to be chaos.

Although Sun Ra signaled the performers as to what they should do next, they did not always pick up the correct cue:

> Sometimes when I think that a poem ought to be said by one of them I say a word or two of it to them. I begin, for example, to say the first verse of a poem. It has happened that I have said just one word and one of them has misunderstood the poem—what does it matter? The program has been slightly modified, a part of the program has come on before another which will follow, but the same spirit of creation is always there.

In any case, different nights had a different focus, according to Danny Thompson, determined by occasion and location:

> We have as many as fifteen different arrangements of the same piece— such as "El Is the Sound of Joy"—and any one might be used. It was adjusted to the time, the city, to what people need to hear.

Sun Ra said that he was now following the outlines of constellations in his stage marches and shuffle dances.

Though the opening of the show usually began with Jacson alone on the thunder drum, some nights Sun Ra would call for something else. Sometimes the whole band would begin to play before the audience was allowed to enter the theater (and sometimes they continued to play after the curtain had gone down and the lights had come up, sending the audience out in the streets singing "Space is the place"). Once in Germany he asked Jacson to open with a bassoon solo. "This," said Jacson, "was not something I wanted to do; the Germans were the people who had invented the bassoon." So when he walked onto the stage he was shaky, and just as he began to play, he split the reed, unleashing a howl. But the audience responded with applause and shouts of encouragement, and Jacson continued to play, coaxing screams and shrieks out of the horn.

Sun Ra liked to open performances with a shock, hoping to drive out the hopeless and awaken the rest:

> I like all the sounds that upset people, because they're too complacent, and there are some sounds that really upset them, and man, you need to

shock them out of their complacency, 'cause it's a very bad world in a lot of aspects. They need to wake to how bad it is: then maybe they'll do something about it. It is really a far chance to take, but I think they should take it.

He stressed spontaneity over everything else. Once during "Shadow World," Marshall Allen, Danny Thompson, and Danny Davis were playing collectively when two of Thompson's baritone saxophone keys came loose and flew out into the audience. But he continued to play, stuffing his fingers into the holes to maintain the sound flow. Then his thumb got stuck in one of the holes. When Davis and Allen got tired, Thompson kept playing, not knowing how to get his hand out of his horn. Afterwards Sun Ra said to Marshall, "You need to be creative like that; he was so creative he tore the keys off; he was like that little Dutch boy and the dike!"

Some of this music and the way it was sequenced sounded very strange on record, but it made a kind of visual sense when seen live, even though it was apparent that there was little agreement in the audience as to what they were seeing. Even the Arkestra members did not share the same interpretation of the cosmo drama. Of their marches and dances through the audience at the end of the shows, trumpeter Ahmed Abdullah said that since what they were playing was essentially folk music, leaving the bandstand as they did was a statement about that; similarly, others said that it was a way of getting close to the audience. But Sun Ra said, "My musicians leaving the stage at the end symbolize leaving the planet while alive, rather than dead. You hear the voices leaving. I also use this on records, but live the sound diminishes gradually."

The atmosphere created in the latter part of the performance seemed churchlike, calling up to some people memories of Baptist pageants and Sunday services, sermons, and hymns, the interplay of preacher, choir, and congregation which leads to ecstasy. "Rocket Number Nine" (which may have been written as early as 1943 while Sun Ra was still in Birmingham) closely follows the spiritual "No Hiding Place":

The space age is here to stay
Ain't no place that you can run away

If you run to the rock to hide your face
The rock'll cry out, no hiding place

It's gonna be just like your ancestors said
Even though they're cold and dead

Many of his chants alluded to "All God's Chillun Got Wings," "Ezek'el Saw the Wheel," "Swing Low, Sweet Chariot," "This World Is Not My Home" and other hymns and spirituals, evoking a world in which people fly all over heaven, ride chariots in the sky, and are reunited in the Promised Land. One of his chants exhorted his listeners to comprehend the seriousness of their situation and prepare to leave with him:

You're on the spaceship Earth
And you're outward bound
Out among the stars
Destination unknown
But you haven't met the captain of the spaceship
    yet, have you?
You'd better pay your fare now
You'll be left behind
You'll be left hangin'
In the empty air
You won't be here and you won't be there

Its roots lie in the Baptist hymn "The Old Ship of Zion":

Tis the old ship of Zion
She has landed many thousand
King Jesus is her captain
O, get your ticket ready
She is coming in the harbor
She will land safe in heaven

but also in "The Downward Road is Crowded with Unbelieving Souls":

You can't ride the empty air
And get to heaven that day

These chants were usually done with the Arkestra shuffling, making little jumps, and clapping in a counterclockwise circle as in the old Negro shouts; and, as in the folk form, these events unified this world with the next and provided a sense of their true "home," to which they were "climbing up," "moving on up," or "climbin' the mountain."

Yet no one in the Arkestra appeared to be in ecstatic possession, or in deep mimesis; rather they seemed to be modeling a certain kind of social and spiritual order, eclectically drawing theatrics from many sources other than the Afro-Baptist church: the flash of black cabaret, bar-walking saxophonists, nightclub routines, vaudeville and tent shows, as well as from the big bands themselves, which often had their own resident comics, dancers, skits, and parodies which reflected their early experiences in vaudeville and tent shows. Sun Ra certainly knew opera, with its echoes of Greek tragedy, its frequent settings in ancient cultures or other worlds, its lavishness, the hyperbole of texts, the use of recitatives and arias; and he was acquainted with Richard Wagner's concept of the total work of art with its operatic technology of stereophonic effects, acoustic hallucinations, cries, moans, screams, echoes, wind; the use of fire, total darkness in the theater, the astronomy of *Tristan,* mythical dramaturgy, and the orchestra as army, as emblem of power.

The synesthetic quality of the cosmo dramas also had many sources: barrooms, clubs, and dance halls, of course, many of which used colored lights, prisms, and mirrors for effects. The light shows of the sixties also converged on Sun Ra's productions. They had begun on the West Coast in the Beat colony of San Francisco in the late 1950s, and by the early 1960s they had been mixed with films in rock clubs, and didn't reach the East Coast and London until the midsixties. But there were older sources to these displays as well, which Sun Ra was aware of: the color-producing organs of Europe which had been conceived as early as the eighteenth century, and Scriabin's use of colored lights to reinforce and correlate with specific sounds.

Though Sun Ra seldom offered information on his effects, he said that he used lights and dancers because they made the music more real; and in later years he explained projecting video clips of African dancers behind the band as a way of showing that his music worked with any form of dance.

SPACE FELLOW TRAVELERS

Stefan Brecht had exaggerated when he said that Sun Ra was not ironic. But Sun Ra was going to need a lot more irony to protect himself from what was about to happen, for at the end of the sixties he was destined to be connected to a massive symbolic convergence of drugs, space, and rock and roll that was too global for even him to control.

In London Steve Stollman, the brother of the founder of ESP, was putting on "Spontaneous Underground" sessions weekends at the Marquee Club where free jazz was played, happenings were staged, films were shown on the walls behind performers, and where a new group called Pink Floyd made its debut in the spring of 1966. They were a band influenced by AMM, a theatrical group of experimental jazz musicians organized in 1965, who used stage lighting, costumes, and homemade instruments, and from time to time added experimental composers like Cornelius Cardew and Christian Wolff to their group. Soon Pink Floyd became the first British group to use a full light show on stage, with the individual players subordinated by the lighting. And by 1966 they were simulating space with pieces such as "Astronomy Dominé," "Set the Controls for the Heart of the Sun," or "Interstellar Overdrive," long, free-form instrumentals that would soon be labeled "freak-outs" by the cognoscenti. It would all culminate in their 1973 recording, *Dark Side of the Moon*.

Right behind them came other space-oriented bands: Hawkwind, whose "Space Ritual" tour got under way in November 1971, using slide projections of planets, bleak landscapes, strobe lights, and a saxophonist who played in the free style; the Grateful Dead (whose "Dark Star" seemed to acknowledge Sun Ra indirectly), Jefferson Airplane (later Starship), David Bowie, Gong, Soft Machine, George Clinton, and a horde of German space musicians such as Can, Amon Duul, Tangerine Dream, and Klaus Schulze. Perhaps the strangest of the lot was Bobby Beausoleil (the lover of filmmaker Kenneth Anger, now serving a life sentence for murder), who created a band modeled after Sun Ra's called the Orkustra which played throughout California in the mid-1960s.

But none of the space bands were as lavishly outrageous as Parliament-Funkadelic, a postdisco funk band whose leader George Clinton arrived on stage in white ermine and feathers in his own version of the Mothership. Populated by a cast of characters which included Sir Nose D'Void of Funk, Star Child, and Dr. Funkenstein, Clinton's cartoon-cosmic epic unfolded on the stage: early scenes announced the Earth was out of touch with the One, without funk, and Earth people were suffering from Placebo Syndrome, the lack of the Real Thing. Then Dr. Funkenstein managed to retrieve the funk from Sir Nose (who lives in the Nose Zone, or the Zone of Zero Funkativity, and who had been shot by Star Child's Bop Gun) and was once again spreading funk across the Earth. Near the end of the performance guitarist Gary Shider sailed over the audience, dressed as a diapered angel, and Clinton boarded his ship again and took off. The liner notes to the 1974 album *Standing on the Verge of Gettin' It On* offer a synopsis of Clinton's message:

On the Eighth Day, the Cosmic Strumpet of Mother Nature was spawned to envelope this Third Planet in FUNKADELICAL VIBRA-TIONS. And she birthed Apostles Ra, Hendrix, Stone, and CLINTON to preserve all funkiness of man unto eternity.... But! Fraudulent forces of obnoxious JIVATION grew; Sun Ra strobed back to Saturn to await his next reincarnation. Jimi was forced back into his basic atoms; Sly was co-opted into a jester monolith and ... only seedling GEORGE remained! As it came to be, he did indeed begat FUNKADELIC to restore order Within the Universe. And, nourished from the pamgrierian mammaristic melodpops of Mother Nature, the followers of FUNKADELIA multi-plied incessantly!

Clinton's astral ritual seems as inspired by the Nation of Islam as it is by Sun Ra, and when he was asked about the Ra in 1979, Clinton said, "This boy was definitely out to lunch—the same place I eat at."

Other bands showed the influence of ancient Egypt: Arthur Brown (who wore "Sun God robes" on stage), Rameses, Sphynx (who dressed as mummies on stage and used a portable pyramid as a prop, as did the Glastonbury Fayre, who in June of 1973 had a large replica of the Great Pyramid in their stage shows); Earth, Wind and Fire's cosmic Egyptology, who by 1974 had musicians flying over the audience in harnesses or suddenly disappearing, and later began to wear both space suits and Egyptian robes on stage, the band dancing together with the singers.

But Sun Ra also had his detractors by this time, especially among older African-American musicians, many of whom were mercilessly nasty in their comments. Singer Betty Carter, for instance, once dismissed Sun Ra in an interview that bothered him for years afterwards:

> Sun Ra. They play Europe a lot. He's got his metallic clothes on, his lights flashing back and forth, and he's got the nerve to spell orchestra a-r-k-e-s-t-r-a. It's supposed to have something to do with stars and Mars, but it's nothing but bullshit. Sun Ra has got whitey going for it. He couldn't go uptown and do that to blackie. He would be chased off the stage in Harlem or in Bedford-Stuyvesant.

In the pages of *Down Beat* Brooks Johnson, a Chicago promoter, criticized Sun Ra for precisely the opposite reason, for driving whites away by being a "neo-neo-Tom"—one who makes a career out of being black, one for whom "everything musical is ultimately the product of, or reduces itself to the color of his skin":

> ... Sun Ra is tomming. He's helping and encouraging the very thing he abhors, the closed clique of power that controls his musical life. He does this not because he is too daring and creative in the sound he produces but because his view about life and how to beat it is distorted. Success is not based on alienation, but on accommodation. Even success in the purest artistic sense (i.e., removed from pecuniary considerations) is based upon accommodating the ideas and impulses of the artist to his manual and physical talents. Sun Ra, in attempting to alienate from his

own work the white man, stunts his own potential. In short, he Toms as part of his contribution to jazz.

But Sun Ra also found defenders in strange quarters: his myth-ritual would years later be seen by music writer Martha Bayles as part of the "positive" efforts of Jimi Hendrix, Sly Stone, and James Brown at "celebration and survival," not a part of what she perceived as George Clinton's camp cynicism, a music lacking spirituality, a part of the anarchistic, nihilistic impulses of the European avant-garde's influence on pop culture.

As New York City became aware of the shift of demographics taking place in the East Village, the police began to pay more attention to the area, and the Arkestra was regularly being warned about the noise at rehearsals. So when the landlord decided to put the house up for sale Sun Ra saw that it was time for a move. Marshall Allen's father owned some property in Philadelphia and offered to rent them a row house at 5626 Morton Street in Germantown. So in the fall of 1968 Sun Ra moved to what he called "the city of Brotherly shove," the "worst place in America," "the headquarters of the devil in disguise"). It was certainly a city with more than its share of cults, unorthodox religions, prophets, and dissidents: the site of the founding of the Rosicrucians in the United States; the final earthly home of Father Divine and Prophet Cherry; and over the next two decades it would yield up corporate hippie New Age guru-turned-murderer Ira Einhorn and religio-political cults like Move (both of whom pursued Sun Ra), and a variety of other bizarre figures. And though Sonny was never specific about the devil in Philadelphia, he did take notice of the fact that Morton Street was the same street on which then Police Commissioner Frank Rizzo had once lived.

Despite his hyperbole, the relocation to Philadelphia was actually a move on up: the house was a sandstone row house typical of the area, but because of the peculiar siting of the houses across the street, the Arkestra's house faced a parklike group of trees. (One of those trees was a few years later struck by lightning just after Sun Ra told Jacson that he should have a new drum; Jacson then hollowed the tree trunk out and carved it with an Egyptian bas-relief.) They adapted the house to their spirits, painted the front window frames blue ("haint blue" they would have called it in South Carolina, to ward off evil); covering the window glass with aluminum foil (to reflect light and symbolize life, according to those of spiritual bent; to keep the narcs from seeing in, said the hippies who drove past, looking for who knows what); and they covered the front door with de rigueur psychedelic swirls of color. In the 1960s Germantown was still integrated, but whites and middle-class blacks were beginning to move out to northeast Philadelphia or New Jersey, and as they did, Germantown was lumped together with the rest of this new black area—with neighborhoods like Mount Airy and Cheltenham—as "North Philadelphia."

But there were problems with the move. Philadelphia had only one or two jazz clubs, and even they were beginning to tilt towards pop music; and in any case the Arkestra was almost unknown in Philadelphia, so finding work was going to be tough. On top of this, the Arkestra's musicians were now spread between New York and Philadelphia (and Chicago and Birmingham, for that matter) and Sun Ra had to begin recruiting some local players to take up the slack at rehearsals in the crowded front room of the house. When they lacked enough musicians to make the compositions sound right he hoped that the few who were there would be enough to carry them when they played with the full group. But in spite of now having their own house, they seldom had enough musicians at rehearsals to do what he wanted, and often had to fall back on older pieces to carry them in performances where some of the musicians did not know the new music. The swing re-creations especially began to suffer from younger players who were not raised in that tradition and got very little rehearsal on them. And with time, even Sun Ra's older arrangements had to be simplified to accommodate new musicians on the gig.

Rehearsals created a few complaints from their new neighbors, but when the police arrived Sonny told them they were merely making a joyous noise to the Lord in the city as the Good Book required. And gradually they became known as good neighbors, especially liked by the kids. Within a year there was a record by the Arkestra on the juke box in the neighborhood laundromat and Sonny was listed in the Philadelphia phone book as "Ra, Sun." (The phone was sometimes answered by an ominous voice which proclaimed, "You have reached Outer Space." "I was afraid to look at my phone bill at the end of the month," said one journalist who dared to call.)

Despite the distance from Philadelphia, the Arkestra traveled back and forth to New York for long Monday nights at Slug's and various other gigs. For years, early-morning commuters were startled as they boarded the Metroliner to Philadelphia to find spacemen sleeping among their fellow passengers.

CHAPTER FIVE

When winter arrived in Philadelphia in 1968 the Arkestra drove out West for a series of jobs they had cobbled together in California even though they were virtually unknown there. Still, the rise of black nationalism had laid a kind of groundwork for them where their performances could be viewed by those who cared to do so as part of a renewal of bonds with Africa. They set out across the country in a van, these cosmic adventurers, most of whom had never been west of Illinois. Driving straight through, day and night, they reached California just in time for their first performance at the College of Marin on December 6, where a banner over the door reading "Soul Is Takin' Over" greeted them. The Arkestra had eleven musicians, June Tyson, four dancers, and Richard Wilkinson, who Sun Ra had been teaching to use mirrors, pieces of cloth, art works, slides, and films for the cosmo drama. They were dressed in capes, vests, and brightly colored shirts, with bells on their ankles. The dancers carried paintings around the stage, stepping carefully over dozens of instruments; the whole saxophone section rose from their seats and descended into the audience, strolling, conversing musically, then returning to the stage to surround the conga drum player and urge him on; the two alto saxophonists, Danny Davis and Marshall Allen, sparred in a duet of howls and screams, climaxed by the two of them rolling on the floor while still playing; the dancers were dressed in capes so long they formed trains, and Sun Ra strolled about the stage with a crystal ball. The evening concluded with the whole band marching around the theater, a few musicians dueling in the back of the auditorium with a member of the audience. Sun Ra's museum without walls was on the road.

And on they went, to San Jose State College the next day, the Oakland Auditorium Theater the next week, and on December 14, the San Francisco Art Institute. John Burks wrote up the show as a funky fashion event (not surprisingly, as it was for *Rolling Stone*):

Sun Ra himself is usually the most resplendent, attired in floor-length robes that sparkle and shimmer, in a tiger-skin sun hat, ornamented with several pendants and sunbursts draped here and there. Sun Ra is forever splitting from the stage to do costume changes. He's got robes of every color in the spectrum. Sometimes as many as twenty changes per concert.

"It's constant change, see," he explains. "We keep the lights changing ... and the costumes changing. ..." At first he designed all his own, and the band's, apparel. But having set the style, he found that people all over the country were making stuff and giving it to them. So now they lovingly accept and wear everything that comes their way. All these dashikis and togas and hats of every dimension and badges and crests and sparkles and dangles. The two chicks who sing (rather badly) with the band are especially spacey in their skintight playsuits, draped with filminess and full capes and beads and sun jewelry, with their turquoise boots and golden hoods and space shades.

Almost everybody in the band wears shades while they play, but the space shades... Sun Ra and the girls wear are really *too* much. They're opaque lenses—the outsized eyepieces—with semicircular vertical slits to see through ... Sun Ra's got every color.

Those shades were snow-glasses of orange and yellow which were bought from a street merchant on the Lower East Side; and in spite of being imported from Europe, they suggested the heavy-lidded look of some West African sculpture. All of America saw those glasses, for there on the April 19, 1969, blue-tinted cover of *Rolling Stone* was Sun Ra staring out impassively at the world.

Another person in the audience in San Francisco that night was Damon Choice, a third-year art student at the institute who was overwhelmed by what he heard. He told Sonny that he played vibraphone, and asked if could sit in. At first he thought they were just a "cadre of weirdness":

> But playing with Sun Ra was a total experience. That first time with the Arkestra I felt so *in tune;* I could no longer be satisfied with just being out of tune. Sun Ra could tune the audience up; and after the Arkestra left the concert was still on!
>
> It was amazing. Laughter would break out on the bandstand or in the audience for no reason at all. What the individuals played eclipsed the process. I'd look at a guy and ask myself, "How could a person this ridiculous play like that?" We found ourselves playing in ways that couldn't be duplicated, in no known style.

After returning to Philadelphia, they came back to the West Coast in April of 1969, this time with seventeen musicians, first to the University of Santa Cruz, and on to the Dorsey High School Auditorium for their first appearance in Los Angeles. A series of concerts had been scheduled at Dorsey presenting some of the younger black musicians in the new music, so it was a promising venue in which to debut. But half the audience walked out during the opening number. By now, Sun Ra had treated such receptions as accomplishments—as having cleared the hopeless from the event—and undaunted, they went on to play Cowell College and Merrill College, both at the University of California at Santa Clara, then up to the San Francisco Art Institute, and finally to the University of California at Davis.

On their drive back east on Route 80 through Nevada they stopped in Fernley when it began to snow. Back on the road again they hit a stretch of black ice, and something—some said the tremors of an H-bomb test—sent their truck flying off the road to land upside down. No one was injured, but some of the delicate string instruments used on *Strange Strings* were destroyed. They managed to get the truck back on the road and stopped at the next town, Lovelock, where they rented a whole motel for the night. Clifford Jarvis wandered off and disappeared into a bar, yelling, "Howdy, pardners," to the locals. Later, after he hadn't returned to the hotel, Sun Ra went looking for him, and as he entered the bar, he saw Jarvis being held at gunpoint by the owner. When he asked what was up, the locals told him that "we have nothing in common with niggers." Sun Ra disputed that. "Name *one* thing," they said. "You and them are all going to die some day." However the town folks interpreted that, it gave them pause enough for Sun Ra to hustle Jarvis back to the motel. But later that night someone in the band saw men in pickup trucks with rifles beginning to assemble in front of the motel. The Arkestra quickly packed up the truck out back, and left Lovelock, lights and motor off, rolling silently downhill until they were well out of town and on their way back home.

Sonny's sense of money and finances was truly otherworldly. He took in money and paid it out without any concern for the consequences, and kept no records. When they finally began to make some real money the IRS demanded taxes. But since he paid the musicians and expenses in cash, it was impossible for him to establish his costs. He let bills pile up and seemed to have no concern for how they would be paid—he was known to sometimes walk out of Manny's Music in New York City with a new keyboard, leaving Richard Wilkinson scrambling to make arrangements for paying for it later. He acquired a Cadillac, and when one of the drivers used someone else's credit card and it was traced to the car, Sun Ra put the car in storage in New York City to conceal it. Then he forgot to make payments on it, and it was sold by the storage company. His phone bills were huge, not only because he made many long-distance calls, but because it was his habit to put the phone down during calls, wander off, and come back later. But he never hesitated to ask anyone he knew for money. Somewhere in the early 1970s, his sister said she heard from him for the first time in over twenty years: he was calling to ask her to help him pay his phone bills before they cut off his service. And once she had given it to him, "He never even said 'thank you.' "

With Sun Ra's finances out of control, he became concerned that Saturn records were not selling as well as they should, and put Richard Wilkinson and later Danny Thompson in charge of records produced in New York and Philadelphia. Increasingly he gave Thompson more and more responsibility for the band until Thompson was in effect player-manager. Sonny thought of records as a hedge against slack periods for the band, and sometimes they were their sole musical means of economic survival. Singles were particularly quick and easy to produce, and with their carefully refined approach to cheap production, also very profitable (Variety Recording Studio's records show that the mastering and the creation of metal parts for pressing Saturn 9/1954—"Daddy's Gonna Tell You No Lie"/"A Foggy Day"—cost only $220 in September of 1983). Most of their record sales were made from the bandstand during breaks in performances, but the records were also bought by a few distributors like Roundup in Cambridge, Massachusetts, and selected record stores such as Jerry Gordon's Third Street Jazz & Blues in Philadelphia.

Since the Arkestra was wary of conventional record business practices, they developed a system of sales which Thompson called "no bullshit C.O.D.": everything was done by hand, face to face, cash on the barrelhead, even if it meant flying to upstate New York or even Utrecht or Amsterdam to trade records for American dollars, on the tarmac if possible, and catching the return flight home. It could mean loading five or six boxes of records onto tiny commuter flights where the ticket seller might also be the baggage handler; or talking their way through customs on a bus driving from West Germany through East Germany to get to Berlin; or more often than not, flying to Europe with records in one box, covers in a another, labels in a third, and meeting purchasers in hotel lobbies after staying up all night assembling the records and hand-lettering the labels and covers.

Danny Thompson's approach to the sale of records was what he called improvisation, and what others might call shtick: a mixture of messianic zeal, hustle, and moxie. When he entered Third Street Jazz & Blues with handfuls of 45s, some of which looked warped, handmade, maybe not even recorded on, he launched into a pitch that assured the sales staff that no other store would be getting these records, that they were a unique product, collectors' items, that they would immediately sell out...then, more ominously, that they were dangerous. After such a spiel, who could say to him only, "We'll take a couple"? When asked what the returns policy was for defective records, Thompson would answer, "The Creator works in mysterious ways."

Thompson took charge of arranging tours, booking hotels, driving the bus, negotiating terms, and collecting money. At a time in which the big band was said to be obsolete because of the cost of maintaining and moving so many musicians, he found ways to cut corners and keep them on the road. He was asked once if traveling was a financial hardship for the band: "The only hard part is getting home." Sun Ra's habit was to get the band wherever they were going by the best means possible, to live as well as they could while they were there, and to prolong the trip until the money ran out. They were consummate tourists, buying musical instruments, clothes, and souvenirs wherever they went (in New Mexico Sonny asked to be taken to a Western hat shop: "Do you have a Tom Mix model in my size?"), living as true artists *should* live. They spread out across every city they visited and in their costumes they were as conspicuous as Shriners (lacking only the little cars). You might find the whole band glittering and shining at breakfast in the middle of the night at Denny's; or see them strolling through Disneyland. This meant, of course, that they could be stranded even after successful gigs. With not enough money for tickets home, the musicians might have to leave their instruments behind with someone until some scheme could be worked out. More often than not the someone was Thompson. There he'd be, maybe standing alone on a corner outside a hotel in Milan with piles of instruments and electronic gear, looking to flag three cabs at once to move them somewhere else, hoping that the other two cabs wouldn't take off on their own. Or he might be attempting to talk an airline ticket agent into letting him ship them now and pay later.

Thompson also organized other business ventures such as a mom-and-pop grocery store in Philadelphia's Germantown called "Pharaoh's Den" which his mother financed. The idea was to bring high culture into the community by means of art work and historical posters on display at the store, and to make some money from the neighborhood kids at the same time. Thompson's skills were such that Sonny became so dependent on him for practical matters that at one point he announced to the band that he had "adopted" him as his son, converting even financial dealings into a family matter.

■ ■ ■

John Sinclair booked the Arkestra into the Detroit Rock and Roll Revival on May 30–31 at the Michigan State Fairgrounds for a show which included Chuck Berry, the MC-5, Dr. John, the Psychedelic Stooges (with Iggy Pop), Terry Reid, Ted Nugent, and the Amboy Dukes. After the Arkestra had played for a few minutes half the audience was cheering, the other half booing. The same response met them at the Newport Jazz Festival on July 3 before 4,000 people. They were scheduled to appear in an outdoor concert in the middle of a string of mainstream jazz groups such as Phil Woods, Young-Holt Ltd., and Kenny Burrell, and when their turn came it had been raining for over three hours. Even though they were accompanied by the Joshua Light Show (from the San Francisco psychedelic rock scene) and the rain stopped when they came on, the audience was audibly ambivalent. Dan Morgenstern in *Down Beat* said it was a sloppy performance, but affecting; he found their "tribal ritual" metaphysically naive, but admitted that whatever it was, it seemed to work for the performers.

In midsummer *Apollo 11* was poised to send the first men to the moon, and Americans had time to reflect on the meaning of the event for their lives. *Esquire* spent its July issue pondering the appropriate words for Armstrong and Aldrin to speak on their landing, and asked a horde of notables for their suggestions. There, among Hubert Humphrey, Vladimir Nabokov, Marianne Moore, Robert Graves, Senator George McGovern, William Safire, Isaac Asimov, Timothy Leary, Muhammad Ali, Bob Hope, Truman Capote, Ayn Rand, W. H. Auden, Marshall McLuhan, Justice William O. Douglas, Ed Koch, Gwendolyn Brooks, and Kurt Vonnegut, Jr., was Sun Ra. While most of the others ruminated pondorously on the lonely responsibility of the achievement, Sun Ra wrote a cheery poem inaugurating the new age:

Reality has touched against myth
Humanity can move to achieve the impossible
Because when you've achieved one impossible the others
Come together to be with their brother, the first impossible
Borrowed from the rim of the myth
Happy Space Age to You. . . .

The first side of what would be called *My Brother the Wind, Vol. II* was recorded in late 1969, with Sun Ra's recently purchased Farfisa organ featured on every track, most of which were minor blues or neoswing tunes. "Walking on the Moon" was dedicated to Neil Armstrong, and had a distant affinity to "Dem Bones Gonna Rise Again." But it was his new synthesizer on the second side of the record which was the surprise. Sonny had been hearing about the idea of the synthesizer for years. It was just the sort of thing he had dreamed about: a self-contained system which generated sounds out of electricity, sounds which could be musical in a conventional sense, but was also capable of producing sounds which had never been heard before, unearthly sounds, he thought. He first heard Robert Moog's synthesizer in 1966. Shortly after Raymond Scott and Walter Carlos began to use synthesizers as novelties. Paul Bley then showed that it was possible to use a synthesizer in jazz, recording in 1969 on a large model that he also somehow managed to tour with. But to Sonny it was above all a space-age instrument; and except for the keyboard, it did look like the control panel of a rocket ship.

He traveled up to Moog's studios in 1969 and saw his experimental models, one of which was a theremin that was activated by touching a band of metal. Later at a rehearsal, he told the band that when he couldn't make one of these models work, Moog's people said that it responded differently to different people's skin: "You *know* what that means," Sonny joked. "Even machines can be racist! We got to be ready for the space age."

Late in the year Sun Ra bought a preproduction model of the new Mini-Moog, a relatively portable unit, and immediately scheduled time at Variety Studio to record with it. Gershon Kingsley was called in to program it for him. Kingsley was a classically trained pianist, an early Moog enthusiast who had performed on synthesizer at a happening in the early 1960s where Merce Cunningham danced and John Cage read Buckminster Fuller, and who had recorded on Moog with Jean-Jacques Perry on *The In Sound from Way Out* in 1964. In between takes, Kingsley struggled to set the instrument up to get the variety of sounds that Sun Ra wanted. The solos for Mini-Moog on the second side of *My Brother the Wind, Vol. II* use none of the tricks or clichés of the other first users of the instrument: Sun Ra seemed to be testing it for its melodic possibili-

ties, working on its sliding chromatic capacities, trying out whole tone
runs, and for the moment he seemed happy just to be able to get a celeste
or marimba-like tone out of the instrument.

Within a few months he recorded a second *My Brother the Wind* (thus
becoming Volume I by default) and used two Mini-Moogs in order to
play polyphonically. It was a crude and fascinating record, containing
some eccentric funk propelled by John Gilmore on drums (an instrument he had taken up when the band found themselves short of a
percussionist). The high moment was side B, "The Code of Interdependence," on which Sun Ra set the synthesizer for a sound something like
damped steel drums and played so fast that it seems to be recorded at the
wrong speed. Truly, no one had ever gotten sounds like this out of an instrument of any kind. Yet when he was asked by *Down Beat* to comment
on the instrument's place in music, he suggested that at least for the moment he was not looking for dramatic sonic effects:

> The Moog Synthesizer in its potential and application to and for the fu-
> ture is tremendous in scope, particularly for those who are creative natu-
> rals. It most certainly is worthy of a place in music. There are many
> effects on it which at present are not upon any other instrument. On one
> of my compositions, *My Brother the Wind*, the Moog is a perfect projective
> voice. Of course, like other electronic keyboard instruments, it will re-
> quire a different technical approach, touch and otherwise in most efforts
> of behavior. It is a challenge to the music scene.... The main point con-
> cerning the synthesizer is the same as in all other instruments, that is, its
> capacity for the projection of feeling. This will not be determined in a
> large degree just by the instrument itself, but always in music, by the mu-
> sician who plays the instrument.

His experiments on the Moog also appeared on "Scene I, Take 1" and
"Seen III, Took 4" on *The Solar-Myth Approach, Vols. I and II*, records Sun
Ra sold to the French company BYG. The tapes for these two records
were recorded between 1967 and 1970 in various places with different
groupings of musicians and show Sun Ra rigorously exploring intervals,
timbres, and small ranges of musical material to uncover their possibilities. In "Spectrum," for instance, horns are placed in dissonant relation

to each other so that "beats" can be heard from clashes of semitones; in "Legend" trombones quietly duet a capella and then are swallowed up by fluttering reeds and hyperspeed Clavinet; and the piano's bass keys rumble and rattle in "They'll Come Back" (a composition inspired by watching the motion of waves).

THE GRAND TOUR

Early in 1970 the Arkestra was booked into a variety of new places, such as the Red Garter, a swing-oriented dance club where the bandstand was a fire engine in which the musicians sat, and the Opera House at the Brooklyn Academy of Music. The Arkestra was beginning to be known as a "show" which could draw a crowd.

Willis Conover had been urging Sun Ra to take the Arkestra to Europe for some time, and assured him that the way had been paved for him over Voice of America and the time was right. So when an offer came for them to play a pair of concerts at the Fondation Maeght in the south of France, they began making preparations.

First there were the passports. When they filled out the forms at the passport office in New York City, the clerk at the desk said to Sun Ra, "Sir, you're going to have to give us better information than this. We need your parents' names, your birth date...." Verta Mae Grosvenor recalled that Sun Ra said, " 'That *is* the correct information.' After a few minutes the clerk went back to speak to her supervisor. Sun Ra was only wearing his day wear, but it was still pretty out! The supervisor was no-nonsense, but after talking to Sun Ra she said, 'Sir, why don't you come back in a few hours.' When we came back there was another person there and he knew about it, and he said, 'We'll just give you the passport.' It just got so *out* that they just gave it to him!"

That passport gained talismanic force over the years, and musicians shook their heads when they saw it. Talvin Singh, an English tabla player, said:

His philosophy was that either you be part of the society or you don't. And he wasn't part of it. He created his own. I mean, I actually saw his passport and there was some weird shit on it. It had some different stuff.

The gig at the Fondation Maeght in Saint-Paul-de-Vence announced that Sun Ra had been accepted by the international avant-garde. The Maeght was one of the premier small museums in the world, and its sculpture gardens and halls had received Picasso, John Cage, and many of the world's most influential artists since its opening in 1964.

Nineteen musicians and dancers were on the stage on the evening of August 3. The audience had little or no knowledge of Sun Ra's music, since his records weren't widely distributed in France, and when they arrived they saw the Arkestra spread out before them like elaborate decor: musicians in red tunics, seated in a forest of instruments on stage, dancers in red dresses. On a screen behind them was projected a sky full of stars, then planets, children in Harlem, Indians on hunting trips, and newsreel footage of protests; a ball of "magic fire" rose slowly up to the ceiling; saxophonists began to battle like samurai, then came together like brothers; and in the still center of it all, Sun Ra sat behind the Moog, creating the sounds of gales, storms, and waves crashing. From the very first note, an agitated woman stood up and cried out, "What is *this*?" Afterwards she came up and insisted on seeing the written music. Europeans seemed to want to know whether there was music behind what they were hearing, as if it would assure them that this was rational activity, and Sonny was always happy to show them the scores. A man once blurted out that his "five-year-old daughter could play that!" Sun Ra readily agreed: "She could play it, but could she *write* it?"

Two of the most striking pieces of the Maeght concerts were "Shadow World" with its hocketed saxophone ostinato, Gilmore's howling solo, and Sun Ra's frightening organ assault (his right arm repeatedly crushing the keys as if it was stuck there, his left hand thrashing the bass keys), and "Friendly Galaxy No. 2," where six flutes improvised in harmony against piano, Alan Silva's bowed bass, and a tiny, barely audible trumpet figure which rose to the surface lightly again and again like a recurrent dream. Sun Ra's comments on this piece show how far he went to make adjustments for the circumstances of specific performances:

One of the things which most impressed listeners at the Fondation Maeght is the passage for six flutes ad lib, six flutes playing in harmony. I could say improvising in harmony. I'm inspired by it to do something else which would be totally different. I believe it's a musical idea which would be totally different. I believe it's a new way of using flutes. It's at once both very melodic and harmonious and at the same time so distant, as if the music was heard in the distance through a sort of mist. It's so "out of this world."

Curious thing, the flutes had never played this passage with the piano, but because of the peculiar acoustics in the room I knew that it would be absolutely necessary that I play at the same time because the flutes would be bothered by an echo that the audience fortunately wouldn't hear at all. So above this the trumpets entered in, played a sort of ad lib riff because this light echo didn't allow them to understand the rhythm.

Just as they got back to Philadelphia, a loose confederation of European promoters offered to bring them back: Victor Schonfield and Music Now, a nonprofit production company in the UK, Joachim Berendt in Germany and Claude Delcloo in France, helped by radio station SWF in Germany, and Sabena Airlines. The plan was to send them on tour across the three countries and record them in London for Black Lion and for SABA/MPS in Germany. There were even efforts made to get them booked in Africa.

Sun Ra took twenty people this time, and picked up two African dancers in Paris, Math Samba and Roger Aralamon Hazoumé (who was also a fire-eater) and, in an era before spectacular productions became the norm, they shipped a small mountain of equipment, lights, films, slides, and costumes. Sonny alone had the Mini-Moog, a Farfisa organ, a Rocksichord, a Hohner Clavinet, a Hohner Electra, and the Spacemaster. For the trip he added Eloe Omoe (Leroy Taylor), a bass clarinetist who loved classic bebop melodies, a former member of one of the toughest gangs on the South Side of Chicago. He was Sonny's "Chicago gangster," but also what Sonny considered a very "intuitive person" like himself. He liked to test Eloe's abilities by asking him who the next person coming to see them might be, or who was knocking at the door. And most of the time he was right. If audiences sometimes confused alto saxophonists Danny Davis and Marshall Allen, they were equally convinced that Eloe and James Jacson were brothers. Two tiers of musicians were developing in the band now, an older group of established professionals, and those of a younger, more aggressive post–civil rights generation, and each had their own expectations and distinct stage personas.

Sonny worked the band furiously before the tour, lecturing them on what they would be doing in Europe and what to expect, and rehearsed them up until three hours before they left for the plane. Once they arrived in Paris they went straight to the hotel where Sonny began to inspect hotel rooms, selecting them for each musician, weighing the color potential of each, and if necessary even changing the color of the room by putting blue, yellow, and red swatches of cloth on the walls. These rooms were used well, for meeting the press there, hanging out, eating, and sometimes softly rehearsing for ten to twelve hours at a stretch.

On October 9, 1970, they opened the tour in Nanterre, at the Théâtre des Amandiers, where afterwards the jazz reviewers in effect also asked, "What is this?" A performance of classic pantomime, maybe, with staged battles, parades, and kings? Or a Punch and Judy show of the absurd? But jazz . . . ?

After a stop in Lyons on the twelfth they went back to Paris where they were booked to play in a theater on the circus grounds in the old neighborhood of Les Halles on Friday the thirteenth, a bitterly cold day with a full moon rising. But two days before they were to appear, a dance club which was filled beyond capacity and without adequate exits burned down, killing numbers of people, so the police declared at the last minute that less than half of the 4,000 people who had bought tickets would be allowed into Sun Ra's concert. The crowd began to gather in front of the theater well in advance, and when the time came for the show to begin the doors did not open. An hour went by, and the cold began to get to them. Then when the doors opened and it became apparent that only some would be allowed in, the angry and disappointed remaining ticket holders refused to leave. It had all the makings of the riot for the 1913 premiere of Stravinsky's *Le Sacré du Printemps.* The spirit of the May 1968 upheavals was still fresh in the minds of the young of France, and lest they forget them, the police arrived on cue, not only the police, but the *maréchaussée,* the elite mounted police corps, and other forces—many of whom were formidably tall Senegalese—appeared in riot gear and placed themselves between the theater and the crowd. Another half hour or so passed and nobody moved, but when chants of "*Libérez Sun Ra*" began to rise, the police started to push the crowd back with sticks . . .

Meanwhile, in the theater the show was about to begin when the crowd began to call out to the Arkestra that it was not fair for them to play when their brothers and sisters were still out there on the barricades. Sun Ra considered the situation, then grabbed the sign of the Sun, held it above his head, and started towards the exit, the Arkestra and the audience following the leader.

Out of the theater they came, shedding heat as they walked, banners streaming, Sun Ra, the Solar Arkestra, and the chosen few, marching straight through the police phalanx and down the street. And the crowds followed as they all circled around the block. When the procession returned to the front of the theater the police officials gave Sun Ra a salute as he passed their shattered ranks and marched into the theater, this time with the Les Halles 4,000 (now plus fellow travelers and cops), and the Arkestra mounted the stage again.

The theater inside was almost as cold as outside. There were now too many people, the sound system was poor, the lighting bad, the projection faint; the synthesizer broke down, and the police strolled up and down the aisles as if they were part of the cosmo drama. But when dancer Ife Tayo promenaded across the stage with the glowing globe held high, Hazoumé began beating an African drum while dressed in a warrior's suit of chain mail, and Math Samba leaped into the air dressed only in a loincloth, the audience was in their pocket. Only a critic or two was disappointed: "naive Baroque," they grumbled; "the triumph of glitter and gilded cardboard."

Of a later trip to France, Damon Choice said:

In Paris they thought the Arkestra was a bunch of *enfants terribles*. And we thought we were disciplined gentlemen! But then we had a strange relationship between discipline in rehearsal and a childlike partying on stage. On stage we talked together, joked, and laughed. We were family.

To have even played the Donaueschingen Festival for New Music was a triumph, since it was the center of new German experimental and avant-garde music, the site at which Karlheinz Stockhausen had first come to world notice. But Joachim Berendt had found a way to slip jazz in, and on October 17 the Arkestra made its first appearance in Germany. Seizing the moment, Sun Ra unleashed some of his most advanced music: "Black Forest Myth," a work of animal cries, wind, and an organ so thunderous that it seemed that Sun Ra had never needed a synthesizer in the first place. The audience received them well, but the German critics dismissed them, and the Arkestra went on to Barcelona and then to Amsterdam to play the Paridiso. Back in Paris, but without work for over two weeks, they hung on, barely getting by.

The audience on November 7 at Berlin Jazz Days at the Kongresshalle in West Berlin was not ready for what they saw. The Arkestra opened for the premier European-based free jazz big band Globe Unity Orchestra, led by Alexander von Schippenbach, a German pianist. Globe Unity had established itself as a grimly serious representative of the new jazz, but one which also owed less to American musical tradition than European jazz groups of the past. The audience was not sure that what they were witnessing with the Arkestra wasn't a parody. The sermonizing and call-and-response declamations on outer space were unsettling to begin with, but the final blow came when Sun Ra peered through a telescope aimed at the roof of the hall, and claimed he could see his native Saturn. When some in the crowd began to boo, Sonny stunned them into silence when he told them that the noise they were making was the sound of the "subhumans" (the English equivalent of the word used by the Nazis to describe the Jews): "I don't see any subhumans in the hall, but I hear them." Then he turned back to the band "with fire in his eyes and signaled for a kick-ass space chord," said Jacson. "And he hit the same chord on the organ. Blam!" Then he called out Pat Patrick, and baritone screams echoed through the theater, growing wilder with each chorus, producing the essence of what New York musicians were calling "energy music," until the audience was subdued, if not entirely overcome.

They arrived in London just before their concert on November 9, and again they were plagued by problems: shortly before the date of the performance once again the location had to be changed, this time from the larger Rainbow Theatre to Queen Elizabeth Hall, which cut the number of seats from 2,000 to 1,000, and the remaining tickets sold out days before the concert. So hours before on the night of the performance there were hundreds of people in line for tickets, angry that they couldn't get in. Then the sound crew arrived too late to set up for recording. But this time, the performance was a genuine triumph. David Toop recalls the shock of that evening;

> His first UK performance...was one of the most spectacular concerts ever held in this country. Not spectacular so much in terms of effects, which were low on budget but high on strange atmosphere; spectacular in terms of presenting a complete world view, so occult, so *other*, to all of us in the audience that the only possible responses were outright dismissal or complete intuitive empathy with a man who had chosen to discard all the possibilities of a normal life, even a normal jazz life, in favour of an unremitting alien identity. Fire-eaters, a golden-robed dancer carrying a sun symbol, tornadoes of percussion, eerie cello glissandi, ferocious blasts and tendrils of electronic sound from Sun Ra on Farfisa organ and Moog synthesizer, futuristic lyrics of the advertising age sung by June Tyson—"If you find earth boring, just the same old thing, come on sign up for Outer Spaceways Incorporated"—saxophone riffs repeated over and over by Pat Patrick and Danny Thompson as they moved down the seating aisles towards the stage while John Gilmore shredded and blistered a ribbon of multiphonics from his tenor, film images of Africa and outer space.... As depictions of archaic futures, shamanistic theatre, images of divined worlds, these devices of cumulative sensory overload were regarded at the time as distractions from the music. But those who concentrated solely on the music ignored Ra's role as a political messenger.

A second performance was arranged for them at Seymour Hall by Tam Fiofori, Pat Griffiths, and a black cultural group called Placenta Arts. The Arkestra shared the program with Chris McGregor's Quintet from South Africa and Osibisa, a Ghanaian rock group. A party which many Africans and West Indians attended was arranged for the band afterwards at a house in northwest London. Ademola Johnson remembered,

> It was an African party because the African boys—they were very *African* in those days. We had African food and there was music, of course, but background music, no one played "live." Sun Ra was there and all the band. It was a lot of question-and-answer, a lot of thought. He was "hold-

ing court" but a lot of us argued with him. His image of Africa is different from the real Africa that people are living in today. But he was respected: he's an elder to start with so you've got to respect.

A third performance was arranged at Liverpool University where a
large and energetic crowd attempted to reverse the usual stage-to-
audience direction of the Arkestra's performances by surging out of
their seats towards the stage, stomping and chanting, "Ra, Ra, Ra." When
it was all over promoter Victor Schonfield had lost thousands, but the
European connection had been made. Sun Ra was now a world musician.

The overseas tour had put them on the map in New York City as well.
Now there were a couple of prestigious gigs to start off 1971—the Vil-
lage Gate and a concert at the Metropolitan Museum of Art's "Com-
posers in Performance" series in February. Then the call came for the
University of California Jazz Festival in Berkeley on April 23, and for
two nights at the Harding Theater in San Francisco. While they were in
California, Sonny started to work on a series of compositions he called
"Disciplines," in which "the slightest variation would destroy the thing."
"The Discipline series goes up to 99..." [they actually passed that num-
ber]. These compositions, he said, would be built on hocketed horn lines,
with each horn playing within a two- to three-note range, a cyclical
melody developing out of the fragments, each person playing his parts
scrupulously with no deviation whatsoever. His description did not fit all
of the Discipline series as it evolved, but they clearly were tightly conceived exercises using minimal material.

On June 11, the Arkestra went south to play a concert in Los Angeles
at the J. P. Widney Junior High School that a cousin of Danny Thompson's, Alden Kimbrough, had arranged. Sun Ra's reputation was spreading rapidly now, and this should have been a moment of conquest, but
things turned ugly when the custodial staff—not knowing Sun Ra's
practice of playing without regard for time—interrupted the concert by
turning off the lights. Sun Ra was furious and lectured the guard and the
audience on injustice, race, leadership, and civil order, and ended by
putting a curse on the City of Angels.

How dare you turn the light out on me! I am not afraid of the dark. My people have lived in darkness. I'm a part of nature. The birds don't have to stop playing at 1 o'clock; why should I? You just had one earthquake...you might expect another.

Perhaps he also knew that the school bore the name of one of the first presidents of the University of Southern California, a man who had written a book called *Race Life of the Aryan People* in which he predicted Los Angeles would one day become the center of world Aryan supremacy.

The Arkestra then moved to Oakland at the invitation of Bobby Seale to live in a house owned by the Black Panther Party. Sonny was impressed by the practical side of the Panthers—their ideas for schools, a breakfast program for children, providing groceries for the needy, building a community—and though he did not share their theoretical underpinnings and their violent implications, he thought they had the best program he had heard of for black people. The Arkestra was now at least remotely connected to the group that J. Edgar Hoover declared the biggest threat to American internal security. So as benign as the Arkestra's activities were—they played a local mental hospital, performed at a wedding at the Rosicrucian Museum in San Jose, worked at clubs like the Native Son, and gave free concerts in the parks—they found themselves under surveillance by both the FBI and the Oakland police.

One of the first people Sun Ra met in Oakland was Marvin X Jackmon, a young Black Muslim writer who had been convicted for draft resistance and who Amiri Baraka had worked with four years before when Baraka had been a visiting professor at San Francisco State College. Marvin X's poem "Burn, Baby, Burn" had turned the Watts street cry into art, and Baraka had published his work in his Jihad series. Sun Ra played Marvin X's wedding and later did incidental music for a performance of his short play, "The Black Bird," a parable of black freedom inspired by Black Muslim beliefs.

In the late fall, they set out for their second tour of Europe, from October through December. Now with six dancers, two singers, and twenty-two musicians (including eleven woodwinds, four drummers, and Pat

Patrick doubling on bass guitar), they played concerts in Stockholm (where Tommy Hunter rejoined them) and Aarbus, Denmark, in October, then in Delft, in the Netherlands, in November. The performances were spread so far apart that the money they were receiving ran thin, and three of the musicians began demanding to be paid. After the Delft concert one of them tried to take the money by force in Sonny's hotel room, and was stopped only when other band members came by and heard what was going on. Sonny fired the three of them, and over the next three weeks eleven more left, including all the dancers except June Tyson.

On November 29 they returned to Paris to play the Théâtre du Chatelet. Paris reminded Sonny of Montreal, and he loved to walk the streets and visit the museums, especially the Egyptian section of the Louvre. Verta Mae Grosvenor said, "Walking with Sun Ra in France was something else! Everyone stared at us. We were a sensation...like Josephine Baker's arrival in Paris." And of all the European cities they played, Paris was the one which took them most seriously, that saw something challenging and perhaps disturbing in their music. It was the latest episode in Paris's long history of encounters with black music and a new chapter in its running discourse on its meaning.

L'ART NÉGRE

Jazz first reached Paris just after World War I and revitalized French popular culture and provided the spark which helped ignite the dadaist and surrealist impulses. Jazz was almost literally the *frisson*, the shock to the system the French had been waiting for. First there was the "noise," the loudness of it all, though in retrospect it is easy to see that what they were hearing was a combination of a modest increase in volume mixed with the polyphony of collective improvisation, the polymetric layering of one rhythm on top of another and "unmusical effects" such as horns imitating human, animal, and mechanical sounds (barnyard noise, shouts and laughing, sirens). But part of the "noise" was visual, for they were also encountering black bodies—*les corps autres*—in a performance setting. Drummers juggled sticks, instruments were held at spectacular angles, soloists bobbed up and down from the group, dancing while they played. Tappers and shake dancers subdivided their bodies, using their hips and their trunks independently and—in a grand break with French terpsichore—made noises with their feet. They were synesthetic performances, one sensory perception operating in a context reserved for another, as if dance, sculpture, theater, and music were all at work at once; and in a time when the phonograph was the rage, there was something here which escaped mechanical reproduction. Intellectuals and journalists talked of "trance" and the "sacred," of erotics and exoticism. It was the perfect bridging of Descartes' higher and lower mind, a mixture of what they perceived of as simultaneously primitive and modern.

Now, after the Arkestra's second appearance in Paris, that shock was being felt in certain circles all over again. The French had already experienced the theatrics and historical sweep of the Art Ensemble of Chicago and had read them as aggressively nationalist and threatening, as representatives of the black American political vanguard. But with Sun Ra they needed to account for anachronisms, the alternation between free collectivity and the rigorously orchestrated passages, the cult of personality pushed all the way to the cosmos, the sheer wonderland of the cosmo drama—this was something else!

Jazz Magazine of Paris gathered together a group of critics, artists, and intellectuals to come to terms with what they had seen. As the discussion unfolded, they puzzled over a series of contradictions in what they had heard on records versus what they had seen on different stages, and primitivism and modernism were much on their minds.

PHILIPPE CARLES: The concert that Sun Ra gave at Chatelet was very different from what we've heard of his music on records, wasn't it?

JEAN-ROBERT MASSON: I was perplexed listening to the records from Saint-Paul-de-Vence (*Nuits de Fondation Maeght*): nothing was happening, so to speak. How could the same orchestra who had made the orchestrally rich ESP records be the same one who made the *Nuits* records, which were almost immobile, and which reduced itself to a crude and simple rhythmic event. I had to conclude that the gestural and visual element had a very large place in the spectacles of Sun Ra which wasn't evident from listening to the ESP records. The evening at Chatelet just underlined this, going all the way to caricature.

DENIS CONSTANT: In the ESP album *Nothing Is,* the element of spectacle is already perceptible.

FRANCIS MARMANDE: The question didn't pose itself in this way until after I had been to the Nanterre concert in 1970, since I hadn't yet heard his live recordings.

PC: Were the references to Africa so evident at Nanterre?

FM: In the costumes, yes, they were very different from the Superman costumes we saw at Chatelet. On the other hand, the African references were less clear in the dances.

JEAN-LOUIS COMOLLI: It was interesting precisely for this invention of Africa by blacks from Harlem and elsewhere. But it was a mythic Africa, a bricolage.

DC: A drugstore-styled Africa.

JLC: That was it. A vision of Africa wholly invented by Western culture, by the dominant ideology of the United States, by the way whites represent Africa to themselves. These dances, for example, are just the opposite of African dances, because they had no sacred, initiatory, or mystical context....

FM: ... myths without mythology, or mysticism without religion ...

JLC: What was equally noticeable in the dances was that there was an absence of choreography, at least in the classical sense of the term. Dance governed by rules was here opposed by gesticulation and crude movement.

DC: Like music, the dance was improvised. It seemed to me, however, that the dancers must have received classical training.

JLC: It was in any case very far removed from the preoccupations with rigor of contemporary ballet. Each dancer arrived on stage and gave a more or less loose exhibition of the music. Without being pejorative, I would say that they weren't doing anything at all....

FM: What they were dancing was the death of the sign.

They were also disturbed by what seemed to be discontinuity in the performance:

DC: But what differentiates Sun Ra's music from much African music is that this dominant rhythm isn't constant. It doesn't maintain a musical continuity. There were polyrhythmic passages to accompany dances, but as soon as they came back to the "orchestral language" the percussionists became more discreet—the jazz drummers took the lead again....

FM: I insist on believing that the discontinuity was the principal characteristic of the spectacle. The "flag waving" of the saxophonists was very controlled and the continual "noise-making" of the percussionists seemed to me two different realities connected by a dialectic of the contraries which the musicians themselves illustrated. One of the saxophonists after having played—rather admirably, I might add, in a trancelike state—left the orchestra, came up to the front with a camera in his hand, and with the curiosity of a tourist, started to photograph the musicians. It was as if the actors of this sonorous fresco came to double themselves completely, and, then the instruments became the witness of the spectacle, which the others continued to create. They were the orchestra's shadow, carried on its own voice.

FM: The discontinuity of spectacle was highlighted by the place. The stage at Chatelet restricted the ambulatory nature of this music. For example, when the baritones left their stands to play while walking around you couldn't hear them anymore...

JLC: One could say, in short, that there was an attempt to break up the scene, but this was first of all contradicted by Chatelet itself, the classic character of Italian-style theatre.

FM: Insofar as we heard nothing of this very original attempt at orchestral restructuring, which consisted of people with the same instruments walking around, quartets or quintets of flutes or baritones, reminiscent of some sort of sect of dervishes.

Next they fretted over the spectacular nature of the music, the dancing musicians, the lighting...

JLC: What remains interesting is this attempt to make music spectacular in and of itself. The musicians don't disappear behind it. They are no longer buried beneath their instruments. They are no longer able to be reabsorbed into their instruments, and then overcome them. Their dialectical relationship to the instrument becomes more complicated. They play, but while walking or dancing, while representing the music. This attempt was spoiled at Chatelet so you couldn't really feel the weight of it.

DC: This phenomenon of the musical spectacular belongs to the tradition of popular Afro-American music. We've already seen musicians dancing with their instruments at the Olympia in the Sam and Dave Orchestra.

J-RM: In effect Sun Ra uses very old practices. Musicians walking outside the traditional scenic space is something you find in New Orleans bands and also in Duke Ellington. The theatrical use of lighting belongs to the shows of Harlem....

FM: But it is really not a question of regression at all. What we see with Sun Ra is rather the deconstruction of a music that could include the gestural, and the deconstruction is exhibited, presented itself on the stage at Chatelet, a theater that is at the same time privileged and censoring. He has redoubled the deconstruction. This integration of the gestural and the musical we've already seen with the Art Ensemble of Chicago, and to a certain extent, in the marching-in-place of Albert Ayler....

J-RM: It's important to mention that either voluntarily or by happenstance, the orchestra destroyed the notion of closed work. There was neither a beginning nor an end....

FM: You could even ask yourself if the Sun Ra concert had an ending. We left at a point where the curtain had gone down, while the music was continuing to play. That underlined our position as voyeurs. We were only allowed a moment's access to this music.

Discussions like this happened everywhere. Even before the Arkestra came to France for the first time, *Jazz Magazine* assembled a panel of the country's most distinguished critics to discuss *The Heliocentric World of Sun Ra*. But they argued so much over how to approach Sun Ra's music—whether to see it in exclusively political or musical terms, whether to read the titles programmatically, etc.—that they never got around to discussing the record, except for calling it "violently expressionist." And it was worse when live performances were involved. If you first saw Sun Ra and the Arkestra live, you saw a multidimensional event, a performance which broke the laws of Northern European performance, and you were affected by it one way or the other. But when you heard them on record you heard myth without the ritual, and the words took on a weight that the multimedia had balanced and lightened. And if you saw them at an inconventional venue like the Maeght Foundation and then at a traditional theater like Chatelet you saw a different group entirely, one constrained by the limited space.

SUNSET ON THE NILE

In December they went on to Odense and Copenhagen in Denmark. When they finished the Copenhagen concert on December 5 they decided at the last minute to go on to Egypt instead of straight back to New York. Sun Ra sold some concert tape to Black Lion Records to pay for the tickets and they left on December 7, not knowing anyone in Egypt and not sure of where they would stay or how they would pay for it.

When they landed they were held up at Egyptian customs because of the unlikelihood of an entire orchestra arriving as tourists and because of the name on Sun Ra's passport. To be named after the sun god twice was really a bit too much. On the latter objection Sun Ra resourcefully suggested the guard call the curator of the National Museum of Antiquities with whom he was ready to discuss Egyptology. They let them in, but customs kept most of their instruments just in case. The band took cabs to the Mena House Hotel outside of Cairo, and they woke up the next day to see the morning fog slowly lifting to reveal the pyramid of Giza. A day later Tommy Hunter began taking motion pictures of members of the Arkestra as they faced the pyramids, while the wind made their costumes billow so it appeared they were flying. These were films that Sun Ra would later project behind the band at Slug's and at concerts.

It was a lifetime's dream come true for Sun Ra, but yet things did not seem quite right. As he had feared, many of the modern Egyptians did not appear to be *his* people, not a Hamitic people. When he told some locals about his racial theories of ancient Egypt, they suggested he read Freud's *Moses and Monotheism*. And when he couldn't find it in bookstores he concluded that the Egyptian government had banned it.

With the help of Hartmut Geerken, a writer and free musician who was teaching at the Goethe Institute in Cairo, the Arkestra cobbled together a kind of local mini-tour. First there was a concert on December 12 at Geerken's home in Heliopolis where the guests paid seventy-five dollars each to attend. Most of the Arkestra's luggage had not yet cleared customs, but they were loaned instruments by Salah Ragab, a brigadier general and the head of military music in the Egyptian army and himself a jazz drummer. Though he was later disciplined for the contact, he continued to meet with the band under various disguises, including once when he came with the son of Gamal Abdel Nasser, also a jazz musician. Musicians and dancers were jammed into the house with several dozen guests, but they still managed a light show and dancing, and a march throughout the house and into the garden (while the Egyptian secret police kept watch from outside).

One of the guests that evening arranged a performance for them on television on December 16, and the next night, after the Ministry of Culture canceled a scheduled ballet, they played a concert at the Balloon Theater (a theater which burned down shortly after they played there, as did the Mena House Hotel). They then played a concert at American University, where only their cab fare across Cairo was paid for; and when they worked the Versailles Club (where they had been asked to play for dancers), Sun Ra unleashed the Moog and sent a woman screaming out of the club (he later said she had tried to jump in the Nile).

They intended to stay only a few days, but as usual it turned into two weeks, as they rode camels, shopped, hitchhiked, and went sight-seeing. Geerken tried to talk Sun Ra into going into the great pyramid, but at first he resisted—he seemed afraid, and said that it was too dangerous (though he later said that he wanted to go into the pyramids without Geerken so that they could take pictures without getting permission). Finally he and a small group decided to go. They climbed the staircase, crawled through the low entrances, and slipped through the narrow corridors in order to reach the King's Chamber, and as they did the lights suddenly went out. Sun Ra later said that he had chanted the name of Ra nine times when it happened, although Geerken remembered only Sun Ra saying, "Why do we need light, Sun Ra, the sun is here." Whatever, they managed to walk back out through the darkness. (When Sun Ra recounted this story to writer Robert Palmer in 1978 at the Beacon Theater in New York, the lights went out in the theater, leaving a dead spot in the middle of the tape recording as evidence.)

One night near the end of their stay in Cairo, Geerken saw Sun Ra seated at a table in the hotel with a candle and a piece of paper covered with long rows of numbers. It was not numerology; they were again out of money, with not even enough to pay the hotel bill. This was becoming a regular occurrence on tours, as Sonny loved traveling and became depressed when they returned to Philadelphia. Geerken once saw Sun Ra pay for a $1000 phone bill by selling the rights to a master tape of the band. This time, members of the band sold personal items to get the money. And Sonny left his Sun harp with Geerken as security against money he loaned him.

Back in Oakland, by means which were only conceivable in the late 1960s and early 1970s, Sun Ra was appointed a lecturer at the University of California at Berkeley through the Regents' Program and the Department of Afro-American Studies. Every week during the spring quarter of 1971 he met his class, Afro-American Studies 198: "The Black Man in the Cosmos," in a large room in the music department building. Although a respectable number of students signed up, after a couple of classes it was down to a handful ("What could you expect with a course named like that," Sun Ra once chortled). But a large number of local black folks regularly attended, always distinguishable from the students by their party dress. The classes ran like rehearsals: first came the lecture, followed by a half hour of solo keyboard or Arkestra performance. But it was a proper course—Sun Ra had after all trained to be a teacher in college—with class handouts, assignments, and a reading list which made even the most au courant sixties professors' courses pale. There was *The Egyptian Book of the Dead*; Bill Looney's *Radix*, a book of astrology; Alexander Hislip's *Two Babylons*; the theosophical works of Madame Blavatsky; spiritually channeled tomes like *The Book of Oahspe*; Henry Dumas's *Ark of Bones* and *Poetry for My People*; LeRoi Jones's and Larry Neal's, *Black Fire*; David Livingston's *Missionary Travels and Researches in South Africa*; Theodore P. Ford's, *God Wills the Negro*; Archibald Rutledge's, *God's Children*; the Spring 1971 issue of *Stylus*, the literary magazine of the black students of Temple University (which contained poetry by Sun Ra); John S. Wilson's *Jazz: Where It Came From, Where It's At* (published by the United States Information Agency); Yosef A. A. Ben-Jochannan's, *Black Man of the Nile and His Family*; Count Volney's *Ruins of Empire*; the King James version of the Bible (listed on the syllabus only as "The Source Book of Man's Life and Death"); P. D. Ouspensky's, *A New Model of the Universe*; Frederick Bodmer's, *The Loom of Language*;

Blackies Etymology; and other recommended books on hieroglyphics, color therapy, the Rosicrucians, Afro-American folklore, and ex-slaves' writings. When students returned after the first class to tell Sun Ra that the books were not available in the bookstores and were either missing from the library or had never been there in the first place, he merely smiled knowingly.

His list of suggested topics for student term papers summed up his interests at the time, but it also showed an astute sense of what universities expect their student's papers to deal with: "The Striving of the Black Bourgeoisie," "Negritude," "Planning for the Future," "The Role of Technology in Music," and "Developing Relevant Culture."

In a typical lecture, Sun Ra wrote biblical quotes on the board and then "permutated" them—rewrote and transformed their letters and syntax into new equations of meaning, while members of the Arkestra passed through the room, preventing anyone from taping the class. His lecture subjects included Neoplatonic doctrines; the application of ancient history and religious texts to racial problems; pollution and war; and a radical reinterpretation of the Bible in light of Egyptology. Sun Ra the southern black man, the jazz musician, the reluctant leader, the recipient of outer-space wisdom, the messenger, the militant, the hippie icon, the avant-gardist, was now Sun Ra, visiting lecturer.

I'm talking about something that's so impossible, it can't possibly be true. But it's the only way the world's gonna survive, this impossible thing. My job is to change five billion people to something else. Totally impossible. But everything that's possible's been done by man, I have to deal with the impossible. And when I deal with the impossible and am successful, it makes me feel good because I know that I'm not bullshittin'.

SUN RA

Other gods have I known...

SUN RA

It ain't necessarily so that it ain't necessarily so.

SUN RA

A lecture might begin with Sun Ra saying that the Creator is the ultimate god. Like the Cannaites' El, the Creator is the oldest of gods, the god of gods, the one that made all gods possible, the oldest known extraterrestrial being. Yet, the Creator is not a god as Christians understand their God, but infinite, the *omni-presence*, the highest form imaginable; the God of the living, and like the Sun, the purest state of being. He never dies. He always *is*. We should seek to *be* like the sun. Though the Creator *is*, he is also in evolution, a natural being, a superior being ("superior" can always get better and better and better; "supreme" is finished, not changing). When someone once modestly suggested that God was love, Sun Ra responded, "Fool, God is more than love will ever be! God is beyond human projections!" He was going well beyond a paraphrase of an old Baptist homily, "God is more than any problem I have": God, he would say, doesn't require human love nor does he guarantee to return it. God is neither good nor evil, though he can be demanding; he can beat you up if he wants to. The God that humans acknowledge is actually more than a person; in a sense he's more like a government. He—or It—is a league of gods and nonhuman entities which watches over all conceivable and inconceivable reality. People talk about dying, resting in peace and going to heaven. But there is no peace in heaven: it's a war zone. It was there that war first began.

The distinction between the Creator and God was not always clear, and Sonny sometimes used them interchangeably, but it was the Creator who was most important to him. The Creator allows for creative thought. The Creator is nature's God, the God of the early romantics, or the eighteenth-century deists' conception of God, as mentioned in the Declaration of Independence.

Nature is more than they say nature is: an English garden is not nature; because weeds are nature too; more than the preconceived notion of a nice rose. Ants, snakes, and slugs are all part of nature, too. Anything you can control gets relegated to religion, to the gods. But nature's god is terrifying... they call all catastrophes "acts of god."

If you're in trouble, it's the Creator, not God, who can help you:

> A fellow who was sort of managing me, he went down the subway in New York City—14th Street. The police came down, said he jumped the turnstile. He said, "I didn't jump over the turnstile. I paid." So they took him back, up to the booth. The woman said, "Oh, no, that was two white fellows jumped over the turnstile—it wasn't him." So he said to the police, "See, you embarrassed me and I haven't done anything. You see how all you all do things if someone's a black man?" So one of the police got behind him, on his knees, the other—like little boys—pushed him over. They did that, and somehow the nightstick hit the pavement. So here come the other police. They didn't ask no questions. They formed a ring around him and tried to hit him with their sticks, but they couldn't hit him. He moved his head about and moved his head about. They surrounded him, and all at once, he said, "Creator, help me!" And then this voice came out of nowhere and said, "Leave the motherfucker alone!" So, now, they stopped and looked around. They didn't see nothing, but they didn't continue.
>
> So Jackson [Jacson], our conga player was telling them in Philadelphia about that incident. He said, "The Creator talks like that? He talks our language?" The other fellows said, "Yeah, he talks whatever language that you understand. He won't tell you something that you don't understand, 'cause you won't get the message."

Who was the Creator? To some he cautiously hinted that it might be Lucifer, the light-bringer, the leader of the angelic choir. The source of the idea that jazz is the devil's music, he laughed. To others he was more definite. The Creator *was* Lucifer, one and the same, though not the Lucifer that we know from *Paradise Lost* or the *Qur'an*, more the demiurge, the artificer of the Gnostics. Then who was God? There were different answers to the question. He once had a dream in which Jesus and Lucifer were friends and and each had their own jobs. He saw them at something like a union call-up, where each god got picked for a task. "God" was something like that, more like a committee or a government. The god that people on Earth worshipped, however, was usually their own projection—each person might have a different god. Sometimes he said that the god that people on Earth worshipped might even be white people themselves, who had taught black people to worship them. The point was that people have been worshipping the wrong god.

The key to understanding, Sonny believed, is through the spirit, not through the body or the mind ... but by allowing your spirit to take control and guide your actions. The spirit is part of the Creator, a small spark of that originating force. Creativity was expected of man. The god within you that refuses to create perishes. Human beings are in the state they are in because they have allowed the physical self to destroy the spiritual self. The body fools you: it is naturally ungrateful and lazy; it demands destructive, earthly obsessions like liquor, drugs, and sex. And even after you've spent a "lifetime" caring for it and feeding it, it'll lie down on you, die on you. Humans' bodies aren't even real, they're copies of bodies, reproductions, from the reproductive system. Yet we still have the capacity to become creators, not copiers. Darwin had the right idea with evolution (rather than revolution, which is strictly physical), but it is evolution of the spirit, not the body, that we should be concerned with.

"What Sun Ra had to do," said James Jacson, "was reverse that state of bodily control, and he would demonstrate it with music and the Arkestra." The spirits of people on Earth are starved for beauty, and so spirituality was the domain in which he was prepared to work.

> He proved you could do it by taking individuals and teaching them to do it—even people with no experience, no ideals, no intelligence ... and once you achieved what the spirit could lead you to, you were hooked ... you wanted to do it forever.

The spirit can be located by stopping thought, abandoning knowledge, trusting intuition. You can't do it with your mind alone. Ignorance, in fact, is a form of spirit. Human beings have more ignorance than knowledge, so if you let ignorance take over, release yourself from your defenses, release the animal side of you, the spirit will take over ... and you'll make beautiful music. You won't make mistakes. To err is human, to be human is to make mistakes; but the spirit never errs. Everything should be done with the spirit because the mind can't be trusted: you can always lose your mind, but never your spirit ... the spirit can help you to be what you really are.

At times he talked as if nature and spirit were the same: history repeats itself, nature never does. Every sunset is different. Nature is always new. Human beings repeat the same bad things. They're in a groove. He thought of himself as a natural—a natural learner, sight-reader, arranger, composer, scholar—as natural as the birds sing in praise of the Creator.

The spirit is pure energy (as is the Creator)—a kind of electricity, and that electricity is diffused throughout the body, which can be tapped. For a battery to work there must be a negative and positive. There's an arc between them, and in the arc there's a small space—the "narrow." That's the place you should be, so as not to make positive or negative judgments to the spirit, for a positive action can have negative consequences or vice versa. He wanted the Arkestra to be that arc in electricity, he would say, at the balance point, in the middle of polarities.

Nor can the spirit die, because it was never born. It is not even part of the created world, but is as old as the Creator of which it is a part.

Life and death were both put into question by Sun Ra. From childhood he had wondered why it was necessary to die. Nature teaches us how beautiful things can be, so death is not logical. What did God want anyway? He let those who served him and believed in him die just like those who ignored him. The Bible says: find me just one pure-hearted person. And at least two people in the Bible—Enoch and Elijah—didn't die. It also says that the last enemy to be destroyed shall be death (1 Corinthians 15:26), and that should give us some hope.

Earth now stands in the shadow of the valley of death. Death is what all nations and all peoples have in common, not money or language. But instead of trying to defeat death, people want to be amused. But sex, drugs, money, politics, religion, none of them have ever saved anyone from death. Death is weak, not strong, but weakness is powerful, the power which conquers people: you die because you get weaker and weaker until you are the equal of death.

If death is to be defeated, then life itself must be denied, because those who weren't born will not have to die. Even Christ said, "You must hate your life in order to live forever" (John 12:25). Sonny wrote a poem about it:

> I hate myself.
> Most of all I hate,
> I hate me.

A publisher once said to him, "You can't print that." He said, "Can't I hate myself? That's the only right I have."

This "life" is death pretending to be life. It ought to be abolished since it is meaner for people than death could ever be. But life and death didn't interest him; he was talking about "being," a third state, which forms a triangle with life and death. Being gave life and death permission to exist.

This is the only planet with "life." Life is not the same as being, and a human life and a human being aren't the same, because a human being can never die. "Being" is a better term—beings don't die. The eternal part has no name. Being is eternal, while life is a prison. To be is the thing: if you be, you is, forever, into infinity. "To be or not to be: that is the question," as simple as that, from Shakespeare. Sonny agreed: "To be or not to be: That's the question." It's about being, then; it's not about life; it's not about death; it's about being. Even when they speak of a Supreme Being, they don't say "Supreme Life." To him, the best thing about jazz was that the idea or being of jazz is based upon the spontaneous improvisation principle. Pure jazz is that which is without preconceived notion, or that which is just being, and that was really his definition of jazz.

"So people should take a good look at life and see if it's good, you know. But if you got one person who's dead or dying or crippled or blind, then you have to say, 'It's bad . . . life is bad,' because you have to judge a tree by the fruit, and the fruit of life is a lot of people crippled, paralyzed, dead and dying, diseased. That's the fruit of life. So you should hate it. Death, too. It doesn't really offer anybody anything, and no one has really come out boldly on TV and said, 'Here I am. Death is all right.' So, then, being a scientist, Sonny would say neither one of them is any good until it proves to be effective, but then that's totally unnecessary. If people are going to be immortal or live, they don't really have to die. They've already got life, so why can't they just extend it? It's very simple, you know: it either is or it ain't."

This is the only planet where death is a reality. Nowhere else has death. There's been nowhere else that death has been pronounced the destiny. If you get off this planet, you are no longer under its laws. It's just like anything else. If you get off planet Earth, and wherever you go, you are under that law. Sonny said he wouldn't want to be caught dead on this planet.

We talk about people having "departed" from this world, but never say they "arrived" here. The birthday should be the arrival day, and what you call death should be the departure day.

Death is an empire that is incredibly large. Nobody's really dead; they are over there in captivity. The body is not the person. The body is like a car: it can't go anywhere without a driver. Death was talked into existence and can be talked out of it. Words affect the living *and* the dead. One man brought death into existence, and one man can destroy it [Romans 5:12].

This may seem weird to some, a philosophy, a religion, a science built on the denial of death. But aren't most religions built on a fear and denial of death? At least this one is humane: we have to bring back the dead. We have to help our ancestors. We have their bodies here already, but not their spirits.

I don't deal with life, Sonny would declaim: death is a curse, as the Bible says; people aren't ready for my music, but they're ready for death. The white race is based on Pauline theories, for Paul said, "Who shall deliver me from the body of this death?" ... "If a man that I taught to live, lives to death." It says elsewhere in the Bible: "Their whole life through is nothing but death."

Nietzsche said God is dead. He should've said god is death. That's just like saying God doesn't exist, a foolish statement. Man can't even prove that *he* exists—he dies more than he exists, and more quickly, more quickly than in the rest of nature. If there's something which doesn't exist, it's man.

"I gave up my so-called life by never living it," Sonny said.

Man's acceptance of the Bible at face value as guidance is a fatal error. The Bible *is* a book of instructions, a blueprint, an instruction manual for the spirit over the animal. But it has to be decoded, because it tells you what *not* to do ("thou shalt not...") rather than what *to* do. The Bible is a code book rather than a good book. It's man-made, a story by men which God made come true. God made man eat his words.

Much of Sun Ra's work and thinking begins with the interpretation and reinterpretation of biblical texts, refuting fundamentalism, really, living to prove the Bible was written in symbols and metaphors with no room for literalism. It has to be interpreted in other ways, and not be limited to one phonetic reading.

In the beginning was the word, the word was made flesh; we are all made from words. And we create with words. Words are like seeds: when you speak you throw words in the air and the universe throws them back at you. You reap what you sow. To say "so" is to say "amen" to something. Saying something makes it so. The problem is we don't know how to talk to the Creator, to ask for what we want or need or how the words should go together, so we don't get what we want. Words are like chemicals; there are some that show no reaction when brought together; others react together; new words can be discovered by putting them together, turning them around, breaking them apart; making equations between words—like "live" and "evil"—and thus discovering new possibilities:

> The elasticity of words
> The phonetic-dimension of words
> The multi-self of words
> Is energy for thought—If it is a reality.
> The idea that words
> Can form themselves into the impossible
> Is through the words.
>
> The fate of humanity is determined
> By the word they so or approve
> Because they reap what they so
> Even if it is the fruit of their lies
>   ("Words and the Impossible")

The crucifixion is an example: "Let's look at the plan, judge the tree by the fruit.... A world that believes that, whatever they're studying, believes in it straight to the graveyard. Now, they don't deny that, they can't, because it's true—whatever they're doing ends up in the graveyard. Even the Son of God ended up in the graveyard. Now, how could they teach a limited philosophy or a limited position like that...? Somebody came on this planet and showed them, 'This is where you're going, where you're going to end up; I'm going show you what's going to happen to you,'...and He came and showed them. That's all that was, a play.... 'Now, I'm going to show you what's going to happen to you if you believe the Word of God, and I'm going to play the part of Son of God and show you what God is.'

"So He came and he went right to the cross and said, 'This is what God wants you to do: follow me.' Ever since then they've been dying. If the Son of God died, well, God didn't save His own son; how can anybody think He's gonna save anybody else? His Son had to buy death; so will everybody else. He just came and showed them the way...the way *not* to go."

The cross represents death, the worship of the god of death as opposed to the ever-living god. A whole civilization has been created establishing the values of death as good. So the cross is something sinister, a reminder of a trick and failure. It reminds Christ and all messiahs that if you return, you'll get it again. "When Simon, Peter, and Andrew were fishing with nets, Jesus called to them, and told them he would make them fishers of men" [Matthew 4:19]. "Net" reversed is "ten"; X is the Roman numeral for "ten." The net is Christ, he is being used to trap humans. "X-mas" is a mass for the dead.... The confederate flag has an X on it....

"He died for the ungodly and unrighteous, he didn't die for the righteous, so that's why the righteous have such a hard time...people who don't have any sins—they don't get saved. I call it a weird doctrine!"

The problem began with the Tower of Babylon, where the languages were confused. God sets traps for men with words, by creating confusion by phonetic tricks, and writing perpetuates the confusion. Intellectuals and theocrats haven't seen the source of this confusion, and people are dying for want of words. "He switched the languages. 'The first should be last; the last should be first'; that means the "a" to the "z," "b" to "y," see that? Switched the alphabet subtly, very subtly. Then He said, 'Forgive them, Father. They know not what they do.' The Bible says, 'The dead don't know anything.' So He killed them with one sentence: 'They know not what they do.' And so that's because they're dead in their heads. That's what it is. And to this day they don't know what they do, because they're dead."

But the Bible also provides the means for reversing our backward state on this planet. "Take with you words, and turn to the Lord" in Hosea 14:2, a particularly obscure book, tells us what we must do. The keys to the languages are the roots of words to put things back in place to where it was at first, and then you'll have the whole story ... people are nothing but jigsaw puzzles now ... it doesn't make sense, because some of the pieces are cut just slightly off, and you have to be able to put it over in the right place and you see the whole picture.

> Proper evaluation of words and letters in their phonetic and associated sense can bring the people of earth into the clear light of pure cosmic wisdom.
>
> ("Cosmic Tones for Mental Therapy")

The English language above all is especially a language of duplicity, though that's not necessarily a bad thing: it is also the language of the angels (i.e., the Angles).

In order to restore languages, equations have to be balanced, because equations are the natural state of the universe. Grammatically, an equation is a balanced statement, bridged by a copula, a form of the verb "to be": am, are, is, was, were. But he saw other possibilities. In a class handout, for instance, he had written:

> It is said that tomorrow never comes. Here is an equation with the word never. The equation should read *Tomorrow comes never* or *Never comes tomorrow*. Tomorrow here is associated with never. It is all about the never never land ... read the story (myth) of Peter Pan. Every myth is a mathematical parable. Myth is another form of truth, a parable is a myth; it is a

parallel assertion. Myth in Greek is mythos, a word meaning a word, speech, legend.

TOMORROW NEVER COMES
COMES TOMORROW NEVER
NEVER COMES TOMORROW
TOMORROW COMES NEVER
NEVER TOMORROW COMES
COMES NEVER TOMMOROW

That is the equation, a touch of myth.

There were also equations of words with the same numerological value (there is a universal value of words, and by counting letters, equivalents can be seen across languages); but '"wordology"—recognizing words of the same phonetic equivalence, as in homonyms and homophones, and recognizing euphemistic equivalence—is more important than numerology. So wordplay and puns are also equations, equations of sound: you can find equivalence in formations like funeral "home" or funeral "parlor"; or you can equate raise=race=raze=rays; or word=were'd=world=would=weird. We are caught up in a war of the words!

"I'll be running across some amazing things...some incredible things about the Bible, Sun Ra would say, like 'He who seeks to save his life shall lose it.' That has always worried me. A lot of people will go on and give up their life to try and get life. When you're dealing with the Bible you're dealing with a law book. And with the law you have to be exact. It could be "lose it" as "loose it." Very close, you see. Or maybe "L-U-Z." Then a word flashes through my mind...blam! Then I knew what it meant. It's supposed to be spelled "L-U-C-I-D." 'He who seeks to save his life shall lucid.' It's close. It almost defies the brain to think that it could be that. Put it in an equation and it fits. "Lucid" means to make it clear. I'm fascinated by words because they are pathways."

In Germany Sun Ra told a group of students that *tod* ("death") spelled backwards is "dot," "period," "the end," something finished; a person who is late is tardy (someone you could then call the late Mr. X). In a Kalamazoo classroom he tested students with "virgin" and "version" and found that they confused the words when they heard them spoken. What you hear and what is said are sometimes different.

"Mathematics is balanced; it proves itself. That's what that means: when you deal with equilibrium, balance, when a person loses their equilibrium, he can't even stand up. So if this planet lost equilibrium, it would do a flip. You got to have equilibrium; that's why you got a right leg and a left leg, so you can stand up, you know. Really, a person's not really single, he's built in duality, got two arms, you see, he got to balance himself, and that's the way it should be with doctrines and religions and philosophy. It should balance itself. If it can't balance itself, you shouldn't believe it, shouldn't follow it, because then *you'd* be unbalanced.

" 'Unbalanced' also means mentally ill, so then it comes down to balance, and that's equation. It proves itself, you see. All you have to do is use intuition and reason, and you can see yourself what is needed: they need equilibrium, balance. They need sound truths that deal with sound.... That's why you can hear it. If you hear sound that's not balanced or something, it not only hurts the ear; it hurts the body."

In a poem, "A Blueprint/Declaration," he discussed equations even as he illustrated their use:

One part of an equation
Is a blueprint/declaration of the other part
Similar
Yet differentially not...

It is nothing
If it is all
Still there are different alls
The end is all

But all is everything
Yet if everything is all/the end
It denies the other side of the end
For some ends

Have many points leading to their respective selves
And there is/is each/their many points
Leading out from their
Respective selves

In another poem, "Cosmic Equation," he tells how he learned of
equations, and why they are important:

Then another tomorrow
They never told me of
Came with the abruptness of a fiery dawn
And spoke of Cosmic Equations:
The equations of sight-similarity
The equations of sound-similarity
Subtle Living Equations
Clear only to those
Whose wish is to be attuned
To the vibrations of the Outer Cosmic Worlds
Subtle Living Equations of the outer-realms
Dear only to those
Who wish fervently the greater life.
Sight and sound similarities
    are "keys to the cosmic puzzle

The Bible is filled with equations which need interpretation, and
more often than not he found that what he read was disturbing. "A friend
of the world is an enemy of God" [James 4:4], for example, which he
read to mean if anyone helps Earth he is an enemy of God, thus putting
himself in jeopardy. Or, "God is delighted when his children defeat him
in battle." What did that mean? Though he was not clear, he thought that
as in a friendly chess game, when you take the opponent's men, you put
them in a box. And when God and Satan are playing, the men get taken
and put in a box. The thing to do is not be taken.

The Bible could be rewritten to offer a correct blueprint, an alter-
destiny for earth, alter to the altar. "They've got this bible that says God
rested on the seventh day. They got to write another book to say He woke

up. They just say He went to sleep. So some force comes along and makes people rest, too. They rest right in the cemetery because they said that."

Music offered a means for dealing with words. After Babylon there was confusion in languages, but not in music, which was now the universal language—the language of the universe. Music operates like a language. Musical notes represent sounds, just as letters of the alphabet symbolize sounds. And just as there is confusion when several sounds are represented by the same letter of the alphabet, some notes—like Db and C#—for example, are the same sound when played, though different musicians can derive different interpretations from them. Music provides a model for understanding language: you can read notes backwards or upside down; they can be put together one after the other or on top of each other. And even though music theory might tell you otherwise, they are all interchangeable (while they remain different and yet the same). Words can be treated like music, by taking a sentence and moving the words around within it. Or by moving the letters around in a word. Permutating. Just as in music, where dissonance can be rationalized, you can make apparent nonsense meaningful. If musicians are tone scientists they can hear the reality of what is being played *and* said. Politics, religion, philosophy have all been tried, but music has not been given a chance. A living music could be used to decode even the Bible.

Music also provides a model for government. From the music he had experienced, big bands were living microcosms of government; the big bands best represented society, and harmonious relations between people. The bands' history showed what could be done. But bands also showed what could go wrong. When soloists were lured away from bands by promoters and turned into "stars" of small combos it promoted self-sufficiency and destroyed initiative, creating chaos in black communities. By taking musical metaphors literally, he was able to conceive of a utopia based on models of musical principles.

I've studied different philosophies, different religions, and different people, and in my study I have acquired a conviction that something is lack-

ing in most cultures, in each country, in each religion, in each philosophy.... I discovered the flaw. These people are never in tune with nature.
And when these people are in power and have responsibilities and need
to act, well, of course they're going to act with too much spirit, they're
completely out of tune, and nothing is going to work.

My music is an example of what I have just said, and the solutions I am
proposing. In effect, in music, even if your instrument is slightly out of
tune, and that happens a certain amount of time, if you are the musician
which you should be, and you intervene where it is necessary, and you
were to play with a maximum of precision and discipline, you're never
lost or panicked. You can lean on something that is firm and the music
will come out good enough. In other words, if you take two guys, one of
whom is a little sharp and one of whom is a little flat, these two might just
play well together, but if you insist on playing alone and you are out of
tune, it's terrible.

So, today people are completely out of tune, but the people...could
sound magnificent if they had the correct composer or arranger, who
would know how to judiciously use them and to make them play together
and obtain a certain sound.

His concern with precision and discipline took shape against what he
saw as an American addiction to freedom and liberty. Freedom had
proved itself a plague, a curse, especially for black people, a false idol
which they had chased after but which has remained unattainable and
ultimately unnatural. Freedom from what? Freedom from eternal life?
Freedom from being? The Bible warns you: "But take heed lest by any
means this liberty of yours become a stumbling block to them that are
weak" [1 Corinthians 8:9]. Freedom is a code word for death, and the
only truly free people are in the cemetery, where they rest in peace (another trick word, by the way). Patrick Henry said give me liberty or give
me death—and he got both.

The people of Earth, he said, have been free of the universe long
enough—they've been isolationist and Earth-centered. But there are
other people and governments. Freedom is a double-edged sword. "Look
at the kind of people who say, 'I'm free, white, and 21.' Are they free? I
see myself as P-H-R-E but not F-R-E-E. That's the name of the sun in

ancient Egypt." But a balance is needed: freedom with discipline. Freedom must give way to interplanetary discipline. We should have discipline, discipline, discipline, twenty-four hours a day. There should be programs where you can turn to a station called "Discipline" and they can present the people on this planet who deal with discipline.

Liberty, too, is not all it's cracked up to be: even the liberty bell is cracked, for that matter, and it was liberty that led people to the use of crack.

Equality is another false goal. There is no equality in nature, no democracy, only hierarchy, where you are judged by your quality. Music is not based on equality—the chords and notes are all different. Equality means nothing to God: everyone he sent here is unique. I have to rise above liberty and freedom and equality.

Sun Ra's views on race and the role of black people on Earth changed strikingly over the years. A few years before he began teaching at Berkeley, he could say: "Now, when I speak of Black, I am speaking of more than what others speak of. I am speaking of ancient black people and ancient black Wisdom people, who are the natural government of nature by the oath of their ancestors."

Blacks were originally in direct contact with God, and other races had to reach Him through them. But black people did something wrong, lost contact, fell, for spiritual reasons, leaving them with little but music, a gift of the Creator. And when the white man bought that, they were left with nothing of their own. Look at the big bands: black people had the best ones, and whites lured the arrangers away for their own bands and signed the star musicians up to play in combos, destroying black people's models of discipline and precision and generosity and beauty. (It was not a matter of prejudice, though: white people destroyed their own bands the same way.) Now blacks are trying to re-create their ties to the Creator through church services and ecstatic rituals. Whites never had this contact, and are new and evolutionarily immature in spiritual matters. So integration is not such a good idea.

Sun Ra's life on Earth bridged a period in which he felt that desegregation had weakened the black community and made the idea of a community less possible: The Bible said, "Separate yourself, O, my people. Do not partake of a sin" [2 Corinthians 6:17]. Rome itself had been conquered by intermarriage and integration. It was not that he blamed whites alone for slavery—Africans and Arabs were also involved; and in any case he did not believe that one race can be saved at the expense of another. The entire whole planet needs help.

In earlier years he had addressed himself almost completely to the problems of black people: "I'm concerned with blacks because to me black people are not in tune with their natural selves. So I have to start with them because if they're not reconciled to the equation, then the world never will be anything.... The rest of the nations have had some sort of discipline or order or government. But they haven't...I...have to set up some sort of discipline program for black people."

Black people, above all, suffer under the spell of the idea of death. In *The Fire Next Time,* James Baldwin wrote:

Life is tragic simply because the earth turns and the sun inexorably rises and sets, and one day, for each of us, the sun will go down for the last time. Perhaps the whole root of our trouble, the human trouble, is that we will sacrifice all the beauty of our lives, will imprison ourselves in totems, taboos, crosses, blood sacrifices, steeples, mosques, races, armies, flags, nations, in order to deny the fact of death, which is the only fact we have.

Sun Ra understood him as saying that the only truth blacks know is death; and since whites can't face death, they hate blacks for it.

As black nationalism took hold in the 1960s he was often acclaimed as one of its aesthetic theorists. But he never espoused all or even most of the main tenants of the orthodoxy. He agreed that black people should have their own culture, and he favored cultural centers for blacks at one point, and later even urged emigration to space, thus solving the nationalists' "land question" (what Baraka called the "space question") on an intergalactic level. Yet he also began with the assumption that they were no longer African peoples, and had very little in common with Africans. And since American blacks had come from different ethnic groups in

Africa, it was difficult to see them as unified by heritage. In any case here they had been isolated, without their own language, their own government.

He had little sympathy for the popular solutions proposed in the 1960s. He mocked them viciously: black pride? It goeth before the fall. Black power? I prefer black weakness, he'd say, black cosmo weakness. Power gets absorbed, but weakness unleashed could destroy the whole earth. The question for him was whether white people had enough imagination and sincerity to want a better world. If they did, they could do what the black man had failed to do. Once the black man had had the same chance, had been at the tip-top of civilization in the world, and had had a choice, and made the wrong one. The white race is at that point now. They've got a choice: they either move forward to greater things, greater things than have ever been done on this planet, or else they follow the way of the rest of civilization that came up, and then they die. But America doesn't have to do that, despite the prophets of doom, despite the Bible itself, despite anything. There's always a better way. Things are at a point where the world needs America to do something else that hasn't been done, some impossible things. America achieved becoming the richest country in the world, and when you achieve one thing, the way is always open for another thing.

White people have set themselves up as god, he said, taught black people to worship them for the power they have. Then white people chose inferior blacks to be on top; and then they talk about blacks being inferior! I have no interest in black supremacy, but in spiritual superiority.

"I couldn't approach black people with the truth because they like lies. They live lies. They say, 'Love they neighbor as thyself,' but I don't see them doing that. I don't think of Negroes as my brothers... I'm a demon. They respect that. I'm going to beat the superficiality out of them.... At one time I felt that white people were to blame for everything, but then I found out they're just puppets and pawns of some greater force, which has been using them. And giving them money and giving them everything to make them feel, 'Oh well, I'm supreme.' It fooled them—made a fool out of *them* too—and also made a fool out of black people. Some force is having a good time off both of them, and looking, enjoying itself in a reserved seat, wondering, 'I wonder when they're going to wake up.' "

He began to distance himself from all races, and resorted to verbal shock tactics to make the point. In England he said that he was not "an African American, but an English American...I don't know any African languages." Later, when Francis Davis asked him how black people should be referred to, he answered, "I say 'dark'—I like the word 'dark' better than I do 'black.' Black folk used to be darkies. 'That's Why Darkies Were Born.' 'Without a Song.' I take that as my song. God didn't give black folks nothin' except the music. I used to be interested in saving black people. Now, they're expendable as far as I'm concerned."

One night at the Knitting Factory Jazz Festival in 1988 he startled even the Arkestra by announcing that he wanted to begin by talking about niggers. He opened his bandstand lecture by deriving "nigger" (especially as white people in the South pronounce it) from Hebrew, where "*ger*" means "stranger" or "alien." Then he went on to suggest that America is a nation of niggers: we have English niggers, Jewish niggers, Irish niggers, Chinese niggers, a whole country of niggers; only Indians are not niggers. Was this a twist on D. H. Lawrence's vision of America as a nation of escaped slaves? On Jean Toomer's idea of Americans as a new race, "The Blue Men"? Perhaps, but his notion of race and races and his place among them reached further:

"Because of segregation, I have only a vague knowledge of the white world and that knowledge is superficial. Because I know more about black than white, I know my needs and naturalness, I know my intuition is to be what it is natural for me to be—that is the law of nature everywhere. There are different orders of being, for each order has its own way and weigh of being, just as each color has its own vibration. My measurement of race is rate of vibration—beams, rays.... In the scheme of things even the least of the brothers has his day, and when you realize the meaning of that day, you will feel the presence of an angel in disguise."

He said he was not a man, not a mortal, but part of the angel race, the dark spirit/angel race (an archangel, of course), a different order of

being. Angels are pure spirit, so they don't make mistakes. He referred
Berkeley students to Geoffrey Hodson's *The Brotherhood of Angels and of
Men,* in which angels were taxonomized as those of power, of the healing
arts, of the house, of building, of nature, of beauty and art, and of music.
Angels of music are God's instrument: they glow with the color of their
song, and every light and sound is an echo of God's voice and eyes. All
men are the instruments they play on. ("Angels" he derived from the
Greek "angelos," or "messenger," thus making him a jazz messenger.)

Angels managed to enter the country through slavery, Sun Ra said,
because blacks were taken in through the Department of Commerce
rather than Justice (demons got in as well, since there were no passports
required for slavery). So therefore mixed up among humans you have
angels. "They come here and act like poor people, they come in and act
like slaves, and they have control, and people didn't even know
it...there's a lot of people who said, 'Oh, yeah, they ain't nothing, they
beasts,' and they brought them on in, and in doing that they allowed anything to come in here. They allowed people who were emperors and
kings and nobles...now they're all down here together, so you couldn't
tell which was what."

In the liner notes to the Saturn record *Discipline 27–II,* he wrote:

Sunbursts appear in dark disguises
Bringing to fore
The strange truth of Eternal myth
Is the Sound, It is the
Sound truth...Music Sound
And there always is music
The music always is
Whatever is
Always whatever is the music is
The sound pure
The sound symmetry
Equational values: vibrational
Differentiations: rhythms,
Harmonies, thought moods, Pattern
Silences that speak

Cohesive points bridges connect
opposites.......
There is black sound
The code
Projector sensitivity
Force reach decision
Perpendicular spirals
Galaxies, planets, earth
Man and his world
And the other world of man
Comprehension response
To the world of angels

Angels and demons: the demonic is the terrifying, but as the ancients knew, not necessarily bad; besides, everything on Earth is bad, so if being good means Earth, he wanted to be bad. He took Pearl Buck's title *The Good Earth* to be ironic.

> I am not ruled like a man: the measure of a man is what he rules; the sun never sets on the British Empire, a hell of a measurement. If you can rule yourself, no one else can rule you; or measure you.

Part of the answer is to create myths of the future, since some truths are too difficult and threatening to be expressed openly; truth is not malleable, whereas myth can be shaped. The future people are talking about is no good; we need to do the impossible. Calling on his dream experiences, he said, "I've been told by these forces that it can be done, a substitute future, a vice-future (though not a bad one), an alter-destiny can be developed, a substitution in an equation, for the future, too, is an equation. I would say that the synonym for myth is happiness—because that's why they go to the show, to the movies, and they sit up there under these myths trying to get themselves some happiness. And if the actors can indulge in myth, why can't the musicians? They might be actors in sound...."

Astro-Black mythology was what he had to develop: black people are not real in this society. They exist here as myths, but other people's myths. "I really prefer mythocracy to democracy. Before history. Anything before history is a myth.... That's where black people are. Reality equals death, because everything which is real has a beginning and an end. Myth speaks of the impossible, of immortality. And since everything that's possible has been tried, we need to try the impossible."

He held a special wrath for certain terms the Bible honors—"the righteous," "the good," and "the bad" and "truth," for example. He mockingly deployed them in extravagant wordplay: "the righteous fight for the right; nobody fights for the wrong. So right must be so good. With me [my way], you lose the freedom to die (if I'm right). I've seen a lot of righteous people didn't make it, but I'm neither righteous nor otherwise, because I don't have no standards to go by what 'righteous' is. But I might be pure evil, I don't know, since I can't be pure good, I have no alternative but to say I'm pure evil, and I don't be doin' nothin' to harm people or to help them all the time. That makes me doubly evil, though.... I'm doing wrong by doing good for people, but I make the name 'evil' nice because it's compared to those who say they're 'good.'... They say they're righteous and they never do anything that's right; I can say I'm evil and never do anything that's bad. It works both ways. But then my way can win."

Sometimes it seemed merely a practical distinction: The righteous don't make mistakes, he said, so they can't learn from their mistakes; the righteous have not supported beauty and art; and if the righteous were to be the saved, he thought it was unfair—immortality should be for everyone, including the unrighteous and the already dead. Sometimes he found counter-evidence in the Bible: "Be not righteous over much; neither make thyself over wise: why shouldest thou destroy thyself?" [Ecclesiastes 8:17].

"Good" and "bad" likewise he gave special scrutiny: "My mind refuses to believe there are any bad people now, even though a lot of people have tried to do things to me, talk about me so bad. But I really don't have any animosity toward humanity. They have my sympathy. They've done a good job in ignorance to be as far as they are.

"... Death takes everybody, so anything that's greater than that would also have to do that. But it would be quite wrong to just save all the good

people and not give the bad ones a chance. Bad people are quite interesting sometimes. They have a lot of imagination."

When Mayor Wilson Goode of Philadelphia authorized the dropping
of an incendiary bomb during a raid on the headquarters of MOVE in
Philadelphia in the 1980s, setting off on a fire which destroyed blocks of
houses and killing many, Sun Ra simply said, "It's not about how good
you are. Mayor Goode was bad.

" 'Truth' can also be bad, as when a man says 'I'll kill you' and he does.
The moment of truth in a bullfight is the time of the bull's death. A bull
is an announcement of truth nailed to a tree. Jesus was nailed to a tree.
The Bible is made of trees and has leaves. It is the tree of knowledge.
'You shall know a tree by its fruit.' And the Bible is a source of trouble to
those who don't understand it.

"Those who live by reality are slaves of truth. It's a kind of narcotic, a
dope. When the police find out the truth about you, they say they get the
'dope' on you; they talk about a drug that can make you truthful, 'truth
serum.' So the dope will make you free. Truth can be bad."

In fact, people who tell the real truth are the ones who suffer.... People have been misled, he said, they're in deep ignorance, the more they
learn the worse the planet gets, so they get to killing a lot of people who
said the world was round and burning up some poor soul for telling the
truth, and they got rid of a lot of people who really were telling the
truth to help the planet. And now they need them, but they killed them.
And they're wanting to follow what they thought was true. And the
world is in this condition it's in today because of them killing these people that were telling the truth. It's time to try myth.

This all may seem strange, but they say that truth is stranger than
fiction.

"They say that history repeats itself; but history is only his-story. You
haven't heard my story yet. My story is different from his story. My story
is not part of history because history repeats itself. But my story is endless, it never repeats itself. Why should it? The sunset does not repeat itself. Neither does a sunrise. Nature never repeats itself. My story is
close to mystery. My story is better for man than history. Mystery is better than history. What's your story?"

So his lectures went. Any word might be the subject of investigation and play. "USA" turned up in "JerUSAlem," for example; "liberal" might be connected to "churl" etymologically; or he might identify himself not as "occult," but as "ninth cult." Or class discussion might focus on the importance of music to order and morality. And in a typical class handout, such as one titled "The Other Side of Music," several of these concerns surfaced together:

Some music is of specialized interpretation. Some music is of synchronization precision. Every light is a vibrational sight and sound: It is rhythm in harmony with beams/rays/intensification and projection visibility. Music is light and darkness... precedent of vitality... stimulation extraordinary.

EVERY PLACE THERE IS MUSIC. CHAOS IS MUSIC AND HARMONIOUS PEACE IS MUSIC.

.....

..... Silence is music. There are different kinds of silences, each silence is a world all of it's own. In a lesser but not least important sense, silence is an integral part of all music: in a fractional sense when judged metrically.

We must not forget transposition. Transposition always results in a change of color. Behold the vastness of music, it is as vast as the greater allness and the greater neverness... and too music in its meta-phases must not be ignored. Are you thinking of metaphysics alone? Well don't. In the future and even as of now, you will have to contend with and recognize METAMENTAL and METASPIRIT, also you will come face to face with oblique METATHESIS

Black is space: THE OUTER DARKNESS, the void direction to the heavens. Each spaceport planet is a heaven/haven. Planet earth is erth (permutation thre/three), planet #3 from the sun. From this reckoning, it is the third heaven. The music of the outer darkness is the music of the void. The opening is the void; but the opening is synonym to the beginning. This is an indication interpretation.

... Some music is of specialized interpretation.... Some music is of synchronization precision. Sometimes music becomes more than music, and this thought reach is of the incredible plane.

POETRY

Though musicians or journalists seldom asked Sonny about his poetry, it was one of his principal activities in this period and often supplemented his lectures. He had begun writing poetry when he was nine years old. And when he did, he told writer James Spady, "I wasn't influenced by Paul Laurence Dunbar's poetry. He was a sentimentalist. I'm a scientist.... I take the position of a scientist who comes from another dimension." "They're all scientific equations. I am dealing outside conventional wisdom. I want to explore the ultra dimensions of being. We must move beyond life and death considering they are not essential in the universe. I know more about other regions than this planet."

He made a point of including his poetry on his album covers, concert programs, and record sales brochures: "... in a certain sense it's not really poetry. Sometimes the verses rhyme, sometimes they don't." He even on occasion said that the poetry was the most important part of his work, and that the music was just a pretext to make it possible and to get people's attention. He had read the southern poet Sidney Lanier's *The Science of English Verse* when it was argued that sound could serve as artistic material, the body as a musical instrument. Poetry offered him a chance to compose with language as he did with music:

What I want to do is associate words so they produce a certain fact. If you mix two chemical products you produce a reaction. In the same way if you put together certain words you'll obtain a reaction which will have a value for people on this planet. That's why I continue to put words together. Einstein said he was looking for an equation for eternal life. But we built the atomic bomb, and his project has never materialized. But I'm sure he was right. To put words together, or, even if you could, to paint the image that is necessary to put out the vibrations that we need, that would change the destiny of the whole planet.

His poems were heavily Neoplatonic in content, the music of the spheres playing in the background, poetry as music as divine order; he toys with number symbolism, focuses on creativity and incarnation. This is not "jazz poetry," raising rhythm like a flag triumphantly over the poetic landscape; nor is it a poetry susceptible to the vernacular style dominant in black writing of the 1960s and 1970s, one open only to cries of anger, or celebrations of the ghetto or the ghetto warrior. As he said, he was not a sentimentalist. "Sun Ra took the high post," Amiri Baraka said. "He spoke from the pulpit, essentially as minister, but also as a prophet. He was always preaching; and though his preachments were not of this world, they were there for those who needed to be ministered to." The preacher's high style is one point of reference, the blues singer another, for there is always the first-person singularity of his location in these poems, a deep identification with his subject, even if it calls on him to play the "bad man" for a higher moral purpose.

In the rush to meet the demand for black literature at the end of the 1960s, Doubleday expressed interest in publishing Sun Ra's work. Sonny and several others went to work preparing a manuscript for publication, Sonny typing on his own typewriter with "cursive" fonts, with others helping. But the book never appeared, some saying it was because of Alton Abraham's lack of approval, others saying Doubleday felt it was closer to philosophy than poetry. Still, Sun Ra went ahead on his own, and he and Alton Abraham published *The Immeasurable Equation* and *Extensions Out. The Immeasurable Equation, Vol. II* through Ihnfinity, Inc./Saturn Research of Chicago in 1972, though both books got very poor distribution.

On Christmas Day, 1976, Sun Ra read a selection of his poems accompanied by music on the program "Blue Genesis" over the University of Pennsylvania's radio station WXPN. The choice of poems and their sequencing offers a sense of what Sun Ra thought was most important in his writing. Here are key words like "cosmos," "truth," "bad," "myth," and "the impossible,"; attention to phonetic equivalence; the universality of music and its metaphysical status; allusions to black fraternal orders and secret societies; biblical passages and their interpretation; and even a few autobiographical glimpses. The poems were read softly, with little expression, the music punctuating the words, with the heavy echo and delay in the studio sometimes reducing the words to pure sound without meaning:

PLANES OF NATURE

If they would rise above their wisdom
They could see nature as it is
And they would understand
That there are other planes of nature
Greater than the plane they know.

All around them
See the other measure
To the other wisdom-ignorance-myth.

COSMOS QUERY

Why should a god visit earth
If to be only a slave to man
Why should a man be a slave to man
If only to be a slave to man
Or a man to God
Or a god to man?
If only to be within a state
Unnatural to his natural self
Or alter-self

COSMOS EVOLUTION

When men are brothers
They are brothers because they
know they are.
They walk the initiate bridge
degree of pointlessness.....

Friends of pointless.....
Intuition companionship.
Sincere understandingness.....
of/on angelic planes of being.
That is why I have said they are
not my brothers if they are not
brothers.

WHEN YOU MEET A MAN

When you meet a man
You meet a scheme of words
Patterns of concept
A concepted being
Whose very birth conception is called.

TRUTH IS BAD/GOOD

Truth is bad
Or truth is good
It depends upon where
And how and who you are.
The word truth must be considered carefully
And the precepts of that which is called truth
Must be equationized and balanced

And understood.
Or else, it must be abandoned
And another truth placed in its place.
This is the idea of the greater age
The outer worlds of etherness
This is the word from the Cosmic-Cosmo-Tomorrow.

THE SOUND IMAGE

That's what the music says, that is how to say the music...
The music is a journey, the journey is endless
It is sound endlessly communication language point.
Endless sound is a universal because that is what the music is
That is what the music is, the universal language
The bridge-communication sound
There is no other way to speak to everyone in language each can
Feel and understand except through the music.

How can you speak to other worlds except through the music, the
music lets them know, where you are at and what you are.
If you are pure, the music's pure.
The music is the testing ground, it is your choice that tells the tale,
When all else fails.

Pure music is what you must face.
If you limit, if you reject, if you do not consider
If you are selfish-earthly bound,
Pure music is your nemesis.

You cannot pretend: you will accept or you will reject.
There is no middle ground.
The mirror of pure sound is a negative field/feel that photographs
The image-mind impression soul and psychic-self even the
potential
immediate alter-destiny/destinies.

The music is the image is the music is the image
The sound image.

The living image of sound......Image
Sound of the Cosmo-World approach journey.
The waves of sound are like the waves of water in the ocean
There is a tide and time of sound
This the music is like a journey
Which is endless
Unscheduled directions are suddenly necessary
Now and then to synchronize the code momentum dimension
To environmental light or darkness equation-balance image
Or improvisational alter counterpoint blueprint sound.
The music is not only just music.
It touches and projects other dimensions
Time-zone eternities and cosmo-infinity spiral-parallels
The parallels are feels/fields of parables, which are instruments
For the instruments are not only just instruments
The people are the instrument.
That's how the music goes, that's what the music is.....

That is the mirror on the wall, above the handwriting there.
It is invisible to all
It is a mirror that you must hear
Vibration...rhythm...harmonic sound is hidden in each melody.
It is never what it seems to be
You can only hear what the mirror sees. No more, nor less is ever
    allowed
The sound mirror is what you see of you that's sound.
       If you're not sound,
       Then you're not pure
Pure is real-sincerity
    and pure knows pure is sound and true.
            It's all what the music says of you
            It's not what the music you say of it.
IT'S ALL WHAT THE MUSIC SAYS OF YOU
   The music is the living mirror of the universe.

   The Pivoting Planes
When the word was spoken,

IT WAS BALANCED ON THE
    PIVOTING PLANES OF SOUND,
When it was written, it reflected one plane of sight
    And the triple meaning with its multi-divisions
Was no longer apparent,
    Because the meaning of the balanced word
on the PIVOTING PLANES
            cannot be written as revealingly as it
            can be thought and felt
        Because the idea of the PIVOTING PLANES
      is like a touch of vibrating magic
        And the magic is the wisdom-ignorance
          Of unspeakable understanding
          intuition.
Thus is the idea of the PIVOTING PLANES
    of the
      greater impossible
      and the
    Immeasurable
      equation
    SPACE-VOID
      reality
        on
        the
        outer reach
          of the unending
          On
          ONNESS "O   N."

THE POTENTIAL

Beyond other thought and other worlds
Are the things that seem not to be
And yet are.
How impossible is the impossible
Yet the impossible is a thought

And every thought is real
An idea, a flash of intuition's fire
A seed of fire that can bring to be
The reality of itself.
Beyond other thought and other words
Are the potentials....
That hidden circumstance
And pretentious chance
Cannot control.

THE FOOLISH FOE

There were some things I never tried to do
And most of them were things I wanted to do
... There were opposing forces
   Why should they oppose me?
   Why? Why?
Now and then I thought, there is
No such enemy as I think they are.
But then, it is beyond thought ... it is beyond thought ...
I feel
These opposing forces whose power is their weakness
The power they grant to their servants/subjects
They exist, Indeed they do.
I feel and always have felt
It is, it always was true
Since this plane of existent I came to be, to know
They are are/were here!
I never resisted them,
They think I did
It was only pretense desires I projected to them
Were my non-resistance weapon/shield of defense.
I do not desire what they thought I desire
Neither now nor ever then
Non-resistance became my resistance

My resistance is non-resistance. Do they challenge?
I resist the challenge
Foolish foe!
I have already won the victory
How? You will never know.
I have forgotten the how I did
I only know I know only
I only know....
It was never your game,
It is always mine
I resist the challenge
Foolish Foe
I always win the victory
You did not know the secret code
If I win, I win and if I lose I win!
You did not know

You do not know!

THE ENDLESS UNIVERSE

This universe is endless
And everything in it is endless
How can it be an endless universe, if everything is not endless
That is a part of it?
Every beginning is an end
Look back and see, it's in the past
Every beginning is the end of some endlessness

But the past is an eternity all its own
It is not a part of the endless Universe
Because the past had an end, it is a realm of the ended...

Look backward at the past
And you will see all the beginnings are there

If you have an end in view, what's your aim/desire?
Be careful!
Do not make the end you seek
The end.
There are different kinds of ends
Like bookends are
And bookends are
But Book ends end.
What does the law of bookings say?
That is the answer of the way . . .
When they are booked, they're in the book.
What does the Good BOOK say?
The planet earth is booked
Within the BOOK
The GUIDE BOOK leads the world,
"I will be their guide," it says . . .
Whence does earth go?
And whither man?
"I will be their guide even unto _____ ."

Let's say It said, *the end,* instead.
For what are words but words to use
Let's take words and return,
The Bad Guide Book Good says that too.
A simple thing, it's simple true
TAKE WORDS AND RETURN . . . . . .
There's no way other left for you.
"TAKE WORDS AND RETURN" . . . .

from

THE AIR SPIRITUAL MAN

All creative art is music. Art . . . choreography . . . sculpture . . . portraits . . .
art works, photography, painting, architectural designs, the forms of na-

ture: trees, flowers, grass. Everything vibrational is of different degrees of music. There is music everywhere infinite...infinity is the language of endearing impression.

Rhythm, melody, and harmony: melody is of rhythm as rhythm is of melody: while a harmony is often concealed melody when it moves with the compositional theme/melody. Variety is a key to movement in composition.

The potentials of music in its relationship to people is still as if untouched in any of the spheres such as mental, spiritual, physical, psychic nature.... Musicians of great worth to this planet have too often been frustrated out of doing what nature intended for them to do; as a result, all too often the substitute of a more aggressive but less talented person has taken the place of the natural musician-artist, thus bypassing the masters.

The beauty of music is that it can reach across the border of reality into the myth...impressions never known before can be conveyed immediately. A sincere universal mind can universalize the world by the simple act of doing so. But that idea is of the myth and it is of the myth which I speak. The potential of the myth is inexpressible because it is of the realm of the impossible.

Myth demands another type of music. It is all because of the necessities of another age which needs another type of music which has not been of the known reality before. Music then will have a different place in the sun.

The earth cannot move without music. The earth moves in a certain rhythm, a certain sound, a certain note. When the music stops the earth will stop and everything upon it will die.

The Berkeley job offered a comfortable arrangement for Sonny and the band. They had free housing, the University of California loaned them a station wagon, and there was a ready supply of gigs, paying and non-paying: they worked at local clubs like the Native Son, and presented a chaotic concert at Ho Chi Minh Park in Berkeley with 100 saxophonists. Sun Ra became a well-known local figure, and could be seen almost anywhere—in the bookstores, teaching a master class at San Francisco State College, or in the supermarket, rolling a cart filled with nothing but cabbage and toilet paper.

But then things started to go bad: an ideological split within the Panthers resulted in the Arkestra being evicted from their house ("we got kicked out by Eldridge Cleaver or somebody"); and Sun Ra said he was not paid for two months that he taught at Berkeley. Sonny said it was because of the controversial content of his lectures (noting the deposing of Haile Selassie, and heaping blame on Ethiopia for the slave trade, he said the Black House had fallen, and anticipating Watergate, predicted that the White House and Nixon were the next to fall—" 'Nix' means 'no,' you know; and 'on' backwards is 'no,' too"); or because Berkeley assumed that he was in Egypt that term. Governor Ronald Reagan was at the time building his presidential bid by attacking the state colleges and universities for having Angela Davis, "a known Communist," on the payroll of the State of California. If Reagan had only known that Sun Ra was teaching at Berkeley, who knows how different American history might have been.

With no place to live, and having been stiffed for the Berkeley gig, Sun Ra took the Arkestra back East. But while the Arkestra was still living in Oakland, Sun Ra had been approached by film producer Jim Newman with an idea of making a half-hour documentary of the Arkestra for PBS. Newman thought they might shoot with a true "cosmic light show" at the planetarium in San Francisco, the band seated in the audience. And though that particular plan never materialized, with John Coney as director, a new kind of film was conceived: *Space Is the Place*, part documentary, part science fiction, part blaxploitation, part revisionist biblical epic. Strange enough in its own time, as the years passed it assumed an even stranger aura of 1970s ideas and affectations and what appears to be the genuinely timeless in Sun Ra's dress and manner.

The final version of the film is easy enough to summarize (if not so easy to understand): having been traveling in space for some years in a rocket ship propelled by music as fuel, Sun Ra locates a planet which he deems suitable for the resuscitation of the black race. He returns to earth and lands in Oakland, circa 1972 (where in real life the Arkestra was staying and where the Black Panthers were under attack by the police and the FBI). Throughout the film Ra battles with the Overseer, a supernatural pimp who profits from the degradation of black people. Sun Ra offers those who would follow him into space an "alter-destiny," but the Overseer, the FBI, and NASA ultimately force him to return to space prematurely.

It would be a mistake to take the film too literally as a reflection of Sun Ra's ideas. Though he did make many suggestions during the filming which were ultimately incorporated—the scenes at the Rosicrucian building in L.A.; the arrival in the spaceship; the flashback to a Chicago club in 1943 (representing an incident that took place in the Club DeLisa when a mobster threatened him); his costumes, etc. But producer Newman says that no one was sure of all of the meanings of the film, as it was collectively written and considerably re-edited (Joshua Smith, the writer, was added after shooting had started; and Sun Ra—though he took directions well—kept leaving the script behind, or ignoring it). The Overseer, for example, started out as the mirror-faced, hooded figure seen first near the beginning of the film. But the name soon became used for the devil-like card player who contends with Sun Ra for dominion over the earth. Throughout the filming, Sun Ra was reading daily in *The Urantia Book,* the same 2,000-page channeled tome which Karlheinz Stockhausen was also given in 1971, setting off his monster composition, "Licht," which he has been working on ever since. *The Urantia Book* is an account of the history and nature of the universe (of which Urantia, or Earth, is only a small part), and which predicts that a celestial musician will appear on Earth one day who could change the world. The Overseer may have been inspired by the Celestial Overseers of this book, but may also derive from plantation foremen like Simon Legree in the literature of American slavery. Perhaps Sun Ra's overriding concern was that NASA had launched a program which would guarantee the segregation of space; and, in a twist on the Great Society Programs of Lyndon Johnson, he wanted to offer black youth something through the space program.

Since some of the actors were high-visibility characters from other films (like Johnny Keys, who was in *Behind the Green Door* and Ray Johnson from *Dirty Harry*), there was a sense of the mélange in the casting alone. It's possible to identify allusions to LeRoi Jones's *A Black Mass* or to the ideas of various black nationalist groups and artists, but the influence of recent black films like *Cotton Comes to Harlem, Shaft, Hit Man,* and *Superfly* are also clear. Too clear, Sun Ra, thought, and though he seemed to enjoy the humor in some of the sex scenes at first, after he and Tommy Hunter came back in 1973 to complete a few sequences, he demanded they be cut. Finally, the film was reduced from ninety minutes to sixty-three minutes with several scenes removed, including two sexual situations; a pool-hall scene with a junkie who, after hearing space music, forgoes drugs and enters the spaceship at the end; and a scene in which Sun Ra saves some white people ("We can't do that! The NAACP will be after us!").

Sun Ra's contract earned him 50 percent of the gross, and he became very involved in the final product. He began to spend a lot of time at the movies in order to get ideas. But many of the suggestions he came up with were impossible to execute or difficult for Newman to understand. After Sonny went back East they spent hours on the phone talking about his concerns: then Sonny said he would edit it himself, and Newman sent him a copy of the footage. Sun Ra began to think the whole film should be remade: it needed more beauty; it should be a spiritual film; a blueprint for a better world:

> In anything there's a barter system, you know. You give something to get something. That's what I'm saying in this movie. Put what you have to offer in exchange for immortality. What do you have to offer me? And then I said, you have one thing that you can give me that's priceless in exchange for your life. You got one thing that you can give me in exchange for the life of this planet. It's priceless. It has no price on it. And I said that's black folks because they're priceless. They have no price. They're worthless. Which makes them priceless. They ain't worth nothing. Priceless. Give them to me. That's in the film.

After a couple of showings in San Francisco and New York, *Space Is the Place* disappeared, leaving behind only an album of that name on Blue Thumb Records, and thus became the consummate underground film. Pieces of it were sometimes projected behind the Arkestra without sound, like shards from some vanished civilization, but it was gone. Sonny later said that elements of his ideas and the film were used both in *Star Wars* and *Close Encounters of the Third Kind* (the intervals of the 1960 melody "Lights on a Satellite" in fact evoke the spaceship tones of *Close Encounters*). And by 1988 he bitterly talked about putting even the objectionable scenes back in ("I want to put earth things back in there so I deceive people a little bit. I want them to think that I'm a phony.").

Distribution of Saturn Records had improved over the last couple of years after a Chicago record firm agreed to handle their records, but now that that company was being taken over by another one, the remaining records were cut out and sold just above cost. But even this helped Sun Ra to become better known, as the records wound up for sale in small-town drugstores and five-and-dime stores.

In 1972 Ed Michel, the producer of the recording *Space Is the Place,* offered Sun Ra and Alton Abraham a lucrative contract on behalf of ABC/Impulse to rerelease the bulk of the Saturn catalog and to go into the studio and make new records. Thirty reissues were prepared for release, an introductory sampler called *Welcome to Saturn,* and four new albums were recorded, *Astro Black* (1972), *Pathways to Unknown Worlds* (1975), *Crystal Spears,* and *Cymbals* (both possibly 1972). Over the next three years Impulse issued two of the new recordings, *Astro Black* (in quadraphonic sound) and *Pathways to Unknown Worlds,* and reissued *Angels and Demons at Play, Super-Sonic Jazz* (under the title *Supersonic Sounds*), *Jazz in Silhouette, The Nubians of Plutonia, Fate in a Pleasant Mood, Bad and Beautiful, The Magic City,* and *Atlantis,* all with new art work and press announcements.

But then ABC abruptly canceled the project, cutting out the records already issued and leaving the rest of the reissues and *Crystal Spears* and *Cymbals* unreleased. With the records cut out and dumped into sale bins of record stores Sun Ra received no more payment for sales:

> I finally consented to make some for them and what did they do? They cut the ends off so I don't get any royalties. Impulse was going to spend almost a million dollars in publicity. They were going to put out fourteen LPs at one time. Something happened where they didn't keep their contract.

Nonetheless, Impulse was the one major label with a commitment to the new jazz, having recorded John Coltrane, Archie Shepp, and most of the major figures, so their embrace of Sun Ra saw to it that his records reached a much greater audience and gave him new press attention and reviews.

CHAPTER SIX

hen Slug's closed in late 1972 it liberated the Arkestra from a dependency on New York City, closing that episode in their history and forcing them to look for new kinds of work. They had already picked up a few dates at the Monterey Jazz Festival and the Ann Arbor Blues & Jazz Festival, and Sun Ra had just won the *Down Beat* Critic's Poll for Talent Deserving of Wider Recognition, so they felt some kind of momentum developing, even though any particular day might still find them scuffling, worrying about the next week's food.

But in 1973 things began to happen, and for the next seventeen years they would be living in a blur of travel, fulfilling their destiny, as Sonny put it, to lead the lives of troubadours. There were more colleges to play, and the Newport Jazz Festival in New York. In September they returned to Europe for the third time, starting their tour on September 9 in France at the Communist Party–supported Fête de l'Humanité. When they arrived at the festival grounds they found the audience in an especially ugly mood, having already driven Jerry Lee Lewis off the stage, and Chuck Berry was leaving fast (the word was that their arrival in limos had been enough to set that volatile post–May '68 crowd off). When the Arkestra reached the stage a moratorium began as the crowd froze in amazement: audience and critics alike were bewildered by what they saw, then won over. But what had they seen? A particularly arcane black nationalist paramilitary display? A ridiculous parody of European avant-garde theater? One critic wrote that it was a quasireligious phenomenon, and like the Church itself, the band used cheap props and *son et lumière* effects. But, he asked in all seriousness, could a secular group like this move forward and progress, or would they be trapped forever in their rituals like the Church? Whatever they were, the Arkestra was disrupting critical predispositions and habits, their show calling attention to the critics' limitations. A performance like this would require multiple levels of readings, and a fuller understanding of different genres, different forms of media, and different styles of playing.

But for whatever reason—shock, delight, puzzlement—the Arkestra brought the audience to its feet seven times that day, clapping and cheering. "Music," Sonny said matter-of-factly, "soothes the savage beast." It soothed them enough, in fact, that the Ballet Folklórico de Mexico which followed next was also received well, for which the dancers and the Minister of Culture of Mexico credited the Arkestra.

They played the Olympia in Paris on September 30, but poor advance press put them into a hall three-quarters empty. The critics were there, though, and overflowing with praise and interpretations: other critics were wrong, they said, Sun Ra was about laughter, fun. His Egypt was the Egypt of Laurel and Hardy, the Egypt of the bazaar (someone actually called it "an Africa made in Chicago"); it was tradition without the Oedipal complex, a burlesque subversion of borrowed cultural and ideological elements. The Arkestra was, as the French would say, a rich text.

Over the next few days they worked a discotheque in Nancy ("I play for people on the left and the right: to me it's the same thing") and then went back to Paris to The Gibus for an appearance which was recorded for French Atlantic Records. Next on to the United States for a free concert organized by ESP Records for Jennings Hall, a temporary shelter for boys, in an effort to call attention to New York City's failed youth services program; and they followed that on December 22 by an ESP-sponsored "Celebration for the Comet Kohoutek" at Town Hall in New York a few weeks before the comet passed close to the earth on its once-in-127-years' journey.

Throughout 1973 and 1974 many of Sun Ra's performances were called "Space Is the Place," a program in which much of the music heard in abbreviated versions on the film soundtrack was played at full length, while portions of the film were shown behind the band. The *Soundtrack to the Film "Space Is the Place"* (recorded in 1972 but not released until 1993) samples their working repertory at the time. There were Sun Ra spirituals like "Satellites Are Spinning" and space chants and marches such as "Calling Planet Earth," "Space Is the Place," "We'll Wait for You," "Outer Spaceways, Inc.," and "Along Came Ra," the piece with which the Arkestra was now regularly introducing Sun Ra. They returned to the epiphanies of *Strange Strings* and great percussion expositions like "Watusa" and "When the Black Man Ruled the World"; there were the sawtooth melodies of Ra's Moog on "Cosmic Forces" and "We'll Wait for You"; free-improvised, collective "cells" or bursts of sound ("I Am the Brother of the Wind"); and solos which were added to, one instrument after the other, until the weight of the sonics obliterated conventional musical forms (as on "The Overseer").

Free jazz is sometimes mistakenly described as great displays of ego, or said to be nothing more than loud, undisciplined free-for-alls, as if the music should bear the weight of all of the social excesses of the late 1960s and early 1970s; but records of performances like this one show that with Sun Ra, at least, collective, open improvisation involved a patience and a willingness to wait for things to happen, the use of subtle dynamics, and even the old-fashioned discipline of turn taking.

Sun Ra was also beginning to increase the number of swing recreations he used in every program. The recording from The Gibus had included Fletcher Henderson's "King Porter Stomp." The recent deaths of Duke Ellington and Louis Armstrong had him reflecting about the forgotten masterworks of that era. Well before the modern interest in jazz repertory ensembles in jazz, Sonny began to produce mini-concerts of swing classics within his shows. As he chanted in one piece,

> They tried to fool you
> Now I've got to school you
> About jazz
> About jazz
> Louis Armstrong, now that's jazz
> Billie Holiday, now that's jazz
> It don't mean a thing
> If it ain't got that swing

It was a move both oppositional and prescient: he had seen the limits of the avant-garde, and sensing a shift beginning in American sensibilities, he was unwilling to give up the large audiences he had drawn. And even if he moved toward the middle, his goals were still the same: "My music is self-underground—that is, it is out of the music industry: I've made records with no titles, primitive, natural and pure. I'm also recording standards so that people can compare what I do with those in the past. The avant-garde can't play other people's music because they're not mature enough."

In 1974, shortly before Sun Ra turned sixty, he accepted an invitation from the Ministry of Culture of Mexico that dated back to their meeting at the Fête de l'Humanité, and took the Arkestra on a tour of Mexico in February and March. But as soon as they arrived they ran afoul of the Musicians Union which barred them from playing; the Actors Union then interceded, and they managed to perform as actors—not that much of a stretch, after all—with the band billed as Sun Ra and his Cosmo Drama. Sun Ra told the band that an earthquake would even the score, and later it was said that the Union's office building had been leveled.

They performed at the Palacio de Bellas Artes, the Teatro Hidalgo, Chapultepec Park (where they played on a little island while people rowed around them in boats), at the University of Mexico, outdoors at housing projects, and in front of pyramids again, this time at Teotihuacan. While staying in plush accommodations, they made appearances on television and radio, visited archaeological sites, and wandered the neighborhoods.

International experiences like these encouraged Sun Ra to assert his own authority over his work. For the first time he issued his own Saturn Records from Philadelphia, records that Alton Abraham in Chicago would call "unauthorized." (The two final Saturns from Chicago were *The Soul Vibrations of Man* and *Taking a Chance on Chances* (both 1977), the last a mistitling of *Taking a Chance on Chancey*, a reference to the French hornist, Vincent Chancey.) The Philadelphia Saturns were at first only available at performances, and so some of them are known to exist today in only in a few copies each, and debate continues over whether some ever existed at all (such as the probably apocryphal *Celebrations for Dial Tones* or *The Eternal Flame of Youth*). As if more mystery was needed, some of the first Philadelphia Saturns issued (*Space Probe, Outer Spaceways Incorporated,* and *The Invisible Shield*) all appeared in the same cover, but with the records pressed chaotically, the B sides of some appearing with several different A sides. The next batch of Saturns were all hand-lettered and designed by the band, with brightly printed stickers bearing images of Thoth, Horus, and Sun Ra; the labels showed pyramids, hieroglyphs, monograms, sunbursts, Egyptian boats, Sun Ra's head, unicorns, an ankh over the eye of Horus; and some had psychedelic swirls and what appear to be rubbings from stone carvings.

Sun Ra's hesitance to assume all of the weight of the leader/performer had vanished, and though he joked about his failure to break through to stardom as part of his plan to keep a "low profile," he drew on all the theatrics and performance skills he had observed in a life of club-, theater-, and churchgoing. At the Beacon Theater in New York City, for example, he did a creditable soft-shoe dance to Billie Holiday's song, "God Bless the Child." At Gino's Empty Foxhole, the basement of a church on the edge of the University of Pennsylvania campus in Philadelphia, he used lighting combined with industrial fans to create solar storms that sent the musicians' capes billowing as if the Arkestra was in flight. Then Sun Ra disappeared into his own cape, his face outlined against the windblown fabric, and, while a space chord howled, he tore a hole in the cape and poked his head through, as if he were ripping an opening in space itself. To members of the audience who came prepared by hallucinogens and stimulants—as they did more and more often nowadays—the spectacle was magnified beyond belief.

He and the band now interacted more directly and sometimes even threateningly with the audience: more audience members were singled out for individualized cosmic treatment, the verbal messages directed face to face. Sonny added "Face the Music" to their closing moments, which they chanted over and over as they strolled the stage:

> What do you do when you know that you know
> that you know that you're wrong?

You've got to face the music
You've got to listen to the cosmo song.

It was one of the first of a series of message-songs each of which expanded the meaning of proverbial expressions on music such as "a sound
music for sound bodies and minds" or "you've got to pay the piper."

During a concert at Hunter College on June 16 they recorded *Out
Beyond the Kingdom Of,* on which Sonny returned to the piano for "Discipline 99," which was in effect a concerto which begins slowly and
erupts into double-time explosions in free tempo. Sun Ra had begun
performing carefully measured vocal declamations in this period,
which were then usually repeated by June Tyson and the other singers
(sometimes billed as the Space Ethnic Voices) or the whole band.
Though surprisingly formal, they were well within the range of what
was considered acceptable among Baptist preachers, but still far from
what jazz people would consider as "vocals."

By 1975 the Arkestra's roster of musicians included people in all parts of
the country, and they could draw on sympathetic performers wherever
they played without moving a full band. But without regular rehearsals,
new material was not always well played, and the swing re-creations especially suffered. Yet since virtually the whole saxophone section—Eloe
Omoe, James Jacson, John Gilmore, Marshall Allen, and Danny Thompson (Pat Patrick was now teaching at the State University of New York
at Old Westbury)—was living in the house in Philadelphia, they at least
were familiar with the book. Two new trumpet players, Ahmed Abdullah and Michael Ray, had joined the band: Abdullah had worked with
many of the younger players in free jazz, and Ray was a very theatrical
lead trumpet capable of a wide range of sonic tricks, humor, and physical contortions (he had played for a time in the 1980s with Kool and the
Gang).

By now they could play almost any major university or college—
places like the University of Pittsburgh, Antioch College, Kent State

University, York University in Toronto, the University of Virginia—as well as be able to get engagements as far afield as the Keystone Corner in San Francisco, the Smiling Dog Saloon in Cleveland, the Bottom Line in New York, the Jazz Showcase in Chicago, the Stables in East Lansing, Michigan, or the Minnesota Institute of Art. The crowds were not always as big as his reputation (as when a concert at La Salle College in Philadelphia drew seven people), but Sun Ra was beginning to receive respect which went beyond that given to mere performers: he was made a member of the Honorary Advisory Committee of the Black Music Center at Indiana University; and he won the *Down Beat* Critic's Poll again, this time in both the organ and synthesizer categories, and again in the Talent Deserving of Wider Recognition award.

In the summer of 1976 the Arkestra began their fourth tour of Europe with twenty-eight people and ended with fourteen, playing all the major festivals, Paris, Montreux (where they recorded *Live at Montreux*), Pescara, Nîmes, Northsea, Juan-les-Pins, and Arles, and were greeted everywhere as celebrities. Yet once they returned home to Philadelphia they still sank back into semiobscurity, the band playing down the block at the Red Carpet Lounge to a neighborhood audience of twenty, or at outdoor free concerts in the parks of North Philadelphia, to which sometimes no one came.

At the end of 1976 the Arkestra was invited to participate at the last minute in FASTEC 77 (the World Black and African Festival of Arts and Culture) in January 1977 in Lagos, a huge four-week diasporic celebration promoted by the newly oil-rich government of Nigeria. With only a few days' notice and no money up front, the band thought it was ridiculous to even consider it, but Sonny was adamant: "Your ancestors came into America without a cent. How much money do you have?" When one of the musicians answered fifty cents, he said, "That's fifty cents more than your ancestors had." They were going.

Sun Ra noticed that very few musicians had been invited to the festival—a mistake, he thought—and he assumed that having been asked at the last minute meant that music had been an afterthought, and that "only those who weren't tied up to the white man could make it." Still, he said it was important for them to go to help destroy the African's stereotype of the American black man. From the moment of their arrival he was in a combative mood. When a Nigerian at the airport called out, "Welcome home, Sun Ra," Sonny answered, "Home? Your people sold mine. This is no longer my home!" At each performance the artists displayed flags from their own countries; but when Sun Ra got on stage he raised a purple and black banner that he called "the flag of death." He was annoyed that they were only allowed to play at the festival twice, and it was made worse when the Arkestra played overtime as usual and a large number of people left to catch the last buses back from the hall: misunderstanding their exit for rejection, Sonny saw it as typical of blacks to not respect one another. But at their second performance the lighting man was so impressed by the music that he lowered the lights after they left the stage and refused to turn them back on as the Miriam Makeba set began: "The Master has spoken!" he proclaimed. Sonny interceded, and insisted that she, too, was an artist, and should be treated with respect.

Over the four weeks, there was time to visit outside the city, to hear local music and to play for Africans and see them dancing to the Arkestra's music at informal performances. The band was invited to visit the flamboyant and politically rebellious performer Fela Anikulapo-Kuti at his house and nightclub where he was staging a counter-FASTEC, but Sonny thought it was unwise and told the band not to go—a decision which he said was justified later when Fela's place was attacked and burned down by troops of the Nigerian army. The trip ended on a bitter note when the Arkestra was not allowed to march in the final grand parade because Sun Ra would not agree to give the raised fist salute of Black Power. Then afterwards, when National Public Radio reported on the festival, one woman interviewed said his music didn't represent black people in the United States.

After the festival was over they returned by way of Egypt, and this time traveled in that country more widely, and wound up playing for the multinational troops in the Sinai Peninsula.

Just as his reputation on the synthesizer was growing, Sun Ra began to play more piano again, and in a style that reached back further in jazz tradition than most would have suspected. But those who had known him for years understood that his origins were in the blues, and assumed that side of his playing: "Sun Ra could play the blues for twenty four hours without repeating a phrase," they claimed. Though many recognized him as capable of playing bombastically, and of using the piano for color, few thought of him as a major player. But Paul Bley, one of the two or three leading pianists of free jazz, believed that Sonny was a great piano player, so great that he didn't need a band. If anything, he felt, the band was a cover for his insecurity. Early in 1977 Bley convinced Sonny to do a series of piano duo performances with him in New York and Europe and to record for Bley's new audio and video company, Improvising Artists. In Europe Bley was surprised to see that once he was alone on stage, "Sonny was a ham who liked to clown and surprise the audience—as at Lake Como, where he shocked them by playing a cake walk!" On May 20 Sun Ra went into the studio to record *Solo Piano*, and played a mixture of his own compositions and some unusually conceived standards, such as a very freely played "Sometimes I Feel Like a Motherless Child," or "Yesterdays" done in a brisk stride. On July 3 he was recorded solo (*St. Louis Blues*) while playing at Axis-in-Soho as part of the Newport Jazz Festival, and again there were surprises: his "St. Louis Blues" aluded to Earl Hines's famous boogie-woogie version and a cheerful little love song like "Three Little Words" got turned into a melodrama. But there were modest experiments in keyboard resources as well, such as "Sky and Sun," which stayed almost entirely within a small range at the top of the keyboard.

Now emboldened, he played alone more often. Only a few days later he gave another solo concert on radio for WKCR at Columbia. And in later years he did a few more piano records for Saturn, *God Is More than Love* in 1979 with a trio (where in a group setting he seems freer, more expansive) and *Aurora Borealis* in 1980. In years to come he would solo more and more frquently during the Arkestra's performances, as in the live recording, "Cosmo Journey Blue" in *Cosmo Sun Connection* in 1984, where the rhythm disappears, leaving him alone to play a slow boogie. There was a solo concert at Carnegie Hall in 1979 and one at Lincoln Center in 1988 where he premiered "New York Town," a tone poem which included sections labeled "Twilight in Central Park," "Greenwich Village: East and West," "Twin Towers," "Times Square and Columbus

Circle," "Rivers Two: East and Hudson," "Jazz and Manhattan Skyscrapers," and "Harlem Myths and Mystics."

THE INTERVIEW AS JEREMIAD

If Sun Ra now felt more at ease as a leader and performer, he also seemed willing to reveal at least a few elements of his past, offering brief glimpses of his life in Chicago, his work with other musicians before the Arkestra that were enough to locate him in the jazz tradition. Every interviewer sooner or later got around to asking about Birmingham and Jupiter—both equally mysterious as far as they were concerned. Journalists from across the world found their way to the Morton Street address, expecting who knows what, but always finding a subject who told them more than they wanted to know about subjects they didn't want to write about. For outside of music and poetry, his medium was the interview, his form the jeremiad; and like other African-American Jeremiahs—Frederic Douglass, Booker T. Washington, Ida B. Wells, W.E.B. Du Bois, and Martin Luther King, Jr.—his message included the familiar motifs of Exodus and America as a promised land, the chronicles of human sinfulness, dire threats, and prophecies mixed with hope and optimism. But there were other elements: the importance of creativity, the traps of freedom and equality, the neglect of leadership, the need to defeat death, the deception of the Bible, and the necessity to decode it by means of "equations." For some, at least, the peak of his concerts came after the music, in interviews with journalists and conversations with fans in dressing rooms, in the hall, or leaning against the bus. And though the band might be tired and hungry or waiting to be paid, they stuck with him, sometimes for hours, an appreciative chorus signaling clueless listeners on whether to laugh or to be amazed. Or they were there to simply hold the line against skeptics and debunkers. He often worked from ambiguous biblical passages, like a country preacher moving from written text to oral pyrotechnics; or he might plumb the meaning of a single word or pairs of words, exploring dead metaphors for neglected meanings, reviving clichés and proverbs to see what they might yet yield.

Sometimes these interviews and semipublic lectures were published with ideas abruptly introduced, without context, or left hanging and undeveloped. In part this was Sun Ra's style: his ideas were almost never complete, parts of them were dropped in one conversation to be continued in an interview the same night, or another night, with another interviewer. The meaning might only become obvious after hearing ten or twenty lectures, or after reading thirty interviews. In any case, he detested completeness—things which were complete were "finished," "ended," dead. But in large part the difficulty in understanding Sun Ra was the result of him being edited and abbreviated, inaccurately transcribed, or poorly translated.

He talked in an unceasing monotonic flow which absorbed everything in its path—questions, comments, objections, distractions. He soloed with words, calling and responding to himself, using pet licks or falling back on patented phrases when memory or creativity failed him, riffing, keeping the music of his words moving forward in a stream of energy which propelled him and maintained his strength and helped bring a hint of danger into his performances. Threaded through all of his talk was the literature of the world, references to daily news events or what he had just seen on television. And he never strayed far from the Christian scripture which he sometimes used ironically, sometimes literally. He had the preacher's love of the extended metaphor, pushing a single figure to its breaking point, revising and shifting direction in midsentence:

People are just like receivers, they're like speakers, too, like amplifiers. They're also like instruments because they got a heart that beats and that's a drum. They've got eardrums, too, and they got some strings in there, so they actually got harps on each side of their head. If you play certain harmonies, these strings will vibrate in people's ears and touch different nerves in the body. When the proper things are played in each person, these strings will automatically tune themselves properly and then the person will be in tune. There will be no discord, they will be tuned up perfectly, just like each automobile have to be tuned according to what kind of automobile it is. My music does have a vibration somewhere within it that can reach every person in the audience through feeling.

If he was never easy to follow, whether in person or in reading a transcript of what he said, he was nonetheless fascinating, even compelling, and on reflection what he said made a peculiar sense, though one that might not be easy to convey to others.

He denied that he was a philosopher, said he was not about religion or politics, that he was a creator who worked for the Creator, running a "selective service to find those who understand the Creator."

> I'm a messenger to, from, and of.... You can listen to me if you want to or not. I'm like the birds who sing in the trees.

Journalists used to dealing with Jesus freaks and Indian mystics in the 1960s approached him with certain predispositions, which he promptly deflated: did he practice meditation? "I don't deal with meditation—it's too passive. I'm interested in cogitation and retrospection." What did he think about the Rastafarians? "They don't know anything about Ra!" Did he believe that the world was going to come to an end with the millennium? We already passed one millennium, in fact, we passed the apocalypse: we are living in End Time, all right, but in the last daze. It's *after* the end of the world. Don't you know that yet?

Much of what he said in public conversation and in interviews was for shock value, especially when journalists were involved, and he enjoyed reading about the ripples which followed the outlandish quotes attributed to him. But behind the tricksterism and the jokes there was a shrewd purposefulness. He reveled in ambiguity and duality, his Gemini quality, and he erased or blurred all oppositions: earth/space, black/white, angel/demon, good/evil, male/female, sacred/secular, blues/spirituals.

Though it never occurred to them in the beginning, interviewers in later years wanted to know about his sexuality. A group of black men living together in the 1960s was seen as a collective, as a statement of blackness, or a defensive posture beyond question. An apparently ascetic and celibate lifestyle was a legitimate black male choice, one understood to be a means of gathering strength for the cataclysm to come. By the 1980s a paradigmatic shift had occurred from group to self, and questions of individual identity had to be raised, essentialist questions. When asked directly about why he had never married, Sun Ra answered, "They neither marry nor are given in marriage but are like angels that shine forth like the sun" (an elaborated paraphrase of Matthew 22:30, where Jesus also says that God is God of the living, not the dead). Or he said that children didn't think about sex, why should he? He had transcended it. He disavowed the use of music for sexual enticement or stimulation; and though the performances at Slug's had the patina of being wild and licentious displays, once when a woman who was dancing drunkenly began to remove her clothes Sun Ra stopped the band and refused to go on until she was put out of the club.

It came as a surprise to many to learn that Sun Ra was a conservative person, in many ways a southern person. Those who had known him for years attest to his celibacy and his moderation in most things. He drew the line hard on drugs, for others and himself. His objection was practical—they slowed him down: "I'm trying to increase my natural capacity, and move faster and faster without limitations. Technology is progress, but the human spirit is static." It was widely reported that he was not a drinker, but he did enjoy an occasional glass of wine or Old Granddad, though he was strict about his musicians drinking before or during performances. He once ordered the great bassist Jaco Pastorius off the stage when he saw the condition he was in. He liked to eat, and though he could be adventuresome, his tastes tended toward fruits, vegetables, and the fundamentals of down-home southern cuisine. He was wary of doctors and even more so of medicines which interfered with what he felt to be his natural state, preferring traditional herbs for healing. He believed that hoodoo and voodoo were effective, and once bought what he was told was a voodoo doll in Amsterdam and used it to threaten certain members of the Arkestra.

He thought voting was the most important part of citizenship and tried to encourage others to vote. When Richard Nixon left office during the Watergate scandal what concerned Sun Ra most was the disrespect which leaders were shown and the ease with which they were disposed of. He voted for George Bush in 1988 and was considering voting for Ross Perot in 1992, though his reasons for doing so were not conservative party line: Bush's "duplicity would help in dealing with the chaos of the world" and of Perot, he said "go with the man with the money." He felt that much of the trouble with children in America began when the Bible was taken out of the classroom (though he said it had nothing to do with *reading* the Bible: it should just be left in the class-room). Strictness was necessary in child raising, and he favored spanking as the natural form of discipline ("we all come into the world with a smack on the booty, anyway").

If his interviews were beginning to throw some light on his past, the Arkestra's performances were also becoming less mysterious, less threatening, and even more invitational and participatory for audiences. In a concert in Central Park he passed out small whistles to the crowd, invited anyone with an instrument to come on stage, and led everyone around the bandshell at the end. He presented frequent tributes to the masters of early jazz—Jelly Roll Morton, Duke Ellington, Fletcher Henderson. The Arkestra began placing a mini-tribute to *Star Wars* in their performances, with a midget dressed as Darth Vader dueling with light sabers with characters dressed like aliens from the bar scene. (*Star Wars* and *Close Encounters of the Third Kind* had just been released and Sun Ra had became an enthusiastic fan. "Did you see *Star Wars?*" Sonny once asked writer Francis Davis. "It was very accurate.") The band also began a long-running series of Halloween gigs in which they wore Frankenstein masks and played novelty pieces like his composition "Halloween in Harlem." A few years later Sonny began to incorporate two souvenir paddles (one marked "Attitude Adjuster," the other "Fanny Fanner") that he had bought in a gift shop in Virginia as business in his shows, teasing the audience that he might use it on them, and occasionally lightly tapping a willing victim on the booty. James Jacson began doing a convincing impression of Louis Armstrong's vocal on "Mack the Knife." And at Christmas Eve performances they played Christmas songs and had sing-alongs.

On May 21, 1978, the Arkestra were guests on *Saturday Night Live*, perhaps the only television show which could contain Sun Ra at the time, much less invite him. It was the biggest audience they would ever have, and Sonny intended to get as much on as possible, even though they would only have fifteen minutes to play. But as they rehearsed he was told they would have no more than six minutes. He complained that they had already appeared on television in Egypt, Mexico, the Netherlands, Sweden, Germany, and Spain, and had never been so restricted. "But they said 'television moves so fast here'; so we will have to move fast, and to condense our whole show into six minutes." Introduced by Buck Henry as "Sun Ra and his Jazz from Another Planet Arkestra," it turned out to be only a little over four minutes, though they managed to fit in "Space Is the Place," "The Sound Mirror," and "Watusa." The lighting was wrong, the band squeezed together as tightly on the set as they had been at Slug's, the dancers moving as little as possible to stay on camera, the Arkestra's mystique effectively wiped away as only television can do. Afterwards NBC said they received many calls of protest about this weirdness during the show, but that the letters which followed Sun Ra's appearance ran fifty-fifty.

Sonny took a quartet to Italy early in 1978 with Michael Ray, John Gilmore, and Luqman Ali on drums, and despite his misgivings about small bands, they produced some concert and studio recordings there which are some of the most interesting and little known of the Sun Ra output. Two of them, *New Steps* and *Other Voices,* were for the Italian label Horo which had very little distribution in the United States, and the other three—all from live performances—were on Saturn. Both Horos contain a number of ballads and medium-tempo pieces which tend toward funk, but *New Steps* had "My Favorite Things," which pitches John Gilmore's carefully wrought, close-to-the-chords, low-key reading against John Coltrane's famous modal interpretation; "Moon People," a conversation of squeaky cartoon-synthesizer voices; and "When There Is No Sun," a softly chanted mournful dirge which would turn up at many Sun Ra performances hereafter:

> The sky is a sea of darkness
> When there is no sun
> The sky is a sea of darkness
> When there is no sun to light the way
> When there is no sun to light the way

> There is no day
> There is no day
> There's only darkness
> Eternal sea of darkness...

Media Dream is an organ record with no obvious points of reference to the jazz organ tradition. On much of it Sun Ra simply built simple melodies around single chords and obligatti, suggesting a more interesting direction in which minimalism might have gone had Sun Ra been interested in that movement in the 1970s. *Disco 3000* has Sun Ra playing organ against sound loops and drum machine, producing a heavy ambient wash (though not so heavy that he could not still insert "Sometimes I Feel Like a Motherless Child" into "Dance of the Cosmo-Aliens") that points out another stylistic road not taken.

In Philadelphia again, *Lanquidity* was recorded for Philly Jazz, a small company with great ambitions (it was they who attempted to form the Ra-legion Cosmo-Fan Club), and its silver metallic cover hinted that the Arkestra was playing catch-up in the year of Abba's "Dancing Queen" and KC and the Sunshine Band's "I'm Your Boogie Man." If *Lanquidity* was disco-inspired (Sun Ra was playing a Fender Rhodes, electric guitars ran through sound processors, the whole work multitracked), it was revisionist disco, dance music transformed in the same way he had rechanneled Les Baxter, making the music simultaneously easy to ignore and vaguely disquieting. "Lanquid," to be sure: on "There Are Other Worlds," the Space Ethnic Voices almost inaudibly whisper, "There are other worlds they have not told you of/They wish to speak to you" in shifting layers of sound, producing a true dream state; and the dance beat—as with much of this recording—gives the listener a false sense of security, for the music seems to have nothing to do with periodicity. And when the beat drops away—as it does in "There Are Other Worlds"—the music winds down like a music box.

There were other media projects to come. Film director Bob Mugge began shooting *Sun Ra: A Joyful Noise* in 1979, which for the first time showed the Arkestra at home and at work. And in December the

Arkestra played the Modern Theater in Boston with the Spacescape music-color machine, a keyboard device invented and played by media artist Bill Sebastian which matched colors and three-dimensional shapes to the music being played by the Arkestra (a performance they repeated a year later at Soundscape in New York). (In 1986 Sebastian made two videos with the Arkestra, *Calling Planet Earth* and *Sunset on the Nile*, which continued some of the same effects he had created on the Spacescape keyboard.)

By 1979 Sun Ra was becoming the world musician he had aimed to be. He now traveled into the Deep South for the first time since he left, playing the Atlanta Jazz Festival ("There was a standing ovation in the middle of 'Days of Wine and Roses' because they could taste the wine and smell the roses") where he was also made an honorary citizen of the city of Atlanta. But one honor he failed to receive was tied to NASA's launching of *Voyager I* into space to orbit Saturn. The satellite was equipped with a gold-plated metal-alloy recording of musical selections said by experts to best represent the people of Earth: Bach, Beethoven, Mozart, Stravinsky, Louis Armstrong, Chuck Berry, among them. Writer Michael Shore called Sun Ra to see what he thought about being left off the record:

> Aside from pointing out that Saturn could teach Earthlings a lot, especially Jews—"Jews worship a six-pointed star," he said, "and Saturn's the sixth planet from the Sun; also Jews worship on Saturday, which is really Saturn's Day"—he's not angry about the omission. In fact, he's blissfully unperturbed. "The outer space beings," he said, "are my brothers. They *sent* me here. They *already* know my music."*

In the fall they began a series of performances at Squat Theater in New York which lasted off and on over the next three years. Squat was established by a group of Hungarian refugees in a dingy storefront in the

---

*(When the Challenger space shuttle exploded in January 1986, Sun Ra said that NASA lacked discipline and a knowledge of music.)

Chelsea area at 23rd Street and 8th Avenue, where they presented some of the most radical theater and performance the city had ever seen. At one point the Arkestra did two nights of concerts with 100 musicians jammed into the tiny space, and in order to coordinate so many musicians Sun Ra rehearsed in shifts for twenty-four hours straight, with different musicians and instrumental sections one after another. On another occasion Dorothy Donegan and Sun Ra did double concerts at Squat, first playing together and then both with the Arkestra at another time. If anything, Squat drew audiences more diverse than Slug's: Amiri Baraka came, as did John Cage, actors from the TV soaps, artists, and the B-52's and other musicians from the new punk scene in the city, many of whom later claimed Ra as an inspiration.

Nine records came out of 1979, and together they document the enormous range of the band's repertory at that point. Three examples are enough to grasp their scope: on *Sleeping Beauty*'s "Springtime Again" the band languorously chants "It's spring, it's springtime again" over lush, dreamy textures going nowhere; "UFO" (from *On Jupiter*), frankly, was a disco record, with big-band riffs over disco rhythms. (When they were rehearsing, some of the musicians complained when Sonny asked them to listen to examples of currently popular disco records: "This is some hokey shit, Sonny." "This hokey shit is somebody's hopes and dreams," he chided them. "Don't be so hip!") The title piece on *I Pharaoh* has Sun Ra returning to his Egyptian interests, declaring over flutes and drums that the modern Egyptians are not his people; that the world has destroyed his kingdom: "I am Pharaoh, I should know; the only thing I have left is immortality. Why don't you be my people now. Give up your death for me." Meanwhile, the chanting becomes multilayered and polyphonic, and the whole project seems to come loose from its moorings.

On March 28, 1979, a nuclear accident occurred in the reactor at Three Mile Island, less than 100 miles upwind from Philadelphia, and for a week there were evacuations and talk of nuclear disaster. Sun Ra became very concerned that nuclear energy had gotten out of hand and in a rare antitechnological moment, he told everyone who would listen that solar power was the only sane and cheap form of energy, one that he had been proposing ever since he was a child. His interviews over the next

few years show his growing fear of the possibilities of nuclear apocalypse, and in the late 1980s he added pollution to his apprehensions,
though it often served more as a metaphor for Earth's evils than as part
of a political movement ("the planet's landlord will extract revenge for
the misuse of the planet"). In 1982 he recorded "Nuclear War," becoming one of the first instances of protest rap:

> Nuclear war...
> They're talking about
> Nuclear war...
>
> It's a motherfucker
> Don't you know
> If they push that button
> Your ass got to go

Convinced he had a hit single, he took it to Columbia Records who
showed no interest in it, and he finally sold it to Y Records in London
who produced a twelve-inch single aimed at disco jocks.

Now in his late sixties, Sonny was writing and performing fewer new
compositions. And with less rehearsal time the band's shows were more
standardized, with fewer surprises in an evening's selections. New
recordings continued to appear at the rate of two or three a year, and if
they were sometimes casually pieced together and not always as innovative as in the past, they still could hold surprises. *A Fireside Chat with Lucifer* was recorded in 1982 at a session at Variety Sound which produced
an unusually wide array of music: Charlie Chaplin's "Smile," Ellington's
"Drop Me Off in Harlem" and "Sophisticated Lady," but also the long
title work, a free composition organized around space chords and Sun
Ra's organ cues, a piece which sustains a lyrical edge in spite of an open
framework and textures which encourage sonorities to surface and
emerge from the band as if there was no human intention behind them.
And Ra's organ playing here was built less on bombast and sonic terror
than it is on whispers, stutters, shivers, and swells.

Sun Ra was given an American Jazz Master award by the National En-
dowment of the Arts in 1982 along with Count Basie, Kenny Clarke,
Sonny Rollins, Dizzy Gillespie, and Roy Eldridge, and on December 5

he was made a member of "The All-Time Great Chicago Jazz Band" by the *Chicago Tribune Magazine*. Sun Ra had reached an extraordinary position at which he could at least in theory play almost any venue in the United States. In the early 1980s he worked avant-garde niches like the Squat or Art on the Beach in New York; he was in demand at universities like the University of Wisconsin, Princeton, Temple, Brandeis, and at Harvard (where, like Malcolm X, he gave a lecture); or at mainstream art shrines like the Kennedy Center in Washington or the Whitney Museum in New York; he could play dance halls in Kansas City, country-and-western bars in North Hollywood, or the Chicago Jazz Festival; he toured Europe every summer; and even in Philadelphia, where he had always had to scuffle, he was now welcome at city-run sites like Penn's Landing or the Afro-American Museum. He had found a way in which he could present traditional jazz values and free jazz explorations, some pop songs and even some classical works (including Chopin and Rachmaninoff among others) while still keeping the cosmo drama and the message it contained intact. It was a delicate act that is difficult to explain. "Sun Ra kept the sixties going a long time," John Sinclair said, a spirit which balanced populist inclusion with an elitist weirdness which could have easily driven away an audience. But he also kept the 1930s, '40s, and '50s going as well. They were practicing Afro-modernism, as art historian Robert Farris Thompson put it; playing, as the Art Ensemble of Chicago said, "great black music, ancient to the future." Zora Neale Hurston would probably have said that the Arkestra were simply blacks who kept on being black.

But America was changing in the early 1980s, had been changing for seven or eight years, and though the Arkestra now had many places in which to play, there were fewer audiences to whom their music would not appear as anything but eccentric or even slightly defective divertissements—memorable, but one-time experiences for most, part of the disposable rituals of late adolescence for others. The swing retrospectives and comedy material were popular with audiences, as was the group singing at the end of shows (25,000 people at the 1984 Chicago Jazz Festival cheerfully chanting "We are the children of the sun"); but it was the kind of anonymous popularity of a Preservation Hall Jazz Band. And in a sense, by being everywhere, their invisibility was guaranteed.

Though work was plentiful, jobs which paid enough to transport a big band around the country were beginning to became harder to find in the mid-1980s, and the Arkestra often depended on friends to find them work and to promote them, especially out of town. In Los Angeles they called on Alden Kimbrough; in the Bay Area there were John and Peter Hinds, two young musicians who befriended the band and became devoted to them, helped them with bookings, and printed up abridged versions of *The Immeasurable Equation* for the band to sell after gigs (and also recorded hundreds of hours of talks with Sun Ra and the band, and later published them as *Sun Ra Research* and *Sun Ra Quarterly*); in Kansas City it was the Rev. Dwight Frizzell (minister in the Universal Life Church, Bachelor of Fine Arts, Doctor of Metaphysics, musician, artist, and photographer); on the East Coast Phil Schaap at WKCR and later, Trudy Morse; and in Europe it was Victor Schonfield, Joachim Berendt, Hartmut Geerken, and the Trinidadian fellow mystic Frank Haffa. And it was Europe and its festivals that they now counted on to sustain them in the long haul. Europe, not coincidentally, was the only place where Sonny felt his music was treated respectfully, where he was provided with big halls, good pianos and sound systems, and where the media were sincere. Once in a while some theater in the United States would go all out, as when in the fall of 1984, the Lydia Mendelsohn Theater in Ann Arbor enabled Sun Ra and June Tyson to appear on stage on thrones which appeared and disappeared through trapdoors. But more often they were given a second-class piano and haphazard amplification setups. No matter how discouraging the circumstances he never flinched, even when some told him that jazz was dead: "Jazz is not dead. Jazz can't die. It's the musicians who are dead . . . they've been dead for the last twenty years!"

There was another trip to Egypt in 1983, during which they recorded *Sun Ra Meets Salah Ragab in Egypt*, where Ragab and the Cairo Jazz Band play on one side and the Arkestra plays Ragab's compositions "Egypt Strut" and "Dawn" on the other. At the end of the year they did a three-month tour of Europe, where Sun Ra left the Arkestra in Paris in late October and for one week played Milan, the Zurich Jazz Festival, the Berlin Jazz Festival, Montreux, Brussels, and Nancy with a group called the Sun Ra All Stars which included Archie Shepp, Marshall Allen, and John Gilmore on saxophones, Don Cherry and Lester Bowie on trumpets, Richard Davis, bass, and Philly Joe Jones, Don Moye, and Clifford Jarvis on drums, what the press might have called a "supergroup" of free jazz players at the time.

But the supergroup of them all occurred when John Cage and Sun Ra, the musical architects who independently invented modern noise, were both invited by Rick Russo and Bronwyn Rucker to perform at the Coney Island Museum on June 8, 1986, for the benefit of the newly formed Meltdown Records. Beyond what they shared in their roles in musical history, Cage and Sun Ra were both great talkers, masters of anecdotal wisdom, as well as self-mystifiers and priests of small but very influential musical cults. And when once asked for ten words that defined his life's work, Cage included "discipline" as one of them. Whatever Cage thought about the meeting, Sun Ra told the band that Cage was the most important Euro-American composer, and he wondered why he was being asked to appear with him.

When the day came, a pitchman and a "snake woman" worked the crowds on the boardwalk to entice the audience inside, where pizza and beverages were being served while they waited for the big show to begin. Sun Ra and Cage talked briefly beforehand, but most of what they had to say was not heard by others. Ra entered first, preceded by dancer Ted Thomas sanctifying the space before them with a censer; and then Marshall Allen playing a fanfare on a wind synthesizer, followed by John Cage. Sun Ra, dressed in a purple tunic with silver foil sleeves, seated himself behind a Yamaha DX-7 keyboard and played softly for a few minutes, while Thomas danced about with tendrils of incense trailing. Then Cage, dressed in denim as usual, made soft mouth noises for a few minutes. And so it went, back and forth. Only once, for the briefest of seconds, did they play together, when Sonny added some soft bell tones behind Cage, but then quit, perhaps feeling a draft, sensing that Cage was somewhere else. Then Sun Ra read from his poetry, accompanying himself on keyboard, and June Tyson sang "Enlightenment" and danced with two male dancers and it was over. Afterwards, Cage told Sun Ra that a writer friend had said to him that if he wanted to take another step in music and didn't want to be behind the times he ought to listen to Sun

Ra. Sun Ra smiled, and like a straight man in a comedy team said, "I've been in the same position myself." Sometime later when someone asked Cage about playing with Sun Ra he corrected them: they had not played together.

Despite the routinization in the band's performances Sun Ra could still on occasion surprise even his oldest fans, sometimes with totally new material or with even the subtlest of shifts in the old. On their way back from Egypt in 1989, the Arkestra appeared at the Orpheus Theater in Athens, Greece, where Hartmut Geerken said they "played as if in a trance. Sonny had colored his face bright red, his tunic was red, too, and the Arkestra was dressed in blue and black" under the influence of Scorpio.

An evening with Sun Ra and the 100-piece Omniversal Symphonic was advertised for the Lennox Chalet on the Lower East Side for July 19 and 20, 1984; and even though only eighty musicians actually played on one night, and fifty the other, it was still a happy gathering of free musicians of New York such as Gary Bartz, Kalaparusha, Rashied Ali, and Charles Tyler, an evening soured only by the musicians having to stand in line for hours afterwards to receive the forty dollars that Sun Ra insisted on distributing to them personally.

Production of Saturn recordings was slowing down, but a series of well-produced records were recorded by other companies between 1986 and 1988 which showed Sun Ra's preoccupation with older swing styles: *Reflections in Blue, Hours After, Blue Delight,* and *Somewhere Else.* Yet each of the records worked some angle, some small element of conceptual enrichment or irritation capable of keeping them out of the nostalgia bins. *Reflections in Blue,* for example, had Jerome Kern's "I Dream Too Much," an odd eighty-bar ballad to begin with, which Sonny sang so that he landed on quarter tones at the end of phrases, an idea he said was suggested by the movement in the harmony of the original; "State Street Chicago" from the same album was an unequivocal riff-type swing tune, but with Sun Ra providing toy-piano sonorities on the synthesizer it had an uneasy cast to it; "Say It Isn't So," a well-played, straight swing arrangement in which Carl LeBlanc's guitar obligatos were nonetheless played sharp enough to suggest bitonality; and for that matter, any number of smooth pop melodies on these records on their fourth or fifth listening could reveal some angular counter-melody which could unsettle the listener.

Phil Alvin of the pop group the Blasters hired the Arkestra to back him on three songs for an album of nostalgia called *Un "Sung Stories"* which they recorded at Variety Studios in a session which began at 8:30 in the morning after a night of playing at Sweet Basil and lasted seventeen hours. Sonny left the piano only three times, otherwise writing the arrangements and rehearsing the band. They recorded Cab Calloway's "The Ballad of Smokey Joe," "The Old Man of the Mountain," and "Buddy, Can You Spare a Dime?"

Formal recognition of Sun Ra's work continued when, for the first time in thirty-three years, he returned to his home state to be inducted into the Alabama Music Hall of Fame, along with Jo Jones and other musicians, and afterwards to be a guest at Governor George Wallace's home. In 1987 WKCR at Columbia presented a weeklong, twenty-four-hour-a-day festival of his work which included long interviews with the band and Sun Ra, and obscure and private recordings such as the 45-rpm singles, most of which had scarcely been heard by anyone. Listeners who fell asleep with the radio on sometimes were awakened by the chilling sound of Sun Ra's synthesizer whirring behind his flattened poetry readings in the middle of the night.

In 1988 he was inducted into the Alabama Jazz Hall of Fame in Birmingham. This triumphal return home meant a great deal to him, and he talked about it as a vindication. Yet when he was requested to provide biographical information for a display which would be set up in their new building, he offered no help, nor did he tell them what not to write. So Herman S. Blount (aka Sun Ra) was permanently enshrined in a display case. When he flew in for the induction he avoided old friends or family, except for trumpeter Jothan Callins, who he called and asked to accompany him to dinner and to the various festivities. Though he made no concession for hometown provinciality and came dressed in full stage costume, he wanted Callins with him just in case. The ceremony was elaborate, conducted in the Boutwell Auditorium in Birmingham. And here, in the epicenter of the civil rights movement, Sonny made a point of saying that his music had accomplished what the movement's leaders had not: that he—unlike Nat Cole, whose concert had been disrupted by segregationists in this very building some twenty years before—had been welcomed there.

The Arkestra visited Japan for the first time in 1988, when they were spectacularly filmed at the Aurex Festival ("Live Under the Sky") in Tokyo, and recorded at the Pit-Inn, which resulted in an elaborate multirecord set and a picture disk. And then there was their annual tour of Europe. If the music was not always as startling as it once was, life with Sun Ra was never dull. While they were in Berlin, Sun Ra was kidnapped. He was leaning on a car, when several men he was talking to inside pulled him in, the car driving off into the night with the door still open. The band looked for him for hours, and they began to panic. Then suddenly he was back. He said he had been taken to a planetarium for an interview by people who had said they were a reviewer and a photographer. They wanted to know the secret of the black space program. "They started asking me questions, strange questions, like how did I intend to get black folks off the planet. What kind of ship was I going to use? What kind of fuel was I going to use in the ship? What kind of material would the ship be made of?" He told them: "I wasn't using any gasoline. I'm using sound. You haven't reached that stage on this planet yet where you can use sound to run your ships and run your cars and heat your house. Your scientists haven't reached that yet. But it will happen. Where you can take a cassette and put it in your car and it will run it—with the right kind of music, of course. And it won't explode..."

In a sense it was business as usual with Sun Ra, but some of the band complained that it was a setup, another of his jokes. But who could be sure? The line between the mundane and the theatrical was sometimes very fine with Sonny. And when it came to money matters especially, there was always some question. It was not that Sonny lived so well, but that the finances of a collective enterprise such as this one, operating at the margins of music, were difficult at best—impossible, he would say— and the mystification of finances was more real than fabricated. So, once when they came back from Italy and Sun Ra suddenly disappeared, returning days later to say that he had been robbed of the money they had made on the tour, some suspected that he had been hiding out at an airport hotel in Baltimore to avoid telling them there was not enough money to pay them. But who could be sure?

Whatever happened on that occasion, Sun Ra *was* being robbed as bootleg recordings of their performances were turning up all over the world; and without regular management and accounting it was easy for the Arkestra to be underpaid and the money they did make to slip away from them. Sun Ra became concerned about the mechanical royalties on his compositions, as he suspected that he was not being credited properly in the United States and that others were collecting his royalties overseas. One day he announced that he wanted to check his copyrights in the Library of Congress, and hired a limousine to drive him and road manager Spencer Weston to Washington ("Scholars should travel at least as well as entertainers"). On the way they picked up some burgers, cheese fries, and milk shakes to go, and he was disappointed when he was not allowed to take them into the library.

They returned to Birmingham again in 1988, now for a paying gig, a performance at the Nick, and followed it up with the Cotton Club in Atlanta, Nightstage in Cambridge, the Kuumbwa Jazz Center in Santa Cruz, Slim's in San Francisco, the Montreux/Detroit Festival, and the Chicago Jazz Festival. For the festivals Sonny deepened the percussion section with three jazz drummers (Buster Smith, Luqman Ali, and Samurai Celestial), Kwasi Asare on African drums, and a Brazilian capoeira troop from New York which included dancer/percussionists Lorimil Machado and Gato, and two drummers, Elson (Dos Santos) Nascimento and Jorge Silva. Nascimento stayed on with the band and continued to play the *surdo* with the Arkestra.

Now seventy-four, Sun Ra began to think about any venue, outlet, and musical genre that he had not yet tapped. One night, after watching the David Letterman Show he sent Danny Thompson to New York City to see if he could get them on. The producers asked to see something by the band and Danny gave them the *Calling Planet Earth* video with Bill Sebastian's psychedelic optical effects, but Letterman's people decided it was too over the top for them. Just as casually he tried to see the Russian ambassador in Washington to see if it was possible for the Arkestra to play in Russia ("I told them that we were playing world music, and they should be interested in that").

Maybe it was synchronicity when Hal Wilmer conceived of a jazz-and-pop tribute to Walt Disney's film music to be called *Stay Awake* and asked the Arkestra to record "Pink Elephants on Parade" from *Dumbo*. It was precisely the kind of thing Sonny was looking for. He took the assignment seriously, bought a video copy of *Dumbo*, and was delighted when he saw that Dumbo was a kindly elephant who had the ability to fly but was nonetheless considered a freak. In his loneliness Dumbo spent time staring sadly into the night skies. On top of this there were some pyramids and Middle Eastern themes and some prepsychedelia and outer-space references in the film, as well as some hipster crows, so Sun Ra announced that he could relate to Dumbo. But when he saw the arrangement that Wilmer had prepared he said it was all wrong and began rewriting it. It meant another eighteen-hour stint in the studio before it was done. But film critic J. Hoberman wrote of that short track:

> A near normal arrangement of the ditty heralding Dumbo's psychedelic freak-out, it is sung with such falsetto enthusiasm that it might almost be about something—like maybe the segment of the population you don't see on *Soul Train*.

Now that he was familiar with the whole Disney songbook, over the next year Sun Ra prepared enough of the film music that he could take the band on tour as the Disney Odyssey Arkestra, playing a whole evening's worth of the songs with what one could charitably call broad humor: there was lots of falsetto and *basso profundo* singing, mouse-ears hats, saxophonist Noel Scott doing back flips, a dancer in a Dumbo costume. The program was heavy with songs from *Sleeping Beauty* and *Snow White and the Seven Dwarfs*, all of which were humorous treatments except for "The Forest of No Return," the words of which sounded like something Sun Ra himself would have written as a cautionary song about life on Earth. Walt Disney now had the status of a Fletcher Henderson or an Ellington in the Ra canon:

> I felt that America had not given proper status—or proper honor—to those who do something worthwhile. I felt that it recognized those who do something bad, and it puts them in jail, but it had not recognized those who did something good. So I felt I could balance the equation—by doing something to recognize those who came before, who did something nice. I'd been doing Duke Ellington, Fletcher Henderson, Basie—first I did that. The black folks still asleep, they didn't help me with that. So then I did George Gershwin, Irving Berlin, Cole Porter—and then finally I did the Walt Disney thing.... this way I can show the cosmic forces that there have been some people who came this way who were very nice. Because if they look at the world the way it is today, they could actually come and destroy people, because they say, "They're not intellectually proper." But if I put up Fletcher Henderson or Walt Disney, it's a shield of beauty.

There were two last Saturn records to come, both recorded at concerts at the Knitting Factory between January 29 and 31, 1988. It was an unusual pair of concerts which made for strange records, both of which shattered the audience's assumptions about what Sun Ra was capable of at this point—and which mock the biographer's attempt to draw a coherent evolutionary line connecting his work over time. Sonny used particularly hard-edged settings on the keyboards that evening, and kept the music going almost nonstop, pushing soloists hard and managing to get them to match the electronic sonorities of the keyboard. With the exception of Ra's chanted epic "This World Is Not My Home," most of the material was either new or improvised: a brisk metallic waltz, some pulse-free drifts of sound, a high-tech but old-time blues. Art Jenkins's vocals through metal megaphone especially echoed Sonny's synthesizer settings, buzzing, gurgling, and sliding between tones: outer space, but with one foot always in the gutter. When the two records were packaged, the hand-lettered covers were titled *Hidden Fire 1* and *2* (and in the tradition, some got marked *3* and *4*, even though they were the same records); and since they were sold only from the bandstand, they immediately became collectors' items.

MODERN LIVING

Life in the Morton Street house was shaped by the necessities of everyday affairs: shopping, cleaning, and cooking, the logistics of members working outside of the Arkestra to supplement income in such a way that it did not conflict with playing and rehearsals. They watched television (Sun Ra especially liked the cartoons—Roadrunner was a favorite). They celebrated Thanksgiving and Christmas, had festive dinners and exchanged gifts. Sonny, in fact, could be generous and enjoyed buying gifts for others. He enjoyed the Mummers Parade, and sometimes was in the crowds along the streets on New Year's Day.

He was often seen taking the train from Germantown Station to Center City, and most people took him for granted. Gail Hawkins, a neighbor, remembers seeing him one day with headphones on, and sitting down next to him, asked him what he was listening to. When he handed her the headphones she realized they weren't plugged in to anything. Downtown he might visit record stores (where he is remembered as buying organ trios and Fletcher Henderson reissues) or clothing shops; or get a transfer and go to West Philadelphia to visit the Egyptian Hall at the University of Pennsylvania Museum. Or he might stop at Temple University and visit the library. He developed contacts with student groups at Temple and student radio station WXPN at the University of Pennsylvania where he often appeared on programs. He became well known enough that he was invited to give lectures at the Free Library of Philadelphia and for a number of community groups.

The musicians who lived in the house counted on him to organize their daily schedules and to provide the means for their survival, but they also expected him to enlighten them, entertain them, and lead them from adventure to adventure, all the while assuring them that they were on the right path. Some felt that he had extraordinary gifts: that he could predict at least some part of the future, see into other dimensions (where

the Shadow People dwelled, for example, in a parallel wld); that he
was in touch with forces on other planets, in other univses, that he
might know the secret to conquer death. It was a heavy bien to carry,
and when he turned out to be wrong about something, orien a member of the Archestra died, he was obliged to explain the ccradictions.

It was not always easy for him to be happy. He had put hife into this
music, and it was often ignored, or worse, treated as a jokThey would
travel to some European festival and be treated lavishly, a then it was
over and time to come back to a house that needed a new lting system
and structural repair in a declining neighborhood. And wh he was sad
he could bring everyone around him down. He had goibeyond the
horizon and had seen the beauty and potential which layefore them.
Only by means of music could he stave off the squalomd disorder
which surrounded him: "I hate everyday life. This planet ike a prison.
I'm trying to free people. I've observed this planet fromher planets
and I've experienced what I saw in my music."

Insomnia had long since become a way of life, sleep cong to him in
unexpected places, never complete, not always convenierbut permit-
ting him half-dream states in which he experienced life orher planets,
sometimes as a tourist where he went on shopping spre buying ex-
pensive (but tax-free) socks and pants in astounding colornd fabrics. It
was in one of these dreams—which he readily called p:hic experiences—that he came to feel most attuned to Saturn. Thewere recognizable historical figures in other dreams, such as one inhich he saw
Lucifer and Christ as friends, both waiting to be called toork—a kind
of union call-up, he said—in which they both had their m jobs to do
in the universe. What he had been shown above all elseas what was
wrong with the people on the planet Earth:

> Something is wrong with the way man defines his life. The vld is going
> through a destructive phase, and the universe is watching tolp people,
> not destroy them. In a supermarket you have a right to choosverything,
> all of which isn't good for you—same with the universe.

"People on Earth ought make a mistake and do somethiniight; people
have been doing wrong so long that if they did somethingght it would
be a mistake."

"He didn't want human beings in their usual state," Jacson said.

> ...what had human beings accomplished? Sometimes he would say "There was a fork in the road and they hadn't taken it." Or he'd say, "They were on the right road, but going in the wrong direction."

Yet above all, he knew his destiny was to be a leader, a role he disclaimed and regretted almost constantly. At times he hinted that he appeared on Earth on a day of cosmic significance, but he never considered himself the messiah—in fact, he believed that there were many messiahs, maybe thousands, appearing over human history, some evil, some good. But to know one's own messianic status would assure one's own death. For Earth had no respect for leaders, was contemptuous of them; leaders were especially distrusted in the United States, where the Declaration of Independence declared that it was a country of the people, by the people, and for the people, and not a word about leaders.

He had never wanted to be a leader—of a band, of a religion, of a people. Even the call to be a messenger—the UFO experience—was hedged. He was forced by the Creator into the job of Troubleshooter for the Universe. "I'm not a leader, a philosopher, a religious person, only a person who wants to present something that can change humans. I'm an adjuster, a coordinator.... I'm ready and able, but I'm not willing. I won't preach to the people of earth...let them come to me!"

Throughout everything he said, there was a deep disdain for humanity, and the cosmic hurt that lay behind it. No interview went by without a disavowal of the human race: " 'Man' is a horrible word to galactic beings. So horrible they spell it out, 'M-A-N' ":

> I am not seeking leadership.... I will lead nothing like humans. The only reason I'm here is that the Creator got me here against my will. If I can get out of in any way enlightening this planet I'll do so with the greatest of pleasure and let them stay in their darkness, cruelty, hatred, ignorance, and the other things they got in their houses of deceit.

When his efforts on behalf of black people were ignored, he went further:

Someone said there was a conspiracy of silence against me.... It seemed
that it came from black people too, who did things to try to block me.
Most amazing. But it's true—they did. And it's true that they're still doing
it. Therefore I have to separate from black people. And not call them my
people. Because your own people do not try to block you. So I'm saying
that you've got some block people....

Leadership was a special affliction, a kind of isolation; he sensed that
all leaders had been made to suffer for their work. Duke Ellington was a
lonely man who had not been able to accomplish everything he wanted.
And Sun Ra had never heard his music played correctly: "Nobody plays
it right. The music's not good enough." Sun Ra's disappointment extended even to his followers, to his efforts with the Arkestra. "Sometimes
I meet musicians who are emotionally out of it," said Sun Ra. "Maybe
their wife left them or something. I took in a lot of musicians who were
nothing, and I helped them get themselves together. They went on and
they always left. As long as they didn't have any money, as long as they
needed my help, my demands were never too heavy. Then after they got
on their feet, they would forget about me." The latest disappointment
was the break with Danny Thompson. He said that Danny had kept his
marriage a secret from him, and now was planning to move away to
Texas. It was a blow to the organization, and Sonny viewed it as betrayal
by the heir apparent.

"I did never want to be successful. I want to be the only thing I could
be without anybody stopping me in America—that is, to be a failure.
So I feel pretty good about it, I'm a total failure.... So now as I've been
successful as a failure, I can be successful."

In June of 1989 they were invited back to Birmingham to perform at
City Stages, a festival held on the grounds of the old Sloss iron plant, on
a stage surrounded by the ghostly megaliths of defunct blast furnaces.
Before the concert the Arkestra led the Sun Strut, a parade though
downtown Birmingham, carrying banners and symbols of the sun. When
they reached Kelley Ingram Park where firehoses and dogs had once
been turned on civil rights demonstrators he was asked to bless the park.

He was visibly embarrassed: "I was on the spot. I'm not a minister or something, so I gave it a cosmo-blessing." There was a reuniting of sorts with family members, even with some distant relatives who drove up from South Alabama. They had dinner at Dreamland, the *haut* barbecue establishment of Alabama (where the vegetarians of the band ended up eating white bread with barbecue sauce). And after the concert they squeezed in a last-minute subscription-only concert at the Southern Dance Works Studio. They left the next day for a series of festivals in Canada, and slipped in a July 4 benefit performance at Battery Park with Don Cherry for the New Wilderness Foundation.

In September, *Miami Vice* star Philip Michael Thomas brought the band to his theater in North Miami. Thomas had come to know Sun Ra through some of the West Coast Arkestra dancers he knew when he was in *Hair*. There was another ceremony of recognition, with the mayor of North Miami declaring it Sun Ra Day, and Thomas giving him a small engraved pyramid.

In October, while playing in Yugoslavia, they finally found a way to the Soviet Union, though surprisingly to Tbilisi, in Georgia, where Jason had sought the Golden Fleece; there they appeared at a festival along with a reunion of the alumni of Art Blakey's Jazz Messengers for his seventy-fifth birthday. For five days they played, visited a local winery, met with local musicians, and were astonished to see how well known their music was there. They returned to the United States just in time to appear on David Sanborn's CBS-TV show *Night Music* on December 10, where late-night viewers saw Sun Ra interviewed for the first time on television; and shortly afterwards he was also featured on NBC TV's *Nightwatch*.

The Arkestra's performance schedule for the first ten months of 1990 would have been daunting to any performer, but for a seventy-six-year-old man and an aging band it was somewhere on the scale of the miraculous: Nightstage in Boston; a residency at Dartmouth College for a week; to Europe and Wuppertal in Germany, Leeuwarden in the Netherlands, Stuttgart, and Istanbul; St. Joseph's College in Philadelphia, Wolf Trap in Virginia, Slim's in San Francisco, and three other gigs in northern Cali-

fornia; followed by the Palomino Club in North Hollywood, Club Lin-
gerie in Los Angeles, and then Denver; a wedding in Central Park, back
to Europe to the First Moscow International Jazz Festival, then back to
the United States; and almost immediately a return to Europe and the
Bluecoat Arts Centre in Liverpool, the University of London Students'
Union, The Mean Fiddler in London; Grundy's Music Room and the
City Stages Festival again in Birmingham, the Frog Island Jazz/Blues
Festival, Ypsilanti, Michigan, and Orchestra Hall in Detroit; to Europe
again to Lausanne, Switzerland, the Lugano Jazz Festival, another festival
at Skeppsholmen in Switzerland, Restaurant Kaufleuten in Zurich, the
Wigan Festival in England, and then Milan, where they recorded *Mayan
Temples;* an African street festival in Brooklyn, the Bottom Line in New
York City; to Europe (for the fifth time that year) to Wales and the Edinburgh Jazz Festival; the Cat Club in New York City, Portland, Maine,
Town Hall in New York City, and Maxwell's in Hoboken; and Europe
one more time to the Théâtre-Carré Saint-Vincent in Orléans, France,
and the Hackney Empire in London; back in Philadelphia, a recording of
Sun Ra's poetry for Blast First Records of London accompanying himself
on "thrash harp." These were the principal gigs, which for the most part
were well paying, but there were others in between which sometimes
barely paid for the transportation. (In the Sun Ra School of Touring,
once an engagement had been accepted which paid, say, $3,000 for one
night, they'd also look around for a local bar in which to play for a few
hundred dollars the next night, to the annoyance of bookers and club
managers.) Any man Sun Ra's age would find a schedule like this exhausting and might look for ways to coast, ride on his age and the fact that
he had merely survived. But Sonny refused to let up.

When Don Glasgo invited Sun Ra to a week's residency at Dartmouth
College he asked him to send ahead eight or ten arrangements which the
Barbary Coast Jazz Ensemble, the student jazz group, could be working
on. But first Sonny asked to see a photo of the band. Then he sent ten
lead sheets for different instruments, one for each composition, but no
arrangements. When Glasgo called Sonny and asked him what they
should do with these sheets, Sonny told him they should transpose each

of them for all the instruments so that they could all practice them in unison, slowly. Once he arrived at the school he set about rehearsing the students as he did the Arkestra, spending much of the time with them writing out parts to suit each player while they sat and waited.

At Wolf Trap he seemed faint, and at one point almost fell off the piano bench. When they returned to Philadelphia the Arkestra talked him into going by the emergency room at Germantown Hospital. This was not easy, because Sun Ra had never seemed concerned about his health, and he had not seen a doctor or been in a hospital for years except for once when his thumb was mashed in a car door—and even then it was the band who made him go. In fact very few in the band could keep up with him: he still slept only a few hours a night, didn't need glasses; he was overweight, but by any standard he still seemed to be in remarkable health. Until now. When the doctor saw his high blood pressure and his irregular heartbeat he immediately put him in the hospital. But he was back out in a few days with some medicine and advice about his diet. A few engagements in the state of Washington had to be canceled, but within two weeks they were back on the road, traveling by train the only change in his routine. And he truly seemed revived.

While on a tour of Europe in April they played a festival in Istanbul where the promoters had them play on a flatbed truck as they drove from the airport to the hotel, and crowds of people filled the street and welcomed them as if they were liberators. It was in Turkey that Sun Ra was approached by some mystics who gave him *The Book of Information,* another channeled work from forces beyond, only this one had been dictated from a satellite to a computer. There were forty chapters in a manuscript of over 500 pages, all in English, written in the familiar register of New Age, much of it concerning space travel and advice for survival, an explanation of the higher forces watching Earth and evidence of secret knowledge held by a select few on Earth. And in spite of the ominous messages within, it concluded cheerfully by predicting that things would improve on Earth after 1990. Wherever Sonny went over the next few months he gave away parts of the book—to critics, fans, and old friends, anyone he felt had the spirit to understand and use it well, hand-ing them a few pages at random—just like he talked—broadcasting it, sowing it, he might say, so the world would know he wasn't bullshitting.

Before they left for Moscow in May he decided that he would dedicate the concert there to cosmonaut Yuri Gagarin, and he set to work on a suite for him. When they arrived they were offered their choice of three hotels, so he chose the Hotel Kosmos, of course. They spent their five days there sightseeing, jamming with local musicians, greeting people who they had met at Tbilisi who had come to see them, guessing at who around them was KGB, and marveling at the scale of the city.

For the Edinburgh Festival he had agreed to write arrangements for another band to play, but he never completed them, and his fee was substantially reduced. He brushed it off, but it was clear that he was not up to the work he had scheduled. While he was in Scotland he bought an Inverness cape in what for him was an uncharacteristic gray...lead-colored, really ("the Saturn color"), and a Glengarry hat to replace the Basque beret with a piece of velvet sewed onto it which he usually wore.

The second City Stages Festival in Birmingham was an even bigger deal than the last one. Michael Shore of MTV News brought a crew to document it and filmed a lengthy interview with Sonny and reunited him with some of his former musicians and one or two schoolmates. When Frank Adams came backstage to greet him after not having seen him for forty-four years, he walked up behind him, and said, "Bet you don't know who I am"; and without turning around, Sonny identified him. Adams went on to explain that since he had last seen him he had been in the army, had gone on to college and graduate school, where he had received a Ph.D., had taught school, been a principal, and was now director of music instruction for the city of Birmingham. "What a waste," Sonny said. "You were a good saxophone player."

Following City Stages they had another gig in Tuscaloosa, and afterwards, on the way to Montgomery they stopped in Oxford, Alabama, true center of Klan country, where one of the band was arrested and handcuffed on suspicion of using a controlled substance. In an act of courage which elevated him to new heights of respect—especially among the Arkestra members from Alabama—Sonny headed straight to the high sheriff's office and began a peroration: "You have no right to arrest this man! He hasn't done anything wrong. He just stopped to get a hamburger. Nobody here knows anything about him. He's not even a citizen of the United States. Don't try that Rev. King stuff on me! Don't even try it! I don't like the way you disgrace this state. There's going to be an international incident over this. I go all over the world and I'll be ashamed to tell people I'm from Alabama...." On and on he went, for maybe twenty minutes. When he stopped the sheriff asked, "What do you want me to do, Sonny?" And in the end they released him in Sun Ra's custody. "They said they liked my attitude...."

At the Cat Club they played for the New York Swing Dance Society, a group which held monthly swing extravaganzas where those who had mastered the high-energy popular dances of the 1930s and '40s displayed their art before bands which played authentic music of the period. But Sonny's angular takes on those tunes drove half the dancers angrily out of the club. Then, as the live set ended, a DJ put on a Fletcher Henderson record of the real thing and the crowd was astounded when the Arkestra joined in, playing along with it note for note from memory.

The Théâtre-Carré Saint-Vincent event in Orléans, France, was billed as a "Jazz Symphonique" concert, and Sun Ra had nineteen classical musicians made available to him to add to the sixteen musicians he was bringing, which already included two violins and a cello. He threw himself into the project and bought a computer to help him produce the instruments' parts. But once they reached Paris, Sun Ra confided to Jothan Callins that he didn't have the arrangements ready for the larger ensemble. And though he didn't ask for help, he seemed distraught, his hands shaking. So for the next fifty hours Callins worked with Sun Ra on the parts, transcribing and Xeroxing day and night, even adding his own composition, "Alabama," to the list, and then when the night of the performance came, Callins conducted the Arkestra for Sonny. "When I finished he thanked me for it. It was the first time I'd ever heard him thank anyone for anything."

About two years before, Sun Ra had bought June Tyson a violin, and she had been teaching herself to play and slowly working herself into performances. But when she seated herself in the violin section for a rehearsal in Paris, it was obvious to the classical players that she was not a trained musician. When she began to read another violinist's music, he pulled the music stand away from her, saying it was "his music." After another violinist did the same thing, she went out and bought a huge pile of music—standards, transcriptions of Thelonious Monk tunes, some Miles Davis—and when she returned at the next rehearsal she piled all of it in front of her on a music stand and announced to the string players that this was "her music."

For this performance and the upcoming Hackney Empire engagement in London Sun Ra also added Talvin Singh on tablas. When Singh went to meet Sun Ra where he was staying (at a private residence outside Paris) to discuss his part, the house was filled with burning frankincense and myrrh. Asked about rehearsing with the group, Sun Ra told him there was no need for it, just sit close to him and watch. "He never told me what to play: just actions, hand signals, orchestrating the whole vibe with his aura. The energy was amazing. I knew exactly what to play: I couldn't jam all over the music, and I had thought it was going to be like that."

THE TEST

One November morning in Philadelphia, Sun Ra found himself gasping for breath, his heart beating fast, then dropping away to a slow fade. Again they took him to the emergency room, and when the nurse saw his blood-pressure readings they put him back in the hospital once more. He came back out in a few days, but one morning he woke up unable to walk. The band tells the story that the doctor in the emergency room went through the procedures for establishing the nature of the injury, the degree of damage: How many fingers do you see? What year is this? Who's the president of the United States? Where were you born? That was it: he called for a specialist. When the neurologist arrived there was a whispered conference at the door to the room, and the second doctor looked in and said, "Oh, it's Sun Ra. He *is* from Saturn!"

But this time it was serious. Serious enough that his sister came up from Birmingham to see him. The diagnosis was a series of strokes, yet

Sun Ra—like Bob Marley a few years before him—denied it was a stroke, and said it was something done to him by his enemies. "There are forces trying to hold me back. And other forces trying to help me onward. And I'm the battleground!"

One side was affected, his legs, his left hand hardly functioned. He asked to be released from the hospital so the band wouldn't miss any work. But they kept him there and later moved him to a rehabilitation center. While in rehabilitation he asked to have a keyboard beside his bed and continued to play with one hand. He made calls to friends to reassure them and made plans for his return. One of the calls was to Warren Smith at Variety Recording Studio to say that he had heard that Smith's partner Vargas had died, and he was touched to find out that Smith had played part of the Cage/Sun Ra recording at Vargas's funeral.

> To his metaphysical surprise, I informed him that Fred was still at the studio. "Still at the studio? What do you mean?" he asked. "Well," I explained, "I took most of his cremains along with my luggage to Costa Rica, having them buried next to his parents and other family members. But I saved a little tube for my apartment and I saved another tube for the studio." "You did *what*?" Sun Ra asked in disbelief. "Yes," I explained, "when the workers were constructing the new Studio A control booth and no one was looking I slipped the cremains into a part of one of the walls. So Fred is *still* in his studio!" Sun Ra thought that was just the most beautifully metaphysical thing I had ever told him about, and before he hung up he said, "I love you both." The emphasis was on *both*. "I love you, too," was all I could respond, and the fact that he called just before his death adds to my indelible memories of the guy who once denied to me the London *Times*'s report about his real birthplace and his real name...but we both knew otherwise, and he knew I knew. One newspaper, he laughed, even wrote that he had green blood in his veins...

A benefit was held for Sun Ra at the Village Gate at the end of November where Charles Davis, Junior Cook, Michael Weiss, Dewey Redman, and others led their own groups. In January there was another benefit at Sweetwater's with John Gilmore leading the Arkestra. And there was even talk of a tribute to Sun Ra at Lincoln Center's new jazz department, but nothing came of it.

Though he was discharged from the hospital, he was supposed to continue rehabilitation and medication, both of which he let slide. He tried each medicine, one at a time, and if it made him feel strange, he put it aside. Yet somehow he got himself into condition to continue working, and scarcely three months after his stroke, he was back on the road to Toronto in February 1991. He had to be lifted out of the van in the wheelchair onto the stage and placed before the keyboard; but far from the pathos that one expected, he looked like a portly African king in a translucent green cloak with hood. But there was a distance now in his presence; he seemed barely aware of the audience. A change had occurred in his voice, and he never sang or spoke from the stage again.

Yet he refused to cancel gigs. " 'The show must go on' is a very important statement. People are disturbed and need your help 24 hours a day," he told the band. And he went on: Minneapolis, the Bottom Line, Europe in April for the Banlieues Bleues in Montreuil, France (a performance recorded as *Friendly Galaxy*); four concerts at colleges in New York State, Chattanooga, Atlanta, Rochester, the Royal Northern College of Music in Manchester, England, Koncepts in Oakland, Tubingen, Germany, the Painted Bride in Philadelphia.

He took his physical frailty to be a test, another block to be overcome. His spirit refused to surrender, and there seemed to be a new urgency about him. He was hungry to see signs of his success. When he was elected to the *Down Beat* Hall of Fame in the Thirty-Second Annual International Critic's Poll, he told everyone that he was now in three halls of fame; he boasted of playing in Russia and at a country-and-western bar in Texas; he talked of writing a book, a cosmo-autobiography. But the bitterness and disappointment which always lay near the surface was now visible:

I've been bypassed for a lot of things. That's why they sent the Art Ensemble to Europe before they sent for me. They've invited Ornette Coleman to write symphonies and things but not me, because I talk about space and things so they think I'm a kook. That's what they think. I think so too for even bothering to explain it. We do not disagree.

He later said that he was never going to write his book. When he was asked how, if he didn't write an autobiography, would his story be known in 4,000 years, he replied, "They ain't supposed to know it. If they ain't going to live forever, they don't need to know it."

John Gilmore was slated to be the leader for a small band gig at the Village Vanguard in November, as Sonny thought Gilmore had earned it, but at the last second he turned it back to Sun Ra, and they appeared without costumes under the name of Sun Ra and his All-Star Inventions (Buster Smith, Bruce Edwards, John Ore, Gilmore, Sun Ra on synthesizers, and Chris Anderson, a blind pianist Sonny had known in Chicago). It was a strange and slightly melancholy event.

Though traveling and working less, Sonny began thinking of doing new work: He wanted to prepare a "Moonwalker" set of songs written by Van Morrison and Michael Jackson; he worked on an extended piece for solo Synclavier, part of which was debuted at a master class which he gave (without speaking) at the New England Conservatory of Music in Boston in February. They worked the Knitting Factory in New York, the Pumpehuset in Copenhagen, the Jazzkeller in Frankfurt, the Moonwalker Club in Aarburg, Switzerland, Munich: then they drove down to Tuscaloosa in April to the Chukker for three concerts, the first billed as "Homage to Duke Ellington and Fletcher Henderson," the second as "Homage to the Flowers and Trees," and the third as "From Saturn to Alabama: Travels in Outer Space," and as the titles suggest they were the closest thing to a retrospective Sun Ra would ever give.

They appeared at the Barrymore Theater in Baltimore in May, and went to New York City for the "Knitting Factory Goes Uptown" concert at Town Hall. Saxophonist Roy Nathanson recalls that backstage before the concert Sun Ra was sitting quietly in his wheelchair, an old man, ignored by those making preparations around him. Ted Epstein of Blind Idiot God was tuning up his drums right next to where Sonny had been left. "I said to Ted, 'Keep it down, you're playing right in his ear.' But I felt like an asshole: I mean, this was the man who invented noise!"

On July 4 the Arkestra played at Summerstage in Central Park, opening for the popular noise band Sonic Youth. Guitarist Thurston Moore
was knowledgeable about the history of free jazz and was honored to
work with Sun Ra. "Before the concert," he said, "Sun Ra was withdrawn,
obviously in pain. He sat staring at himself in a mirror, like a magician
doubling his powers before battle." Thousands of teenagers were there
to see Sonic Youth, and few even knew the name Sun Ra. A girl standing
on tiptoes to see over the crowd asked no one in particular who it was on
stage. When somebody told her, she said, "They look like homeless people." And to be honest the exotic clothing and impenetrable sunglasses
that once marked the leading edge of Afrocentric display now seemed
tired and worn—the metallic skullcaps looked like shower caps, the mis-
matched jerkins like something from thrift shops.

It was also June Tyson's last performance with the band. By November she was dead from breast cancer.

There were two other performances at the Bottom Line in July and
August, where Sun Ra seemed increasingly detached, with Gilmore,
himself growing weaker with emphysema, directing the band. The performance was by rote, lacking energy. Still, just when the band might be
drifting off, Sonny's synthesizer would punch in with that ball-peen
hammer-on-I-beam sound that could freeze conversation at the tables;
or there were moments where disembodied riffs could rise up to save a
listless solo, or dissonant swells could threaten to drown the listeners in
sheer sonic density.

Just after winning *Down Beat's* Fortieth Annual International Critic's
Poll in the synthesizer and big-band categories, Sun Ra played the Village Vanguard the week of November 14 with violinist Billy Bang, doing
material he had recorded with Bang's group in September as *A Tribute
to Stuff Smith*. Drummer Andrew Cyrille said, "It was very interesting
because he was partially paralyzed.... [W]hen you're playing those
straight up and down tunes, they have coordinates that are preplanned
and you're supposed to meet at certain places, sometimes he wouldn't be
there. He'd be someplace else. But [bassist] John Ore and I, and also
Billy Bang when he was playin', had to be at these places. But because

Sun Ra was slightly ahead or behind...made for a certain kind of tension on that recording."

There was another performance at S.O.B.'s in New York City on October 21, where they were billed as Sun Ra and his Intergalactic Harmonic Divergent Jazz Arkestra, and a few days later he had another stroke, and was hospitalized again. A few dates were canceled, and when it became clear that he was not able to play or travel he told the Arkestra to go on without him, with John Gilmore as the leader. Gilmore himself was failing, and he ceased taking solos and could barely be heard in the saxophone section. They played a couple of Jewish weddings, one of them at the posh National Arts Club on Gramercy Park in New York, where they played show tunes, some swing favorites, and "Hava Nagila." Then on December 23 through 26 Sun Ra traveled with the band to the Knitting Factory, but did not play.

Evidence Records, a new company cofounded by Jerry Gordon who had sold Sonny's records for many years in his record store, struck a deal with Sun Ra and Alton Abraham and announced a plan of extensive reissues of the early Saturn Records on CD. The reissues drew the attention of the press, and reporters—many of whom had only a faint idea of who Sun Ra was—began calling and coming to the house. But he was skipping his medication and only sporadically attending physical therapy sessions, and was becoming increasingly distant and depressed. When National Public Radio came to the house to record an interview he kept repeating, "First comes the glory, then comes the shame...just like Mike Tyson." They treated it as an enigma, like the line from *Citizen Kane*. But it was part of a lecture he had given to the band many times over the years:

This kingdom is the kingdom of death. It's a shadow world. It's a make-believe world. It's a scenario of being inactive. They play it over and over. The passion play. First comes the glory, then comes the shame. I told the band about six months ago that Mike Tyson's got a lot of glory. I wondered when the shame was going to come. And then the shame came. Anybody. Malcolm X—glory, shame. Napoleon—glory, shame. Joan of Arc—glory, shame. So it all comes down to the Christ thing. They call that good. They call that Good Friday.

There were times when he mentioned others of the ritual of glory and shame: Paul Robeson, Josephine Baker, Martin Luther King, Elijah Muhammad, Charles Mingus. . . . And once he got started he would keep on moving backwards in time, listing those whom he said had ultimately accomplished nothing, such as Solomon and Abraham, "those who were good, but good for nothing!" And now he feared he might be added to the list.

The living room was turned into a bedroom for Sun Ra, so that he could greet visitors more easily and rehearse the band whenever he wanted to. There he sat in his wheelchair, scarcely moving now, surrounded by his framed awards, portraits of himself and the Arkestra, a Yamaha keyboard, piles of unmarked tapes, copies of *Popular Mechanics,* several editions of the Bible, banners and symbols and paintings which celebrated the sun; but there were also the accoutrements of the elderly and the fragile: a portable toilet, walking sticks, a Life Alert system.

When the band was playing out of town and no one was there to help him, a housekeeper and cook came in once a day; but without someone around all day things began to disappear from the house—a computer, keyboards, and tapes. The furnace now broke down completely, and they were forced to get by with space heaters. Gilmore was growing feeble, and himself was in bed much of the time. When Sun Ra became weaker he was returned to a rehabilitation center, and among him, the social workers, and the band, they agreed that he should be sent home to Birmingham to be taken care of by his family. There *was* a family after all: a sister, Mary Jenkins; a nephew, Thomas Jenkins, Jr.; and two nieces, Lillie B. King and Marie Holston. Sun Ra raised no objections. "He never came straight out and said it," Gilmore said, "but he knew it was his time. He said, 'I'm going back to Birmingham.' I guess that's where he came into this world and that's where he wanted to leave it. But Sonny never talked about death. . . . As far as I'm concerned, Sun Ra just moved on to another place."

He came back to Morton Street in mid-January 1993 for one last time, and for seven or eight hours he talked to the people in the house in a cautionary mode—"This world is made up of spoiled children. It's a world of mad bears; feed them honey, and they'll do whatever you want them to do." He stressed that the important thing was the job ahead, being ready for the gig, reaching the people. He reminded them that the important thing was "cogitation," by which he meant turning inward to make yourself part of the world: "You project your spirit outward and *become* everyone else—you understand them and their needs...I've given you all the information I can; now it's up to you." Then Jothan Callins took Sun Ra to the 30th Street Station in Philadelphia and together they rode the train back to Birmingham.

Some said it was his way of making up with his sister. Or that he simply knew that there were no other options. He returned to her house, where she and his niece, Wilma Jean Scott, tried to take care of him. But his sister was eighty-nine and his niece was herself in poor health. He was there a few days when he began running a fever and was taken to the Baptist Medical Center–Princeton where they diagnosed him as having pneumonia. After a week or so of care and medication, he seemed better and was sitting up in his room talking. The hernia which had helped define his whole life was corrected by surgery. Then his niece suddenly died of a heart attack. And in March he too had a heart attack: a pacemaker was installed, and he was placed in intensive care for over three weeks, still partially paralyzed and now only able to mumble. He had reached the seventy-ninth anniversary of his arrival on earth, but he had stopped trying to speak and now only grabbed the hands of those who reached out to him, gripping them so hard that it sometimes took two people to pry his fingers loose. Jothan brought in a tape player so he could hear his own music and Duke Ellington's. Trudy Morse read and chanted his poems to him, especially "This World Is Not My Home":

Is this a planet of life?
Then why do people die?
This is not life, this is death.
Can't you understand?

You're only dreaming.
You're not real here.
You're only dreaming
    you did all the things
    you did before you died.

You're asleep.
Wake up before it's too late
   and you die in a dream.

This world is not the real world.
It's all illusion. It's not real.
Can't you feel that this world is not real?
Someone cast a magic spell
   on the people of planet Earth.

If you do right they put you in jail.
If you do wrong they put you in jail.
You can't win.
You got to do something else.
You got to get away from here.

You make death your master.
You're not free.
If you're free, why do you bow to death?
Is that what you mean by liberty?
Stop bowing down to your master called death.
If you're free, prove it.

On May 30, 1993, a Sunday, towards whatever destiny, he left the planet. The man who had attempted to define death out of existence, to undo it with the force of words, to rescue all of the dead of history, was now himself being tested.

If death is the absence of life,
then death's death is life.

SUN RA

Sun Ra left the planet in a pyramid
made of metal keys.

JAYNE CORTEZ

To Mr. Ra: Rest in Space

MAIN, *Dry Stone Feed*

The church arrangements would have been made by Mary Jenkins, as she had been active in Baptist church affairs in Birmingham and was involved in gospel singing for many years; but since she was not well her daughter Marie planned the memorial service for June 4 at the Sixth Avenue Baptist Church, and a graveside service to follow the next day. June 5 was also the day set for a memorial concert by the Arkestra at the Bottom Line in New York, but the Arkestra made some phone calls and decided that some of them at least could fly down and back in time to make both engagements.

He was placed in a powder-blue metal coffin (which some, of course, said looked like a spaceship), laid to rest dressed in a white robe and cap trimmed in black, an ankh made of interwoven strips of copper and brass resting on his chest. At the evening service there was music by the Arkestra, testimonials by old friends; his poems were read and a few songs were sung, and the assembled mourners left singing "Space Is the Place."

The graveside service was held at Elmwood Cemetery on Martin Luther King Drive in the West End of Birmingham (the same cemetery in which Bear Bryant, Alabama's fabled football coach, also lay). Reverend Pherelle Fowler read from the twenty-third Psalm and called on those assembled to ask the Lord that Sun Ra be raised on eagle wings and taken on high where he might shine like the sun. Then the Reverend

John T. Porter drew on Ecclesiastes 3 and Tennyson's "Crossing the Bar" and offered his own reading of death, a reading with which Sun Ra would largely have agreed: "Death does not discriminate... it rises above race, creed, and social circumstance." The Arkestra then sang.

They'll come back in ships of gold
With wisdom never told
A touch of myth-world's splendor
Then they'll take back the others
Who are not of earth's dimension one
The others who are ready
Melody harmonic rhythmic planes,
Chromatic magic is eternal,
Outward on pleasant spheres,
Nothing is, yet everything is all
A splendid neverness...

The footstone simply read, "Herman Blount (aka Le Son'y Ra)."

Blacks thought I was talking about whites.
But I was talking about everybody.

SUN RA

How should Sun Ra be remembered? Some may recall him as one of the great avant-gardists of the second half of the twentieth century, a period in which the avant-garde often seemed lost or in hiding. Others may remember his larger project as merely a product of the racial unrest of his time, an extreme form of black nationalism, where Afrocentricity is extended from Egypt to the heavens. But Sun Ra's spirit was too universalistic to stop at the wretched limits of race in human history, too inclusive to settle for art-shock for art-shock's sake (if anything, he made the outrages of the avant-garde seem vapid, thin, and full of despair). His concern was the confusion and disorder which waste the potential for

beauty and happiness in our world, and the possibilities for seeing beyond the limits of anger, immediate gratification, and even death. Having been cast in the role of a person of color in this country, he studied
that part closely, and found within it the possibility of witnessing for all
of the peoples of Earth.

He might also be remembered as a composer in the grand tradition,
one who was driven by a hunger for totality that only music could express. To him poetry, dance, and music were linked together as arts of the
highest order, and music—especially instrumental music—was the most
immediate means for engaging the emotions with a higher reality. Music
could provide a metaphysical experience through which one could enter
the sublime, and come to know the cosmos. He understood music to be a
universal language, and something akin to religion. Music could convey
more than feelings about phenomena, it could express its essence, and
thus could disclose secrets of nature not available to reason, secrets
which reveal the true nature of the world. Sun Ra saw that music sym-
bolized the unity in diversity that is the cosmos, and the big band was his
space vehicle, African-American aesthetics his culture-synthesizing
principle. He was the bandleader as prophetic leader, the music arranger
as arranger of the world.

Such a program was enough to qualify him as a European romantic.
But his was also an African-American romanticism, its goal a collective
metaphysical experience. Though like the Europeans he began with a
conception of the body as an individual instrument sympathetically vi-
brating to music—thus linking the body to the celestial, the harmony of
the spheres, the experience of the flight of music, the hovering of music
in space—he saw it not as private experience, the artist alone, cut off
from other artists. In Sun Ra's romanticism, art is capable of constituting
a community which mirrors the universe, an artist's vision of the black
sacred cosmos. It is a music which is made collectively (and that is part
of his meaning of "precision"), an emergent form in which even a mistake will be corrected by the group.

As teacher, he worked to awaken his followers. Like Nietzsche, he un-
flinchingly assaulted received Christianity (especially those two great
interlocutors, Moses and Paul), as he did history's proudest achievements, freedom and democracy. He questioned the polarities of good
and evil, transvalued many of the basic terms of Western culture,

putting them in question, mocking their pomposity. "Truth" was not to be seen as a good, or even neutral: it was always the consequences of language and the result of some exercise of power—and both of the latter were in a state of babble.

Nonetheless, he preserved a few absolutes from attack: beauty, discipline, space, the Creator, infinity, even while he left them undefined and empty of fixed meaning, floating independent of each other, and in any case always in a kind of future with a dreamlike horizon.

> When I say space music, I'm dealing with the void, because that is of space too; but I'm dealing with the outer void, because somehow man is trapped in playing roles into the haven or heaven of the inner void, but I am not in that. That particular aim/goal does not interest my spirit-mind and because of that it moves out to something else where the word space is the synonym for a multi-dimension of different things other than what people might at present think it means. So I leave the word space open, like space is supposed to be, when I say space-music.

His message was ambiguous, humorous, continually revised and renewed, amusing to himself. He scattered ideas like he did the parts of *The Book of Information*. And his music was often like that as well, melodies rising up from surprising sources, only to be discarded or alternated with others, or made up of brief fragments which nonetheless seem to form into polyphony; or horns and instruments whose sonorities were ill fitted to each other, but which nevertheless finally cohere at some point. His music seemed ahistorical, resisting dating and stylistic categorization, but by the same token also resisting dismissal as old-fashioned. When in the later years he returned to the blues and the pop songs and swing of his youth he seemed to be doing just what he said he was doing—"schooling" us on his music's origins, showing us the links we had missed so that we could make sense of what we were hearing.

To be sure, some thought him insane, or at least eccentric in the extreme, or a put-on of a low order. But he effectively stayed one step ahead of any of his doubters and questioners, absorbing their criticisms, surprising even himself with his own constructions, his wordplay, his conjunctions. He spent so much more time talking about what was wrong and so little about what his message was, that he sometimes even ominously joked that he wasn't sure *what* the answer was. But meanwhile he had the floor.

He invited those who listened to write on the surface he provided, to respond by completing the picture. And in a period in which all institutions and occupations were in the process of being discredited or being put into question, he was for some the perfect spokesman for his times. Most reasonable people would have said that he was a demanding master, a selfish, overbearing, self-serving teacher, a guru, in a word; but not the idea of the guru which Europe had imported from Asia. With Sun Ra it was up to you to make sense of what he said, to find in it what you could use. You had to engage your spirit to understand him, but it was your spirit which was always in control, not Sun Ra. It was that attitude that audiences who responded to Sun Ra's music took to the performances. You accepted what you liked and ignored the too-far-out, the obscure or embarrassing parts. And he in turn ignored the Philistines in his audience. Or transvalued their comments. A teenager once said to him, "This is sixth-grade jazz!" "Yeah," he answered, "because the average American has a sixth-grade education, so thank you, I'm reaching them."

"Sun Ra didn't say you had to believe what he says; you should just check it out for yourself," said Danny Thompson. He seldom told his musicians what was acceptable or unacceptable directly, but steered the Arkestra by indirection and suggestion, working their strengths and weaknesses, weaving one person into another, drawing them out.

> He made you face your own situation, your own realities, not his. He'd say, "Look at X. He has self-esteem, but Y has none." "Jacson," he said to me, "you're supposed to be intelligent, and you can't even spell your name right!" Or, "Eloe, he's a Chicago gangster; only thing is he's not in Chicago anymore." And then he'd find a way to work the two together.

Jacson had studied Zen philosophy before he had met Sun Ra, and he recognized paradoxical communication at work in his teaching. "So like a smart ass, I asked him, 'Sonny, what's the sound of one hand clapping?' 'The breeze, Jacson,' he answered, 'the breeze.' "

A lot of what he said resisted close scrutiny. He seemed to be flirting with nonsense, but it could worry you for days. Art Jenkins recalls that one day, Sonny said something like:

Sometimes you could be someplace and be out of place, or be no place and be out of place. But when you're somewhere you don't have to be out of place because you might lose your place, and be last, or be left out.

Verta Mae Grosvenor saw him a bit differently:

He didn't spell everything out, but it was a way he talked. Once Marshall fell down the stairs. He had told Marshall not to do something or other, so we were then all subjected to this long lecture on what happens if we don't obey, or follow the Cosmic Path, the teachings of Sonny. The talk, the teachings, the music, it was all one...

Like his old teacher 'Fess Whatley, he blurred the lines between the lecture and the gig.

Nothing he did was without meaning, even the seating on the buses, the rooms at the hotel. We were never sure whether we were being punished or rewarded. It was part of the discipline. If you think of an abstract painting, to the eye it's abstract; but the painter tells you how the parts fit together. Maybe he did it for a different look or a different sound.

We had the confidence of knowing we were doing something new. And the audience knew and understood it. So if you ask me what it meant, I just knew that I understood it. It was like receiving those records and poems from Jacson before I knew much about the Arkestra or Sun Ra...I just accepted it. Later, I might ask myself, am I crazy?

When he told you things, you *knew*. But you couldn't necessarily explain it to others.

Musicians outside the Arkestra had a range of responses to his talk, and drummer Andrew Cyrille encompassed them all when he said:

Sun Ra would rap about what he thought of the Cosmos in terms of his philosophy and it would be some very interesting stuff he would say,

whether you believed it or not. And a lot of times it was humorous, and a
lot of times it was ridiculous, and a lot of times it was right on the money.

Vernon Davis saw him as unceasingly in the process of change:

You never knew what he might say or who he might be when you went up
to see him in his room. He might say he was Lucifer, or God. And by the
time you left he'd be *both* Lucifer and God!

It was the openness of his structure that reached dancer Judith
Holten:

We all projected our dreams onto Sun Ra. I thought we were going to save
the black race and I thought the music was magical and thought that
somehow we would all live forever or leave the planet. I projected my
own myth onto Sun Ra and then I found out that it wasn't my myth, his
myth was different than my myth, and then I had to make an adjustment.
It was also like a mirror and you saw what you wanted to project but people do that all the time, but his mirror was so rich! You could get lost in
there, like a hall of mirrors.

There was nothing surprising about his mysticism per se: scratch any
musician and you find a crypto-Pythagorean. Scratch music history and
you find a line which stretches back at least as far as Marsilio Ficino in
the fifteenth century and his belief that music is formed of the same substance as the spirit, that it has the power to bring individuals into line
with the heavens; or to Henry Cornelius Agrippa, who thought music
had the power to raise the spirits of the dead. Sun Ra was in a long line
of composer-mystics which included Ives, Schoenberg, and Stockhausen, to name only a few moderns; and Ornette Coleman, Cecil Taylor, and Anthony Braxton within the jazz tradition.

Sun Ra's ideas might seem strange, sometimes silly, but much of what
he said seems to have parallels with the Gnostics, particularly those of
the twelfth-century Catherist religion practiced by a series of ascetic
and heretical groups in the south of France, a group incidentally which
had great influence on the troubadours of that era; but since some elements of it could also be found in various branches of African-American

religion, his ideas lie perhaps in some even older spiritual teachings. If he had located his synthesis of these ideas strictly in the past (as he did with Egypt), he could have slipped by as a run-of-the-mill mystic. But when he positioned it in the ultramodern, in technology, in space travel, the warning signals went up.

Sun Ra refused to accept a fixed identity, or a locatable historical position; he resisted closure: Who was he? Where did he come from? How many records had he made? What was the meaning of his teachings? He effaced his biography and then built a structure to sustain his shifting identity. As messenger he expanded ever outward, from black South to urban North, to the nation, Earth, Saturn, the universe, the omniverse; from Southern Baptist to ancient Egyptian to the Angel race. Face to face he was impressive, if difficult to follow and hard to believe. But in cosmo drama and the *Gesamtkunstwerk* of his shows it was hard to dismiss him lightly. He assembled elements of music, dance, and art which had never been witnessed together, and yet at the same time seemed to distantly allude to tent shows, dance halls, and country churches, as well as to real or forgotten empires. And he did it with a level of intention and seriousness which seemed no longer possible.

A finely tuned if tortured moral sensibility pervaded all of his work, and his myth-ritual statements could wake you to the void in our lives even where it was impossible to accept his solution. "Sun Ra's consistent statement," Baraka said, "musically and spoken is that this is a primitive world. Its practices, beliefs, religions, are uneducated, unenlightened, savage, destructive, already in the past... That's why Sun Ra returned only to say he left. Into the Future. Into Space."

NOTES

UNLESS OTHERWISE NOTED, all quotes are from interviews conducted by the author between 1993 and 1996. Since some quotations come from interviews given by Sun Ra which were published in French, German, Dutch, and Italian periodicals, considerable variation of tone and style may appear in the translation into English. In translating these texts I was aided by Amy Reid, Anti Bax, Dorothea Schulz, and Christina Lombardi, but the responsibility for the versions given here rests with the author.

INTRODUCTION

xv The reconstruction of the Swarthmore College concert was done from memory, so some conflation with other concerts of the period may have occurred.

xvi "Along came Ra": Transcribed from concerts circa 1988.

xvi "Mongo" and "Arboria": Review of Chicago Jazz Showcase performance by J. B., *Jazz Magazine* (Paris) 251 (January 1977), p. 53.

xvii "Genius or Charlatan?": Rolf-Ulrich Kaiser, "Sun Ra: Scharlaten oder Weltverbesserer?" *Jazz Podium*, June 1968.

CHAPTER ONE

4 May 22, 1914: promotion record: Herman P. Blount.

4 "Black Herman": Gerald Early, "Black Herman Comes Through Only Once Every Seven Tears: Black Magic, White Magic, and American Culture," in

The Culture of Brusing, p. 209; Black Herman, *Secrets of Magic, Mystery and Legerdemain.*

5   "You can't ask me to be specific about time": Michael Shore, "Sun Ra," *Musician, Player and Listener,* no. 24 (April–May 1980), p. 49.

6   "At three, the Creator": Phil Schaap, "An Interview with Sun Ra," *WKCR* v, no. 5 (January–February 1989), p. 31.

6   "I'm not a human": Rich Theis, "Sun Ra," *Option,* September–October 1983, p. 48.

6   "I've separated myself": Rolf-Ulrich Kaiser, "Sun Ra: Scharlaten oder Weltverbesserer?," *Jazz Podium,* June 1968, p. 183.

7   "[Man] has to rise": Sun Ra interview with Gerry Clark, September 14, 1990.

7   "It's not good for me": Karen Bennett, "The Brother from Another Planet," *Philadelphia Inquirer Sunday Magazine,* September 25, 1988, p. 12.

7   "He was born at my mother's": Kathy Kemp, "Aboard the Spaceship Sun Ra," *Birmingham Post-Herald Kudzu Magazine,* April 17, 1992, p. 6.

8   Lionel Hampton, *Hamp: An Autobiography,* pp. 3–4.

9   "she said you make your own heaven": Robert D. Rusch, "Sun Ra: Interview," *Jazztalk,* 1984, p. 64.

9   "I never could understand if Jesus died": Francis Davis interview with Sun Ra, Philadelphia, January 29, 1990.

9   Ann Adams interviews with W. C. Patton and Melvin Caswell, Birmingham, 1995.

10   *Manual of Drills to be Used in the Exemplification of the Ritualistic Work of Modern Woodmen of America; Official Ritual of the Modern Woodmen of America 1915.*

10   Clinic study, Warren State Hospital, Warren, Pennsylvania, February 12, 1943.

10   "It was a setup": Theis, "Sun Ra," p. 48.

11   "I've never been part of the planet": John Litweiler, *The Freedom Principle,* p. 144.

11   "When I was a child I sang melodies": Jean-Louis Noames, "Visite au Dieu Soleil," *Jazz Magazine* (Paris) 125 (December 1969), p. 74.

12   "My grandmother liked church music": Eddy Determeyer, "Sun Ra: verleden, heden, toekomost," *Jazz Nu* 4, no. 10 (July 1982), p. 402.

12   "I had read about poets and writers": Rusch, "Sun Ra," p. 64.

15   "I played for social clubs": Sun Ra interview with Phil Schaap on WKCR, New York, December 12, 1988.

16   "When I heard Charlie Parker": Determeyer, "Sun Ra," p. 404.

17   "I never missed a band": Tam Fiofori, "Sun Ra's Space Odyssey," *Down Beat,* May 14, 1970, p. 14.

17 "What happened is that, in the Deep South": Phil Schaap, "An Interview with Sun Ra," *WKCR* 5, no. 6 (March 1989), p. 28.

17 "My grandmother called this music 'reels' ": Determeyer, "Sun Ra," p. 403.

18 Bertrand Demusy, "John Tuggle 'Fess' Whatley: A Maker of Musicians," *Jazz Monthly,* 1966, pp. 6–9.

19 Jothan Callins, "The Birmingham Jazz Community," 1982.

19 "If I had an appointment": Author interview with Frank Adams.

20 "brilliant" and "apt": Industrial High School cumulative card records.

20 "The Value of an Ideal Theme": *The Industrial High School Record* XI, no. III (March 13, 1931), p. 1.

23 Ann Adams interview with J. L. Lowe, Birmingham, 1995.

24 Clarence Williams: Sun Ra interview with John and Peter Hinds, May 30, 1990, *Sun Ra Research* 8 (September 1996), p. 3.

25 "I said don't use my name": Determeyer, "Sun Ra," p. 403.

27 "So there they were": Bert Primack, "Captain Angelic: Sun Ra," *Down Beat,* May 4, 1978, p. 15.

27 "you could major in everything": Ibid.

27 "I think I studied everything": Len Lyons, "Sun Ra: Interstellar Prophet of Jazz," *The Great Jazz Pianists,* p. 85.

27 "At the end of the first term": *The Normal Index,* vol. 15, no. 3 (January 1936), p. 2.

28 "She was so nice": Primack, "Captain Angelic," p. 15.

28 "I studied Chopin": Lyons, "Sun Ra," p. 85; *Bulletin of the State A. & M. Institute, Normal, Alabama* 15, no. 8 (August 1936).

28 "The next thing, I decided since I was making": Primack, "Captain Angelic."

28 "Then I decided to try and reach God": Davis interview with Sun Ra.

29 "They were having a good time.": Ibid.

32 "This was in Huntsville": Determeyer, "Sun Ra," p. 403.

33 "Forbes had never": Ann Adams interview with George Pruitt, 1995.

37 Discussion of Birmingham is informed by Robin Kelly, *Race Rebels: Culture, Politics, and the Black Working Class,* pp. 55–100; and *Hammer and Hoe: Alabama Communists during the Great Depression.*

40 "I don't have the right": Sun Ra quoted by Walter Miller in an interview with the author.

41 "At the present moment": Questionnaire, National Service Board for Religious Objectors, November 18, 1942.

41 "I have never been able": Ibid.

42 "The local board would not": Letter from Herman P. Blount to J. N. Weaver, National Service Board for Religious Objectors, November 28, 1942.

43 "Enclosed please find": Ibid.

44 "I've never seen": Sun Ra quoted by John Gilmore in interview with the author.

44 "I write you this begging": Letter from Herman P. Blount to the U.S. Marshall, Birmingham, Alabama, from Walker County Jail, Jasper, Alabama, January 31, 1943.

45 "This morning": Ibid.

46 "a psychopathic personality": Clinic study, Warren State Hospital.

47 "A white man heard me play": Sun Ra quoted by Gilmore.

47 "a fellow from camp": Letter from Herman P. Blount to the National Service Board, November 9, 1943.

47 "At all my band rehearsals": Ibid.

49 "Sun Ra would go into": Bennett, "The Brother from Another Planet," p. 14.

CHAPTER TWO

53 For background of the Club DeLisa I was helped by Dempsey J. Travis, *An Autobiography of Black Jazz*. Chicago: Urban Research Institute, 1983, pp. 123–43.

53 "After we'd get": Robert Palmer, "Sun Ra: 'The Creator of the Universe Got a Sense of Humor.'" *The Real Paper,* November 6, 1974, p. 18.

55 "That band": Len Lyons, "Sun Ra: Interstellar Prophet of Jazz," *The Great Jazz Pianists,* 1983, p. 86.

55 "...but I told him": Ibid.

56 "All of the people": Ira Steingroot, "Sun Ra's Magical Kingdom," *Reality Hackers,* no. 6 (Winter 1988), p. 51.

56 "...Fletcher didn't say anything": Phil Schaap, "An Interview with Sun Ra," *WKCR* 5, no. 5 (January–February 1989), p. 5.

57 "Fletcher was really": John C. Reid, "It's After the End of the World," *Coda* 231 (April–May 1990), p. 30.

57 "I give you": Red Sanders quoted by Tommy Hunter in an interview with the author.

58 "Yes, he had that": C. O. Simpkins, *Coltrane: A Biography,* p. 96.

59 "when Sun Ra was on it": Val Wilmer, "Sun Ra—Pictures of Infinity," in *As Serious As Your Life,* 1980, p. 83.

61 Robert Rusch, "Interview: Yusef Lateef," *Cadence,* January 1989, p. 23.

61 "Yes, that's the only": Robert Palmer, "Sun Ra," p. 18.

61 "Their first night": Ibid.

62 "You might say": Graham Lock interview with Sun Ra, London, 1990.

67 C. F. Volney. *The Ruins, or, Meditation on the Revolutions of Empires: and The Law of Nature.* Baltimore: Black Classic Press, 1991.

68 "Just imagine": Volney quoted by St. Clair Drake, *Black Folks Here and There,* vol. 1, 1987, p. 133.

69 Archibald Rutledge, *God's Children,* 1947; *Home by the River,* 1941.

69 Godfrey Higgins, *Anacalypsis: An Attempt to Draw Aside the Veil of the Saitic Isis: An Inquiry into the Origin of Language, Nation and Religion,* 1833.

70 Wilhelm Worringer, *Egyptian Art,* p. 1.

70 This discussion is informed by Michael Barkun, *Race and the Radical Right,* 1994.

72 Alexander Hislip, *The Two Babylons, or Papal Worship Proved to Be the Worship of Nimrod and His Wife,* 1945.

73 "all that Bud Powell": Paul B. Matthews, "Junior Mance Interview, Part 1," *Cadence* 20, no. 7 (July 1994), p. 13.

76 C. O. Simpkins, *Coltrane: A Biography,* 1975, pp. 99–100.

78 "When I was in Chicago": Sun Ra, "Your Only Hope Now Is a Lie," *Hambone,* no. 2 (Fall 1982), p. 110.

79 Mark Ribowsky, *Don't Look Back: Satchel Paige in the Shadows of Baseball,* 1994, pp. 24–25.

80 "That's the way Fletcher": Robert D. Rusch, "Sun Ra: Interview," *Jazztalk,* 1984, p. 68.

80 R. W. B. Lewis, "Ritual Naming: Ralph Ellison and Toni Morrison," in *Literary Reflections,* 1993, pp. 177–94; Kimberly W. Benston, " 'I Yam What I Yam': Naming and Unnaming in Afro-American Literature," *Black American Literature Forum,* vol. 16, no. 1 (Spring 1982), pp. 3–11; J. L. Dillard, *Black Names,* 1976.

80 Cynthia Eal Kerman, *The Lives of Jean Toomer: A Hunger for Wholeness,* 1987, pp. 28–29.

81 "My poor blind": Elijah Muhammad, *Message to the Black Man,* 1965, p. 55.

81 Claudia Dreifus, "Chloe Wofford Talks About Toni Morrison," *New York Times Magazine,* September 11, 1994, pp. 72–75.

82 Alan Light, "The Man Who Won't Be Prince," *Vibe,* August 1994, p. 45.

83 "cosmology and planets": Tam Fiofori, "Sun Ra's Duality," *Melody Maker,* February 5, 1972, p. 28.

83 "related to immortality": Ibid.

83 "I have many names": Declaration by Sun Ra from stage performances c. 1988.

83 "You see, on this planet": John Corbett, "Sun Ra: Gravity and Levity," *Extended Play*, 1994, p. 316.

84 "Sun Ra is not a person": Ibid.

85 "How did you get": Rolf-Ulrich Kaiser, "Sun Ra: Scharlaten oder Weltverbesserer?" *Jazz Podium*, June 1968, p. 184.

85 "Ra is my spirit name": Art Sato, "Sun Ra: In the Spirit of the Universe," *Konceptualizations* 9, nos. 1 & 2 (Winter/Spring 1993), pp. 2–5.

85 "When I moved to Chicago": Eddy Determeyer, "Sun Ra: verleden, heden, toekomost," *Jazz Nu* 4, no. 10 (July 1982), p. 403.

85 "the x pronounced": Lyons, "Sun Ra," p. 85.

85 "God said he'd send": Sun Ra, "Your Only Hope Now Is a Lie," p. 111.

86 " 'Herman' reversed": Ira Steingroot, "Sun Ra's Magical Kingdom," *Reality Hackers*, no. 6 (Winter 1988), pp. 46–47, 50–51.

86 "My mama always called me 'son' ": Anson Kenny, "Play It Again, Sun Ra," *Philadelphia Magazine*, April 1977, pp. 75–79, 81.

86 "I always called myself": *Souvenir Booklet of the 1970 Tour*, compiled by Victor Schonfield for Music Now.

86 "on my side": Kenny, Ibid.

86 "I'm very interested in names": Philippe Carles, "Il sera temps d'édifier la maison noire . . . Sun Ra," *Jazz Magazine* (Paris) 217 (December 1973), p. 24.

88 "It was for my own edification": Phil Schaap, "An Interview with Sun Ra," *WKCR* 5, no. 6 (March 1989), p. 26.

89 "Sun Ra was another": Phil Schaap's interview with Pat Patrick on WKCR, April 16, 1987.

90 On the background to doowop, see Anthony J. Gribin and Matthew M. Schiff, *Doo-Wop*. Iola, Wis.: Krause Publications, 1992.

91 "He taught us": Robert Pruter, "The Doowop Years" in the notes to *Sun Ra: The Singles*, Evidence Records ECD 22164 (1996).

91 "Lucifer": Ibid.

91 "Dreaming": Lyrics transcribed from *Sun Ra: The Singles*, Evidence Records ECD 22164 (1996).

92 "When you would": Robert Campbell interview with John Gilmore, June 7, 1993.

94 " 'Arkestra' has a 'ra' ": Franco Fayenz, "Sun Ra: Vo dico qual è la mia galassia," in *Jazz & Jazz*, 1988, p. 145.

94 "Ra can be written": Robert Palmer, "Sun Ra: 'The Creator of the Universe Got a Sense of Humor,' " *The Real Paper*, November 6, 1974, p. 18.

94 "I read that in Sanskrit": Fayenz, "Sun Ra."

95 Bert Vuijsje, "Sun Ra nar van de schepper," *Haagse Post*, November 25, 1970.

98 Discussion of Moog's studio from rehearsal tape, c. 1970.

100 "I wanted them to": Bert Vuijsje, "Sun Ra Spreekt," *Jazz Wereld,* October 1968, p. 17.

105 This discussion has been aided by Peter Lamborn Wilson, "Lost/Found Moorish Time Lines in the Wilderness of North America," in *Sacred Drift: Essays on the Margins of Islam,* 1993, pp. 15–50; Leon Forrest, "Elijah," *Relocations of the Spirit,* 1994, pp. 16–66.

CHAPTER THREE

111 "Sun Ra taught me": Rudie Kagie, "Het sterfhuis vande jazz," *Vrij Nederland,* February 3, 1996, p. 52.

111 "Ignorance": Sun Ra quoted by James Jacson in an interview with the author, 1995.

113 "Play that apple.": W. Kim Heron, "Sun Ra Sets His Own Strange World to Music," *Detroit Free Press,* October 24, 1980.

113 "It's probably this precision": Daniel Soutif, "Sun Ra: un beau soleil sous le bonnet," *Claviers* (Paris), no. 1 (May 1981), p. 43.

114 "Anyone can make sense": Sun Ra quoted by Jacson, 1995.

114 "Sonny gave you": Robert Campbell interview with Lucious Randolph, February 7, 1993.

115 "In the army": Philippe Carles, "Il sera temps d'édifier la maison noire...Sun Ra," *Jazz Magazine* (Paris) 217 (December 1973), p. 24.

115 "Now, in rehearsal": Robert Palmer, "Sun Ra: 'The Creator of the Universe Got a Sense of Humor,'" *The Real Paper,* November 6, 1974, p. 18.

115 "We rehearsed one way": Robert Campbell interview with Lucious Randolph, March 14, 1993.

115 "you start a four": Ibid., February 2, 1993.

116 "*Jazz Magazine*": Philippe Carles, "L'impossible liberté: Entretien avec Sun Ra, John Gilmore, Marshall Allen et Pat Patrick," *Jazz Magazine* (Paris) 196 (January 1972), p. 12.

116 "Why does the Creator": Sun Ra quoted by Jacson, 1995.

117 "Those who broke the rules": Ibid.

118 "You never knew": Verta Mae Grosvenor in an interview with the author.

119 "Once after a gig": Author interview with Michael Ray, 1995.

119 "Guys like Monk": Robert Barry in an interview with John Litweiler.

120 "I realized": Bert Vuijsje, "Sun Ra nar van de schepper," *Haagse Post,* November 25, 1970.

121 "Can't nobody": C. O. Simpkins, *Coltrane: A Biography,* 1975, p. 97.

121 "First I need to know": Ibid.

122 "... in my music": Mark Dery, "Sun Ra," *Keyboard*, March 1991, p. 43.

122 "It was really": Phil Schaap, "An Interview with Sun Ra," *WKCR* 5, no. 6 (March 1989), pp. 3–4.

123 "Sun Ra writes": John Burks, "Sun Ra," *Rolling Stone*, no. 31 (April 19, 1969), p. 18.

123 "according to the day, the minute": Val Wilmer, *As Serious As Your Life*, 1980, p. 75.

124 "He would throw you": Campbell interview with Randolph, February 7, 1993.

124 "Sun Ra was an enigma": Mark Crooks, "Julius Priester: Interview," *Cadence*, April 1978.

124 "One day": Campbell interview with Randolph.

125 "I could feel the heat": Quoted in Karl Heinz Kessler, "Sun Ra: Music as Means for Social Transformation," in *Omniverse Sun Ra*, Hartmut Geerken and Bernhard Hefele, eds., 1994, p. 116.

126 On titles, see Winston Smith, "Let's Call This: Race, Writing and Difference in Jazz," *Public* 4/5 1990, pp. 71–85.

126 "The music up till": Wilmer, *As Serious As Your Life*, p. 87.

127 "I have always thought orchestra": Rev. Dwight Frizzell interview with Sun Ra, Kansas City, April 1982.

127 "[When I compose]": Soutif, "Sun Ra," p. 46.

127 Robert Campbell interview with Art Hoyle, May 31, 1993.

128 "if the harmony is just": Schaap, 1989, p. 7.

128 "We're not concerned with the world": Simpkins, p. 97.

129 "So I found myself talking": Mark Sinker, "Sun Ra Talks to Mark Sinker," *Different Cats: Stride Magazine*, no. 37 (1995), p. 24.

131 "[This is] not science": Giacomo Pellicciotti, "Parla Sun Ra," *Musica Jazz* 30, no. 2 (February 1974), p. 12.

131 "They make strange and horrible ones": Jean-Louis Noames, "Visite au dieu soleil," *Jazz* 125 (December 1965), p. 75.

133 Elijah Muhammad, *The Theology of Time*, Abass Rassoull, ed., 1992.

133 Khalid Alif Muhammad, *Elaborations of (Allah's Lessons)*, 1984, p. 44.

134 "The White Flyer to Heaven": Paul Oliver, *Songsters & Saints: Vocal Traditions on Race Records*, 1980, pp. 151–52.

134 "black sacred cosmos": Mechal Sobel, *Trabelin' On*, 1988, passim.

135 "I have an intimation": Jean Toomer quoted in James Webb, *The Harmonic Circle*, 1980, pp. 341–42.

136 "The main thing": Arthur Taylor, *Notes and Tones*, 1982, pp. 69–70.

137 "Space is perfect": notes to King Pleasure, *Golden Days,* Hifi Jazz Records (1960).

137 Mark Dery, "Black to the Future: Interviews with Samuel R. Delany, Greg Tate, and Tricia Rose," in *Flame Wars: The Discourse of Cyberculture,* Mark Dery, ed., *The South Atlantic Quarterly* 92, no. 4 (Fall 1993), pp. 735–89.

138 "putting the interstellar carriage": Greg Tate quoted in Dery, "Black to the Future," p. 766.

138 "I think that man": Carles, "Sun Ra," p. 12.

139 "So, this is my view": Mark Tucker, ed., *The Duke Ellington Reader,* 1993, p. 296.

139 Norman Mailer, *Of a Fire on the Moon,* 1971.

140 "According to my research": Bert Vuijsje, "Sun Ra Spreekt," *Jazz Wereld,* October 1968, p. 17.

140 Joe Gonçalves, "Sun Ra at the End of the World," *The Cricket,* no. 4 (1969), p. 11.

141 "Imagination": Liner notes to *Nothing Is,* ESP-Disk 1017 (1966).

141 "Space was Sonny's medium": John Litweiler, notes to *Sun Ra Visits Planet Earth/Interstellar Low Ways,* Evidence Records 22039 (1992).

142 "[There are] many different": Simpkins, pp. 96–97.

142 "So that's what we did": Ibid.

143 "Sonny gave his drummers": Campbell interview with Randolph, February 7, 1993.

144 "Sonny wanted the drummers": Robert Campbell interview with Alvin Fielder, April 26, 1993.

144 "so they could rest": Ibid.

144 "Basie had to lay it aside": Eddy Determeyer, "Sun Ra: verleden, heden, toekomost," *Jazz Nu* 4, no. 10 (July 1982), p. 406.

145 "Sun Ra was going through a change": Campbell interview with Randolph, February 7, 1993.

145 "When we play concerts": Sun Ra, "Sun Ra 2," *Jazz* 266 (November 1970), p. 24.

146 "Every evening I move": Vuijsje, "Sun Ra Spreekt."

146 "I always know": Determeyer, "Sun Ra," p. 403.

147 "What I play": Vuijsje, "Sun Ra Spreekt."

148 For background to the Compass Players, see Donna McCrohan, *The Second City,* 1987; Janet Coleman, *The Compass,* 1990.

149 "Sometimes we do that": Jean-Louis Noames, "Visite au dieu soleil," *Jazz* 125 (December 1965), p. 74.

153 Don Gold, *Down Beat Record Reviews* 2 (1958), pp. 183–84.

154 Norman Mailer in *Cannibals and Christians,* 1966, p. 116; Norman Mailer interview with author.

155 Booklet enclosed with *Jazz by Sun Ra,* Transition Records TRLP J-10.

158 Nat Hentoff, *Down Beat Record Reviews* 2 (1958), pp. 183–84.

159 Martin Williams, "Still Changing the Avant Garde," *Saturday Review,* October 12, 1968, reprinted in Martin Williams, ed. *Jazz Masters in Transition 1957–1969.* New York: Macmillan, 1970, pp. 264–66.

159 Miles Davis blindfold test, reprinted in Leonard Feather and Ira Gitler, eds., *The Encyclopedia of Jazz in the '70's,* 1976, pp. 34–35.

159 Wynton Marsalis in Ben Sidran, *Talking Jazz,* p. 349.

159 Philippe Carles, "L'opera cosmique de Sun Ra," *Jazz Magazine* (Paris) 159 (October 1968), p. 43.

160 Jack Cooke, Review of *Sound of Joy, Jazz Monthly,* May 1970, p. 23.

161 Edward Bland, "On 'The Cry of Jazz'," *Film Culture,* Summer 1960, pp. 28–32.

164 "It was a big package thing": Robert Campbell interview with Hattie Randolph, June 26, 1993.

167 "Today is the shadow": notes to *Jazz in Silhouette,* Saturn 5786 (1958).

167 "Enlightenment": Ibid.

172 "We'd come out": Bert Primack, "Sun Ra: Captain Angelic," *Down Beat,* May 4, 1978, p. 16.

173 "Sometimes the musicians": Campbell interview with Randolph, February 7, 1993.

173 "Don't wear that color": Ibid.

173 "We started [wearing space costumes] back in Chicago": Vuijsje, "Sun Ra Spreekt," p. 18.

174 "I had a special space hat": Primack, "Sun Ra,": p. 16.

174 "A costume *is* music": John Corbett, Jez Nelson, "Up and Coming."

175 "*show* Negroes, cannot *tell* them": quoted by Robert A. Hill, "Making Music: Marcus Garvey, *Dada,* August 1922," in Deborah Willis, ed., *Picturing Me,* 1994, pp. 180–205.

175 "[I]n the early days in every nation": John Corbett, "Sun Ra: Gravity and Levity," *Extended Play,* 1994, p. 313.

175 "All police, all militaries": Sun Ra quoted by James Jacson in interview by the author.

178 "Interplanetary Music": transcribed from *We Travel the Spaceways,* Saturn HK 5445 (1966).

179 "thick-fingered piano": William Russo, review of *Fate in a Pleasant Mood, Down Beat,* October 6, 1966, p. 32.

179 Account of the Arkestra's appearance at the Mocambo from a letter to the author from Pat Reardon, September 26, 1994.

181 "They said I was playing God's music": Ray Townley, "Sun Ra," *Down Beat,* December 20, 1973, p. 18.

CHAPTER FOUR

184 "Sun Ra had this big sunburst": Art Hoyle interview with Robert Campbell, May 31, 1992.

184 "Sonny showed": Ibid.

185 "Yo, Sun Ra!": Michael Zwerin, *Close Enough for Jazz,* 1983, p. 239.

187 "I wasn't sure what Sun Ra": Michael Shore's liner notes to *Cosmic Tones for Mental Therapy,* Evidence Records 22036 (1992).

189 "I couldn't get my thing going": Val Wilmer, "John Gilmore," *The Wire* 17 (July 1985), p. 14.

189 Doug Miller, "The Moan Within the Tone: African Retentions in Rhythm and Blues Saxophone Style in Afro-American Popular Music," *Popular Music,* 14/2 (1995), pp. 155–74.

191 "The Sun Also Rises," *Down Beat,* March 29, 1962, p. 15.

191 "If nothing else": John S. Wilson, "Space Jazz Lacks Boosters: Cosmic Group Fails to Orbit with Rhythmic Propulsion," *New York Times,* February 29, 1962.

192 "Here's a music": notes to *Secrets of the Sun,* Saturn 208 (1967).

193 "Sun Ra asked me to sing": Art Jenkins interview on WKCR, April 17, 1987.

193 For description of life on the Lower East Side in the early 1960s, see the special issue of *African-American Review,* vol. 27, no. 4 (1993).

194 Apartment descriptions drawn from J. C. Thomas, "Sun Ra's Space Probe," *Down Beat,* June 13, 1968, pp. 19–20; John S. Wilson, "Sun Ra: I'm Talking About Cosmic Things," *New York Times,* April 7, 1968, p. 18; Bert Vuijsje, "Sun Ra Spreekt," *Jazz Wereld,* October 1968, p. 16.

196 "You can't say": Bob Young and Al Stankus, *Jazz Cooks,* 1992, p. 177.

197 "Sun Ra had this loft": Darius James, *That's Blaxploitation!* 1995, p. 76.

199 "When Angels Speak": notes to *When Angels Speak of Love,* Saturn 1966 (1966).

202 "I am in Birmingham": Martin Luther King, Jr., "Letter from the Birmingham Jail," in *Why We Can't Wait,* 1963.

203 Gary Stewart, *Breakout: Profiles in African Rhythm,* 1992, pp. 87–96.

203 "so that people who are worshipping": Cole Gagne, ed., "Sun Ra" in *Soundpieces 2: Interviews with American Composers,* 1993, p. 377.

204 "I criticized him": Robert D. Rusch, "Art Blakey: Interview," *Cadence* 7, no. 7 (July 1981), p. 11.

205 On the October Revolution, see John F. Szwed, liner note to *The October Revolution,* Evidence Records ECD 22166 (1996).

206 "they present a reviewer": A. B. Spellman, "Jazz at the Judson," *The Nation,* February 8, 1965, pp. 149–51.

209 "Ra was so far out": Amiri Baraka, *Eulogies,* 1996, p. 171.

209 "Study the history": LeRoi Jones, "Meanings of Nationalism," *Raise Race Rays Raze,* 1971, p. 109.

211 "Ra held court": Ibid.

212 Larry Neal, *Views of a Liberated Future,* p. 73; Elijah Muhammad, *Message to the Blackman,* 1965, pp. 110–11, 112, 119.

212 "The Magic City": Sun Ra, *Extensions Out. Immeasurable Equation, Vol. II,* 1972, p. 30.

213 "the purest sound I ever got": Philippe Carles, "L'impossible liberté," *Jazz Magazine* (Paris) 196 (January 1972), p. 13.

214 "It's really saying": Sun Ra interviewed by Greg Ross on WXPN, Philadelphia, 1981.

215 "it quits in strange places": Phil Schaap, "An Interview with Sun Ra," *WKCR* 5, no. 6 (March 1989), p. 15.

216 "Sun Ra would go to the studio": Edwin Pouncey, " 'It Makes You Booomph!' " *Resonance* 4, no. 1 (1995), p. 24.

218 Ronald Sukenick, *Down and In: Life in the Underground,* 1987, pp. 167–68.

218 Descriptions of Slug's drawn from Michael Zwerin, "Jazz Journal: A Little Sample of Something Bad," *Village Voice,* August 15, 1968, p. 21; J. C. Thomas, "Sun Ra's Space Probe," *Down Beat,* June 13, 1968, p. 20; and author's memory.

219 "That's too far out": Charles Blass, "Le Sun Ra, The Village Vanguard, NYC, November 1991," *Different Cats: Stride Magazine,* no. 37 (1995), p. 14.

221 "I look for the incorrigibles": "The New Jazz," *Newsweek,* December 12, 1966, p. 106.

221 "You just played the forbidden sacred music!": Sun Ra interview with Francis Davis, Philadelphia, January 29, 1990.

222 "Costumed and jeweled": A. B. Spellman, "Oral Challenges to the Written Word: The Poetry of Yusef Rahman and Amus Mor," *Sagala* 2 (Washington, D.C.), 1981, pp. 8–9.

222 Ishmael Reed, "I Am a Cowboy in the Boat of Ra," in *Conjure: Selected Poems, 1963–1970,* 1971, pp. 17–18. For a discussion of Reed's poem, see

Shamoon Zamir, "The Artist as Prophet, Priest, and Gunslinger: Ishmael Reed's 'Cowboy in the Boat of Ra,' " *Calllaloo* 17, no. 4 (1994), pp. 1205–35. Henry Dumas's "Ark of Bones" is in *Goodbye, Sweetwater: New & Selected Stories,* 1988, pp. 3–18, and "Outer Space Blues," is in *Knees of a Natural Man: The Selected Poetry of Henry Dumas,* 1989, pp. 66–67. For more on Dumas see the special issue of *Black American Literature Forum* 22, no. 2 (Summer 1988).

224 "He was Gene Ammons": Michael Zwerin, "Jazz Journal: One for Two," *Village Voice,* May 25, 1967.

224 "He wasn't frustrated": James Jacson's interview with the author, 1996.

225 "America never heard the beauty": Sun Ra interview with Paul Robicheau, Boston, December 1987.

226 "By infinity Mr. Ra": John S. Wilson, "Sun Ra: 'I'm Talking About Cosmic Things,' *New York Times,* April 7, 1968, sec. 2, p. 17.

227 "These piano solos": Stefan Brecht, "Sun Ra," *Evergreen Review,* no. 54 (May 1968), p. 90.

228 Luigi Russolo, *The Art of Noises,* 1986 [1913].

229 I am indebted to the discussion of noise and distortion in Brian Eno, *A Year with Swollen Appendices,* 1996, pp. 14–194, 277.

230 Michael Nyman, *Experimental Music,* 1974, pp. 27–70.

230 "in which any sound": John Cage, *For the Birds,* 1981, p. 77.

231 I have benefited here enormously from Sally Banes, *Greenwich Village 1963,* 1993.

235 "What I do is based": Jean-Louis Noames, "Visite au dieu soleil," *Jazz* 125 (December 1965), p. 74.

235 Bert Vuijsje, "Sun Ra Spreekt," *Jazz Wereld,* October 1968, pp. 16–19.

240 "Oh, yeah, I'm using these intervals": Mark Dery, "Sun Ra," *Keyboard,* March 1991, p. 43.

241 "The idea of Ihnfinity": John S. Wilson, "Sun Ra: I'm Talking About Cosmic Things," *New York Times,* April 7, 1968, sec. 2, pp. 17–18.

241 "To perform works": Articles of Incorporation, State of Illinois, Certificate Number 20948, April 10, 1967.

242 "To perform": Articles of Incorporation, State of Illinois, Certificate Number 21981, January 16, 1974.

243 "Statement for the White Panther Arm": Jonathan Eisen, ed., *Twenty-Minute Fandangos and Forever Changes,* 1971, p. 225.

244 Edwin Pouncey, "Motor City Burning," *The Wire* 136 (June 1995), pp. 26–30.

246 Transcribed from a recording of the Alan Burke show.

251 "There comes a point": Len Lyons, "Sun Ra: Interstellar Prophet of Jazz," *The Great Jazz Pianists,* 1983, p. 90.

254 "So what happened?": John Hinds and Peter Hinds. "Conversation with Sun Ra, San Francisco, CA, November 1, '88," *Sun Ra Quarterly* 2 (September 1996), pp. 2–7.

254 John S. Wilson, "Sun Ra and His Arkestra Give a Show with Mixed Media," *New York Times,* April 13, 1968, p. 30.

255 Michael Zwerin, "Jazz Journal: A Little Sample of Something Bad," *Village Voice,* August 15, 1968, pp. 20–21.

255 Paul Richard, "Corcoran Opens Atrium to Sun Ra," *Washington Post,* August 25, 1968.

256 ". . . something that's greater than the truth": Sun Ra interview by Graham Lock, London, 1990.

258 George Mostoller, "Sun Ra," *The Improvisor,* 1993, p. 35.

259 "Sometimes when I think that a poem": Sun Ra, "Sun Ra 2," *Jazz* 266 (November 1970), p. 24.

259 "I like all the sounds that upset people": Sun Ra interview with Lock, 1990.

260 Graham Lock kindly pointed out these specific parallels to the author.

262 Charles Perry, *The Haight-Ashbury: A History,* 1984, pp. 66–70.

262 Faubion Bowers, *Scriabin,* vol. 1, 1969, p. 204.

263 Dave Thompson, *Sun Daze: The History and Mystery of Electric Ambient Space Rock,* 1994.

264 "On the Eighth Day": Quoted in Scott Hacker, "P-Funk," in Pagan Kennedy, *Platforms: A Microwaved Cultural Chronicle of the 1970's,* 1994, pp. 150–51.

265 "Sun Ra. They play Europe": Arthur Taylor, *Notes and Tones,* 1982, p. 279.

265 "Sun Ra is tomming": Brooks Johnson, "Toms and Tomming: A Contemporary Report," *Down Beat,* June 16, 1966, p. 24.

266 Martha Bayles, *Hole in My Soul,* 1994, pp. 276–77.

CHAPTER FIVE

270 "Sun Ra himself": John Burks, "Sun Ra," *Rolling Stone,* no. 31 (April 19, 1969), p. 16.

271 "But playing with Sun Ra": Damon Choice interview on WKCR, April 20, 1987.

274 "Do you have a Tom Mix model?": Steve Feld interview with the author.

275 Dan Morgenstern, *Down Beat,* August 21, 1969, pp. 26–27, 45.

275 William Honan, "*Le mot juste* for the Moon," *Esquire,* July 1969, p. 54.

277 Rehearsal tape, c. 1970.

277 "The Moog synthesizer": Tam Fiofori, "Moog Modulations: A Symposium," *Down Beat,* July 23, 1970, pp. 34, 39.

278 "His philosophy was": Rob Young, "Hands-on Experience," *The Wire* 144 (February 1996), p. 26.

279 "One of the things": Sun Ra, "Sun Ra 2," *Jazz* 266 (November 1970), p. 24.

280 Cris Flicker, "Les Halles: Piège à Ra," *Jazz* 269 (December 1970), p. 9; Alain Tercinet, "Le soleil n'a pas brille pour nous ou comment je n'ai pas entendu Sun Ra," *Jazz* 269 (December 1970), p. 9.

281 Damon Choice interview with Charles Blass on WKCR, Arrival Day Festival, May 1995.

284 David Toop, *Oceans of Sound,* 1995, pp. 23–24.

284 Ademola Johnson, as told to Val Wilmer, 1995.

285 "The Discipline series": Robert Palmer, "Sun Ra: 'The Creator of the Universe Got a Sense of Humor,' " *The Real Paper,* November 6, 1974, p. 19.

286 "How dare you": performance tape June 11, 1971.

286 "The Black Bird": In Ed Bullins, *New Plays from the Black Theater,* 1969, pp. 109–18.

287 Michel Leiris, "Jazz," *Sulfur* 15 (1986), pp. 97–104.

288 "Un Soir au Chatelet," *Jazz Magazine* 196 (January 1972), pp. 14–17.

291 Lucien Malson, ed., "Les cahiers de jazz," *Jazz Magazine* (Paris) 176 (March 1970), pp. xxiv–xxvi.

292 My sources for the Egyptian expedition were Hartmut Geerken, "Sun Ra Meets Sun Ra. Facets of a Visitation: Egypt, December 1971," in Hartmut Geerken and Bernhard Hefele, *Omniverse Sun Ra,* pp. 121–29; and my interview with Richard Wilkinson and Tommy Hunter, June 1995.

293 "Beacon Theater": Robert Palmer interview with the author, 1994.

294 Reading lists reconstructed from the class notes of Paul Sanion.

295 "I'm talking about": John Corbett, *Extended Play,* 1994, p. 311.

296 The following section draws on dozens of interviews with Sun Ra by myself and others (especially Graham Lock's interviews with Sun Ra in London, 1990), and paraphrases his ideas extensively.

296 "Nature is more than": Sun Ra quoted by James Jacson in interview with the author.

297 "A fellow who was sort of": Sun Ra interview with Francis Davis, Philadelphia, January 29, 1990.

300 "So people should": Sun Ra interview with Lock.

302 "Words and the Impossible": Sun Ra, *The Immeasurable Equation,* 1972, p. 27.

303 "let's look at the plans": Sun Ra interview with Lock.

304 "He switched the languages": Ibid.

304 "Proper evaluation": reproduced from a class handout from Paul Sanion.

305 "I'll be running across": Sun Ra interview with Rev. Dwight Frizzell, Kansas City, April 1982.

306 "Mathematics is balanced": Sun Ra interview with Lock.

306 "Unbalanced": Ibid.

306 "A Blueprint/Declaration": reprinted from one of *The Immeasurable Equation* booklets sold at concerts.

307 "Cosmic Equation": notes to *The Heliocentric Worlds of Sun Ra, Vol. 1* ESP-Disc 1014 (1965).

308 "I've studied different philosophies": Sun Ra, "Sun Ra 1," *Jazz* 265 (October 1970), p. 31.

309 "Look at the Kind": Sun Ra interview with Lock.

310 "Now, when I speak": Tam Fiofori, "Sun Ra's Space Oddyssey," 1970, p. 15.

311 J. Baldwin, *The Fire Next Time,* in *The Price of the Ticket: Collected Nonfiction 1948–1985,* 1985, p. 373; and Sun Ra interview with Davis.

312 "I couldn't approach black people": Sun Ra, "Humanity," *Jazz Monthly* 189 (November 1970), pp. 7–8.

313 "I say 'dark' ": Sun Ra interview with Davis.

313 "Because of segregation": Sun Ra, "Humanity.

314 Geoffrey Hodson, *The Brotherhood of Angels and of Men,* 1927.

314 "So therefore mixed up among humans": Paraphrased from Sun Ra interview with Rich Theis, January 27, 1983.

314 "Sunbursts appear in dark disguises": notes to *Discipline 27-II,* Saturn 538 (1973).

315 "I am not ruled like a man": Sun Ra quoted by James Jacson in an interview with the author.

315 "I've been told": Sun Ra, "Words from Sun Ra," Vibrations 1, no. 1 (July 1967), p. 16.

316 "the righteous fight for the right": Sun Ra interview with Wilfried Rutter, Berlin, October 29, 1983.

316 "I've seen a lot": Sun Ra interview with Graham Lock, London, 1990.

316 "My mind refuses": Sun Ra interview with Greg Ross on WXPN, Philadelphia, 1981.

316 "... Death takes everybody": Ibid.

318 Class handout provided by Paul Sanion.

319 "I wasn't influenced": James Spady, "Sun Ra Brings Solar Precepts to Phree Music and Black Arts Movement," *Philadelphia New Observer,* June 9, 1993, p. 17.

319 "They're all scientific equations": James G. Spady, "Indigene=Folkski: Equations in the Black Arts," *The Black Scholar* 10, nos. 3/4 (November–December 1978), pp. 24–33.

319 "... in a certain sense": Ibid.

319 "What I want to do": Jean-Louis Noames, "Visite au dieu soleil," *Jazz* 125 (December 1965), p. 75.

321 "Planes of Nature": notes to *Discipline 27-II*, Saturn 538 (1973).

321 "Cosmos Query": Sun Ra, *The Immeasurable Equation*, 1972.

322 "Cosmos Evolution": notes to *The Heliocentric Worlds of Sun Ra, Vol. 1* ESP-Disc 1014 (1965).

322 "When You Meet a Man": Sun Ra, *Extensions Out. Immeasurable Equation, Vol. II*, 1972.

322 "Truth Is Bad/Good": Ibid.

323 "The Sound Image": Ibid.

325 "The Potential": Ibid.

326 "The Foolish Foe": Ibid.

327 "The Endless Universe": Ibid.

328 from "The Air Spiritual Man": Ibid.

331 *The Urantia Book*, 1955.

332 "In anything there's": Sun Ra interview with Peter and John Hinds, November 1, 1988, *Sun Ra Research*, issue 4 (September 1995), pp. 4–5.

333 "I want to put earth": Ibid.

333 "I finally consented": Robert D. Rusch, "Sun Ra: Interview," *Jazztalk*, 1984, p. 70.

CHAPTER SIX

335 Philippe Carles, "Sun Ra and his Arkestra," *Jazz Magazine*, no. 216 (October–November 1973), p. 60; Lucien Malson, "Bagarres et désenchantement pour Chuck Berry et Sun Ra," *Le Monde*, September 11, 1973, p. 10; François Postif, "Sun Ra existe: je l'ai rencontre," *Jazz* 298 (October 1973), p. 31.

336 Daniel Soutif, "Olympia, 30 septembre," *Jazz Magazine* (Paris) 216 (October–November 1973), p. 60; Jean Delmas, "Le Ra a l'Olympia," *Jazz-Hot* 299 (November 1973), p. 23.

337 "They tried to fool you": transcribed from live performances c. 1984.

339 "... that you know that you're wrong?": "Face the Music" transcribed from live performances c. 1991.

341 "Your ancestors": James Jacson interview with the author, 1995.

345 "People are just like receivers": W. Royal Stokes, *The Jazz Scene*, 1991, pp. 232–35.

345 Jacson interview with the author.

346 "meditation" and "Rastafarians": Sun Ra quoted by Jacson in interview with the author.

347 "They neither marry": Kathy Kemp, "Aboard the Spaceship Sun Ra," *Birmingham Post-Herald Kudzu Magazine*, April 17, 1992, p. 8.

347 "I'm trying to increase my natural capacity": Franco Fayenz, "Sun Ra: Vodico qual è la mia galassia," in *Jazz & Jazz*, 1988, pp. 136–45.

347 Bush's "duplicity": Phast Phreddy, "Sun Ra Has a Master Plan," *Contrast*, Spring 1990, p. 46.

347 "go with the man": Spencer Weston interview with the author.

348 Sun Ra interview with Francis Davis, Philadelphia, January 29, 1990.

349 "When there is no sun": transcribed from original score.

351 "Aside from pointing out": Michael Shore, "Saturnalia," *Soho Weekly News*, November 19, 1980.

352 "This is some hokey": author interview with Jacson.

353 "Nuclear War": transcribed from live performances c. 1983.

354 Robert Farris Thompson, "Afro-Modernism," *Artforum*, 1996.

356 John Cage and Sun Ra: Howard Mandel, "John Cage Meets Sun Ra: Coney Island of the Minds," *EAR* 2, no. 1 (August–September 1986), pp. 20–21.

359 "They started asking me questions": Davis interview.

360 "Scholars should travel": author interview with Spencer Weston.

361 "Hal Wilmer Plays Disney: Never Mind the Mouse Ears," in *Vulgar Materialism*, 1991, p. 261.

362 "I felt that America had not": Mark Sinker, "Sun Ra Talks to Mark Sinker," *Different Cats: Stride Magazine*, no. 37 (1995), p. 25.

364 "I hate everyday life": Fayenz, "Sun Ra: Vodico qual è la mia galassia."

365 " 'Man' is a horrible word": Graham Lock interview, London, 1990.

366 "Someone said there was a conspiracy of silence": Ibid.

366 "Nobody plays it right": Victor Schonfield interview with the author.

366 "Sometimes I meet": Val Wilmer, "Sun Ra—In Search of Space," *Melody Maker*, November 4, 1972, p. 48.

366 "I did never want to be successful": Robert D. Rusch, "Sun Ra: Interview," *Jazztalk*, 1984, p. 70.

367 "I was on the spot": Sun Ra interview with Francis Davis, 1990.

368 Cat Club: John J. Maimone interview with the author.

371 "You have no right": Jothan Callins interview with the author.

372 "He never told me": Rob Young, "Hands-on Experience," *The Wire* 144 (February 1996), p. 26.

373 "There are forces": Sun Ra quoted by Victor Schonfield in interview with the author.

373 Letter to the author from Warren Smith.

374 " 'The show must go on' ": Jacson interview with the author.

375 "They ain't supposed": James Spady, "Sun Ra Brings Solar Precepts to Phree Music and Black Arts Movement," *Philadelphia New Observer,* June 9, 1993, p. 18.

376 "It was very interesting": Bob Rusch, "Andrew Cyrille: Interview (Part Two)," *Cadence* 21, no. 2 (February 1995), p. 27.

377 "This kingdom is the kingdom of death": Graham Lock interview.

378 "He never came straight out": Tony Norman, "Space Is the Place," *Pittsburgh Post-Gazette Sunday Magazine,* October 24, 1993, pp. 8–10.

379 "Is this a planet of life?": "This World Is Not My Home" transcribed in part from *Hidden Fire I,* Saturn Sun Ra 13188III (1988).

381 "If death is the absence of life": Sun Ra quoted by Jacson in interview with the author.

382 "They'll come back": transcribed from live performances c. 1993.

384 "When I say space music": Tam Fiofori, "Sun Ra's Space Odyssey," *Down Beat,* May 14, 1970, p. 13.

385 "This is sixth-grade jazz": Davis interview.

385 "He made you face": Jacson interview.

386 Art Jenkins interview on WKCR, April 17, 1987.

386 "Sun Ra would rap": Rusch, "Andrew Cyrille."

387 "We all projected": Judith Holten quoted in Art Sato, "In the Spirit of the Universe—Sun Ra," *Konceptualizations* 9, nos. 1 & 2 (Winter/Spring 1993), pp. 2–5.

388 "Sun Ra's consistent statement": Amiri Baraka, *Eulogies,* 1996, p. 171.

SELECTED BIBLIOGRAPHY

Aldinger, Werner. "Sun Ra: Space Is the Place oder ein Sommer ohne Sonne." *Skug,* no. 16 (1993), pp. 24–27.

Alessandrini, Paul. "L'Afrique a Broadway." *Rock & Folk,* 1972.

Baraka, Amiri. *Eulogies.* New York: Marsilio, 1996.

Bartlett, Andrew. "Saturn Rising: Charting the Life and Legacy of Sun Ra." *The Rocket* (Seattle), July 10–24, 1996, p. 9.

Bayles, Martha. *Hole in My Soul: The Loss of Beauty and Meaning in American Popular Music.* New York: The Free Press, 1994.

Berendt, Joachim Ernst. "Sun Ra und sein Schwarzen Kosmos." In *Ein Fenster aud Jazz.* Frankfurt am Main: S. Fischer, 1977, pp. 107–14.

Bland, Edward. "On 'The Cry of Jazz.' " *Film Culture,* Summer 1960, pp. 28–32.

Brecht, Stefan. "Sun Ra." *Evergreen Review,* no. 54 (May 1968), pp. 88, 90.

Burks, John. "Sun Ra." *Rolling Stone,* no. 31 (April 19, 1969), pp. 16–17, 19.

Campbell, Robert L. "Sun Ra: Supersonic Sounds from Saturn." *Goldmine,* January 22, 1993, pp. 22, 24, 26, 28, 30, 32, 34, 36, 38, 40, 42, 125, 132–33.

Cane, Giampiero. *Canto nero.* 2d ed. Bologna: Cooperative Libraria Universaria, 1982.

Carles, Philippe. "L'opera cosmique de Sun Ra." *Jazz Magazine* (Paris) 159 (October 1968), pp. 26–30, 43–46.

Castaldo, Gino. "Il Caso Sun Ra." *Musica Jazz* (Italy), 28, no. 5 (May 1972), pp. 8–14.

Caux, Daniel. "Sun Ra." *Actuel* (Paris), no. 2 (November 1970), pp. 8–10.

Chenard, Marc. "Swing and a Myth." *Coda,* issue 231 (April–May 1990), pp. 24–25.

Chilton, John. *Jazz.* New York: David McKay, 1979, pp. 135–36.

Clark, Gerry. "Saturn, Swing and Stars: Sun Ra's Outer Space Odyssey." *Relix* 21, no. 3 (Summer 1994), pp. 18–19.

Cohen, S. "Faces: Sun Ra." *Musician, Player and Listener,* no. 19 (July–August 1979), p. 27.

Comolli, Jean-Louis. "Out to Lunch: L'Hypothèse du Temps sans Durée." *Jazz Magazine* (Paris) 427 (June 1993), p. 25.

Cooke, Jack. Review of *Sound of Joy. Jazz Monthly,* May 1970, p. 23.

Corbett, John. "The Heaven Is on Earth." *Option* 49 (March/April 1993), pp. 58–64.

———. "Inherit the Sun." *Down Beat,* September 1993, pp. 26–29.

———. "Sun Ra Legacy Still Up in the Air." *Down Beat,* February 1994, p. 16.

———. "Alton Abraham: Brother's Keeper." In John Corbett, *Extended Play.* Durham, NC: Duke University Press, 1994, pp. 218–27.

———. "Brothers from Another Planet: The Space Madness of Lee 'Scratch' Perry, Sun Ra, and George Clinton." In Corbett, *Extended Play,* pp. 7–24.

———. "Sun Ra: Gravity and Levity." In Corbett, *Extended Play,* pp. 308–17 (see also "The Heaven Is on Earth").

Crouch, Stanley. "Last of the Great Bandleaders." *Village Voice,* June 1, 1982, p. 65.

Cutler, Chris. "The Realm of Lightning/Black Music in a White World." In *File Under Popular: Theoretical and Critical Writings on Music.* London: November Books, 1985, pp. 29–79.

Davis, Francis. "Unveiling the Mystery of Sun Ra." *Philadelphia Evening Bulletin,* October 19, 1980.

———. "Hotentot Potentate." In *Outcats.* New York: Oxford University Press, 1990, pp. 24–27 (reprinted from *Village Voice,* 1988).

Diliberto, John. "Orbiting with Sun." *Down Beat,* February 1993, pp. 22–25.

Farne, Libero. "Sun Ra: La Grande Utopia di un'Orchestra-Comunita." *Musica Jazz,* nos. 8–9 (August–September 1993), pp. 24–26.

Feather, Leonard, and Ira Gitler, eds. *The Encyclopedia of Jazz in the '70's.* New York: Da Capo, 1976.

Fiofori, Tam. "Music: Sun Ra, When the Sun Comes Out." *Arts Magazine* 41, no. 8 (Summer 1967), pp. 21–22.

———. "The Illusion of Sun Ra." *Liberator,* vol. 7, no. 12 (December 1967), pp. 12–15.

———. "The Space Music of Sun Ra." *Jazz and Pop* 7, no. 1 (January 1968), pp. 17–19.

———. "The Space Music of Sun Ra and His Space Arkestra." *IT* (London), no. 59 (July 4–17, 1969), p. 18.

———. "The Music of Sun Ra: Space Age Music." *Negro Digest* 19, no. 3 (1970), pp. 23–28.

————. "Sun Ra's Space Music: The InterGalactic Reach." *Friends* (London), June 12, 1970.

————. "Sun Ra & l'extension intergalactique." *Jazz Magazine* (Paris) 185 (January 1971), pp. 20–25, 50–51.

Fiofori, Tam, and Charles Shabacon. "Sun Ra: Sun Screens and Sound Images." *Artscanada* 25, no. 2 (118–119) (June 1968), pp. 8–9.

Flemming, Robert. "Sun Ra's Soul Food Music." *Encore American and Worldwide News* (April 16, 1979), pp. 40–41.

Franco, Maurizio. "Una Giornata sul Planeta." *Musica Jazz,* February 1987, pp. 14–18.

Geerken, Hartmut. "Sun Ra in Agypten." *Jazz Podium* 21, no. 4 (March 1972), pp. 72–74.

————. *Oduktionsprotokoll.* Lichtenberg: Klaus Ramm, 1975.

————. *Sun Ra.* Arlesheim: Schweizer Jazz Museum, 1994.

Geerken, Hartmut, and Bernhard Hefele. *Omniverse Sun Ra.* Germany: Wait-awhile, 1994.

Gold, Don. *Down Beat Record Reviews,* Vol. 2. Chicago: Maher, 1958, pp. 183–84.

Gonçalves, Joe. "Sun Ra at the End of the World." *The Cricket,* no. 4 (1969), pp. 9–11.

Gourgouris, Stathis. "Adorno After Sun Ra." *Strategies,* no. 6 (1991), pp. 198–216.

Griffiths, Pat. "A Space Warning from Sun Ra to the Planet Earth." *Friends* (London), February 2, 1971, p. 2.

Hauff, Sigrid. "Omniverse Sun Ra." *Jazz Podium* 43 (March 1994), pp. 10–14 (reprinted and translated in Geerken and Hefele).

Hennessey, Michael. "Sun Ra: Von Boogie Woogie uber Popsongs bis zu Avant-garde Jazz." *Jazz Podium* 39, no. 4 (April 1990), p. 42.

Hentoff, Nat. *Down Beat Record Reviews,* Vol. 2. Chicago: Maher, 1958, pp. 183–84.

Heron, W. Kim. "Sun Ra Sets His Own Strange World to Music." *Detroit Free Press,* October 24, 1980.

Hoberman, J., ed. *Vulgar Materialism.* Philadelphia: Temple University Press, 1991.

Høegh, Thorsten. "Salsagnge fra Sydsiden." *MM* (Copenhagen), May 1978, pp. 40–43.

Honan, William H. "*Le mot juste* for the Moon." *Esquire,* July 1969, pp. 53–55, 138–41.

Hughes, Michael. "Sun Ra's Avant-Garde Music Reaches Toward the Planets." *Portland Press Herald* [Maine], September 13, 1990.

Ibrahim, B. "Sun Ra in Egypt." *Egyptian Television Magazine,* January 29, 1972, pp. 38–39.

J. B. [Review of Jazz Showcase performance in 1976] *Jazz Magazine* (Paris) 251 (January 1977), p. 53.

Jarrett, Michael. "Sun Ra Supplement." *Jazziz,* May 1993, p. 94.

Johnson, Brooks. "Toms and Tomming: A Contemporary Report." *Down Beat,* June 16, 1966, pp. 24, 44.

Jones, LeRoi. "Apple Cores #3." *Black Music.* New York: William Morrow, 1967, pp. 128–30.

Jost, Ekkehard. "Sun Ra." In *Free Jazz.* Graz: Universal, 1974, pp. 180–99.

Kagie, Rudie. "Het sterfhuis van de jazz." *Veij Nederland* 3 (February 3, 1996), pp. 52–56.

Kenny, Anson. "Play It Again, Sun Ra." *Philadelphia Magazine,* April 1977, pp. 75–79, 81.

Kobe, Reiner. "Rekapituliert die Geschichte der schwarzen Muzik: Sun Ra Arkestra." *Jazz Podium* 37, no. 7 (1988).

Kopelowiez, Guy. "II Autumn in New York." *Jazz* 215 (December 1965), pp. 38–47.

Landwehr, Uschi. "Sun Ra." *Jazz Podium* 18 (1969), pp. 288–89.

Litweiler, John. *The Freedom Principle.* New York: William Morrow, 1984, pp. 140–49.

Lock, Graham. *Forces in Motion.* London: Quartet Books, 1988, pp. 11–23, 152–55.

Loupias, Bernard. "Sun System." *Jazz Magazine* (Paris) 428 (July–August 1993), p. 30.

Macnie, Jim. "Sun Ra Is the Heaviest Man in This Galaxy . . . But He's Just Passing Through." *Musician,* no. 99 (January 1987), pp. 60–62, 70.

Mailer, Norman. *Cannibals and Christians.* New York: Dell, 1966.

Malson, Lucien, ed. "Les cahiers de jazz: IV. de Sun Ra." *Jazz Magazine* (Paris) 176 (March 1970), pp. xxiv–xxvi.

Mandel, Howard. "John Cage Meets Sun Ra: Coney Island of the Minds." *EAR* 2, no. 1 (August–September 1986), pp. 20–21.

Matthews, Paul B. "Interview: Junior Mance, Part 1." *Coda* 20, no. 7 (July 1994), pp. 5–25.

McNally, Owen. "The Mystic Appeal of Sun Ra's Travels into the Spaceways." *The Hartford Courant,* June 24, 1992.

McRae, Barry. "Sun Ra." *Jazz Journal,* 19, no. 8 (August 1966), pp. 15–16.

———. *Jazz Cataclysm.* South Brunswick, NJ: A. S. Barnes, 1967, pp. 166–68.

———. "Avant Courier: Certain Blacks." *Jazz Journal* 25 no. 12 (December 1972), pp. 20–21.

———. "Avant Courier: Another Look at Sun Ra." *Jazz Journal* 28, no. 12 (December 1975), pp. 14–15, 41.

———. "Arena." *Jazz Journal* 30, no. 2 (February 1977), pp. 20–21.

————. "Avant Courier: Intergalactics in SW1." *Jazz Journal International*, October 1982, p. 11.

Mostoller, George. "Sun Ra A.6.1." *The Improvisor* 10 (Birmingham), 1993, pp. 34–39.

Neal, Larry. *Views of a Liberated Future.* New York: Thunder's Mouth Press, 1989.

Nelson, Jez. "Close Encounters of the Ra Kind." *Straight No Chaser*, Autumn 1990, pp. 54–55.

The Normal Index (Alabama A & M), vol. 15, no. 3 (January 1936).

Norman, Tony. "Space Is the Place." *Pittsburgh Post-Gazette Sunday Magazine*, October 24, 1993, pp. 8–10.

Oakland, Veryl. "Le soleil dans sa maison." *Jazz Magazine* (Paris) 322 (October 1983), pp. 20–23.

Oldfield, Mike. "Prophet of the Planets." *The Guardian*, June 6, 1990, p. 36.

Palmer, Robert. "Jazz on Records." *Rolling Stone*, August 5, 1971, p. 46.

————. "Sun Ra Casts Special Light on Jazz." *New York Times*, December 29, 1978, p. C23.

Pekar, Harvey. "Sun Ra." *Coda* 12, issue 139, no. 7 (June–July 1975), pp. 2–11.

Pouncey, Edwin. " 'It Makes You Booomph!' " *Resonance* 4, no. 1 (1995), pp. 22–25.

Powell, J. Otis. "Making Sense of Sun Ra: Philosophy as Music." *Colors* 2, issue 5 (Minneapolis) (September–October 1993), pp. 18–21.

Reich, Howard. "Out of This World." *Chicago Tribune*, February 24, 1991, sec. 13, p. 10.

Richard, Paul. "Corcoran Opens Atrium to Sun Ra." *Washington Post*, August 25, 1968.

Rodrigues, Diego A. "Sun Ra's Prophesy." *Jazz Forum*, no. 32 (December 1974), pp. 35–37.

Rowland, Mark. "Ra Ra, Sun Ra." *The Real Paper* (Boston), December 23, 1978.

Rusch, Robert D. "Art Blakey: Interview." *Cadence* 7, no. 7 (July 1981), pp. 8–12.

Russo, William. Review of *Fate in a Pleasant Mood. Down Beat*, October 6, 1966, p. 32.

Sato, Art. "In the Spirit of the Universe—Sun Ra." *Konceptualizations* 9, nos. 1 & 2 (Winter/Spring 1993), pp. 2–5.

Schmitt, Michel, and Philippe Cardet. "Sun Ra." *Jazz*, no. 303 (March 1974), pp. 22–23.

Sessa, Claudio. "Nel Labirinto Discografico." *Musica Jazz*, nos. 8–9 (August–September 1993), pp. 26–27.

Shoemaker, Bill. "Sun Ra" (part of "Twenty-Five Who Mattered Most"). *Jazz Times*, September 1995, p. 70.

————. "Interview: Yusef Lateef." *Cadence*, January 1989, pp. 5–26.

————. "Andrew Cyrille: Interview (Part Two)." *Cadence* 21, no. 2 (February 1995).

Shore, Michael. "The Big Bands Are Back." *Soho Weekly News*, February 20–21, 1980.

————. "Sun Ra." *Musician, Player and Listener*, no. 24 (April–May 1980), pp. 48–51, 66.

————. "Saturnalia." *Soho Weekly News*, November 19, 1980.

Siclier, Sylvain. "La Planet du Ra-Soleil." *L'Affice*, no. 39 (June 1992), p. 21.

Sidran, Ben. *Talking Jazz*. New York: Da Capo, 1995.

Simpkins, C. O. *Coltrane: A Biography*. New York: Herndon House, 1975, pp. 94–100.

Sinclair, John. "Sun Ra and His Myth-Science Arkestra." *Ann Arbor Sun*, September 6–20, 1974, supplement, p. 8.

————. "A Strange and Celestial Road: Sun Ra & His Band from Outer Space." (Detroit) *Metro Times*, August 31, 1988, pp. 22, 51.

————. "Space Is the Place: Sun Ra's Musical Orbit." *Metro Times*, October 1988.

"Un soir au Chatelet." *Jazz Magazine* (Paris) 196 (January 1972), pp. 10–17.

Spellman, A. B. "Oral Challenges to the Written Word: The Poetry of Yusef Rahman and Amus Mor." *Sagala* 2 (Washington, D.C.), 1981.

Sundin, Bertil. "Sun Ra Arets Konstupplevelse." *Orkester Journalen* (Stockholm), no. 39 (November 1971), pp. 12–13, 18.

"Sun Ra." *Re Search* (San Francisco), no. 1 (1980), p. 15.

"Sun Ra: A Change of Laws." *Soul*, February 18, 1974, p. 10.

"Sun Ra Reveals His Cosmic Music." *Soul*, July 9, 1973, p. 11.

"Sun Ra: un été sans soleil." *Jazz Magazine* (Paris) 428 (July–August 1993), pp. 23–35.

Szwed, John F. "Props: Sun Ra." *Vibe* (September 1993), p. 140.

Taylor, Arthur. *Notes and Tones*. New York: Perigee, 1982.

Thomas, J. C. "Sun Ra's Space Probe." *Down Beat*, June 13, 1968, pp. 19–20.

————. *Chasin' the Trane*. New York: Doubleday, 1975, pp. 180–88.

Thomas, Lorenzo. "The Mathematic of Sun Ra." *Ann Arbor Sun*, April 5–19, 1974, pp. 16–17.

Toop, David. *Ocean of Sound: Aether Talk, Ambient Sound and Imaginary Worlds*. London: Serpent's Tail, 1995, pp. 23–32.

Trent, Chris. "Sun Ra on Record." *Different Cats: Stride Magazine* (Exeter) 37 (1995).

Viklicky, Emil. "Kak Jsem Videl Sun Ra." *Jazz* (Czech.), no. 19 (1977), p. 28.

Vuijsje, Bert. "Sun Ra en de Verwarring." *Jazz Wereld*, no. 19 (1968), pp. 5–9.

Walsh, Mike. "Sun Ra: The Lost Years." *Welcomemat* (Philadelphia), June 22, 1994, pp. 24–27.

Walters, Michael. "Sun Ra and Infinity Music." *Sounds* (UK), 5, December 1970.

Williams, Martin. "Still Changing the Avant Garde." *Saturday Review*, October 12, 1968 (reprinted in Martin Williams, *Jazz Masters in Transition 1957–1969*. New York: Macmillan, 1970, pp. 264–66.

Wilmer, Val. "Red Holloway: Whatever Suits the Occasion." *Coda* 164/165 (February 1979), pp. 46–48.

———. "Sun Ra—Pictures of Infinity." In *As Serious As Your Life*. Rev. ed. Westport: Lawrence Hill, 1980, pp. 74–92.

———. "John Gilmore." *The Wire* 17 (July 1985), pp. 14–17, 19.

———. *Mama Said There'd Be Days Like This: My Life in the Jazz World*. London: The Women's Press, 1989.

Wilson, John S. " 'Space Age Jazz' Lacks Boosters," *New York Times*, February 19, 1962.

———. "Sun Ra and His Arkestra Give a Show with Mixed Media." *New York Times*, April 13, 1968, p. 30.

Yanow, Scott. "Sun Ra." *Jazziz*, May 1993, pp. 66–70.

Young, Bob, and Al Stannus. *Jazz Cooks: Portraits and Recipes of the Greats*. New York: Stewart, Tabori and Chang, 1992, pp. 176–77.

Zenni, Stefano. "Sun Ra: Piaceri e Orrori Intergalattici." *Musica Jazz* 48, no. 4 (April 1992), pp. 23–26.

Zwerin, Michael. "Jazz Journal: A Little Sample of Something Bad." *Village Voice*, August 15, 1968, pp. 20–21.

———. *Close Enough for Jazz*. London: Quartet Books, 1983, pp. 237–39.

INTERVIEWS WITH SUN RA

Aldinger, Werner. "Sun Ra: Ein Monolog." *Jazz*, no. 2, 1985.

Barber, Lynden. "The Joy of Life." *Melody Maker*, November 19, 1983, pp. 30–31.

Bennett, Karen. "The Brother from Another Planet. *Philadelphia Inquirer Sunday Magazine*, September 25, 1988, pp. 12–15, 27–29.

Blass, Charles. "Sun Ra Conversation with Charles Blass" (November 15–16, 1991) *Sun Ra Research* (Milbrae, CA) 1 (May 1995), pp. 1–3 [see also *Different Cats: Stride Magazine* (Exeter) 37 (1995).

Bledsoe, Wayne. "A Close Encounter with Sun Ra." *Detour* (*Knoxville News-Sentinel*), December 30, 1988, p. 8.

Bordowitz, Hank. "Sun Ra: More in Touch with the Heavens Than the Earth." *Jazziz,* May 1989.

Brown, Joe. "Improvising with Sun Ra." *Washington Post,* Weekend Section, Friday, October 5, 1990.

Butler, Mike. "The Strange Celestrial Road to Wigan Pier." *City Limits* [UK], 1990, pp. 16–17.

Carles, Philippe. "L'impossible liberté." *Jazz Magazine* (Paris) 196 (January 1972), pp. 9–13 (with Sun Ra, John Gilmore, Marshall Allen, and Pat Patrick).

———. " 'Il sera temps d'édifier la maison noire…' Sun Ra." *Jazz Magazine* (Paris) 217 (December 1973), pp. 24–26.

Carlton, Bob. "Jazz Man from 'Out There'." *Birmingham News,* June 18, 1989, pp. 1F, 11F.

Caux, Daniel. "Free Jazz." *Chroniques de L'Art Vivant* (Paris), no. 7 (January 1970), p. 30.

———. "The Strange World of Sun Ra." *Chroniques de L'Art Vivant* (Paris), no. 16 (December 1970), pp. 32–33.

Choice, Harriet. "Rah, Rah… Sunny Mr. Ra." *Chicago Tribune,* September 10, 1972, sec. 11, pp. 8–9.

Clark, Gerry. "Sun Ra Spins Out in His Own Orbit." *Chicago Sun-Times,* September 10, 1972, sec. 11, pp. 8–9.

Corbett, John. "From the Vaults: Sun Ra's Celestrial Seasoning, 1985." *Butt Rag* (Chicago), No. 5, c. 1989, pp. 21–28.

Dambrofsky, Gwen. "Stranger in a Strange Band." *Kitchener-Waterloo Record* (Canada), July 13, 1989, p. C7.

Davis, Francis. "Sun Ra Himself." *Philadelphia Inquirer,* February 16, 1990, pp. D1, D5.

Delebo, Claude. "Sun Ra." *Actuel,* no. 11, 1970.

Dery, Mark. "Sun Ra." *Keyboard,* March 1991, pp. 39–40, 43, 46.

Determeyer, Eddy. "Sun Ra: verleden, heden, toekomost." *Jazz Nu* 4, no. 10 (July 1982), pp. 402–8 (Sun Ra on cover).

Doerschuk, Bob. "Sun Ra: Jazz from Another Planet." *Keyboard* 13, no. 1 (January 1987), p. 65.

Dollar, Steven. "Cruisin' Through the Continuum in Sun Ra's Cosmic Chariot." *EightRock* (Atlanta) 2, no. 3 (1993).

Farris, John. "Space Is the Place." *Spin* (April 1989), pp. 98–99.

Fayenz, Franco. "Sun Ra: Vo dico qual è la mia galassia." In *Jazz & Jazz.* Milan: Laterza, 1988, pp. 136–45.

Fiofori, Tam. "Sun Ra." *New York Free Press,* April 18, 1965.

———. "A Statement by Sun Ra on the Planet Earth." *New York Free Press,* April 18, 1968.

———. "Sun Ra's Space Odyssey." *Down Beat,* May 14, 1970, pp. 14–17.

———. "Moog Modulations: A Symposium." *Down Beat,* July 23, 1970, pp. 14–16, 34, 39.

———. "Sun Ra & L'odyssee spatiale." *Jazz Magazine* (Paris) 185 (January 1971), pp. 26–32, 51–52.

———. "Sun Ra." *Orkester Journalen,* October 1971, p. 6.

———. "Sun Ra's Duality." *Melody Maker,* February 5, 1972, p. 28.

———. "Sun Ra's African Roots." *Melody Maker,* February 12, 1972, p. 32.

Franckling, Ken. "Sun Ra." *Jazz Times,* April 1988, p. 23.

Frizzell, Dwight. "The Ancient Egyptian Reader: Some Time with Sun Ra & the Rev." *The Penny Pitch* (Kansas City), December 1980, p. 13.

———. "The Ancient Egyptian Reader: Enfolding the Cosmo-Drama (Part 2)." *The Penny Pitch* (Kansas City), April 1981, p. 13.

Gagne, Cole. "Sun Ra." Cole Gagne, ed. *Soundpieces 2: Interviews with American Composers.* Metuchen, NJ: Scarecrow Press, 1993, pp. 367–88.

Garvin, Rex, and Alistair Indge. "The Sun Has Got His Hat On." *Zig-Zag* (UK), December 1983.

Gill, Andy. "Space Is the Place." *New Musical Express,* August 7, 1982, pp. 24–26.

Harmon, Rick. "A Rising Sun: Influential Jazz Musician Is Catching On." *Montgomery [Alabama] Journal and Advertiser,* June 16, 1989.

Harrington, Richard. "Jazz & Astral Visions." *Washington Post,* January 23, 1982, p. C6.

Hauff, Sigrid. "Der Mythos Sun Ra." *Jazz Podium* 32, no. 4 (April 1984), pp. 10–11.

Hinds, John, and Peter Hinds. "Conversation with Sun Ra, San Francisco, CA, November 1, '88." *Sun Ra Quarterly* 2 (September 1996), pp. 2–7.

Hodara, Philippe. "Sun Ra." *Le Pont des Arts,* no. 3 (Beaubourg), 1977.

"Intergalactic Gig." *St. Paul Pioneer Press-Dispatch,* March 6, 1991.

Jensen, Jorn R. "An Entirely New Reality: Interview with Sun Ra." *Jazz Forum,* no. 32 (December 1974), p. 37.

Jung, Daryl. "Attempting the Impossible." *Now Magazine* (Toronto), February 12, 1986.

Kaiser, Rolf-Ulrich. "Sun Ra: Scharlaten oder Weltverbesserer?" *Jazz Podium,* (June 1968), pp. 182–84.

Katz, Alan. "Musician Picks Denver for His End-of-World Gig." *Denver Post,* November 6, 1988.

Kemp, Kathy. "Aboard the Spaceship Sun Ra." *Birmingham Post-Herald, Kudzu Magazine,* April 17, 1992, pp. 6–8 (Sun Ra on cover).

Kessler, Karl. "That Ra Ra Spirit: A Trip to Sun Ra's Germantown Home and Musical Commune on the Eve of an Arkestra Concert at Memphis." *Philadelphia City Paper,* May 29, 1987, p. 9.

Kumpf, Hugo. "Sun Ra: Zwischen Gott und Teufel, Gargarin und Cosmos. Interview in Moskau." *Jazz Podium* 40, no. 1 (January 1991), pp. 6–7.

Levenson, Jeff. "The Celestial Connection: Sun Ra." *Hot House* (NYC) 4, no. 11 (November 1985), p. 14.

Lock, Graham. "Along Came Ra!" *The Wire* 6 (Spring 1984), pp. 2–3, 5–6.

———. "The Mysteries of Mr. Ra." *The Wire* 78 (August 1990), pp. 34–40.

———. *Chasing the Vibration: Meetings with Creative Musicians.* Exeter (UK): Stride Publications, 1994, pp. 144–55 (reprint of "Along Came Ra!").

Loop, Dwight F. "Sun Ra to Bring Arkestra to UMN for Jazz Concert." *Albuquerque Journal,* March 22, 1981.

Luzzi, Mario. "Sun Ra." In *Uomini e Avaguardie Jazz.* Milan: Gammalibri, 1980, pp. 14–33 (cover photo).

Lyons, Len. "Sun Ra: Interstellar Prophet of Jazz." *Contemporary Keyboard,* December 1978, pp. 16–17, 50 (reprinted in Lyons, *The Great Jazz Pianists.* New York: Quill, 1983, pp. 83–91).

Macnie, Jim. "Space Is the Place." *Elle,* September 1989, pp. 228, 230.

McLeish, Martin. "Sun Ra and Relative Dimensions." *Rubberneck* (UK), 15 (November 1993), pp. 18–22.

McNally, Owen. "Sun Ra: The High Priest of Avant Garde Jazz." *Hartford Courant,* March 3, 1988.

Nelson, Jez. "Up and Coming." *Jazz FM* (London), no. 2, 1990, pp. 8–9.

Neto, Manuel. "Uma Bizarra Viagem Atraves do Jazz." *Sexta-Fera* (Portugal), August 2, 1985.

Noames, Jean-Louis. "Visite au Dieu Soleil." *Jazz Magazine* (Paris) 125 (December 1969), pp. 70–77.

Osborne, Hoyle. "Sun Ra Longs to Play the Music of Infinity." *Philadelphia Daily News,* May 21, 1970.

Palmer, Robert. "Sun Ra: 'The Creator of the Universe Got a Sense of Humor.' " *The Real Paper,* November 6, 1974, pp. 18–19.

Pellicciotti, Giacomo. "Parla Sun Ra." *Musica Jazz* 30, no. 2 (February 1974), pp. 11–16.

Perlich, Tim. "Shows Cosmic View." *Now Magazine* (Toronto), February 1991.

Phreddie, Phast. "Sun Ra Has a Master Plan." *Contrast,* Spring 1990, pp. 39–44.

Primack, Bert. "Captain Angelic: Sun Ra." *Down Beat,* May 4, 1978, pp. 14–16, 40–41.

Reid, John C. "It's After the End of the World." *Coda,* issue 231 (April–May 1990), pp. 30–32.

Rotenstein, David S. "Jazz Pianist Sun Ra Attuned to the 'Music of the Cosmos.' " *Gwinnett Daily News* (Atlanta), April 17, 1992.

Rusch, Bob. "Sun Ra: Interview." *Cadence* 4, no. 4 (June 1978), pp. 3–8, 24 (reprinted in Robert D. Rusch, *Jazztalk*. Secaucus, NJ: Lyle Stuart, 1984, pp. 61–72).

Sale, Bryan. "Sun Ra." *Option*, "M" Issue (March–April 1987), pp. 54–56.

Santoro, Gene. "Space Is the Place." *Dancing in Your Head: Jazz, Blues, Rock and Beyond*. New York: Oxford University Press, 1994, pp. 228–34.

Sato, Art. "Sun Ra Interview." *Konceptualizations* 5, no. 2 (1989), pp. 18–20.

Schaap, Phil. "An Interview with Sun Ra." *WKCR* 5, no. 5 (January–February 1989), pp. 2–8, 25–32; 5, no. 6 (March 1989), pp. 9–15, 25–29.

Shore, Michael. "Calling Planet Earth." *Soho Weekly News*, July 19, 1979, pp. 48–49.

Sinclair, John. "The InterGalactic Discipline of Sun Ra." *Ann Arbor Sun*, September 5–19, 1973, p. 58 (reprinted from the *Warren-Forest Sun*, no. 1, Summer 1967).

Sinker, Mark. "Sun Ra Talks to Mark Sinker, Philadelphia, Spring, 1989." *Different Cats: Stride Magazine* (Exeter) 37 (1995).

Soutif, Daniel. "Sun Ra: un beau soleil sous le bonnet." *Claviers* (Paris), no. 1 (May 1981), pp. 40–46, 90.

Spady, James. "Indigene=Folkski: Equations in the Black Arts." *The Black Scholar* 10, nos. 3/4, Nov./Dec. 1978, pp. 24–33.

————. "Sun Ra Brings Solar Precepts to Phree Music and Back." *Philadelphia New Observer*, June 9, 1993, pp. 17, 22.

Sprague, David. "Sun Ra: Not of This Earth." *Reel to Real* (Raleigh, NC), September 1989, pp. 4–5, 18.

Steingroot, Ira. "Sun Ra's Magical Kingdom." *Reality Hackers* (Berkeley), no. 6 (Winter 1988), pp. 46–47, 50–51.

Stokes, W. Royal. *The Jazz Scene*. New York: Oxford University Press, 1991, pp. 232–35.

Sun Ra. "The KC-Ra Connection." *The Pitch* (Kansas City), February 1983.

"Sun Ra Journeys from Jazz to Spectacle (with Stops at Humor)," [Newark] *Star-Ledger*, February 6, 1989.

"Sun Sets at Dartmouth." *Concord Monitor*, February 9, 1990.

Theis, Rich. "Sun Ra." *Option*, September–October 1983, pp. 48–51.

Tinder, Clifford S. "Sun Ra Talks About Cosmic Space." *Indiana Daily Student* (Bloomington), July 7, 1977, pp. 5, 9.

Townley, Ray. "Sun Ra." *Down Beat*, December 20, 1973, pp. 18, 38.

Varga, George. "Sun Ra: A Musical Prophet." *San Diego Union*, October 3, 1986.

Vuijsje, Bert. "Sun Ra Spreekt." *Jazz Wereld*, October 1968, pp. 16–19 (reprinted in Bert Vuijsje, *De Nieuwe Jazz*. Baarn: Bosch & Keuning, 1978, pp. 67–79).

————. "Sun Ra nar van de schepper." *Haagse Post*, November 25, 1970 [German].

Wasserman, John L. "On the Town: Sun Ra—A Man for the Space Age." *San Francisco Chronicle*, April 30, 1971, p. 47.

Weiss, David. "This Planet Needs Harmony and Love." *Los Angeles Herald Examiner*, November 21, 1981.

West, Hollie I. "Here Comes the Sun Ra." *New York Daily News*, December 3, 1988.

White, Charles. "The People Are the Instrument: Interview with Sun Ra." *Lightworks* (Ann Arbor, MI), no. 11/12 (Fall 1979), pp. 16–18.

Wilmer, Val. "Sun Ra: Flying Saucers Coming to Take Me Away, Ha Ha!" *Melody Maker*, October 29, 1966, p. 8.

————. "Sun Ra—In Search of Space." *Melody Maker*, November 4, 1972, p. 13.

Wilson, John S. "Sun Ra: I'm Talking About Cosmic Things," *New York Times*, April 7, 1968, sec. 2, pp. 17–18.

Young, Bob. "Bandleader Tunes into Dawn of New Century." *Boston Herald*, January 4, 1990.

Zwerin, Michael. "Jazz Journal: A Little Sample of Something Bad." *Village Voice*, August 15, 1968, pp. 20–21.

————. "Jazzman Sun Ra and His Arkestra Keep on Glowing." *International Herald Tribune*, December 1986.

Note: A source for many remarkable interviews given by Sun Ra over the years is *Sun Ra Research*, published by John and Peter Hinds of Omni Press, P.O. Box 787, Millbrae, CA 94030.

ARTICLES AND LECTURES BY SUN RA

Herman P. Blount. "The Value of an Ideal Theme." *The Industrial High School Record* XI, no. III (March 13, 1931), p. 1.

"Words from Sun Ra." *Vibrations* 1 (New York), no. 1 (July 1967), pp. 16–18, 21.

"My Music Is Words." *The Cricket*, no. 1 (1968), pp. 4–11.

"Roses for Satchmo." *Down Beat*, June 2, 1970, pp. 16–17.

"Sun Ra 1." *Jazz* 265 (October 1970), pp. 30–31.

"Sun Ra 2." *Jazz* 266 (November 1970), pp. 22–24.

"Humanity." *Jazz Monthly* 189 (November 1970), pp. 7–8.

Souvenir Program for Sun Ra and the Intergalactic Research Arkestra at Queen

Elizabeth Hall, London, November 9, 1970 (first UK visit). Compiled by Victor Schonfield, published by Music Now.

"Sun Ra." *Research* 1 (1980), p. 15.

"Your Only Hope Now Is a Lie." *Hambone*, no. 2 (1982), pp. 98–114.

"Ein Monolog." *Jazz* (Basel), vol. 2 (1985).

"Music to Seduce a Monster By." *The Guardian*, August 23, 1990.

POETRY BY SUN RA

Comments and Poetry by Sun Ra. Chicago: Saturn Research.

Selected poetry in *Black Fire*, LeRoi Jones and Larry Neal, eds. New York: William Morrow, 1968, pp. 212–20; *Stylus* 13 (Temple University) no. 1 (Spring 1971), pp. 50–55; Notes to *Jazz by Sun Ra*, Vol. 1, Transition Records 10 (1956) (reprinted in *Changes*, no. 1, 1965, pp. 44–46); "The Outer Bridge," *The Cricket*, no. 4 (1969), p. 19.

Extensions Out: The Immeasurable Equation, Vol. II. Chicago: Ihnfinity, Inc./Saturn Research, 1972.

The Immeasurable Equation, Vol. I. Chicago: Ihnfinity, Inc./Saturn Research, 1972.

The Immeasurable Equation. Philadelphia: Le Sony'r Ra, 1980. 72 pp.

The Immeasurable Equation. Philadelphia: Le Sony'r Ra, 1980. 88 pp.

The Immeasurable Equation. Philadelphia: El Saturn/Millbrae, CA: Omni Press, 1985 (in several different forms).

DISSERTATIONS AND THESES

Chase, Alan. "Sun Ra: Musical Change and Musical Ideas in the Life and Work of a Jazz Composer." M.A. thesis, Department of Music, Tufts University, 1992.

Kessler, Karl. "Jazz and Spirituality: Music as Means to Ultimate Transformation." M.A. thesis, Temple University, 1987.

Martinelli, David A. "The Cosmic Myth-Equations of Sun Ra: An Examination of the Unity of Music and Philosophy of an American Creative Improvising Musician." M.A. thesis, Ethnomusicology, UCLA, 1991.

Rycenga, Jennifer Joanne. "The Composer as a Religious Person in the Context of Pluralism." Ph.D. dissertation, Graduate Theological Seminary, Berkeley, CA, 1992.

GENERAL

Baldwin, James. *The Fire Next Time,* in *The Price of the Ticket: Collected Nonfiction 1948–1985.* New York: St. Martin's Press, 1985.

Banes, Sally. *Greenwich Village 1963.* Durham, NC: Duke University Press, 1993.

Barkum, Michael. *Religion and the Racist Right.* Chapel Hill: University of North Carolina Press, 1994.

Benston, Kimberly W. " 'I Yam What I Yam': Naming and Unnaming in Afro-American Literature." *Black American Literature Forum* 16, no. 1 (Spring 1982), pp. 3–11.

Black Herman. *Secrets of Magic, Mystery and Legerdemain.* Dallas: Doren Publishing Company, 1938.

Bowers, Faubion. *Scriabin,* 2 vols. 1. Tokyo and Palo Alto: Kodansha International, 1969.

Cage, John. *For the Birds.* Boston: Marion Boyars, 1981.

Callins, Jothan. "The Birmingham Jazz Community." M.A. thesis, Ethnomusicology, University of Pittsburgh, 1982.

Coleman, Janet. *The Compass.* New York: Knopf, 1990.

Crooks, Mark. "Julius Priester: Interview." *Cadence,* April 1978, pp. 12–15, 19.

Demusy, Bertrand. "John Tuggle 'Fess' Whatley: A Maker of Musicians." *Jazz Monthly,* 1966, pp. 6–9.

Dery, Mark. "Black to the Future: Interviews with Samuel R. Delany, Greg Tate, and Tricia Rose." In *Flame Wars: The Discourse of Cyberculture,* Mark Dery, ed. *The South Atlantic Quarterly* 92, no. 4 (Fall 1993), pp. 735–89.

Dillard, J. L. *Black Names.* The Hague: Mouton, 1976.

Drake, St. Clair. *Black Folks Here and There.* 2 vols. Los Angeles: Center for Afro-American Studies, UCLA, 1987.

Dreifus, Claudia. "Chloe Wofford Talks About Toni Morrison." *New York Times Magazine,* September 11, 1994, pp. 72–75.

Dumas, Henry. *Goodbye, Sweetwater: New & Selected Stories.* New York: Thunder's Mouth Press, 1988.

———. *Knees of a Natural Man: The Selected Poetry of Henry Dumas.* New York: Thunder's Mouth Press, 1989.

Early, Gerald. *The Culture of Brusing.* Hopewell, NJ: Ecco, 1994.

Eisen, Jonathan, ed. *Twenty-Minute Fandangos and Forever Changes.* New York: Random House, 1971.

Eno, Brian. *A Year with Swollen Appendices.* London: Faber and Faber, 1996.

Forrest, Leon. *Relocations of the Spirit.* Wakefield, RI: Asphodel Press, 1994.

Hacker, Scott. "P-Funk." In *Platforms: A Microwaved Cultural Chronicle of the 1970's,* Pagan Kennedy, ed. New York: St. Martin's 1994, pp. 150–51.

Hampton, Lionel. *Hamp: An Autobiography.* New York: Warner, 1989.

Hentoff, Nat. *Down Beat Record Reviews,* Vol. 2. Chicago: Maher, 1958, pp. 183–84.

Higgins, Godfrey. *Anacalypsis: An Attempt to Draw Aside the Veil of the Saitic Isis: An Inquiry into the Origin of Language, Nation and Religion,* 1833.

Hislip, Alexander. *The Two Babylons or Papal Worship Proved to Be the Worship of Nimrod and His Wife.* New York: Loizeaux, 1945.

Hodson, Geoffrey. *The Brotherhood of Angels and of Men.* London: The Theosophical Publishing House, 1927.

Jackson, John G. *Ethiopia and the Origin of Civilization.* Baltimore: Black Classic Press, n.d.

James, Darius. *That's Blaxploitation!* New York: St. Martin's (Griffin), 1995.

James, George M. *Stolen Legacy: The Greeks Were Not the Authors of Greek Philosophy.* San Francisco: Julian Richardson Associates, 1954.

Jones, LeRoi. *Raise Race Rays Raze.* New York: Random House, 1971.

Kelly, Robin. *Hammer and Hoe: Alabama Communists during the Great Depression.* Chapel Hill: University of North Carolina Press, 1990.

————. *Race Rebels: Culture, Politics, and the Black Working Class.* New York: The Free Press, 1994.

Kerman, Cynthia Eal. *The Lives of Jean Toomer: A Hunger for Wholeness.* Baton Rouge: Louisiana State University Press, 1987.

King, Jr., Martin Luther. "Letter from the Birmingham Jail."

Leiris, Michel. "Jazz." *Sulfur* 15 (1986), pp. 97–104.

Lewis, R.W.B. *Literary Reflections.* Boston: Northeastern University Press, 1993.

Light, Alan. "The Man Who Won't Be Prince." *Vibe,* August 1994.

McCrohan, Donna. *The Second City.* New York: Perigee Books, 1987.

Marvin X. "The Black Bird." In *New Plays from the Black Theater,* Ed Bullins, ed., New York: Bantam, 1969, pp. 109–18.

Massey, Gerald. *A Book of Beginnings.* London: Williams and Norgate, 1881.

Miller, Doug. "The Moan Within the Tone: African Retentions in Rhythm and Blues Saxophone Style in Afro-American Popular Music." *Popular Music* 14/2 (1995), pp. 155–74.

Modern Woodmen of America. *Official Ritual of the Modern Woodmen of America 1915.* Modern Woodmen of America, 1915.

————. *Manual of Drills to be Used in the Exemplification of the Ritualistic Work of Modern Woodmen of America.* Modern Woodmen of America, 1920.

Muhammad, Elijah. *Message to the Black Man*. Philadelphia: Hakim's Publications, 1965.

————. *The Theology of Time*, Abass Rassoull, ed. Hampton, VA: U.B. and U.S. Communications Systems, 1992.

Muhammad, Khalid Alif. *Elaborations of (Allah's Lessons)*, 1984.

Nyman, Michael. *Experimental Music*. New York: Schirmer Music, 1974.

Oliver, Paul. *Songsters & Saints: Vocal Traditions on Race Records*. Cambridge: Cambridge University Press, 1980, pp. 151–52.

Perry, Charles. *The Haight-Ashbury: A History*. New York: Random House, 1984.

Pouncey, Edwin. "Motor City Burning." *The Wire* 136 (June 1995), pp. 26–30.

Reed, Ishmael. *Conjure: Selected Poems, 1963–1970*. Amherst: University of Massachusetts Press, 1971.

Ribowsky, Mark. *Don't Look Back: Satchel Paige in the Shadows of Baseball*. New York: Simon & Schuster, 1994.

Russolo, Luigi. *The Art of Noises*. New York: Pendragon Press, 1986 [1913].

Rutledge, Archibald. *Home by the River*. Indianapolis: Bobbs-Merrill, 1941.

————. *God's Children*. Indianapolis: Bobbs-Merrill, 1947.

Smith, Winston. "Let's Call This: Race, Writing and Difference in Jazz." *Public* 4/5 (1990), pp. 71–85.

Sobel, Mechal. *Trabelin' On: The Slave Journey to an Afro-Baptist Faith*. Princeton: Princeton University Press, 1988.

Stewart, Gary. *Breakout: Profiles in African Rhythm*. Chicago: University of Chicago Press, 1992.

Sukenick, Ronald. *Down and In: Life in the Underground*. New York: Beech Tree Books, 1987.

Thompson, Dave. *Sun Daze: The History and Mystery of Electric Ambient Space Rock*. Los Angeles: Cleopatra Press, 1994.

Thompson, Robert Farris. "Afro-Modernism," Artforum, vol. 30, no. 1 (1991), pp. 91–92.

Travis, Dempsey J. *An Autobiography of Black Jazz*. Chicago: Urban Research Institute, 1983.

Tucker, Mark, ed. *The Duke Ellington Reader*. New York: Oxford University Press, 1993.

The Urantia Book. Chicago: Urantia Foundation, 1955.

Volney, C. F. *The Ruins, or, Meditation on the Revolutions of Empires: and The Law of Nature*. Baltimore: Black Classic Press, 1991.

Webb, James. *The Harmonic Circle*. New York: Putnam, 1980.

Willis, Deborah, ed. *Picturing Me*. New York: New Press, 1994.

Wilson, Peter Lamborn. "Lost/Found Moorish Time Lines in the Wilderness of North America." In *Sacred Drift: Essays on the Margins of Islam*. San Francisco: City Lights, 1993, pp. 15–50.

Worringer, Wilhelm. *Egyptian Art*. London: G. P. Putnam, 1928.

Zamir, Shamoon. "The Artist as Prophet, Priest, and Gunslinger: Ishmael Reed's 'Cowboy in the Boat of Ra.' " *Callaloo* 17, no. 4 (1994), pp. 1205–35.

DISCOGRAPHY

Campbell, Robert L. *The Earthly Recordings of Sun Ra*. Redwood, NY: Cadence Jazz Books, 1994.

DISCOGRAPHY

BY ROBERT L. CAMPBELL

ALBUMS

Note. Albums indicated with a * have been issued in hybrid pressings that combine a side A originally from one LP with a side B that originated on another. In this discography, only the original LP titles and couplings are listed.

1948

Saturn 485: **Deep Purple.** *Deep Purple.* Recorded at Sun Ra's apartment, Chicago, late 1948 or early 1949. [Available on Evidence 22014.]

1955

Saturn 485: **Deep Purple.** *Piano Interlude / Can This Be Love?* Sun Ra's apartment, Chicago, 1955. [Available on Evidence 22014.]

1956

Saturn SR-9956-2 O/P: **Angels and Demons at Play.** *Urnack / Medicine for a Nightmare / A Call for All Demons / Demon's Lullaby.* RCA Studios, Chicago, early 1956. [Available on Evidence 22066.]

Saturn H70P0216: **Super-Sonic Jazz.** *Super Blonde / Soft Talk / Springtime in Chicago / Medicine for a Nightmare.* RCA Studios, Chicago, early 1956. [Available on Evidence 22015.]

Saturn HK 5445: **We Travel the Spaceways.** *New Horizons.* RCA Studios, Chicago, early 1956. [Available on Evidence 22038.]

Transition TRLP J-10: **Jazz by Sun Ra.** *Brainville / A Call for All Demons / Transition / Possession / Street Named Hell / Lullaby for Realville / Future / New Horizons / Fall off the Log / Sun Song.* Universal Studios, Chicago, July 12, 1956. [Now available as Delmark DD-411, **Sun Song.**]

Transition TRLP J-30. **Jazz in Transition.** *Swing a Little Taste.* Same session and date. [Ra and Arkestra contributed one track to a various artists' collection; this track also included in Delmark DD-411, **Sun Song.**]

Saturn H70P0216: **Super-Sonic Jazz.** *India / Sunology / Advice to Medics / Sunology part II / Kingdom of Not / Portrait of the Living Sky / Blues at Midnight / El Is a Sound of Joy.* RCA Studios, Chicago, September–December 1956. [Available on Evidence 22015.]

Saturn 9956-11-A/B: **Sun Ra Visits Planet Earth.** *Two Tones / Saturn / Reflections in Blue / El Viktor.* Unidentified studio, Chicago, September–December 1956. [Available on Evidence 22039.]

Delmark DS 414: **Sound of Joy.** *El Is a Sound of Joy / Overtones of China / Two Tones / Paradise / Planet Earth / Ankh / Saturn / Reflections in Blue / El Viktor / As You Once Were^ / Dreams Come True.^* Same session, Chicago, September–December 1956. [^ included in the 1995 CD issue only, Delmark DD-414.]

Saturn 485: **Deep Purple.** *Dreams Come True.* Same version as above.

Saturn XI: **Just Friends.** *Dreams Come True.* Same version as above.

1957

Saturn 485: **Dreams Come True.** *Don't Blame Me / 'SWonderful / Lover Come Back to Me.* Budland, Chicago, early 1957. [Available on Evidence 22014.]

Saturn LP 9956-11-A/B: **Sun Ra Visits Planet Earth.** *Planet Earth / Eve / Overtones of China.* Rehearsals, Chicago, late 1957 or early 1958. [Available on Evidence 22039.]

1958

Saturn K70P3590/K70P3591: **Jazz in Silhouette.** *Hours After / Horoscope / Images / Blues at Midnight / Enlightenment / Saturn / Velvet / Ancient Aiethopia.* Possibly RCA Studios, Chicago, late 1958. [Available on Evidence 22012.]

Saturn SR 512: **Sound Sun Pleasure!!** *'Round Midnight / You Never Told Me That You Care / Hour of Parting / Back in Your Own Backyard / I Could Have Danced All Night.* Possibly RCA Studios, Chicago, late 1958. [The album also contained *Enlightenment* from the preceding session; all cuts available on Evidence 22014.]

Saturn XI: **Just Friends.** *Back in Your Own Backyard.* Same version as above.

1959

Saturn 9956-11E/F. **Lady with the Golden Stockings.** *Plutonian Nights / The Lady with the Golden Stockings / Star Time / Nubia / Africa / Watusa / Aiethopia.* Rehearsals, Chicago, 1958 and 1959. [Available on Evidence 22066.]

Saturn HK 5445: **We Travel the Spaceways.** *Eve.* Rehearsal, Chicago, 1959. [Available on Evidence 22038.]

Saturn SR 9956-2-M/N: **Rocket Number Nine Take off for the Planet Venus.** *Interstellar Low Ways.* Rehearsal, Chicago, 1959. [Available on Evidence 22039.]

1960

Saturn HK 5445: **We Travel the Spaceways.** *Interplanetary Music / Tapestry from an Asteroid.* Rehearsals, Chicago, 1960. [Available on Evidence 22038.]

Saturn 9956-2-O/P: **Angels and Demons at Play.** *Between Two Worlds / Music from the World Tomorrow.* Rehearsals, Chicago, 1960. [Available on Evidence 22066.]

Saturn 9956-2/A/B: **Fate in a Pleasant Mood.** *The Others in Their World / Space Mates / Lights on a Satellite / Fate in a Pleasant Mood / Ankhnaton.* RCA Studios, Chicago, around June 17, 1960. [Available on Evidence 22068.]

Saturn ESR 508: **Holiday for Soul Dance.** *But Not for Me / Day by Day / Holiday for Strings / Dorothy's Dance / I Loves You, Porgy / Body and Soul / Keep Your Sunny Side Up.* Same session. [Available on Evidence 22011.]

Saturn 9956-2-O/P: **Angels and Demons at Play.** *Tiny Pyramids / Angels and Demons at Play.* Same session. [Available on Evidence 22066.]

Saturn SR 9956-2-M/N: **Rocket Number Nine Take off for the Planet Venus.** *Somewhere in Space / Interplanetary Music / Space Loneliness / Rocket Number Nine Take off for the Planet Venus.* Same session. [Available on Evidence 22039.]

Saturn HK 5445: **We Travel the Spaceways.** *Velvet.* Same session. [Available on Evidence 22038.]

Saturn 9956-2/A/B: **Fate in a Pleasant Mood.** *Kingdom of Thunder.* Probably rehearsal, Chicago, 1960. [Available on Evidence 22068.]

Saturn ESR 508: **Holiday for Soul Dance.** *Early Autumn.* Wonder Inn, Chicago, late 1960. [Available on Evidence 22011.]

Saturn 9956-2/A/B: **Fate in a Pleasant Mood.** *Distant Stars.* Rehearsal, Chicago, late 1960. [Available on Evidence 22068.]

Saturn SR 9956-2/M/N: **Rocket Number Nine Take off for the Planet Venus.** *Onward / Space Aura.* Rehearsals, Chicago, late 1960. [Available on Evidence 22039.]

Saturn HK 5445: **We Travel the Spaceways.** *We Travel the Spaceways / Space Loneliness.* Rehearsals, Chicago, late 1960. [Available on Evidence 22038.]

1961

Savoy MG 12169: **The Futuristic Sounds of Sun Ra.** *Bassism / Of Sounds and Something Else / What's That? / Where Is Tomorrow? / The Beginning / China Gate / New Day / Tapestry from an Asteroid / Jet Flight / Looking Outward / Space Jazz Reverie.* Medallion Studio, Newark, NJ, October 10, 1961. [Available on Savoy SV 0213.]

Saturn 532: **Bad and Beautiful.** *The Bad and the Beautiful / Ankh / Search Light Blues / Exotic Two / On the Blue Side / And This Is My Beloved.* Choreographers Workshop, NYC, November–December 1961. [Available on Evidence 22038.]

Saturn 9956: **Art Forms of Dimensions Tomorrow.** *Lights on a Satellite / Kosmos in Blue.* Choreographers Workshop, NYC, November–December 1961. [Available on Evidence 22036.]

1962

Saturn 9956: **Art Forms of Dimensions Tomorrow.** *Cluster of Galaxies / Ankh / Solar Drums / The Outer Heavens / Infinity of the Universe.* Choreographers Workshop, NYC, 1962. [Available on Evidence 22036.]

Saturn GH 9954-E/F: **Secrets of the Sun.** *Friendly Galaxy / Solar Differentials / Space Aura / Love in Outer Space / Reflects Motion / Solar Symbols.* Choreographers Workshop, NYC, 1962.

Blast First BFFP 42 [CD]: **Out There a Minute.** *Somewhere in Space / Dark Clouds with Silver Linings / Journey Outward.* Choreographers Workshop, NYC, 1962.

Saturn 539: **What's New?*** *What's New? / Wanderlust / Jukin' / Autumn in New York.* Choreographers Workshop, NYC, late 1962.

Saturn 529: **The Invisible Shield.*** *State Street / Sometimes I'm Happy / Time after Time 1 / Time after Time 2 / Easy to Love / Sunnyside Up.* Choreographers Workshop, NYC, late 1962.

Saturn 2066: **When Sun Comes Out.** *Circe / The Nile / Brazilian Sun / We Travel the Spaceways / Calling Planet Earth / Dancing Shadows / The Rainmaker / When Sun Comes Out.* Choreographers Workshop, NYC, late 1962 or early 1963. [Available on Evidence 22068.]

Blast First BFFP 42 [CD]: **Out There a Minute.** *Out There a Minute.* Choreographers Workshop, NYC, late 1962 to early 1964.

1963

Saturn 14200A: **Space Probe.*** *Primitive* / *The Conversion of J. P.* Choreographers Workshop, NYC, 1963. ["Primitive" is the end of a performance whose beginning was misplaced for years; the initial portion finally appeared as "Dimensions in Time" on Evidence CD 22068.]

Saturn 1966: **When Angels Speak of Love.** *Celestial Fantasy* / *The Idea of It All* / *Ecstasy of Being* / *When Angels Speak of Love* / *Next Stop Mars.* Choreographers Workshop, NYC, 1963. ["When Angels Speak of Love" and an edited version of "Next Stop Mars" were reissued on Blast First BFFP 42, **Out There a Minute.**]

Saturn 408: **Cosmic Tones for Mental Therapy.** *And Otherness* / *Thither and Yon.* Choreographers Workshop, NYC, late 1963. [Available on Evidence 22036.]

Saturn 408: **Cosmic Tones for Mental Therapy.** *Adventure-Equation* / *Moon Dance* / *Voice of Space.* Tip Top Club, Brooklyn, NY, late 1963. [Available on Evidence 22036.]

1964

Saturn KH 98766: **Other Planes of There.** *Other Planes of There* / *Sound Spectra* / *Sketch* / *Pleasure* / *Spiral Galaxy.* Choreographers Workshop, NYC, early 1964. [Available on Evidence 22037.]

Saturn JHNY 165: **Featuring Pharoah Sanders and Black Harold.** *Gods on a Safari* / *The World Shadow* / *The Voice of Pan* / *Dawn over Israel.* Four Days in December, Judson Hall, NYC, December 31, 1964.

1965

ESP-Disk' 1014: **The Heliocentric Worlds of Sun Ra Volume 1.** *Heliocentric* / *Outer Nothingness* / *Other Worlds* / *The Cosmos* / *Of Heavenly Things* / *Nebulae* / *Dancing in the Sun.* RLA Studio, NYC, April 20, 1965. [Available on ESP 1014.]

Saturn LPB 711: **The Magic City.** *The Shadow World* / *Abstract "I"* / *Abstract Eye.* Rehearsals, NYC, April–May 1965. [Available on Evidence 22069.]

Blast First BFFP 42 [CD]: **Out There a Minute.** *Other Worlds.* Rehearsal, NYC, April–May 1965.

Saturn LPB 711: **The Magic City.** *The Magic City.* Rehearsal, NYC, around September 24, 1965. [Available on Evidence 22069.]

ESP-Disk' 1017: **The Heliocentric Worlds of Sun Ra Volume 2.** *The Sun Myth / A House of Beauty / Cosmic Chaos.* RLA Studio, NYC, November 16, 1965. [Available on ESP 1017.]

MGM E 4358 [Walt Dickerson Quartet]: **Impressions of a Patch of Blue.** *A Patch of Blue Part 1 / A Patch of Blue Part 2 / Bacon and Eggs / High Hopes / Alone in the Park Part 1 / Alone in the Park Part 2 / Selina's Fantasy / Thataway.* Studio recording, NYC, late 1965 or early 1966.

1966

Tifton S-78002 [The Sensational Guitars of Dan & Dale]: **Batman and Robin.** *Batman Theme / Batman's Batmorang / Batman and Robin over the Roofs / The Penguin Chase / Flight of the Batman / Robin's Theme / Penguin's Umbrella / Batman and Robin Swing / Batmobile Wheels / The Riddler's Retreat / The Bat Cave.* Studio recording, Newark, NJ, January 1966.

ESP-Disk' 1045: **Nothing Is.** *Dancing Shadows / Imagination / Exotic Forest / Sun Ra and His Band from Outer Space / Shadow World / Theme of the Stargazers / Outer Spaceways Incorporated / Next Stop Mars.* Buffalo, Syracuse, and other points in upstate NY, May 1966. [Available on ESP 1045.]

Thoth Intergalactic KH-5472: **Strange Strings.** *Worlds Approaching / Strange Strings.* Rehearsals, NYC, 1966.

Saturn SR 509: **Monorails and Satellites.** *Space Towers / Cogitation / Skylight / The Alter-Destiny / Easy Street / Blue Differentials / Monorails and Satellites / The Galaxy Way.* Sun Studios, NYC, 1966. [Available on Evidence 22013.]

Saturn 519: **Monorails and Satellites Vol. II.** *Astro Vision / The Ninth Eye / Solar Boats / Perspective Prisms of Is / Calundronius.* Sun Studios, NYC, 1966.

Saturn 143000A/B: **Outer Spaceways Incorporated.** *Chromatic Shadows / The Wind Speaks / Outer Spaceways Incorporated.* Live, NYC, 1966 or 1967.

1967

Black Lion 30103: **Pictures of Infinity.** *Spontaneous Simplicity.* Rehearsal, NYC, 1967. [Available on Black Lion BLCD 760191, misleadingly retitled **Outer Spaceways Incorporated.**]

Saturn ESR 507: **Atlantis.** *Atlantis.* Olatunji Center of African Culture, NYC, May–December 1967. [Available on Evidence 220067.]

BYG Actuel 529.340: **The Solar-Myth Approach Volume I.** *Spectrum / Realm of Lightning / Legend / They'll Come Back / Adventures of Bugs Hunter.* Sun Studios, NYC, 1967 or 1968.

BYG Actuel 529.341: **The Solar-Myth Approach Volume II.** *Interpretation /
Ancient Ethiopia.* Sun Studios, NYC, 1967 or 1968.

Saturn ESR 507: **Atlantis.** *Mu / Lemuria / Yucatan [Saturn version] / Yucatan [Im-
pulse version^] / Bimini.* Sun Studios, NYC, 1967 or 1968. [^The second version of "Yucatan" replaced the first one on an LP reissue, Impulse 9239; both
versions now included in Evidence 22067.]

Saturn 487: **Song of the Stargazers.** *Cosmo Dance.* Live, unknown location,
1967 or 1968.

1968

Jihad 1968 [Imamu Amiri Baraka and the Black Arts Theater Troupe with Sun
Ra and his Myth Science Arkestra]: **A Black Mass.** *A Black Mass.* Studio
recording, NYC, 1968.

BYG Actuel 529.340: **The Solar-Myth Approach Volume I.** *The Satellites Are
Spinning.* Sun Studios, NYC, early 1968.

BYG Actuel 529.341: **The Solar-Myth Approach Volume II.** *Outer Spaceways
Incorporated / The Utter Nots.* Sun Studios, NYC, early 1968.

Saturn 14300A/B: **Outer Spaceways Incorporated.*** *The Satellites Are Spinning.*
Live, NYC, 1968.

Black Lion 30103: **Pictures of Infinity.** *Somewhere There / Outer Spaceways Incorporated / Intergalactic Motion^ / Saturn / Song of the Sparer.* Live, NYC, 1968.
[^"Intergalactic Motion" (actually "Ankhnaton") was added to the reissue,
Black Lion BLCD 760191, which was misleadingly retitled **Outer Spaceways Incorporated.**]

Saturn ESR 520: **Continuation.** *Biosphere Blues / Intergalactic Research / Earth
Primitive Earth / New Planet.* Rehearsals, Sun Studios, NYC, early 1968. [The
last two pieces were reissued on Blast First BFFP 42, **Out There a Minute,**
under the titles "Cosmo Enticement" and "Song of Tree and Forest."]

1969

Saturn ESR 520: **Continuation.** *Continuation To / Jupiter Festival.* The East,
Brooklyn, NY, 1969.

Saturn 521: **My Brother the Wind.** *My Brother the Wind / Intergalactic II / To
Nature's God / The Code of Interdependence.* Variety Recording Studios, NYC,
late 1969 or early 1970.

BYG Actuel 529.341: **The Solar-Myth Approach Volume II.** *Strange Worlds.*
Live, unknown location, 1969 or 1970.

BYG Actuel 529.341: **The Solar-Myth Approach Volume II.** *Pyramids.* The House of Ra, Philadelphia, 1969 or 1970.

1970

Saturn 523: **My Brother the Wind Volume II.*** *Somewhere Else / Contrast / The Wind Speaks / Sun Thoughts / Journey to the Stars / World of the Myth "I" / The Design-Cosmos II / Otherness Blue / Somebody Else's World / Pleasant Twilight / Walking on the Moon.* Variety Recording Studios, NYC, early 1970. [Available on Evidence 22140. On this CD "Walking on the Moon" is unedited.]

Saturn XI: **Just Friends.** *Otherness Blue / Pleasant Twilight / Walking on the Moon.* Same versions as above.

Blast First BFFP 42 [CD]: **Out There a Minute.** *Jazz and Romantic Sounds.* Studio recording, early 1970.

Thoth Intergalactic IR 1972: **The Night of the Purple Moon.** *Sun-Earth Rock / The All of Everything / Impromptu Festival / Blue Soul / Narrative / Outside the Time Zone / The Night of the Purple Moon / A Bird's Eye View of Man's World / 21st Century Romance / Dance of the Living Image / Love in Outer Space.* Variety Recording Studios, NYC, mid-1970. [An alternate version of "Love in Outer Space" from this session was issued on Blast First BFFP 42, **Out There a Minute.**]

BYG Actuel 529.341: **The Solar-Myth Approach Volume II.** *Scene 1, Take 1.* Variety Recording Studios, NYC, 1970.

BYG Actuel 529.340: **The Solar-Myth Approach Volume I.** *Seen III, Took 4.* Variety Recording Studios, NYC, 1970.

Saturn 142000B: **Space Probe*.** *Space Probe.* Variety Recording Studios, NYC, 1970.

Saturn 14400B: **The Invisible Shield.*** *Island in the Sun / The Invisible Shield / Janus.* Studio recordings, c. 1970.

Shandar 10.003: **Nuits de la Fondation Maeght Volume II.** *Spontaneous Simplicity / Friendly Galaxy No. 2 / The World of the Lightning / Black Myth: The Shadows Took Shape—This Strange World—Journey through the Outer Darkness / Sky.* St.-Paul-de-Vence, France, August 3, 1970.

Shandar 10.001: **Nuits de la Fondation Maeght Volume I.** *Enlightenment / The Stargazers / Shadow World / The Cosmic Explorer.* St.-Paul-de-Vence, France, August 5, 1970.

MPS 2120748: **It's after the End of the World.** *Duos / Strange Dreams / Strange Worlds / Black Myth / It's after the End of the World / Black Forest Myth.* Donaueschingen, West Germany, October 17, 1970.

MPS 2120748: **It's after the End of the World.** *The Myth-Science Approach: Myth versus Reality—Angelic Proclamation—Out in Space / Watusi, Egyptian March.* West Berlin, West Germany, November 7, 1970.

1971

Saturn 200: **Universe in Blue.** *Universe in Blue Part I / Universe in Blue Part II / Blackman / In a Blue Mood / Another Shade of Blue.* Probably live in California, around August 1971.

Thoth Intergalactic KH-1272: **Live in Egypt Volume 1.** *Friendly Galaxy No. 2 / To Nature's God / Why Go to the Moon?* Hartmut Geerken's house, Heliopolis, Egypt, December 12, 1971.

Thoth Intergalactic 7771: **Nidhamu.** *Nidhamu.* Hartmut Geerken's house, Heliopolis, Egypt, December 12, 1971.

Thoth Intergalactic KH-1272: **Live in Egypt Volume 1.** *Discipline 27 / Interview with Ra / Solar Ship Voyage / Interview with Ra (concluded) / Cosmo-Darkness / The Light Thereof.* Egyptian TV broadcast, Cairo, December 16, 1971.

Saturn 1217718: **Horizon.** *Starwatchers / Discipline 2 / The Shadow World / Third Planet / Space Is the Place / Horizon / Discipline 8.* Ballon Theatre, Cairo, December 17, 1971.

Thoth Intergalactic 7771: **Nidhamu.** *Space Loneliness No. 2 / Discipline 11 / Discipline 15.* Ballon Theatre, Cairo, December 17, 1971.

1972

Evidence 22070 [CD]: **Soundtrack to the Film Space Is the Place.** *It's after the End of the World / Under Different Stars / Discipline 33 / Watusi / Calling Planet Earth / I Am the Alter-Destiny / The Satellites Are Spinning take 1 / Cosmic Forces / Outer Spaceways Incorporated take 3 / We Travel the Spaceways / The Overseer / Blackman—Love in Outer Space / Mysterious Crystal / I Am the Brother of the Wind / We'll Wait for You / Space Is the Place.* Studio recording, San Francisco, early 1972.

Impulse AS-9255: **Astro Black.** *Astro Black / Discipline "99" / Hidden Spheres / The Cosmo-Fire (Parts I, II, and III).* Studio recording, Chicago, supposedly May 7, 1972.

Atlantic SD2-502: **Ann Arbor Blues and Jazz Festival 1972.** *Life Is Splendid.* Ann Arbor, MI, September 9, 1972. [The Arkestra contributed one track to this various artists' compilation.]

Blue Thumb BTS-41: **Space Is the Place.** *Space Is the Place / Images / Discipline 33 / Sea of Sounds.* Streeterville Studios, Chicago, October 19, 1972.

Saturn 538: **Discipline 27-II.** *Pan Afro* / *Discipline 8* / *Neptune* / *Discipline 27-II.*
Same session.

1973

Impulse ASD-9298: **Pathways to Unknown Worlds.** *Pathways to Unknown Worlds* / *Extension Out* / *Cosmo-Media.* Studio recording, Chicago, 1973.

Saturn 485: **Deep Purple.** *The World of the Invisible* / *The Order of the Pharaonic Jesters* / *The Land of the Day Star.* Variety Recording Studios, NYC, 1973.

Atlantic 40450 [France only]: **Live at the Gibus.** *Spontaneous Simplicity* / *Lights on a Satellite* / *Ombre Monde #2* / *King Porter Stomp* / *Salutation from the Universe* / *Calling Planet Earth.* The Gibus, Paris, October 1973.

ESP 3033 [CD]: **Concert for the Comet Kohoutek.** *Kohoutek Intro* / *Astro Black* / *Discipline 27* / *Journey through the Outer Darkness* / *Enlightenment* / *Love in Outer Space* / *Discipline 15* / *Life Is Splendid—Outer Space Employment Agency* / *Space Is the Place.* Town Hall, NYC, December 22, 1973. [Many titles were given incorrectly on the CD.]

1974

Saturn 61674: **Out Beyond the Kingdom of.** *Solar Ship* / *Discipline 99* / *How Am I to Know?* / *Sunnyside Up* / *Out Beyond the Kingdom of* / *Cosmos Synthesis* / *Outer Space Employment Agency* / *Journey to Saturn.* Hunter College, NYC, June 16, 1974.

Saturn 81774: **The Antique Blacks.** *Song No. 1* / *There Is Change in the Air* / *The Antique Blacks* / *This Song Is Dedicated to Nature's God* / *The Ridiculous "I" and the Cosmos Me* / *Would I for All that Were* / *Space Is the Place.* Radio broadcast, Philadelphia, August 17, 1974.

Saturn 92074: **Sub Underground.** *Cosmo-Earth Fantasy.* Variety Recording Studios, NYC, September 1974.

Saturn 92074: **Sub Underground.** *Love Is for Always* / *The Song of Drums* / *The World of Africa.* Temple University, Philadelphia, September 20, 1974.

1975

Saturn 752: **What's New?** *We Roam the Cosmos.* Live, unknown location, May 23, 1975. [This B side was coupled with Saturn 539, **What's New?** for the first pressing only. All subsequent editions of **What's New?** used a different B side.]

1976

Saturn MS 87976: **Live at Montreux.** *For the Sunrise / Of the Other Tomorrow / From Out Where Others Dwell / On Sound Infinity Spheres / The House of Eternal Being / Gods of the Thunder Realm / Lights on a Satellite / Take the A Train / Prelude [Cascade] / El Is a Sound of Joy / Encore 1 and 2 [The People Are].* Montreux, Switzerland, July 9, 1976.

Cobra COB 37001: **Cosmos.** *The Mystery of Two / Interstellar Low Ways / Neo Project No. 2 / Cosmos / Moonship Journey / Journey among the Stars / Jazz from an Unknown Planet.* Studio Hautefeuille, Paris, August 1976.

Horo HDP 19-20: **Unity.** *The Satellites Are Spinning / Rose Room.* Châteauvallon Festival, Châteauvallon, France, August 25, 1976.

1977

Leo LR 198 [CD]: **A Quiet Place in the Universe.** *A Quiet Place in the Universe / Friendly Galaxy No. 2—I, Pharaoh / Images / Love in Outer Space / I'll Never Be the Same / Space Is the Place.* Live in the USA, early 1977.

Improvising Artists 37.38.50: **Solo Piano Volume 1.** *Sometimes I Feel Like a Motherless Child / Cosmo Rhythmatic / Yesterdays / Romance of Two Planets / Irregular Galaxy / To a Friend.* Generation Sound Studio, NYC, May 20, 1977. [Available on Improvising Artists 123850.]

Improvising Artists 37.38.58: **St. Louis Blues: Solo Piano.** *Ohosnisixaeht / St. Louis Blues / Three Little Words / Sky and Sun / I Am We Are I / Thoughts on Thoth.* The Axis-in-SoHo, NYC, July 3, 1977. [Available on Improvising Artists 123858.]

Saturn 7877: **Somewhere over the Rainbow.** *We Live to Be / Gone with the Wind / Make Another Mistake / Take the A Train / Amen Amen / Over the Rainbow / I'll Wait for You.* The Bluebird, Bloomington, IN, around July 18, 1977.

Saturn 101477: **Some Blues but Not the Kind That's Blue.** *Some Blues but Not the Kind That's Blue / I'll Get By / My Favorite Things / Nature Boy / Tenderly / Black Magic.* Variety Recording Studios, NYC, October 14, 1977.

Horo HDP 19-20: **Unity.** *Yesterdays / Lightnin' / How Am I to Know? / Lights on a Satellite / Yeah Man! / King Porter Stomp / Images / Penthouse Serenade / Lady Bird—Half Nelson / Halloween in Harlem / My Favorite Things / Enlightenment.* Storyville, NYC, October 24 and 29, 1977.

Saturn 771: **The Soul Vibrations of Man.** *Sometimes the Universe Speaks / Pleiades / Third Heaven—When There Is No Sun / Halloween in Harlem / Untitled Improvisation—The Shadow World.* Jazz Showcase, Chicago, November 1977.

Saturn 772: **Taking a Chance on Chances.** *Taking a Chance on Chances / Lady Bird—Half Nelson / Over the Rainbow / St. Louis Blues / What's New? / Take the A Train.* Same sessions.

1978

Horo HDP 25-26: **New Steps.** *My Favorite Things / Moon People / Sun Steps / Exactly Like You / Friend and Friendship / Rome at Twilight / When There Is No Sun / The Horo.* Horo Voice Studio, Rome, January 2 and 7, 1978.

Horo HDP 23-24: **Other Voices, Other Blues.** *Springtime and Summer Idyll / One Day in Rome / Bridge on the Ninth Dimension / Along the Tiber / Sun, Sky, and Wind / Rebellion / Constellation / The Mystery of Being.* Horo Voice Studio, Rome, January 8 and 13, 1978.

Saturn 1978: **Media Dream.** *Saturn Research / Constellation / Year of the Sun / Media Dreams / Twigs at Twilight / An Unbeknowneth Love.* Live in Italy, January 1978.

Saturn 19782: **Sound Mirror.** *Jazzisticology / Of Other Tomorrows Never Known.* Live in Italy, January 1978.

Saturn CMIJ78: **Disco 3000.** *Disco 3000 / Third Planet / Friendly Galaxy [reprise] / Dance of the Cosmo-Aliens.* Teatro Ciak, Milan, January 23, 1978.

Saturn 19782: **Sound Mirror.** *The Sound Mirror.* Probably Variety Recording Studios, NYC, 1978.

Philly Jazz PJ 1007: **Of Mythic Worlds.** *Mayan Temples / Over the Rainbow / Inside the Blues / Intrinsic Energies / Of Mythic Worlds.* Live, supposedly in Chicago, 1978.

Steeplechase SCS 1126 [Walt Dickerson and Sun Ra]: **Visions.** *Astro / Utopia / Visions / Constructive Neutrons / Space Dance / Light Years^ / Prophecy.^* Studio recording, NYC, July 11, 1978. [^"Light Years" and "Prophecy" first issued on the CD version, SCCD 31126.]

Philly Jazz PJ 666: **Lanquidity.** *Lanquidity / Where Pathways Meet / That's How I Feel / Twin Stars of Thence / There Are Other Worlds (They Have Not Told You Of).* Blank Tapes, NYC, July 17, 1978.

Sweet Earth SER 1003: **The Other Side of the Sun.** *Space Fling / Flamingo / Space Is the Place / The Sunny Side of the Street / Manhattan Cocktail.* Blue Rock Studios, NYC, November 1, 1978, and January 4, 1979.

1979

Saturn 487: **Song of the Stargazers.** *Somewhere Out / Distant Stars / Duo / Seven Points.* Various sessions, up through late 1970s.

Saturn 487: **Song of the Stargazers.** *The Others in Their World / Galactic Synthesis.* Live, unknown location, probably 1979.

Saturn 101679: **On Jupiter.** *UFO.* Variety Recording Studios, NYC, early 1979.

Saturn 79: **Sleeping Beauty.** *Springtime Again / Door of the Cosmos / Sleeping Beauty.* Variety Recording Studios, NYC, probably June 1979.

Rounder 3035: **Strange Celestial Road.** *Celestial Road / Say / I'll Wait for You.* Variety Recording Studios, NYC, probably June 1979. [Available on Rounder CD 3035.]

Saturn 72579: **God Is More than Love Can Ever Be.** *Days of Happiness / Magic City Blue / Tenderness / Blithe Spirit Dance / God Is More than Love Can Ever Be.* Variety Recording Studios, NYC, July 25, 1979.

Saturn 91379: **Omniverse.** *The Place of Five Points / West End Side of Magic City / Dark Lights in a White Forest / Omniverse / Visitant of the Ninth Ultimate.* Variety Recording Studios, NYC, September 13, 1979.

Saturn 101679: **On Jupiter.** *On Jupiter / Seductive Fantasy.* Variety Recording Studios, NYC, October 16, 1979.

Saturn 6680: **I, Pharaoh.** *Rumpelstiltskin / Images / I, Pharaoh.* Live, unknown location, 1979.

DIW 388B [CD]: **Live from Soundscape.** *The Possibility of Altered Destiny.* Soundscape, NYC, November 10, 1979, 9:00P.M. [This lecture by Sun Ra was included as a second disk in the first pressing of DIW 388.]

DIW 388 [CD]: **Live from Soundscape.** *Astro Black / Pleiades / We're Living in the Space Age / Keep Your Sunny Side Up / Discipline 27 / Untitled Improvisation / Watusi / Space Is the Place / We Travel the Spaceways / Angel Race / Destination Unknown / On Jupiter.* Soundscape, NYC, November 11, 1979.

1980

hat Hut 2R17: **Sunrise in Different Dimensions.** *Light from a Hidden Sun / Pin-Points of Spiral Prisms / Silhouettes of the Shadow World / Cocktails for Two / 'Round Midnight / Lady Bird—Half Nelson / Big John's Special / Yeah Man! / Love in Outer Space / Provocative Celestials / Disguised Gods in Skullduggery Rendezvous / Queer Notions / Limehouse Blues / King Porter Stomp / Take the A Train / Lightnin' / On Jupiter / A Helio-hello! and Goodbye Too!* Gasthof Mohren, Willisau, Switzerland, February 24, 1980. [The CD reissue on hat Art 6099 omits "Provocative Celestials," "Love in Outer Space," and "On Jupiter."]

Saturn 91780: **Voice of the Eternal Tomorrow.** *Voice of the Eternal Tomorrow / Approach of the Eternal Tomorrow / The Rose Hue Mansions of the Sun.* Squat Theater, NYC, September 17, 1980.

Saturn 10480/12480: **Aurora Borealis.** *Prelude in C# Minor / Quiet Ecstasy.* Live, unknown location, October 4, 1980.

Saturn Sun Ra 1981: **Dance of Innocent Passion.** *Intensity / Cosmo Energy / Dance of Innocent Passion / Omnisonicism.* Squat Theater, NYC, 1980.

Saturn 10480/12480: **Aurora Borealis.** *Aurora Borealis / Omniscience.* Live, unknown location, December 4, 1980.

Saturn 123180: **Beyond the Purple Star Zone.** *Beyond the Purple Star Zone / Rocket Number Nine / Immortal Being / Romance on a Satellite / Planetary Search.* Jazz Center, Detroit, December 29, 30, and 31, 1980.

Saturn IX SR 72881: **Oblique Parallax.** *Oblique Parallax / Vista Omniverse / Celestial Realms / Journey Stars Beyond.* Jazz Center, Detroit, December 29, 30, and 31, 1980.

1982

Saturn IX/ 1983-220: **Ra to the Rescue.** *Ra to the Rescue Chapter 1 / Ra to the Rescue Chapter 2 / Fate in a Pleasant Mood / When Lights Are Dark / They Plan to Leave / Back Alley Blues.* Squat Theater, NYC, 1982.

Saturn XI: **Just Friends.** *Just Friends / Under the Spell of Love.* Live, unknown locations, around 1982.

Saturn Gemini 19841: **A Fireside Chat with Lucifer.** *Nuclear War / Retrospect / Makeup / A Fireside Chat with Lucifer.* Variety Recording Studios, NYC, September 1982.

Saturn Gemini 19842: **Celestial Love.** *Celestial Love / Interstellarism [Interstellar Low Ways] / Blue Intensity / Sophisticated Lady / Nameless One #2 / Nameless One #3 / Smile.* Same session.

Y RA 2: **Nuclear War.** *Nuclear War / Retrospect / Celestial Love / Sometimes I'm Happy / Blue Intensity / Nameless One #2 / Smile / Drop Me off in Harlem.* Same session, same versions (except "Drop Me off in Harlem" was not released on Saturn).

1983

Praxis CM 106: **Sun Ra Arkestra Meets Salah Ragab in Egypt.** *Egypt Strut / Dawn.* El Nahar Studio, Heliopolis, Egypt, May 1983. [The other side of the album consists of three tracks performed by Salah Ragab and the Cairo Jazz Band.]

Saturn 10-11-85: **Stars that Shine Darkly.*** *Stars that Shine Darkly Part 1.* Montreux, Switzerland, between November 2 and 5, 1983.

Saturn 9-1213-85: **Stars that Shine Darkly Volume 2.*** *Stars that Shine Darkly Part 2.* Same concert.

Saturn 10-11-85: **Stars that Shine Darkly.** *Hiroshima.* Live in Europe, November 1983.

Leo LR 154 [CD]: **Love in Outer Space: Live in Utrecht.** *Along Came Ra / Discipline 27 / Blues Ra / Big John's Special / Fate in a Pleasant Mood / 'Round Midnight / Love in Outer Space—Space Is the Place.* Utrecht, Netherlands, December 11, 1983.

1984

Praxis CM 108: **Live at Praxis '84 Vol. I.** *Untitled Improvisation / Discipline 27-II—Children of the Sun / Nuclear War / Untitled Blues / Fate in a Pleasant Mood / Yeah Man! / Space Is the Place—We Travel the Spaceways—Outer Spaceways Incorporated—Next Stop Mars.* Orpheus Theater, Athens, Greece, February 27, 1984.

Praxis CM 109: **Live at Praxis '84 Vol. II.** *Untitled Improvisation / Untitled Improvisation / Discipline 27 / Mack the Knife / Cocktails for Two / Over the Rainbow / Satin Doll.* Same concert.

Praxis CM 110: **Live at Praxis '84 Vol. III.** *Big John's Special / Carefree / Days of Wine and Roses / Theme of the Stargazers—The Satellites Are Spinning / They'll Come Back / Enlightenment—Strange Mathematic Rhythmic Equations.* Same concert.

Saturn Gemini 9-1213-85: **Stars that Shine Darkly Volume 2.** *Outer Reach Intensity-Energy / Cosmos Rendezvous / Barbizon / The Double That... / The Ever Is...* Live performances, unknown locations, probably 1984.

Saturn/ Recommended SRRRD 1: **Cosmo Sun Connection.** *Fate in a Pleasant Mood / Cosmo Journey Blues / Cosmo Sun Connection / Cosmonaut Astronaut Rendezvous / As Space Ships Approach / Pharaoh's Den.* Live in the USA, 1984.

Saturn 101485: **When Spaceships Appear.** *Drummerlistics / Children of the Sun / Cosmo-Party Blues.* Live concerts, unknown locations, 1984 or 1985. [The rest of this album consists of tracks from **Ra to the Rescue,** some under new titles.]

1986

Slash 25481 [Phil Alvin]: **Un "Sung Stories."** *The Ballad of Smokey Joe / The Old Man of the Mountain / Buddy, Can You Spare a Dime?* Variety Recording Studios, NYC, probably March 1986. [The Arkestra backed Alvin on three Cab Calloway tributes; the rest of the album features other bands.]

Meltdown MPA-1: **John Cage Meets Sun Ra.** *John Cage Meets Sun Ra.* Sideshows by the Sea, Coney Island, Brooklyn, NY, June 8, 1986. [Reissued on CD in January 1997.]

Saturn (no number, cassette): **A Night in East Berlin.** *Mystic Prophecy / Beyond the Wilderness of Shadows / Prelude to a Kiss / Insterstellar Low Ways / Space Is the Place—We Travel the Spaceways / The Shadow World / Rocket Number Nine— Second Stop Is Jupiter.* Friedrichstadtpalast, East Berlin, East Germany, June 28, 1986. [This material was reissued, with different couplings, on two different versions of the CD Leo LR 149.]

Black Saint 120 101 [CD]: **Reflections in Blue.** *State Street Chicago / Nothin' from Nothin' / Yesterdays / Say It Isn't So / I Dream Too Much / Reflections in Blue.* Jingle Machine Studio, Milan, December 18–19, 1986.

Black Saint 120 111 [CD]: **Hours After.** *But Not for Me / Hours After / Beautiful Love / Dance of the Extra Terrestrians / Love on a Faraway Planet.* Same session.

1987

Opus 9115 2080-81: **Bratislava Jazz Days 1987.** *Limehouse Blues.* Bratislava, Czechoslovakia, October 25, 1987. [A two-LP various artists collection.]

1988

Saturn 13188III/12988II: **Hidden Fire 1.** *Untitled Improvisation / Untitled Blues.* The Knitting Factory, NYC, January 29, 1988.

Saturn 13088A/12988B: **Hidden Fire 2.** *2 unidentified titles.* The Knitting Factory, NYC, January 29, 1988.

Saturn 13088A/12988B: **Hidden Fire 2.** *My Brothers the Wind and Sun #9.* The Knitting Factory, NYC, January 30, 1988. ["My Brothers the Wind and Sun #9" was reissued on the second version of the CD Leo LR 149, **A Night in East Berlin.**]

Saturn 13188III/12988II: **Hidden Fire 1.** *Retrospect—This World Is Not My Home.* The Knitting Factory, NYC, January 31, 1988.

A&M AMA 3918 [CD]: **Stay Awake.** *Pink Elephants on Parade.* Variety Recording Studios, NYC, early 1988. [This is a various artists' collection of songs from Walt Disney movies.]

DIW 824 [CD]: **Cosmo Omnibus Imaginable Illusion: Live at Pit-Inn.** *Introduction—Cosmo Approach Prelude / Angel Race—I'll Wait for You / Can You Take It? / If You Came from Nowhere Here / Astro Black / Prelude to a Kiss / Interstellar Low Ways.* Pit-Inn, Tokyo, August 8, 1988.

A&M 5260 [CD]: **Blue Delight.** *Blue Delight / Out of Nowhere / Sunrise / They Dwell on Other Planes / Gone with the Wind / Your Guest Is as Good as Mine / Nashira / Days of Wine and Roses.* Variety Recording Studios, NYC, December 5, 1988.

Rounder 3036 [CD]: **Somewhere Else.** *Love in Outer Space / Everything Is Space / Priest / Tristar.* Same session.

1989

Leo LR 230 [CD]: **Second Star to the Right (Salute to Walt Disney).** *The Forest of No Return / Someday My Prince Will Come / Frisco Fog / Wishing Well / Zip-A-Dee-Doo-Dah / Second Star to the Right / Heigh Ho! Heigh Ho! / Whistle While You Work.* Jazzatelier, Ulrichsberg, Austria, April 29, 1989.

Leo LR 235/236 [CD]: **Stardust from Tomorrow.** *Mystery Intro / Untitled / Blue Low / Prelude in A-Major / Untitled II / Discipline 27 / Back Alley Blues / Prelude to a Kiss / Stardust from Tomorrow / Yeah Man! / We Travel the Spaceways–Space Chants Medley: Outer Spaceways Incorporated / Rocket Number Nine / Take off for the Planet Venus / Second Stop is Jupiter / Pluto / Saturn / Saturn Rings.* Same session.

A&M 75021 5324 [CD]: **Purple Night.** *Journey towards Stars / Friendly Galaxy / Love in Outer Space / Stars Fell on Alabama / Of Invisible Them / Neverness / Purple Night Blues.* BMG Studios, NYC, mid-November 1989.

Rounder 3036 [CD]: **Somewhere Else.** *Discipline—Tall Trees in the Sun / 'SWonderful / Hole in the Sky / Somewhere Else Part 1 / Somewhere Else Part 2 / Stardust from Tomorrow.* Same session.

1990

Blast First BFFP 60 [CD]: **Live in London 1990.** *Frisco / Shadow World / For the Blue People / Prelude to a Kiss / Down Here on the Ground / Blue Delight / Cosmo Song / Space Chants.* The Mean Fiddler, London, June 11, 1990.

Elemental/t.e.c. 90902 [CD]: **Beets: A Collection of Jazz Songs.** *Egyptian Fantasy.* Probably Skeppsholmen, Stockholm, early July 1990. [**Beets** is a various artists' compilation; on the LP edition, Elemental/t.e.c. 90901, this track was heavily edited.]

Black Saint 120 121 [CD]: **Mayan Temples.** *Dance of the Language Barrier / Bygone / Discipline No. 1 / Alone Together / Prelude to Stargazers / Mayan Temples / I'll Never Be the Same / Stardust from Tomorrow / El Is a Sound of Joy / Time after Time / Opus in Springtime / Theme of the Stargazers / Sunset on the Nile.* Mondial Sound, Milan, July 24–25, 1990.

Leo LR 210/211 [CD]: **Pleiades.** *Pleiades / Mythic 1 / Sun Procession / Lights on a Satellite / Love in Outer Space / Planet Earth Day / Mythic 2 / Blue Lou / Prelude #7 in A Major.* Théâtre-Carré Saint-Vincent, Orléans, France, October 27, 1990.

Leo LR 214/215 [CD]: **Live at the Hackney Empire.** *Astro Black / Other Voices / Planet Earth Day / Prelude to a Kiss / Hocus Pocus / Love in Outer Space / Blue Lou / Face the Music / Strings Singhs / Discipline 27-II / I'll Wait for You / East of the Sun / Somewhere over the Rainbow / Frisco Fog / Sunset on the Nile / Skimming and Loping / Yeah Man! / We Travel the Spaceways / They'll Come Back.* Hackney Empire Theatre, London, October 28, 1990.

1991

Leo LR 188 [CD]: **Friendly Galaxy.** *Intro Percussion / Prelude to a Kiss / Blue Lou / Lights on a Satellite / Alabama / Fate in a Pleasant Mood / We Travel the Spaceways / Space Is the Place / Saturn Rings / Friendly Galaxy / They'll Come Back.* Banlieues Bleues, Salles des Fêtes-Mairie, Montreuil, France, April 11, 1991.

Rounder 3124 [CD]: **At the Village Vanguard.** *'Round Midnight / Sun Ra Blues / Autumn in New York / 'SWonderful / Theme of the Stargazers.* Village Vanguard, NYC, November 14 or 17, 1991.

1992

Enja 7071 [CD]: **Destination Unknown.** *Carefree / Echoes of the Future / Prelude to a Kiss / Hocus Pocus / Theme of the Stargazers / Interstellar Low Ways / Destination Unknown / The Satellites Are Spinning / 'SWonderful / Space Is the Place—We Travel the Spaceways.* Moonwalker Club, Aarburg, Switzerland, March 29, 1992.

Soul Note 121 216 [Billy Bang, CD]: **A Tribute to Stuff Smith.** *Only Time Will Tell / Satin Doll / Deep Purple / Bugle Blues / A Foggy Day / April in Paris / Lover Man / Yesterdays.* Sear Sound, NYC, September 20–22, 1992.

SINGLES

These are seven-inch 45-rpm unless otherwise stated.

1946

Bullet 251 [Wynonie Harris, 78 rpm]: *Dig This Boogie* b/w *Lightnin' Struck the Poorhouse.* Studio recording, Nashville, March 1946.

Bullet 252 [Wynonie Harris, 78 rpm]: *My Baby's Barrelhouse* b/w *Drinking by Myself.* Same session. ["Drinking by Myself" available on Route 66 RBD 3, **Mr. Blues Is Coming to Town.**]

1948

Aristocrat 3001 [The Dozier Boys with Gene Wright, 78 rpm]: *St. Louis Blues* b/w *She Only Fools with Me.* Universal Studios, Chicago, October or November 1948.

Aristocrat 3002 [The Dozier Boys with Gene Wright, 78 rpm]. *Big Time Baby* b/w *Music Goes Round and Round.* Same session.

Aristocrat 11001 [Eugene Wright and his Dukes of Swing]: *Pork 'n' Beans* b/w *Dawn Mist.* Same session.

1954

Saturn 9/1954 [The Nu Sounds]: *A Foggy Day.* Club Evergreen, Chicago, 1954 or 1955.

Saturn 9/1954 [The Cosmic Rays]: *Daddy's Gonna Tell You No Lie.* Rehearsal, Chicago, 1954 or 1955.

1955

Saturn SR-401/402 [The Cosmic Rays]: *Dreaming* b/w *Daddy's Gonna Tell You No Lie.* Studio recording, Chicago, 1955.

Saturn B222/B223 [The Cosmic Rays with Le Sun Ra and his Arkestra]: *Bye Bye* b/w *Somebody's in Love.* Studio recording, Chicago, late 1955.

1956

Heartbeat H-3-45/H-4-45 [Billie Hawkins with Sun Ra and his Arkestra]: *I'm Coming Home* b/w *Last Call for Love.* RCA Studios, Chicago, January 1956.

Satur M08W4052/M08W4053 [The Qualities]: *Happy New Year to You!* b/w *It's Christmas Time.* Rehearsal, Chicago, 1956.

Saturn Z222 [Le Sun-Ra and his Arkestra]: *Medicine for a Nightmare* b/w *Urnack.* RCA Studios, Chicago, early 1956. [A previously unissued alternate take of "Medicine for a Nightmare" is included in **The Singles,** Evidence 22164.]

Saturn (unknown #): *A Call for All Demons* b/w *Demon's Lullaby.* RCA Studios, Chicago, early 1956.

Saturn (unknown #): *Saturn* b/w *Supersonic Jazz.* RCA Studios, Chicago, early 1956.

Saturn Z1111: *Super Blonde* b/w *Soft Talk.* RCA Studios, Chicago, early 1956.

1957

Saturn 4236/4237 [Yochannan, The Space Age Vocalist]: *Muck Muck* b/w *Hot Skillet Mama.* Studio recording, Chicago, 1957.

1958

Saturn J08W0245/J08W0246: *Hours After.* Rehearsal, Chicago, early 1958.

Saturn J08W0245/J08W0246: *Great Balls of Fire.* Rehearsal, Chicago, around September 1958.

Saturn (unknown #): *Saturn* b/w *Velvet.* Probably RCA Studios, Chicago, late 1958.

Saturn (unknown #): *'Round Midnight* b/w *Back in Your Own Backyard.* Probably RCA Studios, Chicago, late 1958.

Pink Clouds 333 [Juanita Rogers and Lynn Hollings with Mr. V's Five Joys]: *Teenager's Letter of Promises* b/w *I'm So Glad You Love Me.* Somebody's living room, Chicago, 1958 or 1959.

1959

Saturn 1502 [Yochannan with Sun Ra and his Arkestra]: *The Sun One* b/w *Message to Earthman.* Studio sessions, Chicago, 1959.

Saturn 986 [Yochannan with Sun Ra and his Arkestra]: *The Sun Man Speaks* b/w *Message to Earthman.* Studio sessions, Chicago, 1959. [Evidence 22164, **The Singles,** also includes previously unreleased alternate takes of both sides of this single.]

Saturn 874: *October* b/w *Adventur[e] in Space.* Rehearsals, Chicago, 1959.

1960

Saturn SA-1001: *The Blue Set* b/w *Big City Blues.* RCA Studios, Chicago, around June 17, 1960.

Saturn L08W-0114/L08W-0115: *Space Loneliness* b/w *State Street.* Same session.

1962

Saturn 144M [Little Mack]: *Tell Her to Come on Home* b/w *I'm Making Believe.* Studio recording, NYC, 1962.

1966

Tifton 45-125 [The Sensational Guitars of Dan & Dale]: *Batman Theme* b/w *Robin's Theme.* Studio recording, Newark, NJ, January 1966.

1967

Saturn 3066: *The Bridge* b/w *Rocket Number Nine*. Rehearsals, Sun Studios, NYC, 1967.

Saturn 911-AR: *Blues on Planet Mars* b/w *Saturn Moon*. Rehearsals, Sun Studios, NYC, 1967 or 1968.

1970

Saturn ES 538B: *Enlightenment*. The House of Ra, Philadelphia, 1970 to 1974.

1972

Saturn ES 538A: *Journey to Saturn*. Live, unknown location, 1972 to 1974.

1973

Saturn ES 537B: *The Perfect Man*. Variety Recording Studios, NYC, May 24, 1973.

1974

Saturn ES 537B: *I'm Gonna Unmask the Batman*. WXPN-FM, Philadelphia, possibly July 4, 1974.

1975

Saturn 256: *Love in Outer Space*. Vocal dubbed in 1975 over an instrumental track recorded at Variety Recording Studios, NYC, 1970.

Saturn 256: *Mayan Temple*. Variety Recording Studios, NYC, June 27, 1975.

1978

Saturn 2100: *Disco 2100* b/w *Sky Blues*. Teatro Ciak, Milan, January 23, 1978. ["Disco 2100" is an edited version of "Disco 3000" from the Saturn album of the same name.]

1979

Saturn SR 51879: *Rough House Blues* b/w *Cosmo-Extensions*. Unidentified locations, early 1979.

1982

Saturn Gemini 1982Z: *Quest.* Unidentified location, 1982.

Saturn Gemini 1982Z: *Outer Space Plateau.* The House of Ra, Philadelphia, 1982.

Y RA 1 [12″ 45 rpm]: *Nuclear War* b/w *Sometimes I'm Happy.* Variety Recording Studios, NYC, September 1982.

1988

DIW DEP1-1 [7″ 33 rpm]: *Queer Notions* b/w *Prelude No. 7.* Pit-Inn, Tokyo, August 8, 1988.

DIW DEP1-2 [7″ 33 rpm]: *East of the Sun* b/w *Frisco Fog.* Same session.

DIW DEP1-3 [7″ 33 rpm]: *Opus Springtime* b/w *Cosmos Swing Blues.* Same session.

1991

Blast First BFFP CD 101: **Cosmic Visions.** *I Am the Instrument.* The House of Ra, Philadelphia, October 27, 1991. [This CD single was part of a multimedia Sun Ra memorial package, along with two videos.]

Note: All Saturn singles that were not included in Saturn albums are currently available on Evidence 22164, **The Singles.** The singles on Pink Clouds and Satur are also included in this 2-CD set.

INDEX

Other titles of interest

DANCE OF THE INFIDELS
A Portrait of Bud Powell
Francis Paudras
Foreword by Bill Evans
432 pp., 191 photos
80816-1 $18.95

BLACK MUSIC
LeRoi Jones (Amiri Imamu Baraka)
288 pp., 4 photos
80814-5 $14.95

MILESTONES
The Music and Times of
Miles Davis
Jack Chambers
New introduction by the author
816 pp., 40 photos
80849-8 $21.95

ASCENSION
John Coltrane and His Quest
Eric Nisenson
298 pp.
80644-4 $14.95

BIRD: The Legend
of Charlie Parker
Edited by Robert Reisner
256 pp., 50 photos
80069-1 $13.95

BIRD LIVES!
The High Life and Hard Times
of Charlie (Yardbird) Parker
Ross Russell
431 pp., 32 photos
80679-7 $15.95

BLACK TALK
Ben Sidran
New foreword by Archie Shepp
228 pp., 16 photos
80184-1 $10.95

CHASIN' THE TRANE
The Music and Mystique
of John Coltrane
J. C. Thomas
256 pp., 16 pp. of photos
80043-8 $12.95

DEXTER GORDON
A Musical Biography
Stan Britt
192 pp., 32 photos
80361-5 $13.95

FORCES IN MOTION
The Music and Thoughts
of Anthony Braxton
Graham Lock
412 pp., 16 photos, numerous illus.
80342-9 $15.95

FREE JAZZ
Ekkehard Jost
214 pp., 70 musical examples
80556-1 $13.95

THE FREEDOM PRINCIPLE
Jazz After 1958
John Litweiler
324 pp., 11 photos
80377-1 $13.95

IMPROVISATION
Its Nature and Practice in Music
Derek Bailey
172 pp., 12 photos
80528-6 $13.95

JOHN COLTRANE
Bill Cole
278 pp., 25 photos
80530-8 $14.95

MILES DAVIS
The Early Years
Bill Cole
256 pp.
80554-5 $13.95

MINGUS
A Critical Biography
Brian Priestley
320 pp., 25 photos
80217-1 $13.95

ORNETTE COLEMAN
A Harmolodic Life
John Litweiler
266 pp., 9 photos
80580-4 $14.95

'ROUND ABOUT MIDNIGHT
A Portrait of Miles Davis
Updated Edition
Eric Nisenson
336 pp., 27 photos
80684-3 $14.95

STRAIGHT LIFE
The Story of Art Pepper
Updated Edition
Art and Laurie Pepper
Introduction by Gary Giddins
616 pp., 48 photos
80558-8 $17.95

Available at your bookstore

OR ORDER DIRECTLY FROM 1-800-386-5656

VISIT OUR WEBSITE AT WWW.PERSEUSBOOKS.COM